HEART OF DARKNESS AND OTHER WORKS

COLLECTED NOVELLAS AND SHORT STORIES

By JOSEPH CONRAD

Heart of Darkness and Other Works
By Joseph Conrad

Print ISBN 13: 978-1-4209-5310-7
eBook ISBN 13: 978-1-4209-5311-4

This edition copyright © 2016. Digireads.com Publishing.

Cover Image: A detail of an illustration by Dan Syre Groesbeck to "The Duel" which was published under the title of "The Point of Honor" by The McClure Company, New York, 1908.

Please visit *www.digireads.com*

CONTENTS

An Outpost of Progress

I

There were two white men in charge of the trading station. Kayerts, the chief, was short and fat; Carlier, the assistant, was tall, with a large head and a very broad trunk perched upon a long pair of thin legs. The third man on the staff was a Sierra Leone nigger, who maintained that his name was Henry Price. However, for some reason or other, the natives down the river had given him the name of Makola, and it stuck to him through all his wanderings about the country. He spoke English and French with a warbling accent, wrote a beautiful hand, understood bookkeeping, and cherished in his innermost heart the worship of evil spirits. His wife was a Negress from Loanda, very large and very noisy. Three children rolled about in sunshine before the door of his low, shedlike dwelling. Makola, taciturn and impenetrable, despised the two white men. He had charge of a small clay storehouse with a dried-grass roof, and pretended to keep a correct account of beads, cotton cloth, red kerchiefs, brass wire, and other trade goods it contained. Besides the storehouse and Makola's hut, there was only one large building in the cleared ground of the station. It was built neatly of reeds, with a verandah on all the four sides. There were three rooms in it. The one in the middle was the living room, and had two rough tables and a few stools in it. The other two were the bedrooms for the white men. Each had a bedstead and a mosquito net for all furniture. The plank floor was littered with the belongings of the white men; open half-empty boxes, torn wearing apparel, old boots; all the things dirty, and all the things broken, that accumulate mysteriously round untidy men. There was also another dwelling place some distance away from the buildings. In it, under a tall cross much out of the perpendicular, slept the man who had seen the beginning of all this; who had planned and had watched the construction of this outpost of progress. He had been, at home, an unsuccessful painter who, weary of pursuing fame on an empty stomach, had gone out there through high protections. He had been the first chief of that station. Makola had watched the energetic artist die of fever in the just finished house with his usual kind of "I told you so" indifference. Then, for a time, he dwelt alone with his family, his account books, and the Evil Spirit that rules the lands under the equator. He got on very well with his god. Perhaps he had propitiated him by a promise of more white men to play with, by and by. At any rate the director of the Great Trading Company, coming up in a steamer that resembled an enormous sardine box with a flat-roofed shed erected on it, found the station in good order, and Makola as usual quietly diligent. The director had the cross put up over the first agent's grave, and appointed Kayerts to the post. Carlier was told off as second in charge. The director was a man ruthless and efficient, who at times, but very imperceptibly, indulged in grim humour. He made a speech to Kayerts and Carlier, pointing out to them the promising aspect of their station. The nearest trading post was about three hundred miles away. It was an exceptional opportunity for them to distinguish themselves and to earn percentages on the trade. This appointment was a favour done to beginners. Kayerts was moved almost to tears by his director's kindness. He would, he said, by doing his best, try to justify the flattering confidence, &c., &c. Kayerts had been in the Administration of the Telegraphs, and knew how to express himself correctly. Carlier, an exnoncommissioned officer of cavalry in an army guaranteed from harm by several European powers, was less impressed. If there were commissions to get, so much the better; and, trailing a sulky glance over the river, the forests, the impenetrable bush that seemed to cut off the station from the rest of the world, he muttered between his teeth, "We shall see, very soon."

Next day, some bales of cotton goods and a few cases of provisions having been thrown on shore, the sardine-box steamer went off, not to return for another six months. On the deck the director touched his cap to the two agents, who stood on the bank waving their hats, and turning to an old servant of the Company on his passage to headquarters, said, "Look at those two imbeciles. They must be mad at home to send me such specimens. I told those fellows to plant a vegetable garden, build new storehouses and fences, and construct a landing-stage. I bet nothing will be done! They won't know how to begin. I always thought the station on this river useless, and they just fit the station!"

"They will form themselves there," said the old stager with a quiet smile.

"At any rate, I am rid of them for six months," retorted the director.

The two men watched the steamer round the bend, then, ascending arm in arm the slope of the bank, returned to the station. They had been in this vast and dark country only a very short time, and as yet always in the midst of other white men, under the eye and guidance of their superiors. And now, dull as they were to the subtle influences of surroundings, they felt themselves very much alone, when suddenly left unassisted to face the wilderness; a wilderness rendered more strange, more incomprehensible by the mysterious glimpses of the vigorous life it contained. They were two perfectly insignificant and incapable individuals, whose existence is only rendered possible through the high organization of civilized crowds. Few men realize that their life, the very essence of their character, their capabilities and their audacities, are only the expression of their belief in the safety of their surroundings. The courage, the composure, the confidence; the emotions and principles; every great and every insignificant thought belongs not to the individual but to the crowd: to the crowd that believes blindly in the irresistible force of its institutions and of its morals, in the power of its police and of its opinion. But the contact with pure unmitigated savagery, with primitive nature and primitive man, brings sudden and profound trouble into the heart. To the sentiment of being alone of one's kind, to the clear perception of the loneliness of one's thoughts, of one's sensations—to the negation of the habitual, which is safe, there is added the affirmation of the unusual, which is dangerous; a suggestion of things vague, uncontrollable, and repulsive, whose discomposing intrusion excites the imagination and tries the civilized nerves of the foolish and the wise alike.

Kayerts and Carlier walked arm in arm, drawing close to one another as children do in the dark; and they had the same, not altogether unpleasant, sense of danger which one half suspects to be imaginary. They chatted persistently in familiar tones. "Our station is prettily situated," said one. The other assented with enthusiasm, enlarging volubly on the beauties of the situation. Then they passed near the grave. "Poor devil!" said Kayerts. "He died of fever, didn't he?" muttered Carlier, stopping short. "Why," retorted Kayerts, with indignation, "I've been told that the fellow exposed himself recklessly to the sun. The climate here, everybody says, is not at all worse than at home, as long as you keep out of the sun. Do you hear that, Carlier? I am chief here, and my orders are that you should not expose yourself to the sun!" He assumed his superiority jocularly, but his meaning was serious. The idea that he would, perhaps, have to bury Carlier and remain alone, gave him an inward shiver. He felt suddenly that this Carlier was more precious to him here, in the centre of Africa, than a brother could be anywhere else. Carlier, entering into the spirit of the thing, made a military salute and answered in a brisk tone, "Your orders shall be attended to, Chief!" Then he burst out laughing, slapped Kayerts on the back and shouted, "We shall let life run easily here! Just sit still and gather in the ivory those savages will bring. This country has its good points, after all!" They both laughed loudly while Carlier thought: "That poor Kayerts; he is so fat and unhealthy. It would be awful if I had to bury him here. He is a man I respect." . . . Before they reached the verandah of their house they called one another "my dear fellow."

The first day they were very active, pottering about with hammers and nails and red calico, to put up curtains, make their house habitable and pretty; resolved to settle down comfortably to their new life. For them an impossible task. To grapple effectually with even purely material problems requires more serenity of mind and more lofty courage than people generally imagine. No two beings could have been more unfitted for such a struggle. Society, not from any tenderness, but because of its strange needs, had taken care of those two men, forbidding them all independent thought, all initiative, all departure from routine; and forbidding it under pain of death. They could only live on condition of being machines. And now, released from the fostering care of men with pens behind the ears, or of men with gold lace on the sleeves, they were like those lifelong prisoners who, liberated after many years, do not know what use to make of their freedom. They did not know what use to make of their faculties, being both, through want of practice, incapable of independent thought.

At the end of two months Kayerts often would say, "If it was not for my Melie, you wouldn't catch me here." Melie was his daughter. He had thrown up his post in the Administration of the Telegraphs, though he had been for seventeen years perfectly happy there, to earn a dowry for his girl. His wife was dead, and the child was being brought up by his sisters. He regretted the streets, the pavements, the cafes, his friends of many years; all the things he used to see, day after day; all the thoughts suggested by familiar things—the thoughts effortless, monotonous, and soothing of a Government clerk; he regretted all the gossip, the small enmities, the mild venom, and the little jokes of Government offices. "If I had had a decent brother-in-law," Carlier would remark, "a fellow with a heart, I would not be here." He had left the army and had made himself so obnoxious to his family by his laziness and impudence, that an exasperated brother-in-law had made superhuman efforts to procure him an appointment in the Company as a second-class agent. Having not a penny in the world he was compelled to accept this means of livelihood as soon as it became quite clear to him that there was nothing more to squeeze out of his relations. He, like Kayerts, regretted his old life. He regretted the clink of sabre and spurs on a fine afternoon, the barrack room witticisms, the girls of garrison towns; but, besides, he had also a sense of grievance. He was evidently a much ill-used man. This made him moody, at times. But the two men got on well together in the fellowship of their stupidity and laziness. Together they did nothing, absolutely nothing, and enjoyed the sense of the idleness for which they were paid. And in time they came to feel something resembling affection for one another.

They lived like blind men in a large room, aware only of what came in contact with them (and of that only imperfectly), but unable to see the general aspect of things. The river, the forest, all the great land throbbing with life, were like a great emptiness. Even the brilliant sunshine disclosed nothing intelligible. Things appeared and disappeared before their eyes in an unconnected and aimless kind of way. The river seemed to come from nowhere and flow nowhither. It flowed through a void. Out of that void, at times, came canoes, and men with spears in their hands would suddenly crowd the yard of the station. They were naked, glossy black, ornamented with snowy shells and glistening brass wire, perfect of limb. They made an uncouth babbling noise when they spoke, moved in a stately manner, and sent quick, wild glances out of their startled, never-resting eyes. Those warriors would squat in long rows, four or more deep, before the verandah, while their chiefs bargained for hours with Makola over an elephant tusk. Kayerts sat on his chair and looked down on the proceedings, understanding nothing. He stared at them with his round blue eyes, called out to Carlier, "Here, look! look at that fellow there—and that other one, to the left. Did you ever such a face? Oh, the funny brute!"

Carlier, smoking native tobacco in a short wooden pipe, would swagger up twirling his moustaches, and surveying the warriors with haughty indulgence, would say:

"Fine animals. Brought any bone? Yes? It's not any too soon. Look at the muscles of that fellow third from the end. I wouldn't care to get a punch on the nose from him. Fine arms, but legs no good below the knee. Couldn't make cavalry men of them." And after glancing down complacently at his own shanks, he always concluded: "Pah! Don't they stink! You, Makola! Take that herd over to the fetish" (the storehouse was in every station called the fetish, perhaps because of the spirit of civilization it contained) "and give them up some of the rubbish you keep there. I'd rather see it full of bone than full of rags."

Kayerts approved.

"Yes, yes! Go and finish that palaver over there, Mr. Makola. I will come round when you are ready, to weigh the tusk. We must be careful." Then turning to his companion: "This is the tribe that lives down the river; they are rather aromatic. I remember, they had been once before here. D'ye hear that row? What a fellow has got to put up with in this dog of a country! My head is split."

Such profitable visits were rare. For days the two pioneers of trade and progress would look on their empty courtyard in the vibrating brilliance of vertical sunshine. Below the high bank, the silent river flowed on glittering and steady. On the sands in the middle of the stream, hippos and alligators sunned themselves side by side. And stretching away in all directions, surrounding the insignificant cleared spot of the trading post, immense forests, hiding fateful complications of fantastic life, lay in the eloquent silence of mute greatness. The two men understood nothing, cared for nothing but for the passage of days that separated them from the steamer's return. Their predecessor had left some torn books. They took up these wrecks of novels, and, as they had never read anything of the kind before, they were surprised and amused. Then during long days there were interminable and silly discussions about plots and personages. In the centre of Africa they made acquaintance of Richelieu and of d'Artagnan, of Hawk's Eye and of Father Goriot, and of many other people. All these imaginary personages became subjects for gossip as if they had been living friends. They discounted their virtues, suspected their motives, decried their successes; were scandalized at their duplicity or were doubtful about their courage. The accounts of crimes filled them with indignation, while tender or pathetic passages moved them deeply. Carlier cleared his throat and said in a soldierly voice, "What nonsense!" Kayerts, his round eyes suffused with tears, his fat cheeks quivering, rubbed his bald head, and declared, "This is a splendid book. I had no idea there were such clever fellows in the world." They also found some old copies of a home paper. That print discussed what it was pleased to call "Our Colonial Expansion" in high-flown language. It spoke much of the rights and duties of civilization, of the sacredness of the civilizing work, and extolled the merits of those who went about bringing light and faith and commerce to the dark places of the earth. Carlier and Kayerts read, wondered, and began to think better of themselves. Carlier said one evening, waving his hand about, "In a hundred years, there will be perhaps a town here. Quays, and warehouses, and barracks, and—and—billiard-rooms. Civilization, my boy, and virtue—and all. And then, chaps will read that two good fellows, Kayerts and Carlier, were the first civilized men to live in this very spot!" Kayerts nodded, "Yes, it is a consolation to think of that." They seemed to forget their dead predecessor; but, early one day, Carlier went out and replanted the cross firmly. "It used to make me squint whenever I walked that way," he explained to Kayerts over the morning coffee. "It made me squint, leaning over so much. So I just planted it upright. And solid, I promise you! I suspended myself with both hands to the crosspiece. Not a move. Oh, I did that properly."

At times Gobila came to see them. Gobila was the chief of the neighbouring villages. He was a grey-headed savage, thin and black, with a white cloth round his loins and a mangy panther skin hanging over his back. He came up with long strides of his skeleton legs, swinging a staff as tall as himself, and, entering the common room of the station, would squat on his heels to the left of the door. There he sat, watching Kayerts, and now and then making a speech which the other did not understand. Kayerts, without interrupting his occupation, would from time to time say in a friendly manner: "How goes it, you old image?" and they would smile at one another. The two whites had a liking for that old and incomprehensible creature, and called him Father Gobila. Gobila's manner was paternal, and he seemed really to love all white men. They all appeared to him very young, indistinguishably alike (except for stature), and he knew that they were all brothers, and also immortal. The death of the artist, who was the first white man whom he knew intimately, did not disturb this belief, because he was firmly convinced that the white stranger had pretended to die and got himself buried for some mysterious purpose of his own, into which it was useless to inquire. Perhaps it was his way of going home to his own country? At any rate, these were his brothers, and he transferred his absurd affection to them. They returned it in a way. Carlier slapped him on the back, and recklessly struck off matches for his amusement. Kayerts was always ready to let him have a sniff at the ammonia bottle. In short, they behaved just like that other white creature that had hidden itself in a hole in the ground. Gobila considered them attentively. Perhaps they were the same being with the other—or one of them was. He couldn't decide—clear up that mystery; but he remained always very friendly. In consequence of that friendship the women of Gobila's village walked in single file through the reedy grass, bringing every morning to the station, fowls, and sweet potatoes, and palm wine, and sometimes a goat. The Company never provisions the stations fully, and the agents required those local supplies to live. They had them through the goodwill of Gobila, and lived well. Now and then one of them had a bout of fever, and the other nursed him with gentle devotion. They did not think much of it. It left them weaker, and their appearance changed for the worse. Carlier was hollow-eyed and irritable. Kayerts showed a drawn, flabby face above the rotundity of his stomach, which gave him a weird aspect. But being constantly together, they did not notice the change that took place gradually in their appearance, and also in their dispositions.

Five months passed in that way.

Then, one morning, as Kayerts and Carlier, lounging in their chairs under the verandah, talked about the approaching visit of the steamer, a knot of armed men came out of the forest and advanced towards the station. They were strangers to that part of the country. They were tall, slight, draped classically from neck to heel in blue fringed cloths, and carried percussion muskets over their bare right shoulders. Makola showed signs of excitement, and ran out of the storehouse (where he spent all his days) to meet these visitors. They came into the courtyard and looked about them with steady, scornful glances. Their leader, a powerful and determined-looking Negro with bloodshot eyes, stood in front of the verandah and made a long speech. He gesticulated much, and ceased very suddenly.

There was something in his intonation, in the sounds of the long sentences he used, that startled the two whites. It was like a reminiscence of something not exactly familiar, and yet resembling the speech of civilized men. It sounded like one of those impossible languages which sometimes we hear in our dreams.

"What lingo is that?" said the amazed Carlier. "In the first moment I fancied the fellow was going to speak French. Anyway, it is a different kind of gibberish to what we ever heard."

"Yes," replied Kayerts. "Hey, Makola, what does he say? Where do they come from? Who are they?"

But Makola, who seemed to be standing on hot bricks, answered hurriedly, "I don't know. They come from very far. Perhaps Mrs. Price will understand. They are perhaps bad men."

The leader, after waiting for a while, said something sharply to Makola, who shook his head. Then the man, after looking round, noticed Makola's hut and walked over there. The next moment Mrs. Makola was heard speaking with great volubility. The other strangers— they were six in all—strolled about with an air of ease, put their heads through the door of the storeroom, congregated round the grave, pointed understandingly at the cross, and generally made themselves at home.

"I don't like those chaps—and, I say, Kayerts, they must be from the coast; they've got firearms," observed the sagacious Carlier.

Kayerts also did not like those chaps. They both, for the first time, became aware that they lived in conditions where the unusual may be dangerous, and that there was no power on earth outside of themselves to stand between them and the unusual. They became uneasy, went in and loaded their revolvers. Kayerts said, "We must order Makola to tell them to go away before dark."

The strangers left in the afternoon, after eating a meal prepared for them by Mrs. Makola. The immense woman was excited, and talked much with the visitors. She rattled away shrilly, pointing here and there at the forests and at the river. Makola sat apart and watched. At times he got up and whispered to his wife. He accompanied the strangers across the ravine at the back of the station-ground, and returned slowly looking very thoughtful. When questioned by the white men he was very strange, seemed not to understand, seemed to have forgotten French—seemed to have forgotten how to speak altogether. Kayerts and Carlier agreed that the nigger had had too much palm wine.

There was some talk about keeping a watch in turn, but in the evening everything seemed so quiet and peaceful that they retired as usual. All night they were disturbed by a lot of drumming in the villages. A deep, rapid roll near by would be followed by another far off—then all ceased. Soon short appeals would rattle out here and there, then all mingle together, increase, become vigorous and sustained, would spread out over the forest, roll through the night, unbroken and ceaseless, near and far, as if the whole land had been one immense drum booming out steadily an appeal to heaven. And through the deep and tremendous noise sudden yells that resembled snatches of songs from a madhouse darted shrill and high in discordant jets of sound which seemed to rush far above the earth and drive all peace from under the stars.

Carlier and Kayerts slept badly. They both thought they had heard shots fired during the night—but they could not agree as to the direction. In the morning Makola was gone somewhere. He returned about noon with one of yesterday's strangers, and eluded all Kayerts' attempts to close with him: had become deaf apparently. Kayerts wondered. Carlier, who had been fishing off the bank, came back and remarked while he showed his catch, "The niggers seem to be in a deuce of a stir; I wonder what's up. I saw about fifteen canoes cross the river during the two hours I was there fishing." Kayerts, worried, said, "Isn't this Makola very queer to-day?" Carlier advised, "Keep all our men together in case of some trouble."

II

There were ten station men who had been left by the Director. Those fellows, having engaged themselves to the Company for six months (without having any idea of a month in particular and only a very faint notion of time in general), had been serving the cause of progress for upwards of two years. Belonging to a tribe from a very distant part of the land of darkness and sorrow, they did not run away, naturally supposing that as wandering strangers they would be killed by the inhabitants of the country; in which they were right. They lived in straw huts on the slope of a ravine overgrown with reedy grass, just behind the station buildings. They were not happy, regretting the festive incantations, the sorceries, the human sacrifices of their own land; where they also had parents, brothers, sisters, admired chiefs, respected magicians, loved friends, and other ties supposed generally to be human. Besides, the rice rations served out by the Company did not agree with them, being a food unknown to their land, and to which they could not get used. Consequently they were unhealthy and miserable. Had they been of any other tribe they would have made up their minds to die—for nothing is easier to certain savages than suicide—and so have escaped from the puzzling difficulties of existence. But belonging, as they did, to a warlike tribe with filed teeth, they had more grit, and went on stupidly living through disease and sorrow. They did very little work, and had lost their splendid physique. Carlier and Kayerts doctored them assiduously without being able to bring them back into condition again. They were mustered every morning and told off to different tasks—grass-cutting, fence-building, tree-felling, &c., &c., which no power on earth could induce them to execute efficiently. The two whites had practically very little control over them.

In the afternoon Makola came over to the big house and found Kayerts watching three heavy columns of smoke rising above the forests. "What is that?" asked Kayerts. "Some villages burn," answered Makola, who seemed to have regained his wits. Then he said abruptly: "We have got very little ivory; bad six months' trading. Do you like get a little more ivory?"

"Yes," said Kayerts, eagerly. He thought of percentages which were low.

"Those men who came yesterday are traders from Loanda who have got more ivory than they can carry home. Shall I buy? I know their camp."

"Certainly," said Kayerts. "What are those traders?"

"Bad fellows," said Makola, indifferently. "They fight with people, and catch women and children. They are bad men, and got guns. There is a great disturbance in the country. Do you want ivory?"

"Yes," said Kayerts. Makola said nothing for a while. Then: "Those workmen of ours are no good at all," he muttered, looking round. "Station in very bad order, sir. Director will growl. Better get a fine lot of ivory, then he say nothing."

"I can't help it; the men won't work," said Kayerts. "When will you get that ivory?"

"Very soon," said Makola. "Perhaps tonight. You leave it to me, and keep indoors, sir. I think you had better give some palm wine to our men to make a dance this evening. Enjoy themselves. Work better tomorrow. There's plenty palm wine—gone a little sour."

Kayerts said "yes," and Makola, with his own hands carried big calabashes to the door of his hut. They stood there till the evening, and Mrs. Makola looked into every one. The men got them at sunset. When Kayerts and Carlier retired, a big bonfire was flaring before the men's huts. They could hear their shouts and drumming. Some men from Gobila's village had joined the station hands, and the entertainment was a great success.

In the middle of the night, Carlier waking suddenly, heard a man shout loudly; then a shot was fired. Only one. Carlier ran out and met Kayerts on the verandah. They were both startled. As they went across the yard to call Makola, they saw shadows moving in the night. One of them cried, "Don't shoot! It's me, Price." Then Makola appeared close to them. "Go back, go back, please," he urged, "you spoil all." "There are strange men about," said Carlier. "Never mind; I know," said Makola. Then he whispered, "All right. Bring ivory. Say nothing! I know my business." The two white men reluctantly went back to the house, but did not sleep. They heard footsteps, whispers, some groans. It seemed as if a lot of men came in, dumped heavy things on the ground, squabbled a long time, then went away. They lay on their hard beds and thought: "This Makola is invaluable." In the morning Carlier came out, very sleepy, and pulled at the cord of the big bell. The station hands mustered every morning to the sound of the bell. That morning nobody came. Kayerts turned out also, yawning. Across the yard they saw Makola come out of his hut, a tin basin of soapy water in his hand. Makola, a civilized nigger, was very neat in his person. He threw the soapsuds skilfully over a wretched little yellow cur he had, then turning his face to the agent's house, he shouted from the distance, "All the men gone last night!"

They heard him plainly, but in their surprise they both yelled out together: "What!" Then they stared at one another. "We are in a proper fix now," growled Carlier. "It's incredible!" muttered Kayerts. "I will go to the huts and see," said Carlier, striding off. Makola coming up found Kayerts standing alone.

"I can hardly believe it," said Kayerts, tearfully. "We took care of them as if they had been our children."

"They went with the coast people," said Makola after a moment of hesitation.

"What do I care with whom they went—the ungrateful brutes!" exclaimed the other. Then with sudden suspicion, and looking hard at Makola, he added: "What do you know about it?"

Makola moved his shoulders, looking down on the ground. "What do I know? I think only. Will you come and look at the ivory I've got there? It is a fine lot. You never saw such."

He moved towards the store. Kayerts followed him mechanically, thinking about the incredible desertion of the men. On the ground before the door of the fetish lay six splendid tusks.

"What did you give for it?" asked Kayerts, after surveying the lot with satisfaction.

"No regular trade," said Makola. "They brought the ivory and gave it to me. I told them to take what they most wanted in the station. It is a beautiful lot. No station can show such tusks. Those traders wanted carriers badly, and our men were no good here. No trade, no entry in books; all correct."

Kayerts nearly burst with indignation. "Why!" he shouted, "I believe you have sold our men for these tusks!" Makola stood impassive and silent. "I—I—will—I," stuttered Kayerts. "You fiend!" he yelled out.

"I did the best for you and the Company," said Makola, imperturbably. "Why you shout so much? Look at this tusk."

"I dismiss you! I will report you—I won't look at the tusks. I forbid you to touch them. I order you to throw them into the river. You—you!"

"You very red, Mr. Kayerts. If you are so irritable in the sun, you will get fever and die—like the first chief!" pronounced Makola impressively.

They stood still, contemplating one another with intense eyes, as if they had been looking with effort across immense distances. Kayerts shivered. Makola had meant no more than he said, but his words seemed to Kayerts full of ominous menace! He turned sharply and went away to the house. Makola retired into the bosom of his family; and the tusks, left lying before the store, looked very large and valuable in the sunshine.

Carlier came back on the verandah. "They're all gone, hey?" asked Kayerts from the far end of the common room in a muffled voice. "You did not find anybody?"

"Oh, yes," said Carlier, "I found one of Gobila's people lying dead before the huts—shot through the body. We heard that shot last night."

Kayerts came out quickly. He found his companion staring grimly over the yard at the tusks, away by the store. They both sat in silence for a while. Then Kayerts related his conversation with Makola. Carlier said nothing. At the midday meal they ate very little. They hardly exchanged a word that day. A great silence seemed to lie heavily over the station and press on their lips. Makola did not open the store; he spent the day playing with his children. He lay full-length on a mat outside his door, and the youngsters sat on his chest and clambered all over him. It was a touching picture. Mrs. Makola was busy cooking all day as usual. The white men made a somewhat better meal in the evening. Afterwards, Carlier smoking his pipe strolled over to the store; he stood for a long time over the tusks, touched one or two with his foot, even tried to lift the largest one by its small end. He came back to his chief, who had not stirred from the verandah, threw himself in the chair, and said—

"I can see it! They were pounced upon while they slept heavily after drinking all that palm wine you've allowed Makola to give them. A put-up job! See? The worst is, some of Gobila's people were there, and got carried off too, no doubt. The least drunk woke up, and got shot for his sobriety. This is a funny country. What will you do now?"

"We can't touch it, of course," said Kayerts.

"Of course not," assented Carlier.

"Slavery is an awful thing," stammered out Kayerts in an unsteady voice.

"Frightful—the sufferings," grunted Carlier with conviction.

They believed their words. Everybody shows a respectful deference to certain sounds that he and his fellows can make. But about feelings people really know nothing. We talk with indignation or enthusiasm; we talk about oppression, cruelty, crime, devotion, self-sacrifice, virtue, and we know nothing real beyond the words. Nobody knows what suffering or sacrifice means—except, perhaps the victims of the mysterious purpose of these illusions.

Next morning they saw Makola very busy setting up in the yard the big scales used for weighing ivory. By and by Carlier said: "What's that filthy scoundrel up to?" and lounged out into the yard. Kayerts followed. They stood watching. Makola took no notice. When the balance was swung true, he tried to lift a tusk into the scale. It was too heavy. He looked up helplessly without a word, and for a minute they

stood round that balance as mute and still as three statues. Suddenly
Carlier said: "Catch hold of the other end, Makola—you beast!" and
together they swung the tusk up. Kayerts trembled in every limb. He
muttered, "I say! O! I say!" and putting his hand in his pocket found
there a dirty bit of paper and the stump of a pencil. He turned his back
on the others, as if about to do something tricky, and noted stealthily
the weights which Carlier shouted out to him with unnecessary
loudness. When all was over Makola whispered to himself: "The sun's
very strong here for the tusks." Carlier said to Kayerts in a careless
tone: "I say, chief, I might just as well give him a lift with this lot into
the store."

As they were going back to the house Kayerts observed with a
sigh: "It had to be done." And Carlier said: "It's deplorable, but, the
men being Company's men the ivory is Company's ivory. We must
look after it." "I will report to the Director, of course," said Kayerts.
"Of course; let him decide," approved Carlier.

At midday they made a hearty meal. Kayerts sighed from time to
time. Whenever they mentioned Makola's name they always added to it
an opprobrious epithet. It eased their conscience. Makola gave himself
a half-holiday, and bathed his children in the river. No one from
Gobila's villages came near the station that day. No one came the next
day, and the next, nor for a whole week. Gobila's people might have
been dead and buried for any sign of life they gave. But they were only
mourning for those they had lost by the witchcraft of white men, who
had brought wicked people into their country. The wicked people were
gone, but fear remained. Fear always remains. A man may destroy
everything within himself, love and hate and belief, and even doubt; but
as long as he clings to life he cannot destroy fear: the fear, subtle,
indestructible, and terrible, that pervades his being; that tinges his
thoughts; that lurks in his heart; that watches on his lips the struggle of
his last breath. In his fear, the mild old Gobila offered extra human
sacrifices to all the Evil Spirits that had taken possession of his white
friends. His heart was heavy. Some warriors spoke about burning and
killing, but the cautious old savage dissuaded them. Who could foresee
the woe those mysterious creatures, if irritated, might bring? They
should be left alone. Perhaps in time they would disappear into the
earth as the first one had disappeared. His people must keep away from
them, and hope for the best.

Kayerts and Carlier did not disappear, but remained above on this
earth, that, somehow, they fancied had become bigger and very empty.
It was not the absolute and dumb solitude of the post that impressed
them so much as an inarticulate feeling that something from within
them was gone, something that worked for their safety, and had kept
the wilderness from interfering with their hearts. The images of home;
the memory of people like them, of men that thought and felt as they

used to think and feel, receded into distances made indistinct by the glare of unclouded sunshine. And out of the great silence of the surrounding wilderness, its very hopelessness and savagery seemed to approach them nearer, to draw them gently, to look upon them, to envelop them with a solicitude irresistible, familiar, and disgusting.

Days lengthened into weeks, then into months. Gobila's people drummed and yelled to every new moon, as of yore, but kept away from the station. Makola and Carlier tried once in a canoe to open communications, but were received with a shower of arrows, and had to fly back to the station for dear life. That attempt set the country up and down the river into an uproar that could be very distinctly heard for days. The steamer was late. At first they spoke of delay jauntily, then anxiously, then gloomily. The matter was becoming serious. Stores were running short. Carlier cast his lines off the bank, but the river was low, and the fish kept out in the stream. They dared not stroll far away from the station to shoot. Moreover, there was no game in the impenetrable forest. Once Carlier shot a hippo in the river. They had no boat to secure it, and it sank. When it floated up it drifted away, and Gobila's people secured the carcass. It was the occasion for a national holiday, but Carlier had a fit of rage over it and talked about the necessity of exterminating all the niggers before the country could be made habitable. Kayerts mooned about silently; spent hours looking at the portrait of his Melie. It represented a little girl with long bleached tresses and a rather sour face. His legs were much swollen, and he could hardly walk. Carlier, undermined by fever, could not swagger any more, but kept tottering about, still with a devil-may-care air, as became a man who remembered his crack regiment. He had become hoarse, sarcastic, and inclined to say unpleasant things. He called it "being frank with you." They had long ago reckoned their percentages on trade, including in them that last deal of "this infamous Makola." They had also concluded not to say anything about it. Kayerts hesitated at first—was afraid of the Director.

"He has seen worse things done on the quiet," maintained Carlier, with a hoarse laugh. "Trust him! He won't thank you if you blab. He is no better than you or me. Who will talk if we hold our tongues? There is nobody here."

That was the root of the trouble! There was nobody there; and being left there alone with their weakness, they became daily more like a pair of accomplices than like a couple of devoted friends. They had heard nothing from home for eight months. Every evening they said, "To-morrow we shall see the steamer." But one of the Company's steamers had been wrecked, and the Director was busy with the other, relieving very distant and important stations on the main river. He thought that the useless station, and the useless men, could wait. Meantime Kayerts and Carlier lived on rice boiled without salt, and cursed the Company, all Africa, and the day they were born. One must have lived on such diet to discover what ghastly trouble the necessity of swallowing one's food may become. There was literally nothing else in the station but rice and coffee; they drank the coffee without sugar. The last fifteen lumps Kayerts had solemnly locked away in his box, together with a half-bottle of Cognac, "in case of sickness," he explained. Carlier approved. "When one is sick," he said, "any little extra like that is cheering."

They waited. Rank grass began to sprout over the courtyard. The bell never rang now. Days passed, silent, exasperating, and slow. When the two men spoke, they snarled; and their silences were bitter, as if tinged by the bitterness of their thoughts.

One day after a lunch of boiled rice, Carlier put down his cup untasted, and said: "Hang it all! Let's have a decent cup of coffee for once. Bring out that sugar, Kayerts!"

"For the sick," muttered Kayerts, without looking up.

"For the sick," mocked Carlier. "Bosh! . . . Well! I am sick."

"You are no more sick than I am, and I go without," said Kayerts in a peaceful tone.

"Come! Out with that sugar, you stingy old slave-dealer."

Kayerts looked up quickly. Carlier was smiling with marked insolence. And suddenly it seemed to Kayerts that he had never seen that man before. Who was he? He knew nothing about him. What was he capable of? There was a surprising flash of violent emotion within him, as if in the presence of something undreamt-of, dangerous, and final. But he managed to pronounce with composure:

"That joke is in very bad taste. Don't repeat it."

"Joke!" said Carlier, hitching himself forward on his seat. "I am hungry—I am sick—I don't joke! I hate hypocrites. You are a hypocrite. You are a slave-dealer. I am a slave-dealer. There's nothing but slave-dealers in this cursed country. I mean to have sugar in my coffee today, anyhow!"

"I forbid you to speak to me in that way," said Kayerts with a fair show of resolution.

"You!—What?" shouted Carlier, jumping up.

Kayerts stood up also. "I am your chief," he began, trying to master the shakiness of his voice.

"What?" yelled the other. "Who's chief? There's no chief here. There's nothing here: there's nothing but you and I. Fetch the sugar—you potbellied ass."

"Hold your tongue. Go out of this room," screamed Kayerts. "I dismiss you—you scoundrel!"

Carlier swung a stool. All at once he looked dangerously in earnest. "You flabby, good-for-nothing civilian—take that!" he howled.

Kayerts dropped under the table, and the stool struck the grass inner wall of the room. Then, as Carlier was trying to upset the table, Kayerts in desperation made a blind rush, head low, like a cornered pig would do, and over-turning his friend, bolted along the verandah, and into his room. He locked the door, snatched his revolver, and stood panting. In less than a minute Carlier was kicking at the door furiously, howling, "If you don't bring out that sugar, I will shoot you at sight, like a dog. Now then—one—two—three. You won't? I will show you who's the master."

Kayerts thought the door would fall in, and scrambled through the square hole that served for a window in his room. There was then the whole breadth of the house between them. But the other was apparently not strong enough to break in the door, and Kayerts heard him running round. Then he also began to run laboriously on his swollen legs. He ran as quickly as he could, grasping the revolver, and unable yet to understand what was happening to him. He saw in succession Makola's house, the store, the river, the ravine, and the low bushes; and he saw all those things again as he ran for the second time round the house. Then again they flashed past him. That morning he could not have walked a yard without a groan.

And now he ran. He ran fast enough to keep out of sight of the other man.

Then as, weak and desperate, he thought, "Before I finish the next round I shall die," he heard the other man stumble heavily, then stop. He stopped also. He had the back and Carlier the front of the house, as before. He heard him drop into a chair cursing, and suddenly his own legs gave way, and he slid down into a sitting posture with his back to the wall. His mouth was as dry as a cinder, and his face was wet with perspiration—and tears. What was it all about? He thought it must be a horrible illusion; he thought he was dreaming; he thought he was going mad! After a while he collected his senses. What did they quarrel about? That sugar! How absurd! He would give it to him—didn't want it himself. And he began scrambling to his feet with a sudden feeling of security. But before he had fairly stood upright, a commonsense reflection occurred to him and drove him back into despair. He thought: "If I give way now to that brute of a soldier, he will begin this horror again tomorrow—and the day after—every day—raise other pretensions, trample on me, torture me, make me his slave—and I will be lost! Lost! The steamer may not come for days—may never come." He shook so that he had to sit down on the floor again. He shivered forlornly. He felt he could not, would not move any more. He was completely distracted by the sudden perception that the position was without issue—that death and life had in a moment become equally difficult and terrible.

All at once he heard the other push his chair back; and he leaped to his feet with extreme facility. He listened and got confused. Must run again! Right or left? He heard footsteps. He darted to the left, grasping his revolver, and at the very same instant, as it seemed to him, they came into violent collision. Both shouted with surprise. A loud explosion took place between them; a roar of red fire, thick smoke; and Kayerts, deafened and blinded, rushed back thinking: "I am hit—it's all over." He expected the other to come round—to gloat over his agony. He caught hold of an upright of the roof—"All over!" Then he heard a crashing fall on the other side of the house, as if somebody had tumbled headlong over a chair—then silence. Nothing more happened. He did not die. Only his shoulder felt as if it had been badly wrenched, and he had lost his revolver. He was disarmed and helpless! He waited for his fate. The other man made no sound. It was a stratagem. He was stalking him now! Along what side? Perhaps he was taking aim this very minute!

After a few moments of an agony frightful and absurd, he decided to go and meet his doom. He was prepared for every surrender. He turned the corner, steadying himself with one hand on the wall; made a few paces, and nearly swooned. He had seen on the floor, protruding past the other corner, a pair of turned-up feet. A pair of white naked feet in red slippers. He felt deadly sick, and stood for a time in profound darkness. Then Makola appeared before him, saying quietly: "Come along, Mr. Kayerts. He is dead." He burst into tears of gratitude; a loud, sobbing fit of crying. After a time he found himself sitting in a chair and looking at Carlier, who lay stretched on his back. Makola was kneeling over the body.

"Is this your revolver?" asked Makola, getting up.

"Yes," said Kayerts; then he added very quickly, "He ran after me to shoot me—you saw!"

"Yes, I saw," said Makola. "There is only one revolver; where's his?"

"Don't know," whispered Kayerts in a voice that had become suddenly very faint.

"I will go and look for it," said the other gently. He made the round along the verandah, while Kayerts sat still and looked at the corpse. Makola came back empty-handed, stood in deep thought, then stepped quietly into the dead man's room, and came out directly with a revolver, which he held up before Kayerts. Kayerts shut his eyes. Everything was going round. He found life more terrible and difficult than death. He had shot an unarmed man.

After meditating for a while, Makola said softly, pointing at the dead man who lay there with his right eye blown out:

"He died of fever." Kayerts looked at him with a stony stare. "Yes," repeated Makola, thoughtfully, stepping over the corpse, "I think he died of fever. Bury him to-morrow."

And he went away slowly to his expectant wife, leaving the two white men alone on the verandah.

Night came, and Kayerts sat unmoving on his chair. He sat quiet as if he had taken a dose of opium. The violence of the emotions he had passed through produced a feeling of exhausted serenity. He had plumbed in one short afternoon the depths of horror and despair, and now found repose in the conviction that life had no more secrets for him: neither had death! He sat by the corpse thinking; thinking very actively, thinking very new thoughts. He seemed to have broken loose from himself altogether. His old thoughts, convictions, likes and dislikes, things he respected and things he abhorred, appeared in their true light at last! Appeared contemptible and childish, false and ridiculous. He revelled in his new wisdom while he sat by the man he had killed. He argued with himself about all things under heaven with that kind of wrong-headed lucidity which may be observed in some lunatics. Incidentally he reflected that the fellow dead there had been a noxious beast anyway; that men died every day in thousands; perhaps in hundreds of thousands—who could tell?—and that in the number, that one death could not possibly make any difference; couldn't have any importance, at least to a thinking creature. He, Kayerts, was a thinking creature. He had been all his life, till that moment, a believer in a lot of nonsense like the rest of mankind—who are fools; but now he thought! He knew! He was at peace; he was familiar with the highest wisdom! Then he tried to imagine himself dead, and Carlier sitting in his chair watching him; and his attempt met with such unexpected success, that in a very few moments he became not at all sure who was dead and who was alive. This extraordinary achievement of his fancy startled him, however, and by a clever and timely effort of mind he saved himself just in time from becoming Carlier. His heart thumped, and he felt hot all over at the thought of that danger. Carlier! What a beastly thing! To compose his now disturbed nerves—and no wonder!—he tried to whistle a little. Then, suddenly, he fell asleep, or thought he had slept, but at any rate there was a fog, and somebody had whistled in the fog.

He stood up. The day had come, and a heavy mist had descended upon the land: the mist penetrating, enveloping, and silent; the morning mist of tropical lands; the mist that clings and kills; the mist white and deadly, immaculate and poisonous. He stood up, saw the body, and threw his arms above his head with a cry like that of a man who, waking from a trance, finds himself immured forever in a tomb. "*Help!* . . . *My God!*"

A shriek inhuman, vibrating and sudden, pierced like a sharp dart the white shroud of that land of sorrow. Three short, impatient screeches followed, and then, for a time, the fog-wreaths rolled on, undisturbed, through a formidable silence. Then many more shrieks, rapid and piercing, like the yells of some exasperated and ruthless creature, rent the air. Progress was calling to Kayerts from the river. Progress and civilization and all the virtues. Society was calling to its accomplished child to come, to be taken care of, to be instructed, to be judged, to be condemned; it called him to return to that rubbish heap from which he had wandered away, so that justice could be done.

Kayerts heard and understood. He stumbled out of the verandah, leaving the other man quite alone for the first time since they had been thrown there together. He groped his way through the fog, calling in his ignorance upon the invisible heaven to undo its work. Makola flitted by in the mist, shouting as he ran:

"Steamer! Steamer! They can't see. They whistle for the station. I go ring the bell. Go down to the landing, sir. I ring."

He disappeared. Kayerts stood still. He looked upwards; the fog rolled low over his head. He looked round like a man who has lost his way; and he saw a dark smudge, a cross-shaped stain, upon the shifting purity of the mist. As he began to stumble towards it, the station bell rang in a tumultuous peal its answer to the impatient clamour of the steamer.

The Managing Director of the Great Civilizing Company (since we know that civilization follows trade) landed first, and incontinently lost sight of the steamer. The fog down by the river was exceedingly dense; above, at the station, the bell rang unceasing and brazen.

The Director shouted loudly to the steamer:

"There is nobody down to meet us; there may be something wrong, though they are ringing. You had better come, too!"

And he began to toil up the steep bank. The captain and the engine driver of the boat followed behind. As they scrambled up the fog thinned, and they could see their Director a good way ahead. Suddenly they saw him start forward, calling to them over his shoulder: "Run! Run to the house! I've found one of them. Run, look for the other!"

He had found one of them! And even he, the man of varied and startling experience, was somewhat discomposed by the manner of this finding. He stood and fumbled in his pockets (for a knife) while he faced Kayerts, who was hanging by a leather strap from the cross. He had evidently climbed the grave, which was high and narrow, and after tying the end of the strap to the arm, had swung himself off. His toes were only a couple of inches above the ground; his arms hung stiffly down; he seemed to be standing rigidly at attention, but with one purple cheek playfully posed on the shoulder. And, irreverently, he was putting out a swollen tongue at his Managing Director.

Youth

A NARRATIVE

". . . But the Dwarf answered: No; something human is dearer to me than the wealth of all the world." GRIMM'S TALES.

TO MY WIFE

This could have occurred nowhere but in England, where men and sea interpenetrate, so to speak—the sea entering into the life of most men, and the men knowing something or everything about the sea, in the way of amusement, of travel, or of breadwinning.

We were sitting round a mahogany table that reflected the bottle, the claret glasses, and our faces as we leaned on our elbows. There was a director of companies, an accountant, a lawyer, Marlow, and myself. The director had been a *Conway* boy, the accountant had served four years at sea, the lawyer—a fine crusted Tory, High Churchman, the best of old fellows, the soul of honor—had been chief officer in the P. & O. service in the good old days when mailboats were square-rigged at least on two masts, and used to come down the China Sea before a fair monsoon with stun'sails set alow and aloft. We all began life in the merchant service. Between the five of us there was the strong bond of the sea, and also the fellowship of the craft, which no amount of enthusiasm for yachting, cruising, and so on can give, since one is only the amusement of life and the other is life itself.

Marlow (at least I think that is how he spelt his name) told the story, or rather the chronicle, of a voyage:

"Yes, I have seen a little of the Eastern seas; but what I remember best is my first voyage there. You fellows know there are those voyages that seem ordered for the illustration of life, that might stand for a symbol of existence. You fight, work, sweat, nearly kill yourself, sometimes do kill yourself, trying to accomplish something—and you can't. Not from any fault of yours. You simply can do nothing, neither great nor little—not a thing in the world—not even marry an old maid, or get a wretched 600-ton cargo of coal to its port of destination.

"It was altogether a memorable affair. It was my first voyage to the East, and my first voyage as second mate; it was also my skipper's first command. You'll admit it was time. He was sixty if a day; a little man, with a broad, not very straight back, with bowed shoulders and one leg more bandy than the other, he had that queer twisted-about appearance you see so often in men who work in the fields. He had a nutcracker face—chin and nose trying to come together over a sunken mouth—and it was framed in iron-gray fluffy hair, that looked like a chin strap of cotton-wool sprinkled with coal-dust. And he had blue eyes in that old face of his, which were amazingly like a boy's, with that candid expression some quite common men preserve to the end of their days by a rare internal gift of simplicity of heart and rectitude of soul. What induced him to accept me was a wonder. I had come out of a crack Australian clipper, where I had been third officer, and he seemed to have a prejudice against crack clippers as aristocratic and high-toned. He said to me, 'You know, in this ship you will have to work.' I said I had to work in every ship I had ever been in. 'Ah, but this is different, and you gentlemen out of them big ships; . . . but there! I dare say you will do. Join tomorrow.'

"I joined tomorrow. It was twenty-two years ago; and I was just twenty. How time passes! It was one of the happiest days of my life. Fancy! Second mate for the first time—a really responsible officer! I wouldn't have thrown up my new billet for a fortune. The mate looked me over carefully. He was also an old chap, but of another stamp. He had a Roman nose, a snow-white, long beard, and his name was Mahon, but he insisted that it should be pronounced Mann. He was well connected; yet there was something wrong with his luck, and he had never got on.

"As to the captain, he had been for years in coasters, then in the Mediterranean, and last in the West Indian trade. He had never been round the Capes. He could just write a kind of sketchy hand, and didn't care for writing at all. Both were thorough good seamen of course, and between those two old chaps I felt like a small boy between two grandfathers.

"The ship also was old. Her name was the *Judea*. Queer name, isn't it? She belonged to a man Wilmer, Wilcox—some name like that; but he has been bankrupt and dead these twenty years or more, and his name don't matter. She had been laid up in Shadwell basin for ever so long. You may imagine her state. She was all rust, dust, grime—soot aloft, dirt on deck. To me it was like coming out of a palace into a ruined cottage. She was about 400 tons, had a primitive windlass, wooden latches to the doors, not a bit of brass about her, and a big square stern. There was on it, below her name in big letters, a lot of scroll work, with the gilt off, and some sort of a coat of arms, with the motto 'Do or Die' underneath. I remember it took my fancy immensely. There was a touch of romance in it, something that made me love the old thing—something that appealed to my youth!

"We left London in ballast—sand ballast—to load a cargo of coal in a northern port for Bankok. Bankok! I thrilled. I had been six years at sea, but had only seen Melbourne and Sydney, very good places, charming places in their way—but Bankok!

"We worked out of the Thames under canvas, with a North Sea pilot on board. His name was Jermyn, and he dodged all day long about the galley drying his handkerchief before the stove. Apparently he never slept. He was a dismal man, with a perpetual tear sparkling at the end of his nose, who either had been in trouble, or was in trouble, or expected to be in trouble—couldn't be happy unless something went wrong. He mistrusted my youth, my common sense, and my seamanship, and made a point of showing it in a hundred little ways. I dare say he was right. It seems to me I knew very little then, and I know not much more now; but I cherish a hate for that Jermyn to this day.

"We were a week working up as far as Yarmouth Roads, and then we got into a gale—the famous October gale of twenty-two years ago. It was wind, lightning, sleet, snow, and a terrific sea. We were flying light, and you may imagine how bad it was when I tell you we had smashed bulwarks and a flooded deck. On the second night she shifted her ballast into the lee bow, and by that time we had been blown off somewhere on the Dogger Bank. There was nothing for it but go below with shovels and try to right her, and there we were in that vast hold, gloomy like a cavern, the tallow dips stuck and flickering on the beams, the gale howling above, the ship tossing about like mad on her side; there we all were, Jermyn, the captain, everyone, hardly able to keep our feet, engaged on that gravedigger's work, and trying to toss shovelfuls of wet sand up to windward. At every tumble of the ship you could see vaguely in the dim light men falling down with a great flourish of shovels. One of the ship's boys (we had two), impressed by the weirdness of the scene, wept as if his heart would break. We could hear him blubbering somewhere in the shadows.

"On the third day the gale died out, and by and by a north-country tug picked us up. We took sixteen days in all to get from London to the Tyne! When we got into dock we had lost our turn for loading, and they hauled us off to a tier where we remained for a month. Mrs. Beard (the captain's name was Beard) came from Colchester to see the old man. She lived on board. The crew of runners had left, and there remained only the officers, one boy, and the steward, a mulatto who answered to the name of Abraham. Mrs. Beard was an old woman, with a face all wrinkled and ruddy like a winter apple, and the figure of a young girl. She caught sight of me once, sewing on a button, and insisted on having my shirts to repair. This was something different from the captains' wives I had known on board crack clippers. When I brought her the shirts, she said: 'And the socks? They want mending, I am sure, and John's—Captain Beard's—things are all in order now. I would be glad of something to do.' Bless the old woman! She overhauled my outfit for me, and meantime I read for the first time *Sartor Resartus* and Burnaby's *Ride to Khiva*. I didn't understand much of the first then; but I remember I preferred the soldier to the philosopher at the time; a preference which life has only confirmed. One was a man, and the other was either more—or less. However, they are both dead and Mrs. Beard is dead, and youth, strength, genius, thoughts, achievements, simple hearts—all dies. . . . No matter.

"They loaded us at last. We shipped a crew. Eight able seamen and two boys. We hauled off one evening to the buoys at the dock gates, ready to go out, and with a fair prospect of beginning the voyage next day. Mrs. Beard was to start for home by a late train. When the ship was fast we went to tea. We sat rather silent through the meal—Mahon, the old couple, and I. I finished first, and slipped away for a smoke, my cabin being in a deckhouse just against the poop. It was high water, blowing fresh with a drizzle; the double dockgates were opened, and the steam colliers were going in and out in the darkness with their lights burning bright, a great plashing of propellers, rattling of winches, and a lot of hailing on the pier-heads. I watched the procession of headlights gliding high and of green lights gliding low in the night, when suddenly a red gleam flashed at me, vanished, came into view again, and remained. The fore end of a steamer loomed up close. I shouted down the cabin, 'Come up, quick!' and then heard a startled voice saying afar in the dark, 'Stop her, sir.' A bell jingled. Another voice cried warningly, 'We are going right into that bark, sir.' The answer to this was a gruff 'All right,' and the next thing was a heavy crash as the steamer struck a glancing blow with the bluff of her bow about our forerigging. There was a moment of confusion, yelling, and running about. Steam roared. Then somebody was heard saying, 'All clear, sir.' . . . 'Are you all right?' asked the gruff voice. I had jumped forward to see the damage, and hailed back, 'I think so.' 'Easy astern,' said the gruff voice. A bell jingled. 'What steamer is that?' screamed Mahon. By that time she was no more to us than a bulky shadow maneuvering a little way off. They shouted at us some name—a woman's name, Miranda or Melissa—or some such thing. 'This means another month in this beastly hole,' said Mahon to me, as we peered with lamps about the splintered bulwarks and broken braces. 'But where's the captain?'

"We had not heard or seen anything of him all that time. We went aft to look. A doleful voice arose hailing somewhere in the middle of the dock, '*Judea* ahoy!' . . . How the devil did he get there? . . . 'Hallo!' we shouted. 'I am adrift in our boat without oars,' he cried. A belated waterman offered his services, and Mahon struck a bargain with him for a half crown to tow our skipper alongside; but it was Mrs. Beard that came up the ladder first. They had been floating about the dock in that mizzly cold rain for nearly an hour. I was never so surprised in my life.

"It appears that when he heard my shout 'Come up,' he understood at once what was the matter, caught up his wife, ran on deck, and across, and down into our boat, which was fast to the ladder. Not bad for a sixty-year-old. Just imagine that old fellow saving heroically in his arms that old woman—the woman of his life. He set her down on a thwart, and was ready to climb back on board when the painter came adrift somehow, and away they went together. Of course in the confusion we did not hear him shouting. He looked abashed. She said cheerfully, 'I suppose it does not matter my losing the train now?' 'No, Jenny—you go below and get warm,' he growled. Then to us: 'A sailor has no business with a wife—I say. There I was, out of the ship. Well, no harm done this time. Let's go and look at what that fool of a steamer smashed.'

"It wasn't much, but it delayed us three weeks. At the end of that time, the captain being engaged with his agents, I carried Mrs. Beard's bag to the railway station and put her all comfy into a third-class carriage. She lowered the window to say, 'You are a good young man. If you see John—Captain Beard—without his muffler at night, just remind him from me to keep his throat well wrapped up.' 'Certainly, Mrs. Beard,' I said. 'You are a good young man; I noticed how attentive you are to John—to Captain—' The train pulled out suddenly; I took my cap off to the old woman: I never saw her again . . . Pass the bottle.

"We went to sea next day. When we made that start for Bankok we had been already three months out of London. We had expected to be a fortnight or so—at the outside.

"It was January, and the weather was beautiful—the beautiful sunny winter weather that has more charm than in the summertime, because it is unexpected, and crisp, and you know it won't, it can't, last long. It's like a windfall, like a godsend, like an unexpected piece of luck.

"It lasted all down the North Sea, all down Channel; and it lasted till we were three hundred miles or so to the westward of the Lizards; then the wind went round to the sou'west and began to pipe up. In two days it blew a gale. The *Judea*, hove to, wallowed on the Atlantic like an old candle-box. It blew day after day: it blew with spite, without interval, without mercy, without rest. The world was nothing but an immensity of great foaming waves rushing at us, under a sky low enough to touch with the hand and dirty like a smoked ceiling. In the stormy space surrounding us there was as much flying spray as air. Day after day and night after night there was nothing round the ship but the howl of the wind, the tumult of the sea, the noise of water pouring over her deck. There was no rest for her and no rest for us. She tossed, she pitched, she stood on her head, she sat on her tail, she rolled, she groaned, and we had to hold on while on deck and cling to our bunks when below, in a constant effort of body and worry of mind.

"One night Mahon spoke through the small window of my berth. It opened right into my very bed, and I was lying there sleepless, in my boots, feeling as though I had not slept for years, and could not if I tried. He said excitedly:

"'You got the sounding rod in here, Marlow? I can't get the pumps to suck. By God! It's no child's play.'

"I gave him the sounding rod and lay down again, trying to think of various things—but I thought only of the pumps. When I came on deck they were still at it, and my watch relieved at the pumps. By the light of the lantern brought on deck to examine the sounding rod I caught a glimpse of their weary, serious faces. We pumped all the four hours. We pumped all night, all day, all the week—watch and watch. She was working herself loose, and leaked badly—not enough to drown us at once, but enough to kill us with the work at the pumps. And while we pumped the ship was going from us piecemeal: the bulwarks went, the stanchions were torn out, the ventilators smashed, the cabin door burst in. There was not a dry spot in the ship. She was being gutted bit by bit. The longboat changed, as if by magic, into matchwood where she stood in her gripes. I had lashed her myself, and was rather proud of my handiwork, which had withstood so long the malice of the sea. And we pumped. And there was no break in the weather. The sea was white like a sheet of foam, like a caldron of boiling milk; there was not a break in the clouds, no—not the size of a man's hand—no, not for so much as ten seconds. There was for us no sky, there were for us no stars, no sun, no universe—nothing but angry clouds and an infuriated sea. We pumped watch and watch, for dear life; and it seemed to last for months, for years, for all eternity, as though we had been dead and gone to a hell for sailors. We forgot the day of the week, the name of the month, what year it was, and whether we had ever been ashore. The sails blew away, she lay broadside on under a weather cloth, the ocean poured over her, and we did not care. We turned those handles, and had the eyes of idiots. As soon as we had crawled on deck I used to take a round turn with a rope about the men, the pumps, and the mainmast, and we turned, we turned incessantly, with the water to our waists, to our necks, over our heads. It was all one. We had forgotten how it felt to be dry.

"And there was somewhere in me the thought: By Jove! This is the deuce of an adventure—something you read about; and it is my first voyage as second mate—and I am only twenty—and here I am lasting it out as well as any of these men, and keeping my chaps up to the mark. I was pleased. I would not have given up the experience for worlds. I had moments of exultation. Whenever the old dismantled craft pitched heavily with her counter high in the air, she seemed to me to throw up, like an appeal, like a defiance, like a cry to the clouds without mercy, the words written on her stern: '*Judea*, London. Do or Die.'

"O youth! The strength of it, the faith of it, the imagination of it! To me she was not an old rattletrap carting about the world a lot of coal for a freight—to me she was the endeavor, the test, the trial of life. I think of her with pleasure, with affection, with regret—as you would think of someone dead you have loved. I shall never forget her. . . . Pass the bottle.

"One night when tied to the mast, as I explained, we were pumping on, deafened with the wind, and without spirit enough in us to wish ourselves dead, a heavy sea crashed aboard and swept clean over us. As soon as I got my breath I shouted, as in duty bound, 'Keep on, boys!' when suddenly I felt something hard floating on deck strike the calf of my leg. I made a grab at it and missed. It was so dark we could not see each other's faces within a foot—you understand.

"After that thump the ship kept quiet for a while, and the thing, whatever it was, struck my leg again. This time I caught it—and it was a saucepan. At first, being stupid with fatigue and thinking of nothing but the pumps, I did not understand what I had in my hand. Suddenly it dawned upon me, and I shouted, 'Boys, the house on deck is gone. Leave this, and let's look for the cook.'

"There was a deckhouse forward, which contained the galley, the cook's berth, and the quarters of the crew. As we had expected for days to see it swept away, the hands had been ordered to sleep in the cabin—the only safe place in the ship. The steward, Abraham, however, persisted in clinging to his berth, stupidly, like a mule—from sheer fright I believe, like an animal that won't leave a stable falling in an earthquake. So we went to look for him. It was chancing death, since once out of our lashings we were as exposed as if on a raft. But we went. The house was shattered as if a shell had exploded inside. Most of it had gone overboard—stove, men's quarters, and their property, all was gone; but two posts, holding a portion of the bulkhead to which Abraham's bunk was attached, remained as if by a miracle. We groped in the ruins and came upon this, and there he was, sitting in his bunk, surrounded by foam and wreckage, jabbering cheerfully to himself. He was out of his mind; completely and forever mad, with this sudden shock coming upon the fag-end of his endurance. We snatched him up, lugged him aft, and pitched him headfirst down the cabin companion. You understand there was no time to carry him down with infinite precautions and wait to see how he got on. Those below would pick him up at the bottom of the stairs all right. We were in a hurry to go back to the pumps. That business could not wait. A bad leak is an inhuman thing.

"One would think that the sole purpose of that fiendish gale had been to make a lunatic of that poor devil of a mulatto. It eased before morning, and next day the sky cleared, and as the sea went down the leak took up. When it came to bending a fresh set of sails the crew demanded to put back—and really there was nothing else to do. Boats gone, decks swept clean, cabin gutted, men without a stitch but what they stood in, stores spoiled, ship strained. We put her head for home, and—would you believe it? The wind came east right in our teeth. It blew fresh, it blew continuously. We had to beat up every inch of the way, but she did not leak so badly, the water keeping comparatively smooth. Two hours' pumping in every four is no joke—but it kept her afloat as far as Falmouth.

"The good people there live on casualties of the sea, and no doubt were glad to see us. A hungry crowd of shipwrights sharpened their chisels at the sight of that carcass of a ship. And, by Jove! they had pretty pickings off us before they were done. I fancy the owner was already in a tight place. There were delays. Then it was decided to take part of the cargo out and calk her topsides. This was done, the repairs finished, cargo reshipped; a new crew came on board, and we went out—for Bankok. At the end of a week we were back again. The crew said they weren't going to Bankok—a hundred and fifty days' passage—in a something hooker that wanted pumping eight hours out of the twenty-four; and the nautical papers inserted again the little paragraph: '*Judea*. Bark. Tyne to Bankok; coals; put back to Falmouth leaky and with crew refusing duty.'

"There were more delays—more tinkering. The owner came down for a day, and said she was as right as a little fiddle. Poor old Captain Beard looked like the ghost of a Geordie skipper—through the worry and humiliation of it. Remember he was sixty, and it was his first command. Mahon said it was a foolish business, and would end badly. I loved the ship more than ever, and wanted awfully to get to Bankok. To Bankok! Magic name, blessed name. Mesopotamia wasn't a patch on it. Remember I was twenty, and it was my first second mate's billet, and the East was waiting for me.

"We went out and anchored in the outer roads with a fresh crew—the third. She leaked worse than ever. It was as if those confounded shipwrights had actually made a hole in her. This time we did not even go outside. The crew simply refused to man the windlass.

"They towed us back to the inner harbor, and we became a fixture, a feature, an institution of the place. People pointed us out to visitors as 'That 'ere bark that's going to Bankok—has been here six months—put back three times.' On holidays the small boys pulling about in boats would hail, '*Judea*, ahoy!' and if a head showed above the rail shouted, 'Where you bound to?—Bankok?' and jeered. We were only three on board. The poor old skipper mooned in the cabin. Mahon undertook the cooking, and unexpectedly developed all a Frenchman's genius for preparing nice little messes. I looked languidly after the rigging. We became citizens of Falmouth. Every shopkeeper knew us. At the barber's or tobacconist's they asked familiarly, 'Do you think you will ever get to Bankok?' Meantime the owner, the underwriters, and the charterers squabbled amongst themselves in London, and our pay went on. . . . Pass the bottle.

"It was horrid. Morally it was worse than pumping for life. It seemed as though we had been forgotten by the world, belonged to nobody, would get nowhere; it seemed that, as if bewitched, we would have to live for ever and ever in that inner harbor, a derision and a by-word to generations of long-shore loafers and dishonest boatmen. I obtained three months' pay and a five days' leave, and made a rush for London. It took me a day to get there and pretty well another to come back—but three months' pay went all the same. I don't know what I did with it. I went to a music-hall, I believe, lunched, dined, and supped in a swell place in Regent Street, and was back to time, with nothing but a complete set of Byron's works and a new railway rug to show for three months' work. The boatman who pulled me off to the ship said: 'Hallo! I thought you had left the old thing. *She* will never get to Bankok.' 'That's all *you* know about it,' I said scornfully—but I didn't like that prophecy at all.

"Suddenly a man, some kind of agent to somebody, appeared with full powers. He had grog-blossoms all over his face, an indomitable energy, and was a jolly soul. We leaped into life again. A hulk came alongside, took our cargo, and then we went into dry dock to get our copper stripped. No wonder she leaked. The poor thing, strained beyond endurance by the gale, had, as if in disgust, spat out all the oakum of her lower seams. She was recalked, new-coppered, and made as tight as a bottle. We went back to the hulk and reshipped our cargo.

"Then on a fine moonlight night, all the rats left the ship.

"We had been infested with them. They had destroyed our sails, consumed more stores than the crew, affably shared our beds and our dangers, and now, when the ship was made seaworthy, concluded to clear out. I called Mahon to enjoy the spectacle. Rat after rat appeared on our rail, took a last look over his shoulder, and leaped with a hollow thud into the empty hulk. We tried to count them, but soon lost the tale. Mahon said: 'Well, well! don't talk to me about the intelligence of rats. They ought to have left before, when we had that narrow squeak from foundering. There you have the proof how silly is the superstition about them. They leave a good ship for an old rotten hulk, where there is nothing to eat, too, the fools! . . . I don't believe they know what is safe or what is good for them, any more than you or I.'

"And after some more talk we agreed that the wisdom of rats had been grossly overrated, being in fact no greater than that of men.

"The story of the ship was known, by this, all up the Channel from Land's End to the Forelands, and we could get no crew on the south coast. They sent us one all complete from Liverpool, and we left once more—for Bankok.

"We had fair breezes, smooth water right into the tropics, and the old *Judea* lumbered along in the sunshine. When she went eight knots everything cracked aloft, and we tied our caps to our heads; but mostly she strolled on at the rate of three miles an hour. What could you expect? She was tired—that old ship. Her youth was where mine is—where yours is—you fellows who listen to this yarn; and what friend would throw your years and your weariness in your face? We didn't grumble at her. To us aft, at least, it seemed as though we had been born in her, reared in her, had lived in her for ages, had never known any other ship. I would just as soon have abused the old village church at home for not being a cathedral.

"And for me there was also my youth to make me patient. There was all the East before me, and all life, and the thought that I had been tried in that ship and had come out pretty well. And I thought of men of old who, centuries ago, went that road in ships that sailed no better, to the land of palms, and spices, and yellow sands, and of brown nations ruled by kings more cruel than Nero the Roman and more splendid than Solomon the Jew. The old bark lumbered on, heavy with her age and the burden of her cargo, while I lived the life of youth in ignorance and hope. She lumbered on through an interminable procession of days; and the fresh gilding flashed back at the setting sun, seemed to cry out over the darkening sea the words painted on her stern, '*Judea*, London. Do or Die.'

"Then we entered the Indian Ocean and steered northerly for Java Head. The winds were light. Weeks slipped by. She crawled on, do or die, and people at home began to think of posting us as overdue.

"One Saturday evening, I being off duty, the men asked me to give them an extra bucket of water or so—for washing clothes. As I did not wish to screw on the fresh-water pump so late, I went forward whistling, and with a key in my hand to unlock the forepeak scuttle, intending to serve the water out of a spare tank we kept there.

"The smell down below was as unexpected as it was frightful. One would have thought hundreds of paraffin-lamps had been flaring and smoking in that hole for days. I was glad to get out. The man with me coughed and said, 'Funny smell, sir.' I answered negligently, 'It's good for the health, they say,' and walked aft.

"The first thing I did was to put my head down the square of the midship ventilator. As I lifted the lid a visible breath, something like a thin fog, a puff of faint haze, rose from the opening. The ascending air was hot, and had a heavy, sooty, paraffiny smell. I gave one sniff, and put down the lid gently. It was no use choking myself. The cargo was on fire.

"Next day she began to smoke in earnest. You see it was to be expected, for though the coal was of a safe kind, that cargo had been so handled, so broken up with handling, that it looked more like smithy coal than anything else. Then it had been wetted—more than once. It rained all the time we were taking it back from the hulk, and now with this long passage it got heated, and there was another case of spontaneous combustion.

"The captain called us into the cabin. He had a chart spread on the table, and looked unhappy. He said, 'The coast of West Australia is near, but I mean to proceed to our destination. It is the hurricane month too; but we will just keep her head for Bankok, and fight the fire. No more putting back anywhere, if we all get roasted. We will try first to stifle this 'ere damned combustion by want of air.'

"We tried. We battened down everything, and still she smoked. The smoke kept coming out through imperceptible crevices; it forced itself through bulkheads and covers; it oozed here and there and everywhere in slender threads, in an invisible film, in an incomprehensible manner. It made its way into the cabin, into the forecastle; it poisoned the sheltered places on the deck, it could be sniffed as high as the mainyard. It was clear that if the smoke came out the air came in. This was disheartening. This combustion refused to be stifled.

"We resolved to try water, and took the hatches off. Enormous volumes of smoke, whitish, yellowish, thick, greasy, misty, choking, ascended as high as the trucks. All hands cleared out aft. Then the poisonous cloud blew away, and we went back to work in a smoke that was no thicker now than that of an ordinary factory chimney.

"We rigged the force pump, got the hose along, and by and by it burst. Well, it was as old as the ship—a prehistoric hose, and past repair. Then we pumped with the feeble head pump, drew water with buckets, and in this way managed in time to pour lots of Indian Ocean into the main hatch. The bright stream flashed in sunshine, fell into a layer of white crawling smoke, and vanished on the black surface of coal. Steam ascended mingling with the smoke. We poured salt water as into a barrel without a bottom. It was our fate to pump in that ship, to pump out of her, to pump into her; and after keeping water out of her to save ourselves from being drowned, we frantically poured water into her to save ourselves from being burnt.

"And she crawled on, do or die, in the serene weather. The sky was a miracle of purity, a miracle of azure. The sea was polished, was blue, was pellucid, was sparkling like a precious stone, extending on all sides, all round to the horizon—as if the whole terrestrial globe had been one jewel, one colossal sapphire, a single gem fashioned into a planet. And on the luster of the great calm waters the *Judea* glided imperceptibly, enveloped in languid and unclean vapors, in a lazy cloud that drifted to leeward, light and slow: a pestiferous cloud defiling the splendor of sea and sky.

"All this time of course we saw no fire. The cargo smoldered at the bottom somewhere. Once Mahon, as we were working side by side, said to me with a queer smile: 'Now, if she only would spring a tidy leak—like that time when we first left the Channel—it would put a stopper on this fire. Wouldn't it?' I remarked irrelevantly, 'Do you remember the rats?'

"We fought the fire and sailed the ship too as carefully as though nothing had been the matter. The steward cooked and attended on us. Of the other twelve men, eight worked while four rested. Everyone took his turn, captain included. There was equality, and if not exactly fraternity, then a deal of good feeling. Sometimes a man, as he dashed a bucketful of water down the hatchway, would yell out, 'Hurrah for Bankok!' and the rest laughed. But generally we were taciturn and serious—and thirsty. Oh! how thirsty! And we had to be careful with the water. Strict allowance. The ship smoked, the sun blazed. . . . Pass the bottle.

"We tried everything. We even made an attempt to dig down to the fire. No good, of course. No man could remain more than a minute below. Mahon, who went first, fainted there, and the man who went to fetch him out did likewise. We lugged them out on deck. Then I leaped down to show how easily it could be done. They had learned wisdom by that time, and contented themselves by fishing for me with a chain-hook tied to a broom-handle, I believe. I did not offer to go and fetch up my shovel, which was left down below.

"Things began to look bad. We put the longboat into the water. The second boat was ready to swing out. We had also another, a fourteen-foot thing, on davits aft, where it was quite safe.

"Then, behold, the smoke suddenly decreased. We re-doubled our efforts to flood the bottom of the ship. In two days there was no smoke at all. Everybody was on the broad grin. This was on a Friday. On Saturday no work, but sailing the ship of course, was done. The men washed their clothes and their faces for the first time in a fortnight, and had a special dinner given them. They spoke of spontaneous combustion with contempt, and implied *they* were the boys to put out combustions. Somehow we all felt as though we each had inherited a large fortune. But a beastly smell of burning hung about the ship. Captain Beard had hollow eyes and sunken cheeks. I had never noticed so much before how twisted and bowed he was. He and Mahon prowled soberly about hatches and ventilators, sniffing. It struck me suddenly poor Mahon was a very, very old chap. As to me, I was as pleased and proud as though I had helped to win a great naval battle. O Youth!

"The night was fine. In the morning a homeward-bound ship passed us hull down—the first we had seen for months; but we were nearing the land at last, Java Head being about 190 miles off, and nearly due north.

"Next day it was my watch on deck from eight to twelve. At breakfast the captain observed, 'It's wonderful how that smell hangs about the cabin.' About ten, the mate being on the poop, I stepped down on the main deck for a moment. The carpenter's bench stood abaft the mainmast: I leaned against it sucking at my pipe, and the carpenter, a young chap, came to talk to me. He remarked, 'I think we have done very well, haven't we?' and then I perceived with annoyance the fool was trying to tilt the bench. I said curtly, 'Don't, Chips,' and immediately became aware of a queer sensation, of an absurd delusion—I seemed somehow to be in the air. I heard all round me like a pent-up breath released—as if a thousand giants simultaneously had said Phoo!—and felt a dull concussion which made my ribs ache suddenly. No doubt about it—I was in the air, and my body was describing a short parabola. But short as it was, I had the time to think several thoughts in, as far as I can remember, the following order: 'This can't be the carpenter—What is it?—Some accident—Submarine volcano?—Coals, gas!—By Jove! We are being blown up—Everybody's dead—I am falling into the afterhatch—I see fire in it.'

"The coal-dust suspended in the air of the hold had glowed dull-red at the moment of the explosion. In the twinkling of an eye, in an infinitesimal fraction of a second since the first tilt of the bench, I was sprawling full length on the cargo. I picked myself up and scrambled out. It was quick like a rebound. The deck was a wilderness of smashed timber, lying crosswise like trees in a wood after a hurricane; an immense curtain of soiled rags waved gently before me—it was the mainsail blown to strips. I thought: the masts will be toppling over directly; and to get out of the way bolted on all fours towards the poop ladder. The first person I saw was Mahon, with eyes like saucers, his mouth open, and the long white hair standing straight on end round his head like a silver halo. He was just about to go down when the sight of the main deck stirring, heaving up, and changing into splinters before his eyes, petrified him on the top step. I stared at him in unbelief, and he stared at me with a queer kind of shocked curiosity. I did not know that I had no hair, no eyebrows, no eyelashes, that my young moustache was burnt off, that my face was black, one cheek laid open, my nose cut, and my chin bleeding. I had lost my cap, one of my slippers, and my shirt was torn to rags. Of all this I was not aware. I was amazed to see the ship still afloat, the poop deck whole—and, most of all, to see anybody alive. Also the peace of the sky and the serenity of the sea were distinctly surprising. I suppose I expected to see them convulsed with horror. . . . Pass the bottle.

"There was a voice hailing the ship from somewhere—in the air, in the sky—I couldn't tell. Presently I saw the captain—and he was mad. He asked me eagerly, 'Where's the cabin table?' and to hear such a question was a frightful shock. I had just been blown up, you understand, and vibrated with that experience—I wasn't quite sure whether I was alive. Mahon began to stamp with both feet and yelled at him, 'Good God! don't you see the deck's blown out of her?' I found my voice, and stammered out as if conscious of some gross neglect of duty, 'I don't know where the cabin table is.' It was like an absurd dream.

"Do you know what he wanted next? Well, he wanted to trim the yards. Very placidly, and as if lost in thought, he insisted on having the foreyard squared. 'I don't know if there's anybody alive,' said Mahon, almost tearfully. 'Surely,' he said gently, 'there will be enough left to square the foreyard.'

"The old chap, it seems, was in his own berth, winding up the chronometers, when the shock sent him spinning. Immediately it occurred to him—as he said afterwards—that the ship had struck something, and he ran out into the cabin. There, he saw, the cabin table had vanished somewhere. The deck being blown up, it had fallen down into the lazarette of course. Where we had our breakfast that morning he saw only a great hole in the floor. This appeared to him so awfully mysterious, and impressed him so immensely, that what he saw and heard after he got on deck were mere trifles in comparison. And, mark, he noticed directly the wheel deserted and his bark off her course—and his only thought was to get that miserable, stripped, undecked, smoldering shell of a ship back again with her head pointing at her port of destination. Bankok! That's what he was after. I tell you this quiet, bowed, bandy-legged, almost deformed little man was immense in the singleness of his idea and in his placid ignorance of our agitation. He motioned us forward with a commanding gesture, and went to take the wheel himself.

"Yes; that was the first thing we did—trim the yards of that wreck! No one was killed, or even disabled, but everyone was more or less hurt. You should have seen them! Some were in rags, with black faces, like coal heavers, like sweeps, and had bullet heads that seemed closely cropped, but were in fact singed to the skin. Others, of the watch below, awakened by being shot out from their collapsing bunks, shivered incessantly, and kept on groaning even as we went about our work. But they all worked. That crew of Liverpool hard cases had in them the right stuff. It's my experience they always have. It is the sea that gives it—the vastness, the loneliness surrounding their dark stolid souls. Ah! Well! We stumbled, we crept, we fell, we barked our shins on the wreckage, we hauled. The masts stood, but we did not know how much they might be charred down below. It was nearly calm, but a long swell ran from the west and made her roll. They might go at any moment. We looked at them with apprehension. One could not foresee which way they would fall.

"Then we retreated aft and looked about us. The deck was a tangle of planks on edge, of planks on end, of splinters, of ruined woodwork. The masts rose from that chaos like big trees above a matted undergrowth. The interstices of that mass of wreckage were full of something whitish, sluggish, stirring—of something that was like a greasy fog. The smoke of the invisible fire was coming up again, was trailing, like a poisonous thick mist in some valley choked with dead wood. Already lazy wisps were beginning to curl upwards amongst the mass of splinters. Here and there a piece of timber, stuck upright, resembled a post. Half of a fife rail had been shot through the foresail, and the sky made a patch of glorious blue in the ignobly soiled canvas. A portion of several boards holding together had fallen across the rail, and one end protruded overboard, like a gangway leading upon nothing, like a gangway leading over the deep sea, leading to death—as if inviting us to walk the plank at once and be done with our ridiculous troubles. And still the air, the sky—a ghost, something invisible was hailing the ship.

"Someone had the sense to look over, and there was the helmsman, who had impulsively jumped overboard, anxious to come back. He yelled and swam lustily like a merman, keeping up with the ship. We threw him a rope, and presently he stood amongst us streaming with water and very crestfallen. The captain had surrendered the wheel, and apart, elbow on rail and chin in hand, gazed at the sea wistfully. We asked ourselves, What next? I thought, Now, this is something like. This is great. I wonder what will happen. O youth!

"Suddenly Mahon sighted a steamer far astern. Captain Beard said, 'We may do something with her yet.' We hoisted two flags, which said in the international language of the sea, 'On fire. Want immediate assistance.' The steamer grew bigger rapidly, and by and by spoke with two flags on her foremast, 'I am coming to your assistance.'

"In half an hour she was abreast, to windward, within hail, and rolling slightly, with her engines stopped. We lost our composure, and yelled all together with excitement, 'We've been blown up.' A man in a white helmet, on the bridge, cried, 'Yes! All right! all right!' and he nodded his head, and smiled, and made soothing motions with his hand as though at a lot of frightened children. One of the boats dropped in the water, and walked towards us upon the sea with her long oars. Four Calashes pulled a swinging stroke. This was my first sight of Malay seamen. I've known them since, but what struck me then was their unconcern: they came alongside, and even the bowman standing up and holding to our main chains with the boat hook did not deign to lift his head for a glance. I thought people who had been blown up deserved more attention.

"A little man, dry like a chip and agile like a monkey, clambered up. It was the mate of the steamer. He gave one look, and cried, 'O boys—you had better quit!'

"We were silent. He talked apart with the captain for a time— seemed to argue with him. Then they went away together to the steamer.

"When our skipper came back we learned that the steamer was the *Sommerville*, Captain Nash, from West Australia to Singapore via Batavia with mails, and that the agreement was she would tow us to Anjer or Batavia, if possible, where we could extinguish the fire by scuttling, and then proceed on our voyage—to Bankok! The old man seemed excited. 'We will do it yet,' he said to Mahon, fiercely. He shook his fist at the sky. Nobody else said a word.

"At noon the steamer began to tow. She went ahead slim and high, and what was left of the *Judea* followed at the end of seventy fathom of towrope—followed her swiftly like a cloud of smoke with mastheads protruding above. We went aloft to furl the sails. We coughed on the yards, and were careful about the bunts. Do you see the lot of us there, putting a neat furl on the sails of that ship doomed to arrive nowhere? There was not a man who didn't think that at any moment the masts would topple over. From aloft we could not see the ship for smoke, and they worked carefully, passing the gaskets with even turns. 'Harbor furl—aloft there!' cried Mahon from below.

"You understand this? I don't think one of those chaps expected to get down in the usual way. When we did I heard them saying to each other, 'Well, I thought we would come down overboard, in a lump—sticks and all—blame me if I didn't.' 'That's what I was thinking to myself,' would answer wearily another battered and bandaged scarecrow. And, mind, these were men without the drilled-in habit of obedience. To an onlooker they would be a lot of profane scallywags without a redeeming point. What made them do it—what made them obey me when I, thinking consciously how fine it was, made them drop the bunt of the foresail twice to try and do it better? What? They had no professional reputation—no examples, no praise. It wasn't a sense of duty; they all knew well enough how to shirk, and laze, and dodge—when they had a mind to it—and mostly they had. Was it the two pounds ten a month that sent them there? They didn't think their pay half good enough. No; it was something in them, something inborn and subtle and everlasting. I don't say positively that the crew of a French or German merchantman wouldn't have done it, but I doubt whether it would have been done in the same way. There was a completeness in it, something solid like a principle, and masterful like an instinct—a disclosure of something secret—of that hidden something, that gift, of good or evil that makes racial difference, that shapes the fate of nations.

"It was that night at ten that, for the first time since we had been fighting it, we saw the fire. The speed of the towing had fanned the smoldering destruction. A blue gleam appeared forward, shining below the wreck of the deck. It wavered in patches, it seemed to stir and creep like the light of a glowworm. I saw it first, and told Mahon. 'Then the game's up,' he said. 'We had better stop this towing, or she will burst out suddenly fore and aft before we can clear out.' We set up a yell; rang bells to attract their attention; they towed on. At last Mahon and I had to crawl forward and cut the rope with an ax. There was no time to cast off the lashings. Red tongues could be seen licking the wilderness of splinters under our feet as we made our way back to the poop.

"Of course they very soon found out in the steamer that the rope was gone. She gave a loud blast of her whistle, her lights were seen sweeping in a wide circle, she came up ranging close alongside, and stopped. We were all in a tight group on the poop looking at her. Every man had saved a little bundle or a bag. Suddenly a conical flame with a twisted top shot up forward and threw upon the black sea a circle of light, with the two vessels side by side and heaving gently in its center. Captain Beard had been sitting on the gratings still and mute for hours, but now he rose slowly and advanced in front of us, to the mizzen-shrouds. Captain Nash hailed: 'Come along! Look sharp. I have mailbags on board. I will take you and your boats to Singapore.'

"'Thank you!' said our skipper. 'We must see the last of the ship.'

"'I can't stand by any longer,' shouted the other. 'Mails—you know.'

"'Ay! ay! We are all right.'

"'Very well! I'll report you in Singapore. . . . Good-by!'

"He waved his hand. Our men dropped their bundles quietly. The steamer moved ahead, and passing out of the circle of light, vanished at once from our sight, dazzled by the fire which burned fiercely. And then I knew that I would see the East first as commander of a small boat. I thought it fine; and the fidelity to the old ship was fine. We should see the last of her. Oh the glamor of youth! Oh the fire of it, more dazzling than the flames of the burning ship, throwing a magic light on the wide earth, leaping audaciously to the sky, presently to be quenched by time, more cruel, more pitiless, more bitter than the sea— and like the flames of the burning ship surrounded by an impenetrable night.

"The old man warned us in his gentle and inflexible way that it was part of our duty to save for the underwriters as much as we could of the ship's gear. Accordingly we went to work aft, while she blazed forward to give us plenty of light. We lugged out a lot of rubbish. What didn't we save? An old barometer fixed with an absurd quantity of screws nearly cost me my life: a sudden rush of smoke came upon me, and I just got away in time. There were various stores, bolts of canvas, coils of rope; the poop looked like a marine bazaar, and the boats were lumbered to the gunwales. One would have thought the old man wanted to take as much as he could of his first command with him. He was very, very quiet, but off his balance evidently. Would you believe it? He wanted to take a length of old stream-cable and a kedge anchor with him in the longboat. We said, 'Ay, ay, sir,' deferentially, and on the quiet let the thing slip overboard. The heavy medicine chest went that way, two bags of green coffee, tins of paint—fancy, paint!—a whole lot of things. Then I was ordered with two hands into the boats to make a stowage and get them ready against the time it would be proper for us to leave the ship.

"We put everything straight, stepped the longboat's mast for our skipper, who was in charge of her, and I was not sorry to sit down for a moment. My face felt raw, every limb ached as if broken, I was aware of all my ribs, and would have sworn to a twist in the backbone. The boats, fast astern, lay in a deep shadow, and all around I could see the circle of the sea lighted by the fire. A gigantic flame arose forward straight and clear. It flared fierce, with noises like the whirr of wings, with rumbles as of thunder. There were cracks, detonations, and from the cone of flame the sparks flew upwards, as man is born to trouble, to leaky ships, and to ships that burn.

"What bothered me was that the ship, lying broadside to the swell and to such wind as there was—a mere breath—the boats would not keep astern where they were safe, but persisted, in a pigheaded way boats have, in getting under the counter and then swinging alongside. They were knocking about dangerously and coming near the flame, while the ship rolled on them, and, of course, there was always the danger of the masts going over the side at any moment. I and my two boat-keepers kept them off as best we could with oars and boat-hooks; but to be constantly at it became exasperating, since there was no reason why we should not leave at once. We could not see those on board, nor could we imagine what caused the delay. The boat-keepers were swearing feebly, and I had not only my share of the work, but also had to keep at it two men who showed a constant inclination to lay themselves down and let things slide.

"At last I hailed, 'On deck there,' and someone looked over. 'We're ready here,' I said. The head disappeared, and very soon popped up again. 'The captain says, All right, sir, and to keep the boats well clear of the ship.'

"Half an hour passed. Suddenly there was a frightful racket, rattle, clanking of chain, hiss of water, and millions of sparks flew up into the shivering column of smoke that stood leaning slightly above the ship. The cat-heads had burned away, and the two red-hot anchors had gone to the bottom, tearing out after them two hundred fathom of red-hot chain. The ship trembled, the mass of flame swayed as if ready to collapse, and the fore top-gallant mast fell. It darted down like an arrow of fire, shot under, and instantly leaping up within an oar's length of the boats, floated quietly, very black on the luminous sea. I hailed the deck again. After some time a man in an unexpectedly cheerful but also muffled tone, as though he had been trying to speak with his mouth shut, informed me, 'Coming directly, sir,' and vanished. For a long time I heard nothing but the whirr and roar of the fire. There were also whistling sounds. The boats jumped, tugged at the painters, ran at each other playfully, knocked their sides together, or, do what we would, swung in a bunch against the ship's side. I couldn't stand it any longer, and swarming up a rope, clambered aboard over the stern.

"It was as bright as day. Coming up like this, the sheet of fire facing me was a terrifying sight, and the heat seemed hardly bearable at first. On a settee cushion dragged out of the cabin Captain Beard, with his legs drawn up and one arm under his head, slept with the light playing on him. Do you know what the rest were busy about? They were sitting on deck right aft, round an open case, eating bread and cheese and drinking bottled stout.

"On the background of flames twisting in fierce tongues above their heads they seemed at home like salamanders, and looked like a band of desperate pirates. The fire sparkled in the whites of their eyes, gleamed on patches of white skin seen through the torn shirts. Each had the marks as of a battle about him—bandaged heads, tied-up arms, a strip of dirty rag round a knee—and each man had a bottle between his legs and a chunk of cheese in his hand. Mahon got up. With his handsome and disreputable head, his hooked profile, his long white beard, and with an uncorked bottle in his hand, he resembled one of those reckless sea robbers of old making merry amidst violence and disaster. 'The last meal on board,' he explained solemnly. 'We had nothing to eat all day, and it was no use leaving all this.' He flourished the bottle and indicated the sleeping skipper. 'He said he couldn't swallow anything, so I got him to lie down,' he went on; and as I stared, 'I don't know whether you are aware, young fellow, the man had no sleep to speak of for days—and there will be dam' little sleep in the boats.' 'There will be no boats by and by if you fool about much longer,' I said, indignantly. I walked up to the skipper and shook him by the shoulder. At last he opened his eyes, but did not move. 'Time to leave her, sir,' I said quietly.

"He got up painfully, looked at the flames, at the sea sparkling round the ship, and black, black as ink farther away; he looked at the stars shining dim through a thin veil of smoke in a sky black, black as Erebus.

"'Youngest first,' he said.

"And the ordinary seaman, wiping his mouth with the back of his hand, got up, clambered over the taffrail, and vanished. Others followed. One, on the point of going over, stopped short to drain his bottle, and with a great swing of his arm flung it at the fire. 'Take this!' he cried.

"The skipper lingered disconsolately, and we left him to commune alone for awhile with his first command. Then I went up again and brought him away at last. It was time. The ironwork on the poop was hot to the touch.

"Then the painter of the longboat was cut, and the three boats, tied together, drifted clear of the ship. It was just sixteen hours after the explosion when we abandoned her. Mahon had charge of the second boat, and I had the smallest—the fourteen-foot thing. The longboat would have taken the lot of us; but the skipper said we must save as much property as we could—for the underwriters—and so I got my first command. I had two men with me, a bag of biscuits, a few tins of meat, and a breaker of water. I was ordered to keep close to the longboat, that in case of bad weather we might be taken into her.

"And do you know what I thought? I thought I would part company as soon as I could. I wanted to have my first command all to myself. I wasn't going to sail in a squadron if there were a chance for independent cruising. I would make land by myself. I would beat the other boats. Youth! All youth! The silly, charming, beautiful youth.

"But we did not make a start at once. We must see the last of the ship. And so the boats drifted about that night, heaving and setting on the swell. The men dozed, waked, sighed, groaned. I looked at the burning ship.

"Between the darkness of earth and heaven she was burning fiercely upon a disc of purple sea shot by the blood-red play of gleams; upon a disc of water glittering and sinister. A high, clear flame, an immense and lonely flame, ascended from the ocean, and from its summit the black smoke poured continuously at the sky. She burned furiously, mournful and imposing like a funeral pile kindled in the night, surrounded by the sea, watched over by the stars. A magnificent death had come like a grace, like a gift, like a reward to that old ship at the end of her laborious days. The surrender of her weary ghost to the keeping of stars and sea was stirring like the sight of a glorious triumph. The masts fell just before daybreak, and for a moment there was a burst and turmoil of sparks that seemed to fill with flying fire the night patient and watchful, the vast night lying silent upon the sea. At daylight she was only a charred shell, floating still under a cloud of smoke and bearing a glowing mass of coal within.

"Then the oars were got out, and the boats forming in a line moved round her remains as if in procession—the longboat leading. As we pulled across her stern a slim dart of fire shot out viciously at us, and suddenly she went down, head first, in a great hiss of steam. The unconsumed stern was the last to sink; but the paint had gone, had cracked, had peeled off, and there were no letters, there was no word, no stubborn device that was like her soul, to flash at the rising sun her creed and her name.

"We made our way north. A breeze sprang up, and about noon all the boats came together for the last time. I had no mast or sail in mine, but I made a mast out of a spare oar and hoisted a boat-awning for a

sail, with a boat-hook for a yard. She was certainly over-masted, but I
had the satisfaction of knowing that with the wind aft I could beat the
other two. I had to wait for them. Then we all had a look at the
captain's chart, and, after a sociable meal of hard bread and water, got
our last instructions. These were simple: steer north, and keep together
as much as possible. 'Be careful with that jury-rig, Marlow,' said the
captain; and Mahon, as I sailed proudly past his boat, wrinkled his
curved nose and hailed, 'You will sail that ship of yours under water, if
you don't look out, young fellow.' He was a malicious old man—and
may the deep sea where he sleeps now rock him gently, rock him
tenderly to the end of time!

"Before sunset a thick rain-squall passed over the two boats, which
were far astern, and that was the last I saw of them for a time. Next day
I sat steering my cockle-shell—my first command—with nothing but
water and sky around me. I did sight in the afternoon the upper sails of
a ship far away, but said nothing, and my men did not notice her. You
see I was afraid she might be homeward bound, and I had no mind to
turn back from the portals of the East. I was steering for Java—another
blessed name—like Bankok, you know. I steered many days.

"I need not tell you what it is to be knocking about in an open boat.
I remember nights and days of calm when we pulled, we pulled, and the
boat seemed to stand still, as if bewitched within the circle of the sea
horizon. I remember the heat, the deluge of rain-squalls that kept us
baling for dear life (but filled our water-cask), and I remember sixteen
hours on end with a mouth dry as a cinder and a steering oar over the
stern to keep my first command head on to a breaking sea. I did not
know how good a man I was till then. I remember the drawn faces, the
dejected figures of my two men, and I remember my youth and the
feeling that will never come back any more—the feeling that I could
last forever, outlast the sea, the earth, and all men; the deceitful feeling
that lures us on to joys, to perils, to love, to vain effort—to death; the
triumphant conviction of strength, the heat of life in the handful of dust,
the glow in the heart that with every year grows dim, grows cold, grows
small, and expires—and expires, too soon, too soon—before life itself.

"And this is how I see the East. I have seen its secret places and
have looked into its very soul; but now I see it always from a small
boat, a high outline of mountains, blue and afar in the morning; like
faint mist at noon; a jagged wall of purple at sunset. I have the feel of
the oar in my hand, the vision of a scorching blue sea in my eyes. And I
see a bay, a wide bay, smooth as glass and polished like ice,
shimmering in the dark. A red light burns far off upon the gloom of the
land, and the night is soft and warm. We drag at the oars with aching
arms, and suddenly a puff of wind, a puff faint and tepid and laden with
strange odors of blossoms, of aromatic wood, comes out of the still
night—the first sigh of the East on my face. That I can never forget. It

was impalpable and enslaving, like a charm, like a whispered promise of mysterious delight.

"We had been pulling this finishing spell for eleven hours. Two pulled, and he whose turn it was to rest sat at the tiller. We had made out the red light in that bay and steered for it, guessing it must mark some small coasting port. We passed two vessels, outlandish and high-sterned, sleeping at anchor, and, approaching the light, now very dim, ran the boat's nose against the end of a jutting wharf. We were blind with fatigue. My men dropped the oars and fell off the thwarts as if dead. I made fast to a pile. A current rippled softly. The scented obscurity of the shore was grouped into vast masses, a density of colossal clumps of vegetation, probably—mute and fantastic shapes. And at their foot the semicircle of a beach gleamed faintly, like an illusion. There was not a light, not a stir, not a sound. The mysterious East faced me, perfumed like a flower, silent like death, dark like a grave.

"And I sat weary beyond expression, exulting like a conqueror, sleepless and entranced as if before a profound, a fateful enigma.

"A splashing of oars, a measured dip reverberating on the level of water, intensified by the silence of the shore into loud claps, made me jump up. A boat, a European boat, was coming in. I invoked the name of the dead; I hailed: '*Judea* ahoy!' A thin shout answered.

"It was the captain. I had beaten the flagship by three hours, and I was glad to hear the old man's voice, tremulous and tired. 'Is it you, Marlow?' 'Mind the end of that jetty, sir,' I cried.

"He approached cautiously, and brought up with the deep-sea lead line which we had saved—for the underwriters. I eased my painter and fell alongside. He sat, a broken figure at the stern, wet with dew, his hands clasped in his lap. His men were asleep already. 'I had a terrible time of it,' he murmured. 'Mahon is behind—not very far.' We conversed in whispers, in low whispers, as if afraid to wake up the land. Guns, thunder, earthquakes would not have awakened the men just then.

"Looking around as we talked, I saw away at sea a bright light traveling in the night. 'There's a steamer passing the bay,' I said. She was not passing, she was entering, and she even came close and anchored. 'I wish,' said the old man, 'you would find out whether she is English. Perhaps they could give us a passage somewhere.' He seemed nervously anxious. So by dint of punching and kicking I started one of my men into a state of somnambulism, and giving him an oar, took another and pulled towards the lights of the steamer.

"There was a murmur of voices in her, metallic hollow clangs of the engine room, footsteps on the deck. Her ports shone, round like dilated eyes. Shapes moved about, and there was a shadowy man high up on the bridge. He heard my oars.

"And then, before I could open my lips, the East spoke to me, but it was in a Western voice. A torrent of words was poured into the enigmatical, the fateful silence; outlandish, angry words, mixed with words and even whole sentences of good English, less strange but even more surprising. The voice swore and cursed violently; it riddled the solemn peace of the bay by a volley of abuse. It began by calling me Pig, and from that went crescendo into unmentionable adjectives—in English. The man up there raged aloud in two languages, and with a sincerity in his fury that almost convinced me I had, in some way, sinned against the harmony of the universe. I could hardly see him, but began to think he would work himself into a fit.

"Suddenly he ceased, and I could hear him snorting and blowing like a porpoise. I said:

"'What steamer is this, pray?'

"'Eh? What's this? And who are you?'

"'Castaway crew of an English bark burnt at sea. We came here tonight. I am the second mate. The captain is in the longboat, and wishes to know if you would give us a passage somewhere.'

"'Oh, my goodness! I say. . . . This is the *Celestial* from Singapore on her return trip. I'll arrange with your captain in the morning, . . . and, . . . I say, . . . did you hear me just now?'

"'I should think the whole bay heard you.'

"'I thought you were a shoreboat. Now, look here—this infernal lazy scoundrel of a caretaker has gone to sleep again—curse him. The light is out, and I nearly ran foul of the end of this damned jetty. This is the third time he plays me this trick. Now, I ask you, can anybody stand this kind of thing? It's enough to drive a man out of his mind. I'll report him. . . . I'll get the Assistant Resident to give him the sack, by . . . ! See—there's no light. It's out, isn't it? I take you to witness the light's out. There should be a light, you know. A red light on the—'

"'There was a light,' I said mildly.

"'But it's out, man! What's the use of talking like this? You can see for yourself it's out—don't you? If you had to take a valuable steamer along this God-forsaken coast you would want a light too. I'll kick him from end to end of his miserable wharf. You'll see if I don't. I will—'

"'So I may tell my captain you'll take us?' I broke in.

"'Yes, I'll take you. Good night,' he said, brusquely.

"I pulled back, made fast again to the jetty, and then went to sleep at last. I had faced the silence of the East. I had heard some of its languages. But when I opened my eyes again the silence was as complete as though it had never been broken. I was lying in a flood of light, and the sky had never looked so far, so high, before. I opened my eyes and lay without moving.

"And then I saw the men of the East—they were looking at me.

The whole length of the jetty was full of people. I saw brown, bronze, yellow faces, the black eyes, the glitter, the color of an Eastern crowd. And all these beings stared without a murmur, without a sigh, without a movement. They stared down at the boats, at the sleeping men who at night had come to them from the sea. Nothing moved. The fronds of palms stood still against the sky. Not a branch stirred along the shore, and the brown roofs of hidden houses peeped through the green foliage, through the big leaves that hung shining and still like leaves forged of heavy metal. This was the East of the ancient navigators, so old, so mysterious, resplendent and somber, living and unchanged, full of danger and promise. And these were the men. I sat up suddenly. A wave of movement passed through the crowd from end to end, passed along the heads, swayed the bodies, ran along the jetty like a ripple on the water, like a breath of wind on a field—and all was still again. I see it now—the wide sweep of the bay, the glittering sands, the wealth of green infinite and varied, the sea blue like the sea of a dream, the crowd of attentive faces, the blaze of vivid color—the water reflecting it all, the curve of the shore, the jetty, the high-sterned outlandish craft floating still, and the three boats with tired men from the West sleeping, unconscious of the land and the people and of the violence of sunshine. They slept thrown across the thwarts, curled on bottom-boards, in the careless attitudes of death. The head of the old skipper, leaning back in the stern of the longboat, had fallen on his breast, and he looked as though he would never wake. Farther out old Mahon's face was upturned to the sky, with the long white beard spread out on his breast, as though he had been shot where he sat at the tiller; and a man, all in a heap in the bows of the boat, slept with both arms embracing the stemhead and with his cheek laid on the gunwale. The East looked at them without a sound.

"I have known its fascination since; I have seen the mysterious shores, the still water, the lands of brown nations, where a stealthy Nemesis lies in wait, pursues, overtakes so many of the conquering race, who are proud of their wisdom, of their knowledge, of their strength. But for me all the East is contained in that vision of my youth. It is all in that moment when I opened my young eyes on it. I came upon it from a tussle with the sea—and I was young—and I saw it looking at me. And this is all that is left of it! Only a moment; a moment of strength, of romance, of glamour—of youth! . . . A flick of sunshine upon a strange shore, the time to remember, the time for a sigh, and—good-by!—Night—Good-by . . . !"

He drank.

"Ah! The good old time—the good old time. Youth and the sea. Glamor and the sea! The good, strong sea, the salt, bitter sea, that could whisper to you and roar at you and knock your breath out of you."

He drank again.

"By all that's wonderful it is the sea, I believe, the sea itself—or is it youth alone? Who can tell? But you here—you all had something out of life: money, love—whatever one gets on shore—and, tell me, wasn't that the best time, that time when we were young at sea; young and had nothing, on the sea that gives nothing, except hard knocks—and sometimes a chance to feel your strength—that only—that you all regret?"

And we all nodded at him: the man of finance, the man of accounts, the man of law, we all nodded at him over the polished table that like a still sheet of brown water reflected our faces, lined, wrinkled; our faces marked by toil, by deceptions, by success, by love; our weary eyes looking still, looking always, looking anxiously for something out of life, that while it is expected is already gone—has passed unseen, in a sigh, in a flash—together with the youth, with the strength, with the romance of illusions.

Heart of Darkness

I

The *Nellie*, a cruising yawl, swung to her anchor without a flutter of the sails, and was at rest. The flood had made, the wind was nearly calm, and being bound down the river, the only thing for it was to come to and wait for the turn of the tide.

The sea-reach of the Thames stretched before us like the beginning of an interminable waterway. In the offing the sea and the sky were welded together without a joint, and in the luminous space the tanned sails of the barges drifting up with the tide seemed to stand still in red clusters of canvas sharply peaked, with gleams of varnished sprits. A haze rested on the low shores that ran out to sea in vanishing flatness. The air was dark above Gravesend, and farther back still seemed condensed into a mournful gloom, brooding motionless over the biggest, and the greatest, town on earth.

The Director of Companies was our captain and our host. We four affectionately watched his back as he stood in the bows looking to seaward. On the whole river there was nothing that looked half so nautical. He resembled a pilot, which to a seaman is trustworthiness personified. It was difficult to realize his work was not out there in the luminous estuary, but behind him, within the brooding gloom.

Between us there was, as I have already said somewhere, the bond of the sea. Besides holding our hearts together through long periods of separation, it had the effect of making us tolerant of each other's yarns—and even convictions. The Lawyer—the best of old fellows—had, because of his many years and many virtues, the only cushion on deck, and was lying on the only rug. The Accountant had brought out already a box of dominoes, and was toying architecturally with the bones. Marlow sat cross-legged right aft, leaning against the mizzen-mast. He had sunken cheeks, a yellow complexion, a straight back, an ascetic aspect, and, with his arms dropped, the palms of hands outwards, resembled an idol. The Director, satisfied the anchor had good hold, made his way aft and sat down amongst us. We exchanged a few words lazily. Afterwards there was silence on board the yacht. For some reason or other we did not begin that game of dominoes. We felt meditative, and fit for nothing but placid staring. The day was ending in a serenity of still and exquisite brilliance. The water shone pacifically; the sky, without a speck, was a benign immensity of unstained light; the very mist on the Essex marshes was like a gauzy and radiant fabric, hung from the wooded rises inland, and draping the low shores in diaphanous folds. Only the gloom to the west, brooding over the upper reaches, became more somber every minute, as if angered by the approach of the sun.

And at last, in its curved and imperceptible fall, the sun sank low, and from glowing white changed to a dull red without rays and without heat, as if about to go out suddenly, stricken to death by the touch of that gloom brooding over a crowd of men.

Forthwith a change came over the waters, and the serenity became less brilliant but more profound. The old river in its broad reach rested unruffled at the decline of day, after ages of good service done to the race that peopled its banks, spread out in the tranquil dignity of a waterway leading to the uttermost ends of the earth. We looked at the venerable stream not in the vivid flush of a short day that comes and departs for ever, but in the august light of abiding memories. And indeed nothing is easier for a man who has, as the phrase goes, "followed the sea" with reverence and affection, than to evoke the great spirit of the past upon the lower reaches of the Thames. The tidal current runs to and fro in its unceasing service, crowded with memories of men and ships it had borne to the rest of home or to the battles of the sea. It had known and served all the men of whom the nation is proud, from Sir Francis Drake to Sir John Franklin, knights all, titled and untitled—the great knights-errant of the sea. It had borne all the ships whose names are like jewels flashing in the night of time, from the *Golden Hind* returning with her round flanks full of treasure, to be visited by the Queen's Highness and thus pass out of the gigantic tale, to the *Erebus* and *Terror*, bound on other conquests—and that never returned. It had known the ships and the men. They had sailed from Deptford, from Greenwich, from Erith—the adventurers and the settlers; kings' ships and the ships of men on 'Change; captains, admirals, the dark "interlopers" of the Eastern trade, and the commissioned "generals" of East India fleets. Hunters for gold or pursuers of fame, they all had gone out on that stream, bearing the sword, and often the torch, messengers of the might within the land, bearers of a spark from the sacred fire. What greatness had not floated on the ebb of that river into the mystery of an unknown earth! . . . The dreams of men, the seed of commonwealths, the germs of empires.

The sun set; the dusk fell on the stream, and lights began to appear along the shore. The Chapman lighthouse, a three-legged thing erect on a mud-flat, shone strongly. Lights of ships moved in the fairway—a great stir of lights going up and going down. And farther west on the upper reaches the place of the monstrous town was still marked ominously on the sky, a brooding gloom in sunshine, a lurid glare under the stars.

"And this also," said Marlow suddenly, "has been one of the dark places of the earth."

He was the only man of us who still "followed the sea." The worst that could be said of him was that he did not represent his class. He was a seaman, but he was a wanderer, too, while most seamen lead, if one may so express it, a sedentary life. Their minds are of the stay-at-home order, and their home is always with them—the ship; and so is their country—the sea. One ship is very much like another, and the sea is always the same. In the immutability of their surroundings the foreign shores, the foreign faces, the changing immensity of life, glide past, veiled not by a sense of mystery but by a slightly disdainful ignorance; for there is nothing mysterious to a seaman unless it be the sea itself, which is the mistress of his existence and as inscrutable as Destiny. For the rest, after his hours of work, a casual stroll or a casual spree on shore suffices to unfold for him the secret of a whole continent, and generally he finds the secret not worth knowing. The yarns of seamen have a direct simplicity, the whole meaning of which lies within the shell of a cracked nut. But Marlow was not typical (if his propensity to spin yarns be excepted), and to him the meaning of an episode was not inside like a kernel but outside, enveloping the tale which brought it out only as a glow brings out a haze, in the likeness of one of these misty halos that sometimes are made visible by the spectral illumination of moonshine.

His remark did not seem at all surprising. It was just like Marlow. It was accepted in silence. No one took the trouble to grunt even; and presently he said, very slow:

"I was thinking of very old times, when the Romans first came here, nineteen hundred years ago—the other day. . . . Light came out of this river since—you say Knights? Yes; but it is like a running blaze on a plain, like a flash of lightning in the clouds. We live in the flicker—may it last as long as the old earth keeps rolling! But darkness was here yesterday. Imagine the feelings of a commander of a fine—what d'ye call 'em?—trireme in the Mediterranean, ordered suddenly to the north; run overland across the Gauls in a hurry; put in charge of one of these craft the legionaries,—a wonderful lot of handy men they must have been too—used to build, apparently by the hundred, in a month or two, if we may believe what we read. Imagine him here—the very end of the world, a sea the color of lead, a sky the color of smoke, a kind of ship about as rigid as a concertina—and going up this river with stores, or orders, or what you like. Sandbanks, marshes, forests, savages,— precious little to eat fit for a civilized man, nothing but Thames water to drink. No Falernian wine here, no going ashore. Here and there a military camp lost in a wilderness, like a needle in a bundle of hay— cold, fog, tempests, disease, exile, and death,—death skulking in the air, in the water, in the bush. They must have been dying like flies here. Oh yes—he did it. Did it very well, too, no doubt, and without thinking much about it either, except afterwards to brag of what he had gone through in his time, perhaps. They were men enough to face the darkness. And perhaps he was cheered by keeping his eye on a chance of promotion to the fleet at Ravenna by-and-by, if he had good friends in Rome and survived the awful climate. Or think of a decent young citizen in a toga—perhaps too much dice, you know—coming out here in the train of some prefect, or tax-gatherer, or trader even, to mend his fortunes. Land in a swamp, march through the woods, and in some inland post feel the savagery, the utter savagery, had closed round him,—all that mysterious life of the wilderness that stirs in the forest, in the jungles, in the hearts of wild men. There's no initiation either into such mysteries. He has to live in the midst of the incomprehensible, which is also detestable. And it has a fascination, too, that goes to work upon him. The fascination of the abomination— you know. Imagine the growing regrets, the longing to escape, the powerless disgust, the surrender, the hate."

He paused.

"Mind," he began again, lifting one arm from the elbow, the palm of the hand outwards, so that, with his legs folded before him, he had the pose of a Buddha preaching in European clothes and without a lotus-flower—"Mind, none of us would feel exactly like this. What saves us is efficiency—the devotion to efficiency. But these chaps were not much account, really. They were no colonists; their administration was merely a squeeze, and nothing more, I suspect. They were conquerors, and for that you want only brute force—nothing to boast of, when you have it, since your strength is just an accident arising from the weakness of others. They grabbed what they could get for the sake of what was to be got. It was just robbery with violence, aggravated murder on a great scale, and men going at it blind—as is very proper for those who tackle a darkness. The conquest of the earth, which mostly means the taking it away from those who have a different complexion or slightly flatter noses than ourselves, is not a pretty thing when you look into it too much. What redeems it is the idea only. An idea at the back of it; not a sentimental pretense but an idea; and an unselfish belief in the idea—something you can set up, and bow down before, and offer a sacrifice to. . . ."

He broke off. Flames glided in the river, small green flames, red flames, white flames, pursuing, overtaking, joining, crossing each other—then separating slowly or hastily. The traffic of the great city went on in the deepening night upon the sleepless river. We looked on, waiting patiently—there was nothing else to do till the end of the flood; but it was only after a long silence, when he said, in a hesitating voice, "I suppose you fellows remember I did once turn fresh-water sailor for a bit," that we knew we were fated, before the ebb began to run, to hear about one of Marlow's inconclusive experiences.

"I don't want to bother you much with what happened to me personally," he began, showing in this remark the weakness of many tellers of tales who seem so often unaware of what their audience would best like to hear; "yet to understand the effect of it on me you ought to know how I got out there, what I saw, how I went up that river to the place where I first met the poor chap. It was the farthest point of navigation and the culminating point of my experience. It seemed somehow to throw a kind of light on everything about me—and into my thoughts. It was somber enough too—and pitiful—not extraordinary in any way—not very clear either. No, not very clear. And yet it seemed to throw a kind of light.

"I had then, as you remember, just returned to London after a lot of Indian Ocean, Pacific, China Seas—a regular dose of the East—six years or so, and I was loafing about, hindering you fellows in your work and invading your homes, just as though I had got a heavenly mission to civilize you. It was very fine for a time, but after a bit I did get tired of resting. Then I began to look for a ship—I should think the hardest work on earth. But the ships wouldn't even look at me. And I got tired of that game too.

"Now when I was a little chap I had a passion for maps. I would look for hours at South America, or Africa, or Australia, and lose myself in all the glories of exploration. At that time there were many blank spaces on the earth, and when I saw one that looked particularly inviting on a map (but they all look that) I would put my finger on it and say, 'When I grow up I will go there.' The North Pole was one of these places, I remember. Well, I haven't been there yet, and shall not try now. The glamour's off. Other places were scattered about the Equator, and in every sort of latitude all over the two hemispheres. I have been in some of them, and . . . well, we won't talk about that. But there was one yet—the biggest, the most blank, so to speak—that I had a hankering after.

"True, by this time it was not a blank space any more. It had got filled since my boyhood with rivers and lakes and names. It had ceased to be a blank space of delightful mystery—a white patch for a boy to dream gloriously over. It had become a place of darkness. But there was in it one river especially, a mighty big river, that you could see on the map, resembling an immense snake uncoiled, with its head in the sea, its body at rest curving afar over a vast country, and its tail lost in the depths of the land. And as I looked at the map of it in a shop-window, it fascinated me as a snake would a bird—a silly little bird. Then I remembered there was a big concern, a Company for trade on that river. Dash it all! I thought to myself, they can't trade without using some kind of craft on that lot of fresh water—steamboats! Why shouldn't I try to get charge of one? I went on along Fleet Street, but could not shake off the idea. The snake had charmed me.

"You understand it was a Continental concern, that Trading society; but I have a lot of relations living on the Continent, because it's cheap and not so nasty as it looks, they say.

"I am sorry to own I began to worry them. This was already a fresh departure for me. I was not used to get things that way, you know. I always went my own road and on my own legs where I had a mind to go. I wouldn't have believed it of myself; but, then—you see—I felt somehow I must get there by hook or by crook. So I worried them. The men said 'My dear fellow,' and did nothing. Then—would you believe it?—I tried the women. I, Charlie Marlow, set the women to work—to get a job. Heavens! Well, you see, the notion drove me. I had an aunt, a dear enthusiastic soul. She wrote: 'It will be delightful. I am ready to do anything, anything for you. It is a glorious idea. I know the wife of a very high personage in the Administration, and also a man who has lots of influence with,' &c., &c. She was determined to make no end of fuss to get me appointed skipper of a river steamboat, if such was my fancy.

"I got my appointment—of course; and I got it very quick. It appears the Company had received news that one of their captains had been killed in a scuffle with the natives. This was my chance, and it made me the more anxious to go. It was only months and months afterwards, when I made the attempt to recover what was left of the body, that I heard the original quarrel arose from a misunderstanding about some hens. Yes, two black hens. Fresleven—that was the fellow's name, a Dane—thought himself wronged somehow in the bargain, so he went ashore and started to hammer the chief of the village with a stick. Oh, it didn't surprise me in the least to hear this, and at the same time to be told that Fresleven was the gentlest, quietest creature that ever walked on two legs. No doubt he was; but he had been a couple of years already out there engaged in the noble cause, you know, and he probably felt the need at last of asserting his self-respect in some way. Therefore he whacked the old nigger mercilessly, while a big crowd of his people watched him, thunderstruck, till some man,—I was told the chief's son,—in desperation at hearing the old chap yell, made a tentative jab with a spear at the white man—and of course it went quite easy between the shoulder-blades. Then the whole population cleared into the forest, expecting all kinds of calamities to happen, while, on the other hand, the steamer Fresleven commanded left also in a bad panic, in charge of the engineer, I believe. Afterwards nobody seemed to trouble much about Fresleven's remains, till I got out and stepped into his shoes. I couldn't let it rest, though; but when an opportunity offered at last to meet my predecessor, the grass growing through his ribs was tall enough to hide his bones. They were all there. The supernatural being had not been touched after he fell. And the village was deserted, the huts gaped black, rotting, all askew within the fallen enclosures. A calamity had come to it, sure enough. The people had vanished. Mad terror had scattered them, men, women, and children, through the bush, and they had never returned. What became of the hens I don't know either. I should think the cause of progress got them, anyhow. However, through this glorious affair I got my appointment, before I had fairly begun to hope for it.

"I flew around like mad to get ready, and before forty-eight hours I was crossing the Channel to show myself to my employers, and sign the contract. In a very few hours I arrived in a city that always makes me think of a whited sepulcher. Prejudice no doubt. I had no difficulty in finding the Company's offices. It was the biggest thing in the town, and everybody I met was full of it. They were going to run an over-sea empire, and make no end of coin by trade.

"A narrow and deserted street in deep shadow, high houses, innumerable windows with venetian blinds, a dead silence, grass sprouting between the stones, imposing carriage archways right and left, immense double doors standing ponderously ajar. I slipped through one of these cracks, went up a swept and ungarnished staircase, as arid as a desert, and opened the first door I came to. Two women, one fat and the other slim, sat on straw-bottomed chairs, knitting black wool. The slim one got up and walked straight at me—still knitting with downcast eyes—and only just as I began to think of getting out of her way, as you would for a somnambulist, stood still, and looked up. Her dress was as plain as an umbrella-cover, and she turned round without a word and preceded me into a waiting-room. I gave my name, and looked about. Deal table in the middle, plain chairs all round the walls, on one end a large shining map, marked with all the colors of a rainbow. There was a vast amount of red—good to see at any time, because one knows that some real work is done in there, a deuce of a lot of blue, a little green, smears of orange, and, on the East Coast, a purple patch, to show where the jolly pioneers of progress drink the jolly lager-beer. However, I wasn't going into any of these. I was going into the yellow. Dead in the center. And the river was there—fascinating—deadly—like a snake. Ough! A door opened, a white-haired secretarial head, but wearing a compassionate expression, appeared, and a skinny forefinger beckoned me into the sanctuary. Its light was dim, and a heavy writing-desk squatted in the middle. From behind that structure came out an impression of pale plumpness in a frock-coat. The great man himself. He was five feet six, I should judge, and had his grip on the handle-end of ever so many millions. He shook hands, I fancy, murmured vaguely, was satisfied with my French. *Bon voyage.*

"In about forty-five seconds I found myself again in the waiting-room with the compassionate secretary, who, full of desolation and sympathy, made me sign some document. I believe I undertook amongst other things not to disclose any trade secrets. Well, I am not going to.

"I began to feel slightly uneasy. You know I am not used to such ceremonies, and there was something ominous in the atmosphere. It was just as though I had been let into some conspiracy—I don't know—something not quite right; and I was glad to get out. In the outer room the two women knitted black wool feverishly. People were arriving, and the younger one was walking back and forth introducing them. The old one sat on her chair. Her flat cloth slippers were propped up on a foot-warmer, and a cat reposed on her lap. She wore a starched white affair on her head, had a wart on one cheek, and silver-rimmed spectacles hung on the tip of her nose. She glanced at me above the glasses. The swift and indifferent placidity of that look troubled me. Two youths with foolish and cheery countenances were being piloted over, and she threw at them the same quick glance of unconcerned wisdom. She seemed to know all about them and about me too. An eerie feeling came over me. She seemed uncanny and fateful. Often far away there I thought of these two, guarding the door of Darkness, knitting black wool as for a warm pall, one introducing, introducing continuously to the unknown, the other scrutinizing the cheery and foolish faces with unconcerned old eyes. *Ave!* Old knitter of black wool. *Morituri te salutant.* Not many of those she looked at ever saw her again—not half, by a long way.

"There was yet a visit to the doctor. 'A simple formality,' assured me the secretary, with an air of taking an immense part in all my sorrows. Accordingly a young chap wearing his hat over the left eyebrow, some clerk I suppose,—there must have been clerks in the business, though the house was as still as a house in a city of the dead,—came from somewhere up-stairs, and led me forth. He was shabby and careless, with ink-stains on the sleeves of his jacket, and his cravat was large and billowy, under a chin shaped like the toe of an old boot. It was a little too early for the doctor, so I proposed a drink, and thereupon he developed a vein of joviality. As we sat over our vermouths he glorified the Company's business, and by-and-by I expressed casually my surprise at him not going out there. He became very cool and collected all at once. 'I am not such a fool as I look, quoth Plato to his disciples,' he said sententiously, emptied his glass with great resolution, and we rose.

"The old doctor felt my pulse, evidently thinking of something else the while. 'Good, good for there,' he mumbled, and then with a certain eagerness asked me whether I would let him measure my head. Rather surprised, I said Yes, when he produced a thing like calipers and got the dimensions back and front and every way, taking notes carefully. He was an unshaven little man in a threadbare coat like a gaberdine, with his feet in slippers, and I thought him a harmless fool. 'I always ask leave, in the interests of science, to measure the crania of those going out there,' he said. 'And when they come back, too?' I asked. 'Oh, I never see them,' he remarked; 'and, moreover, the changes take place inside, you know.' He smiled, as if at some quiet joke. 'So you are going out there. Famous. Interesting too.' He gave me a searching glance, and made another note. 'Ever any madness in your family?' he asked, in a matter-of-fact tone. I felt very annoyed. 'Is that question in the interests of science too?' 'It would be,' he said, without taking notice of my irritation, 'interesting for science to watch the mental changes of individuals, on the spot, but . . .' 'Are you an alienist?' I interrupted. 'Every doctor should be—a little,' answered that original, imperturbably. 'I have a little theory which you Messieurs who go out there must help me to prove. This is my share in the advantages my country shall reap from the possession of such a magnificent dependency. The mere wealth I leave to others. Pardon my questions, but you are the first Englishman coming under my observation. . . .' I hastened to assure him I was not in the least typical. 'If I were,' said I, 'I wouldn't be talking like this with you.' 'What you say is rather profound, and probably erroneous,' he said, with a laugh. 'Avoid irritation more than exposure to the sun. Adieu. How do you English say, eh? Good-by. Ah! Good-by. Adieu. In the tropics one must before everything keep calm.' . . . He lifted a warning forefinger. . . . '*Du calme, du calme. Adieu.*'

"One thing more remained to do—say good-by to my excellent aunt. I found her triumphant. I had a cup of tea—the last decent cup of tea for many days—and in a room that most soothingly looked just as you would expect a lady's drawing-room to look, we had a long quiet chat by the fireside. In the course of these confidences it became quite plain to me I had been represented to the wife of the high dignitary, and goodness knows to how many more people besides, as an exceptional and gifted creature—a piece of good fortune for the Company—a man you don't get hold of every day. Good heavens! and I was going to take charge of a two-penny-halfpenny river-steamboat with a penny whistle attached! It appeared, however, I was also one of the Workers, with a capital—you know. Something like an emissary of light, something like a lower sort of apostle. There had been a lot of such rot let loose in print and talk just about that time, and the excellent woman, living right in the rush of all that humbug, got carried off her feet. She talked about 'weaning those ignorant millions from their horrid ways,' till, upon my word, she made me quite uncomfortable. I ventured to hint that the Company was run for profit.

"'You forget, dear Charlie, that the laborer is worthy of his hire,' she said, brightly. It's queer how out of touch with truth women are. They live in a world of their own, and there had never been anything like it, and never can be. It is too beautiful altogether, and if they were to set it up it would go to pieces before the first sunset. Some confounded fact we men have been living contentedly with ever since the day of creation would start up and knock the whole thing over.

"After this I got embraced, told to wear flannel, be sure to write often, and so on—and I left. In the street—I don't know why—a queer feeling came to me that I was an impostor. Odd thing that I, who used to clear out for any part of the world at twenty-four hours' notice, with less thought than most men give to the crossing of a street, had a moment—I won't say of hesitation, but of startled pause, before this commonplace affair. The best way I can explain it to you is by saying that, for a second or two, I felt as though, instead of going to the center of a continent, I were about to set off for the center of the earth.

"I left in a French steamer, and she called in every blamed port they have out there, for, as far as I could see, the sole purpose of landing soldiers and custom-house officers. I watched the coast. Watching a coast as it slips by the ship is like thinking about an enigma. There it is before you—smiling, frowning, inviting, grand, mean, insipid, or savage, and always mute with an air of whispering, 'Come and find out.' This one was almost featureless, as if still in the making, with an aspect of monotonous grimness. The edge of a colossal jungle, so dark-green as to be almost black, fringed with white surf, ran straight, like a ruled line, far, far away along a blue sea whose glitter was blurred by a creeping mist. The sun was fierce, the land seemed to glisten and drip with steam. Here and there grayish-whitish specks showed up, clustered inside the white surf, with a flag flying above them perhaps. Settlements some centuries old, and still no bigger than pin-heads on the untouched expanse of their background. We pounded along, stopped, landed soldiers; went on, landed custom-house clerks to levy toll in what looked like a God-forsaken wilderness, with a tin shed and a flag-pole lost in it; landed more soldiers—to take care of the custom-house clerks, presumably. Some, I heard, got drowned in the surf; but whether they did or not, nobody seemed particularly to care. They were just flung out there, and on we went. Every day the coast looked the same, as though we had not moved; but we passed various places—trading places—with names like Gran' Bassam Little Popo, names that seemed to belong to some sordid farce acted in front of a sinister backcloth. The idleness of a passenger, my isolation amongst all these men with whom I had no point of contact, the oily and languid sea, the uniform somberness of the coast, seemed to keep me away from the truth of things, within the toil of a mournful and senseless delusion. The voice of the surf heard now and then was a positive pleasure, like the speech of a brother. It was something natural, that had its reason, that had a meaning. Now and then a boat from the shore gave one a momentary contact with reality. It was paddled by black fellows. You could see from afar the white of their eyeballs glistening. They shouted, sang; their bodies streamed with perspiration; they had faces like grotesque masks—these chaps; but they had bone, muscle, a wild vitality, an intense energy of movement, that was as natural and true as the surf along their coast. They wanted no excuse for being there. They were a great comfort to look at. For a time I would feel I belonged still to a world of straightforward facts; but the feeling would not last long. Something would turn up to scare it away. Once, I remember, we came upon a man-of-war anchored off the coast. There wasn't even a shed there, and she was shelling the bush. It appears the French had one of their wars going on thereabouts. Her ensign dropped limp like a rag; the muzzles of the long eight-inch guns stuck out all over the low hull; the greasy, slimy swell swung her up lazily and let her down, swaying her thin masts. In the empty immensity of earth, sky, and water, there she was, incomprehensible, firing into a continent. Pop, would go one of the eight-inch guns; a small flame would dart and vanish, a little white smoke would disappear, a tiny projectile would give a feeble screech—and nothing happened. Nothing could happen. There was a touch of insanity in the proceeding, a sense of lugubrious drollery in the sight; and it was not dissipated by somebody on board assuring me earnestly there was a camp of natives—he called them enemies!—hidden out of sight somewhere.

"We gave her her letters (I heard the men in that lonely ship were dying of fever at the rate of three a day) and went on. We called at some more places with farcical names, where the merry dance of death and trade goes on in a still and earthy atmosphere as of an overheated catacomb; all along the formless coast bordered by dangerous surf, as if Nature herself had tried to ward off intruders; in and out of rivers, streams of death in life, whose banks were rotting into mud, whose waters, thickened into slime, invaded the contorted mangroves, that seemed to writhe at us in the extremity of an impotent despair. Nowhere did we stop long enough to get a particularized impression, but the general sense of vague and oppressive wonder grew upon me. It was like a weary pilgrimage amongst hints for nightmares.

"It was upward of thirty days before I saw the mouth of the big river. We anchored off the seat of the government. But my work would not begin till some two hundred miles farther on. So as soon as I could I made a start for a place thirty miles higher up.

"I had my passage on a little sea-going steamer. Her captain was a Swede, and knowing me for a seaman, invited me on the bridge. He was a young man, lean, fair, and morose, with lanky hair and a shuffling gait. As we left the miserable little wharf, he tossed his head contemptuously at the shore. 'Been living there?' he asked. I said, 'Yes.' 'Fine lot these government chaps—are they not?' he went on, speaking English with great precision and considerable bitterness. 'It is funny what some people will do for a few francs a month. I wonder what becomes of that kind when it goes up country?' I said to him I expected to see that soon. 'So-o-o!' he exclaimed. He shuffled athwart, keeping one eye ahead vigilantly. 'Don't be too sure,' he continued. 'The other day I took up a man who hanged himself on the road. He was a Swede, too.' 'Hanged himself! Why, in God's name?' I cried. He kept on looking out watchfully. 'Who knows? The sun too much for him, or the country perhaps.'

"At last we opened a reach. A rocky cliff appeared, mounds of turned-up earth by the shore, houses on a hill, others, with iron roofs, amongst a waste of excavations, or hanging to the declivity. A continuous noise of the rapids above hovered over this scene of inhabited devastation. A lot of people, mostly black and naked, moved about like ants. A jetty projected into the river. A blinding sunlight drowned all this at times in a sudden recrudescence of glare. 'There's your Company's station,' said the Swede, pointing to three wooden barrack-like structures on the rocky slope. 'I will send your things up. Four boxes did you say? So. Farewell.'

"I came upon a boiler wallowing in the grass, then found a path leading up the hill. It turned aside for the boulders, and also for an undersized railway-truck lying there on its back with its wheels in the air. One was off. The thing looked as dead as the carcass of some animal. I came upon more pieces of decaying machinery, a stack of rusty rails. To the left a clump of trees made a shady spot, where dark things seemed to stir feebly. I blinked, the path was steep. A horn tooted to the right, and I saw the black people run. A heavy and dull detonation shook the ground, a puff of smoke came out of the cliff, and that was all. No change appeared on the face of the rock. They were building a railway. The cliff was not in the way or anything; but this objectless blasting was all the work going on.

"A slight clinking behind me made me turn my head. Six black men advanced in a file, toiling up the path. They walked erect and slow, balancing small baskets full of earth on their heads, and the clink kept time with their footsteps. Black rags were wound round their loins, and the short ends behind wagged to and fro like tails. I could see every rib, the joints of their limbs were like knots in a rope; each had an iron collar on his neck, and all were connected together with a chain whose bights swung between them, rhythmically clinking. Another report from the cliff made me think suddenly of that ship of war I had seen firing into a continent. It was the same kind of ominous voice; but these men could by no stretch of imagination be called enemies. They were called criminals, and the outraged law, like the bursting shells, had come to them, an insoluble mystery from over the sea. All their meager breasts panted together, the violently dilated nostrils quivered, the eyes stared stonily uphill. They passed me within six inches, without a glance, with that complete, deathlike indifference of unhappy savages. Behind this raw matter one of the reclaimed, the product of the new forces at work, strolled despondently, carrying a rifle by its middle. He had a uniform jacket with one button off, and seeing a white man on the path, hoisted his weapon to his shoulder with alacrity. This was simple prudence, white men being so much alike at a distance that he could not tell who I might be. He was speedily reassured, and with a large, white, rascally grin, and a glance at his charge, seemed to take me into partnership in his exalted trust. After all, I also was a part of the great cause of these high and just proceedings.

"Instead of going up, I turned and descended to the left. My idea was to let that chain-gang get out of sight before I climbed the hill. You know I am not particularly tender; I've had to strike and to fend off. I've had to resist and to attack sometimes—that's only one way of resisting—without counting the exact cost, according to the demands of such sort of life as I had blundered into. I've seen the devil of violence, and the devil of greed, and the devil of hot desire; but, by all the stars! these were strong, lusty, red-eyed devils, that swayed and drove men— men, I tell you. But as I stood on this hillside, I foresaw that in the blinding sunshine of that land I would become acquainted with a flabby, pretending, weak-eyed devil of a rapacious and pitiless folly. How insidious he could be, too, I was only to find out several months later and a thousand miles farther. For a moment I stood appalled, as though by a warning. Finally I descended the hill, obliquely, towards the trees I had seen.

"I avoided a vast artificial hole somebody had been digging on the slope, the purpose of which I found it impossible to divine. It wasn't a quarry or a sandpit, anyhow. It was just a hole. It might have been connected with the philanthropic desire of giving the criminals something to do. I don't know. Then I nearly fell into a very narrow ravine, almost no more than a scar in the hillside. I discovered that a lot of imported drainage-pipes for the settlement had been tumbled in there. There wasn't one that was not broken. It was a wanton smash-up. At last I got under the trees. My purpose was to stroll into the shade for a moment; but no sooner within than it seemed to me I had stepped into a gloomy circle of some Inferno. The rapids were near, and an uninterrupted, uniform, headlong, rushing noise filled the mournful stillness of the grove, where not a breath stirred, not a leaf moved, with a mysterious sound—as though the tearing pace of the launched earth had suddenly become audible.

"Black shapes crouched, lay, sat between the trees, leaning against the trunks, clinging to the earth, half coming out, half effaced within the dim light, in all the attitudes of pain, abandonment, and despair. Another mine on the cliff went off, followed by a slight shudder of the soil under my feet. The work was going on. The work! And this was the place where some of the helpers had withdrawn to die.

"They were dying slowly—it was very clear. They were not enemies, they were not criminals, they were nothing earthly now,—nothing but black shadows of disease and starvation, lying confusedly in the greenish gloom. Brought from all the recesses of the coast in all the legality of time contracts, lost in uncongenial surroundings, fed on unfamiliar food, they sickened, became inefficient, and were then allowed to crawl away and rest. These moribund shapes were free as air—and nearly as thin. I began to distinguish the gleam of eyes under the trees. Then, glancing down, I saw a face near my hand. The black bones reclined at full length with one shoulder against the tree, and slowly the eyelids rose and the sunken eyes looked up at me, enormous and vacant, a kind of blind, white flicker in the depths of the orbs, which died out slowly. The man seemed young—almost a boy—but you know with them it's hard to tell. I found nothing else to do but to offer him one of my good Swede's ship's biscuits I had in my pocket. The fingers closed slowly on it and held—there was no other movement and no other glance. He had tied a bit of white worsted round his neck—Why? Where did he get it? Was it a badge—an ornament—a charm—a propitiatory act? Was there any idea at all connected with it? It looked startling round his black neck, this bit of white thread from beyond the seas.

"Near the same tree two more bundles of acute angles sat with their legs drawn up. One, with his chin propped on his knees, stared at nothing, in an intolerable and appalling manner: his brother phantom rested its forehead, as if overcome with a great weariness; and all about others were scattered in every pose of contorted collapse, as in some picture of a massacre or a pestilence. While I stood horror-struck, one of these creatures rose to his hands and knees, and went off on all-fours towards the river to drink. He lapped out of his hand, then sat up in the sunlight, crossing his shins in front of him, and after a time let his woolly head fall on his breastbone.

"I didn't want any more loitering in the shade, and I made haste towards the station. When near the buildings I met a white man, in such an unexpected elegance of get-up that in the first moment I took him for a sort of vision. I saw a high starched collar, white cuffs, a light alpaca jacket, snowy trousers, a clear necktie, and varnished boots. No hat. Hair parted, brushed, oiled, under a green-lined parasol held in a big white hand. He was amazing, and had a penholder behind his ear.

"I shook hands with this miracle, and I learned he was the Company's chief accountant, and that all the bookkeeping was done at this station. He had come out for a moment, he said, 'to get a breath of fresh air.' The expression sounded wonderfully odd, with its suggestion of sedentary desk-life. I wouldn't have mentioned the fellow to you at all, only it was from his lips that I first heard the name of the man who is so indissolubly connected with the memories of that time. Moreover, I respected the fellow. Yes; I respected his collars, his vast cuffs, his brushed hair. His appearance was certainly that of a hairdresser's dummy; but in the great demoralization of the land he kept up his appearance. That's backbone. His starched collars and got-up shirt-fronts were achievements of character. He had been out nearly three years; and, later on, I could not help asking him how he managed to sport such linen. He had just the faintest blush, and said modestly, 'I've been teaching one of the native women about the station. It was difficult. She had a distaste for the work.' This man had verily accomplished something. And he was devoted to his books, which were in apple-pie order.

"Everything else in the station was in a muddle,—heads, things, buildings. Strings of dusty niggers with splay feet arrived and departed; a stream of manufactured goods, rubbishy cottons, beads, and brass-wire set into the depths of darkness, and in return came a precious trickle of ivory.

"I had to wait in the station for ten days—an eternity. I lived in a hut in the yard, but to be out of the chaos I would sometimes get into the accountant's office. It was built of horizontal planks, and so badly put together that, as he bent over his high desk, he was barred from neck to heels with narrow strips of sunlight. There was no need to open the big shutter to see. It was hot there too; big flies buzzed fiendishly, and did not sting, but stabbed. I sat generally on the floor, while, of faultless appearance (and even slightly scented), perching on a high stool, he wrote, he wrote. Sometimes he stood up for exercise. When a truckle-bed with a sick man (some invalided agent from up-country) was put in there, he exhibited a gentle annoyance. 'The groans of this sick person,' he said, distract my attention. And without that it is extremely difficult to guard against clerical errors in this climate.'

"One day he remarked, without lifting his head, 'In the interior you will no doubt meet Mr. Kurtz.' On my asking who Mr. Kurtz was, he said he was a first-class agent; and seeing my disappointment at this information, he added slowly, laying down his pen, 'He is a very remarkable person.' Further questions elicited from him that Mr. Kurtz was at present in charge of a trading post, a very important one, in the true ivory-country, at 'the very bottom of there. Sends in as much ivory as all the others put together. . . .' He began to write again. The sick man was too ill to groan. The flies buzzed in a great peace.

"Suddenly there was a growing murmur of voices and a great tramping of feet. A caravan had come in. A violent babble of uncouth sounds burst out on the other side of the planks. All the carriers were speaking together, and in the midst of the uproar the lamentable voice of the chief agent was heard 'giving it up' tearfully for the twentieth time that day. . . . He rose slowly. 'What a frightful row,' he said. He crossed the room gently to look at the sick man, and returning, said to me, 'He does not hear.' 'What! Dead?' I asked, startled. 'No, not yet,' he answered, with great composure. Then, alluding with a toss of the head to the tumult in the station-yard, 'When one has got to make correct entries, one comes to hate those savages—hate them to the death.' He remained thoughtful for a moment. 'When you see Mr. Kurtz,' he went on, 'tell him from me that everything here'—he glanced at the desk—'is very satisfactory. I don't like to write to him—with those messengers of ours you never know who may get hold of your letter—at that Central Station.' He stared at me for a moment with his mild, bulging eyes. 'Oh, he will go far, very far,' he began again. 'He will be a somebody in the Administration before long. They, above—the Council in Europe, you know—mean him to be.'

"He turned to his work. The noise outside had ceased, and presently in going out I stopped at the door. In the steady buzz of flies the homeward-bound agent was lying flushed and insensible; the other, bent over his books, was making correct entries of perfectly correct transactions; and fifty feet below the doorstep I could see the still tree-tops of the grove of death.

"Next day I left that station at last, with a caravan of sixty men, for a two-hundred-mile tramp.

"No use telling you much about that. Paths, paths, everywhere; a stamped-in network of paths spreading over the empty land, through long grass, through burnt grass, through thickets, down and up chilly ravines, up and down stony hills ablaze with heat; and a solitude, a solitude, nobody, not a hut. The population had cleared out a long time ago. Well, if a lot of mysterious niggers armed with all kinds of fearful weapons suddenly took to traveling on the road between Deal and Gravesend, catching the yokels right and left to carry heavy loads for them, I fancy every farm and cottage thereabouts would get empty very soon. Only here the dwellings were gone too. Still I passed through several abandoned villages. There's something pathetically childish in the ruins of grass walls. Day after day, with the stamp and shuffle of sixty pair of bare feet behind me, each pair under a 60-lb. load. Camp, cook, sleep, strike camp, march. Now and then a carrier dead in harness, at rest in the long grass near the path, with an empty water-gourd and his long staff lying by his side. A great silence around and above. Perhaps on some quiet night the tremor of far-off drums, sinking, swelling, a tremor vast, faint; a sound weird, appealing, suggestive, and wild—and perhaps with as profound a meaning as the sound of bells in a Christian country. Once a white man in an unbuttoned uniform, camping on the path with an armed escort of lank Zanzibaris, very hospitable and festive—not to say drunk. Was looking after the upkeep of the road, he declared. Can't say I saw any road or any upkeep, unless the body of a middle-aged negro, with a bullet-hole in the forehead, upon which I absolutely stumbled three miles farther on, may be considered as a permanent improvement. I had a white companion too, not a bad chap, but rather too fleshy and with the exasperating habit of fainting on the hot hillsides, miles away from the least bit of shade and water. Annoying, you know, to hold your own coat like a parasol over a man's head while he is coming-to. I couldn't help asking him once what he meant by coming there at all. 'To make money, of course. What do you think?' he said, scornfully. Then he got fever, and had to be carried in a hammock slung under a pole. As he weighed sixteen stone I had no end of rows with the carriers. They jibbed, ran away, sneaked off with their loads in the night—quite a mutiny. So, one evening, I made a speech in English with gestures, not one of which was lost to the sixty pairs of eyes before me, and the next morning I started the hammock off in front all right. An hour afterwards I came upon the whole concern wrecked in a bush—man, hammock, groans, blankets, horrors. The heavy pole had skinned his poor nose. He was very anxious for me to kill somebody, but there wasn't the shadow of a carrier near. I remembered the old doctor,—'It would be interesting for science to watch the mental changes of individuals, on the spot.' I felt I was becoming scientifically interesting. However, all that is to no purpose. On the fifteenth day I came in sight of the big river again, and hobbled into the Central Station. It was on a back water surrounded by scrub and forest, with a pretty border of smelly mud on one side, and on the three others enclosed by a crazy fence of rushes. A neglected gap was all the gate it had, and the first glance at the place was enough to let you see the flabby devil was running that show. White men with long staves in their hands appeared languidly from amongst the buildings, strolling up to take a look at me, and then retired out of sight somewhere. One of them, a stout, excitable chap with black mustaches, informed me with great volubility and many digressions, as soon as I told him who I was, that my steamer was at the bottom of the river. I was thunderstruck. What, how, why? Oh, it was 'all right.' The 'manager himself' was there. All quite correct. 'Everybody had behaved splendidly! splendidly!'—'you must,' he said in agitation, 'go and see the general manager at once. He is waiting!'

"I did not see the real significance of that wreck at once. I fancy I see it now, but I am not sure—not at all. Certainly the affair was too stupid—when I think of it—to be altogether natural. Still. . . . But at the moment it presented itself simply as a confounded nuisance. The steamer was sunk. They had started two days before in a sudden hurry up the river with the manager on board, in charge of some volunteer skipper, and before they had been out three hours they tore the bottom out of her on stones, and she sank near the south bank. I asked myself what I was to do there, now my boat was lost. As a matter of fact, I had plenty to do in fishing my command out of the river. I had to set about it the very next day. That, and the repairs when I brought the pieces to the station, took some months.

"My first interview with the manager was curious. He did not ask me to sit down after my twenty-mile walk that morning. He was commonplace in complexion, in features, in manners, and in voice. He was of middle size and of ordinary build. His eyes, of the usual blue, were perhaps remarkably cold, and he certainly could make his glance fall on one as trenchant and heavy as an ax. But even at these times the rest of his person seemed to disclaim the intention. Otherwise there was only an indefinable, faint expression of his lips, something stealthy—a smile—not a smile—I remember it, but I can't explain. It was unconscious, this smile was, though just after he had said something it got intensified for an instant. It came at the end of his speeches like a seal applied on the words to make the meaning of the commonest phrase appear absolutely inscrutable. He was a common trader, from his youth up employed in these parts—nothing more. He was obeyed, yet he inspired neither love nor fear, nor even respect. He inspired uneasiness. That was it! Uneasiness. Not a definite mistrust—just uneasiness—nothing more. You have no idea how effective such a . . . a . . . faculty can be. He had no genius for organizing, for initiative, or for order even. That was evident in such things as the deplorable state of the station. He had no learning, and no intelligence. His position had come to him—why? Perhaps because he was never ill . . . He had served three terms of three years out there . . . Because triumphant health in the general rout of constitutions is a kind of power in itself. When he went home on leave he rioted on a large scale—pompously. Jack ashore—with a difference—in externals only. This one could gather from his casual talk. He originated nothing, he could keep the routine going—that's all. But he was great. He was great by this little thing that it was impossible to tell what could control such a man. He never gave that secret away. Perhaps there was nothing within him. Such a suspicion made one pause—for out there there were no external checks. Once when various tropical diseases had laid low almost every 'agent' in the station, he was heard to say, 'Men who come out here should have no entrails.' He sealed the utterance with that smile of his, as though it had been a door opening into a darkness he had in his keeping. You fancied you had seen things—but the seal was on. When annoyed at meal-times by the constant quarrels of the white men about precedence, he ordered an immense round table to be made, for which a special house had to be built. This was the station's mess-room. Where he sat was the first place—the rest were nowhere. One felt this to be his unalterable conviction. He was neither civil nor uncivil. He was quiet. He allowed his 'boy'—an overfed young negro from the coast—to treat the white men, under his very eyes, with provoking insolence.

"He began to speak as soon as he saw me. I had been very long on the road. He could not wait. Had to start without me. The up-river stations had to be relieved. There had been so many delays already that he did not know who was dead and who was alive, and how they got on—and so on, and so on. He paid no attention to my explanations, and, playing with a stick of sealing-wax, repeated several times that the situation was 'very grave, very grave.' There were rumors that a very important station was in jeopardy, and its chief, Mr. Kurtz, was ill. Hoped it was not true. Mr. Kurtz was . . . I felt weary and irritable. Hang Kurtz, I thought. I interrupted him by saying I had heard of Mr. Kurtz on the coast. 'Ah! So they talk of him down there,' he murmured to himself. Then he began again, assuring me Mr. Kurtz was the best agent he had, an exceptional man, of the greatest importance to the Company; therefore I could understand his anxiety. He was, he said, 'very, very uneasy.' Certainly he fidgeted on his chair a good deal, exclaimed, 'Ah, Mr. Kurtz!' broke the stick of sealing-wax and seemed dumbfounded by the accident. Next thing he wanted to know 'how long it would take to' . . . I interrupted him again. Being hungry, you know, and kept on my feet too, I was getting savage. 'How could I tell,' I said. 'I hadn't even seen the wreck yet—some months, no doubt.' All this talk seemed to me so futile. 'Some months,' he said. 'Well, let us say three months before we can make a start. Yes. That ought to do the affair.' I flung out of his hut (he lived all alone in a clay hut with a sort of veranda) muttering to myself my opinion of him. He was a chattering idiot. Afterwards I took it back when it was borne in upon me startlingly with what extreme nicety he had estimated the time requisite for the 'affair.'

"I went to work the next day, turning, so to speak, my back on that station. In that way only it seemed to me I could keep my hold on the redeeming facts of life. Still, one must look about sometimes; and then I saw this station, these men strolling aimlessly about in the sunshine of the yard. I asked myself sometimes what it all meant. They wandered here and there with their absurd long staves in their hands, like a lot of faithless pilgrims bewitched inside a rotten fence. The word 'ivory' rang in the air, was whispered, was sighed. You would think they were praying to it. A taint of imbecile rapacity blew through it all, like a whiff from some corpse. By Jove! I've never seen anything so unreal in my life. And outside, the silent wilderness surrounding this cleared speck on the earth struck me as something great and invincible, like evil or truth, waiting patiently for the passing away of this fantastic invasion.

"Oh, these months! Well, never mind. Various things happened. One evening a grass shed full of calico, cotton prints, beads, and I don't know what else, burst into a blaze so suddenly that you would have thought the earth had opened to let an avenging fire consume all that trash. I was smoking my pipe quietly by my dismantled steamer, and saw them all cutting capers in the light, with their arms lifted high, when the stout man with mustaches came tearing down to the river, a tin pail in his hand, assured me that everybody was 'behaving splendidly, splendidly,' dipped about a quart of water and tore back again. I noticed there was a hole in the bottom of his pail.

"I strolled up. There was no hurry. You see the thing had gone off like a box of matches. It had been hopeless from the very first. The flame had leaped high, driven everybody back, lighted up everything—and collapsed. The shed was already a heap of embers glowing fiercely. A nigger was being beaten near by. They said he had caused the fire in some way; be that as it may, he was screeching most horribly. I saw him, later on, for several days, sitting in a bit of shade looking very sick and trying to recover himself: afterwards he arose and went out—and the wilderness without a sound took him into its bosom again. As I approached the glow from the dark I found myself at the back of two men, talking. I heard the name of Kurtz pronounced, then the words, 'take advantage of this unfortunate accident.' One of the men was the manager. I wished him a good evening. 'Did you ever see anything like it—eh? it is incredible,' he said, and walked off. The other man remained. He was a first-class agent, young, gentlemanly, a bit reserved, with a forked little beard and a hooked nose. He was stand-offish with the other agents, and they on their side said he was the manager's spy upon them. As to me, I had hardly ever spoken to him before. We got into talk, and by-and-by we strolled away from the hissing ruins. Then he asked me to his room, which was in the main building of the station. He struck a match, and I perceived that this young aristocrat had not only a silver-mounted dressing-case but also a whole candle all to himself. Just at that time the manager was the only man supposed to have any right to candles. Native mats covered the clay walls; a collection of spears, assegais, shields, knives was hung up in trophies. The business intrusted to this fellow was the making of bricks—so I had been informed; but there wasn't a fragment of a brick anywhere in the station, and he had been there more than a year—waiting. It seems he could not make bricks without something, I don't know what—straw maybe. Anyways, it could not be found there, and as it was not likely to be sent from Europe, it did not appear clear to me what he was waiting for. An act of special creation perhaps. However, they were all waiting—all the sixteen or twenty pilgrims of them—for something; and upon my word it did not seem an uncongenial occupation, from the way they took it, though the only thing that ever came to them was disease—as far as I could see. They beguiled the time by backbiting and intriguing against each other in a foolish kind of way. There was an air of plotting about that station, but nothing came of it, of course. It was as unreal as everything else—as the philanthropic pretense of the whole concern, as their talk, as their government, as their show of work. The only real feeling was a desire to get appointed to a trading-post where ivory was to be had, so that they could earn percentages. They intrigued and slandered and hated each other only on that account,—but as to effectually lifting a little finger—oh, no. By heavens! there is something after all in the world allowing one man to steal a horse while another must not look at a halter. Steal a horse straight out. Very well. He has done it. Perhaps he can ride. But there is a way of looking at a halter that would provoke the most charitable of saints into a kick.

"I had no idea why he wanted to be sociable, but as we chatted in there it suddenly occurred to me the fellow was trying to get at something—in fact, pumping me. He alluded constantly to Europe, to the people I was supposed to know there—putting leading questions as to my acquaintances in the sepulchral city, and so on. His little eyes glittered like mica discs—with curiosity,—though he tried to keep up a bit of superciliousness. At first I was astonished, but very soon I became awfully curious to see what he would find out from me. I couldn't possibly imagine what I had in me to make it worth his while. It was very pretty to see how he baffled himself, for in truth my body was full of chills, and my head had nothing in it but that wretched steamboat business. It was evident he took me for a perfectly shameless prevaricator. At last he got angry, and to conceal a movement of furious annoyance, he yawned. I rose. Then I noticed a small sketch in oils, on a panel, representing a woman, draped and blindfolded, carrying a lighted torch. The background was somber—almost black. The movement of the woman was stately, and the effect of the torchlight on the face was sinister.

"It arrested me, and he stood by civilly, holding a half-pint champagne bottle (medical comforts) with the candle stuck in it. To my question he said Mr. Kurtz had painted this—in this very station more than a year ago—while waiting for means to go to his trading-post. 'Tell me, pray,' said I, 'who is this Mr. Kurtz?'

"'The chief of the Inner Station,' he answered in a short tone, looking away. 'Much obliged,' I said, laughing. 'And you are the brickmaker of the Central Station. Everyone knows that.' He was silent for a while. 'He is a prodigy,' he said at last. 'He is an emissary of pity, and science, and progress, and devil knows what else. We want,' he began to declaim suddenly, 'for the guidance of the cause intrusted to us by Europe, so to speak, higher intelligence, wide sympathies, a singleness of purpose.' 'Who says that?' I asked. 'Lots of them,' he replied. 'Some even write that; and so *he* comes here, a special being, as you ought to know.' 'Why ought I to know?' I interrupted, really surprised. He paid no attention. 'Yes. To-day he is chief of the best station, next year he will be assistant-manager, two years more and . . . but I dare say you know what he will be in two years' time. You are of the new gang—the gang of virtue. The same people who sent him specially also recommended you. Oh, don't say no. I've my own eyes to trust.' Light dawned upon me. My dear aunt's influential acquaintances were producing an unexpected effect upon that young man. I nearly burst into a laugh. 'Do you read the Company's confidential correspondence?' I asked. He hadn't a word to say. It was great fun. 'When Mr. Kurtz,' I continued severely, 'is General Manager, you won't have the opportunity.'

"He blew the candle out suddenly, and we went outside. The moon had risen. Black figures strolled about listlessly, pouring water on the glow, whence proceeded a sound of hissing; steam ascended in the moonlight, the beaten nigger groaned somewhere. 'What a row the brute makes!' said the indefatigable man with the mustaches, appearing near us. 'Serve him right. Transgression—punishment—bang! Pitiless, pitiless. That's the only way. This will prevent all conflagrations for the future. I was just telling the manager . . .' He noticed my companion, and became crestfallen all at once. 'Not in bed yet,' he said, with a kind of servile heartiness; 'it's so natural. Ha! Danger—agitation.' He vanished. I went on to the river-side, and the other followed me. I heard a scathing murmur at my ear, 'Heap of muffs—go to.' The pilgrims could be seen in knots gesticulating, discussing. Several had still their staves in their hands. I verily believe they took these sticks to bed with them. Beyond the fence the forest stood up spectrally in the moonlight, and through the dim stir, through the faint sounds of that lamentable courtyard, the silence of the land went home to one's very heart,—its mystery, its greatness, the amazing reality of its concealed life. The hurt nigger moaned feebly somewhere near by, and then fetched a deep sigh that made me mend my pace away from there. I felt a hand introducing itself under my arm. 'My dear sir,' said the fellow, 'I don't want to be misunderstood, and especially by you, who will see Mr. Kurtz long before I can have that pleasure. I wouldn't like him to get a false idea of my disposition. . . .'

"I let him run on, this papier-mâché Mephistopheles, and it seemed to me that if I tried I could poke my forefinger through him, and would find nothing inside but a little loose dirt, maybe. He, don't you see, had been planning to be assistant-manager by-and-by under the present man, and I could see that the coming of that Kurtz had upset them both not a little. He talked precipitately, and I did not try to stop him. I had my shoulders against the wreck of my steamer, hauled up on the slope like a carcass of some big river animal. The smell of mud, of primeval mud, by Jove! was in my nostrils, the high stillness of primeval forest was before my eyes; there were shiny patches on the black creek. The moon had spread over everything a thin layer of silver—over the rank grass, over the mud, upon the wall of matted vegetation standing higher than the wall of a temple, over the great river I could see through a somber gap glittering, glittering, as it flowed broadly by without a murmur. All this was great, expectant, mute, while the man jabbered about himself. I wondered whether the stillness on the face of the immensity looking at us two were meant as an appeal or as a menace. What were we who had strayed in here? Could we handle that dumb thing, or would it handle us? I felt how big, how confoundedly big, was that thing that couldn't talk, and perhaps was deaf as well. What was in there? I could see a little ivory coming out from there, and I had heard Mr. Kurtz was in there. I had heard enough about it too—God knows! Yet somehow it didn't bring any image with it—no more than if I had been told an angel or a fiend was in there. I believed it in the same way one of you might believe there are inhabitants in the planet Mars. I knew once a Scotch sailmaker who was certain, dead sure, there were people in Mars. If you asked him for some idea how they looked and behaved, he would get shy and mutter something about 'walking on all-fours.' If you as much as smiled, he would—though a man of sixty— offer to fight you. I would not have gone so far as to fight for Kurtz, but I went for him near enough to a lie. You know I hate, detest, and can't bear a lie, not because I am straighter than the rest of us, but simply because it appalls me. There is a taint of death, a flavor of mortality in lies,—which is exactly what I hate and detest in the world—what I want to forget. It makes me miserable and sick, like biting something rotten would do. Temperament, I suppose. Well, I went near enough to it by letting the young fool there believe anything he liked to imagine as to my influence in Europe. I became in an instant as much of a pretense as the rest of the bewitched pilgrims. This simply because I had a notion it somehow would be of help to that Kurtz whom at the time I did not see—you understand. He was just a word for me. I did not see the man in the name any more than you do. Do you see him? Do you see the story? Do you see anything? It seems to me I am trying to tell you a dream—making a vain attempt, because no relation of a dream can convey the dream-sensation, that commingling of absurdity, surprise, and bewilderment in a tremor of struggling revolt, that notion of being captured by the incredible which is of the very essence of dreams. . . ."

He was silent for a while.

". . . No, it is impossible; it is impossible to convey the life-sensation of any given epoch of one's existence,—that which makes its truth, its meaning—its subtle and penetrating essence. It is impossible. We live, as we dream—alone. . . ."

He paused again as if reflecting, then added—"Of course in this you fellows see more than I could then. You see me, whom you know. . . ."

It had become so pitch dark that we listeners could hardly see one another. For a long time already he, sitting apart, had been no more to us than a voice. There was not a word from anybody. The others might have been asleep, but I was awake. I listened, I listened on the watch for the sentence, for the word, that would give me the clew to the faint uneasiness inspired by this narrative that seemed to shape itself without human lips in the heavy night-air of the river.

". . . Yes—I let him run on," Marlow began again, "and think what he pleased about the powers that were behind me. I did! And there was nothing behind me! There was nothing but that wretched, old, mangled steamboat I was leaning against, while he talked fluently about 'the necessity for every man to get on.' 'And when one comes out here, you conceive, it is not to gaze at the moon.' Mr. Kurtz was a 'universal genius,' but even a genius would find it easier to work with 'adequate tools—intelligent men.' He did not make bricks—why, there was a physical impossibility in the way—as I was well aware; and if he did secretarial work for the manager, it was because 'no sensible man rejects wantonly the confidence of his superiors.' Did I see it? I saw it. What more did I want? What I really wanted was rivets, by heaven! Rivets. To get on with the work—to stop the hole. Rivets I wanted. There were cases of them down at the coast—cases—piled up—burst—split! You kicked a loose rivet at every second step in that station yard on the hillside. Rivets had rolled into the grove of death. You could fill your pockets with rivets for the trouble of stooping down—and there wasn't one rivet to be found where it was wanted. We had plates that would do, but nothing to fasten them with. And every week the messenger, a lone negro, letter-bag on shoulder and staff in hand, left our station for the coast. And several times a week a coast caravan came in with trade goods,—ghastly glazed calico that made you shudder only to look at it, glass beads value about a penny a quart, confounded spotted cotton handkerchiefs. And no rivets. Three carriers could have brought all that was wanted to set that steamboat afloat.

"He was becoming confidential now, but I fancy my unresponsive attitude must have exasperated him at last, for he judged it necessary to inform me he feared neither God nor devil, let alone any mere man. I said I could see that very well, but what I wanted was a certain quantity of rivets—and rivets were what really Mr. Kurtz wanted, if he had only known it. Now letters went to the coast every week. . . . 'My dear sir,' he cried, 'I write from dictation.' I demanded rivets. There was a way—for an intelligent man. He changed his manner; became very cold, and suddenly began to talk about a hippopotamus; wondered whether sleeping on board the steamer (I stuck to my salvage night and day) I wasn't disturbed. There was an old hippo that had the bad habit of getting out on the bank and roaming at night over the station grounds. The pilgrims used to turn out in a body and empty every rifle they could lay hands on at him. Some even had sat up o' nights for him. All this energy was wasted, though. 'That animal has a charmed life,' he said; 'but you can say this only of brutes in this country. No man— you apprehend me?—no man here bears a charmed life.' He stood there for a moment in the moonlight with his delicate hooked nose set a little askew, and his mica eyes glittering without a wink, then, with a curt Good night, he strode off. I could see he was disturbed and considerably puzzled, which made me feel more hopeful than I had been for days. It was a great comfort to turn from that chap to my influential friend, the battered, twisted, ruined, tin-pot steamboat. I clambered on board. She rang under my feet like an empty Huntley & Palmer biscuit-tin kicked along a gutter; she was nothing so solid in make, and rather less pretty in shape, but I had expended enough hard work on her to make me love her. No influential friend would have served me better. She had given me a chance to come out a bit—to find out what I could do. No, I don't like work. I had rather laze about and think of all the fine things that can be done. I don't like work—no man does—but I like what is in the work,—the chance to find yourself. Your own reality—for yourself, not for others—what no other man can ever know. They can only see the mere show, and never can tell what it really means.

"I was not surprised to see somebody sitting aft, on the deck, with his legs dangling over the mud. You see I rather chummed with the few mechanics there were in that station, whom the other pilgrims naturally despised—on account of their imperfect manners, I suppose. This was the foreman—a boiler-maker by trade—a good worker. He was a lank, bony, yellow-faced man, with big intense eyes. His aspect was worried, and his head was as bald as the palm of my hand; but his hair in falling seemed to have stuck to his chin, and had prospered in the new locality, for his beard hung down to his waist. He was a widower with six young children (he had left them in charge of a sister of his to come out there), and the passion of his life was pigeon-flying. He was an enthusiast and a connoisseur. He would rave about pigeons. After work hours he used sometimes to come over from his hut for a talk about his children and his pigeons; at work, when he had to crawl in the mud under the bottom of the steamboat, he would tie up that beard of his in a kind of white serviette he brought for the purpose. It had loops to go over his ears. In the evening he could be seen squatted on the bank rinsing that wrapper in the creek with great care, then spreading it solemnly on a bush to dry.

"I slapped him on the back and shouted, 'We shall have rivets!' He scrambled to his feet exclaiming 'No! Rivets!' as though he couldn't believe his ears. Then in a low voice, 'You . . . eh?' I don't know why we behaved like lunatics. I put my finger to the side of my nose and nodded mysteriously. 'Good for you!' he cried, snapped his fingers above his head, lifting one foot. I tried a jig. We capered on the iron deck. A frightful clatter came out of that hulk, and the virgin forest on the other bank of the creek sent it back in a thundering roll upon the sleeping station. It must have made some of the pilgrims sit up in their hovels. A dark figure obscured the lighted doorway of the manager's hut, vanished, then, a second or so after, the doorway itself vanished too. We stopped, and the silence driven away by the stamping of our feet flowed back again from the recesses of the land. The great wall of vegetation, an exuberant and entangled mass of trunks, branches, leaves, boughs, festoons, motionless in the moonlight, was like a rioting invasion of soundless life, a rolling wave of plants, piled up, crested, ready to topple over the creek, to sweep every little man of us out of his little existence. And it moved not. A deadened burst of mighty splashes and snorts reached us from afar, as though an ichthyosaurus had been taking a bath of glitter in the great river. 'After all,' said the boiler-maker in a reasonable tone, 'why shouldn't we get the rivets?' Why not, indeed! I did not know of any reason why we shouldn't. 'They'll come in three weeks,' I said confidently.

"But they didn't. Instead of rivets there came an invasion, an infliction, a visitation. It came in sections during the next three weeks, each section headed by a donkey carrying a white man in new clothes and tan shoes, bowing from that elevation right and left to the impressed pilgrims. A quarrelsome band of footsore sulky niggers trod on the heels of the donkeys; a lot of tents, camp-stools, tin boxes, white cases, brown bales would be shot down in the courtyard, and the air of mystery would deepen a little over the muddle of the station. Five such installments came, with their absurd air of disorderly flight with the loot of innumerable outfit shops and provision stores, that, one would think, they were lugging, after a raid, into the wilderness for equitable division. It was an inextricable mess of things decent in themselves but that human folly made look like the spoils of thieving.

"This devoted band called itself the Eldorado Exploring Expedition, and I believe they were sworn to secrecy. Their talk, however, was the talk of sordid buccaneers: it was reckless without hardihood, greedy without audacity, and cruel without courage; there was not an atom of foresight or of serious intention in the whole batch of them, and they did not seem aware these things are wanted for the work of the world. To tear treasure out of the bowels of the land was their desire, with no more moral purpose at the back of it than there is in burglars breaking into a safe. Who paid the expenses of the noble enterprise I don't know; but the uncle of our manager was leader of that lot.

"In exterior he resembled a butcher in a poor neighborhood, and his eyes had a look of sleepy cunning. He carried his fat paunch with ostentation on his short legs, and during the time his gang infested the station spoke to no one but his nephew. You could see these two roaming about all day long with their heads close together in an everlasting confab.

"I had given up worrying myself about the rivets. One's capacity for that kind of folly is more limited than you would suppose. I said Hang!—and let things slide. I had plenty of time for meditation, and now and then I would give some thought to Kurtz. I wasn't very interested in him. No. Still, I was curious to see whether this man, who had come out equipped with moral ideas of some sort, would climb to the top after all, and how he would set about his work when there."

II

"One evening as I was lying flat on the deck of my steamboat, I heard voices approaching—and there were the nephew and the uncle strolling along the bank. I laid my head on my arm again, and had nearly lost myself in a doze, when somebody said in my ear, as it were: 'I am as harmless as a little child, but I don't like to be dictated to. Am I the manager—or am I not? I was ordered to send him there. It's incredible.' . . . I became aware that the two were standing on the shore alongside the forepart of the steamboat, just below my head. I did not move; it did not occur to me to move: I was sleepy. 'It *is* unpleasant,' grunted the uncle. 'He has asked the Administration to be sent there,' said the other, 'with the idea of showing what he could do; and I was instructed accordingly. Look at the influence that man must have. Is it not frightful?' They both agreed it was frightful, then made several bizarre remarks: 'Make rain and fine weather—one man—the Council—by the nose'—bits of absurd sentences that got the better of my drowsiness, so that I had pretty near the whole of my wits about me when the uncle said, 'The climate may do away with this difficulty for you. Is he alone there?' 'Yes,' answered the manager; 'he sent his assistant down the river with a note to me in these terms: "Clear this poor devil out of the country, and don't bother sending more of that sort. I had rather be alone than have the kind of men you can dispose of with me." It was more than a year ago. Can you imagine such impudence!' 'Anything since then?' asked the other, hoarsely. 'Ivory,' jerked the nephew; 'lots of it—prime sort—lots—most annoying, from him.' 'And with that?' questioned the heavy rumble. 'Invoice,' was the reply fired out, so to speak. Then silence. They had been talking about Kurtz.

"I was broad awake by this time, but, lying perfectly at ease, remained still, having no inducement to change my position. 'How did that ivory come all this way?' growled the elder man, who seemed very vexed. The other explained that it had come with a fleet of canoes in charge of an English half-caste clerk Kurtz had with him; that Kurtz had apparently intended to return himself, the station being by that time bare of goods and stores, but after coming three hundred miles, had suddenly decided to go back, which he started to do alone in a small dug-out with four paddlers, leaving the half-caste to continue down the river with the ivory. The two fellows there seemed astounded at anybody attempting such a thing. They were at a loss for an adequate motive. As to me, I seemed to see Kurtz for the first time. It was a distinct glimpse: the dug-out, four paddling savages, and the lone white man turning his back suddenly on the headquarters, on relief, on thoughts of home—perhaps; setting his face towards the depths of the wilderness, towards his empty and desolate station. I did not know the motive. Perhaps he was just simply a fine fellow who stuck to his work for its own sake. His name, you understand, had not been pronounced once. He was 'that man.' The half-caste, who, as far as I could see, had conducted a difficult trip with great prudence and pluck, was invariably alluded to as 'that scoundrel.' The 'scoundrel' had reported that the 'man' had been very ill—had recovered imperfectly. . . . The two below me moved away then a few paces, and strolled back and forth at some little distance. I heard: 'Military post—doctor—two hundred miles—quite alone now—unavoidable delays—nine months—no news—strange rumors.' They approached again, just as the manager was saying, 'No one, as far as I know, unless a species of wandering trader—a pestilential fellow, snapping ivory from the natives.' Who was it they were talking about now? I gathered in snatches that this was some man supposed to be in Kurtz's district, and of whom the manager did not approve. 'We will not be free from unfair competition till one of these fellows is hanged for an example,' he said. 'Certainly,' grunted the other; 'get him hanged! Why not? Anything—anything can be done in this country. That's what I say; nobody here, you understand, *here*, can endanger your position. And why? You stand the climate—you outlast them all. The danger is in Europe; but there before I left I took care to—' They moved off and whispered, then their voices rose again. 'The extraordinary series of delays is not my fault. I did my possible.' The fat man sighed, 'Very sad.' 'And the pestiferous absurdity of his talk,' continued the other; 'he bothered me enough when he was here. "Each station should be like a beacon on the road towards better things, a center for trade of course, but also for humanizing, improving, instructing." Conceive you—that ass! And he wants to be manager! No, it's—' Here he got choked by excessive indignation, and I lifted my head the least bit. I was surprised to see how near they were—right under me. I could have spat upon their hats. They were looking on the ground, absorbed in thought. The manager was switching his leg with a slender twig: his sagacious relative lifted his head. 'You have been well since you came out this time?' he asked. The other gave a start. 'Who? I? Oh! Like a charm—like a charm. But the rest—oh, my goodness! All sick. They die so quick, too, that I haven't the time to send them out of the country—it's incredible!' 'H'm. Just so,' grunted the uncle. 'Ah! my boy, trust to this—I say, trust to this.' I saw him extend his short flipper of an arm for a gesture that took in the forest, the creek, the mud, the river,—seemed to beckon with a dishonoring flourish before the sunlit face of the land a treacherous appeal to the lurking death, to the hidden evil, to the profound darkness of its heart. It was so startling that I leaped to my feet and looked back at the edge of the forest, as though I had expected an answer of some sort to that black display of confidence. You know the foolish notions that come to one sometimes. The high stillness confronted these two figures with its ominous patience, waiting for the passing away of a fantastic invasion.

"They swore aloud together—out of sheer fright, I believe—then pretending not to know anything of my existence, turned back to the station. The sun was low; and leaning forward side by side, they seemed to be tugging painfully uphill their two ridiculous shadows of unequal length, that trailed behind them slowly over the tall grass without bending a single blade.

"In a few days the Eldorado Expedition went into the patient wilderness, that closed upon it as the sea closes over a diver. Long afterwards the news came that all the donkeys were dead. I know nothing as to the fate of the less valuable animals. They, no doubt, like the rest of us, found what they deserved. I did not inquire. I was then rather excited at the prospect of meeting Kurtz very soon. When I say very soon I mean it comparatively. It was just two months from the day we left the creek when we came to the bank below Kurtz's station.

"Going up that river was like traveling back to the earliest beginnings of the world, when vegetation rioted on the earth and the big trees were kings. An empty stream, a great silence, an impenetrable forest. The air was warm, thick, heavy, sluggish. There was no joy in the brilliance of sunshine. The long stretches of the waterway ran on, deserted, into the gloom of overshadowed distances. On silvery sandbanks hippos and alligators sunned themselves side by side. The broadening waters flowed through a mob of wooded islands; you lost your way on that river as you would in a desert, and butted all day long against shoals, trying to find the channel, till you thought yourself bewitched and cut off for ever from everything you had known once—

somewhere—far away—in another existence perhaps. There were moments when one's past came back to one, as it will sometimes when you have not a moment to spare to yourself; but it came in the shape of an unrestful and noisy dream, remembered with wonder amongst the overwhelming realities of this strange world of plants, and water, and silence. And this stillness of life did not in the least resemble a peace. It was the stillness of an implacable force brooding over an inscrutable intention. It looked at you with a vengeful aspect. I got used to it afterwards; I did not see it any more; I had no time. I had to keep guessing at the channel; I had to discern, mostly by inspiration, the signs of hidden banks; I watched for sunken stones; I was learning to clap my teeth smartly before my heart flew out, when I shaved by a fluke some infernal sly old snag that would have ripped the life out of the tin-pot steamboat and drowned all the pilgrims; I had to keep a look-out for the signs of dead wood we could cut up in the night for next day's steaming. When you have to attend to things of that sort, to the mere incidents of the surface, the reality—the reality, I tell you— fades. The inner truth is hidden—luckily, luckily. But I felt it all the same; I felt often its mysterious stillness watching me at my monkey tricks, just as it watches you fellows performing on your respective tight-ropes for—what is it? half-a-crown a tumble—"

"Try to be civil, Marlow," growled a voice, and I knew there was at least one listener awake besides myself.

"I beg your pardon. I forgot the heartache which makes up the rest of the price. And indeed what does the price matter, if the trick be well done? You do your tricks very well. And I didn't do badly either, since I managed not to sink that steamboat on my first trip. It's a wonder to me yet. Imagine a blindfolded man set to drive a van over a bad road. I sweated and shivered over that business considerably, I can tell you. After all, for a seaman, to scrape the bottom of the thing that's supposed to float all the time under his care is the unpardonable sin. No one may know of it, but you never forget the thump—eh? A blow on the very heart. You remember it, you dream of it, you wake up at night and think of it—years after—and go hot and cold all over. I don't pretend to say that steamboat floated all the time. More than once she had to wade for a bit, with twenty cannibals splashing around and pushing. We had enlisted some of these chaps on the way for a crew. Fine fellows—cannibals—in their place. They were men one could work with, and I am grateful to them. And, after all, they did not eat each other before my face: they had brought along a provision of hippo-meat which went rotten, and made the mystery of the wilderness stink in my nostrils. Phoo! I can sniff it now. I had the manager on board and three or four pilgrims with their staves—all complete. Sometimes we came upon a station close by the bank, clinging to the skirts of the unknown, and the white men rushing out of a tumble-down hovel, with great gestures of joy and surprise and welcome, seemed very strange,—had the appearance of being held there captive by a spell. The word ivory would ring in the air for a while—and on we went again into the silence, along empty reaches, round the still bends, between the high walls of our winding way, reverberating in hollow claps the ponderous beat of the stern-wheel. Trees, trees, millions of trees, massive, immense, running up high; and at their foot, hugging the bank against the stream, crept the little begrimed steamboat, like a sluggish beetle crawling on the floor of a lofty portico. It made you feel very small, very lost, and yet it was not altogether depressing, that feeling. After all, if you were small, the grimy beetle crawled on— which was just what you wanted it to do. Where the pilgrims imagined it crawled to I don't know. To some place where they expected to get something, I bet! For me it crawled toward Kurtz—exclusively; but when the steam-pipes started leaking we crawled very slow. The reaches opened before us and closed behind, as if the forest had stepped leisurely across the water to bar the way for our return. We penetrated deeper and deeper into the heart of darkness. It was very quiet there. At night sometimes the roll of drums behind the curtain of trees would run up the river and remain sustained faintly, as if hovering in the air high over our heads, till the first break of day. Whether it meant war, peace, or prayer we could not tell. The dawns were heralded by the descent of a chill stillness; the woodcutters slept, their fires burned low; the snapping of a twig would make you start. We were wanderers on a prehistoric earth, on an earth that wore the aspect of an unknown planet. We could have fancied ourselves the first of men taking possession of an accursed inheritance, to be subdued at the cost of profound anguish and of excessive toil. But suddenly, as we struggled round a bend, there would be a glimpse of rush walls, of peaked grass-roofs, a burst of yells, a whirl of black limbs, a mass of hands clapping, of feet stamping, of bodies swaying, of eyes rolling, under the droop of heavy and motionless foliage. The steamer toiled along slowly on the edge of a black and incomprehensible frenzy. The prehistoric man was cursing us, praying to us, welcoming us—who could tell? We were cut off from the comprehension of our surroundings; we glided past like phantoms, wondering and secretly appalled, as sane men would be before an enthusiastic outbreak in a madhouse. We could not understand, because we were too far and could not remember, because we were traveling in the night of first ages, of those ages that are gone, leaving hardly a sign—and no memories.

"The earth seemed unearthly. We are accustomed to look upon the shackled form of a conquered monster, but there—there you could look at a thing monstrous and free. It was unearthly, and the men were—No, they were not inhuman. Well, you know, that was the worst of it—this suspicion of their not being inhuman. It would come slowly to one.

They howled, and leaped, and spun, and made horrid faces; but what thrilled you was just the thought of their humanity—like yours—the thought of your remote kinship with this wild and passionate uproar. Ugly. Yes, it was ugly enough; but if you were man enough you would admit to yourself that there was in you just the faintest trace of a response to the terrible frankness of that noise, a dim suspicion of there being a meaning in it which you—you so remote from the night of first ages—could comprehend. And why not? The mind of man is capable of anything—because everything is in it, all the past as well as all the future. What was there after all? Joy, fear, sorrow, devotion, valor, rage—who can tell?—but truth—truth stripped of its cloak of time. Let the fool gape and shudder—the man knows, and can look on without a wink. But he must at least be as much of a man as these on the shore. He must meet that truth with his own true stuff—with his own inborn strength. Principles? Principles won't do. Acquisitions, clothes, pretty rags—rags that would fly off at the first good shake. No; you want a deliberate belief. An appeal to me in this fiendish row—is there? Very well; I hear; I admit, but I have a voice too, and for good or evil mine is the speech that cannot be silenced. Of course, a fool, what with sheer fright and fine sentiments, is always safe. Who's that grunting? You wonder I didn't go ashore for a howl and a dance? Well, no—I didn't. Fine sentiments, you say? Fine sentiments, be hanged! I had no time. I had to mess about with white-lead and strips of woolen blanket helping to put bandages on those leaky steam-pipes—I tell you. I had to watch the steering, and circumvent those snags, and get the tin-pot along by hook or by crook. There was surface-truth enough in these things to save a wiser man. And between whiles I had to look after the savage who was fireman. He was an improved specimen; he could fire up a vertical boiler. He was there below me, and, upon my word, to look at him was as edifying as seeing a dog in a parody of breeches and a feather hat, walking on his hind-legs. A few months of training had done for that really fine chap. He squinted at the steam-gauge and at the water-gauge with an evident effort of intrepidity—and he had filed teeth too, the poor devil, and the wool of his pate shaved into queer patterns, and three ornamental scars on each of his cheeks. He ought to have been clapping his hands and stamping his feet on the bank, instead of which he was hard at work, a thrall to strange witchcraft, full of improving knowledge. He was useful because he had been instructed; and what he knew was this—that should the water in that transparent thing disappear, the evil spirit inside the boiler would get angry through the greatness of his thirst, and take a terrible vengeance. So he sweated and fired up and watched the glass fearfully (with an impromptu charm, made of rags, tied to his arm, and a piece of polished bone, as big as a watch, stuck flatways through his lower lip), while the wooded banks slipped past us slowly, the short noise was left behind, the interminable miles of silence—and we crept on, towards Kurtz. But the snags were thick, the water was treacherous and shallow, the boiler seemed indeed to have a sulky devil in it, and thus neither that fireman nor I had any time to peer into our creepy thoughts.

"Some fifty miles below the Inner Station we came upon a hut of reeds, an inclined and melancholy pole, with the unrecognizable tatters of what had been a flag of some sort flying from it, and a neatly stacked woodpile. This was unexpected. We came to the bank, and on the stack of firewood found a flat piece of board with some faded pencil-writing on it. When deciphered it said: 'Wood for you. Hurry up. Approach cautiously.' There was a signature, but it was illegible—not Kurtz—a much longer word. 'Hurry up.' Where? Up the river? 'Approach cautiously.' We had not done so. But the warning could not have been meant for the place where it could be only found after approach. Something was wrong above. But what—and how much? That was the question. We commented adversely upon the imbecility of that telegraphic style. The bush around said nothing, and would not let us look very far, either. A torn curtain of red twill hung in the doorway of the hut, and flapped sadly in our faces. The dwelling was dismantled; but we could see a white man had lived there not very long ago. There remained a rude table—a plank on two posts; a heap of rubbish reposed in a dark corner, and by the door I picked up a book. It had lost its covers, and the pages had been thumbed into a state of extremely dirty softness; but the back had been lovingly stitched afresh with white cotton thread, which looked clean yet. It was an extraordinary find. Its title was, '*An Inquiry into some Points of Seamanship*,' by a man Tower, Towson—some such name—Master in his Majesty's Navy. The matter looked dreary reading enough, with illustrative diagrams and repulsive tables of figures, and the copy was sixty years old. I handled this amazing antiquity with the greatest possible tenderness, lest it should dissolve in my hands. Within, Towson or Towser was inquiring earnestly into the breaking strain of ships' chains and tackle, and other such matters. Not a very enthralling book; but at the first glance you could see there a singleness of intention, an honest concern for the right way of going to work, which made these humble pages, thought out so many years ago, luminous with another than a professional light. The simple old sailor, with his talk of chains and purchases, made me forget the jungle and the pilgrims in a delicious sensation of having come upon something unmistakably real. Such a book being there was wonderful enough; but still more astounding were the notes penciled in the margin, and plainly referring to the text. I couldn't believe my eyes! They were in cipher! Yes, it looked like cipher. Fancy a man lugging with him a book of that description into this nowhere and studying it—and making notes—in cipher at that! It was an extravagant mystery.

"I had been dimly aware for some time of a worrying noise, and when I lifted my eyes I saw the wood-pile was gone, and the manager, aided by all the pilgrims, was shouting at me from the river-side. I slipped the book into my pocket. I assure you to leave off reading was like tearing myself away from the shelter of an old and solid friendship.

"I started the lame engine ahead. 'It must be this miserable trader—this intruder,' exclaimed the manager, looking back malevolently at the place we had left. 'He must be English,' I said. 'It will not save him from getting into trouble if he is not careful,' muttered the manager darkly. I observed with assumed innocence that no man was safe from trouble in this world.

"The current was more rapid now, the steamer seemed at her last gasp, the stern-wheel flopped languidly, and I caught myself listening on tiptoe for the next beat of the boat, for in sober truth I expected the wretched thing to give up every moment. It was like watching the last flickers of a life. But still we crawled. Sometimes I would pick out a tree a little way ahead to measure our progress towards Kurtz by, but I lost it invariably before we got abreast. To keep the eyes so long on one thing was too much for human patience. The manager displayed a beautiful resignation. I fretted and fumed and took to arguing with myself whether or no I would talk openly with Kurtz; but before I could come to any conclusion it occurred to me that my speech or my silence, indeed any action of mine, would be a mere futility. What did it matter what anyone knew or ignored? What did it matter who was manager? One gets sometimes such a flash of insight. The essentials of this affair lay deep under the surface, beyond my reach, and beyond my power of meddling.

"Towards the evening of the second day we judged ourselves about eight miles from Kurtz's station. I wanted to push on; but the manager looked grave, and told me the navigation up there was so dangerous that it would be advisable, the sun being very low already, to wait where we were till next morning. Moreover, he pointed out that if the warning to approach cautiously were to be followed, we must approach in daylight—not at dusk, or in the dark. This was sensible enough. Eight miles meant nearly three hours' steaming for us, and I could also see suspicious ripples at the upper end of the reach. Nevertheless, I was annoyed beyond expression at the delay, and most unreasonably too, since one night more could not matter much after so many months. As we had plenty of wood, and caution was the word, I brought up in the middle of the stream. The reach was narrow, straight, with high sides like a railway cutting. The dusk came gliding into it long before the sun had set. The current ran smooth and swift, but a dumb immobility sat on the banks. The living trees, lashed together by the creepers and every living bush of the undergrowth, might have been changed into stone, even to the slenderest twig, to the lightest leaf. It was not sleep—

it seemed unnatural, like a state of trance. Not the faintest sound of any kind could be heard. You looked on amazed, and began to suspect yourself of being deaf—then the night came suddenly, and struck you blind as well. About three in the morning some large fish leaped, and the loud splash made me jump as though a gun had been fired. When the sun rose there was a white fog, very warm and clammy, and more blinding than the night. It did not shift or drive; it was just there, standing all round you like something solid. At eight or nine, perhaps, it lifted as a shutter lifts. We had a glimpse of the towering multitude of trees, of the immense matted jungle, with the blazing little ball of the sun hanging over it—all perfectly still—and then the white shutter came down again, smoothly, as if sliding in greased grooves. I ordered the chain, which we had begun to heave in, to be paid out again. Before it stopped running with a muffled rattle, a cry, a very loud cry, as of infinite desolation, soared slowly in the opaque air. It ceased. A complaining clamor, modulated in savage discords, filled our ears. The sheer unexpectedness of it made my hair stir under my cap. I don't know how it struck the others: to me it seemed as though the mist itself had screamed, so suddenly, and apparently from all sides at once, did this tumultuous and mournful uproar arise. It culminated in a hurried outbreak of almost intolerably excessive shrieking, which stopped short, leaving us stiffened in a variety of silly attitudes, and obstinately listening to the nearly as appalling and excessive silence. 'Good God! What is the meaning—?' stammered at my elbow one of the pilgrims,—a little fat man, with sandy hair and red whiskers, who wore side-spring boots, and pink pajamas tucked into his socks. Two others remained open-mouthed a whole minute, then dashed into the little cabin, to rush out incontinently and stand darting scared glances, with Winchesters at 'ready' in their hands. What we could see was just the steamer we were on, her outlines blurred as though she had been on the point of dissolving, and a misty strip of water, perhaps two feet broad, around her—and that was all. The rest of the world was nowhere, as far as our eyes and ears were concerned. Just nowhere. Gone, disappeared; swept off without leaving a whisper or a shadow behind.

    "I went forward, and ordered the chain to be hauled in short, so as to be ready to trip the anchor and move the steamboat at once if necessary. 'Will they attack?' whispered an awed voice. 'We will all be butchered in this fog,' murmured another. The faces twitched with the strain, the hands trembled slightly, the eyes forgot to wink. It was very curious to see the contrast of expressions of the white men and of the black fellows of our crew, who were as much strangers to that part of the river as we, though their homes were only eight hundred miles away. The whites, of course greatly discomposed, had besides a curious look of being painfully shocked by such an outrageous row. The others had an alert, naturally interested expression; but their faces were essentially quiet, even those of the one or two who grinned as they hauled at the chain. Several exchanged short, grunting phrases, which seemed to settle the matter to their satisfaction. Their headman, a young, broad-chested black, severely draped in dark-blue fringed cloths, with fierce nostrils and his hair all done up artfully in oily ringlets, stood near me. 'Aha!' I said, just for good fellowship's sake. 'Catch 'im,' he snapped, with a bloodshot widening of his eyes and a flash of sharp teeth—'catch 'im. Give 'im to us.' 'To you, eh?' I asked; 'what would you do with them?' 'Eat 'im!' he said curtly, and, leaning his elbow on the rail, looked out into the fog in a dignified and profoundly pensive attitude. I would no doubt have been properly horrified, had it not occurred to me that he and his chaps must be very hungry: that they must have been growing increasingly hungry for at least this month past. They had been engaged for six months (I don't think a single one of them had any clear idea of time, as we at the end of countless ages have. They still belonged to the beginnings of time— had no inherited experience to teach them as it were), and of course, as long as there was a piece of paper written over in accordance with some farcical law or other made down the river, it didn't enter anybody's head to trouble how they would live. Certainly they had brought with them some rotten hippo-meat, which couldn't have lasted very long, anyway, even if the pilgrims hadn't, in the midst of a shocking hullabaloo, thrown a considerable quantity of it overboard. It looked like a high-handed proceeding; but it was really a case of legitimate self-defense. You can't breathe dead hippo waking, sleeping, and eating, and at the same time keep your precarious grip on existence. Besides that, they had given them every week three pieces of brass wire, each about nine inches long; and the theory was they were to buy their provisions with that currency in river-side villages. You can see how *that* worked. There were either no villages, or the people were hostile, or the director, who like the rest of us fed out of tins, with an occasional old he-goat thrown in, didn't want to stop the steamer for some more or less recondite reason. So, unless they swallowed the wire itself, or made loops of it to snare the fishes with, I don't see what good their extravagant salary could be to them. I must say it was paid with a regularity worthy of a large and honorable trading company. For the rest, the only thing to eat—though it didn't look eatable in the least—I saw in their possession was a few lumps of some stuff like half-cooked dough, of a dirty lavender color, they kept wrapped in leaves, and now and then swallowed a piece of, but so small that it seemed done more for the looks of the thing than for any serious purpose of sustenance. Why in the name of all the gnawing devils of hunger they didn't go for us—they were thirty to five—and have a good tuck in for once, amazes me now when I think of it. They were big powerful men, with not much capacity to weigh the consequences, with courage, with strength, even yet, though their skins were no longer glossy and their muscles no longer hard. And I saw that something restraining, one of those human secrets that baffle probability, had come into play there. I looked at them with a swift quickening of interest—not because it occurred to me I might be eaten by them before very long, though I own to you that just then I perceived—in a new light, as it were—how unwholesome the pilgrims looked, and I hoped, yes, I positively hoped, that my aspect was not so—what shall I say?—so—unappetizing: a touch of fantastic vanity which fitted well with the dream-sensation that pervaded all my days at that time. Perhaps I had a little fever too. One can't live with one's finger everlastingly on one's pulse. I had often 'a little fever,' or a little touch of other things—the playful paw-strokes of the wilderness, the preliminary trifling before the more serious onslaught which came in due course. Yes; I looked at them as you would on any human being, with a curiosity of their impulses, motives, capacities, weaknesses, when brought to the test of an inexorable physical necessity. Restraint! What possible restraint? Was it superstition, disgust, patience, fear—or some kind of primitive honor? No fear can stand up to hunger, no patience can wear it out, disgust simply does not exist where hunger is; and as to superstition, beliefs, and what you may call principles, they are less than chaff in a breeze. Don't you know the devilry of lingering starvation, its exasperating torment, its black thoughts, its somber and brooding ferocity? Well, I do. It takes a man all his inborn strength to fight hunger properly. It's really easier to face bereavement, dishonor, and the perdition of one's soul—than this kind of prolonged hunger. Sad, but true. And these chaps too had no earthly reason for any kind of scruple. Restraint! I would just as soon have expected restraint from a hyena prowling amongst the corpses of a battlefield. But there was the fact facing me—the fact dazzling, to be seen, like the foam on the depths of the sea, like a ripple on an unfathomable enigma, a mystery greater—when I thought of it—than the curious, inexplicable note of desperate grief in this savage clamor that had swept by us on the river-bank, behind the blind whiteness of the fog.

"Two pilgrims were quarreling in hurried whispers as to which bank. 'Left.' 'No, no; how can you? Right, right, of course.' 'It is very serious,' said the manager's voice behind me; 'I would be desolated if anything should happen to Mr. Kurtz before we came up.' I looked at him, and had not the slightest doubt he was sincere. He was just the kind of man who would wish to preserve appearances. That was his restraint. But when he muttered something about going on at once, I did not even take the trouble to answer him. I knew, and he knew, that it was impossible. Were we to let go our hold of the bottom, we would be absolutely in the air—in space. We wouldn't be able to tell where we were going to—whether up or down stream, or across—till we fetched against one bank or the other,—and then we wouldn't know at first which it was. Of course I made no move. I had no mind for a smash-up. You couldn't imagine a more deadly place for a shipwreck. Whether drowned at once or not, we were sure to perish speedily in one way or another. 'I authorize you to take all the risks,' he said, after a short silence. 'I refuse to take any,' I said shortly; which was just the answer he expected, though its tone might have surprised him. 'Well, I must defer to your judgment. You are captain,' he said, with marked civility. I turned my shoulder to him in sign of my appreciation, and looked into the fog. How long would it last? It was the most hopeless look-out. The approach to this Kurtz grubbing for ivory in the wretched bush was beset by as many dangers as though he had been an enchanted princess sleeping in a fabulous castle. 'Will they attack, do you think?' asked the manager, in a confidential tone.

"I did not think they would attack, for several obvious reasons. The thick fog was one. If they left the bank in their canoes they would get lost in it, as we would be if we attempted to move. Still, I had also judged the jungle of both banks quite impenetrable—and yet eyes were in it, eyes that had seen us. The river-side bushes were certainly very thick; but the undergrowth behind was evidently penetrable. However, during the short lift I had seen no canoes anywhere in the reach— certainly not abreast of the steamer. But what made the idea of attack inconceivable to me was the nature of the noise—of the cries we had heard. They had not the fierce character boding of immediate hostile intention. Unexpected, wild, and violent as they had been, they had given me an irresistible impression of sorrow. The glimpse of the steamboat had for some reason filled those savages with unrestrained grief. The danger, if any, I expounded, was from our proximity to a great human passion let loose. Even extreme grief may ultimately vent itself in violence—but more generally takes the form of apathy. . . .

"You should have seen the pilgrims stare! They had no heart to grin, or even to revile me; but I believe they thought me gone mad— with fright, maybe. I delivered a regular lecture. My dear boys, it was no good bothering. Keep a look-out? Well, you may guess I watched the fog for the signs of lifting as a cat watches a mouse; but for anything else our eyes were of no more use to us than if we had been buried miles deep in a heap of cotton-wool. It felt like it too—choking, warm, stifling. Besides, all I said, though it sounded extravagant, was absolutely true to fact. What we afterwards alluded to as an attack was really an attempt at repulse. The action was very far from being aggressive—it was not even defensive, in the usual sense: it was undertaken under the stress of desperation, and in its essence was purely protective.

"It developed itself, I should say, two hours after the fog lifted, and its commencement was at a spot, roughly speaking, about a mile and a

half below Kurtz's station. We had just floundered and flopped round a
bend, when I saw an islet, a mere grassy hummock of bright green, in
the middle of the stream. It was the only thing of the kind; but as we
opened the reach more, I perceived it was the head of a long sandbank,
or rather of a chain of shallow patches stretching down the middle of
the river. They were discolored, just awash, and the whole lot was seen
just under the water, exactly as a man's backbone is seen running down
the middle of his back under the skin. Now, as far as I did see, I could
go to the right or to the left of this. I didn't know either channel, of
course. The banks looked pretty well alike, the depth appeared the
same; but as I had been informed the station was on the west side, I
naturally headed for the western passage.

"No sooner had we fairly entered it than I became aware it was
much narrower than I had supposed. To the left of us there was the long
uninterrupted shoal, and to the right a high, steep bank heavily
overgrown with bushes. Above the bush the trees stood in serried ranks.
The twigs overhung the current thickly, and from distance to distance a
large limb of some tree projected rigidly over the stream. It was then
well on in the afternoon, the face of the forest was gloomy, and a broad
strip of shadow had already fallen on the water. In this shadow we
steamed up—very slowly, as you may imagine. I sheered her well
inshore—the water being deepest near the bank, as the sounding-pole
informed me.

"One of my hungry and forbearing friends was sounding in the
bows just below me. This steamboat was exactly like a decked scow.
On the deck there were two little teak-wood houses, with doors and
windows. The boiler was in the fore-end, and the machinery right
astern. Over the whole there was a light roof, supported on stanchions.
The funnel projected through that roof, and in front of the funnel a
small cabin built of light planks served for a pilot-house. It contained a
couch, two camp-stools, a loaded Martini-Henry leaning in one corner,
a tiny table, and the steering-wheel. It had a wide door in front and a
broad shutter at each side. All these were always thrown open, of
course. I spent my days perched up there on the extreme fore-end of
that roof, before the door. At night I slept, or tried to, on the couch. An
athletic black belonging to some coast tribe, and educated by my poor
predecessor, was the helmsman. He sported a pair of brass earrings,
wore a blue cloth wrapper from the waist to the ankles, and thought all
the world of himself. He was the most unstable kind of fool I had ever
seen. He steered with no end of a swagger while you were by; but if he
lost sight of you, he became instantly the prey of an abject funk, and
would let that cripple of a steamboat get the upper hand of him in a
minute.

"I was looking down at the sounding-pole, and feeling much
annoyed to see at each try a little more of it stick out of that river, when

I saw my poleman give up the business suddenly, and stretch himself flat on the deck, without even taking the trouble to haul his pole in. He kept hold on it though, and it trailed in the water. At the same time the fireman, whom I could also see below me, sat down abruptly before his furnace and ducked his head. I was amazed. Then I had to look at the river mighty quick, because there was a snag in the fairway. Sticks, little sticks, were flying about—thick: they were whizzing before my nose, dropping below me, striking behind me against my pilot-house. All this time the river, the shore, the woods, were very quiet—perfectly quiet. I could only hear the heavy splashing thump of the stern-wheel and the patter of these things. We cleared the snag clumsily. Arrows, by Jove! We were being shot at! I stepped in quickly to close the shutter on the land side. That fool-helmsman, his hands on the spokes, was lifting his knees high, stamping his feet, champing his mouth, like a reined-in horse. Confound him! And we were staggering within ten feet of the bank. I had to lean right out to swing the heavy shutter, and I saw a face amongst the leaves on the level with my own, looking at me very fierce and steady; and then suddenly, as though a veil had been removed from my eyes, I made out, deep in the tangled gloom, naked breasts, arms, legs, glaring eyes,—the bush was swarming with human limbs in movement, glistening, of bronze color. The twigs shook, swayed, and rustled, the arrows flew out of them, and then the shutter came to. 'Steer her straight,' I said to the helmsman. He held his head rigid, face forward; but his eyes rolled, he kept on lifting and setting down his feet gently, his mouth foamed a little. 'Keep quiet!' I said in a fury. I might just as well have ordered a tree not to sway in the wind. I darted out. Below me there was a great scuffle of feet on the iron deck; confused exclamations; a voice screamed, 'Can you turn back?' I caught shape of a V-shaped ripple on the water ahead. What? Another snag! A fusillade burst out under my feet. The pilgrims had opened with their Winchesters, and were simply squirting lead into that bush. A deuce of a lot of smoke came up and drove slowly forward. I swore at it. Now I couldn't see the ripple or the snag either. I stood in the doorway, peering, and the arrows came in swarms. They might have been poisoned, but they looked as though they wouldn't kill a cat. The bush began to howl. Our wood-cutters raised a warlike whoop; the report of a rifle just at my back deafened me. I glanced over my shoulder, and the pilot-house was yet full of noise and smoke when I made a dash at the wheel. The fool-nigger had dropped everything, to throw the shutter open and let off that Martini-Henry. He stood before the wide opening, glaring, and I yelled at him to come back, while I straightened the sudden twist out of that steamboat. There was no room to turn even if I had wanted to, the snag was somewhere very near ahead in that confounded smoke, there was no time to lose, so I just crowded her into the bank—right into the bank, where I knew the water was deep.

"We tore slowly along the overhanging bushes in a whirl of broken twigs and flying leaves. The fusillade below stopped short, as I had foreseen it would when the squirts got empty. I threw my head back to a glinting whizz that traversed the pilot-house, in at one shutter-hole and out at the other. Looking past that mad helmsman, who was shaking the empty rifle and yelling at the shore, I saw vague forms of men running bent double, leaping, gliding, distinct, incomplete, evanescent. Something big appeared in the air before the shutter, the rifle went overboard, and the man stepped back swiftly, looked at me over his shoulder in an extraordinary, profound, familiar manner, and fell upon my feet. The side of his head hit the wheel twice, and the end of what appeared a long cane clattered round and knocked over a little camp-stool. It looked as though after wrenching that thing from somebody ashore he had lost his balance in the effort. The thin smoke had blown away, we were clear of the snag, and looking ahead I could see that in another hundred yards or so I would be free to sheer off, away from the bank; but my feet felt so very warm and wet that I had to look down. The man had rolled on his back and stared straight up at me; both his hands clutched that cane. It was the shaft of a spear that, either thrown or lunged through the opening, had caught him in the side just below the ribs; the blade had gone in out of sight, after making a frightful gash; my shoes were full; a pool of blood lay very still, gleaming dark-red under the wheel; his eyes shone with an amazing luster. The fusillade burst out again. He looked at me anxiously, gripping the spear like something precious, with an air of being afraid I would try to take it away from him. I had to make an effort to free my eyes from his gaze and attend to the steering. With one hand I felt above my head for the line of the steam-whistle, and jerked out screech after screech hurriedly. The tumult of angry and warlike yells was checked instantly, and then from the depths of the woods went out such a tremulous and prolonged wail of mournful fear and utter despair as may be imagined to follow the flight of the last hope from the earth. There was a great commotion in the bush; the shower of arrows stopped, a few dropping shots rang out sharply—then silence, in which the languid beat of the stern-wheel came plainly to my ears. I put the helm hard a-starboard at the moment when the pilgrim in pink pajamas, very hot and agitated, appeared in the doorway. 'The manager sends me—' he began in an official tone, and stopped short. 'Good God!' he said, glaring at the wounded man.

"We two whites stood over him, and his lustrous and inquiring glance enveloped us both. I declare it looked as though he would presently put to us some question in an understandable language; but he died without uttering a sound, without moving a limb, without twitching a muscle. Only in the very last moment, as though in response to some sign we could not see, to some whisper we could not hear, he frowned heavily, and that frown gave to his black death-mask an inconceivably somber, brooding, and menacing expression. The luster of inquiring glance faded swiftly into vacant glassiness. 'Can you steer?' I asked the agent eagerly. He looked very dubious; but I made a grab at his arm, and he understood at once I meant him to steer whether or no. To tell you the truth, I was morbidly anxious to change my shoes and socks. 'He is dead,' murmured the fellow, immensely impressed. 'No doubt about it,' said I, tugging like mad at the shoe-laces. 'And, by the way, I suppose Mr. Kurtz is dead as well by this time.'

"For the moment that was the dominant thought. There was a sense of extreme disappointment, as though I had found out I had been striving after something altogether without a substance. I couldn't have been more disgusted if I had traveled all this way for the sole purpose of talking with Mr. Kurtz. Talking with. . . . I flung one shoe overboard, and became aware that that was exactly what I had been looking forward to—a talk with Kurtz. I made the strange discovery that I had never imagined him as doing, you know, but as discoursing. I didn't say to myself, 'Now I will never see him,' or 'Now I will never shake him by the hand,' but, 'Now I will never hear him.' The man presented himself as a voice. Not of course that I did not connect him with some sort of action. Hadn't I been told in all the tones of jealousy and admiration that he had collected, bartered, swindled, or stolen more ivory than all the other agents together? That was not the point. The point was in his being a gifted creature, and that of all his gifts the one that stood out pre-eminently, that carried with it a sense of real presence, was his ability to talk, his words—the gift of expression, the bewildering, the illuminating, the most exalted and the most contemptible, the pulsating stream of light, or the deceitful flow from the heart of an impenetrable darkness.

"The other shoe went flying unto the devil-god of that river. I thought, 'By Jove! it's all over. We are too late; he has vanished—the gift has vanished, by means of some spear, arrow, or club. I will never hear that chap speak after all,'—and my sorrow had a startling extravagance of emotion, even such as I had noticed in the howling sorrow of these savages in the bush. I couldn't have felt more of lonely desolation somehow, had I been robbed of a belief or had missed my destiny in life. . . . Why do you sigh in this beastly way, somebody? Absurd? Well, absurd. Good Lord! mustn't a man ever—Here, give me some tobacco." . . .

There was a pause of profound stillness, then a match flared, and Marlow's lean face appeared, worn, hollow, with downward folds and dropped eyelids, with an aspect of concentrated attention; and as he took vigorous draws at his pipe, it seemed to retreat and advance out of the night in the regular flicker of the tiny flame. The match went out.

"Absurd!" he cried. "This is the worst of trying to tell. . . . Here you all are, each moored with two good addresses, like a hulk with two anchors, a butcher round one corner, a policeman round another, excellent appetites, and temperature normal—you hear—normal from year's end to year's end. And you say, Absurd! Absurd be—exploded! Absurd! My dear boys, what can you expect from a man who out of sheer nervousness had just flung overboard a pair of new shoes. Now I think of it, it is amazing I did not shed tears. I am, upon the whole, proud of my fortitude. I was cut to the quick at the idea of having lost the inestimable privilege of listening to the gifted Kurtz. Of course I was wrong. The privilege was waiting for me. Oh yes, I heard more than enough. And I was right, too. A voice. He was very little more than a voice. And I heard—him—it—this voice—other voices—all of them were so little more than voices—and the memory of that time itself lingers around me, impalpable, like a dying vibration of one immense jabber, silly, atrocious, sordid, savage, or simply mean, without any kind of sense. Voices, voices—even the girl herself—now—"

He was silent for a long time.

"I laid the ghost of his gifts at last with a lie," he began suddenly. "Girl! What? Did I mention a girl? Oh, she is out of it—completely. They—the women, I mean—are out of it—should be out of it. We must help them to stay in that beautiful world of their own, lest ours gets worse. Oh, she had to be out of it. You should have heard the disinterred body of Mr. Kurtz saying, 'My Intended.' You would have perceived directly then how completely she was out of it. And the lofty frontal bone of Mr. Kurtz! They say the hair goes on growing sometimes, but this—ah specimen, was impressively bald. The wilderness had patted him on the head, and, behold, it was like a ball—an ivory ball; it had caressed him, and—lo!—he had withered; it had taken him, loved him, embraced him, got into his veins, consumed his flesh, and sealed his soul to its own by the inconceivable ceremonies of some devilish initiation. He was its spoiled and pampered favorite. Ivory? I should think so. Heaps of it, stacks of it. The old mud shanty was bursting with it. You would think there was not a single tusk left either above or below the ground in the whole country. 'Mostly fossil,' the manager had remarked disparagingly. It was no more fossil than I am; but they call it fossil when it is dug up. It appears these niggers do bury the tusks sometimes—but evidently they couldn't bury this parcel deep enough to save the gifted Mr. Kurtz from his fate. We filled the steamboat with it, and had to pile a lot on the deck. Thus he could see and enjoy as long as he could see, because the appreciation of this favor had remained with him to the last. You should have heard him say, 'My ivory.' Oh yes, I heard him. 'My Intended, my ivory, my station, my river, my—' everything belonged to him. It made me hold my breath in expectation of hearing the wilderness burst into a prodigious peal of laughter that would shake the fixed stars in their places. Everything belonged to him—but that was a trifle. The thing was to know what he belonged to, how many powers of darkness claimed him for their own. That was the reflection that made you creepy all over. It was impossible—it was not good for one either—trying to imagine. He had taken a high seat amongst the devils of the land—I mean literally. You can't understand. How could you?—with solid pavement under your feet, surrounded by kind neighbors ready to cheer you or to fall on you, stepping delicately between the butcher and the policeman, in the holy terror of scandal and gallows and lunatic asylums—how can you imagine what particular region of the first ages a man's untrammeled feet may take him into by the way of solitude—utter solitude without a policeman—by the way of silence, utter silence, where no warning voice of a kind neighbor can be heard whispering of public opinion? These little things make all the great difference. When they are gone you must fall back upon your own innate strength, upon your own capacity for faithfulness. Of course you may be too much of a fool to go wrong—too dull even to know you are being assaulted by the powers of darkness. I take it, no fool ever made a bargain for his soul with the devil: the fool is too much of a fool, or the devil too much of a devil—I don't know which. Or you may be such a thunderingly exalted creature as to be altogether deaf and blind to anything but heavenly sights and sounds. Then the earth for you is only a standing place—and whether to be like this is your loss or your gain I won't pretend to say. But most of us are neither one nor the other. The earth for us is a place to live in, where we must put up with sights, with sounds, with smells too, by Jove!—breathe dead hippo, so to speak, and not be contaminated. And there, don't you see? Your strength comes in, the faith in your ability for the digging of unostentatious holes to bury the stuff in—your power of devotion, not to yourself, but to an obscure, back-breaking business. And that's difficult enough. Mind, I am not trying to excuse or even explain—I am trying to account to myself for—for—Mr. Kurtz—for the shade of Mr. Kurtz. This initiated wraith from the back of Nowhere honored me with its amazing confidence before it vanished altogether. This was because it could speak English to me. The original Kurtz had been educated partly in England, and—as he was good enough to say himself—his sympathies were in the right place. His mother was half-English, his father was half-French. All Europe contributed to the making of Kurtz; and by-and-by I learned that, most appropriately, the International Society for the Suppression of Savage Customs had intrusted him with the making of a report, for its future guidance. And he had written it too. I've seen it. I've read it. It was eloquent, vibrating with eloquence, but too high-strung, I think. Seventeen pages of close writing he had found time for! But this must have been before his—let us say—nerves, went wrong, and caused him to preside at certain midnight dances ending with unspeakable rites, which—as far as I reluctantly gathered from what I heard at various times—were offered up to him—do you understand?—to Mr. Kurtz himself. But it was a beautiful piece of writing. The opening paragraph, however, in the light of later information, strikes me now as ominous. He began with the argument that we whites, from the point of development we had arrived at, 'must necessarily appear to them [savages] in the nature of supernatural beings—we approach them with the might as of a deity,' and so on, and so on. 'By the simple exercise of our will we can exert a power for good practically unbounded,' &c., &c. From that point he soared and took me with him. The peroration was magnificent, though difficult to remember, you know. It gave me the notion of an exotic Immensity ruled by an august Benevolence. It made me tingle with enthusiasm. This was the unbounded power of eloquence—of words—of burning noble words. There were no practical hints to interrupt the magic current of phrases, unless a kind of note at the foot of the last page, scrawled evidently much later, in an unsteady hand, may be regarded as the exposition of a method. It was very simple, and at the end of that moving appeal to every altruistic sentiment it blazed at you, luminous and terrifying, like a flash of lightning in a serene sky: 'Exterminate all the brutes!' The curious part was that he had apparently forgotten all about that valuable postscriptum, because, later on, when he in a sense came to himself, he repeatedly entreated me to take good care of 'my pamphlet' (he called it), as it was sure to have in the future a good influence upon his career. I had full information about all these things, and, besides, as it turned out, I was to have the care of his memory. I've done enough for it to give me the indisputable right to lay it, if I choose, for an everlasting rest in the dust-bin of progress, amongst all the sweepings and, figuratively speaking, all the dead cats of civilization. But then, you see, I can't choose. He won't be forgotten. Whatever he was, he was not common. He had the power to charm or frighten rudimentary souls into an aggravated witch-dance in his honor; he could also fill the small souls of the pilgrims with bitter misgivings: he had one devoted friend at least, and he had conquered one soul in the world that was neither rudimentary nor tainted with self-seeking. No; I can't forget him, though I am not prepared to affirm the fellow was exactly worth the life we lost in getting to him. I missed my late helmsman awfully,—I missed him even while his body was still lying in the pilot-house. Perhaps you will think it passing strange this regret for a savage who was no more account than a grain of sand in a black Sahara. Well, don't you see, he had done something, he had steered; for months I had him at my back—a help—an instrument. It was a kind of partnership. He steered for me—I had to look after him, I worried about his deficiencies, and thus a subtle bond had been created, of which I only became aware when it was suddenly broken. And the intimate profundity of that look he gave me when he received his hurt remains to this day in my memory—like a claim of distant kinship affirmed in a supreme moment.

"Poor fool! If he had only left that shutter alone. He had no restraint, no restraint—just like Kurtz—a tree swayed by the wind. As soon as I had put on a dry pair of slippers, I dragged him out, after first jerking the spear out of his side, which operation I confess I performed with my eyes shut tight. His heels leaped together over the little door-step; his shoulders were pressed to my breast; I hugged him from behind desperately. Oh! he was heavy, heavy; heavier than any man on earth, I should imagine. Then without more ado I tipped him overboard. The current snatched him as though he had been a wisp of grass, and I saw the body roll over twice before I lost sight of it for ever. All the pilgrims and the manager were then congregated on the awning-deck about the pilot-house, chattering at each other like a flock of excited magpies, and there was a scandalized murmur at my heartless promptitude. What they wanted to keep that body hanging about for I can't guess. Embalm it, maybe. But I had also heard another, and a very ominous, murmur on the deck below. My friends the wood-cutters were likewise scandalized, and with a better show of reason—though I admit that the reason itself was quite inadmissible. Oh, quite! I had made up my mind that if my late helmsman was to be eaten, the fishes alone should have him. He had been a very second-rate helmsman while alive, but now he was dead he might have become a first-class temptation, and possibly cause some startling trouble. Besides, I was anxious to take the wheel, the man in pink pyjamas showing himself a hopeless duffer at the business.

"This I did directly the simple funeral was over. We were going half-speed, keeping right in the middle of the stream, and I listened to the talk about me. They had given up Kurtz, they had given up the station; Kurtz was dead, and the station had been burnt—and so on— and so on. The red-haired pilgrim was beside himself with the thought that at least this poor Kurtz had been properly revenged. 'Say! We must have made a glorious slaughter of them in the bush. Eh? What do you think? Say?' He positively danced, the bloodthirsty little gingery beggar. And he had nearly fainted when he saw the wounded man! I could not help saying, 'You made a glorious lot of smoke, anyhow.' I had seen, from the way the tops of the bushes rustled and flew, that almost all the shots had gone too high. You can't hit anything unless you take aim and fire from the shoulder; but these chaps fired from the hip with their eyes shut. The retreat, I maintained—and I was right— was caused by the screeching of the steam-whistle. Upon this they forgot Kurtz, and began to howl at me with indignant protests.

"The manager stood by the wheel murmuring confidentially about the necessity of getting well away down the river before dark at all events, when I saw in the distance a clearing on the river-side and the outlines of some sort of building. 'What's this?' I asked. He clapped his hands in wonder. 'The station!' he cried. I edged in at once, still going half-speed.

"Through my glasses I saw the slope of a hill interspersed with rare trees and perfectly free from undergrowth. A long decaying building on the summit was half buried in the high grass; the large holes in the peaked roof gaped black from afar; the jungle and the woods made a background. There was no enclosure or fence of any kind; but there had been one apparently, for near the house half-a-dozen slim posts remained in a row, roughly trimmed, and with their upper ends ornamented with round carved balls. The rails, or whatever there had been between, had disappeared. Of course the forest surrounded all that. The river-bank was clear, and on the water-side I saw a white man under a hat like a cart-wheel beckoning persistently with his whole arm. Examining the edge of the forest above and below, I was almost certain I could see movements—human forms gliding here and there. I steamed past prudently, then stopped the engines and let her drift down. The man on the shore began to shout, urging us to land. 'We have been attacked,' screamed the manager. 'I know—I know. It's all right,' yelled back the other, as cheerful as you please. 'Come along. It's all right. I am glad.'

"His aspect reminded me of something I had seen—something funny I had seen somewhere. As I maneuvered to get alongside, I was asking myself, 'What does this fellow look like?' Suddenly I got it. He looked like a harlequin. His clothes had been made of some stuff that was brown holland probably, but it was covered with patches all over, with bright patches, blue, red, and yellow,—patches on the back, patches on front, patches on elbows, on knees; colored binding round his jacket, scarlet edging at the bottom of his trousers; and the sunshine made him look extremely gay and wonderfully neat withal, because you could see how beautifully all this patching had been done. A beardless, boyish face, very fair, no features to speak of, nose peeling, little blue eyes, smiles and frowns chasing each other over that open countenance like sunshine and shadow on a windswept plain. 'Look out, captain!' he cried; 'there's a snag lodged in here last night.' What! Another snag? I confess I swore shamefully. I had nearly holed my cripple, to finish off that charming trip. The harlequin on the bank turned his little pug nose up to me. 'You English?' he asked, all smiles. 'Are you?' I shouted from the wheel. The smiles vanished, and he shook his head as if sorry for my disappointment. Then he brightened up. 'Never mind!' he cried encouragingly. 'Are we in time?' I asked. 'He is up there,' he replied, with a toss of the head up the hill, and becoming gloomy all of a sudden. His face was like the autumn sky, overcast one moment and bright the next.

"When the manager, escorted by the pilgrims, all of them armed to the teeth, had gone to the house, this chap came on board. 'I say, I don't like this. These natives are in the bush,' I said. He assured me earnestly it was all right. 'They are simple people,' he added; 'well, I am glad you came. It took me all my time to keep them off.' 'But you said it was all right,' I cried. 'Oh, they meant no harm,' he said; and as I stared he corrected himself, 'Not exactly.' Then vivaciously, 'My faith, your pilot-house wants a clean up!' In the next breath he advised me to keep enough steam on the boiler to blow the whistle in case of any trouble. 'One good screech will do more for you than all your rifles. They are simple people,' he repeated. He rattled away at such a rate he quite overwhelmed me. He seemed to be trying to make up for lots of silence, and actually hinted, laughing, that such was the case. 'Don't you talk with Mr. Kurtz?' I said. 'You don't talk with that man—you listen to him,' he exclaimed with severe exaltation. 'But now—' He waved his arm, and in the twinkling of an eye was in the uttermost depths of despondency. In a moment he came up again with a jump, possessed himself of both my hands, shook them continuously, while he gabbled: 'Brother sailor . . . honor . . . pleasure . . . delight . . . introduce myself . . . Russian . . . son of an arch-priest . . . Government of Tambov . . . What? Tobacco! English tobacco; the excellent English tobacco! Now, that's brotherly. Smoke? Where's a sailor that does not smoke?'

"The pipe soothed him, and gradually I made out he had run away from school, had gone to sea in a Russian ship; ran away again; served some time in English ships; was now reconciled with the arch-priest. He made a point of that. 'But when one is young one must see things, gather experience, ideas; enlarge the mind.' 'Here!' I interrupted. 'You can never tell! Here I have met Mr. Kurtz,' he said, youthfully solemn and reproachful. I held my tongue after that. It appears he had persuaded a Dutch trading-house on the coast to fit him out with stores and goods, and had started for the interior with a light heart, and no more idea of what would happen to him than a baby. He had been wandering about that river for nearly two years alone, cut off from everybody and everything. 'I am not so young as I look. I am twenty-five,' he said. 'At first old Van Shuyten would tell me to go to the devil,' he narrated with keen enjoyment; 'but I stuck to him, and talked and talked, till at last he got afraid I would talk the hind-leg off his favorite dog, so he gave me some cheap things and a few guns, and told me he hoped he would never see my face again. Good old Dutchman, Van Shuyten. I've sent him one small lot of ivory a year ago, so that he can't call me a little thief when I get back. I hope he got it. And for the rest I don't care. I had some wood stacked for you. That was my old house. Did you see?'

"I gave him Towson's book. He made as though he would kiss me, but restrained himself. 'The only book I had left, and I thought I had lost it,' he said, looking at it ecstatically. 'So many accidents happen to a man going about alone, you know. Canoes get upset sometimes—and sometimes you've got to clear out so quick when the people get angry.' He thumbed the pages. 'You made notes in Russian?' I asked. He nodded. 'I thought they were written in cipher,' I said. He laughed, then became serious. 'I had lots of trouble to keep these people off,' he said. 'Did they want to kill you?' I asked. 'Oh no!' he cried, and checked himself. 'Why did they attack us?' I pursued. He hesitated, then said shamefacedly, 'They don't want him to go.' 'Don't they?' I said, curiously. He nodded a nod full of mystery and wisdom. 'I tell you,' he cried, 'this man has enlarged my mind.' He opened his arms wide, staring at me with his little blue eyes that were perfectly round."

III

"I looked at him, lost in astonishment. There he was before me, in motley, as though he had absconded from a troupe of mimes, enthusiastic, fabulous. His very existence was improbable, inexplicable, and altogether bewildering. He was an insoluble problem. It was inconceivable how he had existed, how he had succeeded in getting so far, how he had managed to remain—why he did not instantly disappear. 'I went a little farther,' he said, 'then still a little farther—till I had gone so far that I don't know how I'll ever get back. Never mind. Plenty time. I can manage. You take Kurtz away quick—quick—I tell you.' The glamour of youth enveloped his parti-colored rags, his destitution, his loneliness, the essential desolation of his futile wanderings. For months—for years—his life hadn't been worth a day's purchase; and there he was gallantly, thoughtlessly alive, to all appearance indestructible solely by the virtue of his few years and of his unreflecting audacity. I was seduced into something like admiration—like envy. Glamour urged him on, glamour kept him unscathed. He surely wanted nothing from the wilderness but space to breathe in and to push on through. His need was to exist, and to move onwards at the greatest possible risk, and with a maximum of privation. If the absolutely pure, uncalculating, unpractical spirit of adventure had ever ruled a human being, it ruled this be-patched youth. I almost envied him the possession of this modest and clear flame. It seemed to have consumed all thought of self so completely, that, even while he was talking to you, you forgot that it was he—the man before your eyes—who had gone through these things. I did not envy him his devotion to Kurtz, though. He had not meditated over it. It came to him, and he accepted it with a sort of eager fatalism. I must say that to me it appeared about the most dangerous thing in every way he had come upon so far.

"They had come together unavoidably, like two ships becalmed near each other, and lay rubbing sides at last. I suppose Kurtz wanted an audience, because on a certain occasion, when encamped in the forest, they had talked all night, or more probably Kurtz had talked. 'We talked of everything,' he said, quite transported at the recollection. 'I forgot there was such a thing as sleep. The night did not seem to last an hour. Everything! Everything! . . . Of love too.' 'Ah, he talked to you of love!' I said, much amused. 'It isn't what you think,' he cried, almost passionately. 'It was in general. He made me see things—things.'

"He threw his arms up. We were on deck at the time, and the headman of my wood-cutters, lounging near by, turned upon him his heavy and glittering eyes. I looked around, and I don't know why, but I assure you that never, never before, did this land, this river, this jungle, the very arch of this blazing sky, appear to me so hopeless and so dark, so impenetrable to human thought, so pitiless to human weakness. 'And, ever since, you have been with him, of course?' I said.

"On the contrary. It appears their intercourse had been very much broken by various causes. He had, as he informed me proudly, managed to nurse Kurtz through two illnesses (he alluded to it as you would to some risky feat), but as a rule Kurtz wandered alone, far in the depths of the forest. 'Very often coming to this station, I had to wait days and days before he would turn up,' he said. 'Ah, it was worth waiting for!—sometimes.' 'What was he doing? exploring or what?' I asked. 'Oh yes, of course;' he had discovered lots of villages, a lake too—he did not know exactly in what direction; it was dangerous to inquire too much—but mostly his expeditions had been for ivory. 'But he had no goods to trade with by that time,' I objected. 'There's a good lot of cartridges left even yet,' he answered, looking away. 'To speak plainly, he raided the country,' I said. He nodded. 'Not alone, surely!' He muttered something about the villages round that lake. 'Kurtz got the tribe to follow him, did he?' I suggested. He fidgeted a little. 'They adored him,' he said. The tone of these words was so extraordinary that I looked at him searchingly. It was curious to see his mingled eagerness and reluctance to speak of Kurtz. The man filled his life, occupied his thoughts, swayed his emotions. 'What can you expect?' he burst out; 'he came to them with thunder and lightning, you know—and they had never seen anything like it—and very terrible. He could be very terrible. You can't judge Mr. Kurtz as you would an ordinary man. No, no, no! Now—just to give you an idea—I don't mind telling you, he wanted to shoot me too one day—but I don't judge him.' 'Shoot you!' I cried. 'What for?' 'Well, I had a small lot of ivory the chief of that village near my house gave me. You see I used to shoot game for them.

Well, he wanted it, and wouldn't hear reason. He declared he would shoot me unless I gave him the ivory and then cleared out of the country, because he could do so, and had a fancy for it, and there was nothing on earth to prevent him killing whom he jolly well pleased. And it was true too. I gave him the ivory. What did I care! But I didn't clear out. No, no. I couldn't leave him. I had to be careful, of course, till we got friendly again for a time. He had his second illness then. Afterwards I had to keep out of the way; but I didn't mind. He was living for the most part in those villages on the lake. When he came down to the river, sometimes he would take to me, and sometimes it was better for me to be careful. This man suffered too much. He hated all this, and somehow he couldn't get away. When I had a chance I begged him to try and leave while there was time; I offered to go back with him. And he would say yes, and then he would remain; go off on another ivory hunt; disappear for weeks; forget himself amongst these people—forget himself—you know.' 'Why! he's mad,' I said. He protested indignantly. Mr. Kurtz couldn't be mad. If I had heard him talk, only two days ago, I wouldn't dare hint at such a thing. . . . I had taken up my binoculars while we talked and was looking at the shore, sweeping the limit of the forest at each side and at the back of the house. The consciousness of there being people in that bush, so silent, so quiet—as silent and quiet as the ruined house on the hill—made me uneasy. There was no sign on the face of nature of this amazing tale that was not so much told as suggested to me in desolate exclamations, completed by shrugs, in interrupted phrases, in hints ending in deep sighs. The woods were unmoved, like a mask—heavy, like the closed door of a prison—they looked with their air of hidden knowledge, of patient expectation, of unapproachable silence. The Russian was explaining to me that it was only lately that Mr. Kurtz had come down to the river, bringing along with him all the fighting men of that lake tribe. He had been absent for several months—getting himself adored, I suppose—and had come down unexpectedly, with the intention to all appearance of making a raid either across the river or down stream. Evidently the appetite for more ivory had got the better of the—what shall I say?—less material aspirations. However he had got much worse suddenly. 'I heard he was lying helpless, and so I came up—took my chance,' said the Russian. 'Oh, he is bad, very bad.' I directed my glass to the house. There were no signs of life, but there was the ruined roof, the long mud wall peeping above the grass, with three little square window-holes, no two of the same size; all this brought within reach of my hand, as it were. And then I made a brusque movement, and one of the remaining posts of that vanished fence leaped up in the field of my glass. You remember I told you I had been struck at the distance by certain attempts at ornamentation, rather remarkable in the ruinous aspect of the place. Now I had suddenly a nearer view, and its first result was to make me throw my head back as if before a blow. Then I went carefully from post to post with my glass, and I saw my mistake. These round knobs were not ornamental but symbolic; they were expressive and puzzling, striking and disturbing—food for thought and also for the vultures if there had been any looking down from the sky; but at all events for such ants as were industrious enough to ascend the pole. They would have been even more impressive, those heads on the stakes, if their faces had not been turned to the house. Only one, the first I had made out, was facing my way. I was not so shocked as you may think. The start back I had given was really nothing but a movement of surprise. I had expected to see a knob of wood there, you know. I returned deliberately to the first I had seen—and there it was, black, dried, sunken, with closed eyelids,—a head that seemed to sleep at the top of that pole, and, with the shrunken dry lips showing a narrow white line of the teeth, was smiling too, smiling continuously at some endless and jocose dream of that eternal slumber.

"I am not disclosing any trade secrets. In fact the manager said afterwards that Mr. Kurtz's methods had ruined the district. I have no opinion on that point, but I want you clearly to understand that there was nothing exactly profitable in these heads being there. They only showed that Mr. Kurtz lacked restraint in the gratification of his various lusts, that there was something wanting in him—some small matter which, when the pressing need arose, could not be found under his magnificent eloquence. Whether he knew of this deficiency himself I can't say. I think the knowledge came to him at last—only at the very last. But the wilderness had found him out early, and had taken on him a terrible vengeance for the fantastic invasion. I think it had whispered to him things about himself which he did not know, things of which he had no conception till he took counsel with this great solitude—and the whisper had proved irresistibly fascinating. It echoed loudly within him because he was hollow at the core. . . . I put down the glass, and the head that had appeared near enough to be spoken to seemed at once to have leaped away from me into inaccessible distance.

"The admirer of Mr. Kurtz was a bit crestfallen. In a hurried, indistinct voice he began to assure me he had not dared to take these— say, symbols—down. He was not afraid of the natives; they would not stir till Mr. Kurtz gave the word. His ascendancy was extraordinary. The camps of these people surrounded the place, and the chiefs came every day to see him. They would crawl. . . . 'I don't want to know anything of the ceremonies used when approaching Mr. Kurtz,' I shouted. Curious, this feeling that came over me that such details would be more intolerable than those heads drying on the stakes under Mr. Kurtz's windows. After all, that was only a savage sight, while I seemed at one bound to have been transported into some lightless region of subtle horrors, where pure, uncomplicated savagery was a

positive relief, being something that had a right to exist—obviously—
in the sunshine. The young man looked at me with surprise. I suppose it
did not occur to him Mr. Kurtz was no idol of mine. He forgot I hadn't
heard any of these splendid monologues on, what was it? on love,
justice, conduct of life—or what not. If it had come to crawling before
Mr. Kurtz, he crawled as much as the veriest savage of them all. I had
no idea of the conditions, he said: these heads were the heads of rebels.
I shocked him excessively by laughing. Rebels! What would be the
next definition I was to hear? There had been enemies, criminals,
workers—and these were rebels. Those rebellious heads looked very
subdued to me on their sticks. 'You don't know how such a life tries a
man like Kurtz,' cried Kurtz's last disciple. 'Well, and you?' I said. 'I!
I! I am a simple man. I have no great thoughts. I want nothing from
anybody. How can you compare me to . . . ?' His feelings were too
much for speech, and suddenly he broke down. 'I don't understand,' he
groaned. 'I've been doing my best to keep him alive, and that's enough.
I had no hand in all this. I have no abilities. There hasn't been a drop of
medicine or a mouthful of invalid food for months here. He was
shamefully abandoned. A man like this, with such ideas. Shamefully!
Shamefully! I—I—haven't slept for the last ten nights. . . .'

"His voice lost itself in the calm of the evening. The long shadows
of the forest had slipped down hill while we talked, had gone far
beyond the ruined hovel, beyond the symbolic row of stakes. All this
was in the gloom, while we down there were yet in the sunshine, and
the stretch of the river abreast of the clearing glittered in a still and
dazzling splendor, with a murky and over-shadowed bend above and
below. Not a living soul was seen on the shore. The bushes did not
rustle.

"Suddenly round the corner of the house a group of men appeared,
as though they had come up from the ground. They waded waist-deep
in the grass, in a compact body, bearing an improvised stretcher in their
midst. Instantly, in the emptiness of the landscape, a cry arose whose
shrillness pierced the still air like a sharp arrow flying straight to the
very heart of the land; and, as if by enchantment, streams of human
beings—of naked human beings—with spears in their hands, with
bows, with shields, with wild glances and savage movements, were
poured into the clearing by the dark-faced and pensive forest. The
bushes shook, the grass swayed for a time, and then everything stood
still in attentive immobility.

"'Now, if he does not say the right thing to them we are all done
for,' said the Russian at my elbow. The knot of men with the stretcher
had stopped too, half-way to the steamer, as if petrified. I saw the man
on the stretcher sit up, lank and with an uplifted arm, above the
shoulders of the bearers. 'Let us hope that the man who can talk so well
of love in general will find some particular reason to spare us this

time,' I said. I resented bitterly the absurd danger of our situation, as if to be at the mercy of that atrocious phantom had been a dishonoring necessity. I could not hear a sound, but through my glasses I saw the thin arm extended commandingly, the lower jaw moving, the eyes of that apparition shining darkly far in its bony head that nodded with grotesque jerks. Kurtz—Kurtz—that means short in German—don't it? Well, the name was as true as everything else in his life—and death. He looked at least seven feet long. His covering had fallen off, and his body emerged from it pitiful and appalling as from a winding-sheet. I could see the cage of his ribs all astir, the bones of his arm waving. It was as though an animated image of death carved out of old ivory had been shaking its hand with menaces at a motionless crowd of men made of dark and glittering bronze. I saw him open his mouth wide—it gave him a weirdly voracious aspect, as though he had wanted to swallow all the air, all the earth, all the men before him. A deep voice reached me faintly. He must have been shouting. He fell back suddenly. The stretcher shook as the bearers staggered forward again, and almost at the same time I noticed that the crowd of savages was vanishing without any perceptible movement of retreat, as if the forest that had ejected these beings so suddenly had drawn them in again as the breath is drawn in a long aspiration.

"Some of the pilgrims behind the stretcher carried his arms—two shot-guns, a heavy rifle, and a light revolver-carbine—the thunderbolts of that pitiful Jupiter. The manager bent over him murmuring as he walked beside his head. They laid him down in one of the little cabins—just a room for a bed-place and a camp-stool or two, you know. We had brought his belated correspondence, and a lot of torn envelopes and open letters littered his bed. His hand roamed feebly amongst these papers. I was struck by the fire of his eyes and the composed languor of his expression. It was not so much the exhaustion of disease. He did not seem in pain. This shadow looked satiated and calm, as though for the moment it had had its fill of all the emotions.

"He rustled one of the letters, and looking straight in my face said, 'I am glad.' Somebody had been writing to him about me. These special recommendations were turning up again. The volume of tone he emitted without effort, almost without the trouble of moving his lips, amazed me. A voice! a voice! It was grave, profound, vibrating, while the man did not seem capable of a whisper. However, he had enough strength in him—factitious no doubt—to very nearly make an end of us, as you shall hear directly.

"The manager appeared silently in the doorway; I stepped out at once and he drew the curtain after me. The Russian, eyed curiously by the pilgrims, was staring at the shore. I followed the direction of his glance.

"Dark human shapes could be made out in the distance, flitting indistinctly against the gloomy border of the forest, and near the river two bronze figures, leaning on tall spears, stood in the sunlight under fantastic headdresses of spotted skins, warlike and still in statuesque repose. And from right to left along the lighted shore moved a wild and gorgeous apparition of a woman.

"She walked with measured steps, draped in striped and fringed cloths, treading the earth proudly, with a slight jingle and flash of barbarous ornaments. She carried her head high; her hair was done in the shape of a helmet; she had brass leggings to the knee, brass wire gauntlets to the elbow, a crimson spot on her tawny cheek, innumerable necklaces of glass beads on her neck; bizarre things, charms, gifts of witch-men, that hung about her, glittered and trembled at every step. She must have had the value of several elephant tusks upon her. She was savage and superb, wild-eyed and magnificent; there was something ominous and stately in her deliberate progress. And in the hush that had fallen suddenly upon the whole sorrowful land, the immense wilderness, the colossal body of the fecund and mysterious life seemed to look at her, pensive, as though it had been looking at the image of its own tenebrous and passionate soul.

"She came abreast of the steamer, stood still, and faced us. Her long shadow fell to the water's edge. Her face had a tragic and fierce aspect of wild sorrow and of dumb pain mingled with the fear of some struggling, half-shaped resolve. She stood looking at us without a stir and like the wilderness itself, with an air of brooding over an inscrutable purpose. A whole minute passed, and then she made a step forward. There was a low jingle, a glint of yellow metal, a sway of fringed draperies, and she stopped as if her heart had failed her. The young fellow by my side growled. The pilgrims murmured at my back. She looked at us all as if her life had depended upon the unswerving steadiness of her glance. Suddenly she opened her bared arms and threw them up rigid above her head, as though in an uncontrollable desire to touch the sky, and at the same time the swift shadows darted out on the earth, swept around on the river, gathering the steamer into a shadowy embrace. A formidable silence hung over the scene.

"She turned away slowly, walked on, following the bank, and passed into the bushes to the left. Once only her eyes gleamed back at us in the dusk of the thickets before she disappeared.

"'If she had offered to come aboard I really think I would have tried to shoot her,' said the man of patches, nervously. 'I had been risking my life every day for the last fortnight to keep her out of the house. She got in one day and kicked up a row about those miserable rags I picked up in the storeroom to mend my clothes with. I wasn't decent. At least it must have been that, for she talked like a fury to Kurtz for an hour, pointing at me now and then. I don't understand the dialect of this tribe. Luckily for me, I fancy Kurtz felt too ill that day to

care, or there would have been mischief. I don't understand. . . . No—
it's too much for me. Ah, well, it's all over now.'

"At this moment I heard Kurtz's deep voice behind the curtain,
'Save me!—save the ivory, you mean. Don't tell me. Save *me*! Why,
I've had to save you. You are interrupting my plans now. Sick! Sick!
Not so sick as you would like to believe. Never mind. I'll carry my
ideas out yet—I will return. I'll show you what can be done. You with
your little peddling notions—you are interfering with me. I will return.
I . . .'

"The manager came out. He did me the honor to take me under the
arm and lead me aside. 'He is very low, very low,' he said. He
considered it necessary to sigh, but neglected to be consistently
sorrowful. 'We have done all we could for him—haven't we? But there
is no disguising the fact, Mr. Kurtz has done more harm than good to
the Company. He did not see the time was not ripe for vigorous action.
Cautiously, cautiously—that's my principle. We must be cautious yet.
The district is closed to us for a time. Deplorable! Upon the whole, the
trade will suffer. I don't deny there is a remarkable quantity of ivory—
mostly fossil. We must save it, at all events—but look how precarious
the position is—and why? Because the method is unsound.' 'Do you,'
said I, looking at the shore, 'call it "unsound method"?' 'Without
doubt,' he exclaimed, hotly. 'Don't you?'. . .

'No method at all,' I murmured after a while. 'Exactly,' he exulted.
'I anticipated this. Shows a complete want of judgment. It is my duty to
point it out in the proper quarter.' 'Oh,' said I, 'that fellow—what's his
name?—the brickmaker, will make a readable report for you.' He
appeared confounded for a moment. It seemed to me I had never
breathed an atmosphere so vile, and I turned mentally to Kurtz for
relief—positively for relief. 'Nevertheless I think Mr. Kurtz is a
remarkable man,' I said with emphasis. He started, dropped on me a
cold heavy glance, said very quietly, 'He *was*,' and turned his back on
me. My hour of favor was over; I found myself lumped along with
Kurtz as a partisan of methods for which the time was not ripe: I was
unsound! Ah! but it was something to have at least a choice of
nightmares.

"I had turned to the wilderness really, not to Mr. Kurtz, who, I was
ready to admit, was as good as buried. And for a moment it seemed to
me as if I also were buried in a vast grave full of unspeakable secrets. I
felt an intolerable weight oppressing my breast, the smell of the damp
earth, the unseen presence of victorious corruption, the darkness of an
impenetrable night. . . . The Russian tapped me on the shoulder. I heard
him mumbling and stammering something about 'brother seaman—
couldn't conceal—knowledge of matters that would affect Mr. Kurtz's
reputation.' I waited. For him evidently Mr. Kurtz was not in his grave;
I suspect that for him Mr. Kurtz was one of the immortals. 'Well!' said

I at last, 'speak out. As it happens, I am Mr. Kurtz's friend—in a way.'

"He stated with a good deal of formality that had we not been 'of the same profession,' he would have kept the matter to himself without regard to consequences. 'He suspected there was an active ill-will towards him on the part of these white men that—' 'You are right,' I said, remembering a certain conversation I had overheard. 'The manager thinks you ought to be hanged.' He showed a concern at this intelligence which amused me at first. 'I had better get out of the way quietly,' he said, earnestly. 'I can do no more for Kurtz now, and they would soon find some excuse. What's to stop them? There's a military post three hundred miles from here.' 'Well, upon my word,' said I, 'perhaps you had better go if you have any friends amongst the savages near by.' 'Plenty,' he said. 'They are simple people—and I want nothing, you know.' He stood biting his lips, then: 'I don't want any harm to happen to these whites here, but of course I was thinking of Mr. Kurtz's reputation—but you are a brother seaman and—' 'All right,' said I, after a time. 'Mr. Kurtz's reputation is safe with me.' I did not know how truly I spoke.

"He informed me, lowering his voice, that it was Kurtz who had ordered the attack to be made on the steamer. 'He hated sometimes the idea of being taken away—and then again. . . . But I don't understand these matters. I am a simple man. He thought it would scare you away—that you would give it up, thinking him dead. I could not stop him. Oh, I had an awful time of it this last month.' 'Very well,' I said. 'He is all right now.' 'Ye-e-es,' he muttered, not very convinced apparently. 'Thanks,' said I; 'I shall keep my eyes open.' 'But quiet—eh?' he urged, anxiously. 'It would be awful for his reputation if anybody here—' I promised a complete discretion with great gravity. 'I have a canoe and three black fellows waiting not very far. I am off. Could you give me a few Martini-Henry cartridges?' I could, and did, with proper secrecy. He helped himself, with a wink at me, to a handful of my tobacco. 'Between sailors—you know—good English tobacco.' At the door of the pilot-house he turned round—'I say, haven't you a pair of shoes you could spare?' He raised one leg. 'Look.' The soles were tied with knotted strings sandal-wise under his bare feet. I rooted out an old pair, at which he looked with admiration before tucking it under his left arm. One of his pockets (bright red) was bulging with cartridges, from the other (dark blue) peeped 'Towson's Inquiry,' &c., &c. He seemed to think himself excellently well equipped for a renewed encounter with the wilderness. 'Ah! I'll never, never meet such a man again. You ought to have heard him recite poetry—his own too it was, he told me. Poetry!' He rolled his eyes at the recollection of these delights. 'Oh, he enlarged my mind!' 'Good-by,' said I. He shook hands and vanished in the night. Sometimes I ask myself whether I had ever really seen him—whether it was possible to meet such a phenomenon! . . .

"When I woke up shortly after midnight his warning came to my mind with its hint of danger that seemed, in the starred darkness, real enough to make me get up for the purpose of having a look round. On the hill a big fire burned, illuminating fitfully a crooked corner of the station-house. One of the agents with a picket of a few of our blacks, armed for the purpose, was keeping guard over the ivory; but deep within the forest, red gleams that wavered, that seemed to sink and rise from the ground amongst confused columnar shapes of intense blackness, showed the exact position of the camp where Mr. Kurtz's adorers were keeping their uneasy vigil. The monotonous beating of a big drum filled the air with muffled shocks and a lingering vibration. A steady droning sound of many men chanting each to himself some weird incantation came out from the black, flat wall of the woods as the humming of bees comes out of a hive, and had a strange narcotic effect upon my half-awake senses. I believe I dozed off leaning over the rail, till an abrupt burst of yells, an overwhelming outbreak of a pent-up and mysterious frenzy, woke me up in a bewildered wonder. It was cut short all at once, and the low droning went on with an effect of audible and soothing silence. I glanced casually into the little cabin. A light was burning within, but Mr. Kurtz was not there.

"I think I would have raised an outcry if I had believed my eyes. But I didn't believe them at first—the thing seemed so impossible. The fact is I was completely unnerved by a sheer blank fright, pure abstract terror, unconnected with any distinct shape of physical danger. What made this emotion so overpowering was—how shall I define it?—the moral shock I received, as if something altogether monstrous, intolerable to thought and odious to the soul, had been thrust upon me unexpectedly. This lasted of course the merest fraction of a second, and then the usual sense of commonplace, deadly danger, the possibility of a sudden onslaught and massacre, or something of the kind, which I saw impending, was positively welcome and composing. It pacified me, in fact, so much, that I did not raise an alarm.

"There was an agent buttoned up inside an ulster and sleeping on a chair on deck within three feet of me. The yells had not awakened him; he snored very slightly; I left him to his slumbers and leaped ashore. I did not betray Mr. Kurtz—it was ordered I should never betray him—it was written I should be loyal to the nightmare of my choice. I was anxious to deal with this shadow by myself alone,—and to this day I don't know why I was so jealous of sharing with anyone the peculiar blackness of that experience.

"As soon as I got on the bank I saw a trail—a broad trail through the grass. I remember the exultation with which I said to myself, 'He can't walk—he is crawling on all-fours—I've got him.' The grass was wet with dew. I strode rapidly with clenched fists. I fancy I had some vague notion of falling upon him and giving him a drubbing. I don't know. I had some imbecile thoughts. The knitting old woman with the cat obtruded herself upon my memory as a most improper person to be sitting at the other end of such an affair. I saw a row of pilgrims squirting lead in the air out of Winchesters held to the hip. I thought I would never get back to the steamer, and imagined myself living alone and unarmed in the woods to an advanced age. Such silly things—you know. And I remember I confounded the beat of the drum with the beating of my heart, and was pleased at its calm regularity.

"I kept to the track though—then stopped to listen. The night was very clear: a dark blue space, sparkling with dew and starlight, in which black things stood very still. I thought I could see a kind of motion ahead of me. I was strangely cocksure of everything that night. I actually left the track and ran in a wide semicircle (I verily believe chuckling to myself) so as to get in front of that stir, of that motion I had seen—if indeed I had seen anything. I was circumventing Kurtz as though it had been a boyish game.

"I came upon him, and, if he had not heard me coming, I would have fallen over him too, but he got up in time. He rose, unsteady, long, pale, indistinct, like a vapor exhaled by the earth, and swayed slightly, misty and silent before me; while at my back the fires loomed between the trees, and the murmur of many voices issued from the forest. I had cut him off cleverly; but when actually confronting him I seemed to come to my senses, I saw the danger in its right proportion. It was by no means over yet. Suppose he began to shout? Though he could hardly stand, there was still plenty of vigor in his voice. 'Go away—hide yourself,' he said, in that profound tone. It was very awful. I glanced back. We were within thirty yards from the nearest fire. A black figure stood up, strode on long black legs, waving long black arms, across the glow. It had horns—antelope horns, I think—on its head. Some sorcerer, some witch-man, no doubt: it looked fiend-like enough. 'Do you know what you are doing?' I whispered. 'Perfectly,' he answered, raising his voice for that single word: it sounded to me far off and yet loud, like a hail through a speaking-trumpet. 'If he makes a row we are lost,' I thought to myself. This clearly was not a case for fisticuffs, even apart from the very natural aversion I had to beat that Shadow—this wandering and tormented thing. 'You will be lost,' I said—'utterly lost.' One gets sometimes such a flash of inspiration, you know. I did say the right thing, though indeed he could not have been more irretrievably lost than he was at this very moment, when the foundations of our intimacy were being laid—to endure—to endure—even to the end—even beyond.

"'I had immense plans,' he muttered irresolutely. 'Yes,' said I; 'but if you try to shout I'll smash your head with—' There was not a stick or a stone near. 'I will throttle you for good,' I corrected myself. 'I was on the threshold of great things,' he pleaded, in a voice of longing, with a wistfulness of tone that made my blood run cold. 'And now for this stupid scoundrel—' 'Your success in Europe is assured in any case,' I affirmed, steadily. I did not want to have the throttling of him, you understand—and indeed it would have been very little use for any practical purpose. I tried to break the spell—the heavy, mute spell of the wilderness—that seemed to draw him to its pitiless breast by the awakening of forgotten and brutal instincts, by the memory of gratified and monstrous passions. This alone, I was convinced, had driven him out to the edge of the forest, to the bush, towards the gleam of fires, the throb of drums, the drone of weird incantations; this alone had beguiled his unlawful soul beyond the bounds of permitted aspirations. And, don't you see, the terror of the position was not in being knocked on the head—though I had a very lively sense of that danger too—but in this, that I had to deal with a being to whom I could not appeal in the name of anything high or low. I had, even like the niggers, to invoke him— himself his own exalted and incredible degradation. There was nothing either above or below him, and I knew it. He had kicked himself loose of the earth. Confound the man! he had kicked the very earth to pieces. He was alone, and I before him did not know whether I stood on the ground or floated in the air. I've been telling you what we said— repeating the phrases we pronounced,—but what's the good? They were common everyday words,—the familiar, vague sounds exchanged on every waking day of life. But what of that? They had behind them, to my mind, the terrific suggestiveness of words heard in dreams, of phrases spoken in nightmares. Soul! If anybody had ever struggled with a soul, I am the man. And I wasn't arguing with a lunatic either. Believe me or not, his intelligence was perfectly clear—concentrated, it is true, upon himself with horrible intensity, yet clear; and therein was my only chance—barring, of course, the killing him there and then, which wasn't so good, on account of unavoidable noise. But his soul was mad. Being alone in the wilderness, it had looked within itself, and, by heavens! I tell you, it had gone mad. I had—for my sins, I suppose—to go through the ordeal of looking into it myself. No eloquence could have been so withering to one's belief in mankind as his final burst of sincerity. He struggled with himself, too. I saw it,—I heard it. I saw the inconceivable mystery of a soul that knew no restraint, no faith, and no fear, yet struggling blindly with itself. I kept my head pretty well; but when I had him at last stretched on the couch, I wiped my forehead, while my legs shook under me as though I had carried half a ton on my back down that hill. And yet I had only supported him, his bony arm clasped round my neck—and he was not much heavier than a child.

"When next day we left at noon, the crowd, of whose presence behind the curtain of trees I had been acutely conscious all the time, flowed out of the woods again, filled the clearing, covered the slope with a mass of naked, breathing, quivering, bronze bodies. I steamed up a bit, then swung down-stream, and two thousand eyes followed the evolutions of the splashing, thumping, fierce river-demon beating the water with its terrible tail and breathing black smoke into the air. In front of the first rank, along the river, three men, plastered with bright red earth from head to foot, strutted to and fro restlessly. When we came abreast again, they faced the river, stamped their feet, nodded their horned heads, swayed their scarlet bodies; they shook towards the fierce river-demon a bunch of black feathers, a mangy skin with a pendent tail—something that looked like a dried gourd; they shouted periodically together strings of amazing words that resembled no sounds of human language; and the deep murmurs of the crowd, interrupted suddenly, were like the response of some satanic litany.

"We had carried Kurtz into the pilot-house: there was more air there. Lying on the couch, he stared through the open shutter. There was an eddy in the mass of human bodies, and the woman with helmeted head and tawny cheeks rushed out to the very brink of the stream. She put out her hands, shouted something, and all that wild mob took up the shout in a roaring chorus of articulated, rapid, breathless utterance.

"'Do you understand this?' I asked.

"He kept on looking out past me with fiery, longing eyes, with a mingled expression of wistfulness and hate. He made no answer, but I saw a smile, a smile of indefinable meaning, appear on his colorless lips that a moment after twitched convulsively. 'Do I not?' he said slowly, gasping, as if the words had been torn out of him by a supernatural power.

"I pulled the string of the whistle, and I did this because I saw the pilgrims on deck getting out their rifles with an air of anticipating a jolly lark. At the sudden screech there was a movement of abject terror through that wedged mass of bodies. 'Don't! Don't you frighten them away,' cried someone on deck disconsolately. I pulled the string time after time. They broke and ran, they leaped, they crouched, they swerved, they dodged the flying terror of the sound. The three red chaps had fallen flat, face down on the shore, as though they had been shot dead. Only the barbarous and superb woman did not so much as flinch, and stretched tragically her bare arms after us over the somber and glittering river.

"And then that imbecile crowd down on the deck started their little fun, and I could see nothing more for smoke.

"The brown current ran swiftly out of the heart of darkness, bearing us down towards the sea with twice the speed of our upward progress; and Kurtz's life was running swiftly too, ebbing, ebbing out of his heart into the sea of inexorable time. The manager was very placid, he had no vital anxieties now, he took us both in with a comprehensive and satisfied glance: the 'affair' had come off as well as could be wished. I saw the time approaching when I would be left alone of the party of 'unsound method.' The pilgrims looked upon me with disfavor. I was, so to speak, numbered with the dead. It is strange how I accepted this unforeseen partnership, this choice of nightmares forced upon me in the tenebrous land invaded by these mean and greedy phantoms.

"Kurtz discoursed. A voice! a voice! It rang deep to the very last. It survived his strength to hide in the magnificent folds of eloquence the barren darkness of his heart. Oh, he struggled! he struggled! The wastes of his weary brain were haunted by shadowy images now—images of wealth and fame revolving obsequiously round his unextinguishable gift of noble and lofty expression. My Intended, my station, my career, my ideas—these were the subjects for the occasional utterances of elevated sentiments. The shade of the original Kurtz frequented the bedside of the hollow sham, whose fate it was to be buried presently in the mold of primeval earth. But both the diabolic love and the unearthly hate of the mysteries it had penetrated fought for the possession of that soul satiated with primitive emotions, avid of lying fame, of sham distinction, of all the appearances of success and power.

"Sometimes he was contemptibly childish. He desired to have kings meet him at railway-stations on his return from some ghastly Nowhere, where he intended to accomplish great things. 'You show them you have in you something that is really profitable, and then there will be no limits to the recognition of your ability,' he would say. 'Of course you must take care of the motives—right motives—always.' The long reaches that were like one and the same reach, monotonous bends that were exactly alike, slipped past the steamer with their multitude of secular trees looking patiently after this grimy fragment of another world, the forerunner of change, of conquest, of trade, of massacres, of blessings. I looked ahead—piloting. 'Close the shutter,' said Kurtz suddenly one day; 'I can't bear to look at this.' I did so. There was a silence. 'Oh, but I will wring your heart yet!' he cried at the invisible wilderness.

"We broke down—as I had expected—and had to lie up for repairs at the head of an island. This delay was the first thing that shook Kurtz's confidence. One morning he gave me a packet of papers and a photograph,—the lot tied together with a shoe-string. 'Keep this for me,' he said. 'This noxious fool' (meaning the manager) 'is capable of prying into my boxes when I am not looking.' In the afternoon I saw him. He was lying on his back with closed eyes, and I withdrew quietly, but I heard him mutter, 'Live rightly, die, die . . .' I listened. There was nothing more. Was he rehearsing some speech in his sleep, or was it a fragment of a phrase from some newspaper article? He had been writing for the papers and meant to do so again, 'for the furthering of my ideas. It's a duty.'

"His was an impenetrable darkness. I looked at him as you peer down at a man who is lying at the bottom of a precipice where the sun never shines. But I had not much time to give him, because I was helping the engine-driver to take to pieces the leaky cylinders, to straighten a bent connecting-rod, and in other such matters. I lived in an infernal mess of rust, filings, nuts, bolts, spanners, hammers, ratchet-drills—things I abominate, because I don't get on with them. I tended the little forge we fortunately had aboard; I toiled wearily in a wretched scrap-heap—unless I had the shakes too bad to stand.

"One evening coming in with a candle I was startled to hear him say a little tremulously, 'I am lying here in the dark waiting for death.' The light was within a foot of his eyes. I forced myself to murmur, 'Oh, nonsense!' and stood over him as if transfixed.

"Anything approaching the change that came over his features I have never seen before, and hope never to see again. Oh, I wasn't touched. I was fascinated. It was as though a veil had been rent. I saw on that ivory face the expression of somber pride, of ruthless power, of craven terror—of an intense and hopeless despair. Did he live his life again in every detail of desire, temptation, and surrender during that supreme moment of complete knowledge? He cried in a whisper at some image, at some vision,—he cried out twice, a cry that was no more than a breath—

"'The horror! The horror!'

"I blew the candle out and left the cabin. The pilgrims were dining in the mess-room, and I took my place opposite the manager, who lifted his eyes to give me a questioning glance, which I successfully ignored. He leaned back, serene, with that peculiar smile of his sealing the unexpressed depths of his meanness. A continuous shower of small flies streamed upon the lamp, upon the cloth, upon our hands and faces. Suddenly the manager's boy put his insolent black head in the doorway, and said in a tone of scathing contempt—

"'Mistah Kurtz—he dead.'

"All the pilgrims rushed out to see. I remained, and went on with my dinner. I believe I was considered brutally callous. However, I did not eat much. There was a lamp in there—light, don't you know—and outside it was so beastly, beastly dark. I went no more near the remarkable man who had pronounced a judgment upon the adventures of his soul on this earth. The voice was gone. What else had been there? But I am of course aware that next day the pilgrims buried something in a muddy hole.

"And then they very nearly buried me.

"However, as you see, I did not go to join Kurtz there and then. I did not. I remained to dream the nightmare out to the end, and to show my loyalty to Kurtz once more. Destiny. My destiny! Droll thing life is—that mysterious arrangement of merciless logic for a futile purpose. The most you can hope from it is some knowledge of yourself—that comes too late—a crop of unextinguishable regrets. I have wrestled with death. It is the most unexciting contest you can imagine. It takes place in an impalpable grayness, with nothing underfoot, with nothing around, without spectators, without clamor, without glory, without the great desire of victory, without the great fear of defeat, in a sickly atmosphere of tepid skepticism, without much belief in your own right, and still less in that of your adversary. If such is the form of ultimate wisdom, then life is a greater riddle than some of us think it to be. I was within a hair's-breadth of the last opportunity for pronouncement, and I found with humiliation that probably I would have nothing to say. This is the reason why I affirm that Kurtz was a remarkable man. He had something to say. He said it. Since I had peeped over the edge myself, I understand better the meaning of his stare, that could not see the flame of the candle, but was wide enough to embrace the whole universe, piercing enough to penetrate all the hearts that beat in the darkness. He had summed up—he had judged. 'The horror!' He was a remarkable man. After all, this was the expression of some sort of belief; it had candor, it had conviction, it had a vibrating note of revolt in its whisper, it had the appalling face of a glimpsed truth—the strange commingling of desire and hate. And it is not my own extremity I remember best—a vision of grayness without form filled with physical pain, and a careless contempt for the evanescence of all things—even of this pain itself. No! It is his extremity that I seem to have lived through. True, he had made that last stride, he had stepped over the edge, while I had been permitted to draw back my hesitating foot. And perhaps in this is the whole difference; perhaps all the wisdom, and all truth, and all sincerity, are just compressed into that inappreciable moment of time in which we step over the threshold of the invisible. Perhaps! I like to think my summing-up would not have been a word of careless contempt. Better his cry—much better. It was an affirmation, a moral victory paid for by innumerable defeats, by abominable terrors, by abominable satisfactions. But it was a victory! That is why I have remained loyal to Kurtz to the last, and even beyond, when a long time after I heard once more, not his own voice, but the echo of his magnificent eloquence thrown to me from a soul as translucently pure as a cliff of crystal.

"No, they did not bury me, though there is a period of time which I remember mistily, with a shuddering wonder, like a passage through some inconceivable world that had no hope in it and no desire. I found myself back in the sepulchral city resenting the sight of people hurrying through the streets to filch a little money from each other, to devour their infamous cookery, to gulp their unwholesome beer, to dream their insignificant and silly dreams. They trespassed upon my thoughts. They were intruders whose knowledge of life was to me an irritating pretense, because I felt so sure they could not possibly know the things I knew. Their bearing, which was simply the bearing of commonplace individuals going about their business in the assurance of perfect safety, was offensive to me like the outrageous flauntings of folly in the face of a danger it is unable to comprehend. I had no particular desire to enlighten them, but I had some difficulty in restraining myself from laughing in their faces, so full of stupid importance. I dare say I was not very well at that time. I tottered about the streets—there were various affairs to settle—grinning bitterly at perfectly respectable persons. I admit my behavior was inexcusable, but then my temperature was seldom normal in these days. My dear aunt's endeavors to 'nurse up my strength' seemed altogether beside the mark. It was not my strength that wanted nursing, it was my imagination that wanted soothing. I kept the bundle of papers given me by Kurtz, not knowing exactly what to do with it. His mother had died lately, watched over, as I was told, by his Intended. A clean-shaved man, with an official manner and wearing gold-rimmed spectacles, called on me one day and made inquiries, at first circuitous, afterwards suavely pressing, about what he was pleased to denominate certain 'documents.' I was not surprised, because I had had two rows with the manager on the subject out there. I had refused to give up the smallest scrap out of that package, and I took the same attitude with the spectacled man. He became darkly menacing at last, and with much heat argued that the Company had the right to every bit of information about its 'territories.' And, said he, 'Mr. Kurtz's knowledge of unexplored regions must have been necessarily extensive and peculiar—owing to his great abilities and to the deplorable circumstances in which he had been placed: therefore'—I assured him Mr. Kurtz's knowledge, however extensive, did not bear upon the problems of commerce or administration. He invoked then the name of science. 'It would be an incalculable loss if,' &c., &c. I offered him the report on the 'Suppression of Savage Customs,' with the postscriptum torn off. He took it up eagerly, but ended by sniffing at it with an air of contempt. 'This is not what we had a right to expect,' he remarked. 'Expect nothing else,' I said. 'There are only private letters.' He withdrew upon some threat of legal proceedings, and I saw him no more; but another fellow, calling himself Kurtz's cousin, appeared two days later, and was anxious to hear all the details about his dear relative's last moments. Incidentally he gave me to understand that Kurtz had been essentially a great musician. 'There was the making of an immense success,' said the man, who was an organist, I believe, with lank gray hair flowing over a greasy coat-collar. I had no reason to doubt his statement; and to this day I am unable to say what was Kurtz's profession, whether he ever had any—which was the greatest of his talents. I had taken him for a painter who wrote for the papers, or else for a journalist who could paint—but even the cousin (who took snuff during the interview) could not tell me what he had been— exactly. He was a universal genius—on that point I agreed with the old chap, who thereupon blew his nose noisily into a large cotton handkerchief and withdrew in senile agitation, bearing off some family letters and memoranda without importance. Ultimately a journalist anxious to know something of the fate of his 'dear colleague' turned up. This visitor informed me Kurtz's proper sphere ought to have been politics 'on the popular side.' He had furry straight eyebrows, bristly hair cropped short, an eye-glass on a broad ribbon, and, becoming expansive, confessed his opinion that Kurtz really couldn't write a bit—'but heavens! how that man could talk! He electrified large meetings. He had faith—don't you see?—he had the faith. He could get himself to believe anything—anything. He would have been a splendid leader of an extreme party.' 'What party?' I asked. 'Any party,' answered the other. 'He was an—an—extremist.' Did I not think so? I assented. Did I know, he asked, with a sudden flash of curiosity, 'what it was that had induced him to go out there?' 'Yes,' said I, and forthwith handed him the famous Report for publication, if he thought fit. He glanced through it hurriedly, mumbling all the time, judged 'it would do,' and took himself off with this plunder.

"Thus I was left at last with a slim packet of letters and the girl's portrait. She struck me as beautiful—I mean she had a beautiful expression. I know that the sunlight can be made to lie too, yet one felt that no manipulation of light and pose could have conveyed the delicate shade of truthfulness upon those features. She seemed ready to listen without mental reservation, without suspicion, without a thought for herself. I concluded I would go and give her back her portrait and those letters myself. Curiosity? Yes; and also some other feeling perhaps. All that had been Kurtz's had passed out of my hands: his soul, his body, his station, his plans, his ivory, his career. There remained only his memory and his Intended—and I wanted to give that up too to the past, in a way,—to surrender personally all that remained of him with me to that oblivion which is the last word of our common fate. I don't defend myself. I had no clear perception of what it was I really wanted. Perhaps it was an impulse of unconscious loyalty, or the fulfillment of one of these ironic necessities that lurk in the facts of human existence. I don't know. I can't tell. But I went.

"I thought his memory was like the other memories of the dead that accumulate in every man's life,—a vague impress on the brain of shadows that had fallen on it in their swift and final passage; but before the high and ponderous door, between the tall houses of a street as still and decorous as a well-kept alley in a cemetery, I had a vision of him on the stretcher, opening his mouth voraciously, as if to devour all the earth with all its mankind. He lived then before me; he lived as much as he had ever lived—a shadow insatiable of splendid appearances, of frightful realities; a shadow darker than the shadow of the night, and draped nobly in the folds of a gorgeous eloquence. The vision seemed to enter the house with me—the stretcher, the phantom-bearers, the wild crowd of obedient worshipers, the gloom of the forests, the glitter of the reach between the murky bends, the beat of the drum, regular and muffled like the beating of a heart—the heart of a conquering darkness. It was a moment of triumph for the wilderness, an invading and vengeful rush which, it seemed to me, I would have to keep back alone for the salvation of another soul. And the memory of what I had heard him say afar there, with the horned shapes stirring at my back, in the glow of fires, within the patient woods, those broken phrases came back to me, were heard again in their ominous and terrifying simplicity. I remembered his abject pleading, his abject threats, the colossal scale of his vile desires, the meanness, the torment, the tempestuous anguish of his soul. And later on I seemed to see his collected languid manner, when he said one day, 'This lot of ivory now is really mine. The Company did not pay for it. I collected it myself at a very great personal risk. I am afraid they will try to claim it as theirs though. H'm. It is a difficult case. What do you think I ought to do—resist? Eh? I want no more than justice.' . . . He wanted no more than justice—no more than justice. I rang the bell before a mahogany door on the first floor, and while I waited he seemed to stare at me out of the glassy panel—stare with that wide and immense stare embracing, condemning, loathing all the universe. I seemed to hear the whispered cry, 'The horror! The horror!'

"The dusk was falling. I had to wait in a lofty drawing-room with three long windows from floor to ceiling that were like three luminous and bedraped columns. The bent gilt legs and backs of the furniture shone in indistinct curves. The tall marble fireplace had a cold and monumental whiteness. A grand piano stood massively in a corner, with dark gleams on the flat surfaces like a somber and polished sarcophagus. A high door opened—closed. I rose.

"She came forward, all in black, with a pale head, floating towards me in the dusk. She was in mourning. It was more than a year since his death, more than a year since the news came; she seemed as though she would remember and mourn for ever. She took both my hands in hers and murmured, 'I had heard you were coming.' I noticed she was not very young—I mean not girlish. She had a mature capacity for fidelity, for belief, for suffering. The room seemed to have grown darker, as if all the sad light of the cloudy evening had taken refuge on her forehead. This fair hair, this pale visage, this pure brow, seemed surrounded by an ashy halo from which the dark eyes looked out at me. Their glance was guileless, profound, confident, and trustful. She carried her sorrowful head as though she were proud of that sorrow, as though she would say, 'I—I alone know how to mourn for him as he deserves. But while we were still shaking hands, such a look of awful desolation came upon her face that I perceived she was one of those creatures that are not the playthings of Time. For her he had died only yesterday. And, by Jove! the impression was so powerful that for me too he seemed to have died only yesterday—nay, this very minute. I saw her and him in the same instant of time—his death and her sorrow—I saw her sorrow in the very moment of his death. Do you understand? I saw them together—I heard them together. She had said, with a deep catch of the breath, 'I have survived;' while my strained ears seemed to hear distinctly, mingled with her tone of despairing regret, the summing-up whisper of his eternal condemnation. I asked myself what I was doing there, with a sensation of panic in my heart as though I had blundered into a place of cruel and absurd mysteries not fit for a human being to behold. She motioned me to a chair. We sat down. I laid the packet gently on the little table, and she put her hand over it. . . . 'You knew him well,' she murmured, after a moment of mourning silence.

"'Intimacy grows quick out there,' I said. 'I knew him as well as it is possible for one man to know another.'

"'And you admired him,' she said. 'It was impossible to know him and not to admire him. Was it?'

"'He was a remarkable man,' I said, unsteadily. Then before the appealing fixity of her gaze, that seemed to watch for more words on my lips, I went on, 'It was impossible not to—'

"'Love him,' she finished eagerly, silencing me into an appalled dumbness. 'How true! how true! But when you think that no one knew him so well as I! I had all his noble confidence. I knew him best.'

"'You knew him best,' I repeated. And perhaps she did. But with every word spoken the room was growing darker, and only her forehead, smooth and white, remained illumined by the unextinguishable light of belief and love.

"'You were his friend,' she went on. 'His friend,' she repeated, a little louder. 'You must have been, if he had given you this, and sent you to me. I feel I can speak to you—and oh! I must speak. I want you—you who have heard his last words—to know I have been worthy of him. . . . It is not pride. . . . Yes! I am proud to know I understood him better than anyone on earth—he told me so himself. And since his mother died I have had no one—no one—to—to—'

"I listened. The darkness deepened. I was not even sure whether he had given me the right bundle. I rather suspect he wanted me to take care of another batch of his papers which, after his death, I saw the manager examining under the lamp. And the girl talked, easing her pain in the certitude of my sympathy; she talked as thirsty men drink. I had heard that her engagement with Kurtz had been disapproved by her people. He wasn't rich enough or something. And indeed I don't know whether he had not been a pauper all his life. He had given me some reason to infer that it was his impatience of comparative poverty that drove him out there.

"'. . . Who was not his friend who had heard him speak once?' she was saying. 'He drew men towards him by what was best in them.' She looked at me with intensity. 'It is the gift of the great,' she went on, and the sound of her low voice seemed to have the accompaniment of all the other sounds, full of mystery, desolation, and sorrow, I had ever heard—the ripple of the river, the soughing of the trees swayed by the wind, the murmurs of wild crowds, the faint ring of incomprehensible words cried from afar, the whisper of a voice speaking from beyond the threshold of an eternal darkness. 'But you have heard him! You know!' she cried.

"'Yes, I know,' I said with something like despair in my heart, but bowing my head before the faith that was in her, before that great and saving illusion that shone with an unearthly glow in the darkness, in the triumphant darkness from which I could not have defended her—from which I could not even defend myself.

"'What a loss to me—to us!'—she corrected herself with beautiful generosity; then added in a murmur, 'To the world.' By the last gleams of twilight I could see the glitter of her eyes, full of tears—of tears that would not fall.

"'I have been very happy—very fortunate—very proud,' she went on. 'Too fortunate. Too happy for a little while. And now I am unhappy for—for life.'

"She stood up; her fair hair seemed to catch all the remaining light in a glimmer of gold. I rose too.

"'And of all this,' she went on, mournfully, 'of all his promise, and of all his greatness, of his generous mind, of his noble heart, nothing remains—nothing but a memory. You and I—'

"'We shall always remember him,' I said, hastily.

"'No!' she cried. 'It is impossible that all this should be lost—that such a life should be sacrificed to leave nothing—but sorrow. You know what vast plans he had. I knew of them too—I could not perhaps understand,—but others knew of them. Something must remain. His words, at least, have not died.'

"'His words will remain,' I said.

"'And his example,' she whispered to herself. 'Men looked up to him,—his goodness shone in every act. His example—'

"'True,' I said; 'his example too. Yes, his example. I forgot that.'

"'But I do not. I cannot—I cannot believe—not yet. I cannot believe that I shall never see him again, that nobody will see him again, never, never, never.'

"She put out her arms as if after a retreating figure, stretching them black and with clasped pale hands across the fading and narrow sheen of the window. Never see him! I saw him clearly enough then. I shall see this eloquent phantom as long as I live, and I shall see her too, a tragic and familiar Shade, resembling in this gesture another one, tragic also, and bedecked with powerless charms, stretching bare brown arms over the glitter of the infernal stream, the stream of darkness. She said suddenly very low, 'He died as he lived.'

"'His end,' said I, with dull anger stirring in me, 'was in every way worthy of his life.'

"'And I was not with him,' she murmured. My anger subsided before a feeling of infinite pity.

"'Everything that could be done—' I mumbled.

"'Ah, but I believed in him more than anyone on earth—more than his own mother, more than—himself. He needed me! Me! I would have treasured every sigh, every word, every sign, every glance.'

"I felt like a chill grip on my chest. 'Don't,' I said, in a muffled voice.

"'Forgive me. I—I—have mourned so long in silence—in silence. . . . You were with him—to the last? I think of his loneliness. Nobody near to understand him as I would have understood. Perhaps no one to hear. . . .'

"'To the very end,' I said, shakily. 'I heard his very last words. . . .' I stopped in a fright.

"'Repeat them,' she said in a heart-broken tone. 'I want—I want—something—something—to—to live with.'

"I was on the point of crying at her, 'Don't you hear them?' The dusk was repeating them in a persistent whisper all around us, in a whisper that seemed to swell menacingly like the first whisper of a rising wind. 'The horror! The horror!'

"'His last word—to live with,' she murmured. 'Don't you understand I loved him—I loved him—I loved him!'

"I pulled myself together and spoke slowly.

"'The last word he pronounced was—your name.'

"I heard a light sigh, and then my heart stood still, stopped dead short by an exulting and terrible cry, by the cry of inconceivable triumph and of unspeakable pain. 'I knew it—I was sure!' . . . She knew. She was sure. I heard her weeping; she had hidden her face in her hands. It seemed to me that the house would collapse before I could escape, that the heavens would fall upon my head. But nothing happened. The heavens do not fall for such a trifle. Would they have fallen, I wonder, if I had rendered Kurtz that justice which was his due? Hadn't he said he wanted only justice? But I couldn't. I could not tell her. It would have been too dark—too dark altogether. . . ."

Marlow ceased, and sat apart, indistinct and silent, in the pose of a meditating Buddha. Nobody moved for a time. "We have lost the first of the ebb," said the Director, suddenly. I raised my head. The offing was barred by a black bank of clouds, and the tranquil waterway leading to the uttermost ends of the earth flowed somber under an overcast sky—seemed to lead into the heart of an immense darkness.

The Nigger of the 'Narcissus'

PREFACE

A work that aspires, however humbly, to the condition of art should carry its justification in every line. And art itself may be defined as a single-minded attempt to render the highest kind of justice to the visible universe, by bringing to light the truth, manifold and one, underlying its every aspect. It is an attempt to find in its forms, in its colours, in its light, in its shadows, in the aspects of matter and in the facts of life, what of each is fundamental, what is enduring and essential—their one illuminating and convincing quality—the very truth of their existence. The artist, then, like the thinker or the scientist, seeks the truth and makes his appeal. Impressed by the aspect of the world the thinker plunges into ideas, the scientist into facts—whence, presently, emerging they make their appeal to those qualities of our being that fit us best for the hazardous enterprise of living. They speak authoritatively to our common-sense, to our intelligence, to our desire of peace or to our desire of unrest; not seldom to our prejudices, sometimes to our fears, often to our egoism—but always to our credulity. And their words are heard with reverence, for their concern is with weighty matters: with the cultivation of our minds and the proper care of our bodies; with the attainment of our ambitions; with the perfection of the means and the glorification of our precious aims.

It is otherwise with the artist.

Confronted by the same enigmatical spectacle the artist descends within himself, and in that lonely region of stress and strife, if he be deserving and fortunate, he finds the terms of his appeal. His appeal is made to our less obvious capacities: to that part of our nature which, because of the warlike conditions of existence, is necessarily kept out of sight within the more resisting and hard qualities—like the vulnerable body within the steel armour. His appeal is less loud, more profound, less distinct, more stirring—and sooner forgotten. Yet its effect endures for ever. The changing wisdom of successive generations discards ideas, questions facts, demolishes theories. But the artist appeals to that part of our being which is not dependent on wisdom: to that in us which is a gift and not an acquisition—and, therefore, more permanently enduring. He speaks to our capacity for delight and wonder, to the sense of mystery surrounding our lives; to our sense of pity, and beauty, and pain; to the latent feeling of fellowship with all creation—and to the subtle but invincible, conviction of solidarity that knits together the loneliness of innumerable hearts: to the solidarity in dreams, in joy, in sorrow, in aspirations, in illusions, in hope, in fear, which binds men to each other, which binds together all humanity—the dead to the living and the living to the unborn.

It is only some such train of thought, or rather of feeling, that can in a measure explain the aim of the attempt, made in the tale which follows, to present an unrestful episode in the obscure lives of a few individuals out of all the disregarded multitude of the bewildered, the simple and the voiceless. For, if there is any part of truth in the belief confessed above, it becomes evident that there is not a place of splendour or a dark corner of the earth that does not deserve, if only a passing glance of wonder and pity. The motive, then, may be held to justify the matter of the work; but this preface, which is simply an avowal of endeavour, cannot end here—for the avowal is not yet complete.

Fiction—if it at all aspires to be art—appeals to temperament. And in truth it must be, like painting, like music, like all art, the appeal of one temperament to all the other innumerable temperaments whose subtle and resistless power endows passing events with their true meaning, and creates the moral, the emotional atmosphere of the place and time. Such an appeal, to be effective, must be an impression conveyed through the senses; and, in fact, it cannot be made in any other way, because temperament, whether individual or collective, is not amenable to persuasion. All art, therefore, appeals primarily to the senses, and the artistic aim when expressing itself in written words must also make its appeal through the senses, if its high desire is to reach the secret spring of responsive emotions. It must strenuously aspire to the plasticity of sculpture, to the colour of painting, and to the magic suggestiveness of music—which is the art of arts. And it is only through complete, unswerving devotion to the perfect blending of form and substance; it is only through an unremitting, never-discouraged care for the shape and ring of sentences that an approach can be made to plasticity, to colour; and the light of magic suggestiveness may be brought to play for an evanescent instant over the commonplace surface of words: of the old, old words, worn thin, defaced by ages of careless usage.

The sincere endeavour to accomplish that creative task, to go as far on that road as his strength will carry him, to go undeterred by faltering, weariness or reproach, is the only valid justification for the worker in prose. And if his conscience is clear, his answer to those who, in the fullness of a wisdom which looks for immediate profit, demand specifically to be edified, consoled, amused; who demand to be promptly improved, or encouraged, or frightened, or shocked, or charmed, must run thus:—My task which I am trying to achieve is, by the power of the written word, to make you hear, to make you feel—it is, before all, to make you see. That—and no more, and it is everything. If I succeed, you shall find there according to your deserts: encouragement, consolation, fear, charm—all you demand; and, perhaps, also that glimpse of truth for which you have forgotten to ask.

To snatch in a moment of courage, from the remorseless rush of time, a sapping phase of life is only the beginning of the task. The task approached in tenderness and faith is to hold up unquestioningly, without choice and without fear, the rescued fragment before all eyes and in the light of a sincere mood. It is to show its vibration, its colour, its form; and through its movement, its form, and its colour, reveal the substance of its truth—disclose its inspiring secret: the stress and passion within the core of each convincing moment. In a single-minded attempt of that kind, if one be deserving and fortunate, one may perchance attain to such clearness of sincerity that at last the presented vision of regret or pity, of terror or mirth, shall awaken in the hearts of the beholders that feeling of unavoidable solidarity; of the solidarity in mysterious origin, in toil, in joy, in hope, in uncertain fate, which binds men to each other and all mankind to the visible world.

It is evident that he who, rightly or wrongly, holds by the convictions expressed above cannot be faithful to any one of the temporary formulas of his craft. The enduring part of them—the truth which each only imperfectly veils—should abide with him as the most precious of his possessions, but they all: Realism, Romanticism, Naturalism, even the unofficial sentimentalism (which, like the poor, is exceedingly difficult to get rid of); all these gods must, after a short period of fellowship, abandon him—even on the very threshold of the temple—to the stammerings of his conscience and to the outspoken consciousness of the difficulties of his work. In that uneasy solitude the supreme cry of Art for Art, even, loses the exciting ring of its apparent immorality. It sounds far off. It has ceased to be a cry, and is heard only as a whisper, often incomprehensible, but at times, and faintly, encouraging.

Sometimes, stretched at ease in the shade of a roadside tree, we watch the motions of a labourer in a distant field, and after a time, begin to wonder languidly as to what the fellow may be at. We watch the movements of his body, the waving of his arms, we see him bend down, stand up, hesitate, begin again. It may add to the charm of an idle hour to be told the purpose of his exertions. If we know he is trying to lift a stone, to dig a ditch, to uproot a stump, we look with a more real interest at his efforts; we are disposed to condone the jar of his agitation upon the restfulness of the landscape; and even, if in a brotherly frame of mind, we may bring ourselves to forgive his failure. We understood his object, and, after all, the fellow has tried, and perhaps he had not the strength, and perhaps he had not the knowledge. We forgive, go on our way—and forget.

And so it is with the workman of art. Art is long and life is short, and success is very far off. And thus, doubtful of strength to travel so far, we talk a little about the aim—the aim of art, which, like life itself, is inspiring, difficult—obscured by mists. It is not in the clear logic of a triumphant conclusion; it is not in the unveiling of one of those heartless secrets which are called the Laws of Nature. It is not less great, but only more difficult.

To arrest, for the space of a breath, the hands busy about the work of the earth, and compel men entranced by the sight of distant goals to glance for a moment at the surrounding vision of form and colour, of sunshine and shadows; to make them pause for a look, for a sigh, for a smile—such is the aim, difficult and evanescent, and reserved only for a very few to achieve. But sometimes, by the deserving and the fortunate, even that task is accomplished. And when it is accomplished—behold!—all the truth of life is there: a moment of vision, a sigh, a smile—and the return to an eternal rest.

CHAPTER I

Mr. Baker, chief mate of the ship *Narcissus*, stepped in one stride out of his lighted cabin into the darkness of the quarter-deck. Above his head, on the break of the poop, the night-watchman rang a double stroke. It was nine o'clock. Mr. Baker, speaking up to the man above him, asked:—'Are all the hands aboard, Knowles?'

The man limped down the ladder, then said reflectively:—

'I think so, sir. All our old chaps are there, and a lot of new men has come . . . They must be all there.'

'Tell the boatswain to send all hands aft,' went on Mr. Baker; 'and tell one of the youngsters to bring a good lamp here. I want to muster our crowd.'

The main deck was dark aft, but halfway from forward, through the open doors of the forecastle, two streaks of brilliant light cut the shadow of the quiet night that lay upon the ship. A hum of voices was heard there, while port and starboard, in the illuminated doorways, silhouettes of moving men appeared for a moment, very black, without relief, like figures cut out of sheet tin. The ship was ready for sea. The carpenter had driven in the last wedge of the main-hatch battens, and, throwing down his maul, had wiped his face with great deliberation, just on the stroke of five. The decks had been swept, the windlass oiled and made ready to heave up the anchor; the big tow-rope lay in long bights along one side of the main deck, with one end carried up and hung over the bows, in readiness for the tug that would come paddling and hissing noisily, hot and smoky, in the limpid, cool quietness of the early morning. The captain was ashore, where he had been engaging some new hands to make up his full crew; and, the work of the day over, the ship's officers had kept out of the way, glad of a little breathing-time. Soon after dark the few liberty-men and the new hands began to arrive in shore-boats rowed by white-clad Asiatics, who clamoured fiercely for payment before coming alongside the gangway-ladder. The feverish and shrill babble of Eastern language struggled against the masterful tones of tipsy seamen, who argued against brazen claims and dishonest hopes by profane shouts. The resplendent and bestarred peace of the East was torn into squalid tatters by howls of rage and shrieks of lament raised over sums ranging from five annas to half a rupee; and every soul afloat in Bombay Harbour became aware that the new hands were joining the *Narcissus*.

Gradually the distracting noise had subsided. The boats came no longer in splashing clusters of three or four together, but dropped alongside singly, in a subdued buzz of expostulation cut short by a 'Not a piece more! You go to the devil!' from some man staggering up the accommodation-ladder—a dark figure, with a long bag poised on the shoulder. In the forecastle the newcomers, upright and swaying amongst corded boxes and bundles of bedding, made friends with the old hands, who sat one above another in the two tiers of bunks, gazing at their future shipmates with glances critical but friendly. The two forecastle lamps were turned up high, and shed an intense hard glare; shore-going hard hats were pushed far on the backs of heads, or rolled about on the deck amongst the chain-cables; white collars, undone, stuck out on each side of red faces; big arms in white sleeves gesticulated; the growling voices hummed steady amongst bursts of laughter and hoarse calls. 'Here, sonny, take that bunk! . . . Don't you do it! . . . What's your last ship? . . . I know her. . . . Three years ago, in Puget Sound . . . This here berth leaks, I tell you! . . . Come on; give us a chance to swing that chest! . . . Did you bring a bottle, any of you shore toffs? . . . Give us a bit of 'baccy . . . I know her; her skipper drank himself to death . . . He was a dandy boy! . . . Liked his lotion inside, he did! . . . No! . . . Hold your row, you chaps! . . . I tell you, you came on board a hooker, where they get their money's worth out of poor Jack, by—! . . .'

A little fellow, called Craik and nicknamed Belfast, abused the ship violently, romancing on principle, just to give the new hands something to think over. Archie, sitting aslant on his sea-chest, kept his knees out of the way, and pushed the needle steadily through a white patch in a pair of blue trousers. Men in black jackets and stand-up collars, mixed with men bare-footed, bare-armed, with coloured shirts open on hairy chests, pushed against one another in the middle of the forecastle. The group swayed, reeled, turning upon itself with the motion of a scrimmage, in a haze of tobacco smoke. All were speaking together, swearing at every second word. A Russian Finn, wearing a yellow shirt with pink stripes, stared upwards, dreamy-eyed, from under a mop of tumbled hair. Two young giants with smooth, baby faces—two Scandinavians—helped each other to spread their bedding, silent, and smiling placidly at the tempest of good-humoured and meaningless curses. Old Singleton, the oldest able seaman in the ship, sat apart on the deck right under the lamps, stripped to the waist, tattooed like a cannibal chief all over his powerful chest and enormous biceps. Between the blue and red patterns his white skin gleamed like satin; his bare back was propped against the heel of the bowsprit, and he held a book at arm's length before his big, sunburnt face. With his spectacles and a venerable white beard, he resembled a learned and savage patriarch, the incarnation of barbarian wisdom serene in the blasphemous turmoil of the world. He was intensely absorbed, and, as he turned the pages an expression of grave surprise would pass over his rugged features. He was reading 'Pelham.' The popularity of Bulwer-Lytton in the forecastles of Southern-going ships is a wonderful and bizarre phenomenon. What ideas do his polished and so curiously insincere sentences awaken in the simple minds of the big children who people those dark and wandering places of the earth? What meaning can their rough, inexperienced souls find in the elegant verbiage of his pages? What excitement?—what forgetfulness?—what appeasement? Mystery! Is it the fascination of the incomprehensible?—is it the charm of the impossible? Or are those beings who exist beyond the pale of life stirred by his tales as by an enigmatical disclosure of a resplendent world that exists within the frontier of infamy and filth, within that border of dirt and hunger, of misery and dissipation, that comes down on all sides to the water's edge of the incorruptible ocean, and is the only thing they know of life, the only thing they see of surrounding land—those life-long prisoners of the sea? Mystery?

Singleton, who had sailed to the southward since the age of twelve, who in the last forty-five years had lived (as we had calculated from his papers) no more than forty months ashore—old Singleton, who boasted, with the mild composure of long years well spent, that generally from the day he was paid off from one ship till the day he shipped in another he seldom was in a condition to distinguish daylight—old Singleton sat unmoved in the clash of voices and cries, spelling through 'Pelham' with slow labour, and lost in an absorption profound enough to resemble a trance. He breathed regularly. Every time he turned the book in his enormous and blackened hands the muscles of his big white arms rolled slightly under the smooth skin. Hidden by the white moustache, his lips, stained with tobacco-juice that trickled down the long beard, moved in inward whisper. His bleared eyes gazed fixedly from behind the glitter of black-rimmed glasses. Opposite to him, and on a level with his face, the ship's cat sat on the barrel of the windlass in the pose of a crouching chimera, blinking its green eyes at its old friend. It seemed to meditate a leap on to the old man's lap over the bent back of the ordinary seaman who sat at Singleton's feet. Young Charley was lean and long-necked. The ridge of his backbone made a chain of small hills under the old shirt. His face of a street-boy—a face precocious, sagacious, and ironic, with deep downward folds on each side of the thin, wide mouth—hung low over his bony knees. He was learning to make a lanyard knot with a bit of an old rope. Small drops of perspiration stood out on his bulging forehead; he sniffed strongly from time to time, glancing out of the corners of his restless eyes at the old seaman, who took no notice of the puzzled youngster muttering at his work.

The noise increased. Little Belfast seemed, in the heavy heat of the forecastle, to boil with facetious fury. His eyes danced; in the crimson of his face, comical as a mask, the mouth yawned black, with strange grimaces. Facing him, a half-undressed man held his sides, and throwing his head back, laughed with wet eyelashes. Others stared with amazed eyes. Men sitting doubled up in the upper bunks smoked short pipes, swinging bare brown feet above the heads of those who, sprawling below on sea-chests, listened, smiling stupidly or scornfully. Over the white rims of berths stuck out heads with blinking eyes; but the bodies were lost in the gloom of those places, that resembled narrow niches for coffins in a white-washed and lighted mortuary. Voices buzzed louder. Archie, with compressed lips, drew himself in, seemed to shrink into a smaller space, and sewed steadily, industrious and dumb. Belfast shrieked like an inspired Dervish:—' . . . So I seez to him, boys, seez I, "Beggin' yer pardon, sorr," seez I to that second mate of that steamer—"beggin' your-r-r pardon, sorr, the Board of Trade must 'ave been drunk when they granted you your certificate!" "What do you say, you—!" seez he, comin' at me like a mad bull . . . all in his white clothes; and I up with my tar pot and capsizes it all over his blamed lovely face and his lovely jacket. . . . "Take that!" seez I. "I am a sailor, anyhow, you nosing, skipper-licking, useless, sooperfloos bridge-stanchion, you! That's the kind of man I am!" shouts I . . . You should have seed him skip, boys! Drowned, blind with tar, he was! So . . .'

'Don't 'ee believe him! He never upset no tar; I was there!' shouted somebody. The two Norwegians sat on a chest side by side, alike and placid, resembling a pair of love-birds on a perch, and with round eyes stared innocently; but the Russian Finn, in the racket of explosive shouts and rolling laughter, remained motionless, limp and dull, like a deaf man without a backbone. Near him Archie smiled at his needle. A broad-chested, slow-eyed newcomer spoke deliberately to Belfast during an exhausted lull in the noise:—'I wonder any of the mates here are alive yet with such a chap as you on board! I concloode they ain't that bad now, if you had the taming of them, sonny.'

'Not bad! Not bad!' screamed Belfast. 'If it wasn't for us sticking together . . . Not bad! They ain't never bad when they ain't got a chawnce, blast their black 'arts . . .' He foamed, whirling his arms, then suddenly grinned and, taking a tablet of black tobacco out of his pocket, bit a piece off with a funny show of ferocity. Another new hand—a man with shifty eyes and a yellow hatchet face, who had been listening open-mouthed in the shadow of the midship locker—observed in a squeaky voice:—'Well, it's a 'omeward trip, anyhow. Bad or good, I can do it hall on my 'ed—s'long as I get 'ome. And I can look after my rights! I will show 'em!' All the heads turned towards him. Only the ordinary seaman and the cat took no notice. He stood with arms akimbo, a little fellow with white eyelashes, He looked as if he had known all the degradations and all the furies. He looked as if he had been cuffed, kicked, rolled in the mud; he looked as if he had been scratched, spat upon, pelted with unmentionable filth . . . and he smiled with a sense of security at the faces around. His ears were bending down under the weight of his battered hard hat. The torn tails of his black coat flapped in fringes about the calves of his legs. He unbuttoned the only two buttons that remained and every one saw he had no shirt under it. It was his deserved misfortune that those rags which nobody could possibly be supposed to own looked on him as if they had been stolen. His neck was long and thin; his eyelids were red; rare hairs hung about his jaws; his shoulders were peaked and drooped like the broken wings of a bird; all his left side was caked with mud which showed that he had lately slept in a wet ditch. He had saved his inefficient carcass from violent destruction by running away from an American ship where, in a moment of forgetful folly, he had dared to engage himself; and he had knocked about for a fortnight ashore in the native quarter, cadging for drinks, starving, sleeping on rubbish-heaps, wandering in sunshine: a startling visitor from a world of nightmares. He stood repulsive and smiling in the sudden silence. This clean white forecastle was his refuge; the place where he could be lazy; where he could wallow, and lie and eat—and curse the food he ate; where he could display his talents for shirking work, for cheating, for cadging; where he could find surely some one to wheedle and some one to bully—and where he would be paid for doing all this. They all knew him. Is there a spot on earth where such a man is unknown, an ominous survival testifying to the eternal fitness of lies and impudence? A taciturn long-armed shellback, with hooked fingers, who had been lying on his back smoking, turned in his bed to examine him dispassionately, then, over his head, sent a long jet of clear saliva towards the door. They all knew him! He was the man that cannot steer, that cannot splice, that dodges the work on dark nights; that, aloft, holds on frantically with both arms and legs, and swears at the wind, the sleet, the darkness; the man who curses the sea while others work. The man who is the last out and the first in when all hands are called. The man who can't do most things and won't do the rest. The pet of philanthropists and self-seeking landlubbers. The sympathetic and deserving creature that knows all about his rights, but knows nothing of courage, of endurance, and of the unexpressed faith, of the unspoken loyalty that knits together a ship's company. The independent offspring of the ignoble freedom of the slums full of disdain and hate for the austere servitude of the sea.

Some one cried at him: 'What's your name?'—'Donkin,' he said, looking round with cheerful effrontery.—'What are you?' asked another voice.—'Why, a sailor like you, old man,' he replied, in a tone that meant to be hearty but was impudent.—'Blamme if you don't look a blamed sight worse than a broken-down fireman,' was the comment in a convinced mutter. Charley lifted his head and piped in a cheeky voice: 'He is a man and a sailor'—then wiping his nose with the back of his hand bent down industriously over his bit of rope. A few laughed. others stared doubtfully. The ragged newcomer was indignant.—'That's a fine way to welcome a chap into a fo'c'sle,' he snarled. 'Are you men or a lot of 'artless cannybals?'—'Don't take your shirt off for a word, shipmate,' called out Belfast, jumping up in front, fiery, menacing, and friendly at the same time.—'Is that 'ere bloke blind?' asked the indomitable scarecrow, looking right and left with affected surprise. 'Can't 'ee see I 'aven't got no shirt?'

He held both his arms out crosswise and shook the rags that hung over his bones with dramatic effect.

''Cos why?' he continued very loud. 'The bloody Yankees been tryin' to jump my guts hout 'cos I stood up for my rights like a good 'un. I ham a Henglishman, I ham. They set upon me an' I 'ad to run. That's why. A'n't yer never seed a man 'ard up? Yah!

What kind of blamed ship is this? I'm dead broke. I 'aven't got nothink. No bag, no bed, no blanket, no shirt—not a bloomin' rag but what I stand in. But I 'ad the 'art to stand hup agin' them Yankees. 'As any of you 'art enough to spare a pair of old pants for a chum?'

He knew how to conquer the naive instincts of that crowd. In a moment they gave him their compassion, jocularly, contemptuously, or surlily; and at first it took the shape of a blanket thrown at him as he stood there with the white skin of his limbs showing his human kinship through the black fantasy of his rags. Then a pair of old shoes fell at his muddy feet. With a cry:—'From under,' a rolled-up pair of trousers, heavy with tar stains, struck him on the shoulder. The gust of their benevolence sent a wave of sentimental pity through their doubting hearts. They were touched by their own readiness to alleviate a shipmate's misery. Voices cried:—'We will fit you out, old man.' Murmurs: 'Never seed seech a hard case . . . Poor beggar . . . I've got

an old singlet . . . Will that be of any use to you? . . . Take it, matey . . .'
Those friendly murmurs filled the forecastle. He pawed around with his
naked foot, gathering the things in a heap and looked about for more.
Unemotional Archie perfunctorily contributed to the pile an old cloth
cap with the peak torn off. Old Singleton, lost in the serene regions of
fiction, read on unheeding. Charley, pitiless with the wisdom of youth,
squeaked:—'If you want brass buttons for your new unyforms I've got
two for you.' The filthy object of universal charity shook his fist at the
youngster.—'I'll make you keep this 'ere fo'c'sle clean, young feller,'
he snarled viciously. 'Never you fear. I will learn you to be civil to an
able seaman, you hignorant hass.' He glared harmfully, but saw
Singleton shut his book, and his little beady eyes began to roam from
berth to berth.—'Take that bunk by the door there—it's pretty fair,'
suggested Belfast. So advised, he gathered the gifts at his feet, pressed
them in a bundle against his breast, then looked cautiously at the
Russian Finn, who stood on one side with an unconscious gaze,
contemplating, perhaps, one of those weird visions that haunt the men
of his race. 'Get out of my road, Dutchy,' said the victim of Yankee
brutality. The Finn did not move—did not hear. 'Get out, blast ye,'
shouted the other, shoving him aside with his elbow. 'Get out, you
blanked deaf and dumb fool. Get out.' The man staggered, recovered
himself, and gazed at the speaker in silence.—'Those damned furriners
should be kept hunder,' opined the amiable Donkin to the forecastle. 'If
you don't teach 'em their place they put on you like hanythink.' He
flung all his worldly possessions into the empty bed-place, gauged with
another shrewd look the risks of the proceeding, then leaped up to the
Finn, who stood pensive and dull.—'I'll teach you to swell around,' he
yelled. 'I'll plug your eyes for you, you blooming square-head.' Most
of the men were now in their bunks and the two had the forecastle clear
to themselves. The development of the destitute Donkin aroused
interest. He danced all in tatters before the amazed Finn, squaring from
a distance at the heavy, unmoved face. One or two men cried
encouragingly: 'Go it, Whitechapel!' settling themselves luxuriously in
their beds to survey the fight. Others shouted: 'Shut yer row! . . . Go
an' put yer 'ed in a bag! . . .' The hubbub was recommencing. Suddenly
many heavy blows struck with a handspike on the deck above boomed
like discharges of small cannon through the forecastle. Then the
boatswain's voice rose outside the door with an authoritative note in its
drawl:—'D'ye hear, below there? Lay aft! Lay aft to muster all hands!'
    There was a moment of surprised stillness. Then the forecastle
floor disappeared under men whose bare feet flopped on the planks as
they sprang clear out of their berths. Caps were rooted for amongst
tumbled blankets. Some, yawning, buttoned waistbands. Half-smoked
pipes were knocked hurriedly against woodwork and stuffed under
pillows. Voices growled:—'What's up? . . . Is there no rest for us?'

Donkin yelped:—'If that's the way of this ship, we'll 'ave to change hall that . . . You leave me alone . . . I will soon . . .' None of the crowd noticed him. They were lurching in twos and threes through the doors, after the manner of merchant Jacks who cannot go out of a door fairly, like mere landsmen. The votary of change followed them. Singleton, struggling into his jacket, came last, tall and fatherly, bearing high his head of a weatherbeaten sage on the body of an old athlete. Only Charley remained alone in the white glare of the empty place, sitting between the two rows of iron links that stretched into the narrow gloom forward. He pulled hard at the strands in a hurried endeavour to finish his knot. Suddenly he started up, flung the rope at the cat, and skipped after the black tom that went off leaping sedately over chain compressors, with the tail carried stiff and upright, like a small flagpole.

Outside the glare of the steaming forecastle the serene purity of the night enveloped the seamen with its soothing breath, with its tepid breath flowing under the stars that hung countless above the mastheads in a thin cloud of luminous dust. On the town side the blackness of the water was streaked with trails of light which undulated gently on slight ripples, similar to filaments that float rooted to the shore. Rows of other lights stood away in straight lines as if drawn up on parade between towering buildings; but on the other side of the harbour sombre hills arched high their black spines, on which, here and there, the point of a star resembled a spark fallen from the sky. Far off, Byculla way, the electric lamps at the dock gates shone on the end of lofty standards with a glow blinding and frigid like captive ghosts of some evil moons. Scattered all over the dark polish of the roadstead, the ships at anchor floated in perfect stillness under the feeble gleam of their riding-lights, looming up, opaque and bulky, like strange and monumental structures abandoned by men to an everlasting repose.

Before the cabin door Mr. Baker was mustering the crew. As they stumbled and lurched along past the mainmast, they could see aft his round, broad face with a white paper before it, and beside his shoulder the sleepy head, with dropped eyelids, of the boy, who held, suspended at the end of his raised arm, the luminous globe of a lamp. Even before the shuffle of naked soles had ceased along the decks, the mate began to call over the names. He called distinctly in a serious tone befitting this roll-call to unquiet loneliness, to inglorious and obscure struggle, or to the more trying endurance of small privations and wearisome duties. As the chief mate read out a name, one of the men would answer: 'Yes, sir!' or 'Here!' and, detaching himself from the shadowy mob of heads visible above the blackness of starboard bulwarks, would step barefooted into the circle of light, and in two noiseless strides pass into the shadows on the port side of the quarter-deck. They answered in divers tones: in thick mutters, in clear, ringing voices; and some, as if the whole thing had been an outrage on their feelings, used an injured intonation: for discipline is not ceremonious in merchant ships, where the sense of hierarchy is weak, and where all feel themselves equal before the unconcerned immensity of the sea and the exacting appeal of the work.

Mr. Baker read on steadily:—'Hansen—Campbell—Smith—Wamibo. Now, then, Wamibo. Why don't you answer? Always got to call your name twice.' The Finn emitted at last an uncouth grunt, and, stepping out, passed through the patch of light, weird and gaudy, with the face of a man marching through a dream. The mate went on faster:—'Craik—Singleton—Donkin . . . O Lord!' he involuntarily ejaculated as the incredibly dilapidated figure appeared in the light. It stopped; it uncovered pale gums and long, upper teeth in a malevolent grin.—'Is there anything wrong with me, Mister Mate?' it asked, with a flavour of insolence in the forced simplicity of its tone. On both sides of the deck subdued titters were heard.—'That'll do. Go over,' growled Mr. Baker, fixing the new hand with steady blue eyes. And Donkin vanished suddenly out of the light into the dark group of mustered men, to be slapped on the back and to hear flattering whispers. Round him men muttered to one another:—'He ain't afeard, he'll give sport to 'em, see if he don't . . . Reg'lar Punch and Judy show . . . Did ye see the mate start at him? . . . Well! Damme, if I ever! . . .'

The last man had gone over, and there was a moment of silence while the mate peered at his list.—'Sixteen, seventeen,' he muttered. 'I am one hand short, bosun,' he said aloud. The big west-countryman at his elbow, swarthy and bearded like a gigantic Spaniard, said in a rumbling bass:—'There's no one left forward, sir. I had a look round. He ain't aboard, but he may turn up before daylight.'—'Ay. He may or he may not,' commented the mate; 'can't make out that last name. It's all a smudge . . . That will do, men. Go below.'

The indistinct and motionless group stirred, broke up, began to move forward.

'Wait!' cried a deep, ringing voice.

All stood still. Mr. Baker, who had turned away yawning, spun round open-mouthed. At last, furious, he blurted out:—'What's this? Who said "Wait"? What . . .'

But he saw a tall figure standing on the rail. It came down and pushed through the crowd, marching with a heavy tread towards the light on the quarter-deck. Then again the sonorous voice said with insistence:—'Wait!' The lamplight lit up the man's body. He was tall. His head was away up in the shadows of lifeboats that stood on skids above the deck. The whites of his eyes and his teeth gleamed distinctly, but the face was indistinguishable. His hands were big and seemed gloved.

Mr. Baker advanced intrepidly. 'Who are you? How dare you . . .'

he began.

The boy, amazed like the rest, raised the light to the man's face. It was black. A surprised hum—a faint hum that sounded like the suppressed mutter of the word 'Nigger'—ran along the deck and escaped out into the night. The nigger seemed not to hear. He balanced himself where he stood in a swagger that marked time. After a moment he said calmly:—'My name is Wait—James Wait.'

'Oh!' said Mr. Baker. Then, after a few seconds of smouldering silence, his temper blazed out. 'Ah! Your name is Wait. What of that? What do you want? What do you mean, coming shouting here?'

The nigger was calm, cool, towering, superb. The men had approached and stood behind him in a body. He overtopped the tallest by a half a head. He said: 'I belong to the ship.' He enunciated distinctly, with soft precision. The deep, rolling tones of his voice filled the deck without effort. He was naturally scornful, unaffectedly condescending, as if from his height of six foot three he had surveyed all the vastness of human folly and had made up his mind not to be too hard on it. He went on:—The captain shipped me this morning. I couldn't get aboard sooner. I saw you all aft and I came up the ladder, and could see directly you were mustering the crew. Naturally I called out my name. I thought you had it on your list, and would understand. You misapprehended.' He stopped short. The folly around him was confounded. He was right as ever, and as ever ready to forgive. The disdainful tones had ceased, and breathing heavily, he stood still, surrounded by all these white men. He held his head up in the glare of the lamp—a head vigorously modelled into deep shadows and shining lights—a head powerful and misshapen with a tormented and flattened face—a face pathetic and brutal: the tragic, the mysterious, the repulsive mask of a nigger's soul.

Mr. Baker, recovering his composure, looked at the paper close. 'Oh, yes; that's so. All right, Wait. Take your gear forward,' he said.

Suddenly the nigger's eyes rolled wildly, became all whites. He put his hand to his side and coughed twice, a cough metallic, hollow, and tremendously loud; it resounded like two explosions in a vault; the dome of the sky rang to it, and the iron plates of the ship's bulwarks seemed to vibrate in unison; then he marched off forward with the others. The officers lingering by the cabin door could hear him say: 'Won't some of you chaps lend a hand with my dunnage? I've got a chest and a bag.' The words, spoken sonorously, with an even intonation, were heard all over the ship, and the question was put in a manner that made refusal impossible. The short, quick shuffle of men carrying something heavy went away forward, but the tall figure of the nigger lingered by the main hatch in a knot of smaller shapes. Again he was heard asking: 'Is your cook a coloured gentleman?' Then a disappointed and disapproving 'Ah! h'm!' was his comment upon the information that the cook happened to be a mere white man. Yet, as they went all together towards the forecastle, he condescended to put his head through the galley door and boom out inside a magnificent 'Good evening, doctor!' that made all the saucepans ring. In the dim light the cook dozed on the coal locker in front of the captain's supper. He jumped up as if he had been cut with a whip, and dashed wildly on deck to see the backs of several men going away laughing. Afterwards, when talking about that voyage, he used to say:—'The poor fellow had scared me. I thought I had seen the devil.' The cook had been seven years in the ship with the same captain. He was a serious-minded man with a wife and three children, whose society he enjoyed on an average one month out of twelve. When on shore he took his family to church twice every Sunday. At sea he went to sleep every evening with his lamp turned full up, a pipe in his mouth, and an open Bible in his hand. Some one had always to go during the night to put out the light, take the book from his hand, and the pipe from between his teeth. 'For'— Belfast used to say, irritated and complaining—'some night, you stupid cookie, you'll swallow your ould clay, and we will have no cook.'— 'Ah! sonny, I am ready for my Maker's call . . . wish you all were.' the other would answer with a benign serenity that was altogether imbecile and touching. Belfast outside the galley door danced with vexation. 'You holy fool! I don't want you to die,' he howled, looking up with furious, quivering face and tender eyes. 'What's the hurry? you blessed wooden-headed ould heretic, the divvle will have you soon enough. Think of Us . . . of Us . . . of Us!' And he would go away, stamping, spitting aside, disgusted and worried; while the other, stepping out, saucepan in hand, hot, begrimed, and placid, watched with a superior, cock-sure smile the back of his 'queer little man' reeling in a rage. They were great friends.

Mr. Baker, lounging over the after-hatch, sniffed the humid night in the company of the second mate.—'Those West India niggers run fine and large—some of them . . . Ough! . . . Don't they? A fine, big man that, Mr. Creighton. Feel him on a rope. Hey? Ough! I will take him into my watch, I think.' The second mate, a fair gentlemanly young fellow, with a resolute face and a splendid physique, observed quietly that it was just about what he expected. There could be felt in his tone some slight bitterness which Mr. Baker very kindly set himself to argue away. 'Come, come, young man,' he said, grunting between the words. 'Come! Don't be too greedy. You had that big Finn in your watch all the voyage. I will do what's fair. You may have those two young Scandinavians and I . . . Ough! . . . I get the nigger, and will take that . . . . Ough! that cheeky costermonger chap in a black frock-coat. I'll make him . . . Ough! . . . make him toe the mark, or my . . . Ough! . . . name isn't Baker. Ough! Ough! Ough!'

He grunted thrice—ferociously. He had that trick of grunting so between his words and at the end of sentences. It was a fine, effective grunt that went well with his menacing utterance, with his heavy, bull-necked frame, his jerky, rolling gait; with his big, seamed face, his steady eyes, and sardonic mouth. But its effect had been long discounted by the men. They liked him; Belfast, who was a favourite, and knew it—mimicked him, not quite behind his back. Charley—but with greater caution—imitated his walk. Some of his sayings became established daily quotations in the forecastle. Popularity can go no farther! Besides, all hands were ready to admit that on a fitting occasion the mate could 'jump down a fellow's throat in a reg'lar Western Ocean style.'

Now he was giving his last orders. 'Ough! . . . You, Knowles! Call all hands at four. I want . . . Ough! . . . to heave short before the tug comes. Look out for the Captain. I am going to lay down in my clothes . . . Ough! . . . Call me when you see the boat coming. Ough! Ough! . . . The old man is sure to have something to say when he comes aboard' he remarked to Creighton. 'Well, good-night . . . Ough! A long day before us to-morrow . . . Ough! . . . Better turn in now. Ough! Ough!'

Upon the dark deck a band of light flashed, then a door slammed, and Mr. Baker was gone into his neat cabin. Young Creighton stood leaning over the rail, and looked dreamily into the night of the East. And he saw in it a long country lane, a lane of waving leaves and dancing sunshine. He saw stirring boughs of old trees outspread, and framing in their arch the tender, the caressing blueness of an English sky. And through the arch a girl in a clear dress, smiling under a sunshade, seemed to be stepping out of the tender sky.

At the other end of the ship the forecastle, with only one lamp burning now, was going to sleep in a dim emptiness traversed by loud breathings, by sudden short sighs. The double row of berths yawned black, like graves tenanted by uneasy corpses. Here and there a curtain of gaudy chintz, half drawn, marked the resting-place of a sybarite. A leg hung over the edge very white and lifeless. An arm stuck straight out with a dark palm turned up, and thick fingers half closed. Two light snores, that did not synchronise quarreled in funny dialogue. Singleton stripped again—the old man suffered much from prickly heat—stood cooling his back in the doorway, with his arms crossed on his bare and adorned chest. His head touched the beam of the deck above. The nigger, half undressed, was busy casting adrift the lashing of his box, and spreading his bedding in an upper berth. He moved about in his socks, tall and noiseless, with a pair of braces beating about his heels. Amongst the shadows of stanchions and bowsprit, Donkin munched a piece of hard ship's bread, sitting on the deck with upturned feet and restless eyes; he held the biscuit up before his mouth in the whole fist, and snapped his jaws at it with a raging face. Crumbs fell between his outspread legs. Then he got up.

'Where's our water-cask?' he asked in a contained voice.

Singleton, without a word, pointed with a big hand that held a short smouldering pipe. Donkin bent over the cask, drank out of The tin, splashing the water, turned round and noticed the nigger looking at him over the shoulder with calm loftiness. He moved up sideways.

'There's a blooming supper for a man,' he whispered bitterly. 'My dorg at 'ome wouldn't 'ave it. It's fit enouf for you an' me. 'Ere's a big ship's fo'c'sle . . . Not a bloomin' scrap of meat in the kids I've looked in all the lockers . . .

The nigger stared like a man addressed unexpectedly in a foreign language. Donkin changed his tone:—'Giv' us a bit of 'baccy, mate' he breathed out confidentially, 'I 'aven't 'ad a smoke or chew for the last month. I am rampin' mad for it. Come on, old man'!'

'Don't be familiar,' said the nigger. Donkin started and sat down on a chest near by, out of sheer surprise. 'We haven't kept pigs together.' continued James Wait in a deep undertone. 'Here's your tobacco.' Then, after a pause, he asked:—'What ship?'—'*Golden State*,' muttered Donkin indistinctly, biting the tobacco. The nigger whistled low.—'Ran?' he said curtly. Donkin nodded: one of his cheeks bulged out.—'In course I ran,' he mumbled. 'They booted the life hout of one Dago chap on the passage 'ere, then started on me. I cleared hout 'ere.'—'Left your dunnage behind?'—'Yes, dunnage and money,' answered Donkin, raising his voice a little; 'I got nothink. No clothes, no bed. A bandy-legged little Hirish chap 'ere 'as give me a blanket . . . Think I'll go an' sleep in the fore topmast staysail to-night.'

He went on deck trailing behind his back a corner of the blanket. Singleton, without a glance, moved slightly aside to let him pass. The nigger put away his shore togs and sat in clean working clothes on his box, one arm stretched over his knees. After staring at Singleton for some time he asked without emphasis:—'What kind of ship is this? Pretty fair? Eh?'

Singleton didn't stir. A long while after he said, with unmoved face:—'Ship! . . . Ships are all right. It is the men in them!'

He went on smoking in the profound silence. The wisdom of half a century spent listening to the thunder of the waves had spoken unconsciously through his old lips. The cat purred on the windlass. Then James Wait had a fit of roaring, rattling cough, that shook him, tossed him like a hurricane, and flung him panting with staring eyes headlong on his sea-chest. Several men woke up. One said sleepily out of his bunk: 'Struth! what a blamed row!'—'I have a cold on my chest,' gasped Wait.—'Cold! you call it,' grumbled the man; 'should think 'twas something more . . .'—'Oh! you think so,' said the nigger upright and loftily scornful again. He climbed into his berth and began coughing persistently while he put his head out to glare all round the forecastle. There was no further protest. He fell back on the pillow, and could be heard there wheezing regularly like a man oppressed in his sleep.

Singleton stood at the door with his face to the light and his back to the darkness. And alone in the dim emptiness of the sleeping forecastle he appeared bigger, colossal, very old; old as Father Time himself, who should have come there into this place as quiet as a sepulchre to contemplate with patient eyes the short victory of sleep, the consoler. Yet he was only a child of time, a lonely relic of a devoured and forgotten generation. He stood, still strong, as ever unthinking; a ready man with a vast empty past and with no future, with his childlike impulses and his man's passions already dead within his tattooed breast. The men who could understand his silence were gone—those men who knew how to exist beyond the pale of life and within sight of eternity. They had been strong, as those are strong who know neither doubts nor hopes. They had been impatient and enduring, turbulent and devoted, unruly and faithful. Well-meaning people had tried to represent those men as whining over every mouthful of their food; as going about their work in fear of their lives. But in truth they had been men who knew toil, privation, violence, debauchery—but knew not fear, and had no desire of spite in their hearts. Men hard to manage, but easy to inspire; voiceless men—but men enough to scorn in their hearts the sentimental voices that bewailed the hardness of their fate. It was a fate unique and their own; the capacity to bear it appeared to them the privilege of the chosen! Their generation lived inarticulate and indispensable, without knowing the sweetness of affections or the refuge of a home—and died free from the dark menace of a narrow grave. They were the everlasting children of the mysterious sea. Their successors are the grown-up children of a discontented earth. They are less naughty, but less innocent; less profane, but perhaps also less believing; and if they had learned how to speak they have also learned how to whine. But the others were strong and mute, they were effaced, bowed and enduring, like stone caryatides that hold up in the night the lighted halls of a resplendent and glorious edifice. They are gone now—and it does not matter. The sea and the earth are unfaithful to their children: a truth, a faith, a generation of men goes—and is forgotten, and it does not matter! Except, perhaps, to the few of those who believed the truth confessed the faith—or loved the men.

A breeze was coming. The ship that had been lying tide-rode swung to a heavier puff; and suddenly the slack of the chain cable between the windlass and the hawse-pipe clinked, slipped forward an inch, and rose gently off the deck with a startling suggestion as of unsuspected life that had been lurking stealthily in the iron. In the hawse-pipe The grinding links sent through the ship a sound like a low groan of a man sighing under a burden. The strain came on the windlass, the chain tautened like a string, vibrated—and the handle of the screw-brake moved in slight jerks. Singleton stepped forward. Till then he had been standing meditative and unthinking, reposeful and hopeless, with a face grim and blank—a sixty-year-old child of the mysterious sea. The thoughts of all his lifetime could have been expressed in six words, but the stir of those things that were as much a part of his existence as his beating heart called up a gleam of alert understanding upon the sternness of his aged face. The flame of the lamp swayed, and the old man, with knitted and bushy eyebrows, stood over the brake, watchful and motionless in the wild saraband of dancing shadows. Then the ship, obedient to the call of her anchor, forged ahead slightly and eased the strain. The cable relieved, hung down, and after swaying imperceptibly to and fro dropped with a loud tap on the hard wood planks. Singleton seized the high lever, and, by a violent throw forward of his body, wrung out another half-turn from the brake. He recovered himself, breathed largely, and remained for awhile glaring down at the powerful and compact engine that squatted on the deck at his feet, like some quiet monster—a creature amazing and tame.

'You . . . hold!' he growled at it masterfully, in the incult tangle of his white beard.

CHAPTER II

Next morning, at daylight, the *Narcissus* went to sea.

A slight haze blurred the horizon. Outside the harbour the measureless expanse of smooth water lay sparkling lay sparkling like a floor of jewels, and as empty as the sky. The short black tug gave a pluck to windward, in the usual way, then let go the rope, and hovered for a moment on the quarter with her engines stopped; while the slim, long hull of the ship moved ahead slowly under lower top-sails. The loose upper canvas blew out in the breeze with soft round contours, resembling small white clouds snared in the maze of ropes. Then the sheets were hauled home, the yards hoisted, and the ship became a high and lonely pyramid, gliding, all shining and white, through the sunlit mist. The tug turned short round and went away towards land. Twenty-six pairs of eyes watched her low broad stern crawling languidly over the beating water with fierce hurry. She resembled an enormous and aquatic blackbeetle, surprised by the light, overwhelmed by the sunshine, trying to escape with ineffectual effort into the distant gloom of the land. She left a lingering smudge of smoke on the sky, and two vanishing trails of foam on the water. On the place where she had stopped a round black patch of soot remained undulating on the swell—an unclean mark of the creature's rest.

The *Narcissus* left alone, heading south, seemed to stand resplendent and still upon the restless sea, under the moving sun. Flakes of foam swept past her sides; the water struck her with flashing blows; the land glided away, slowly fading; a few birds screamed on motionless wings over the swaying mastheads. But soon the land disappeared, the birds went away; and to the west the pointed sail of an Arab dhow running for Bombay, rose triangular and upright above the sharp edge of the horizon, lingered, and vanished like an illusion. Then the ship's wake, long and straight, stretched itself out through a day of immense solitude. The setting sun, burning on the level of the water, flamed crimson below the blackness of heavy rain clouds. The sunset squall, coming up from behind, dissolved itself into the short deluge of a hissing shower. It left the ship glistening from trucks to waterline, and with darkened sails. She ran easily before a fair monsoon, with her decks cleared for the night; and, moving along with her, was heard the sustained and monotonous swishing of the waves, mingled with the low whispers of men mustered aft for the setting of watches; the short plaint of some block aloft; or, now and then, a loud sigh of wind.

Mr. Baker, coming out of his cabin, called out the first name sharply before closing the door behind him. He was going to take charge of the deck. On the homeward trip according to an old custom of the sea, the chief officer takes the first night-watch—from eight till midnight. So Mr. Baker, after he had heard the last 'Yes, sir!' said moodily, 'Relieve the wheel and look-out;' and climbed with heavy feet the poop ladder to windward. Soon after Mr. Creighton came down, whistling softly, and went into the cabin. On the doorstep the steward lounged, in slippers, meditative, and with his shirt-sleeves rolled up to the armpits. On the main deck the cook, locking up the galley doors, had an altercation with young Charley about a pair of socks. He could be heard saying impressively, in the darkness amidships: 'You don't deserve a kindness. I've been drying them for you, and now you complain about the holes—and you swear, too! Right in front of me! If I hadn't been a Christian—which you ain't, you young ruffian—I would give you a clout on the head . . . Go away!' Men in couples or threes stood pensive or moved silently along the bulwarks in the waist. The first busy day of a homeward passage was sinking into the dull peace of resumed routine. Aft, on the high poop, Mr. Baker walked shuffling, grunted to himself in the pauses of his thoughts. Forward, the look-out man, erect between the flukes of the two anchors, hummed an endless tune, keeping his eyes fixed dutifully ahead in a vacant stare. A multitude of stars coming out into the clear night peopled the emptiness of the sky. They glittered, as if alive above the sea; they surrounded the running ship on all sides; more intense than the eyes of a staring crowd, and as inscrutable as the souls of men.

The passage had begun; and the ship, a fragment detached from the earth, went on lonely and swift like a small planet. Round her the abysses of sky and sea met in an unattainable frontier. A great circular solitude moved with her, ever changing and ever the same, always monotonous and always imposing. Now and then another wandering white speck, burdened with life, appeared far off—disappeared; intent on its own destiny. The sun looked upon her all day, and every morning rose with a burning, round stare of undying curiosity. She had her own future; she was alive with the lives of those beings who trod her decks; like that earth which had given her up to the sea, she had an intolerable load of regrets and hopes. On her lived timid truth and audacious lies; and, like the earth, she was unconscious, fair to see—and condemned by men to an ignoble fate. The august loneliness of her path lent dignity to the sordid inspiration of her pilgrimage. She drove foaming to the southward, as if guided by the courage of a high endeavour. The smiling greatness of the sea dwarfed the extent of time. The days raced after one another, brilliant and quick like the flashes of a lighthouse, and the nights, eventful and short, resembled fleeting dreams.

The men had shaken into their places, and the half-hourly voice of the bells ruled their life of unceasing care. Night and day the head and shoulders of a seaman could be seen aft by the wheel, outlined high against sunshine or starlight, very steady above the stir of revolving spokes. The faces changed, passing in rotation. Youthful faces, bearded faces, dark faces: faces serene, or faces moody, but all akin with the brotherhood of the sea; all with the same attentive expression of eyes, carefully watching the compass or the sails. Captain Allistoun, serious, and with an old red muffler round his throat all day long pervaded the poop. At night, many times he rose out of the darkness of the companion, such as a phantom above a grave, and stood watchful and mute under the stars, his night-shirt fluttering like a flag—then, without a sound, sank down again. He was born on the shores of the Pentland Firth. In his youth he attained the rank of harpooner in Peterhead whalers. When he spoke of that time his restless grey eyes became still and cold, like the loom of ice. Afterwards he went into the East Indian trade for the sake of change. He had commanded the *Narcissus* since she was built. He loved his ship, and drove her unmercifully; for his secret ambition was to make her accomplish some day a brilliantly quick passage which would be mentioned in nautical papers. He pronounced his owner's name with a sardonic smile spoke but seldom to his officers, and reproved errors in a gentle voice, with words that cut to the quick. His hair was iron-grey, his face hard and of the colour of pump-leather. He shaved every morning of his life—at six—but once (being caught in a fierce hurricane eighty miles south-west of Mauritius) he had missed three consecutive days. He feared naught but an unforgiving God, and wished to end his days in a little house, with a plot of ground attached—far in the country—out of sight of the sea.

He, the ruler of that minute world, seldom descended from the Olympian heights of his poop. Below him—at his feet, so to speak—common mortals led their busy and insignificant lives. Along the main deck Mr. Baker grunted in a manner bloodthirsty and innocuous; and kept all our noses to the grindstone, being—as he once remarked—paid for doing that very thing. The men working about the deck were healthy and contented—as most seamen are, when once well out to sea. The true peace of God begins at any spot a thousand miles from the nearest land; and when He sends there the messengers of His might it is not in terrible wrath against crime, presumption, and folly, but paternally, to chasten simple hearts—ignorant hearts that know nothing of life, and beat undisturbed by envy or greed.

In the evening the cleared decks had a reposeful aspect, resembling the autumn of the earth. The sun was sinking to rest, wrapped in a mantle of warm clouds. Forward, on the end of the spare spurs, the boatswain and the carpenter sat together with crossed arms; two men friendly, powerful, and deep-chested. Beside them the short, dumpy sailmaker—who had been in the Navy—related, between the whiffs of his pipe, impossible stories about Admirals. Couples tramped backwards and forwards, keeping step and balance without effort, in a confined space. Pigs grunted in the big pigsty. Belfast, leaning thoughtfully on his elbow, above the bars communed with them through the silence of his meditation. Fellows with shirts open wide on sunburnt breasts sat upon the mooring bits, and all up the steps of the forecastle ladders. By the foremast a few discussed in a circle the characteristics of a gentleman. One said:—'It's money as does it.' Another maintained:—'No, it's the way they speak.' Lame Knowles stumped up with an unwashed face (he had the distinction of being the dirty man of the forecastle), and, showing a few yellow fangs in a shrewd smile, explained craftily that he 'had seen some of their pants' The backsides of them—he had observed—were thinner than paper from constant sitting down in offices, yet otherwise they looked first-rate and would last for years. It was all appearance. 'It was,' he said, 'bloomin' easy to be a gentleman when you had a clean job for life.' They disputed endlessly, obstinate and childish; they repeated in shouts and with inflamed faces their amazing arguments; while the soft breeze, eddying down the enormous cavity of the foresail, that stood out distended above their bare heads, stirred the tumbled hair with a touch passing and light like an indulgent caress.

They were forgetting their toil, they were forgetting themselves. The cook approached to hear, and stood by, beaming with the inward consciousness of his faith, like a conceited saint unable to forget his glorious reward; Donkin, solitary and brooding over his wrongs on the forecastle-head, moved closer to catch the drift of the discussion below him; he turned his sallow face to the sea, and his thin nostrils moved, sniffing the breeze, as he lounged negligently by the rail. In the glow of sunset faces shone with interest, teeth flashed, eyes sparkled. The walking couples stood still suddenly, with broad grins; a man bending over a washtub, sat up, entranced, with the soapsuds flecking his wet arms. Even the three petty officers listened leaning back, comfortably propped, and with superior smiles. Belfast left off scratching the ear of his favorite pig, and, open-mouthed, tried with eager eyes to have his say. He lifted his arms, grimacing and baffled. From a distance Charley screamed at the ring:—'I know about gentlemen more'n any of you. I've been hintymate with 'em . . . I've blacked their boots.' The cook, craning his neck to hear better, was scandalized. 'Keep your mouth shut when your elders speak, you impudent young heathen—you.' 'All right, old Hallelujah, I'm done,' answered Charley, soothingly. At some opinion of dirty Knowles, delivered with an air of supernatural cunning, a ripple of laughter ran along, rose like a wave, burst with a startling roar. They stamped with both feet; they turned their shouting faces to the sky; many, spluttering, slapped their thighs; while one or two, bent double, gasped hugging themselves with both arms like men in pain. The carpenter and the boatswain, without changing their attitude, shook with laughter where they sat; the sailmaker, charged with an anecdote about a Commodore, looked sulky; the cook was wiping his eyes with a greasy rag; and lame Knowles, astonished at his own success, stood in their midst showing a slow smile.

Suddenly the face of Donkin leaning high-shouldered over the after-rail became grave. Something like a weak rattle was heard through the forecastle door. It became a murmur; it ended in a sighing groan. The washerman plunged both his arms into the tub abruptly; the cook became more crestfallen than an exposed backslider; the boatswain moved his shoulders uneasily; the carpenter got up with a spring and walked away—while the sailmaker seemed mentally to give his story up, and began to puff at his pipe with sombre determination. In the blackness of the doorway a pair of eyes glimmered white, and big and staring. Then James Wait's head protruding, became visible, as if suspended between the two hands that grasped a doorpost on each side of the face. The tassel of his blue woolen nightcap, cocked forward, danced gaily over his left eyelid. He stepped out in a tottering stride. He looked powerful as ever, but showed a strange and affected unsteadiness in his gait; his face was perhaps a trifle thinner, and his eyes appeared rather startlingly prominent. He seemed to hasten the retreat of departing light by his very presence; the setting sun dipped sharply, as though fleeing from our nigger; a black mist emanated from him; a subtle and dismal influence a something cold and gloomy that floated out and settled on all the faces like a mourning veil. The circle broke up. The joy of laughter died on stiffened lips. There was not a smile left among all the ship's company. Not a word was spoken. Many turned their backs, trying to look unconcerned; others, with averted heads, sent half-reluctant glances out of the corners of their eyes. They resembled criminals conscious of misdeeds more than honest. men distracted by doubt; only two or three stared frankly, but stupidly, with lips slightly open. All expected James Wait to say something, and, at the same time, had the air of knowing beforehand what he would say. He leaned his back against the doorpost, and with heavy eyes swept over us a glance domineering and pained, like a sick tyrant overawing a crowd of abject but untrustworthy slaves.

No one went away. they waited in fascinated dread. He said ironically, with gasps between the words:—

'Thank you . . . chaps. You . . . are nice . . . and . . . quiet . . . you are! Yelling so . . . before . . . the door . . .'

He made a longer pause, during which he worked his ribs in an exaggerated labour of breathing. It was intolerable. Feet were shuffled. Belfast let out a groan; but Donkin above blinked his red eyelids with invisible eyelashes, and smiled bitterly over the nigger's head.

The nigger went on again with surprising ease. He gasped no more, and his voice rang, hollow and loud, as though he had been talking in an empty cavern. He was contemptuously angry.

'I tried to get a wink of sleep. You know I can't sleep o'nights. And you come jabbering near the door here like a blooming lot of old women . . . You think yourselves good shipmates. Do you? . . . Much you care for a dying man!'

Belfast swung away from the pigsty. 'Jimmy,' he cried tremulously, 'if you hadn't been sick I would—'

He stopped. The nigger waited awhile, then said, in a gloomy tone:—'You would . . . What? Go an' fight another such one as yourself. Leave me alone. It won't be for long. I'll soon die . . . It's coming right enough!'

Men stood around very still, breathing lightly, and with exasperated eyes It was just what they had expected, and hated to hear, that idea of stalking death, thrust at them many times a day like a boast and like a menace by this obnoxious nigger. He seemed to take a pride in that death which, so far, had attended only upon the ease of his life; he was overbearing about it, as if no one else in the world had ever been intimate with such a companion; he paraded it unceasingly before us with an affectionate persistence that made its presence indubitable, and at the same time incredible. No man should be suspected of such monstrous friendship! Was he a reality—or was he a sham—this ever-expected visitor of Jimmy's? We hesitated between pity and mistrust, while, on the slightest provocation, he shook before our eyes the bones of his bothersome and infamous skeleton. He was for ever trotting him out. He would talk of that coming death as though it had been already there, as if it had been walking the deck outside, as if it would presently come in to sleep in the only empty bunk; as if it had sat by his side at every meal. It interfered daily with our occupations, with our leisure, with our amusements. We had no songs and no music in the evening, because Jimmy (we all lovingly called him Jimmy, to conceal our hate of his accomplice) had managed, with that prospective decease of his, to disturb even Archie's mental balance. Archie was the owner of the concertina; but after a couple of stinging lectures from Jimmy he refused to play any more. He said:—'Yon's an uncanny joker. I dinna ken what's wrang wi' him, but there's something verra wrang, verra wrang. It's nae manner of use asking me. I won't play.' Our singers became mute because Jimmy was a dying man. For the same reason no chap—as Knowles remarked—could 'drive in a nail to hang his few poor rags upon,' without being made aware of the enormity he committed in disturbing Jimmy's interminable last moments. At night, instead of the cheerful yell, 'One bell! Turn out! Do you hear there? Hey! hey! hey! Show leg!' the watches were called man by man, in whispers, so as not to interfere with Jimmy's, possibly, last slumber on earth. True, he was always awake, and managed, as we sneaked out on deck, to plant in our backs some cutting remark that, for the moment, made us feel as if we had been brutes, and afterwards made us suspect ourselves of being fools. We spoke in low tones within that fo'c'sle as though it had been a church. We ate our meals in silence and dread, for Jimmy was capricious with his food, and railed bitterly at the salt meat, at the biscuits, at the tea as at articles unfit for human consumption— 'let alone for a dying man!' He would say:—'Can't you find a better slice of meat for a sick man who's trying to get home to be cured—or buried? But there! if I had a chance, you fellows would do away with it. You would poison me. Look at what you have given me!' We served him in his bed with rage and humility, as if we had been the base couriers of a hated prince; and he rewarded us by his unconciliating criticism. He had found the secret of keeping for ever on the run the fundamental imbecility of mankind; he had the secret of life, that confounded dying men, and he made himself master of every moment of our existence. We grew desperate, and remained submissive. Emotional little Belfast was for ever on the verge of assault or on the verge of tears. One evening he confided to Archie:—'for a ha'penny I would knock his ugly block off the skulking dodger!' And the straightforward Archie pretended to be shocked! Such was the infernal spell which that casual St. Kitt's nigger had cast upon our guileless manhood! But the same night Belfast stole from the galley the officers' Sunday fruit pie, to tempt the fastidious appetite of Jimmy. He endangered not only his long friendship with the cook but also—as is appeared—his eternal welfare. The cook was over-whelmed with grief; he did not know the culprit but he knew that wickedness flourished; he knew that Satan was abroad amongst those men, whom he looked upon as in some way under his spiritual care. Whenever he saw three or four of us standing together he would leave his stove, to run out and preach. We fled from him; and only Charley (who knew the thief) affronted the cook with a candid gaze which irritated the good man. 'It's you, I believe,' he groaned, sorrowful, and with a patch of soot on his chin. 'It's you. You are a brand for burning! No more of your socks in my galley.' Soon, unofficially, the information was spread about that, should there be another case of stealing, our marmalade (an extra allowance: half a pound per man) would be stopped. Mr. Baker ceased to heap jocular abuse upon his favourites, and grunted suspiciously at all. The captain's cold eyes, high up on the poop, glittered mistrustful, as he surveyed us trooping in a small mob from halyards to braces for the usual evening pull at all the ropes. Such stealing in a merchant ship is difficult to check, and may be taken as a declaration by the men of their dislike for their officers. It is a bad symptom. It may end in God knows what trouble. The *Narcissus* was still a peaceful ship, but mutual confidence was shaken. Donkin did not conceal his delight. We were dismayed.

Then illogical Belfast approached our nigger with great fury. James Wait, with his elbow on the pillow, choked, gasped out:—'Did I ask you to bone the dratted thing? Blow your blamed pie. It has made me worse—you little Irish lunatic, you!' Belfast, with scarlet face and trembling lips, made a dash at him. Every man in the forecastle rose with a shout. There was a moment of wild tumult. Some one shrieked piercingly:—'Easy, Belfast! Easy! . . .' We expected Belfast to strangle Wait without more ado. Dust flew. We heard it through the nigger's cough, metallic and explosive like a gong. Next moment we saw Belfast hanging over him. He was saying plaintively:—'Don't! Don't, Jimmy! don't be like that. An angel couldn't put up with ye—sick as ye are.' He looked round at us from Jimmy's bedside, his comical mouth twitching, and through tearful eyes; then he tried to put straight the disarranged blankets. The unceasing whisper of the sea filled the forecastle. Was James Wait frightened, or touched, or repentant? He lay on his back with a hand to his side, and as motionless as if his expected visitor had come at last. Belfast fumbled about his feet, repeating with emotion:—'Yes. We know. Ye are bad, but . . . Just say what ye want done, and . . . We all know ye are bad—very bad . . .' No! Decidedly James Wait was not touched or repentant. Truth to say, he seemed rather startled. He sat up with incredible suddenness and ease. 'Ah, you think I am bad, do you?' he said gloomily, in his clearest baritone voice (to hear him speak sometimes you would never think there was anything wrong with that man). 'Do you? . . . Well, act according! Some of you haven't sense enough to put a blanket shipshape over a sick man. There! Leave it alone'! I can die anyhow!' Belfast turned away limply with a gesture of discouragement. In the silence of the forecastle, full of interested men, Donkin pronounced distinctly:— 'Well, I'm blowed!' and sniggered. Wait looked at him. He looked at him in a quite friendly manner. Nobody could tell what would please our incomprehensible invalid: but for us the scorn of that snigger was hard to bear.

Donkin's position in the forecastle was distinguished but unsafe. He stood on the bad eminence of a general dislike. He was left alone; and in his isolation he could do nothing but think of the gales of the Cape of Good Hope and envy us the possession of warm clothing and waterproofs. Our sea-boots, our oilskin coats, our well-filled sea-chests, were to him so many causes for bitter meditation: he had none of those things, and he felt instinctively that no man, when the need arose, would offer to share them with him. He was impudently cringing to us and systematically insolent to the officers. He anticipated the best results, for himself, from such a line of conduct—and was mistaken. Such natures forget that under extreme provocation men will be just— whether they want to be so or not. Donkin's insolence to long-suffering Mr. Baker became at last intolerable to us, and we rejoiced when the mate, one dark nigh, tamed him for good. I was done neatly, with great decency and decorum, and with little noise. We had been called—just before midnight—to trim the yards, and Donkin—as usual made—as usual, made insulting remarks. We stood sleepily in a row with the forebrace in our hands waiting for the next order, and heard in the darkness a scuffly trampling of feet, an exclamation of surprise, sounds of cuffs and slaps, suppressed, hissing whispers:—'Ah! Will you!' . . . 'Don't! . . . Don't!' . . . 'Then behave.' . . . 'Oh! Oh! . . .' Afterwards there were soft thuds mixed with the rattle of iron things as if a man's body had been tumbling helplessly amongst the main-pump rods. Before we could realise the situation, Mr. Baker's voice was heard very near and a little impatient:—'Haul away, men! Lay back on that rope!' And we did lay back on the rope with great alacrity. As if nothing had happened, the chief mate went on trimming the yards with his usual and exasperating fastidiousness. We didn't at the time see anything of Donkin, and did not care. Had the chief officer thrown him overboard, no man would have said as much as 'Hallo! he's gone!' But, in truth, no great harm was done—even if Donkin did lose one of his front teeth. We perceived this in the morning, and preserved a ceremonious silence: the etiquette of the forecastle commanded us to be blind and dumb in such a case, and we cherished the decencies of our life more than ordinary landsmen respect theirs. Charley, with unpardonable want of savoir vivre, yelled out:—''Ave you been to your dentyst? . . . Hurt ye, didn't it?' He got a box on the ear from one of his best friends. The boy was surprised, and remained plunged in grief for at least three hours. We were sorry for him, but youth requires even more discipline than age. Donkin grinned venomously. From that day he became pitiless; told Jimmy that he was a 'black fraud'; hinted to us that we were an imbecile lot, daily taken in by a vulgar nigger. And Jimmy seemed to like the fellow!

Singleton lived untouched by human emotions. Taciturn and unsmiling, he breathed amongst us—in that alone resembling the rest of the crowd. We were trying to be decent chaps, and found it jolly difficult; we oscillated between the desire of virtue and the fear of ridicule; we wished to save ourselves from the pain of remorse, but did not want to be made the contemptible dupes of our sentiment. Jimmy's hateful accomplice seemed to have blown with his impure breath undreamt-of subtleties into our hearts. We were disturbed and cowardly. That we knew. Singleton seemed to know nothing, understand nothing. We had thought him till then as wise as he looked, but now we dared, at times, suspect him of being stupid—from old age. One day, however, at dinner, as we sat on our boxes round a tin dish that stood on the deck within the circle of our feet, Jimmy expressed his general disgust with men and things in words that were particularly disgusting. Singleton lifted his head. We became mute. The old man, addressing Jimmy, asked:—'Are you dying?' Thus interrogated, James Wait appeared horribly startled and confused. We were all startled. Mouths remained open; hearts thumped; eyes blinked; a dropped tin fork rattled in the dish; a man rose as if to go out, and stood still. In less than a minute Jimmy pulled himself together.—'Why? Can't you see I am?' he answered shakily. Singleton lifted a piece of soaked biscuit ('his teeth'—he declared—'had no edge on them now') to his lips.— 'Well, get on with your dying,' he said with venerable mildness: 'don't raise a blamed fuss with us over that job. We can't help you.' Jimmy fell back in his bunk, and for a long time lay very still wiping the perspiration off his chin. The dinner-tins were put away quickly. On deck we discussed the incident in whispers. Some showed a chuckling exultation. Many looked grave. Wamibo, after long periods of staring dreaminess, attempted abortive smiles; and one of the young Scandinavians, much tormented by doubt, ventured in the second dog- watch to approach Singleton (the old man did not encourage us much to speak to him) and ask sheepishly:—'You think he will die?' Singleton looked up.—'Why, of course he will die.' he said deliberately. This seemed decisive. It was promptly imparted to every one by him who had consulted the oracle. Shy and eager, he would step up and with averted gaze recite his formula:—'Old Singleton says he will die.' It was a relief! At last we knew that our compassion would not be misplaced, and we could again smile without misgivings—but we reckoned without Donkin. Donkin 'didn't want to 'ave no truck with 'em dirty furriners.' When Neillssen came to him with the news: 'Singleton says he will die,' he answered him by a spiteful 'And so will you—you fat-headed Dutchman. Wish you Dutchmen were hall dead— 'stead comin' takin' our money hinto your starvin' country.' We were appalled. We perceived that after all Singleton's answer meant nothing. We began to hate him for making fun of us. All our certitudes were going; we were on doubtful terms with our officers; the cook had given us up for lost; we had overheard the boatswain's opinion that 'we were a crowd of softies' We suspected Jimmy, one another, and even our very selves. We did not know what to do. At every insignificant turn of our humble life we met Jimmy overbearing and blocking the way, arm-in-arm with his awful and veiled familiar. It was a weird servitude.

It began a week after leaving Bombay and came on us stealthily like any other great misfortune. Every one had remarked that Jimmy from the first was very slack at his work; but we thought it simply the outcome of his philosophy of life. Donkin said:—'You put no more weight on a rope than a bloody sparrer.' He disdained him. Belfast, ready for a fight, exclaimed provokingly:—'You don't kill yourself, old man!'——'Would you?' he retorted with extreme scorn—and Belfast retired. One morning, as we were washing decks, Mr. Baker called to him:—'Bring your broom over here, Wait.' He strolled languidly. 'Move yourself! Ough!' grunted Mr. Baker. 'What's the matter with your hind legs?' He stopped dead short. He gazed slowly with eyes that bulged out, with an expression audacious and sad.—'It isn't my legs,' he said, 'it's my lungs.' Everybody listened.—'What's . . . Ough . . . !' 'What's wrong with them?' inquired Mr. Baker. All the watch stood around on the wet deck, grinning, with brooms or buckets in their hands. He said mournfully:—'Going—or gone. Can't you see I'm a dying man? I know it!' Mr. Baker was disgusted.—'Then why the devil did you ship aboard here?—' 'I must live till I die—mustn't I?' he replied. The grins became audible.—'Go off the deck—get out of my sight,' said Mr. Baker. He was nonplussed. It was an unique experience. James Wait, obedient, dropped his broom, and walked slowly forward. A burst of laughter followed him. It was too funny. All hands laughed . . . They laughed! . . . Alas!'

He became the tormentor of all our moments; he was worse than a nightmare. You couldn't see that there was anything wrong with him: a nigger does not show. He was not very fat—certainly—but then he was no leaner than other niggers we had known. He coughed often, but the most prejudiced person could perceive that, mostly, he coughed when it suited his purpose. he wouldn't, or couldn't, do his work—and he wouldn't lie up. One day he would skip aloft with the best of them, and next time we would be obliged to risk our lives to get his limp body down. He was reported, he was examined; he was remonstrated with, threatened, cajoled, lectured. He was called into the cabin to interview the captain. There were wild rumours. It was said he had cheeked the old man; it was said he had frightened him. Charley maintained that the 'skipper, weepin' 'as giv' 'im 'is blessin' an' a pot of jam.' Knowles had it from the steward that the unspeakable Jimmy had been reeling against the cabin furniture; that he had groaned; that he had complained of general brutality and disbelief; and had ended by coughing all over the old man's meteorological journals which were then spread on the table. At any rate, Wait returned forward supported by the steward. who, in a pained and shocked voice, entreated us:—'Here! Catch hold of him, one or you. He is to lie up.' Jimmy drank a tin mugful of coffee, and, after bullying first one and then another, went to bed. He remained there most of the time, but when it suited him would come on deck and appear amongst us. He was scornful and brooding; he looked ahead upon the sea; and no one could tell what was the meaning of that black man sitting apart in a meditative attitude and as motionless as a carving.

He refused steadily all medicine; he threw sago and corn-flour overboard till the steward got tired of bringing it to him. He asked for paregoric. They sent him a big bottle; enough to poison a wilderness of babes. He kept it between his mattress and the deal lining of the ship's side; and nobody ever saw him take a dose. Donkin abused him to his face, jeered at him while he gasped; and the same day Wait would lend him a warm jersey. Once Donkin reviled him for half an hour; reproached him with the extra work his malingering gave to the watch; and ended by calling him 'a black-faced swine.' Under the spell of our accursed perversity we were horror-struck. But Jimmy positively seemed to revel in that abuse. It made him look cheerful—and Donkin had a pair of old sea boots thrown at him. 'Here, you East-end trash,' boomed Wait, 'you may have that.'

At last Mr. Baker had to tell the captain that James Wait was disturbing the peace of the ship. 'Knock discipline on the head—he will, Ough,' grunted Mr. Baker. As a matter of fact, the starboard watch came as near as possible to refusing duty, when ordered one morning by the boatswain to wash out their forecastle. It appears Jimmy objected to a wet floor—and that morning we were in a compassionate mood. We thought the boatswain a brute, and, practically, told him so. Only Mr. Baker's delicate tact prevented an all-fired row: he refused to take us seriously. He came bustling forward, and called us many unpolite names, but in such a hearty and seamanlike manner that we began to feel ashamed of ourselves. In truth, we thought him much too good a sailor to annoy him willingly: and after all Jimmy might have been a fraud—probably was! The forecastle got a clean up that morning; but in the afternoon a sick-bay was fitted up in the deck-house. It was a nice little cabin opening on deck, and with two berths. Jimmy's belongings were transported there, and then—notwithstanding his protests—Jimmy himself. He said he couldn't walk. Four men carried him on a blanket. He complained that he would have to die there alone, like a dog. We grieved for him, and were delighted to have him removed from the forecastle. We attended him as before. The galley was next door, and the cook looked in many times a day. Wait became a little more cheerful. Knowles affirmed having heard him laugh to himself in peals one day. Others had seen him walking about on deck at night. His little place, with the door ajar on a long hook, was always full of tobacco smoke. We spoke through the crack cheerfully, sometimes abusively, as we passed by, intent on our work. He fascinated us. He would never let doubt die. He overshadowed the ship. Invulnerable in his promise of speedy corruption he trampled on our self-respect, he demonstrated to us daily our want of moral courage; he tainted our lives. Had we been a miserable gang of wretched immortals, unhallowed alike by hope and fear, he could not have lorded it over us with a more pitiless assertion of his sublime privilege.

CHAPTER III

Meantime the *Narcissus*, with square yards, ran out of the fair monsoon. She drifted slowly, swinging round and round the compass, through a few days of baffling light airs. Under the patter of short warm showers, grumbling men whirled the heavy yards from side to sine; they caught hold of the soaked ropes with groans and sighs, while their officers, sulky and dripping with rain water, unceasingly ordered them about in wearied voices. During the short respites they looked with disgust into the smarting palms of their stiff hands, and asked one another bitterly:—'Who would be a sailor if he could be a farmer?' All the tempers were spoilt, and no man cared what he said. One black night, when the watch, panting in the heat and half-drowned with the rain, had been through four mortal hours hunted from brace to brace, Belfast declared that he would 'chuck going to sea for ever and go in a steamer.' This was excessive, no doubt. Captain Allistoun, with great self-control, would mutter sadly to Mr. Baker:—'It is not so bad—not so bad.' when he had managed to shove, and dodge, and manoeuvre his smart ship through sixty miles in twenty-four hours. From the doorstep of the little cabin, Jimmy, chin in hand, watched our distasteful labours with insolent and melancholy eyes. We spoke to him gently—and out of his sight exchanged sour smiles.

Then, again, with a fair wind and under a clear sky, the ship went on piling up the South Latitude. She passed outside Madagascar and Mauritius without a glimpse of the land. Extra lashings were put on the spare spars. Hatches were looked to. The steward in his leisure moments and with a worried air tried to fit washboards to the cabin doors. Stout canvas was bent with care. Anxious eyes looked to the westward, towards the cape of storms. The ship began to dip into a south-west swell, and the softly luminous sky of low latitudes took on a harder sheen from day to day above our heads: it arched high above the ship, vibrating and pale, like an immense dome of steel, resonant with the deep voice of freshening gales. The sunshine gleamed cold on the white curls of black waves. Before the strong breath of westerly squalls the ship, with reduced sail, lay slowly over, obstinate and yielding. She drove to and fro in the unceasing endeavour to fight her way through the invisible violence of the winds: she pitched headlong into the dark smooth hollows; she struggled upwards over the snowy ridges of great running seas; she rolled, restless, from side to side, like a thing in pain. Enduring and valiant, she answered to the call of men; and her slim spars waving for ever in abrupt semicircles, seemed to beckon in vain for help towards the stormy sky.

It was a bad winter off the Cape that year. The relieved helmsmen came off flapping their arms, or ran stamping hard and blowing into swollen, red fingers. The watch on deck dodged the sting of cold sprays or, crouching in sheltered corners, watched dismally the high and merciless seas boarding the ship time after time in unappeasable fury. Water tumbled in cataracts over the forecastle doors. You had to dash through a waterfall to get into your damp bed. The men turned in wet and turned out stiff to face the redeeming and ruthless extractions of their glorious and obscure fate. Far aft, and peering watchfully to windward, the officers could be seen through the mist of squalls. They stood by the weather-rail, holding on grimly, straight and glistening in their long coats; then, at times, in the disordered plunges of the hard-driven ship, they appeared high up, attentive, tossing violently above the grey line of a clouded horizon, and in motionless attitudes.

They watched the weather and the ship as men on shore watch the momentous chances of fortune. Captain Allistoun never left the deck, as though he had been part of the ship's fittings. Now and then the steward, shivering, but always in shirt sleeves, would struggle towards him with some hot coffee, half of which the gale blew out of each cup before it reached the master's lips. He drank what was left gravely in one long gulp, while heavy sprays pattered loudly on his oilskin coat, the seas swishing broke about his high boots; and he never took his eyes off the ship. He watched her every motion; he kept his gaze riveted upon here as a loving man who watches the unselfish toil of a delicate woman upon the slender thread of whose existence is hung the whole meaning and joy of the world. We all watched her. She was beautiful and had a weakness. We loved her no less for that. We admired her qualities aloud, we boasted of them to one another, as though they had been our own, and the consciousness of her only fault we kept buried in the silence of our profound affection. She was born in the thundering peal of hammers beating upon iron, in black eddies of smoke, under a gray sky, on the banks of the Clyde. The clamorous and sombre stream gives birth to things of beauty that float away into the sunshine of the world to be loved by men. The *Narcissus* was one of that perfect brood. Less perfect than many perhaps, but she was ours, and consequently, incomparable. We were proud of her. In Bombay, ignorant landlubbers alluded to her as that 'pretty grey ship.' Pretty! A scurvy meed of commendation! We knew she was the most magnificent sea-boat ever launched. We tried to forget that, like many good sea-boats, she was at times rather crank. She was exacting. She wanted care in loading and handling, and no one knew exactly how much care would be enough. Such are the imperfections of mere men! The ship knew, and sometimes would correct the presumptuous human ignorance by the wholesome discipline of fear. We had heard ominous stories about past voyages. The cook (technically a seaman, but in reality no sailor)—the cook, when unstrung by some misfortune, such as the rolling over of a saucepan, would mutter gloomily while he wiped the floor:—'There! Look at what she has done! Some voy'ge she will drown all hands! You'll see if she won't.' To which the steward, snatching in the galley a moment to draw breath in the hurry of his worried life, would remark philosophically:—'Those that see won't tell, anyhow. I don't want to see it.' We derided those fears. Our hearts went out to the old man when he pressed her hard so as to make her hold her own, hold to every inch gained to windward; when he made her under reefed sails, leap obliquely at enormous waves. The men, knitted together aft into a ready group by the first sharp order of an officer coming to take charge of the deck in bad weather:—'Keep handy the watch,' stood admiring her valiance. Their eyes blinked in the wind; their dark faces were wet with drops of water more salt and bitter than human tears; beards and moustaches, soaked, hung straight and dripping like fine seaweed. They were fantastically misshapen; in high boots, in hats like helmets, and swaying clumsily, stiff and bulky in glistening oilskins, they resembled men strangely equipped for some fabulous adventure. Whenever she rose easily to a towering green sea, elbows dug ribs, faces brightened, lips murmured:—'Didn't she do it cleverly,' and all the heads turning like one watched with sardonic grins the foiled wave go roaring to leeward, white with the foam of a monstrous rage. But when she had not been quick enough and, stuck heavily, lay over trembling under the blow, we clutched at the ropes, and looking up at the narrow bands of drenched and strained sails waving desperately aloft, we thought in our hearts—'No wonder. Poor thing!'

The thirty-second day out of Bombay began inauspiciously. In the morning a sea smashed one of the galley doors. We dashed in through lots of steam and found the cook very wet and indignant with the ship:—'She's getting worse every day. She's trying to drown me in front of my own stove!' He was very angry. We pacified him, and the carpenter, though washed away twice from there, managed to repair the door. Through that accident our dinner was not ready till late, but it didn't matter in the end because Knowles, who went to fetch it, got knocked down by a sea and the dinner went over the side. Captain Allistoun, looking more hard and thin-lipped than ever, hung on to full topsails and foresail, and would not notice that the ship, asked to do too much, appeared to lose heart altogether for the first time since we knew her. She refused to rise, and bored her way sullenly through the seas. Twice running, as though she had been blind or weary of life, she put her nose deliberately into a big wave and swept the decks from end to end. As the boatswain observed with marked annoyance, while we were splashing about in a body to try and save a worthless wash-tub:—'Every blooming thing in the ship is going overboard this afternoon.' Venerable Singleton broke his habitual silence and said with a glance aloft:—'The old man's in a temper with the weather, but it's no good bein' angry with the winds of heaven.' Jimmy had shut his door, of course. We knew he was dry and comfortable within his little cabin, and in our absurd say were pleased one moment, exasperated the next, by that certitude. Donkin skulked shamelessly, uneasy and miserable. He grumbled:—'I'm perishin' with cold houtside in bloomin' wet rags, an' that 'ere black sojer sits dry on a blamed chest full of bloomin' clothes; blank his black soul!' We took no notice of him; we hardly gave a thought to Jimmy and his bosom friend. There was no leisure for idle probing of hearts. Sails blew adrift. Things broke loose. Cold and wet, we were washed about the deck while trying to repair damages. The ship tossed about, shaken furiously, like a toy in the hand of a lunatic. Just at sunset there was a rush to shorten sail before the menace of a sombre hail cloud. The hard gust of wind came brutal like the blow of a fist. The ship relieved of her canvas in time received it pluckily: she yielded reluctantly to the violent onset; then, coming up with a stately and irresistible motion, brought her spars to windward in the teeth of the screeching squall. Out of the abysmal darkness of the black cloud overhead white hail streamed on her, rattled on the rigging, leaped in handfuls off the yards, rebounded on the deck—round and gleaming in the murky turmoil like a shower of pearls. It passed away. For a moment a livid sun shot horizontally the last rays of a sinister light between the hills of steep, rolling waves. Then a wild night rushed in—stamped out in a great howl that dismal remnant of a stormy day.

There was no sleep on board that night. Most seamen remember in their life one or two such nights of a culminating gale. Nothing seems left of the whole universe but darkness, clamour, fury—and the ship. And like the last vestige of a shattered creation she drifts, bearing an anguished remnant of sinful mankind, through the distress, tumult, and pain of an avenging terror. No one slept in the forecastle. The tin oil-lamp suspended on a long string, smoking, described wide circles; wet clothing made dark heaps on the glistening floor; a thin layer of water rushed to and fro. In the bed-places men lay booted, resting on elbows and with open eyes. Hung-up suits of oilskin swung out and in, lively and disquieting like reckless ghosts of decapitated seamen dancing in a tempest. No one spoke and all listened. Outside the night moaned and sobbed to the accompaniment of a continuous loud tremor as of innumerable drums beating far off. Shrieks passed through the air. Tremendous dull blows made the ship tremble while she rolled under the weight of the seas toppling on her deck. At times she soared up swiftly as if to leave this earth for ever, than during interminable moments fell through a void with all the hearts on board of her standing still, till a frightful shock, expected and sudden, started them off again with a big thump. After every dislocating jerk of the ship, Wamibo, stretched full length, his face on the pillow, groaned slightly with the pain of his tormented universe. Now and then, for the fraction of an intolerable second, the ship, in the fiercer burst of a terrible uproar, remained on her side, vibrating and still, with a stillness more appalling than the wildest motion. Then upon all those prone bodies a stir would pass, a shiver of suspense. A man would protrude his anxious head and a pair of eyes glistened in the sway of light, glaring wildly. Some moved their legs a little as if making ready to jump out. But several, motionless on their backs and with one hand gripping hard the edge of the bunk, smoked nervously with quick puffs, staring upwards; immobilised in a great craving for peace.

At midnight, orders were given to furl the fore and mizzen topsails. With immense efforts men crawled aloft through a merciless buffeting, saved the canvas, and crawled down almost exhausted, to bear in panting silence the cruel battering of the seas. Perhaps for the first time in the history of the merchant service the watch, told to go below, did not leave the deck, as if compelled to remain there by the fascination of a venomous violence. At every heavy gust men, huddled together, whispered to one another:—'It can blow no harder'—and presently the gale would give them the lie with a piercing shriek, and drive their breath back into their throats. A fierce squall seemed to burst asunder the thick mass of sooty vapours; and above the wrack of torn clouds glimpses could be caught of the high moon rushing backwards with frightful speed over the sky, right into the wind's eye. Many hung their heads, muttering that it 'turned their inwards out' to look at it. Soon the clouds closed up, and the world again became a raging, blind darkness that howled, flinging at the lonely ship salt sprays and sleet.

About half-past seven the pitchy obscurity round us turned a ghastly grey, and we knew that the sun had risen. This unnatural and threatening daylight, in which we could see one another's wild eyes and drawn faces, was only an added tax on our endurance. The horizon seemed to have come on all sides within arm's length of the ship. Into that narrowed circle furious seas leaped in, stuck, and leaped out. A rain of salt, heavy drops flew aslant like mist. The main-topsail had to be goose-winged, and with stolid resignation every one prepared to go aloft once more; but the officers yelled, pushed back, and at last we understood that no more men would be allowed to go on the yard than were absolutely necessary for the work. As at any moment the masts were likely to be jumped out or blown overboard, we concluded that the captain didn't want to see all his crowd go over the side at once. That was reasonable. The watch then on duty, led by Mr. Creighton, began to struggle up the rigging. The wind flattened them against the ratlines; then, easing a little, would let them ascent a couple of steps; and again, with a sudden gust, pin all up the shrouds the whole drawling line in attitudes of crucifixion. The other watch plunged down on the main deck to haul up the sail. Men's heads bobbed up as the water flung them irresistibly from side to side. Mr. Baker grunted encouragingly in our midst, spluttering and blowing amongst the tangled ropes like an energetic porpoise. Favoured by an ominous and untrustworthy lull, the work was done without any one being lost either off the deck or from the yard. For the moment the gale seemed to take off, and the ship, as if grateful for our efforts, plucked up heart and made better weather of it.

At eight the men off duty, watching their chance, ran forward over the flooded deck to get some rest. The other half of the crew remained aft for their turn of 'seeing her through her trouble,' as they expressed if. The two mates urged the master to go below. Mr. Baker grunted in his ear:—'Ough! surely now . . . Ough! . . . confidence in us . . . nothing more to do . . . she must lay it out or go. Ough! Ough!' Tall young Mr. Creighton smiled down at him cheerfully:—'. . . She's right as a trivet! Take a spell, sir.' He looked at them stonily with bloodshot, sleepless eyes. The rims of his eyelids were scarlet, and he moved his jaw unceasingly with a slow effort, as though he had been masticating a lump of india-rubber. He shook his head. He repeated:—'Never mind me. I must see it out—I must see it out,' but he consented to sit down for a moment on the skylight, with his hard face turned unflinchingly to windward. The sea spat at it—and stoical, it streamed with water as though he had been weeping. On the weather side of the poop the watch, hanging on to the mizzen rigging and to one another, tried to exchange encouraging words. Singleton, at the wheel, yelled out:—'Look out for yourselves!' His voice reached them in a warning whisper. They were startled.

A big, foaming sea came out of the mist; it made for the ship, roaring wildly, and in its rush it looked as mischievous and discomposing as a madman with an axe. One or two, shouting, scrambled up the rigging; most, with a convulsive catch of the breath, held on where they stood. Singleton dug his knees under the wheel-box, and carefully eased the helm to the headlong pitch of the ship, but without taking his eyes off the coming wave. It towered close-to and high, like a wall of green glass topped with snow. The ship rose to it as though she had soared on wings, and for a moment rested poised upon the foaming crest, as if she had been a great sea-bird. Before we could draw breath a heavy gust struck her, another roller took her unfairly under the weather bow, she gave a toppling lurch, and filled her decks. Captain Allistoun leaped up, and fell; Archie rolled over him, screaming:—'She will rise!' She gave another lurch to leeward; the lower deadeyes dipped heavily; the men's feet flew from under them, and they hung kicking above the slanting poop. They could see the ship putting her side in the water, and shouted all together:—'She's going!' Forward the forecastle doors flew open, and the watch below were seen leaping out one after another, throwing their arms up; and, falling on hands and knees, scrambled aft on all fours along the high side of the deck, sloping more than the roof of a house. From leeward the seas rose, pursuing them; they looked wretched in a hopeless struggle, like vermin fleeing before a flood; they fought up the weather ladder of the poop one after another, half naked and staring wildly; and as soon as they got up they shot to leeward in clusters, with closed eyes, till they brought up heavily with their ribs against the iron stanchions of the rail; then, groaning, they rolled in a confused mass. The immense volume of water thrown forward by the last scend of the ship had burst the lee door of the forecastle. They could see their chests, pillows, blankets, clothing, come out floating upon the sea. While they struggled back to windward they looked in dismay. The straw beds swam high, the blankets, spread out, undulated; while the chests, waterlogged and with a heavy list, pitched heavily, like dismasted hulks, before they sank; Archie's big coat passed with outspread arms, resembling a drowned seaman floating with his head under water. Men were slipping down while trying to dig their fingers into the planks; others, jammed in corners, rolled enormous eyes. They all yelled unceasingly;—'The masts! Cut! Cut! . . .' A black squall howled over the ship, that lay on her side with the weather yard-arms pointing to the clouds; while the tall masts, inclined nearly to the horizon, seemed to be of an unmeasurable length. The carpenter let go his hold, rolled against the skylight, and began to crawl to the cabin entrance, where a big axe was kept ready for just such an emergency. At that moment the topsail sheet parted, the end of the heavy chain racketed aloft, and sparks of red fire streamed down through the flying sprays. The sail flapped once with a jerk that seemed to tear our hearts out through our teeth, and instantly changed into a bunch of fluttering narrow ribbons that tied themselves into knots and became quiet along the yard. Captain Allistoun struggled, managed to stand up with his face near the deck, upon which men swung on the ends of ropes, like nest robbers upon a cliff. One of his feet was on somebody's chest; his face was purple; his lips moved. He yelled also; he yelled, bending down:—'No! No!' Mr. Baker, one leg over the binnacle-stand, roared out:—'Did you say no? Not cut?' He shook his head madly. 'No! No!' Between his legs the crawling carpenter heard, collapsed at once, and lay full length in the angle of the skylight. Voices took up the shout—'No! No!' Then all became still. They waited for the ship to turn over altogether, and shake them out into the sea; and upon the terrific noise of wind and sea not a murmur of remonstrance came out from those men, who each would have given ever so many years of life to see 'them damned sticks go overboard!' They all believed it their only chance, but a little hard-faced man shook his grey head and shouted 'No!' without giving them as much as a glance. They were silent, and gasped. They gripped rails, they had wound ropes'-ends under their arms; they clutched ring-bolts, they crawled in heaps where there was foothold; they held on with both arms, hooked themselves to any thing to windward with elbows, with chins, almost with their teeth: and some, unable to crawl away from where they had been flung, felt the sea leap up striking against their backs as they struggled upwards. Singleton had stuck to the wheel. His hair flew out in the wind; the gale seemed to take its life-long adversary by the beard and shake his old head. He wouldn't let go, and, with his knees forced between the spokes, flew up and down like a man on a bough. As Death appeared unready, they began to look about. Donkin, caught by one foot in a loop of some rope, hung, head down, below us and yelled, with his face to the deck:—'Cut! Don't mind that murderin' fool! Cut, some of you!' One of his rescuers struck him a back-handed blow over the mouth; his head banged on the deck and he became suddenly very quiet, with a white face, breathing hard, and with a few drops of blood trickling from his cut lip. On the lee side another man could be seen stretched out as if stunned; only the washboard prevented him from going over the side. It was the steward. We had to sling him up like a bale, for he was paralysed with fright. he had rushed up out of the pantry when he felt the ship go over, and had rolled down helplessly, clutching a china mug. It was not broken. With difficulty we tore it from him, and when he saw it in our hands he was amazed. 'Where did you get that thing?' he kept on asking, in a trembling voice. His shirt was blown to shreds; the ripped sleeves flapped like wings. Two men made him fast, and, doubled over the rope that held him, he resembled a bundle of wet rags. Mr. Baker crawled along the line of men, asking:—'Are you all there?' and looking them over. Some blinked vacantly, others shook convulsively; Wamibo's head hung over his breast; and in painful attitudes, cut by lashings, exhausted with clutching, screwed up in corners, they breathed heavily. Their lips twitched, and at every sickening heave of the overturned ship they opened them wide as if to shout. The cook, embracing a wooden stanchion, unconsciously repeated a prayer. In every short interval of the fiendish noises around he could be heard there without cap or slippers, imploring in that storm the Master of our lives not to lead him into temptation. Soon he also became silent. In all that crowd of cold and hungry men, waiting wearily for a violent death, not a voice was heard; they were mute, and in sombre thoughtfulness listened to the horrible imprecations of the gale.

Hours passed. They were sheltered by the heavy inclination of the ship from the wind that rushed in one long unbroken moan above their heads, but cold rain showers fell at times into the uneasy calm of their refuge. Under the torment of that new infliction a pair of shoulders would writhe a little. Teeth chattered. The sky was clearing, and bright sunshine gleamed over the ship. After every burst of battering seas, vivid and fleeting rainbows arched over the drifting hull in the flick of sprays. the gale was ending in a clear blow, which gleamed and cut like a knife. Between two bearded shellbacks Charley, fastened with somebody's long muffler to a deck ring-bolt, wept quietly, with rare tears wrung out by bewilderment, cold, hunger, and general misery. One of his neighbours punched him in the ribs, asking roughly:— 'What's the matter with your cheek? In fine weather there's no holding you, youngster.' Turning about with prudence he worked himself out of his coat and threw it over the boy. The other man closed up, muttering:—'Twill make a bloomin' man of you, sonny.' They flung their arms over and pressed against him. Charley drew his feet up and his eyelids dropped. Sighs were heard, as men, perceiving that they were not to be 'drowned in a hurry,' tried easier positions. Mr. Creighton, who had hurt his leg, lay amongst us with compressed lips. Some fellows belonging to his watch set about securing him better. Without a word or a glance he lifted his arms one after the other to facilitate the operation, and not a muscle moved in his stern, young face. They asked him with solicitude:—

'Easier now, sir?' He answered with a curt:—'That'll do.' He was a hard young officer, but many of his watch used to say they liked him well enough because he had 'such a gentlemanly way of damning us up and down the deck.' Others, unable to discern such fine shades of refinement, respected him for his smartness. For the first time since the ship had gone on her beam ends Captain Allistoun gave a short glance down at his men. He was almost upright—one foot against the side of the skylight, one knee on the deck; and with the end of the vang round his waist swung back and forth with his gaze fixed ahead watchful, like a man looking out for a sign. Before his eyes the ship, with half her deck below water, rose and fell on heavy seas that rushed from under her flashing in the cold sunshine. We began to think she was wonderfully buoyant—considering. confident voices were heard shouting:—'She'll do, boys!' Belfast exclaimed with fervour:—'I would give a month's pay for a draw at a pipe!' One or two, passing dry tongues on their salt lips, muttered something about a 'drink of water.' The cook, as if inspired, scrambled up with his breast against the poop water-cask and looked in. There was a little at the bottom. He yelled, waved his arms, and two men began to crawl backwards and

forwards with the mug. We had a good mouthful all round. The master
shook his head impatiently, refusing. When it came to Charley one of
his neighbours shouted:—'That bloomin' boy's asleep.' He slept as
though he had been dosed with narcotics. They let him be. Singleton
held to the wheel with one hand while he drank, bending down to
shelter his lips from the wind. Wamibo had to be poked and yelled at
before he saw the mug held before his eyes. Knowles said
sagaciously:—'It's better'n a tot o' rum.' Mr. Baker grunted:—'Thank
ye.' Mr. Creighton drank and nodded. Donkin gulped greedily, glaring
over the rim. Belfast made us laugh when with grimacing mouth he
shouted:—'Pass it this way. We're all taytottlers here.' The master,
presented with the mug again by a crouching man, who screamed up at
him:—'We all had a drink, captain,' groped for it without ceasing to
look ahead, and handed it back stiffly as though he could not spare half
a glance away from the ship. Faces brightened. We shouted to the
cook:—'Well done, doctor!' He sat to leeward, propped by the water-
cask and yelled back abundantly, but the seas were breaking in thunder
just then, and we only caught snatches that sounded like: 'Providence'
and 'born again.' He was at his old game of preaching. We made
friendly but derisive gestures at him, and from below he lifted one arm,
holding on with the other, moved his lips, he beamed up to us, straining
his voice—earnest, and ducking his head before the sprays.

Suddenly some one cried:—'Where's Jimmy?' and we were
appalled once more. On the end of the row the boatswain shouted
hoarsely:—'Has anyone seed him come out?' Voices exclaimed
dismally:—'Drowned—is he? . . . No! In his cabin! . . . Good Lord! . . .
Caught like a bloomin' rat in a trap . . . Couldn't open his door . . .
Aye! She went over too quick and the water jammed it . . . Poor
beggar! . . . No help for 'im . . . Let's go and see . . .' 'Damn him, who
could go?' screamed Donkin.—'Nobody expects you to,' growled the
man next to him; 'you're only a thing.'—'Is there half a chance to get
at 'im?' inquired two or three men together. Belfast untied himself with
blind impetuosity, and all at once shot down to leeward quicker than a
flash of lightning. We shouted all together with dismay; but with his
legs overboard he held and yelled for a rope. In our extremity nothing
could be terrible; so we judged him funny kicking there, and with his
scared face. some one began to laugh, and, as if hysterically infected
with screaming merriment, all those haggard men went off laughing,
wild-eyed, like a lot of maniacs tied up on a wall. Mr. Baker swung off
the binnacle-stand and tendered him one leg. He scrambled up rather
scared, and consigning us with abominable words to the 'divvle.' 'You
are . . . Ough! You're a foul-mouthed beggar, Craik,' grunted Mr.
Baker. He answered, stuttering with indignation:—'Look at 'em, sorr.
The bloomin' dirty images! laughing at a chum gone overboard. Call
themselves men, too.' But from the poop the boatswain called out:—

'Come along.' and Belfast crawled away in a hurry to join him. the five men, poised and gazing over the edge of the poop, looked for the best way to get forward. They seemed to hesitate. The others, twisting in their lashings, turning painfully, stared with open lips. Captain Allistoun saw nothing; he seemed with his eyes to hold the ship up in a superhuman concentration of effort. The wind screamed loud in the sunshine; columns of spray rose straight up; and in the glitter of rainbows bursting over the trembling hull the men went cautiously, disappearing from sight with deliberate movements.

They went swinging from belaying-pin to cleat above the seas that beat the half-submerged deck. Their toes scraped the planks. Lumps of cold green water toppled over the bulwark and on their heads. They hung for a moment on strained arms, with the breath knocked out of them, and with closed eyes—then, letting go with one hand, balanced with lolling heads, trying to grab some rope or stanchion further forward. The long-armed and athletic boatswain swung quickly, gripping things with a fist hard as iron, and remembering suddenly snatches of the last letter from his 'old woman.' Little Belfast scrambled rageously, muttering 'cursed nigger.' Wamibo's tongue hung out with excitement; and Archie, intrepid and calm, watched his chance to move with intelligent coolness.

When above the side of the house, they let go one after another, and falling heavily, sprawled, pressing their palms to the smooth teak wood. Round them the backwash of waves seethed white and hissing. All the doors had become trap-doors, of course. The first was the galley door. The galley extended from side to side, and they could hear the sea splashing with hollow noises in there. The next door was that of the carpenter's shop. They lifted it, and looked down. The room seemed to have been devastated by an earthquake. Everything in it had tumbled on the bulkhead facing the door, and on the other side of that bulkhead there was Jimmy, dead or alive. The bench, a half-finished meat-safe, saws, chisels, wire rods, axes, crowbars, lay in a heap besprinkled with loose nails. A sharp adze stuck up with a shining edge that gleamed dangerously down there like a wicked smile. The men clung to one another peering. A sickening, sly lurch of the ship nearly sent them overboard in a body. Belfast howled 'Here goes!' and leaped down. Archie followed cannily, catching at shelves that gave way with him, and eased himself in a great crash of ripped wood. There was hardly room for three men to move. And in the sunshiny blue square of the door, the boatswain's face, bearded and dark, Wamibo's face, wild and pale, hung over—watching.

Together they shouted: 'Jimmy! Jim!' From above the boatswain contributed a deep growl: 'You . . . Wait!' In a pause, Belfast entreated: 'Jimmy, darlin' are ye aloive?' The boatswain said: 'Again! All together boys!' All yelled excitedly. Wamibo made noises resembling loud barks. Belfast drummed on the side of the bulkhead with a piece of iron. All ceased suddenly. The sound of screaming and hammering went on thin and distinct—like a solo after a chorus. He was alive. He was screaming and knocking below us with the hurry of a man prematurely shut up in a coffin. We went to work. We attacked with desperation the abominable heap of things heavy, of things sharp, of things clumsy to handle. The boatswain crawled away to find somewhere a flying end of a rope; and Wamibo, held back by shouts:— 'Don't jump! . . . Don't come in here, muddle-head!'—remained glaring above us—all shining eyes, gleaming fangs, tumbled hair; resembling an amazed and half-witted fiend gloating over the extraordinary agitation of the damned. The boatswain adjured us to 'bear a hand,' and a rope descended. We made things fast to it and they went up spinning, never to be seen by man again. A rage to fling things overboard possessed us. We worked fiercely, cutting our hands, and speaking brutally to one another. Jimmy kept up a distracting row; he screamed piercingly, without drawing breath, like a tortured woman; he banged with hands and feet. The agony of his fear wrung our hearts so terribly that we longed to abandon him, to get out of that place deep as a well and swaying like a tree, to get out of his hearing, back on the poop where we could wait passively for death in incomparable repose. We shouted to him to 'shut up, for God's sake.' He redoubled his cries. He must have fancied we could not hear him. Probably he heard his own clamour but faintly. We could picture him crouching on the edge of the upper berth, letting out with both fists at the wood, in the dark, and with his mouth wide open for that unceasing cry. Those were loathsome moments. A cloud driving across the sun would darken the doorway menacingly. Every movement of the ship was pain. We scrambled about with no room to breathe, and felt frightfully sick. The boatswain yelled down at us:—'Bear a hand! Bear a hand! We two will be washed away from here directly if you ain't quick!' Three times a sea leaped over the high side and flung bucketfuls of water on our heads. Then Jimmy, startled by the shock, would stop his noise for a moment—waiting for the ship to sink, perhaps—and began again, distressingly loud, as if invigorated by the gust of fear. At the bottom the nails lay in a layer several inches thick. It was ghastly. Every nail in the world, not driven in firmly somewhere, seemed to have found its way into that carpenter's shop. There they were, of all kinds, the remnants of stores from seven voyages. Tin-tacks, copper tacks (sharp as needles), pump nails, with big heads, like tiny iron mushrooms; nails without any heads (horrible); French nails polished and slim. They lay in a solid mass more inabordable than a hedgehog. We hesitated yearning for a shovel, while Jimmy below us yelled as though he had been flayed. Groaning, we dug our fingers in, and very much hurt, shook our hands, scattering nails and drops of blood. We passed up our hats full of assorted nails to the boatswain, who, as if performing a mysterious and appeasing rite, cast them wide upon a raging sea. We got to the bulkhead at last. Those were stout planks. She was a ship, well finished in every detail—the *Narcissus* was. They were the stoutest planks ever put into a ship's bulkhead—we thought—and then we perceived that, in our hurry, we had sent all the tools overboard. Absurd little Belfast wanted to break it down with his own weight, and with both feet leaped straight up like a springbok, cursing the Clyde shipwrights for not scamping their work. Incidentally he reviled all North Britain, the rest of the earth, the sea—and all his companions. He swore, as he alighted heavily on his heels, that he would never, never any more associate with any fool that 'hadn't savvy enough to know his knee from him elbow.' He managed by his thumping to scare the last remnant of wits out of Jimmy. We could hear the object of our exasperated solicitude darting to and fro under the planks, now here, now there, in a puzzling manner. He squeaked as he dodged the invisible blows. It was more heartrending even than his yells. Suddenly Archie produced a crowbar. He had kept it back; also a small hatchet. We howled with satisfaction. He struck a mighty blow and small chips flew at our eyes. The boatswain above shouted:—'Look out! Look out there. Don't kill the man. Easy does it!' Wamibo, maddened with the excitement hung head down and insanely urged us:—'Hoo! Strook 'im! Hoo! Hoo!' We were afraid he would fall in and kill one of us and, hurriedly, we entreated the boatswain to 'shove the blamed Finn overboard.' Then, all together, we yelled down at the planks:—'Stand from under! Get forward.' and listened. We only heard the deep hum and moan of the wind above us, the mingled roar and hiss of the seas. The ship, as if overcome with despair, wallowed lifelessly, and our heads swam with that unnatural motion. Belfast clamoured:—'For the love of God, Jimmy, where are ye? . . . Knock! Jimmy darlint! . . . Knock! You bloody black beast! Knock!' He was as quiet as a dead man inside a grave; and, like men standing above a grave, we were on the verge of tears—but with vexation, the strain, the fatigue; with the great longing to be done with it, to get away, and lay down to rest somewhere where we could see our danger and breathe, Archie shouted:—'Gi'e me room!' We crouched behind him, guarding our heads, and he struck time after time in the joint of the planks. They cracked. Suddenly the crowbar went halfway in through a splintered oblong hole. It must have missed Jimmy's head by less than an inch. Archie withdrew it quickly, and that infamous nigger rushed at the hole, put his lips to it, and whispered 'Help' in an almost extinct voice; he pressed his head to it, trying madly to get out through that opening one inch wide and three inches long. In our disturbed state we were absolutely paralysed by his incredible action. It seemed impossible to drive him away. Even Archie at last lost his composure. 'If ye don't clear oot I'll drive the crowbar thro' your head.' he shouted in a determined voice. He meant what he said, and his earnestness seemed to make an impression on Jimmy. He disappeared suddenly, and we set to prising and tearing at the planks with the eagerness of men trying to get at a mortal enemy, and spurred by the desire to tear him limb from limb. The wood split, cracked, gave way. Belfast plunged in head and shoulders and groped viciously. 'I've got 'im! Got 'im,' he shouted. 'Oh! There! . . . He's gone; I've got 'im! . . . Pull at my legs! . . . Pull!' Wamibo hooted unceasingly. The boatswain shouted directions:— 'Catch hold of his hair, Belfast; pull straight up, you two! . . . Pull fair!' We pulled fair. We pulled Belfast out with a jerk, and dropped him with disgust. In a sitting posture, purple-faced, he sobbed despairingly:—'How can I hold on to 'is blooming short wool?'

Suddenly Jimmy's head and shoulders appeared. He stuck half-way, and with rolling eyes foamed at our feet. We flew at him with brutal impatience, we tore the shirt off his back, we tugged at his ears, we panted over him; and all at once he came away in our hands as though somebody had let go his legs. With the same movement, without a pause, we swung him up. His breath whistled, he kicked our upturned faces, he grasped two pairs of arms above his head, and he squirmed up with such precipitation that he seemed positively to escape from our hands like a bladder full of gas. Streaming with perspiration, we swarmed up the rope, and, coming into the blast of cold wind, gasped like men plunged into icy water. With burning faces we shivered to the very marrow of our bones. Never before had the gale seemed to us more furious, the sea more mad, the sunshine more merciless and mocking, and the position of the ship more hopeless and appalling. Every movement of her was ominous of the end of her agony and of the beginning of ours. We staggered away from the door, and, alarmed by a sudden roll, fell down in a bunch. it appeared to us that the side of the house was more smooth than glass and more slippery than ice. There was nothing to hang on to but a long brass hook used sometimes to keep back an open door. Wamibo held on to it and we held on to Wamibo, clutching our Jimmy. He had completely collapsed now. He did not seem to have the strength to close his hand. We stuck to him blindly in our fear. We were not afraid of Wamibo letting go (we remembered that the brute was stronger than any three men in the ship), but we were afraid of the hook giving way, and we also believed that the ship had made up her mind to turn over at last. But she didn't. A sea swept over us. The boatswain spluttered:—'Up and away. There's a lull. Away aft with you, or we will all go to the devil here.' We stood up surrounding Jimmy. We begged him to hold up, to hold on, at least. He glared with his bulging eyes, mute as a fish, and with all the stiffness knocked out of him. He wouldn't stand; he wouldn't even as much as clutch at our necks; he was only a cold black skin loosely stuffed with soft cotton wool; his arms and legs swung jointless and pliable; his head rolled about; the lower lip hung down, enormous and heavy. We pressed round him, bothered and dismayed; sheltering him we swung here and there in a body; and on the very brink of eternity we tottered all together with concealing and absurd gestures, like a lot of drunken men embarrassed with a stolen corpse.

Something had to be done. We had to get him aft. A rope was tied slack under his armpits, and, reaching up at the risk of our lives, we hung him on the foresheet cleat. He emitted no sound; he looked as ridiculously lamentable as a doll that had lost half its sawdust, and we started on our perilous journey over the main deck, dragging along with care that pitiful, that limp, that hateful burden. He was not very heavy, but had he weighed a ton he could not have been more awkward to handle. We literally passed him from hand to hand. Now and then we had to hang him up on a handy belaying-pin, to draw a breath and reform the line. Had the pin broken he would have irretrievably gone into the Southern Ocean, but he had to take his chance of that; and after a little while, becoming apparently aware of it, he groaned slightly, and with a great effort whispered a few words. We listened eagerly. He was reproaching us with our carelessness in letting him run such risks: 'Now, after I got myself from there,' he breathed out weakly. 'There' was his cabin. And he got himself out. We had nothing to do with it apparently! . . . No matter . . . We went on and let him take his chances, simply because we could not help it; for though at that time we hated him more than ever—more than anything under heaven—we did not want to lose him. We had so far saved him; and it had become a personal matter between us and the sea. We meant to stick to him. Had we (by an incredible hypothesis) undergone similar toil and trouble for an empty cask, that cask would have become as precious to us as Jimmy was. More precious, in fact, because we would have had no reason to hate the cask. And we hated James Wait. We could not get rid of the monstrous suspicion that this astounding black-man was shamming sick, had been malingering heartlessly in the face of our toil, of our scorn, of our patience—and now was malingering in the face of our devotion—in the face of death. Our vague and imperfect morality rose with disgust at his unmanly lie. But he stuck to it manfully—amazingly. No! It couldn't be. He was at all extremity. His cantankerous temper was only the result of the provoking invincibleness of that death he felt by his side. Any man may be angry with such a masterful chum. 'But, then, what kind of men were we—with our thoughts! Indignation and doubt grappled within us in a scuffle that trampled upon the finest of our feelings. And we hated him because of the suspicion; we detested him because of the doubt. We could not scorn him safely—neither could we pity him without risk to our dignity. So we hated him, and passed him carefully from hand to hand. We cried, 'Got him?—'Yes, all right. Let go.' and he swung from one enemy to another, showing about as much life as an old bolster would do. His eyes made two narrow white slits in the black face. He breathed slowly, and the air escaped through his lips with a noise like the sound of bellows. We reached the poop ladder at last, and it being a comparatively safe place, we lay for a moment in an exhausted heap to rest a little. He began to mutter. We were always incurably anxious to hear what he had to say. This time he mumbled peevishly. 'It took you some time to come. I began to think the whole smart lot of you had been washed overboard. What kept you back? Hey? Funk?' We said nothing. With sighs we started again to drag him up. The secret and ardent desire of our hearts was to beat him viciously with our fists about the head and we handled him as tenderly as though he had been made of glass.

The return on the poop was like the return of wanderers after many years amongst people marked by the desolation of time. Eyes were turned slowly in their sockets glancing at us. Faint murmurs were heard. 'Have you got 'im after all?' The well-known faces looked strange and familiar; they seemed faded and grimy; they had a mingled expression of fatigue and eagerness. They seemed to have become much thinner during our absence, as if all these men had been starving for a long time in their abandoned attitudes. The captain, with a round turn of a rope on his wrist, and kneeling on one knee, swung with a face cold and stiff but with living eyes he was still holding the ship up heeding no one, as if lost in the unearthly effort of that endeavour. We fastened up James Wait in a safe place. Mr. Baker scrambled along to lend a hand. Mr. Creighton, on his back, and very pale, muttered, 'Well done,' and gave us, Jimmy and the sky, a scornful glance, then closed his eyes slowly. Here and there a man stirred a little, but most remained apathetic, in cramped positions, muttering between shivers. The sun was setting. A sun enormous, unclouded and red, declining low as if bending down to look in their faces. The wind whistled across long sunbeams that, resplendent and cold, struck full on the dilated pupils of staring eyes without making them wink. The wisps of hair and the tangled beards were grey with the salt of the sea. The faces were earthy, and the dark patches under the eyes extended to the ears, smudged into the hollows of sunken cheeks. The lips were livid and thin, and when they moved it was difficulty, as though they had been glued to the teeth. Some grinned sadly in the sunlight, shaking with cold. Others were sad and still. Charley, subdued by the sudden disclosure of the insignificance of his youth, darted fearful glances. The two smooth-faced Norwegians resembled decrepit children, staring stupidly. To leeward, on the edge of the horizon, black seas leaped up towards the glowing sun. It sank slowly, round and blazing, and the crests of waves splashed on the edge of the luminous circle. One of the Norwegians appeared to catch sight of it, and, after giving a violent start, began to speak. His voice, startling the others, made them stir. They moved their heads stiffly, or turning with difficulty, looked at him with surprise, with fear, or in grave silence. He chattered at the setting sun, nodding his head, while the big seas began to roll across the crimson disc; and over miles of turbulent waters the shadows of high waves swept with a running darkness the faces of men. A crested roller broke with a loud hissing roar, and the sun, as if put out disappeared. The chattering voice faltered, went out together with the light. There were sighs. In the sudden lull that follows the crash of a broken sea a man said wearily, 'Here's that bloomin' Dutchman gone off his chump.' A seaman, lashed by the middle, tapped the deck with his open hand with unceasing quick flaps. In the gathering greyness of twilight a bulky form was seen rising aft, and began marching on all fours with the movements of some big cautious beast. It was Mr. Baker passing along the line of men. He grunted encouragingly over every one, felt their fastenings. Some, with half-open eyes, puffed like men oppressed by heat; others, mechanically and in dreamy voices answered him, 'Aye! aye! sir!' He went from one to another grunting, 'Ough! . . . See her through it yet;' and unexpectedly, with loud angry outbursts, blew up Knowles for cutting off a long piece from the fall of the relieving tackle. 'Ough!—Ashamed of yourself—Relieving tackle—Don't you know better!—Ough!—Able seaman! Ough!' The lame man was crushed. He muttered, 'Get som'think for a lashing for myself, sir.'— 'Ough! Lashing—yourself. Are you a tinker or a sailor—What? Ough!—May want that tackle directly—Ough! More use to the ship than your lame carcass. Ough!—Keep it! Keep it, now you've done it.' He crawled away slowly, muttering to himself about some men being 'worse than children.' It had been a comforting row. Low exclamations were heard: 'Hallo . . . Hallo . . .' Those who had been painfully dozing asked with convulsive starts, 'What's up? . . . What is it?' The answers came with unexpected cheerfulness: 'The mate is going bald-headed for lame Jack about something or other.' 'No! . . .' 'What 'as he done?' Some even chuckled. It was like a whiff of hope, like a reminder of safe days. Donkin, who had been stupefied with fear, revived suddenly and began to shout:—''Ear 'im; that's the way they tawlk to hus. Vy donch 'ee 'it 'im—one ov yer? 'It 'im. 'It 'im! Comin' the mate hover hus. We are as good men as 'ee! We're hall goin' to 'ell now. We 'ave been starved in this rotten ship, an' now we're goin' to be drowned for them black-'earted bullies! 'it 'im!' He shrieked in the deepening gloom, he blubbered and sobbed, screaming:—''It 'im! 'It 'im!' The rage and fear of his disregarded right to live tried the steadfastness of hearts more than the menacing shadows of the night that advanced through the unceasing clamor of the gale. From aft Mr. Baker was heard:—'Is one of you men going to stop him—must I come along?

'Shut up! . . .' 'Keep quiet!' cried various voices, exasperated, trembling with cold.—'You'll get one across the mug from me directly.' said an invisible seaman, in a weary tone, 'I won't let the mate have the trouble.' He ceased and lay still with the silence of despair. On the black sky the stars, coming out, gleamed over an inky sea that, speckled with foam, flashed back at them the evanescent and pale light of a dazzling whiteness born from the black turmoil of the waves. Remote in the eternal calm they glittered hard and cold above the uproar of the earth; they surrounded the vanquished and tormented ship on all sides: more pitiless than the eyes of a triumphant mob and as unapproachable as the hearts of men.

The icy south wind howled exultingly under the sombre splendour of the sky. The cold shook the men with a restless violence as though it had tried to shake them to pieces. Short moans were swept unheard off the stiff lips. Some complained in mutters of 'not feeling themselves below the waist'; while those who had closed their eyes, imagined they had a block of ice on their chests. Others, alarmed at not feeling any pain in their fingers, beat the deck feebly with their hands—obstinate and exhausted. Wamibo stared vacant and dreamy. The Scandinavians kept on a meaningless mutter through chattering teeth. The spare Scotchmen, with determined efforts, kept their lower jaws still. The West-country men lay big and stolid in an invulnerable surliness. A man yawned and swore in turns. Another breathed with a rattle in his throat. Two elderly hard-weather shellbacks, fast side by side, whispered dismally to one another about the landlady of a boarding-house in Sunderland, whom they both knew. They extolled her motherliness and her liberality; they tried to talk about the joint of beef and the big fire in the downstairs kitchen. The words dying faintly on their lips, ended in light sighs. A sudden voice cried into the cold night, 'Oh Lord!' No one changed his position or took any notice of the cry. One or two passed, with a repeated and vague gesture, their hand over their faces, but most of them kept very still. In the benumbed immobility of their bodies they were excessively wearied by their thoughts, that rushed with the rapidity and vividness of dreams. Now and then, by an abrupt and startling exclamation, they answered the weird hail of some illusion; then, again, in silence contemplated the vision of known faces and familiar things. They recalled the aspect of forgotten shipmates and heard the voice of dead and gone skippers. They remembered the noise of gaslit streets, the steamy heat of tap-rooms, or the scorching sunshine of calm days at sea.

Mr. Baker left his insecure place, and crawled, with stoppages, along the poop. In the dark and on all fours he resembled some carnivorous animal prowling amongst corpses. At the break, propped to windward of a stanchion, he looked down on the main deck. It seemed to him that the ship had a tendency to stand up a little more. The wind had eased a little, he thought, but the sea ran as high as ever. The waves foamed viciously, and the lee side of the deck disappeared under a hissing whiteness as of boiling milk, while the rigging sang steadily with a deep vibrating note, and, at every upward swing of the ship, the wind rushed with a long-drawn clamour amongst the spars. Mr. Baker watched very still. A man near him began to make a blabbing noise with his lips, all at once and very loud, as though the cold had broken brutally through him. He went on: 'Ba—ba—ba—brrr—brr—ba—ba— ' 'Stop that!' cried Mr. Baker, groping in the dark. 'Stop it!' He went on shaking the leg he found under his hand.—'What is it, sir?' called out Belfast, in the tone of a man awakened suddenly: 'we are looking after that 'ere Jimmy.'—'Are you? Ough! Don't make that row then. Who's that near you?'—'It's me—the boatswain, sir,' growled the West-country man; 'we are trying to keep life in that poor devil.'— 'Aye, aye!' said Mr. Baker, 'Do it quietly, can't you.'—'He wants us to hold him up above the rail,' went on the boatswain, with irritation, 'says he can't breathe here under our jackets.'—'If we lift 'im, we drop 'im overboard,' said another voice, 'we can't feel our hands with cold.'—'I don't care. I am choking!' exclaimed James Wait in a clear tone.—'Oh, no, my son,' said the boatswain, desperately, 'you don't go till we all go on this fine night.'—'You will see yet many a worse,' said Mr. Baker, cheerfully.—'It's no child's play, sir!' answered the boatswain. 'Some of us further aft, here, are in a pretty bad way.'—'If the blamed sticks had been cut out of her she would be running along on her bottom now like any decent ship, an' giv' us all a chance,' said some one, with a sigh.—'The old man wouldn't have it . . . much he cares for us,' whispered another.—'Care for you!' exclaimed Mr. Baker, angrily. 'Why should he care for you? Are you a lot of women passengers to be taken care of? We are here to take care of the ship— and some of you ain't up to that. Ough! . . . What have you done so very smart to be taken care of? Ough! . . . Some of you can't stand a bit of a breeze without crying over it.'—'Come, sorr. We ain't so bad,' protested Belfast, in a voice shaken by shivers; 'we ain't . . . brrr . . .'— 'Again,' shouted the mate, grabbing at the shadowy form; 'again! . . . Why, you're in your shirt! What have you done?'—'I've put my oilskin and jacket over that half-dead nayggur—and he says he chokes,' said Belfast, complainingly.—'You wouldn't call me nigger if I wasn't half dead you Irish beggar!' boomed James Wait, vigorously.—'You . . . brrr . . . You wouldn't be white if you were ever so well . . . I will fight you . . . brrr . . . in fine weather . . . brrr . . . with one hand tied behind my back . . . brrr . . .'—'I don't want your rags—I want air,' gasped out the other faintly, as if suddenly exhausted.

The sprays swept over the whistling and pattering. Men disturbed in their peaceful torpor by the pain of quarrelsome shouts, moaned, muttering curses. Mr. Baker crawled off a little way to leeward where a water-cask loomed up big, with something white against it. 'Is it you, Podmore?' asked Mr. Baker. He had to repeat the question twice before the cook turned, coughing feebly.—'Yes, sir. I've been praying in my mind for a quick deliverance; for I am prepared for any call . . . I—'— 'Look here, cook,' interrupted Mr. baker, 'the men are perishing with cold.'—'Cold!' said the cook, mournfully; 'they will be warm enough before long.'—'What?' asked Mr. Baker, looking along the deck into the faint sheen of frothing water.—'They are a wicked lot,' continued the cook solemnly, but in an unsteady voice, 'about as wicked as any ship's company in this sinful world! Now, I'—he trembled so that he could hardly speak; his was an exposed place, and in a cotton shirt, a thin pair of trousers, and with his knees under his nose, he received, quaking, the flicks of stinging, salt drops; his voice sounded exhausted—'now, I—any time . . . My eldest youngster, Mr. Baker . . . a clever boy . . . last Sunday on shore before this voyage he wouldn't go to church, sir. Says I, "You go and clean yourself or I'll know the reason why!" What does he do? . . . Pond, Mr. Baker—fell into the pond in his best rig, sir! . . . Accident? . . . "Nothing will save you, fine scholar though you are!" says I . . . Accident! . . . I whopped 'im!' he repeated, rattling his teeth; then, after a while, let out a mournful sound that was half a groan, half a snore. Mr. Baker shook him by the shoulders. 'Hey! Cook! Hold up, Podmore! Tell me—is there any fresh water in the galley tank? The ship is lying along less, I think; I would try to get forward. A little water would do them good. Hallo! Look out! Look out!' The cook struggled.—'Not you, sir—not you!' He began to scramble to windward. 'Galley! . . . my business!' he shouted.—

'Cook's going crazy now,' said several voices. He yelled:— 'Crazy, am I? I am more ready to die than any of you, officers incloosive—there! As long as she swims I will cook! I will get you coffee.'—'Cook, ye are a gentleman!' cried Belfast. But the cook was already going over the weather ladder. He stopped for a minute to shout back on the poop:—'as long as she swims I will cook!' and disappeared as though he had gone overboard. The men who had heard sent after him a cheer that sounded like a wail of sick children. An hour or more afterwards some one said distinctly: 'He's gone for good.'—'Very likely,' assented the boatswain; 'even in fine weather he was as smart about the deck as a milch-cow on her first voyage. We ought to go and see.' Nobody moved. As the hours dragged slowly through the darkness Mr. Baker crawled back and forth along the poop several times. Some men fancied they had heard him exchange murmurs with the master, but at that time the memories were incomparably more vivid than anything actual, and they were not certain whether the murmurs were heard now or many years ago. They did not try to find out. A mutter more or less did not matter. It was too cold for curiosity, and almost for hope. They could not spare a moment or a thought from the great mental occupation of wishing to live. And the desire of life kept them alive, apathetic, and enduring, under the cruel persistence of wind and cold; while the bestarred black dome of the sky revolved slowly above the ship, that drifted, bearing their patience and their suffering, through the stormy solitude of the sea.

Huddled close to one another, they fancied themselves utterly alone. They heard sustained loud noises and again bore the pain of existence through long hours of profound silence. In the night they saw sunshine, felt warmth, and suddenly, with a start, thought that the sun would never rise upon a freezing world. Some heard laughter, listened to songs; others, near the end of the poop, could hear loud human shrieks, and, opening their eyes, were surprised to hear them still, though very faint, and far away. The boatswain said:—'Why, it's the cook, hailing from forward I think.' He hardly believed his own words or recognised his own voice. It was a long time before the man next to him gave a sign of life. He punched hard his other neighbour and said:—'The cook's shouting!' Many did not understand, others did not care; the majority further aft did not believe. But the boatswain and another men had the pluck to crawl away forward to see. They seemed to have been gone for hours, and were soon forgotten. Then suddenly men that had been plunged in a hopeless resignation became as if possessed with a desire to hurt. They belaboured one another with fists. In the darkness they struck persistently anything soft they could feel near, and, with a greater effort than for a shout, whispered excitedly:— 'They've got some hot coffee . . . Bosun got it . . .' 'No! . . . Where?' . . . 'It's coming! Cook made it.' James Wait moaned. Donkin scrambled viciously, caring not where he kicked, and anxious that the officers should have none of it. It came in a pot, and they drank in turns. It was hot, and while it blistered the greedy palates, it seemed incredible. The men sighed out parting with the mug:—'How 'as he done it?' Some cried weakly—'Bully for you, doctor!'

He had done it somehow. Afterwards Archie declared that the thing was 'meeraculous.' For many days we wondered, and it was the one ever-interesting subject of conversation to the end of the voyage. We asked the cook, in fine weather, how he felt when he saw his stove 'reared up on end.' We inquired, in the north-east trade and on serene evenings, whether he had to stand on his head to put things right somewhat. We suggested he had used his bread-board for a raft, and from there comfortably had stoked his grate; and we did our best to conceal our admiration under the wit of fine irony. He affirmed not to know anything about it, rebuked our levity, declared himself, with solemn animation, to have been the object of special mercy for the saving of our unholy lives. Fundamentally he was right, no doubt; but he need not have been so offensively positive about it—he need not have hinted so often that it would have gone hard with us had he not been there, meritorious and pure, to receive the inspiration and the strength for the work of grace. Had we been saved by his recklessness or his agility, we could have at length become reconciled to the fact; but to admit our obligation to anybody's virtue and holiness alone was as difficult for us as for any other handful of mankind. Like many benefactors of humanity, the cook took himself too seriously, and reaped the reward of irreverence. We were not ungrateful, however. He remained heroic. His saying—the saying of his life—became proverbial in the mouths of men as are the sayings of conquerors or sages. Later on, whenever one of us was puzzled by a task and advised to relinquish it, he would express his determination to persevere and to succeed by the words:—'As long as she swims I will cook!'

The hot drink helped us through the bleak hours that precede the dawn. The sky low by the horizon took on the delicate tints of pink and yellow like the inside of a rare shell. And higher, where it glowed with a pearly sheen, a small black cloud appeared, like a forgotten fragment of the night set in a border of dazzling gold. The beams of light skipped on the crests of waves. The eyes of men turned to the eastward. The sunlight flooded their weary faces. They were giving themselves up to fatigue as though they had done for ever with their work. On Singleton's black oilskin coat the dried salt glistened like hoar frost. He hung on by the wheel, with open and lifeless eyes. Captain Allistoun, unblinking, faced the rising sun. His lips stirred, opened for the first time in twenty-four hours, and with a fresh firm voice he cried, 'Wear ship!'

The commanding sharp tones made all these torpid men start like a sudden flick of a whip. Then again, motionless where they lay, the force of habit made some of them repeat the order in hardly audible murmurs. Captain Allistoun glanced down at his crew, and several, with fumbling fingers and hopeless movements, tried to cast themselves adrift. He repeated impatiently, 'Wear ship. Now then, Mr. Baker, get the men along. What's the matter with them?'—'Wear ship. Do you hear there?—Wear ship!' thundered out the boatswain suddenly. His voice seemed to break through the deadly spell. Men began to stir and crawl,—'I want the fore-top-mast stay-sail run up smartly,' said the master, very loudly; 'if you can't manage it standing up you must do it lying down—that's all. Bear a hand!'—'Come along! Let's give the old girl a chance.' urged the boatswain.—'Aye! aye! Wear ship!' exclaimed quavering voices. The forecastle men, with reluctant faces, prepared to go forward. Mr. Baker pushed ahead grunting on all fours to show the way, and they followed him over the break. The others lay still with a vile hope in their hearts of not being required to move till they got saved or drowned in peace.

After some time they could be seen forward appearing on the forecastle head, one by one in unsafe attitudes; hanging on to the rails;

clambering over the anchors; embracing the cross-head of the windlass or hugging the fore-capstan. They were restless with strange exertions, waved their arms, knelt, lay flat down, staggered up, seemed to strive their hardest to go overboard. Suddenly a small white piece of canvas fluttered amongst them, grew larger, beating. Its narrow head rose in jerks—and at last it stood distended and triangular in the sunshine.— 'They have done it!' cried the voices aft. Captain Allistoun let go the rope he had round his wrist and rolled to leeward headlong. He could be seen casting the lee main braces off the pins while the backwash of waves splashed over him.—'Square the main yard!' he shouted up to us—who stared at him in wonder. We hesitated to stir. 'The main brace, men. Haul! haul anyhow! Lay on your backs and haul! 'he screeched, half drowned down there. We did not believe we could move the main yard, but the strongest and the less discouraged tried to execute the order. Others assisted half-heartedly. Singleton's eyes blazed suddenly as he took a fresh grip of the spokes. Captain Allistoun fought his way up to the windward.—'Haul men! Try to move it! Haul, and help the ship.' His hard face worked suffused and furious. 'Is she going off, Singleton?' He cried.—'Not a move yet, sir,' croaked the old seaman in a horribly hoarse voice.—'Watch the helm, Singleton.' spluttered the master. 'Haul men! Have you no more strength than rats? Haul, and earn your salt.' Mr. Creighton, on his back, with a swollen leg and a face as white as a piece of paper, blinked his eyes, his bluish lips twitched. In the wild scramble men grabbed at him, crawled over his hurt leg, knelt on his chest. He kept perfectly still, setting his teeth without a moan, without a sigh. The master's ardour, the cries of that silent man inspired us. We hauled and hung in bunches on the rope. We heard him say with violence to Donkin, who sprawled abjectly on his stomach,—'I will brain you with this belaying pin if you don't catch hold of the brace,' and that victim of men's injustice, cowardly and cheeky, whimpered;—'Are you going ter murder hus now?' While, with sudden desperation he grabbed the rope. Men sighed, shouted, hissed meaningless words, groaned. The yards moved, came slowly square against the wind, that hummed loudly on the yard-arms.— 'Going off, sir,' shouted Singleton, 'she's just started.'—'Catch a turn with that brace. Catch a turn!' clamoured the master. Mr. Creighton, nearly suffocated and unable to move, made a mighty effort, and with his left hand managed to nip the rope.—'All fast!' cried someone. He closed his eyes as if going off into a swoon, while huddled together about the brace we watched with scared looks what the ship would do now.

She went off slowly as though she had been weary and disheartened like the men she carried. She paid off very gradually, making us hold our breath till we choked, and as soon as she had brought the wind abaft the beam she started to move, and fluttered our hearts. It was awful to see her, nearly overturned, begin to gather way and drag her submerged side through the water. The dead-eyes of the rigging churned the breaking seas. The lower half of the deck was full of mad whirlpools and eddies; and the long line of the ice rail could be seen showing black now and then in the swirls of a field of foam as dazzling and white as a field of snow. The wind sang shrilly amongst the spars; and at every slight lurch we expected her to slip to the bottom sideways from under our backs. When dead before it she made the first distinct attempt to stand up, and we encouraged her with a feeble and discordant howl. A great sea came running up aft and hung for a moment over us with a curling top; then crashed down under the counter and spread out on both sides into a great sheet of bursting froth. Above its fierce hiss we heard Singleton's croak:—'She is steering!' He had both his feet now planted firmly on the grating, and the wheel spun fast as he eased the helm.—'Bring the wind on the port quarter and steady her!' called out the master, staggering to his feet, the first man up from amongst our prostrate heap. One or two screamed with excitement:—'She rises!' Far away forward, Mr. Baker and three others were seen erect and black on the clear sky, lifting their arms, and with open mouths as though they had been shouting all together. The ship trembled, trying to lift her side, lurched back, seemed to give up with a nerveless dip, and suddenly with an unexpected jerk swung violently to windward, as though she had torn herself out from a deadly grasp. The whole immense volume of water, lifted by her deck, was thrown bodily across to starboard. Loud cracks were heard. Iron ports breaking open thundered with ringing blows. The water topped over the starboard rail with the rush of a river falling over a dam. The sea on deck, and the seas on every side of her, mingled together in a deafening roar. She rolled violently. We got up and were helplessly run or flung about from side to side. Men, rolling over and over, yelled.—'The house will go!'—'She clears herself!' Lifted by a towering sea she ran along with it for a moment, spouting thick streams of water through every opening of her wounded sides. The ice braces having been carried away or washed off the pins, all the ponderous yards on the fore swung from side to side and with appalling rapidity at every roll. The men forward were seen crouching here and there with fearful glances upwards at the enormous spars that whirled about over their heads. The torn canvas and the ends of broken gear streamed in the wind like wisps of hair. Through the clear sunshine, over the flashing turmoil and uproar of the seas, the ship ran blindly, dishevelled and headlong, as if fleeing for her life; and on the poop we spun, we tottered about, distracted and noisy. We all spoke at once in a thin babble; we had the aspect of invalids and the gestures of maniacs. Eyes shone, large and haggard, in smiling, meagre faces that seemed to have been dusted over with powdered chalk. We stamped, clapped our hands, feeling ready to jump and do anything, but in reality hardly able to keep on our feet. Captain Allistoun, hard and slim, gesticulated madly from the poop at Mr. Baker; 'Steady these fore-yards! Steady them the best you can!' On the main deck, men excited by his cries, splashed, dashing aimlessly here and there with the foam swirling up to their waists. Apart, far aft, and alone by the helm, old Singleton had deliberately tucked his white beard under the top button of his glistening coat. Swaying upon the din and tumult of the seas, with the whole battered length of the ship launched forward in a rolling rush before his steady old eyes, he stood rigidly still, forgotten by all, and with an attentive face. In front of his erect figure only the two arms moved crosswise with a swift and sudden readiness, to check or urge again the rapid stir of circling spokes. He steered with care.

CHAPTER IV

On men reprieved by its disdainful mercy, the immortal sea confers in its justice the full privilege of desired unrest. Through the perfect wisdom of its grace they are not permitted to meditate at ease upon the complicated and acrid savour of existence, lest they should remember and, perchance, regret the reward of a cup of inspiring bitterness, tasted so often, and so often withdrawn from before their stiffening but reluctant lips. They must without pause justify their life to the eternal pity that commands toil to be hard and unceasing, from sunrise to sunset, from sunset to sunrise: till the weary succession of nights and days tainted by the obstinate clamour of sages, demanding bliss and an empty heaven, is redeemed at last by the vast silence of pain and labour, by the dumb fear and the dumb courage of men obscure, forgetful, and enduring.

The master and Mr. Baker coming face to face stared for a moment, with the intense and amazed looks of men meeting unexpectedly after years of trouble. Their voices were gone, and they whispered desperately at one another.—'Any one missing?' asked Captain Allistoun.—'No, All there.'—'Anybody hurt?'—'Only the second mate.'—'I will look after him directly. We're lucky.'—'Very,' articulated Mr. Baker, faintly. He gripped the rail and rolled bloodshot eyes. The little grey man made an effort to raise his voice above a dull mutter, and fixed his chief mate with a cold gaze, piercing like a dart.— 'Get sail on the ship,' he said, speaking authoritatively, and with an inflexible snap of his thin lips. 'Get sail on her as soon as you can. This is a fair wind. At once, sir—Don't give the men time to feel themselves. They will get done up and stiff, and we will never . . . We must get her along now' . . . He reeled to a long heavy roll; the rail dipped into the glancing hissing water. He caught a shroud, swung helplessly against the mate . . . 'now we have a fair wind at last.—

Make—sail.' His head rolled from shoulder to shoulder. His eyelids
began to beat rapidly. 'And the pumps—pumps, Mr. Baker.' He peered
as though the face within a foot of his eyes had been half a mile off.
'Keep the men on the move to—to get her along.' he mumbled in a
drowsy tone, like a man going off into a doze. He pulled himself
together suddenly. 'Mustn't stand. Won't do,' he said with a painful
attempt at a smile. He let go his hold, and, propelled by the dip of the
ship, ran aft unwillingly, with small steps, till he brought up against the
binnacle stand. Hanging on there he looked up in an objectless manner
at Singleton, who, unheeding him, watched anxiously the end of the
jib-boom—'Steering gear works all right?' he asked. There was a noise
in the old seaman's throat, as though the words had been rattling there
together before they could come out.—'Steers . . . like a little boat,' he
said, at last, with hoarse tenderness, without giving the master as much
as half a glance—then, watchfully, spun the wheel down, steadied,
flung it back again. Captain Allistoun tore himself away from the
delight of leaning against the binnacle, and began to walk the poop,
swaying and reeling to preserve his balance . . .

The pump-rods, clanking, stamped in short jumps, while the fly-
wheels turned smoothly, with great speed, at the foot of the mainmast,
flinging back and forth with a regular impetuosity two limp clusters of
men clinging to the handles. They abandoned themselves, swaying
from the hip with twitching faces and stony eyes. The carpenter,
sounding from time to time, exclaimed mechanically: 'Shake her up!
Keep her going!' Mr. Baker could not speak, but found his voice to
shout; and under the goad of his objurgations, men looked to the
lashings, dragged out new sails; and thinking themselves unable to
move, carried heavy blocks aloft—overhauled the gear. They went up
the rigging with faltering and desperate efforts. Their heads swam as
they shifted their hold, stepped blindly on the yards like men in the
dark; or trusted themselves to the first rope to hand with the negligence
of exhausted strength. The narrow escape from the falls did not disturb
the languid beat of their hearts; the roar of the seas seething far below
them sounded continuous and faint like an indistinct noise from another
world; the wind filled their eyes with tears, and with heavy gusts tried
to push them off from where they swayed in insecure positions. With
streaming faces and blowing hair they flew up and down between sky
and water, bestriding the ends of yard-arms, crouching on foot-ropes,
embracing lifts to have their hands free, or standing up against chain
ties. Their thoughts floated vaguely between the desire of rest and the
desire of life, while their stiffened fingers cast off head-earrings,
fumbled for knives, or held with tenacious grip against the violent
shocks of beating canvas. They glared savagely at one another, made
frantic signs with one hand while they held their life in the other,
looked down on the narrow strip of flooded deck, shouted along to

leeward:' Light-to!' . . . 'Haul out!' . . . 'Make fast!'. Their lips moved, their eyes started, furious and eager with the desire to be understood, but the wind tossed their words unheard upon the disturbed sea. In an unendurable and unending strain they worked like men driven by a merciless dream to toil in an atmosphere of ice or flame. They burnt and shivered in turns. Their eyeballs smarted as if in the smoke of a conflagration; their heads were ready to burst with every shout. Hard fingers seemed to grip their throats. At every roll they thought; Now I must let go. It will shake us all off—and thrown about aloft they cried wildly: 'Look out there—catch the end.' . . . 'Reeve clear' . . . 'Turn this block . . .' They nodded desperately; shook infuriated faces. 'No! No! From down up.' They seemed to hate one another with a deadly hate. The longing to be done with it all gnawed at their breasts, and the wish to do things well was a burning pain. They cursed their fate, contemned their life, and wasted their breath in deadly imprecations upon one another. The sailmaker, with his bald head bared, worked feverishly, forgetting his intimacy with so many admirals. The boatswain, climbing up with marlinspikes and bunches of spunyarn rovings, or kneeling on the yard and ready to take a turn with the midship-stop, had acute and fleeting visions of his old woman and the youngsters in a moorland village. Mr. Baker, feeling very weak, tottered here and there, grunting and inflexible, like a man of iron. He waylaid those who, coming from aloft, stood gasping for breath. He ordered, encouraged, scolded. 'Now then—to the top mainsail now! Tally on to that gantline. Don't stand about there!'—'Is there no rest for us?' muttered voices. He spun round fiercely, with a sinking heart.—'No! No rest till the work is done. Work till you drop. That's what you're here for.' A bowed seaman at his elbow gave a short laugh.—'Do or die,' he croaked bitterly, then spat into his broad palms, swung up his long arms, and grasping the rope high above his head sent out mournful, wailing cry for a pull all together. A sea boarded the quarter-deck and sent the whole lot sprawling to leeward. Caps, handspikes floated. Clenched hands, kicking legs, with here and there a spluttering face, stuck out of the white hiss of foaming water. Mr. Baker, knocked down with the rest, screamed—'Don't let go that rope! Hold on to it! Hold!' And sorely bruised by the brutal fling, they held on to it, as though it had been the fortune of their life. The ship ran, rolling heavily, and the topping crests glanced past port and starboard flashing their white heads. Pumps were freed. Braces were rove. The three topsails and foresail were set. She spurted faster over the water, outpacing the swift rush of waves. The menacing thunder of distanced seas rose behind her—filled the air with the tremendous vibrations of its voice. And devastated, battered, and wounded she drove foaming to the northward, as though inspired by the courage of a high endeavour . . .

The forecastle was a place of damp desolation. They looked at their dwelling with dismay. It was slimy, dripping; it hummed hollow with the wind, and was strewn with shapeless wreckage like a half-tide cavern in a rocky and exposed coast. Many had lost all they had in the world, but most of the starboard watch had preserved their chests; thin streams of water trickled out of them, however. The beds were soaked; the blankets spread out and saved by some nail squashed under foot. They dragged wet rags from evil-smelling corners, and, wringing the water our, recognised their property. Some smiled stiffly. Others looked round blank and mute.

There were cries of joy over old waistcoats, and groans of sorrow over shapeless things found amongst the black splinters of smashed bed boards. One lamp was discovered jammed under the bowsprit, Charley whimpered a little. Knowles stumped here and there, sniffing, examining dark places for salvage. He poured dirty water out of a boot, and was concerned to find the owner. Those who, overwhelmed by their losses, sat on the forepeak hatch, remained elbows on knees, and, with a fist against each cheek, disdained to look up. He pushed it under their noses. 'Here's a good boot. Yours?' They snarled, 'No—get out.' One snapped at him, 'Take it the hell out of this.' He seemed surprised. 'Why? It's a good boot,' but remembering suddenly that he had lost every stitch of his clothing, he dropped his find and began to swear. In the dim light cursing voices clashed. A man came in and, dropping his arms, stood still, repeating from the doorstep, 'Here's a bloomin' old go! Here's a bloomin' old go!' A few rooted anxiously in flooded chests for tobacco. They breathed hard, clamoured with heads down, 'Look at that, Jack!' . . . 'Here! Sam! Here's my shore-going rig spoilt for ever.' One blasphemed tearfully holding up a pair of dripping trousers. No one looked at him. The cat came out from somewhere. He had an ovation. They snatched him from hand to hand, caressed him in a murmur of pet names. They wondered where he had 'weathered it out;' disputed about it. A squabbling argument began. Two men came in with a bucket of fresh water, and all crowded round it; but Tom, lean and mewing, came up with every hair astir and had the first drink. A couple of men went aft for oil and biscuits.

Then in the yellow light and in the intervals of mopping the deck they crunched hard bread, arranging to 'worry through somehow.' Men chummed as to beds. Turns were settled for wearing boots and having the use of oilskin coats. They called one another 'old man' and 'sonny' in cheery voices. Friendly slaps resounded. Jokes were shouted. One or two stretched on the wet deck, slept with heads pillowed on their bent arms, and several, sitting on the hatch, smoked. Their weary faces appeared through a thin blue haze, pacified and with sparkling eyes. The boatswain put his head through the door. 'Relieve the wheel. one of you'—he shouted inside—'it's six. Blamme if that old Singleton hasn't been there more'n thirty hours. You are a fine lot.' He slammed the door again. 'Mate's watch on deck,' said some one. 'Hey, Donkin, it's your relief!' shouted three or four together. He had crawled into an empty bunk and on wet planks lay still. 'Donkin, your wheel.' He made no sound. 'Donkin's dead,' guffawed some one. 'Sell 'is bloomin' clothes,' shouted another. 'Donkin, if ye don't go to the bloomin' wheel they will sell your clothes—d'ye hear?' jeered a third. He groaned from his dark hole. He complained about pains in all his bones, he whimpered pitifully. 'He won't go,' exclaimed a contemptuous voice, 'your turn, Davies.' The young seaman rose painfully squaring his shoulders. Donkin stuck his head out, and it appeared in the yellow light, fragile and ghastly. 'I will giv' yer a pound of tobaccer,' he whined in a conciliating voice, 'so soon as I can draw it from haft I will—s'elp me . . .' Davies swung his arm backhanded and the head vanished. 'I'll go, he said, but you will pay for it.' He walked unsteady but resolute in the door. 'So I will,' yelped Donkin, popping out behind him. 'So I will—s'elp me . . . three bob they chawrge.' 'You will pay my price . . . in fine weather.' he shouted over his shoulder. One of the men unbuttoned his wet coat rapidly, threw it at his head. 'Here, Taffy—take that, you thief!' 'Thank you!' he cried from the darkness above the swish of rolling water. He could be heard splashing; a sea came on board with a thump. 'He's got his bath already,' remarked a grim shellback. 'Aye, aye!' grunted the others. Then, after a long silence, Wamibo made strange noises. 'Hallo, what's up with you?' said one grumpily. 'He says he would have gone for Davy,' explained Archie, who was the Finn's interpreter generally. 'I believe him!' cried voices . . . 'Never mind, Dutchy . . . You'll do, muddle-head . . . Your turn will come soon enough . . . You don't know when ye're well off.' They ceased, and all together turned their faces to the door. Singleton stepped in, made two paces, and stood swaying slightly. The sea hissed, flowed roaring past the bows, and the forecastle trembled, full of a deep rumour; the lamp flared, swinging like a pendulum. He looked with a dreamy and puzzled stare, as though he could not distinguish the still men from their restless shadows. There were awe-struck murmurs:— 'Hallo, hallo' . . . 'How does it look outside now, Singleton?' Those who sat on the hatch lifted their eyes in silence, and the next oldest seaman in the ship (those two understood one another, though they hardly exchanged three words in a day) gazed up at his friend attentively for a moment, then taking a short clay pipe out of his mouth, offered it without a word. Singleton put out his arm towards it, missed, staggered, and suddenly fell forward, crashing down, stiff and headlong like an uprooted tree. There was a swift rush. Men pushed, crying:— 'He's done!' . . . 'Turn him over!' . . . 'Stand clear there!' Under a crowd of startled faces bending over him he lay on his back, staring upwards in a continuous and intolerable manner. In the breathless silence of a general consternation, he said in a grating murmur:—'I am all right,' and clutched with his hands. They helped him up. He mumbled despondently:—'I am getting old . . . old.'—'Not you,' cried Belfast, with ready tact. Supported on all sides, he hung his head.— 'Are you better?' they asked. He glared at them from under his eyebrows with large black eyes, spreading over his chest the bushy whiteness of a beard long and thick.—'Old! old!' he repeated sternly. Helped along, he reached his bunk. There was in it a slimy soft heap of something that smelt like does at dead low water a muddy foreshore. It was his soaked straw bed. With a convulsive effort he pitched himself on it, and in the darkness of the narrow place could be heard growling angrily, like an irritated and savage animal uneasy in its den:—'Bit of breeze . . . small thing . . . can't stand up . . . old!' He slept at last. He breathed heavily, high-booted, sou'wester on head, and his oilskin clothes rustled, when with a deep sighing groan he turned over. men conversed about him in quiet concerned whispers. 'This will break 'im up' . . . 'Strong as a horse' . . . 'Aye. But he ain't what he used to be' . . . . In sad murmurs they gave him up. Yet at midnight he turned out to duty as if nothing had been the matter, and answered to his name with a mournful 'Here!' He brooded alone more than ever, in an impenetrable silence and with a saddened face. For many years he had heard himself called 'Old Singleton,' and had serenely accepted the qualification, taking it as a tribute of respect due to a man who through half a century had measured his strength against the favours and the rages of the sea. He had never given a thought to his mortal self. He lived unscathed, as though he had been indestructible, surrendering to all the temptations, weathering many gales. He had panted in sunshine, shivered in the cold; suffered hunger, thirst, debauch; passed through many trials— known all the furies. Old! It seemed to him he was broken at last. And like a man bound treacherously while he sleeps, he woke up fettered by the long chain of disregarded years. He had to take up at once the burden of all his existence, and found it almost too heavy for his strength. Old! He moved his arms, shook his head, felt his limbs. Getting old . . . and then? He looked upon the immortal sea with the awakened and groping perception of its heartless might; he saw it unchanged, black and foaming under the eternal scrutiny of the stares; he heard its impatient voice calling for him out of a pitiless vastness full of unrest, of turmoil, and of terror. He looked afar upon it, and he saw an immensity tormented and blind, moaning and furious, that claimed all the days of his tenacious life, and, when life was over, would claim the worn-out body of its slave.

This was the last of the breeze. It veered quickly, changed to a black south-eastern and blew itself out, giving the ship a famous shove to the northward into the joyous sunshine of the trade. Rapid and white she ran homewards in a straight path, under a blue sky and upon the plain of a blue sea. She carried Singleton's completed wisdom, Donkin's delicate susceptibilities, and the conceited folly of us all. The hours of ineffective turmoil were forgotten; the fear and anguish of these dark moments were never mentioned in the glowing peace of fine days. Yet from that time our life seemed to start afresh as though we had died and been resuscitated. All the first part of the voyage, the Indian Ocean on the other side of the Cape, all that was lost in a haze, like an ineradicable suspicion of some previous existence. It had ended—then there were blank hours; a livid blur—and again we lived! Singleton was possessed of sinister truth; Mr. Creighton of a damaged leg; the cook of fame—and shamefully abused the opportunities of his distinction. Donkin had an added grievance. He went about repeating with insistence:—''E said 'e would brain me—did you hear? They hare goin' to murder hus now for the least little thing.' We began at last to think it was rather awful. And we were conceited! We boasted our pluck, of our capacity foe work, of our energy. We remembered honourable episodes: our devotion, our indomitable perseverance—and were proud of them as though they had been the outcome of our unaided impulses. We remembered our danger, our toil—and conveniently forgot our horrible scare. We decried our officer—who had done nothing—and listened to the fascinating Donkin, His care for our rights, his disinterested concern for our dignity, were not discouraged by the invariable contumely of our words, by the disdain of our looks. Our contempt for him was unbounded—and we could unbounded—and we could not but listen with interest to that consummate artist. He told us we were good men—a 'bloomin' condemned lot of good men.' 'Who thanked us? Who took any notice of our wrongs? Didn't we lead a 'dorg's loife for two poun' ten a month?' Did we think that miserable pay enough to compensate us for the risk to our lives and for the loss of our clothes? 'We've lost hevery rag!' he cried. He made us forget that he, at any rate, had lost nothing of his own. The younger men listened, thinking—this 'ere Donkin's a long-headed chap, though no kind of man, anyhow. The Scandinavians were frightened at his audacities; Wamibo did not understand; and the older seamen thoughtfully nodded their heads making the thin gold earrings glitter in the fleshy lobes of hairy ears. Severe, sun-burnt faces were propped meditatively on tattooed forearms. Veined, brown fists held in their grip the dirty white clay of smoldering pipes. They listened, impenetrable, broad-backed, with bent shoulders, and in grim silence. He talked with ardour, despised and irrefutable. His picturesque and filthy loquacity flowed like a troubled stream from a poisoned source. His beady little eyes danced, glancing right and left, ever on the watch for the approach of an officer. Sometimes Mr. Baker going forward to take a look at the head sheets would roll with his uncouth gait through the sudden stillness of the men; or Mr. Creighton limped along, smooth-faced, youthful, and more stern than ever piercing our short silence with a keen glance of his clear eyes. Behind his back Donkin would begin again darting stealthy, sidelong looks.— ''Ere's one of 'em. Some of yer 'as made 'im fast that day. Much thanks yer got for hit. Ain't 'ee a-drivin' yer wusse'n hever? . . . Let 'im slip hover-board . . . Vy not? It would 'ave been less trouble. Vy not?' He advanced confidentially, backed away with great effect; he whispered, he screamed, waved his miserable arms no thicker than pipe-stems—stretched his lean neck—spluttered—squinted. In the pauses of his impassioned orations the wine sighed quietly aloft, the calm sea unheeded murmured in a warning whisper along the ship's side. We abominated the creature and could not deny the luminous truth of his contentions. It was all so obvious. We were indubitably good men; our deserts were great and our pay small. Through our exertions we had saved the ship and the skipper would get the credit of it. What had he done? we wanted to know. Donkin asked:—'What 'ee could do without hus?' and we could not answer. We were oppressed by the injustice of the world, surprised to perceive how long we had lived under its burden without realising our unfortunate state, annoyed by the uneasy suspicion of our undiscerning stupidity. Donkin assured us it was all our 'good 'eartedness,' but we would not be consoled by such shallow sophistry. We were men enough to courageously admit to ourselves our intellectual shortcomings; though from that time we refrained from kicking him, tweaking his nose or from accidentally knocking him about, which last, after we had weathered the Cape, had been rather a popular amusement. Davies ceased to talk at him provokingly about black eyes and flattened noses. Charley, much subdued since the gale, sis not jeer at him. Knowles deferentially and with a crafty air propounded questions such as:—'Could we all have the same grub as the mates? Could we all stop ashore till we got it? What would be the next thing to try for if we got that?' He answered readily with contemptuous certitude; he strutted with assurance in clothes that were much too big for him as though he had tried to disguise himself. These were Jimmy's clothes most—though he would accept anything from anybody; but nobody, except Jimmy, had anything to spare. His devotion to Jimmy was unbounded. He was for ever dodging in the little cabin, ministering to Jimmy's wants, humoring his whims, submitting to his exacting peevishness, often laughing with him. Nothing could keep him away from the pious work of visiting the sick, especially when there was some heavy hauling to be done on deck. Mr. Baker had on two occasions jerked him out of there by the scruff of the neck to our inexpressible scandal. Was a sick chap to be left without attendance? Were we to be ill-used for attending a shipmate?—'What?' growled Mr. Baker, turning menacingly at the mutter, and the whole half-circle like one man stepped back a pace.

'Set the topmast stunsail. Away aloft Donkin, overhaul the gear.' ordered the mate inflexibly. 'Fetch the sail along; bend the down-haul clear. Bear a hand.' Then, the sail set, he would go slowly aft and stand looking at the compass for a long time, careworn, pensive, and breathing hard as if stifled by the taint of unaccountable ill-will that pervaded the ship. 'What's up amongst them?' he thought. 'Can't make out this hanging back and growling. A good crowd, too, as they go nowadays.' On deck the men exchanged bitter words, suggested by a silly exasperation against something unjust and irremediable that would not be denied, and would whisper into their ears long after Donkin had ceased speaking. Our little world went on its curved and unswerving path carrying a discontented and aspiring population. They found comfort of a gloomy kind in an interminable and conscientious analysis of their unappreciated worth; and inspired by Donkin's hopeful doctrines they dreamed enthusiastically of the time when every lonely ship would travel over a serene sea, manned by a wealthy and well-fed crew of satisfied skippers.

It looked as if it would be a long passage. The south-east trades, light and unsteady, were left behind; and then, on the equator and under a low grey sky, the ship, in close heat, floated upon a smooth sea that resembled a sheet of ground glass. Thunder squalls hung on the horizon, circled round the ship, far off and growling angrily, like a troop of wild beasts afraid to charge home. The invisible sun, sweeping above the upright masts, made on the clouds a blurred stain of rayless light, and a similar patch of faded radiance kept pace with it from east to west over the unglittering level of the waters. At night, through the impenetrable darkness of earth and heaven, broad sheets of flame waved noiselessly; and for half a second the becalmed craft stood out with its masts and rigging, with every sail and every rope distinct and black in the centre of a fiery outburst, like a charred ship enclosed in a globe of fire. And, again, for long hours she remained lost in a vast universe of night and silence where gentle sighs wandering here and there like forlorn souls, made the still sails flutter as in sudden fear, and the ripple of a beshrouded ocean whisper its compassion afar—in a voice mournful, immense, and faint . . .

When the lamp was put out, and through the door thrown wide open, Jimmy, turning on his pillow, could see vanishing beyond the straight line of top-gallant rail, the quick, repeated visions of a fabulous world made up of leaping fire and sleeping water. The lightning gleamed in his big sad eyes that seemed in a red flicker to burn themselves out in his black face, and then he would lay blinded and invisible in the midst of an intense darkness. He could hear on the quiet deck soft footfalls, the breathing of some man lounging on the doorstep; the low creak of swaying masts; or the calm voice of the watch-officer reverberating aloft, hard and loud, amongst the unstirring sails. he listened with avidity, taking a rest in the attentive perception of the slightest sound from the fatiguing wanderings of his sleeplessness. He was cheered by the rattling of blocks, reassured by the stir and murmur of the watch, soothed by the slow yawn of some sleepy and weary seaman settling himself deliberately for a snooze on the planks. Life seemed an indestructible thing. It went on in darkness, in sunshine. in sleep; tireless, it hovered affectionately round the imposture of his ready death. It was bright, like the twisted flare of lightning, and more full of surprises than the dark night. It made him safe, and the calm of its overpowering darkness was as precious as its restless and dangerous light.

But in the evening, in the dog-watches, and even far into the first night-watch, a knot of men could always be seen congregated before Jimmy's cabin. They leaned on each side of the door, peacefully interested and with crossed legs; they stood astride the doorstep discoursing, or sat in silent couples on his sea-chest; while against the bulwark along the spare topmast, three or four in a row stared meditatively, with their simple faces lit up by the projected glare of Jimmy's lamp. The little place, repainted white, had, in the night, the brilliance of a silver shrine where a black idol, reclining stiffly under a blanket, blinked its weary eyes and received our homage. Donkin officiated. He had the air of a demonstrator showing a phenomenon, a manifestation bizarre, simple, and meritorious, that, to the beholders, should be a profound and an everlasting lesson. 'Just look at 'im, 'e knows what's what—never fear!' he exclaimed now and then, flourishing a hand hard and fleshless like the claw of a snipe. Jimmy, on his back, smiled with reserve and without moving a limb. He affected the languor of extreme weakness, so as to make it manifest to us that our delay in hauling him out from his horrible confinement, and then that night spent on the poop among out selfish neglect of his needs, had 'done for him.' He rather liked to talk about it, and of course we were always interested. He spoke spasmodically, in fast rushes with long pauses between, as a tipsy man walks . . . 'Cook had just given me a pannikin of hot coffee . . . Slapped it down there, on my chest— banged the door to . . . I felt a heavy roll coming; tried to save my coffee, burnt my fingers . . . and fell out of my bunk . . . She went over so quick . . . Water came in through the ventilator . . . I couldn't move the door to . . . dark as a grave . . . tried to scramble up into the upper berth . . . Rats . . . a rat bit my finger as I got up . . . I could hear him swimming below me . . . I thought you would never come . . . I thought you were all gone overboard . . . of course . . . could hear nothing but the wind . . . Then you came . . . to look for the corpse, I suppose. A little more and . . .'

'Man! but ye made a rare lot of noise in here,' observed Archie, thoughtfully.

'You chaps kicked up such a confounded row above . . . Enough to scare any one . . . I didn't know what you were up to . . . Bash in the blamed planks . . . my head . . . Just what a silly, scary gang of fools would do . . . Not much good to me anyhow . . . Just as well . . . drown . . . Pah.'

He groaned, snapped his big white teeth, and gazed with scorn. Belfast lifted a pair of dolorous eyes, with a broken-hearted smile, clenched his fists stealthily; blue-eyed Archie caressed his red whiskers with a hesitating hand;; the boatswain at the door stared a moment, and brusquely went away with a loud guffaw. Wamibo dreamed . . . Donkin felt all over his sterile chin for the few rare hairs, and said, triumphantly, with a sidelong glance at Jimmy:—'Look at 'im! Wish I was 'arf as 'ealthy has 'e his—I do.' He jerked a short thumb over his shoulder towards the after end of the ship. 'That's the blooming way to do 'em!' he yelped, with forced heartiness. Jimmy said:—'Don't be a dam' fool,' in a pleasant voice. Knowles, rubbing his shoulder against the doorpost, remarked shrewdly:—'We can't all go an' be took sick— it would be mutiny.'—'Mutiny—gawn!' jeered Donkin; 'there's no bloomin' law against bein' sick.'—'There's six weeks' hard for refoosing dooty,' argued Knowles, 'I mind I once seed in Cardiff the crew of an overloaded ship—leastways she weren't overloaded, only a fatherly old gentleman with a white beard and an umbreller came along the quay and talked to the hands. Said as how it was crool hard to be drownded in winter just for the sake of a few pounds more for the owner—he said. Nearly cried over them—he did; and he had a square mainsail coat, and a gaff-topsail hat too—all proper. So they chaps they said they wouldn't go to be drownded in winter—depending upon that 'ere Plimsoll man to see 'em through the court. They thought to have a bloomin' lark and two or three days spree. And the beak giv' 'em six weeks—coss the ship warn't overloaded. Anyways they made it out in court that she wasn't. There wasn't one overloaded ship in Penarth Dock at all. 'Pears that old coon he was only on pay and allowance from some kind people, under orders to look for overloaded ships, and he couldn't see no further than the length of his umbreller. Some of us in the boarding-house, where I live when I'm looking for a ship in Cardiff, stood by to duck that old weeping sponger in the dock. We kept a good look out, too—but he topped his boom directly he was outside the court . . . Yes. They got six weeks' hard . . .'

They listened, full of curiosity, nodding in the pauses their rough pensive faces. Donkin opened his mouth once or twice, but restrained himself. Jimmy lay still with open eyes and not at all interested. A seaman emitted an opinion that after a verdict of atrocious partiality 'the bloomin' beaks go an' drink at the skipper's expense.' Others assented. It was clear, of course, Donkin said:—'Well, six weeks hain't much trouble. You sleep hall night in, reg'lar, in chokey. Do it hon my

'ead.' 'You are used to it ainch'ee, Donkin?' asked somebody. Jimmy
condescended to laugh. It cheered every one wonderfully. Knowles,
with surprising mental agility, shifted his ground. 'If we all went sick
what would happen to the ship? eh?' He posed the problem and grinned
all round.—'Let 'er go to 'ell,' sneered Donkin. 'Damn 'er. She ain't
yourn.'—'What? Just let her drift?' insisted Knowles in a tone of
unbelief.—'Aye! Drift an' be blowed,' affirmed Donkin with fine
recklessness. The other did not see it—meditated.—'The stores would
run out,' he muttered, 'and . . . never get anywhere . . . and what about
pay-day?' he added with greater assurance.—'Jack likes a good pay-
day,' exclaimed a listener on the doorstep. 'Aye, because then the girls
put one arm round his neck an' t'other in his pocket, an' call him
ducky. Don't they, Jack?'—'Jack, you're a terror with the gals.'—'He
takes three of 'em in tow to once, like one of 'em Watkinses two-funnel
tugs waddling away with three schooners behind.'—'Jack, you're a
lame scamp.'—'Jack, tell us about that one with a blue eye and a black
eye. Do'—'There's plenty of girls with one black eye along the
Highway by . . .'—'No, that's a speshul one—come Jack.' Donkin
looked severe and disgusted; Jimmy very bored; a grey-haired sea-dog
shook his head slightly, smiling at the bowl of his pipe, discreetly
amused. Knowles turned about bewildered; stammered first at one, then
at another.—'No! . . . I never! . . . can't talk sensible sense amidst you .
. . Always on the kid.' He retired bashfully—muttering and pleased.
They laughed hooting in the crude light, around Jimmy's bed, where on
a white pillow his hollowed black face moved to and fro restlessly. A
puff of wind came, made the flame of the lamp leap, and outside, high
up, the sails fluttered, while near by the block of the foresheet struck a
ringing blow on the iron bulwark. A voice far off cried, 'Helm up!'
another, more faint, answered, 'Hard up, sir!' They became silent—
waiting expectantly. The grey-haired seaman knocked his pipe on the
doorstep and stood up. The ship leaned over gently and the sea seemed
to wake up, murmuring drowsily. 'Here's a little wind comin',' said
some one very low, Jimmy turned over slowly to face the breeze. The
voice in the night cried loud and commanding:—'Haul the spanker
out.' The group before the door vanished out of the light. They could be
heard tramping aft while they repeated with various intonations:—
'Spanker out! . . .' 'Out spanker, sir!' Donkin remained alone with
Jimmy. There was a silence. Jimmy opened and shut his lips several
times as if swallowing draughts of fresher air; Donkin moved the toes
of his bare feet and looked at them thoughtfully.

  'Ain't you going to give them a hand with the sail?' asked Jimmy.

  'No. Hif six ov 'em hain't 'nough beef to set that blamed, rotten
spanker, they hain't fit to live,' answered Donkin in a bored, faraway
voice, as though he had been talking from the bottom of a hole. Jimmy
considered the conical, fowl-like profile with a queer kind of interest;

he was leaning out of his bunk with the calculating, uncertain expression of a man who reflects how best to lay hold of some strange creature that looks as though it could sting or bite. But he said only:— 'The mate will miss you—and there will be ructions.'

Donkin got up to go. 'I will do for 'im hon some dark night, see hif I don't,' he said over his shoulder.

Jimmy went on quickly:—'You're like a poll-parrot, like a screechin' poll-parrot.' Donkin stopped and cocked his head attentively on one side. His big ears stood our, transparent and veined, resembling the thin wings of a bat.

'Yuss?' he said, with his back towards Jimmy.

'Yes! Chatter out all you know—like . . . like a dirty white cockatoo.'

Donkin waited. He could hear the other's breathing, long and slow; the breathing of a man with a hundredweight or so on the breast-bone. Then he asked calmly:—'What do I know?'

'What? . . . What I tell you . . . not much. What do you want . . . to talk about my health so . . .'

'Hit's a bloomin' himposyshun. A bloomin', stinkin', first-class himposyshun—but hit don't tyke me hin. Not hit.'

Jimmy kept still. Donkin put his hands in his pockets, and in one slouching stride came up to the bunk.

'I talk—what's the hodds. They hain't men here—sheep they hare. A driven lot of sheep. I 'old you hup . . . Vy not? you're well hoff.'

'I am . . . I don't say anything about that . . .'

'Well, Let 'em see hit. Let 'em larn what a man can do. I ham a man. I know hall about yer . . .' Jimmy threw himself further away on the pillow; the other stretched out his skinny neck, jerked his bird face down at him as though pecking at the eyes. 'I ham a man. I've seen the hinside of every chokey in the Colonies rather'n give hup my rights . . .'

'You are a jail-prop,' said Jimmy weakly.

'I ham . . . an' proud of it too. You! You 'aven't the bloomin' nerve—so you hinventyd this 'ere dodge . . .' He paused, then with marked afterthought accentuated slowly:—'Yer ain't sick—hare yer?'

'No,' said Jimmy firmly. 'Been out of sorts now and again this year,' he mumbled with a sudden drop in his voice.

Donkin closed one eye, amicable and confidential. He whispered:—'Ye 'ave done it afore—aven'tchee?' Jimmy smiled— then as if unable to hold back he let himself go:—'Last ship—yes. I was out of sorts on the passage. See? It was easy. They paid me off in Calcutta, and the skipper made no bones about it either . . . I got my money all right. Laid up fifty-eight days! The fools! O Lord! The fools! Paid right off.' He laughed spasmodically. Donkin chummed giggling. Then Jimmy coughed violently. 'I am as well as ever,' he said, as soon as he could draw breath.

Donkin made a derisive gesture. 'In course,' he said profoundly, 'hany one can see that.'—'They don't.' said Jimmy, gasping like a fish.——'They would swallow any yarn,' affirmed Donkin.—'Don't you let on too much,' admonished Jimmy in an exhausted voice.—'Your little gyme? Eh?' commented Donkin jovially. Then with sudden disgust: 'Yer hall for yerself, s'long has ye're right . . .'

So charged with egoism James Wait pulled the blanket up to his chin and lay still for awhile. His heavy lips protruded in an everlasting black pout. 'Why are you so hot on making trouble?' he asked without much interest.

''Cos hit's a bloomin' shayme. We hare put hon . . . bad food, bad pay . . . I want hus to kick up a bloomin' row; a blamed 'owling row that would make 'em remember! Knocking people habout . . . brain hus . . . hindeed! Ain't we men?' His altruistic indignation blazed. Then he said calmly;—'I've been a-hairing of yer clothes'—'All right,' said Jimmy languidly, 'bring them in.'—'Giv' us the key of your chest, I'll put 'em away for yer,' said Donkin with friendly eagerness.—'Bring 'em in, I will put them away myself.' answered James Wait with severity. Donkin looked down, muttering . . . 'What d'you say? What d'you say?' inquired Wait anxiously,—'Nothink. The night's dry, let 'em 'ang out till the morning,' said Donkin, in a strangely trembling voice, as though restraining laughter or rage. Jimmy seemed satisfied.—'Give me a little water for the night in my mug—there,' he said.

Donkin took a stride over the doorstep.—'Git it yerself,' he replied in a surly tone. 'You can do it, hunless you hare sick.'—'Of course I can do it,' said Wait, 'only . . .'—'Well, then, do it.' said Donkin viciously, 'if yer can look hafter yer clothes, yer can look hafter yerself.' He went on deck without a look back.

Jimmy reached out for the mug. Not a drop. He put it back gently with a faint sigh—and closed his eyes. He thought:—That lunatic Belfast will bring me some water if I ask. Fool. I am very thirsty . . . It was very hot in the cabin, and it seemed to turn slowly round, detach itself from the ship, and swing out smoothly into a luminous arid space where a black sun shone, spinning very fast. A place without any water! No water! A policeman with the face of Donkin drank a glass of beer by the side of an empty well, and flew away flapping vigorously. A ship whose mastheads protruded through the sky and could not be seen, was discharging grain, and the wind whirled the dry husks in spirals along the quay of a dock with no water in it. He whirled the dry husks in spirals along with the husks—and more dry. He expanded his hollow chest. The air streamed in carrying away in its rush a lot of strange things that resembled houses, trees, people, lamp-posts . . . No more! There was no more air—and he had not finished drawing his long breath. But he was in gaol! They were locking him up. A door slammed. They turned the key twice, flung a bucket of water over him—Phoo! What for?

He opened his eyes, thinking the fall had been very heavy for an empty man—empty—empty. He was in his cabin. Ah! All right! His face was streaming with perspiration, his arms heavier than lead. He saw the cook standing in the doorway, a brass key in one hand and a bright tin hook-pot in the other.

'I have been locking up for the night,' said the cook, beaming benevolently. 'Eight-bells just gone. I brought you a pot of cold tea for your night's drinking, Jimmy. I sweetened it with some white cabin sugar, too. Well—it won't break the ship.'

He came in, hung the pot on the edge of the bunk, asked perfunctorily, 'How goes it?' and sat down on the box.—'H'm,' grunted Wait inhospitably. The cook wiped his face with a dirty cotton rag, which, afterwards, he tied around his neck.—'That's how them firemen do in steamboats,' he said serenely, and much pleased with himself. 'My work is as heavy as theirs—I'm thinking—and longer hours. did you ever see them down the stokehold? Like fiends they look—firing—firing—firing—down there.'

He pointed his forefinger at the deck. Some gloomy thought darkened his shining face, fleeting, like the shadow of a traveling cloud over the light of a peaceful sea. The relieved watch tramped noisily forward, passing in a body across the sheen of the doorway. Some one cried, 'Good night!' Belfast stopped for a moment and looked in at Jimmy, quivering and speechless as if with repressed emotion. He gave the cook a glance charged with dismal foreboding, and vanished. The cook cleared his throat, Jimmy stared upwards and kept as still as a man in hiding.

The night was clear, with a gentle breeze. The ship heeled over a little, slipping quietly over a sombre sea towards the inaccessible and festal splendor of a black horizon pierced by points of flickering fire. Above the mastheads the resplendent curve of the Milky Way spanned the sky like a triumphant arch of eternal light, thrown over the dark pathway of the earth. On the forecastle head a man whistled with loud precision a lively jig, while another could be heard faintly, shuffling and stamping in time. There came from forward a confused murmur of voices, laughter—snatches of song. The cook shook his head, glanced obliquely at Jimmy, and began to mutter. 'Aye. Dance and sing. That's all they think of. I am surprised the Providence don't get tired . . . They forget the day that's sure to come . . . but you . . .'

Jimmy drank a gulp of tea, hurriedly, as though he had stolen it, and shrank under his blanket, edging away towards the bulkhead. The cook got up, closed the door, then sat down again and said distinctly:—

'Whenever I poke my galley fire I think of you chaps—swearing, stealing, lying, and worse—as if there was no such thing as another world . . . Not bad fellows, either, in a way,' he conceded slowly; then, after a pause of regretful musing he went on in a resigned tone:—'Well, well. they will have a hot time of it. Hot! Did I say? The furnaces of one of them White Star boats ain't nothing to it.'

He kept quiet for a while. There was a great stir in his brain; an addled vision of bright outlines; an exciting row of rousing songs and groans of pain. He suffered, enjoyed, admired, approved. He was delighted, frightened, exalted—like on that evening (the only time in his life—twenty-seven years ago; he loved to recall the number of years) when as a young man he had—through keeping bad company— become intoxicated in an East-end music-hall. A tide of sudden feeling swept him clean out of his body. He soared. He contemplated the secret of the hereafter. It commended itself to him. It was excellent; he loved it, himself, all hands, and Jimmy. His heart overflowed with tenderness with comprehension, with the desire to meddle, with anxiety for the soul of that black man, with the pride of possessed eternity, with the feeling of might. Snatch him up in his arms and pitch him right into the middle of salvation . . . the black soul—blacker—body—rot—Devil. No! Talk—strength—Samson . . . There was a great din as of cymbals in his ears; he flashed through an ecstatic jumble of shining faces, lilies, prayer-books, unearthly joy, white shirts, gold harps, black coats, wings. He saw flowing garments, clean shaved faces, a sea of light—— a lake of pitch. There were sweet scents, a smell of sulphur—red tongues of flame licking a white mist. An awesome voice thundered! . . . It lasted three seconds.

'Jimmy!' he cried in an inspired tone. Then he hesitated. A spark of human pity glimmered yet through the infernal fog of his supreme conceit.

'What?' said James Wait, unwillingly. There was a silence. He turned his head just the least bit and stole a cautious glance. The cook's lips moved inaudibly; his face was rapt his eyes turned up. He seemed to be mentally imploring deck beams, the brass hook of the lamp, two cockroaches.

'Look here,' said James Wait, 'I want to go to sleep. I think I could.'

'This is no time for sleep!' exclaimed the cook, very loud. He had prayerfully divested himself of the last vestige of his humanity. He was a voice—a fleshless and sublime thing, as on that memorable night— the night when he went over the sea to make coffee for perishing sinners. 'This is no time for sleeping,' he repeated with exaltation. 'I can't sleep.'

'Don't care damn,' said Wait, with factitious energy. 'I can. go an' turn in.'

'Swear . . . in the very jaws! . . . In the very jaws! Don't you see the fire . . . don't you feel it? Blind, chock-full of sin! I can see it for you. I can't bear it. I hear the call to save you. Night and day. Jimmy let me save you!' The words of entreaty and menace broke out of him in a roaring torrent. The cockroaches ran away. Jimmy perspired, wriggling stealthily under his blanket. The cook yelled . . . 'Your days are numbered! . . .'—'Get out of this,' boomed Wait, courageously.—'Pray with me! . . .'—'I won't! . . .' the little cabin was as hot as an oven. It contained an immensity of fear and pain; an atmosphere of shrieks and moans; prayers vociferated like blasphemies and whispered curses. Outside, the men called by Charley, who informed them in tones of delight that there was a row going on in Jimmy's place, pushed before the closed door, too startled to open it. All hands were there. The watch below had jumped up, asked:—'What is it?' Others said:—'Listen!' The muffled screaming went on:—'On your knees! On your knees!'— Shut up!—'Never! You are delivered into my hands . . . Your life has been saved . . . Purpose . . . Mercy . . . Repent.'—'You are a crazy fool! . . .'—'Account of you . . . you . . . Never sleep in this world, if I . . .'— 'Leave off.'—'No! . . . stokehold . . . only think! . . .' Then an impassioned screeching babble where words pattered like hail.—'No!' shouted Jim.—'Yes. You are! . . . No help . . . Everybody says so.'— 'You lie!'—'I see you dying this minnyt! . . . before my eyes . . . as good as dead now.'—'Help!' shouted Jimmy, piercingly.—'Not in this valley . . . look upwards,' howled the other.—'Go away! Murder! Help!' clamoured Jimmy. His voice broke. There were moanings, low mutters, a few sobs.

'What's the matter now?' said a seldom-heard voice.—'Fall back, men! Fall back, there!' repeated Mr. Creighton sternly, pushing through—'Here's the old man.' whispered some.—'The cook's in there, sir' exclaimed several, backing away. The door clattered open; a broad stream of light4 darted out on wondering faces; a warm whiff of vitiated air passed. The two mates towered head and shoulders above the spare, grey-headed man who stood revealed between them, in shabby clothes, stiff and angular like a small carved figure, and with a thin, composed face. The cook got up from knees. Jimmy sat high in the bunk, clasping his drawn-up legs. The tassel of the blue nightcap almost imperceptibly trembled over his knees. They gazed astonished at his long, curved back, while the white corner of one eye gleamed blindly at them. He was afraid to turn his head, he shrank within himself; and there was an aspect astounding and animal-like in the perfection of his expectant immobility. A thing of instinct—the unthinking stillness of a scared brute.

'What are you doing here?' asked Mr. Baker, sharply.—'My duty,' said the cook, with ardour.—'Your . . . what?' began the mate. Captain Allistoun touched his arm lightly.—'I know his caper,' he said, in a low voice. 'Come out of that, Podmore,' he ordered aloud.

The cook wrung his hands, shook his fists above his head, and his arms dropped as if too heavy. For a moment he stood distracted and speechless.—'Never,' he stammered, 'I . . . he . . . I.'—'What—do—you—say?' pronounced Captain Allistoun. 'Come out at once—or . . .'—'I am going.' said the cook, with a hasty and sombre resignation. He strode over the doorstep firmly—hesitated—made a few steps. They looked at him in silence.—'I make you responsible!' he cried desperately, turning half round. 'That man is dying. I make you . . .'— 'You there yet?' called the master in a threatening tone.—'No, sir,' he exclaimed hurriedly in a startled voice. The boatswain led him away by the arm; some one laughed; Jimmy lifted his head for a stealthy glance, and in one unexpected leap sprang out of his bunk; Mr. Baker made a clever catch and felt him very limp in his arms; the group at the door grunted with surprise.—'He lies,' gasped Wait. 'He talked about black devils—he is a devil—a white devil—I am all right.' He stiffened himself, and Mr. Baker, experimentally, let him go. He staggered a pace or two; Captain Allistoun watched him with a quiet and penetrating gaze; Belfast ran to his support. He did not appear to be aware of any one near him; he stood silent for a moment, battling single-handed with a legion of nameless terrors amidst the eager looks of excited men who watched him far off, utterly alone in the impenetrable solitude of his fear. Heavy breathings stirred the darkness. The sea gurgled through the scuppers as the ship heeled over to a short puff of wind.

'Keep him away from me,' said James Wait at last in his fine baritone voice, and leaning with all his weight on Belfast's neck. 'I've been better this last week . . . I am well . . . I was going back to duty . . . —now if you like—Captain.' Belfast hitched his shoulders to keep him upright.

'No,' said the master, looking at him fixedly.

Under Jimmy's armpit Belfast's red face moved uneasily. A row of eyes gleaming stared on the edge of light. They pushed one another with elbows, turned their heads, whispered. Wait let his chin fall on his breast and, with lowered eyelids, looked round in a suspicious manner.

'Why not?' cried a voice from the shadows, 'the man's all right, sir.'

'I am all right,' said Wait with eagerness. 'Been sick . . . better . . . turn-to now.' He sighed.—'Howly Mother!' exclaimed Belfast with a heave of the shoulders, 'stand up, Jimmy.'—'Keep away from me then,' said Wait, giving Belfast a petulant push, and reeling against the door-post. His cheek-bones glistened as though they had been varnished. He snatched off his night-cap, wiped his perspiring face with it, flung it on the deck. 'I am coming out,' he said without stirring.

'No. You don't,' said the master curtly. Bare feet shuffled, disapproving voices murmured all round; he went on as if he had not heard:—'You have been skulking nearly all the passage and now you want to come out. You think you are near enough to the pay-table now. Smell the shore, hey?'

'I've been sick . . . now—better,' mumbled Wait glaring in the light.—'You have been shamming sick,' retorted Captain Allistoun with severity: 'Why . . .' he hesitated for less than half a second. 'Why, anybody can see that. There's nothing the matter with you, but you choose to lie-up to please yourself—and now you shall lie-up to please me. Mr. baker, my orders are that this man is not to be allowed on deck to the end of the passage.'

There were exclamations of surprise, triumph, indignation. The dark group of men swung across the light. 'What for?' 'Told you so . . .' 'Bloomin' shame . . .'—'We've got to say something habout that,' screeched Donkin from the rear.—'Never mind, Jim—'—'We'll see you righted,' called several together. An elderly seaman stepped to the front. 'D'ye mean to say, sir,' he asked ominously, 'that a sick chap ain't allowed to get well in this 'ere hooker?' Behind him Donkin whispered excitedly amongst a staring crowd where no one spared him a glance, but Captain Allistoun shook a forefinger at the angry bronzed face of the speaker.—'You—you hold your tongue,' he said warningly.—'This isn't the way,' clamoured two or three younger men. 'Hare we bloomin' masheens?' inquired Donkin in a piercing tone, and dived under the elbows of the front rank.—'Soon show 'im we ain't boys . . .'—'The man's a man if he is black.'—'We ain't goin' to work this bloomin' ship shorthanded if Snowball's all right . . .'—'He says he is.'—'Well then, strike, boys, strike!'—'That's the bloomin' ticket.' Captain Allistoun said sharply to the second mate: 'Keep quiet, Mr. Creighton,' and stood composed in the tumult, listening with profound attention to mixed growls and screeches, to every exclamation and every curse of the sudden outbreak. Somebody slammed the cabin door to with a kick; the darkness full of menacing mutters leaped with a short clatter over the streak of light, and the men became gesticulating shadows that growled, hissed, laughed excitedly. Mr. Baker whispered:—'Get away from them, sir.' The big shape of Mr. Creighton hovered silently about the slight figure of the master.—'We have been hymposed upon all this voyage,' said a gruff voice, 'but this 'ere fancy takes the cake.'—'That man is a shipmate.'—'Are we bloomin' kids?'—'The port watch will refuse duty.' Charley carried away by his feelings whistled shrilly, then yelped:—'Giv' us our Jimmy!' This seemed to cause a variation in the disturbance. There was a fresh burst of squabbling uproar. A lot of quarrels were going on at once.—'Yes'—'No.'—'Never been sick.'—'Go for them to once.'—'Shut yer mouth, youngster—this is men's work.'—'Is it?' muttered Captain Allistoun bitterly. Mr. Baker grunted: 'Ough! They're gone silly. They've been simmering for the last month.'—'I did notice,' said the master.—'They have started a row amongst themselves now,' said Mr. Creighton with disdain, 'better get aft, sir. We will soothe them.'— 'Keep your temper, Creighton,' said the master. And the three men began to move slowly towards the cabin door.

In the shadows of the fore rigging a dark mass stamped eddied, advanced, retreated. There were words of reproach, encouragement, unbelief, execration. The elder seamen, bewildered and angry, growled their determination to go through with something or other; but the younger school of advanced thought exposed their and Jimmy's wrongs with confused shouts, arguing amongst themselves. They clustered round that moribund carcass, the fit emblem of their aspirations. and encouraging one another they swayed, they tramped on one spot, shouting that they would not be 'put upon' Inside the cabin, Belfast, helping Jimmy into his bunk, twitched all over in his desire not to miss all the row, and with difficulty restrained the tears of his facile emotion. James Wait flat on his back under the blanket, gasped complaints.— 'We will back you up, never fear,' assured Belfast, busy about his feet.—'I'll come out tomorrow—skipper or no skipper.' He lifted one arm with great difficulty, passed the hand over his face; 'Don't you let that cook . . .' he breathed out.—'No, no,' said Belfast, turning his back on the bunk, 'I will put a head on him if he comes near you.'—'I will smash his mug!' exclaimed faintly Wait, enraged and weak; 'I don't want to kill a man, but . . .' He panted fast like a dog after a run in sunshine. Some one just outside the door shouted, 'He's as fit as any ov us!' Belfast put his hand on the door-handle.—'Here!' called James Wait hurriedly and in such a clear voice that the other spun round with a start. James Wait, stretched out black and deathlike in the dazzling light, turned his head on the pillow. His eyes stared at Belfast, appealing and impudent. 'I am rather weak from lying-up so long,' he said distinctly. Belfast nodded. 'Getting quite well now,' insisted Wait.—'Yes, I noticed you getting better this . . . last month,' said Belfast looking down. 'Hallo! What's this?' he shouted and ran out.

He was flattened directly against the side of the house by two men who lurched against him. A lot of disputes seemed to be going on all round. He got clear and was three distinct figures standing alone in the fainter darkness under the arched foot of the mainsail, that rose above their heads like a convex wall of a high edifice. Donkin hissed:—'Go for them . . . it's dark!' The crowd took a short run aft in a body—then there was a check. Donkin, agile and thin flitted past with his right arm going like a windmill—and then stood still suddenly with his arm pointing rigidly above his head. The hurtling flight of some small heavy object was heard; it passed between the heads of the two mates, bounded heavily along the deck, stuck the after hatch with a ponderous and deadened blow. The bulky shape of Mr. Baker grew distinct. 'Come to your senses, men!' he cried, advancing at the arrested crowd.

'Come back, Mr. Baker!' called the master's quiet voice. He obeyed unwillingly. There was a minute of silence, then a deafening hubbub arose. Above it Archie was heard energetically:—'If ye do oot ageen I wull tell!' There were shouts. 'Don't!' 'Drop it!'—'We ain't that kind!' The black cluster of human forms reeled against the bulwark, back again towards the house. Shadowy figures could be seen tottering, falling, leaping up. Ringbolts rang under stumbling feet.—'Drop it!' 'Let me!'—'No!'—'Curse you! . . . hah!' Then sounds as of some one's face being slapped; a piece of iron fell on the deck; a short scuffle, and some one's shadowy body scuttled rapidly across the main hatch before the shadow of a kick. A raging voice sobbed out a torrent of filthy language . . . —'Throwing things—good God!' grunted Mr. Baker in dismay.—'That was meant for me,' said the master quietly; 'I felt the wind of that thing; what was it—an iron belaying-pin?'—'By Jove!' muttered Mr. Creighton. The confused voices of men talking amidships mingled with the wash of the sea, ascended between the silent and distended sails—seemed to flow away into the night, further than the horizon, higher than the sky. The stars burned steadily over the inclined mastheads. Trails of light lay on the water, broke before the advancing hull, and, after she had passed, trembled for a long time as if in awe of the murmuring sea.

Meantime the helmsman, anxious to know what the row was about, had let go the wheel, and, bent double, ran with long stealthy footsteps to the break of the poop. The *Narcissus*, left to herself, came up gently to the wind without any one being aware of it. She gave a slight roll, and the sleeping sails woke suddenly, coming all together with a mighty flap against the masts, then filled again one after another in a quick succession of loud reports that ran down the lofty spars, till the collapsed mainsail flew out last with a violent jerk. The ship trembled from trucks to keel; the sails kept on rattling like a discharge of musketry; the chain sheets and loose shackles jingled aloft in a thin peal; the gin blocks groaned. It was as if an invisible hand had given the ship an angry shake to recall the men that peopled her decks to the sense of reality, vigilance and duty.—'Helm up!' cried the master sharply. 'Run aft, Mr. Creighton, and see what that fool there is up to.'—'Flatten in the head sheets. Stand by the weather fore-braces,' growled Mr. Baker. Startled men ran swiftly repeating the orders. The watch below, abandoned all at once by the watch on deck, drifted towards the forecastle in twos and threes, arguing noisily as they went.—'We shall see to-morrow!' cried a loud voice, as if to cover with a menacing hint an inglorious retreat. And then only orders were heard, the falling of heavy coils of rope, the rattling of blocks. Singleton's white head flitted here and there in the night, high above deck, like the ghost of a bird.—'Going off, sir!' shouted Mr. Creighton from aft.—'Full again.'—'All right . . .'—'Ease off the head sheets.

That will do the braces. Coil the ropes,' grunted Mr. Baker, bustling about.

Gradually the tramping noises, the confused sound of voices, died out, and the officers, coming together on the poop discussed events. Mr. Baker was bewildered and grunted; Mr. Creighton was calmly furious; but Captain Allistoun was composed and thoughtful. He listened to Mr. Baker's growling argumentation, to Creighton's interjected and severe remarks, while looking down on the deck he weighed in his hand the iron belaying-pin—that a moment ago had just missed his head—as if it had been the only tangible fact of the whole transaction. He was one of those commanders who speak little, seem to hear nothing, look at no one—and know everything, hear every whisper, see every fleeting shadow of their ship's life. His two big officers towered above his lean, short figure; they talked over his head; they were dismayed, surprised, and angry, while between them the little quiet man seemed to have found his taciturn serenity in the profound depths of a larger experience. Lights were burning in the forecastle; now and then a gust of babbling chatter came from forward, swept over the decks, and became faint, as if the unconscious ship gliding gently through the great peace of the sea, had left behind and for ever the foolish noise of turbulent mankind. But it was renewed again and again. Gesticulating arms, profiles of heads with open mouths appeared for a moment in the illuminated squares of doorways; black fists darted— withdrew . . . 'Yes. It was most damnable to have such an unprovoked row sprung on one,' assented the master . . . A tumult of yells rose in the light, abruptly ceased . . . He didn't think there would be any further trouble just then . . . A bell was struck aft, another, forward, answered in a deeper tone, and the clamour of ringing metal spread round the ship in a circle of wide vibrations that ebbed away into the immeasurable night of an empty sea . . . Didn't he know them! Didn't he! In past years. Better men, too. Real men to stand by one in a tight place. Worse than devils too sometimes—downright, horned devils. Pah! This—nothing. A miss as good as a mile . . . The wheel was being relieved in the usual way.—'Full and by,' said, very loud, the man going off.—'Full and by,' repeated the other, catching hold of the spokes.—'This head wind is my trouble,' exclaimed the master, stamping his foot in sudden anger; 'head wind! all the rest is nothing.' He was calm again in a moment. 'Keep them on the move to-night, gentlemen; just to let them feel we've got hold all the time—quietly, you know. Mind you keep your hands off them, Creighton. To-morrow I will talk to them like a Dutch Uncle. A crazy crowd of tinkers! Yes, tinkers! I could count the real sailors amongst them on the fingers of one hand. Nothing will do but a row—if—you—please.' He paused. 'Did you think I had gone wrong there Mr. Baker?' He tapped his forehead, laughed short. 'When I saw him standing there, three parts dead and so scared—black amongst that gaping lot—no grit to face what's coming to us all—the notion came to me all at once, before I could think. Sorry for him—like you would be for a sick brute. If ever a creature was in a mortal funk to die! . . . I thought I would let him go out in his own way. Kind of impulse. It never came into my head, those fools . . . H'm! Stand to it now—of course.' He stuck the belaying-pin in his pocket, seemed ashamed of himself, then sharply:—'If you see Podmore at his tricks again tell him I will have him put under the pump. Had to do it once before. The fellow breaks out like that now and then. Good cook tho'.' He walked away quickly, came back to the companion. The two mates followed him through the starlight with amazed eyes. He went down three steps, and changing his tone, spoke with his head near the deck:—'I shan't turn in to-night. in case of anything; just call out if . . . Did you see the eyes of that sick nigger, Mr. Baker? I fancied he begged me for something. What? Past all help. One lone black beggar amongst the lot of us, and he seemed to look through me into the very hell. Fancy, this wretched Podmore! Well, let him die in peace. I am master here after all. Say what I like. Let him be. He might have been half a man once . . . Keep a good look-out.' He disappeared below, leaving his mates facing one another, and more impressed than if they had seen a stone image shed a miraculous tear of compassion over the incertitudes of life and death . . .

In the blue mist spreading from twisted threads that stood upright in the bowls of pipes, the forecastle appeared as vast as a hall. Between the beams a heavy cloud stagnated; and the lamps surrounded by halos burned each at the core of a purple glow in two lifeless flames without rays. Wreaths drifted in denser wisps. Men sprawled about on the deck, sat in negligent poses, or, bending a knee, drooped with one shoulder against a bulkhead. Lips moved, eyes flashed, waving arms made sudden eddies in the smoke. The murmur of voices seemed to pile itself higher and higher as if unable to run out quick enough through the narrow doors. The watch below in their shirts, and striding on long white legs resembled raving somnambulists; while now and then one of the watch on deck would rush in, looking strangely over-dressed, listen a moment, fling a rapid sentence into the noise and run out again; but a few remained near the door, fascinated, and with one ear turned to the deck.—'Stick together, boys,' roared Davis. Belfast tried to make himself heard. Knowles grinned in a slow, dazed way. A short fellow with a thick clipped beard kept on yelling periodically:—'Who's afeard? Who's afeard?' Another one jumped up, excited, with blazing eyes, sent out a sting of unattached curses and sat down quietly. Two men discussed familiarly, striking one another's breast in turn, to clinch arguments. Three others, with their heads in a bunch, spoke all together with a confidential air, and at the top of their voices. It was a stormy chaos of speech where intelligible fragments tossing, struck the ear.

One could hear:—'In the last ship'—'Who cares? Try it on any one of us if—.' 'Knock under'—'Not a hand's turn'—'He says he is all right'—'I always thought'—'Never mind . . .' Donkin, crouching all in a heap against the bowsprit, hunched his shoulder-blades as high as his ears, and hanging a peaked nose, resembled a sick vulture with ruffled plumes. Belfast, straddling his legs, had a face red with yelling, and with arms thrown up, figured a Maltese cross. The two Scandinavians, in a corner, had the dumbfounded and distracted aspect of men gazing at a cataclysm. And, beyond the light, Singleton stood in the smoke, monumental, indistinct, with his head touching the beam; like a statue of heroic size in the gloom of a crypt.

He stepped forward, impassive and big. The noise subsided like a broken wave: but Belfast cried once more with uplifted arms:—'The man is dying I tell ye!' then sat down suddenly on the hatch and took his head between his hands. All looked at Singleton, gazing upwards from the deck staring out of dark corners, or turning their heads with curious glances. They were expectant and appeased as if that old man, who looked at no one, had possessed the secret of their uneasy indignations and desires, a sharper vision, a clearer knowledge. And indeed standing there amongst them, he had the uninterested appearance of one who had seen multitudes of ships, had listened many times to voices such as theirs, had already seen all that could happen on the wide seas. They heard his voice rumble in his broad chest as though the words had been rolling towards them out of a rugged past. 'What do you want to do?' he asked. No one answered. Only Knowles muttered—'Aye, aye,' and somebody said low:—'It's a bloomin' shame.' He waited made a contemptuous gesture.—'I have seen rows aboard ship before some of you were born,' he said slowly, 'for something or nothing; but never for such a thing.—' 'The man is dying, I tell ye,' repeated Belfast woefully, sitting at Singleton's feet.—'And a black fellow, too,' went on the old seaman, 'I have seen them die like flies.' He stopped, thoughtful, as if trying to recollect gruesome things, details of horrors, hecatombs of niggers. They looked at him fascinated. He was old enough to remember slavers, bloody mutinies, pirates perhaps; who could tell through what violences and terrors he had lived! What would he say? He said:—'You can't help him; die he must.' He made another pause. His moustache and beard stirred. He chewed words, mumbled behind white hairs; incomprehensible and exciting, like an oracle behind a veil . . . —'Stop ashore—sick.— Instead—bringing all this head wind. Afraid. The sea will have her own.—Die in the sight of land. Always so. They know it—long passage—more days, more dollars.—you keep quiet.—What do you want? Can't help him.' He seemed to wake up from a dream. 'You can't help your selves,' he said austerely, 'Skipper's no fool. He has something in his mind. Look out—I say! I know 'em!' With eyes fixed in front he turned his head from right to left, from left to right, as if inspecting a long row of astute skippers.—'He said 'e would brain me!' cried Donkin in a heartrending tone. Singleton peered downwards with puzzled attention, as though he couldn't find him.—'Damn you!' he said vaguely, giving it up. He radiated unspeakable wisdom, hard unconcern, the chilling air of resignation. Round him all the listeners felt themselves somehow completely enlightened by their disappointment, and, mute, they lolled about with the careless ease of men who can discern perfectly the irremediable aspect of their existence. He, profound and unconscious, waved his arm once, and strode out on deck without another word.

Belfast was lost in a round-eyed meditation. One or two vaulted heavily into upper berths, and, once there, sighed; others dived head first inside lower bunks—swift, and turning round instantly upon themselves, like animals going into lairs. The grating of a knife scraping burnt clay was heard. Knowles grinned no more. Davies said, in a tone of ardent conviction:—'Then our skipper's looney.' Archie muttered:—'My faith! we haven't heard the last of it yet!' Four bells were struck.—'Half our watch below is gone!' cried Knowles in alarm, then reflected, 'Well, two hours sleep is something towards a rest,' he observed consolingly. Some already pretended to slumber; and Charley, sound asleep, suddenly said a few slurred words in an arbitrary, blank voice.—'This blamed boy has worrums!' commented Knowles from under a blanket, and in a learned manner. Belfast got up and approached Archie's berth.—'we pulled him out,' he whispered sadly.—'And now we will have to chuck him overboard,' went on Belfast, whose lower lip trembled.—'Chuck what?' asked Archie.— 'Poor Jimmy,' breathed out Belfast.—'He be blowed!' said Archie with untruthful brutality, and sat up in his bunk; 'It's all through him. If it hadn't been for me, there would have been murder on board this ship!'—'Tain't his fault, is it?' argued Belfast, in a murmur; 'I've put him to bed . . . and he ain't no heavier than an empty beef-cask,' he added, with tears in his eyes. Archie looked at him steadily, then turned his nose to the ship's side with determination. Belfast wandered about as though he had lost his way in the dim forecastle, and nearly fell over Donkin. He contemplated him from on high for awhile. 'Ain't ye going to turn in?' he asked. Donkin looked up hopelessly.—'That black-'earted Scotch son of a thief kicked me!' he whispered from the floor, in a tone of utter desolation.—'And a good job, too!' said Belfast, still very depressed; 'You were as near hanging as damn-it to-night, sonny. Don't you play any of your murthering games around my Jimmy! You haven't pulled him out. You just mind! ''Cos if I start to kick you'—he brightened up a bit—'if I start to kick you, it will be Yankee fashion— to break something!' He tapped lightly with his knuckles the top of the bowed head. 'You moind, me bhoy!' he concluded, cheerily. Donkin

let it pass.—'Will they split on me?' he asked, with pained anxiety.—
'Who—split?' hissed Belfast, coming back a step. 'I would split your
nose this minyt if I hadn't Jimmy to look after! Who d'ye think we
are?' Donkin rose and watched Belfast's back lurch through the
doorway. On all sides men slept, breathing calmly. He seemed to draw
courage and fury from the peace around him. Venomous and thin-
faced, he glared from the ample misfit of borrowed clothes as if looking
for something he could smash. His heart leaped wildly in his narrow
chest. They slept! He wanted to wring necks, gouge eyes, spit on faces.
He shook a dirty pair of meagre fists at the smoking lights. 'Ye're no
men!' he cried, in a deadened tone. No one moved. 'Yer 'aven't the
pluck of a mouse!' His voice rose to a husky screech. Wamibo blinked,
uncomprehending but interested. Donkin sat down heavily; he blew
with force through quivering nostrils, he ground and snapped his teeth,
and, with the chin pressed hard against the breast, he seemed busy
gnawing his way through it, as if to get at the heart within . . .

In the morning the ship, beginning another day of her wandering
life, had an aspect of sumptuous freshness, like the spring-time of the
earth. The washed decks glistened in a long clear stretch; the oblique
sunlight struck the yellow brasses in dazzling splashes, darted over the
polished rods in lines of gold, and the single drops of salt water
forgotten here and there along the rail were as limpid as drops of dew,
and sparkled more than scattered diamonds. The sails slept hushed by a
gentle breeze. The sun, rising lonely and splendid in the blue sky, saw a
solitary ship gliding close-hauled on the blue sea.

The men pressed three deep abreast of the mainmast and opposite
the cabin-door. They shuffled, pushed, had an irresolute mien and stolid
faces. At every slight movement Knowles lurched heavily on his short
leg. Donkin glided behind backs, restless and anxious, like a man
looking for an ambush. Captain Allistoun came out suddenly. He
walked to and fro before the front. He was grey, slight, alert, shabby in
the sunshine, and as hard as adamant. He had his right hand in the side-
pocket of his jacket, and also something heavy in there that made folds
all down that side. One of the seamen cleared his throat ominously.—'I
haven't till now found fault with you men,' said the master, stopping
short. He faced them with his worn, steely gaze, that by an universal
illusion looked straight into every individual pair of the twenty pairs of
eyes before his face. At his back, Mr. baker, bloomy and bull-necked,
grunted low; Mr. Creighton, fresh as paint, had rosy cheeks and a
ready, resolute bearing. 'And I don't now,' continued the master; 'but I
am here to drive this ship and keep every man-jack aboard of her up to
the mark. If you knew your work as well as I do mine, there would be
no trouble. You've been braying in the dark about "See to-morrow
morning!" Well, you see me now. What do you want?' He waited,
stepping quickly to and fro, giving them searching glances. What did

they want? Jimmy was forgotten; no one thought of him, alone forward in his cabin, fighting great shadows, clinging to brazen lies, chuckling painfully over his transparent deceptions. No, not Jimmy; he was more forgotten than if he had been dead. They wanted great things. And suddenly all the simple words they knew seemed to be lost for ever in the immensity of their vague and burning desire. They knew what they wanted, but they could not find anything worth saying. They stirred on one spot, swinging, at the end of muscular arms, big tarry hands with crooked fingers. A murmur died out.—'What is it—food?' asked the master, 'you know the stores had been spoiled off the Cape.'—'We know that, sir,' said a bearded shell-back in the front rank—'Work too hard—eh? Too much for your strength?' he asked again. There was an offended silence.—'We don't want to go shorthanded, sir,' began at last Davies in a wavering voice, 'and this 'ere black— . . .'—'Enough!' cried the master. He stood scanning them for a moment, then walking a few steps this way and that began to storm at them coldly, in gusts violent and cutting like the gales of those icy seas that had known his youth.—'Tell you what's the matter? Too big for your boots. Think yourselves damn good men. Know half your work. Do half your duty. Think it too much. If you did ten times as much it wouldn't be enough.'—'We did our best by her, sir,' cried some one with shaky exasperation.—'Your best,' stormed on the master; 'You here a lot on shore, don't you? They don't tell you there your best isn't much to boast of. I tell you—your best is no better than bad. You can do no more? No, I know, and say nothing. But you stop your caper or I will stop it for you! Stop it!' He shook a finger at the crowd. 'As to that man,' he raised his voice very much; 'as to that man, if he puts his nose out on deck without my leave I will clap him in irons. There!' The cook heard him forward, ran out of the galley lifting his arms, horrified, unbelieving, amazed, and ran in again. There was a moment of profound silence during which a bow-legged seaman, stepping aside, expectorated decorously into the scupper. 'There is another thing,' said the master calmly. He made a quick stride and with a swing took an iron belaying-pin out of his pocket. 'This!' His movement was so unexpected and sudden that the crowd stepped back. He gazed fixedly at their faces, and some at once put on a surprised air as though they had never seen a belaying-pin before. He held it up. 'This is my affair. I don't ask you any questions, but you all know it; it has got to go where it came from.' His eyes became angry. The crowd stirred uneasily. They looked away from the piece of iron, they appeared shy, they were embarrassed and shocked as though it had been something horrid, scandalous, or indelicate, that in common decency should not have been flourished like this in broad daylight. The master watched them attentively. 'Donkin,' he called out in a short, sharp tone.

Donkin dodged behind one, then behind another, but they looked over their shoulders and moved aside. The ranks kept on opening before him, closing behind, till at last he appeared alone before the master as though he had come up through the deck. Captain Allistoun moved close to him. They were much of a size, and at short range the master exchanged a deadly glance with the beady eyes. They wavered,—'You know this,' asked the master.—'No, I don't,' answered the other with cheeky trepidation.—'You are a cur. Take it,' ordered the master. Donkin's arms seemed glued to his thighs; he stood, e yes front, as if drawn on parade. 'Take it,' repeated the master, and stepped closer; they breathed on one another. 'Take it,' said Captain Allistoun again, making a menacing gesture. Donkin tore away one arm from his side.—'Vy hare yer down hon me?' he mumbled with effort as if his mouth had been full of dough.—'If you don't . . .' began the master. Donkin snatched at the pin as though his intention had been to run away with it, and remained stock still holding it like a candle. 'Put it back where you took it from,' said Captain Allistoun, looking at him fiercely. Donkin stepped back opening wide eyes. 'Go, you blackguard, or I will make you,' cried the master, driving him slowly backwards by a menacing advance. He dodged, and with the dangerous iron tried to guard his head from a threatening fist. Mr. Baker ceased grunting for a moment.—'Good! By Jove,' murmured appreciatively Mr. Creighton in the tone of a connoisseur.—'Don't tech me,' snarled Donkin, backing away.—'Then go. Go faster.'—'Don't yer 'it me . . . I will pull yer hup afore the magistryt . . . I'll show yer hup.' Captain Allistoun made a long stride and Donkin, turning his back fairly, ran off a little, then stopped and over his shoulder showed yellow teeth.— 'Further on, fore-rigging,' urged the master, pointing with his arm.— 'Hare yer goin' to stand by and see me bullied,' screamed Donkin at the silent crowd that watched him. Captain Allistoun walked at him smartly. He started off again with a leap, dashed at the fore-rigging, rammed the pin into its hole violently. 'I will be heven with yer yet,' he screamed at the ship at large and vanished beyond the foremast. Captain Allistoun spun round and walked back aft with a composed face, as though he had already forgotten the scene. Men moved out of his way. He looked at no one.—'That will do, Mr. Baker. Send the watch below,' he said quietly. 'And you men try to walk straight for the future,' he added in a calm voice. He looked pensively for a while at the of the impressed and retreating crowd. 'Breakfast, steward,' he called in a tone of relief through the cabin door.—'I didn't like to see you—Ough!—give that pin to that chap, sir,' observed Mr. Baker; 'he could have bust—Ough!—bust your head like an eggshell with it.'— 'O! he!' muttered the master absently. 'Queer lot,' he went on in a low voice. 'I suppose it's all right now. Can never tell tho', nowadays, with such a . . . years ago; I was a young master then—one China voyage I had a mutiny; real mutiny, Baker. Different men tho'. I knew what they wanted: they wanted to broach cargo and get at the liquor. Very simple . . . We knocked them about for two days, and when they had enough— gentle as lambs. Good crew. And a smart trip I made.' He glanced aloft at the yards braced sharp up. 'Head wind day after day,' he exclaimed bitterly. 'Will we never get a decent slant this passage?'—'Ready, sir,' said the steward appearing before them as if by magic and with a stained napkin in his hand.—'Ah! All right. Come along Mr. Baker— it's late—with all this nonsense.'

CHAPTER V

A heavy atmosphere of oppressive quietude pervaded the ship. In the afternoon men went about washing clothes and hanging them out to dry in the unprosperous breeze with the meditative language of disenchanted philosophers. Very little was said. The problem of life seemed too voluminous for the narrow limits of human speech, and by common consent it was abandoned to the great sea that had from the beginning enfolded it in its immense grip; to the sea that knew all, and would in time infallibly unveil to each the wisdom hidden in all the errors, the certitude that lurks in doubts, the realm of safety and peace beyond the frontiers of sorrow and fear. And in the confused current of impotent thoughts that set unceasingly this way and that through bodies of men, Jimmy bobbed up upon the surface, compelling attention, like a black buoy chained to the bottom of a muddy stream. Falsehood triumphed. It triumphed through doubt, through stupidity through pity, through sentimentalism. We set ourselves to bolster it up, from compassion from recklessness, from a sense of fun. Jimmy's steadfastness to his untruthful attitude in the face of the inevitable truth had the proportions of a colossal enigma—of a manifestation grand and incomprehensible that at times inspired a wondering awe; and there was also, to many, something exquisitely droll in fooling him thus to the top of his bent. The latent egoism of tenderness to suffering appeared in the developing anxiety not to see him die. His obstinate non-recognition of the only certitude whose approach we could watch from day to day was as disquieting as the failure of some law of nature. He was so utterly wrong about himself that one could not but suspect him of having access to some source of supernatural knowledge. He was absurd to the point of inspiration. He was unique, and as fascinating as only something inhuman could be; he seemed to shout his denials already from beyond the awful border. He was becoming immaterial like an apparition; his cheekbones rose, the forehead slanted more; the face was all hollows, patches of shade; and the fleshless head resembled a disinterred black skull, fitted with two restless globes of silver in the sockets of eyes. He was demoralising. Through him we were becoming highly humanised, tender, complex, excessively decadent: we understood the subtlety of his fear, sympathised with all his repulsions, shrinkings evasions, delusions—as though we had been over-civilised, and rotten, and without any knowledge of the meaning of life. We had the air of being initiated in some infamous mysteries; we had the profound grimaces of conspirators, exchanged meaning glances, significant short words. We were inexpressibly vile and very much pleased with ourselves. We lied to him with gravity, with emotion, with unction, as if performing some moral trick with a view to an eternal reward. We made a chorus of affirmation to his wildest assertions, as though he had been a millionaire, a politician, or a reformer—and we a crowd of ambitious lubbers. When we ventured to question his statements we did it after the manner of obsequious sycophants. to the end that his glory should be augmented by the flattery of our dissent. He influenced the moral tone of our world as though he had it in his power to distribute honours, treasures, or pain; and he could give us nothing but his contempt. It was immense; it seemed to grow gradually larger, as his body day by day shrank a little more, while we looked. It was the only thing about him—of him—that gave the impression of durability and vigour. It lived within him with an unquenchable life. It spoke through the eternal pout of his black lips; it looked at us through the profound impertinence of his large eyes, that stood far out of his head like the eyes of crabs. We watched them intently. Nothing else of him stirred. He seemed unwilling to move, as if distrustful of his own solidity. The slightest gesture must have disclosed to him (it could not surely be otherwise) his bodily weakness, and caused a pang of mental suffering. He was chary of movements. He lay stretched out, chin on blanket, in a kind of sly, cautious immobility. Only his eyes roamed over faces: his eyes disdainful, penetrating and sad.

It was at that time that Belfast's devotion—and also his pugnacity—secured universal respect. He spent every moment of his spare time in Jimmy's cabin. He tended him, talked to him; was as gentle as a woman, as tenderly gay as an old philanthropist, as sentimentally careful of his nigger as a model slave-owner. But outside he was irritable, explosive as gunpowder, sombre, suspicious, and never more brutal than when most sorrowful. With him it was a tear and a blow: a tear for Jimmy, a blow for any one who did not seem to take a scrupulously orthodox view of Jimmy's case. We talked about nothing else. The two Scandinavians, even, discussed the situation—but it was impossible to know in what spirit, because they quarreled in their own language. Belfast suspected them of irreverence, and in this incertitude thought that there was no option but to fight them both. They became very much terrified by his truculence, and henceforth lived amongst us, dejected, like a pair of mutes. Wamibo never spoke intelligibly, but he was as smileless as an animal—seemed to know much less about it all than the cat—and consequently was safe. Moreover he had belonged to the chosen band of Jimmy's rescuers, and was above suspicion. Archie was silent generally, but often spent an hour or so talking to Jimmy quietly with an air of proprietorship. At any time of the day and often through the night some man could be seen sitting on Jimmy's box. In the evening, between six and eight, the cabin was crowded, and there was an interested group at the door. Every one stared at the nigger.

He basked in the warmth of our interest. His eyes gleamed ironically, and in a weak voice he reproached us with our cowardice. He would say, 'If you fellows had stuck out for me I would be now on deck.' We hung our heads. 'Yes, but if you think I am going to let them put me in irons just to show you sport . . . Well, no . . . It ruins my health, this lying up, it does. You don't care.' We were as abashed as if it had been true. His superb impudence carried all before it. We would not have dared to revolt. We didn't want to really. We wanted to keep him alive till home—to the end of the voyage.

Singleton as usual held aloof, appearing to scorn the insignificant events of an ended life. Once only he came along, and unexpectedly stopped in the doorway. He peered at Jimmy in profound silence, as if desirous to add that black image to the crowd of Shades that peopled his old memory. We kept very quiet and for a long time Singleton stood there as though he had come by appointment to call for some one, or to see some important event. James Wait lay perfectly still and apparently not aware of the gaze scrutinising him with a steadiness full of expectation. There was a sense of tussle in the air. We felt the inward strain of men watching a wrestling bout. At last Jimmy with perceptible apprehension turned his head on the pillow.—'Good evening,' he said in a conciliating tone.—'H'm,' answered the old seaman, grumpily. For a moment longer he looked at Jimmy with severe fixity, then suddenly went away. It was a long time before any one spoke in the little cabin, though we all breathed more freely as men do after an escape from some dangerous situation. We all knew the old man's ideas about Jimmy, and nobody dared to combat them. They were unsettling they caused pain; and, what was worse, they might have been true for all we knew. Only once did he condescend to explain them fully, but the impression was lasting. He said that Jimmy was the cause of head winds. Mortally sick men—he maintained—linger till the first sight of land, and then die; and Jimmy knew that the land would draw his life from him. It is so in every shi. Didn't we know it? He asked us with austere contempt: what did we know? What would we doubt next? Jimmy's desire encouraged by us and aided by Wamibo's spells delayed the ship in the open sea. Only lubberly fools couldn't see it. Whoever heard of such a run of calms and head winds? It wasn't natural . . . We could not deny that it was strange. We felt uneasy. The common saying, 'more days, more dollars,' did not give the usual comfort because the stores were running short. Much had been spoiled off the Cape, and we were on half allowance of biscuit. Peas, sugar and tea had been finished long ago. Salt meat was giving out. We had plenty of coffee but very little water to make it with. We took up another hole in our belts and went on scraping, polishing, painting the ship from morning to night. And soon she looked as though she had come out of a band-box; but hunger lived on board of her. Not dead starvation, but steady, living hunger that stalked about on the decks, slept in the forecastle; the tormentor of waking moments, the disturber of dreams. We looked to windward for signs of change. Every few hours of night and day we put her round with the hope that she would come up on that tack at last! She didn't. She seemed to have forgotten the way home; she rushed to and fro, heading north-west, heading east; she ran backwards and forwards, distracted, like a timid creature at the foot of a wall. Sometimes, as if tired to death, she would wallow languidly for a day in the smooth swell of an unruffled sea. All up to the swinging masts the sails thrashed furiously through the hot stillness of the calm. We were weary, hungry, thirsty; we commenced to believe Singleton, but with unshaken fidelity dissembled to Jimmy. We spoke to him with jocose allusiveness, like cheerful accomplices in a clever plot; but we looked to the westward over the rail with mournful eyes for a sign of hope, for a sign of fair wind; even if its first breath should bring death to our reluctant Jimmy. In vain! The universe conspired with James Wait. Light airs from the northward sprung up again; the sky remained clear; and round our weariness the glittering sea. touched by the breeze, basked voluptuously in the great sunshine, as though it had forgotten our life and trouble.

Donkin looked out for a fair wind along with the rest. No one knew the venom of his thoughts now. He was silent, and appeared thinner, as if consumed slowly by an inward rage at the injustice of men and fate. He was ignored by all and spoke to no one, but his hate for every man looked out through his eyes. He talked with the cook only, having somehow persuaded the good man that he—Donkin—was a much calumniated and persecuted person. Together they bewailed the immorality of the ship's company. There could be no greater criminals than we, who by our lies conspired to send the soul of a poor ignorant black man to ever-lasting perdition. Podmore cooked what there was to cook, remorsefully, and felt all the time that by preparing the food of such sinners he imperilled his own salvation. As to the Captain—he had lived with him for seven years, he said, and would not have believed it possible that such a man . . . 'Well. Well . . . There it is . . . Can't get out of it. Judgment capsized all in a minute . . . Struck in all his pride . . . More like a visitation than anything else.' Donkin, perched sullenly on the coal-locker, swung his legs and concurred. He paid in the coin of spurious assent for the privilege to sit in the galley; he was disheartened and scandalised; he agreed with the cook; could find no words severe enough to criticise our conduct; and when in the heat of reprobation he swore at us, Podmore, who would have liked to swear also if it hadn't been for his principles, pretended not to hear. So Donkin, unrebuked, cursed enough for two, cadged for matches, borrowed tobacco, and loafed for hours, very much at home before the stove. From there he could hear us on the other side of the bulkhead, talking to Jimmy. The cook knocked the pots about, slammed the oven door, muttered prophecies of damnation for all the ship's company; and Donkin, who did not admit of any hereafter, except for the purposes of blasphemy, listened, concentrated and angry, gloating fiercely over a called-up image of infinite torment—like men gloat over the accursed images of cruelty and revenge, of greed, and of power . . .

On clear evenings the silent ship, under the cold sheen of the dead moon, took on the false aspect of passionless repose resembling the winter of the earth. Under her a long band of gold barred the black disc of the sea. Footsteps echoed on her quiet decks. The moonlight clung to her like a frosted mist, and the white sails stood out in dazzling cones as of stainless snow. In the magnificence of the phantom rays the ship appeared pure like a vision of ideal beauty, illusive like a tender dream of serene peace. And nothing in her was real, nothing was distinct and solid but the heavy shadows that filled her decks with their unceasing and noiseless stir; the shadows blacker than the night and more restless than the thoughts of men.

Donkin prowled spiteful and alone amongst the shadows, thinking that Jimmy too long delayed to die. That evening, just before dark, land had been reported from aloft, and the master, while adjusting the tubes of the long glass, had observed with quiet bitterness to Mr. Baker that, after fighting our way inch by inch to the Western Islands there was nothing to expect now but a spell of calm. The sky was clear and the barometer high. The light breeze dropped with the sun, and an enormous stillness, the forerunner of a night without wind, descended upon the heated waters of the ocean. As long as daylight lasted, the hands collected on the forecastle-head watched on the eastern sky the island of Flores, that rose above the level expanse of the sea with irregular and broken outlines like a sombre ruin upon a vast and deserted plain. It was the first land seen for nearly four months. Charley was excited, and in the midst of general indulgence took liberties with his betters. Men strangely elated without knowing why, talked in groups, and pointed with bared arms. For the first time that voyage Jimmy's sham existence seemed for a moment forgotten in the face of a solid reality. We had got so far anyhow. Belfast discoursed, quoting imaginary examples of short homeward passages from the Islands. 'Them smart fruit schooners do it in five days,' he affirmed. 'What do you want?—only a good little breeze.' Archie maintained that seven days was the shortest passage, and they disputed amicably with insulting words. Knowles declared he could already smell home from there, and with a heavy list on his short leg laughed fit to split his sides. A group of grizzled sea-dogs looked out for a time in silence and with grim absorbed faces. One said suddenly—'Tain't far to London now.'—'My first night ashore, blamme if I haven't steak and onions for supper . . . and a pint of bitter,' said another.—'A barrel ye mean,' shouted some one.—'Ham an' eggs three times a day. That's the way I live!' cried an excited voice. There was a stir, appreciative murmurs; eyes began to shine; jaws champed; short nervous laughs were heard. Archie smiled with reserve all to himself. Singleton came up, gave a negligent glance, and went down again without saying a word, indifferent, like a man who had seen Flores an incalculable number of times. The night travelling from the East blotted out of the limpid sky the purple stain of the high land. 'Dead calm,' said somebody quietly. The murmur of lively talk suddenly wavered, died out; the clusters broke up; men began to drift away one by one, descending the ladders slowly and with serious faces as if sobered by that reminder of their dependence upon the invisible. And when the big yellow moon ascended gently above the sharp rim of the clear horizon it found the ship wrapped up in a breathless silence; a fearless ship that seemed to sleep profoundly, dreamlessly, on the bosom of the sleeping and terrible sea.

Donkin chafed at the peace—at the ship—at the sea that stretched away on all sides merged into the illimitable silence of all creation. He felt himself pulled up sharp by unrecognised grievances. He had been physically cowed, but his injured dignity remained indomitable, and nothing could heal his lacerated feelings. Here was land already—home very soon—a bad pay-day—no clothes—more hard work. How offensive all this was. Land. The land draws away life from sick sailors. That nigger there had money—clothes—easy times; and would not die. Land draws life away . . . He felt tempted to go and see whether it did. Perhaps already . . . It would be a bit of luck. There was money in the beggar's chest. He stepped briskly out of the shadows into the moonlight, and, instantly, his craving, hungry face from sallow became livid. He opened the door of the cabin and had a shock. Sure enough, Jimmy was dead! He moved no more than a recumbent figure with clasped hands, carved on the lid of a stone coffin. Donkin glared with avidity. Then Jimmy, without stirring, blinked his eyelids, and Donkin had another shock. Those eyes were rather startling. He shut the door behind his back with gentle care, looking intently the while at James Wait as though he had come in there at great risk to tell some secret of startling importance. Jimmy did not move but glanced languidly out of the corners of his eyes. 'Calm?' he asked.—'Yuss,' said Donkin, very disappointed, and sat down on the box.

Jimmy breathed with composure. He was use to such visits at all times of night or day. Men succeeded one another. They spoke in clear voices, pronounced cheerful words, repeated old jokes, listened to him; and each, going out, seemed to leave behind a little of his own vitality, surrender some of his own strength, renew the assurance of life—the indestructable thing! He did not like to be alone in his cabin, because, when he was alone, it seemed to him as if he hadn't been there at all. There was nothing. No pain. Not now. Perfectly right—but he couldn't enjoy his healthful repose unless some one was by to see it. This man would do as anybody. Donkin watched him stealthily.—'Soon home now,' observed Wait.—'Why d'yer whisper?' asked Donkin with interest, 'can't you speak hup?' Jimmy looked annoyed and said nothing for a while; then in a lifeless unringing voice:—'Why should I shout? You ain't deaf that I know.'—'Oh! I can 'ear right enough,' answered Donkin in a low tone, and looked down. He was thinking sadly of going out when Jimmy spoke again.—'Time we did get home . . . to get something decent to eat . . . I am always hungry.' Donkin felt angry all of a sudden.—'What habout me,' he hissed, 'I am 'ungry too an' got ter work. You, 'ungry!'—'Your work won't kill you,' commented Wait, feebly; 'there's a couple of biscuits in the lower bunk there—you may have one. I can't eat them.' Donkin dived in, groped in the corner and when he came up again his mouth was full. He munched with ardour. Jimmy seemed to doze with open eyes. Donkin finished his hard bread and got up.—'You're not going? asked Jimmy, staring at the ceiling.—'No,' said Donkin impulsively, and instead of going out leaned his back against the closed door. He looked at James Wait, and saw him long, lean, dried up, as though all his flesh had shrivelled on his bones in the heat of a white furnace; the meagre fingers of one hand moved lightly upon the edge of the bunk playing an endless tune. To look at him was irritating and fatiguing; he could last like this for days; he was outrageous—belonging wholly neither to death nor life, and perfectly invulnerable in his apparent ignorance of both. Donkin felt tempted to enlighten him.—'What hare yer thinkin' of?' he asked surlily. James Wait had a grimacing smile that passed over the deathlike impassiveness of his bony face. incredible and frightful as would, in a dream, have been the sudden smile of a corpse.

'There is a girl,' whispered Wait . . . 'Canton Street girl—She chucked a third engineer of a Rennie boat—for me. Cooks oysters just as I like . . . She says—she would chuck—any toff—for a coloured gentleman . . . That's me. I am kind to women.' he added a shade louder.

Donkin could hardly believe his ears. He was scandalised.— 'Would she? Yer wouldn't be hany good to 'er,' he said with unrestrained disgust. Wait was not there to hear him. He was swaggering up the east India Dock Road; saying kindly, 'Come along for a treat.' pushing glass swing-doors,, posing with superb assurance in the gaslight above a mahogany counter.—'D'yer think yer will hever get ashore?' asked Donkin angrily. Wait came back with a start.—'Ten days,' he said promptly, and returned at once to the regions of memory that know nothing of time. He felt untired, calm, and as if safely withdrawn within himself beyond the reach of every grave incertitude. There was something of the immutable quality of eternity in the slow moments of his complete restfulness. He was very quiet and easy amongst his vivid reminiscences which he mistook joyfully for images of an undoubted future. He cared for no one. Donkin felt this vaguely like a blind man may feel in his darkness the fatal antagonism of all the surrounding existences, that to him shall for ever remain irrealisable, unseen and enviable. He had a desire to assert his importance, to break, to crush; to be even with everybody for everything; to tear the veil, unmask expose, leave no refuge—a perfidious desire of truthfulness! He laughed in a mocking splutter and said:

'Ten days. Strike me blind if I hever! . . . You will be dead by this time to-morrow p'r'aps. Ten days!' He waited for a while. 'D'ye 'ear me? Blamme if yer don't look dead halready.'

Jimmy must have been collecting his strength for he said almost aloud—'You're a stinking, cadging liar. Every one knows you.' And sitting up, against all probability, startled his visitor horribly. But very soon Donkin recovered himself. He blustered, 'What? What? Who's a liar? You hare—the crowd hare—the skipper—heverybody. I hain't! Putting on hairs! Who's yer?' He nearly choked himself with indignation. 'Who's yer to put on hairs,' he repeated trembling. ''Ave one—'ave one, says 'ee—an' cawn't heat 'em 'isself. Now I'll 'ave both. By Gawd—I will! Yer nobody!'

He plunged into the lower bunk, rooted in there and brought to light another dusty biscuit. He held it up before Jimmy—then took a bite defiantly.

'What now?' he asked with feverish impatience. 'Yer may take one—says yer. Why not giv' me both? No. I'm a mangy dorg. One for a mangy dorg. I'll tyke both. Can yer stop me? Try. Come on. Try.'

Jimmy was clasping his legs and hiding his face on the knees. His shirt clung to him. Every rib was visible. His emaciated back was shaken in repeated jerks by the panting catches of his breath.

'Yer won't? Yer can't? What did I say?' went on Donkin fiercely. He swallowed another dry mouthful with a hasty effort. The other's silent helplessness, his weakness, his shrinking attitude exasperated him. 'Ye're done!' he cried. 'Who's yer to be lied to; to be waited on 'and and foot like a bloomin' hymperor. Yer nobody. Yer no one at all!' he spluttered with such a strength of unerring conviction that it shook him from head to foot in coming out, and left him vibrating like a released string.

Jimmy rallied again. He lifted his head and turned bravely at Donkin, who saw a strange face, an unknown face, a fantastic and grimacing mask of despair and fury. Its lips moved rapidly; and hollow, moaning, whistling sounds filled the cabin with a vague mutter full of menace, complaint and desolation, like the far-off murmur of a rising wind. Wait shook his head; rolled his eyes; he denied, cursed, menaced—and not a word had the strength to pass beyond the sorrowful pout of those black lips. It was incomprehensible and disturbing; a gibberish of emotions, a frantic dumb show of speech pleading for impossible things, threatening a shadowy vengeance. It sobered Donkin into a scrutinising watchfulness.

'Yer can't holler. See? What did I tell yer?' he said slowly after a moment of attentive examination. The other kept on headlong and unheard, nodding passionately, grinning with grotesque and appalling flashes of big white teeth. Donkin, as if fascinated by the dumb eloquence and anger of that black phantom, approached, stretching his neck out with distrustful curiosity; and it seemed to him suddenly that he was looking only at the shadow of a man crouching high in the bunk on the level with his eyes.—'What? What?' he said. He seemed to catch the shape of some words in the continuous panting hiss. 'Yer will tell Belfast! Will yer? Hare yer a bloomin' kid?' He trembled with alarm and rage. 'Tell yer gran'mother! Yer afeard! Who's yer ter be afeard more'n hanyone?' His passionate sense of his own importance ran away with a last remnant of caution. 'Tell an' be damned! Tell if yer can!' he cried. 'I've been treated worse'n a dorg by your blooming back-lickers. They 'as set me on, honly to turn against me, I ham the honly man 'ere. They choked me, kicked me—an' yer laffed—yer black, rotten hincumbrance, you! You will pay fur it. They giv' yer their grub, their water—yer will pay fur hit to me, by Gawd! Who haxed me ter 'ave a drink of water? They put their bloomin' rags on yer that night, an' what did they giv' ter me—a clout on the bloomin' mouth—blast their . . . S'elp me! . . . Yer will pay fur hit with yer money. Hi'm goin' ter 'ave it in a minyte; has soon has ye're dead, yer bloomin' useless fraud. That's the man I ham. An ye're a thing——a bloody thing. Yah—you corpse!'

He flung at Jimmy's head the biscuit he had been all the time clutching hard, but it only grazed, and striking with a loud crack the bulkhead beyond burst like a hand-grenade into flying pieces. James Wait, as though wounded mortally, fell back on the pillow. His lips ceased to move and the rolling eyes became quiet and stared upwards with an intense and steady persistence. Donkin was surprised; he sat suddenly on the chest, and looked down, exhausted and gloomy. After a moment he began to mutter to himself, 'Die, you beggar—die. Somebody'll come in . . . I wish I was drunk . . . Ten days . . . Hoysters

. . .' He looked up and spoke louder. 'No . . . no more for yer . . . no more bloomin' gals that cook hoysters . . . Who's yer? Hit's my turn now . . . I wish I was drunk; I would soon giv' you a leg up haloft. That's where yer will go. Feet first, through a port . . . Splash! Never see yer hany more. Hoverboard! Good 'nuff fur yer.'

Jimmy's head moved slightly and he turned his eyes to Donkin's face; a gaze unbelieving, desolated and appealing, of a child frightened by the menace of being shut up alone in the dark. Donkin observed him from the chest with hopeful eyes; then without rising he tried the lid. Locked. 'I wish I was drunk.' he muttered and getting up listened anxiously to the distant sound of footsteps on the deck. They approached—ceased. Some one yawned interminably just outside the door, and the footsteps went away shuffling lazily. Donkin's fluttering heart eased its pace, and when he looked towards the bunk again Jimmy was staring as before at the white beam.—''Ow d'yer feel now?' he asked.—'Bad,' breathed out Jimmy.

Donkin sat down patient and purposeful. Every half-hour the bells spoke to one another ringing along the whole length of the ship. Jimmy's respiration was so rapid that it couldn't be counted, so faint that it couldn't be heard. His eyes were terrified as though he had been looking at unspeakable horrors; and by his face one could see that he was thinking of abominable things. Suddenly with an incredibly strong and heart-breaking voice he sobbed out:

'Overboard! . . . I! . . . My God!'

Donkin writhed a little on the box. He looked unwillingly. Jimmy was mute. His two long bony hands smoothed the blanket upwards, as though he had wished to gather it all up under his chin. A tear, a big solitary tear, escaped from the corner of his eye and, without touching the hollow cheek, fell on the pillow, his throat rattled faintly.

And Donkin, watching the end of that hateful nigger, felt the anguishing grasp of a great sorrow on his heart at the thought that he himself, some day, would have to go through it all—just like this—perhaps! His eyes became moist. 'Poor beggar,' he murmured. The night seemed to go by in a flash; it seemed to him he could hear the irremediable rush of precious minutes. How long would this blooming affair last? Too long surely. No luck. He could not restrain himself. He got up and approached the bunk. Wait did not stir. Only his eyes appeared alive and his hands continued their smoothing movement with a horrible and tireless industry. Donkin bent over.

'Jimmy,' he called low. There was no answer, but the rattle stopped. 'D'yer see me?' he asked trembling. Jimmy's chest heaved. Donkin, looking away, bent his ear to Jimmy's lips and heard a sound like the rustle of a single dry leaf driven along the smooth sand of a beach. It shaped itself.

'Light . . . the lamp . . . and . . . go.' breathed out Wait.

Donkin, instinctively, glanced over his shoulder at the blazing flame; then, still looking away, felt under the pillow for a key. he got it at once and for the next few minutes was shakily but swiftly busy about the box. when he got up, his face—for the fist time in his life—had a pink flush—perhaps of triumph.

He slipped the key under the pillow again, avoiding to glance at Jimmy, who had not moved. He turned his back squarely from the bunk and started to the door as though he were going to walk a mile. At his second stride he had his nose against it. He clutched the handle cautiously, but at that moment he received the irresistible impression of something happening behind his back. He spun round as though he had been tapped on the shoulder. He was just in time to see Jimmy's eyes blaze up and go out at once like two lamps overturned together by a sweeping blow. Something resembling a scarlet thread hung down his chin out of the corner of his lips—and he had ceased to breathe.

Donkin closed the door behind him gently but firmly. Sleeping men, huddled under jackets, made on the lighted deck shapeless dark mounds that had the appearance of neglected graves. Nothing had been done all through the night and he hadn't been missed. He stood motionless and perfectly astounded to find the world outside as he had left it; there was the sea, the ship—sleeping men; and he wondered absurdly at it, as though he had expected to find the men dead, familiar things gone for ever; as though, like a wanderer returning after many years, he had expected to see bewildering changes. He shuddered a little in the penetrating freshness of the air, and hugged himself forlornly. The declining moon drooped sadly in the western board as if withered by the cold touch of a pale dawn. The ship slept. And the immortal sea stretched away, immense and hazy, like the image of life with a glittering surface and lightless depths; promising, empty inspiring—terrible. Donkin gave it a defiant glance and slunk off noiselessly as if judged and cast out by the august silence of its might.

Jimmy's death, after all, came as a tremendous surprise. We did not know till then how much faith we had put in his delusions. We had taken his chances of life so much at his own valuation that his death, like the death of an old belief shook the foundations of our society. A common bond was gone; the strong, effective and respectable bond of a sentimental lie. All that day we mooned at our work, with suspicious looks and a disabused air. In our hearts we thought that in the matter of his departure Jimmy had acted in a perverse and unfriendly manner. He didn't back us up, as a shipmate should. In going he took away with himself the gloomy and solemn shadow in which our folly had posed, with human satisfaction, as a tender arbiter of fate. And now we saw it was no such thing. It was just common foolishness; a silly and ineffectual meddling with issues of majestic import—that is, if Podmore was right. Perhaps he was? Doubt survived Jimmy; and, like a community of banded criminals disintegrated by a touch of grace, we were profoundly scandalised with each other. Men spoke unkindly to their best chums. Others refused to speak at all. Singleton only was not surprised. 'Dead—is he? Of course,' he said, pointing at the island right abeam: for the calm still held the ship spell-bound within sight of Flores. Dead—of course. He wasn't surprised. Here was the land, and there, on the forehatch and waiting for the sailmaker—there was that corpse. Cause and effect. And for the fist time that voyage, the old seaman became quite cheery and garrulous, explaining and illustrating from the stores of experience how, in sickness, the sight of an island (even a very small one) is generally more fatal than the view of a continent. But he couldn't explain why.

Jimmy was to be buried at five, and it was a long day till then—a day of mental disquiet and even of physical disturbance. We took no interest in our work and, very properly, were rebuked for it. This, in our constant state of hungry irritation, was exasperating. Donkin worked with his brow bound in a dirty rag, and looked so ghastly that Mr. Baker was touched with compassion at the sight of this plucky suffering.—'Ough! You, Donkin! Put down your work and go lay-up this watch. You look ill.'—'Hi ham, sir—in my 'ead,' he said in a subdued voice, and vanished speedily. This annoyed many, and they thought the mate 'bloomin' soft to-day.' Captain Allistoun could be seen on the poop watching the sky cloud over from the south-west, and it soon got to be known about the decks that the barometer had begun to fall in the night and that a breeze might be expected before long. This, by a subtle association of ideas, led to violent quarrelling as to the exact moment of Jimmy's death. Was it before or after 'that 'ere glass started down'? It was impossible to know and it caused much contemptuous growling at one another. All of a sudden there was a great tumult forward. Pacific Knowles and good-tempered Davies had come to blows over it. The watch below interfered with spirit, and for ten minutes there was a noisy scrimmage round the hatch, where, in the balancing shade of the sails, Jimmy's body, wrapped up in a white blanket, was watched over by the sorrowful Belfast, who, in his desolation, disdained the fray. When the noise had ceased, and the passions had calmed into surly silence, he stood up at the head of the swathed body, and lifting both arms on high, cried with pained indignation:—'You ought to be ashamed of your-selves! . . .' We were.

Belfast took his bereavement very hard. He gave proofs of unextinguishable devotion. It was he, and no other man, who would help the sailmaker to prepare what was left of Jimmy for a solemn surrender to the insatiable sea. He arranged the weights carefully at the feet; two holystones, an old anchor-shackle without its pin, some broken links of a worn-out stream cable. He arranged them this way, then that. 'Bless my soul! you aren't afraid he will chafe his heel?' said the sailmaker, who hated the job. He pushed the needle, puffing furiously, with his head in a cloud of tobacco smoke; he turned the flaps over, pulled at the stitches, stretched the canvas.—'Lift his shoulders . . . Pull to you a bit . . . So—o—o—. Steady.' Belfast obeyed, pulled, lifted, overcame with sorrow, dropping tears on the tarred twine.—'Don't you drag the canvas too taut over his poor face, Sails,' he entreated tearfully.—'What are you fashing yourself for? He will be comfortable enough,' assured the sailmaker, cutting the thread after the last stitch, that came about the middle of Jimmy's forehead. He rolled up the remaining canvas, put away the needles. 'What makes you take on so?' he asked. Belfast looked down at the long package of grey sailcloth.—'I pulled him out,' he whispered, 'and he did not want to go. If I had sat up with him last night he would have kept alive for me . . . but something made me tired.' The sailmaker took vigorous draws at his pipe and mumbled:—'When I . . . West India Station . . . In the *Blanche* frigate . . . Yellow Jack . . . sewed in twenty men a day . . . Portsmouth—Devonport men—townies—knew their fathers, mothers—sisters—the whole boiling of 'em. Thought nothing of it. And these niggers like this one—you don't know where it comes from. Got nobody. No use to nobody. Who will miss him?'—'I do—I pulled him out,' mourned Belfast dismally.

On two planks nailed together, and apparently resigned and still under the folds of the Union Jack with a white border, James Wait, carried aft by four men, was deposited slowly, with his feet pointing at an open port. A swell had set in from the westward, and following on the roll of the ship, the red ensign, at half-mast, darted out and collapsed again on the grey sky, like a tongue of flickering fire; Charley tolled the bell; and at every swing to starboard the whole vast semi-circle of steely waters visible on that side seemed to come up with a rush to the edge of the port, as if impatient to get at our Jimmy. Every one was there but Donkin, who was too ill to come; the Captain and Mr. Creighton stood bareheaded on the break of the poop; Mr. Baker, directed by the master, who had said to him gravely:—'You know more about the prayer book than I do,' came out of the cabin door quickly and a little embarrassed. All the caps went off. He began to read in a low tone, and with his usual harmlessly menacing utterance, as though he had been for the last time reproving confidentially that dead seaman at his feet. The men listened in scattered groups; they leaned on the fife rail, gazing on the deck; they held their chins in their hands thoughtfully, or, with crossed arms and one knee slightly bent, hung their heads in an attitude of upright meditation. Wamibo dreamed. Mr. Baker read on, grunting reverently at the turn of every page. The words, missing the unsteady hearts of men, rolled out to wander without a home upon the heartless sea; and James Wait, silenced forever, lay uncritical and passive under the hoarse murmur of despair and hopes.

Two men made ready and waited for those words that send so many of our brothers to their last plunge. Mr. Baker began the last passage. 'Stand by.' muttered the boatswain. Mr. Baker read out:' To the deep,' and paused. The men lifted the inboard end of the planks, the boatswain snatched off the Union Jack, and James Wait did not move.—'Higher,' muttered the boatswain angrily. All the heads were raised; every man stirred uneasily, but James Wait gave no sign of going. In death and swathed up for all eternity, he yet seemed to hang on to the ship with the grip of an undying fear. 'Higher! Lift!' whispered the boatswain fiercely.—'He won't go,' stammered one of the men shakily, and both appeared ready to drop everything. Mr. Baker waited, burying his face in the book, and shuffling his feet nervously. All the men looked profoundly disturbed, from their midst a faint humming noise spread out—growing louder . . . 'Jimmy!' cried Belfast in a wailing tone, and there was a second of shuddering dismay.

'Jimmy, be a man!' he shrieked passionately. Every mouth was wide open, not an eyelid winked. He stared wildly, twitching all over; he bent his body forward like a man peering at an horror. 'Go, Jimmy!—Jimmy, go! Go!' His fingers touched the head of the body and the grey package started reluctantly to, all at once, whizz off the lifted planks with the suddenness of a flash of lightning. The crowd stepped forward like one man; a deep Ah—h—h! came out vibrating from the broad chests. The ship rolled as if relieved of an unfair burden; the sails flapped. Belfast, supported by Archie, gasped hysterically; and Charley, who anxious to see Jimmy's last dive, leaped headlong on the rail, was too late to see anything but the faint circle of a vanishing ripple.

Mr. Baker, perspiring abundantly, read out the last prayer in a deep rumour of excited men and fluttering sails. 'Amen!' he said in an unsteady growl, and closed the book.

'Square the yards!' thundered a voice above his head. All hands gave a jump; one or two dropped their caps; Mr. Baker looked up surprised. The master, standing on the break of the poop, pointed to the westward. 'Breeze coming,' he said, 'square the yards. Look alive, men!' Mr. Baker crammed the book hurriedly into his pocket.— 'Forward there—let go the foretack!' he hailed joy fully bareheaded and brisk; 'Square the foreyard, you port-watch!'—'Fair wind—fair wind,' muttered the men going to the braces.—'What did I tell you?' mumbled old Singleton, flinging down coil after coil with hasty energy; 'I knowed it!—he's gone, and here it comes.'

It came with the sound of a lofty and powerful sigh. The sails filled, the ship gathered way, and the waking sea began to murmur sleepily of home to the ears of men.

That night, while the ship rushed foaming to the Northward before a freshening gale, the boatswain unbosomed himself to the petty officers' berth:—'The chap was nothing but trouble,' he said, 'from the moment he came aboard—d'ye remember—that night in Bombay? Been bullying all that softy crowd—cheeked the old man—we had to go fooling all over a half-drowned ship to save him. Dam' nigh a mutiny all for him—and now the mate abused me like a pickpocket for forgetting to dab a lump of grease on them planks. So I did, but you ought to have known better too, than to leave a nail sticking up—hey, Chips?' 'And you ought to have known better than to chuck all my tools overboard for 'im, like a skeary greenhorn,' retorted the morose carpenter. 'Well—he's gone after 'em now,' he added in an unforgiving tone. 'On the China Station, I remember once, the Admiral he says to me . . .' began the sailmaker.

A week afterwards the *Narcissus* entered the chops of the Channel.

Under white wings she skimmed low over the blue sea like a great tired bird speeding to its nest. The clouds raced with her mastheads; they rose astern enormous and white, soared to the zenith, flew past, and falling down the wide curve of the sky seemed to dash headlong into the sea—the clouds swifter than the ship, more free, but without a home. The coast to welcome her stepped out of space into the sunshine. The lofty headlands trod masterfully into the sea; the wide bays smiled in the light; the shadows of homeless clouds ran along the sunny plains, leaped over valleys, without a check darted up the hills, rolled down the slopes; and the sunshine pursued them with patches of running brightness. On the brows of dark cliffs white lighthouses shone in pillars of light. The Channel glittered like a blue mantle shot with gold and starred by the silver of the capping seas. The *Narcissus* rushed past the headlands and the bays. Outward-bound vessels crossed her track, lying over, and with their masts stripped for a slogging fight with the hard sou'wester. And, inshore, a string of smoking steamboats waddled, hugging the coast, like migrating and amphibious monsters, distrustful of the restless waves.

At night the headlands retreated, the bays advanced into one unbroken line of gloom. The lights of the earth mingled with the lights of heaven; and above the tossing lanterns of a trawling fleet a great lighthouse shone steadily, such as an enormous riding light burning above a vessel of fabulous dimensions Below its steady glow, the coast, stretching away straight and black, resembled the high side of an indestructible craft riding motionless upon the immortal and unresting sea. The dark land lay alone in the midst of waters, like a mighty ship bestarred with vigilant lights—a ship carrying the burden of millions of lives—a ship freighted with dross and with jewels, with gold and with steel. She towered up immense and strong, guarding priceless traditions and untold suffering, sheltering glorious memories and base forgetfulness, ignoble virtues and splendid transgressions. A great ship!

For ages had the ocean battered in vain her enduring sides; she was there when the was vaster and darker, when the sea was great and mysterious, and ready to surrender the prize of fame to audacious men. A ship mother of fleets and nations! The great flagship of the race; stronger than the storms! and anchored in the open sea.

The *Narcissus*, heeling over to off-shore gusts, rounded the South Foreland, passed through the Downs, and, in tow, entered the river. Shorn of the glory of her white wings, she wound obediently after the tug through the maze of invisible channels. As she passed them the red-painted light-vessels, swung at their moorings seemed for an instant to sail with great speed in the rush of tide, and the next moment were left hopelessly behind. The big buoys on the tails of banks slipped past her sides very low, and, dropping in her wake, tugged at their chains like fierce watch-dogs. The reach narrowed; from both sides the land approached the ship. She went steadily up the river. On the riverside slopes the houses appeared in groups—seemed to stream down the declivities at a run to see her pass, and, checked by the mud of the foreshore, crowded on the banks. Further on, the tall factory chimneys appeared in insolent bands and watched her go by, like a straggling crowd of slim giants swaggering and upright under the black plummets of smoke cavalierly aslant. She swept round the bends; an impure breeze shrieked a welcome between her stripped spars; and the land, closing in, stepped between the ship and the sea.

A low cloud hung before her—a great opalescent and tremulous cloud, that seemed to rise from the steaming brows of millions of men. Long drifts of smoky vapours soiled it with livid trails; it throbbed to the beat of millions of hearts, and from it came an immense and lamentable murmur—the murmur of millions of lips praying, cursing, sighing, jeering—the undying murmur of folly, regret, and hope exhaled by the crowds of the anxious earth. The *Narcissus* entered the cloud; the shadows deepened; on all sides there was the clang of iron, the sound of mighty blows, shrieks, yells. Black barges drifted stealthily on the murky stream. A mad jumble of begrimed walls loomed up vaguely in the smoke, bewildering and mournful, like a vision of disaster. The tugs, panting furiously, backed and filled in the stream, to hold the ship steady at the dock-gates; from her bows two lines went through the air whistling, and struck at the land viciously, like a pair of snakes. A bridge broke in two before her, as if by enchantment; big hydraulic capstans began to turn all by themselves, as though animated by a mysterious and unholy spell. She moved through a narrow lane of water between two low walls of granite, and men with check-ropes in their hands kept pace with her, walking on the broad flagstones. A group waited impatiently on each side of the vanished bridge: rough heavy men in caps; sallow-faced men in high hats; two bareheaded women; ragged children, fascinated and with wide eyes. A cart coming at a jerky trot pulled up sharply. One of the women screamed at the silent ship—'Hallo, Jack!' without looking at any one in particular, and all hands looked at her from the forecastle head.— 'Stand clear! Stand clear of that rope!' cried the dockmen, bending over stone posts. The crowd murmured, stamped where they stood.—'Let go your quarter-checks! Let go!' sang out a ruddy-faced old man on the quay. The ropes splashed heavily falling in the water, and the *Narcissus* entered the dock.

The stony shores ran away right and left in straight lines, enclosing a sombre and rectangular pool. brick walls rose high above the water— soulless walls, staring through hundreds of windows as troubled and dull as the eyes of over-fed brutes. At their base monstrous iron cranes crouched, with chains hanging from their long necks, balancing cruel-looking hooks over the decks of lifeless ships. A noise of wheels rolling over stones, the thump of heavy things falling, the racket of feverish winches, the grinding of strained chains, floated on the air. Between high buildings the dust of all the continents soared in short flights; and a penetrating smell of perfumes and dirt, of spices and hides, of things costly and of things filthy, pervaded the space, made for it an atmosphere precious and disgusting. The *Narcissus* came gently into her berth; the shadows of soulless walls fell upon her, the dust of all the continents leaped upon her deck, and a swarm of strange men, clambering up her sides, took possession of her in the name of the sordid earth. She had ceased to live.

A toff in a black coat and high hat scrambled with agility, came up to the second mate, shook hands, and said:—'Hallo, Herbert.' It was his brother. A lady appeared suddenly. A real lady, in a black dress and with a parasol. She looked extremely elegant in the midst of us, and as strange as if she had fallen there from the sky. Mr. Baker touched his cap to her. It was the master's wife. And very soon the Captain, dressed very smartly and in a white shirt, went with her over the side. We didn't recognise him at all till, turning on the quay, he called to Mr. Baker:—'Remember to wind up the chronometers to-morrow morning.' An underhand lot of seedy-looking chaps with shifty eyes wandered in and out of the forecastle looking for a job—they said— 'More likely for something to steal,' commented Knowles cheerfully. Poor beggars. Who cared? Weren't we home! But Mr. Baker went for one of them who had given him some cheek, and we were delighted. Everything was delightful—'I've finished aft, sir,' called out Mr. Creighton.—'No water in the well, sir,' reported for the last time the carpenter, sounding-rod in hand. Mr. Baker glanced along the decks at the expectant groups of men, glanced aloft at the yards.—'Ough! That will do, men.' he grunted. The groups broke up. The voyage was ended.

Rolled-up beds went flying over the rail; lashed chests went sliding along the gangway—mighty few of both at that. 'The rest is having a cruise off the Cape,' explained Knowles enigmatically to a dock-loafer with whom he had struck a sudden friendship. Men ran, calling to one another, hailing utter strangers to 'lend a hand with the dunnage,' then sudden decorum approached the mate to shake hands before going ashore.—'Good-bye, sir,' they repeated in various tones. Mr. Baker grasped hard palms, grunted in a friendly manner at every one, his eyes twinkled.—'Take care of your money, Knowles. Ough! Soon get a nice wife if you do.' The lame man was delighted.—'Good-bye, sir,' said Belfast with emotion, wringing the mate's hand, and looked up with swimming eyes. 'I thought I would take 'im ashore with me,' he went on plaintively. Mr. Baker did not understand, but said kindly:—'Take care of yourself, Craik,' and the bereaved Belfast went over the rail mourning and alone.

Mr. Baker in the sudden peace of the ship moved about solitary and grunting, trying door handles peering into dark places, never done—a model chief mate! No one waited for him ashore. Mother dead; father and two brothers, Yarmouth fishermen, drowned together on the Dogger Bank; sister married and unfriendly. Quite a lady. Married to the leading tailor of a little town, and its leading politician, who did not think his sailor brother-in-law quite respectable enough for him. Quite a lady, quite a lady, he thought, sitting down for a moment's rest on the quarter-hatch. Time enough to go ashore and get a bite, and sup, and a bed somewhere. He didn't like to part with the ship. No one to think about then. The darkness of a misty evening fell, cold and damp, upon the deserted deck; and Mr. Baker sat smoking, thinking of all the successive ships to whom through many years he had given the best of a seaman's care. And never a command in sight. Not once!—'I haven't somehow the cut of a skipper about me,' he meditated placidly, while the shipkeeper (who had taken possession of the galley), a wizened old man with bleared eyes, cursed him, in whispers for 'hanging about so.'—'Now Creighton,' he pursued the unenvious train of thought. 'quite a gentleman . . . swell friends . . . will get on. Fine young fellow . . . a little more experience.' He got up and shook himself. 'I'll be back first thing to-morrow morning for the hatches. Don't you let them touch anything before I come, shipkeeper,' he called out. Then, at last, he also went ashore—a model chief mate!

The men scattered by the dissolving contract of the land came together once more in the shipping office.—'The *Narcissus* pays off,' shouted outside a glazed door a brass-bound old fellow with a crown and the capitals B. T. on his cap. A lot trooped in at once but many were late. The room was large, white-washed, and bare; a counter surmounted by a brass-wire grating fenced off a third of the dusty space, and behind the grating a pasty-faced clerk, with his hair parted in the middle, had the quick, glittering eyes and the vivacious, jerky movements of a caged bird. Poor Captain Allistoun also in there, and sitting before a little table with piles of gold and notes on it, appeared subdued by his captivity. Another Board of Trade bird was perching on a high stool near the door; an old bird that did not mind the chaff of elated sailors. The crew of the *Narcissus*, broken up into knots, pushed in the corners. They had new shore togs, smart jackets that looked as if they had been shaped with an axe, glossy trousers that seemed made of crumpled sheet-iron, collarless flannel shirts, shiny new boots. They tapped on shoulders, button-holed one another, slapped their thighs, stamped, with bursts of subdued laughter. Most had clean radiant faces; only one or two were dishevelled and sad; the two young Norwegians looked tidy, meek, and altogether of a promising material for the kind ladies that patronize the Scandinavian Home. Wamibo, still in his working clothes, dreamed, upright and burly in the middle of the room, and, when Archie came in, woke up for a smile. But the wide-awake clerk called out a name, and the paying-off business began.

One by one they came up to the pay-table to get the wages of their glorious and obscure toil. They swept the money with care into broad palms, rammed it trustfully into trousers pockets, or, turning their backs on the table, reckoned with difficulty in the hollow of their stiff hands.—'Money right? Sign the release. There—there,' repeated the clerk, impatiently. 'How stupid those sailors are!' he thought. Singleton came up, venerable—and uncertain as to daylight; brown drops of tobacco juice maculated his white beard; his hands, that never hesitated in the great light of the open sea, could hardly find the small pile of gold in the profound darkness of the shore. 'Can't write?' said the clerk, shocked. 'Make a mark, then.' Singleton painfully sketched in a heavy cross, blotted the page. 'What a disgusting old brute,' muttered the clerk. Somebody opened the door for him, and the patriarchal seaman passed through unsteadily, without as much as a glance at any of us.

Archie had a pocket-book. he was chaffed. Belfast, who looked wild, as though he had already luffed up through a public-house or two, gave signs of emotion and wanted to speak to Captain privately. The master was surprised. They spoke through the wires, and we could hear the Captain saying:—'I've given it up to the Board of Trade.' 'I should 've liked to get something of his,' mumbled Belfast. 'But you can't, my man. It's given up, locked and sealed, to the Marine Office,' expostulated the master; and Belfast stood back, with drooping mouth and troubled eyes. In a pause of the business we heard the master and the clerk talking. We caught 'James Wait—deceased—found no papers of any kind—no relations—no trace—the office must hold his wages then.' Donkin entered. He seemed out of breath, was grave, full of business. He went straight to the desk, talked with animation to the clerk, who thought him an intelligent man. They discussed the account, dropping h's against one another as if for a wager—very friendly.

Captain Allistoun paid. 'I give you a bad discharge,' he said, quietly. Donkin raised his voice:—'I don't want your bloomin' discharge— keep it. I'm goin' ter 'ave a job hashore.' He turned to us. 'No more bloomin' sea fur me,' he said, aloud. All looked at him. He had better clothes, had an easy air, appeared more at home than any of us; he stared with assurance, enjoying the effect of his declaration. 'Yuss. I 'ave friends well hoff. That's more'n yer got. But I ham a man. Yer shipmates for all that. Who's comin' fur a drink?'

No one moved. There was a silence; a silence of blank faces and stony looks. He waited a moment, smiled bitterly, and went to the door. There he faced round once more. 'Yer won't? Yer bloomin' lot of 'ypocrites. No? What 'ave I done to yer? Did I bully yer? Did I hurt yer? Did I? . . . Yer won't drink? . . . No! . . . Then may yer die of thirst, hevery mother's son of yer! Not one of yer 'as the sperrit of a bug. Ye're the scum of the world. Work and starve!'

He went out, and slammed the door with such violence that the old Board of Trade bird nearly fell off his perch.

'He's mad,' said Archie. 'No! No! He's drunk,' insisted Belfast, lurching about, and in a maudlin tone. Captain Allistoun sat smiling thoughtfully at the cleared pay-table.

Outside, on Tower Hill, they blinked, hesitated clumsily, as if blinded by the strange quality of the hazy light, as if discomposed by the view of so many men; and they who could hear one another in the howl of gales seemed deafened and distracted by the dull roar of the busy earth.—'To the Black Horse! To the Black Horse!' cried some. 'Let us have a drink together before we part.' They crossed the road, clinging to one another. Only Charlie and Belfast wandered off alone. As I came up I saw a red-faced, blowsy woman, in a grey shawl, and with dusty, fluffy hair, fall on Charley's neck. It was his mother. She slobbered over him:—'O, my boy! My boy!'—'Leggo of me,' said Charley, 'Leggo, mother!' I was passing him at the time, and over the untidy head of the blubbering woman he gave me a humorous smile and a glance ironic, courageous, and profound, that seemed to put all my knowledge of life to shame. I nodded and passed on, but heard him say again, good-naturedly:—'If you leggo of me this minyt—ye shall 'ave a bob for a drink out of my pay.' In the next few steps I came upon Belfast. He caught my arm with tremulous enthusiasm.—'I couldn't go wi' 'em,' he stammered, indicating by a nod our noisy crowd, that drifted slowly along the other sidewalk. 'When I think of Jimmy . . . Poor Jim! When I think of him I have no heart for drink. You were his chum, too . . . but I pulled him out . . . didn't I? Short wool he had . . . Yes. And I stole the blooming pie . . . He wouldn't go . . . He wouldn't go for nobody.' He burst into tears. 'I never touched him—never— never—' he sobbed. 'He went for me like . . . like . . . a lamb.'

I disengaged myself gently. Belfast's crying fits generally ended in a fight with some one, and I wasn't anxious to stand the brunt of his inconsolable sorrow. Moreover, two bulky policemen stood near by, looking at us with a disapproving and incorruptible gaze.—'So long!' I said, and went off.

But at the corner I stopped to take my last look at the crew of the *Narcissus*. They were swaying, irresolute and noisy on the broad flagstones before the Mint. They were bound for the Black Horse, where men, in fur caps, with brutal faces and in shirt sleeves, dispense out of varnished barrels the illusions of strength, mirth, happiness; the illusion of splendour and poetry of life, to the paid-off crews of southern-going ships. From afar I saw them discoursing, with jovial eyes and clumsy gestures, while the sea of life thundered into their ears ceaseless and unheeded. And swaying about there on the white stones, surrounded by the hurry and clamour of men, they appeared to be creatures of another kind—lost, alone, forgetful, and doomed; they were like castaways, like reckless and joyous castaways, like mad castaways making merry in the storm and upon an insecure ledge of a treacherous rock.

The roar of the town resembled the roar of topping breakers, merciless and strong, with a loud voice and cruel purpose; but overhead the clouds broke; a flood of sunshine streamed down the walls of grimy houses. The dark knot of seamen drifted in sunshine. To the left of them the trees in Tower Gardens sighed, the stones of the Tower gleaming, seemed to stir in the play of light, as if remembering suddenly all the great joys and sorrows of the past, the fighting prototypes of these men; press-gangs; mutinous cries; the wailing of women by the riverside, and the shouts of men welcoming victories. The sunshine of heaven fell like a gift of grace on the mud of the earth, on the remembering and mute stones, on greed, selfishness; on the anxious faces of forgetful men. And to the right of the dark group the stained front of the Mint, cleansed by the flood of light, stood out for a moment, dazzling and white like a marble palace in a fairy tale. The crew of the *Narcissus* drifted out of sight.

I never saw them again. The sea took some, the steamers took others, the graveyards of the earth will account for the rest. Singleton has no doubt taken with him the long record of his faithful work into the peaceful depths of an hospitable sea. And Donkin, who never did a decent day's work in his life, no doubt earns his living by discoursing with filthy eloquence upon the right of labour to live. So be it! Let the earth and the sea each have its own.

A gone shipmate, like any other man, is gone for ever; and I never saw one of them again. But at times the spring-flood of memory sets with force up the dark River of the Nine Bends. Then on the waters of the forlorn stream drifts a ship—a shadowy ship manned by a crew of Shades. They pass and make a sign, in a shadowy hall. Haven't we, together and upon the immortal sea, wrung out a meaning from our sinful lives? Good-bye brothers! You were a good crowd. As good a crowd as ever fisted with wild cries the beating canvas of a heavy foresail; or tossing aloft, invisible in the night, gave back yell for yell to a westerly gale.

Amy Foster

Kennedy is a country doctor, and lives in Colebrook, on the shores of Eastbay. The high ground rising abruptly behind the red roofs of the little town crowds the quaint High Street against the wall which defends it from the sea. Beyond the sea-wall there curves for miles in a vast and regular sweep the barren beach of shingle, with the village of Brenzett standing out darkly across the water, a spire in a clump of trees; and still further out the perpendicular column of a lighthouse, looking in the distance no bigger than a lead pencil, marks the vanishing-point of the land. The country at the back of Brenzett is low and flat, but the bay is fairly well sheltered from the seas, and occasionally a big ship, windbound or through stress of weather, makes use of the anchoring ground a mile and a half due north from you as you stand at the back door of the "Ship Inn" in Brenzett. A dilapidated windmill near by lifting its shattered arms from a mound no loftier than a rubbish heap, and a Martello tower squatting at the water's edge half a mile to the south of the Coastguard cottages, are familiar to the skippers of small craft. These are the official seamarks for the patch of trustworthy bottom represented on the Admiralty charts by an irregular oval of dots enclosing several figures six, with a tiny anchor engraved among them, and the legend "mud and shells" over all.

The brow of the upland overtops the square tower of the Colebrook Church. The slope is green and looped by a white road. Ascending along this road, you open a valley broad and shallow, a wide green trough of pastures and hedges merging inland into a vista of purple tints and flowing lines closing the view.

In this valley down to Brenzett and Colebrook and up to Darnford, the market town fourteen miles away, lies the practice of my friend Kennedy. He had begun life as surgeon in the Navy, and afterwards had been the companion of a famous traveller, in the days when there were continents with unexplored interiors. His papers on the fauna and flora made him known to scientific societies. And now he had come to a country practice—from choice. The penetrating power of his mind, acting like a corrosive fluid, had destroyed his ambition, I fancy. His intelligence is of a scientific order, of an investigating habit, and of that unappeasable curiosity which believes that there is a particle of a general truth in every mystery.

A good many years ago now, on my return from abroad, he invited me to stay with him. I came readily enough, and as he could not neglect his patients to keep me company, he took me on his rounds—thirty miles or so of an afternoon, sometimes. I waited for him on the roads; the horse reached after the leafy twigs, and, sitting in the dogcart, I could hear Kennedy's laugh through the half-open door left open of some cottage. He had a big, hearty laugh that would have fitted a man twice his size, a brisk manner, a bronzed face, and a pair of grey, profoundly attentive eyes. He had the talent of making people talk to him freely, and an inexhaustible patience in listening to their tales.

One day, as we trotted out of a large village into a shady bit of road, I saw on our left hand a low, black cottage, with diamond panes in the windows, a creeper on the end wall, a roof of shingle, and some roses climbing on the rickety trellis-work of the tiny porch. Kennedy pulled up to a walk. A woman, in full sunlight, was throwing a dripping blanket over a line stretched between two old apple-trees. And as the bobtailed, long-necked chestnut, trying to get his head, jerked the left hand, covered by a thick dog-skin glove, the doctor raised his voice over the hedge: "How's your child, Amy?"

I had the time to see her dull face, red, not with a mantling blush, but as if her flat cheeks had been vigorously slapped, and to take in the squat figure, the scanty, dusty brown hair drawn into a tight knot at the back of the head. She looked quite young. With a distinct catch in her breath, her voice sounded low and timid.

"He's well, thank you."

We trotted again. "A young patient of yours," I said; and the doctor, flicking the chestnut absently, muttered, "Her husband used to be."

"She seems a dull creature," I remarked listlessly.

"Precisely," said Kennedy. "She is very passive. It's enough to look at the red hands hanging at the end of those short arms, at those slow, prominent brown eyes, to know the inertness of her mind—an inertness that one would think made it everlastingly safe from all the surprises of imagination. And yet which of us is safe? At any rate, such as you see her, she had enough imagination to fall in love. She's the daughter of one Isaac Foster, who from a small farmer has sunk into a shepherd; the beginning of his misfortunes dating from his runaway marriage with the cook of his widowed father—a well-to-do, apoplectic grazier, who passionately struck his name off his will, and had been heard to utter threats against his life. But this old affair, scandalous enough to serve as a motive for a Greek tragedy, arose from the similarity of their characters. There are other tragedies, less scandalous and of a subtler poignancy, arising from irreconcilable differences and from that fear of the Incomprehensible that hangs over all our heads—over all our heads. . . ."

The tired chestnut dropped into a walk; and the rim of the sun, all red in a speckless sky, touched familiarly the smooth top of a ploughed rise near the road as I had seen it times innumerable touch the distant horizon of the sea. The uniform brownness of the harrowed field glowed with a rosy tinge, as though the powdered clods had sweated out in minute pearls of blood the toil of uncounted ploughmen. From the edge of a copse a waggon with two horses was rolling gently along the ridge. Raised above our heads upon the sky-line, it loomed up against the red sun, triumphantly big, enormous, like a chariot of giants drawn by two slow-stepping steeds of legendary proportions. And the clumsy figure of the man plodding at the head of the leading horse projected itself on the background of the Infinite with a heroic uncouthness. The end of his carter's whip quivered high up in the blue. Kennedy discoursed.

"She's the eldest of a large family. At the age of fifteen they put her out to service at the New Barns Farm. I attended Mrs. Smith, the tenant's wife, and saw that girl there for the first time. Mrs. Smith, a genteel person with a sharp nose, made her put on a black dress every afternoon. I don't know what induced me to notice her at all. There are faces that call your attention by a curious want of definiteness in their whole aspect, as, walking in a mist, you peer attentively at a vague shape which, after all, may be nothing more curious or strange than a signpost. The only peculiarity I perceived in her was a slight hesitation in her utterance, a sort of preliminary stammer which passes away with the first word. When sharply spoken to, she was apt to lose her head at once; but her heart was of the kindest. She had never been heard to express a dislike for a single human being, and she was tender to every living creature. She was devoted to Mrs. Smith, to Mr. Smith, to their dogs, cats, canaries; and as to Mrs. Smith's grey parrot, its peculiarities exercised upon her a positive fascination. Nevertheless, when that outlandish bird, attacked by the cat, shrieked for help in human accents, she ran out into the yard stopping her ears, and did not prevent the crime. For Mrs. Smith this was another evidence of her stupidity; on the other hand, her want of charm, in view of Smith's well-known frivolousness, was a great recommendation. Her short-sighted eyes would swim with pity for a poor mouse in a trap, and she had been seen once by some boys on her knees in the wet grass helping a toad in difficulties. If it's true, as some German fellow has said, that without phosphorus there is no thought, it is still more true that there is no kindness of heart without a certain amount of imagination. She had some. She had even more than is necessary to understand suffering and to be moved by pity. She fell in love under circumstances that leave no room for doubt in the matter; for you need imagination to form a notion of beauty at all, and still more to discover your ideal in an unfamiliar shape.

"How this aptitude came to her, what it did feed upon, is an inscrutable mystery. She was born in the village, and had never been further away from it than Colebrook or perhaps Darnford. She lived for four years with the Smiths. New Barns is an isolated farmhouse a mile away from the road, and she was content to look day after day at the same fields, hollows, rises; at the trees and the hedgerows; at the faces of the four men about the farm, always the same—day after day, month after month, year after year. She never showed a desire for conversation, and, as it seemed to me, she did not know how to smile. Sometimes of a fine Sunday afternoon she would put on her best dress, a pair of stout boots, a large grey hat trimmed with a black feather (I've seen her in that finery), seize an absurdly slender parasol, climb over two stiles, tramp over three fields and along two hundred yards of road—never further. There stood Foster's cottage. She would help her mother to give their tea to the younger children, wash up the crockery, kiss the little ones, and go back to the farm. That was all. All the rest, all the change, all the relaxation. She never seemed to wish for anything more. And then she fell in love. She fell in love silently, obstinately—perhaps helplessly. It came slowly, but when it came it worked like a powerful spell; it was love as the Ancients understood it: an irresistible and fateful impulse—a possession! Yes, it was in her to become haunted and possessed by a face, by a presence, fatally, as though she had been a pagan worshipper of form under a joyous sky— and to be awakened at last from that mysterious forgetfulness of self, from that enchantment, from that transport, by a fear resembling the unaccountable terror of a brute. . . ."

With the sun hanging low on its western limit, the expanse of the grass-lands framed in the counter-scarps of the rising ground took on a gorgeous and sombre aspect. A sense of penetrating sadness, like that inspired by a grave strain of music, disengaged itself from the silence of the fields. The men we met walked past slow, unsmiling, with downcast eyes, as if the melancholy of an over-burdened earth had weighted their feet, bowed their shoulders, borne down their glances.

"Yes," said the doctor to my remark, "one would think the earth is under a curse, since of all her children these that cling to her the closest are uncouth in body and as leaden of gait as if their very hearts were loaded with chains. But here on this same road you might have seen amongst these heavy men a being lithe, supple, and long-limbed, straight like a pine with something striving upwards in his appearance as though the heart within him had been buoyant. Perhaps it was only the force of the contrast, but when he was passing one of these villagers here, the soles of his feet did not seem to me to touch the dust of the road. He vaulted over the stiles, paced these slopes with a long elastic stride that made him noticeable at a great distance, and had lustrous black eyes. He was so different from the mankind around that, with his freedom of movement, his soft—a little startled, glance, his olive complexion and graceful bearing, his humanity suggested to me the nature of a woodland creature. He came from there."

The doctor pointed with his whip, and from the summit of the descent seen over the rolling tops of the trees in a park by the side of the road, appeared the level sea far below us, like the floor of an immense edifice inlaid with bands of dark ripple, with still trails of glitter, ending in a belt of glassy water at the foot of the sky. The light blur of smoke, from an invisible steamer, faded on the great clearness of the horizon like the mist of a breath on a mirror; and, inshore, the white sails of a coaster, with the appearance of disentangling themselves slowly from under the branches, floated clear of the foliage of the trees.

"Shipwrecked in the bay?" I said.

"Yes; he was a castaway. A poor emigrant from Central Europe bound to America and washed ashore here in a storm. And for him, who knew nothing of the earth, England was an undiscovered country. It was some time before he learned its name; and for all I know he might have expected to find wild beasts or wild men here, when, crawling in the dark over the sea-wall, he rolled down the other side into a dyke, where it was another miracle he didn't get drowned. But he struggled instinctively like an animal under a net, and this blind struggle threw him out into a field. He must have been, indeed, of a tougher fibre than he looked to withstand without expiring such buffetings, the violence of his exertions, and so much fear. Later on, in his broken English that resembled curiously the speech of a young child, he told me himself that he put his trust in God, believing he was no longer in this world. And truly—he would add—how was he to know? He fought his way against the rain and the gale on all fours, and crawled at last among some sheep huddled close under the lee of a hedge. They ran off in all directions, bleating in the darkness, and he welcomed the first familiar sound he heard on these shores. It must have been two in the morning then. And this is all we know of the manner of his landing, though he did not arrive unattended by any means. Only his grisly company did not begin to come ashore till much later in the day. . . ."

The doctor gathered the reins, clicked his tongue; we trotted down the hill. Then turning, almost directly, a sharp corner into the High Street, we rattled over the stones and were home.

Late in the evening Kennedy, breaking a spell of moodiness that had come over him, returned to the story. Smoking his pipe, he paced the long room from end to end. A reading-lamp concentrated all its light upon the papers on his desk; and, sitting by the open window, I saw, after the windless, scorching day, the frigid splendour of a hazy sea lying motionless under the moon. Not a whisper, not a splash, not a stir of the shingle, not a footstep, not a sigh came up from the earth below—never a sign of life but the scent of climbing jasmine; and Kennedy's voice, speaking behind me, passed through the wide casement, to vanish outside in a chill and sumptuous stillness.

". . . The relations of shipwrecks in the olden time tell us of much suffering. Often the castaways were only saved from drowning to die miserably from starvation on a barren coast; others suffered violent death or else slavery, passing through years of precarious existence with people to whom their strangeness was an object of suspicion, dislike or fear. We read about these things, and they are very pitiful. It is indeed hard upon a man to find himself a lost stranger, helpless, incomprehensible, and of a mysterious origin, in some obscure corner of the earth. Yet amongst all the adventurers shipwrecked in all the wild parts of the world there is not one, it seems to me, that ever had to suffer a fate so simply tragic as the man I am speaking of, the most innocent of adventurers cast out by the sea in the bight of this bay, almost within sight from this very window.

"He did not know the name of his ship. Indeed, in the course of time we discovered he did not even know that ships had names—'like Christian people'; and when, one day, from the top of the Talfourd Hill, he beheld the sea lying open to his view, his eyes roamed afar, lost in an air of wild surprise, as though he had never seen such a sight before. And probably he had not. As far as I could make out, he had been hustled together with many others on board an emigrant-ship lying at the mouth of the Elbe, too bewildered to take note of his surroundings, too weary to see anything, too anxious to care. They were driven below into the 'tween-deck and battened down from the very start. It was a low timber dwelling—he would say—with wooden beams overhead, like the houses in his country, but you went into it down a ladder. It was very large, very cold, damp and sombre, with places in the manner of wooden boxes where people had to sleep, one above another, and it kept on rocking all ways at once all the time. He crept into one of these boxes and laid down there in the clothes in which he had left his home many days before, keeping his bundle and his stick by his side. People groaned, children cried, water dripped, the lights went out, the walls of the place creaked, and everything was being shaken so that in one's little box one dared not lift one's head. He had lost touch with his only companion (a young man from the same valley, he said), and all the time a great noise of wind went on outside and heavy blows fell—boom! boom! An awful sickness overcame him, even to the point of making him neglect his prayers. Besides, one could not tell whether it was morning or evening. It seemed always to be night in that place.

"Before that he had been travelling a long, long time on the iron track. He looked out of the window, which had a wonderfully clear glass in it, and the trees, the houses, the fields, and the long roads seemed to fly round and round about him till his head swam. He gave me to understand that he had on his passage beheld uncounted multitudes of people—whole nations—all dressed in such clothes as the rich wear. Once he was made to get out of the carriage, and slept through a night on a bench in a house of bricks with his bundle under his head; and once for many hours he had to sit on a floor of flat stones dozing, with his knees up and with his bundle between his feet. There was a roof over him, which seemed made of glass, and was so high that the tallest mountain-pine he had ever seen would have had room to grow under it. Steam-machines rolled in at one end and out at the other. People swarmed more than you can see on a feast-day round the miraculous Holy Image in the yard of the Carmelite Convent down in the plains where, before he left his home, he drove his mother in a wooden cart—a pious old woman who wanted to offer prayers and make a vow for his safety. He could not give me an idea of how large and lofty and full of noise and smoke and gloom, and clang of iron, the place was, but some one had told him it was called Berlin. Then they rang a bell, and another steam-machine came in, and again he was taken on and on through a land that wearied his eyes by its flatness without a single bit of a hill to be seen anywhere. One more night he spent shut up in a building like a good stable with a litter of straw on the floor, guarding his bundle amongst a lot of men, of whom not one could understand a single word he said. In the morning they were all led down to the stony shores of an extremely broad muddy river, flowing not between hills but between houses that seemed immense. There was a steam-machine that went on the water, and they all stood upon it packed tight, only now there were with them many women and children who made much noise. A cold rain fell, the wind blew in his face; he was wet through, and his teeth chattered. He and the young man from the same valley took each other by the hand.

"They thought they were being taken to America straight away, but suddenly the steam-machine bumped against the side of a thing like a house on the water. The walls were smooth and black, and there uprose, growing from the roof as it were, bare trees in the shape of crosses, extremely high. That's how it appeared to him then, for he had never seen a ship before. This was the ship that was going to swim all the way to America. Voices shouted, everything swayed; there was a ladder dipping up and down. He went up on his hands and knees in mortal fear of falling into the water below, which made a great splashing. He got separated from his companion, and when he descended into the bottom of that ship his heart seemed to melt suddenly within him.

"It was then also, as he told me, that he lost contact for good and all with one of those three men who the summer before had been going about through all the little towns in the foothills of his country. They would arrive on market days driving in a peasant's cart, and would set

up an office in an inn or some other Jew's house. There were three of
them, of whom one with a long beard looked venerable; and they had
red cloth collars round their necks and gold lace on their sleeves like
Government officials. They sat proudly behind a long table; and in the
next room, so that the common people shouldn't hear, they kept a
cunning telegraph machine, through which they could talk to the
Emperor of America. The fathers hung about the door, but the young
men of the mountains would crowd up to the table asking many
questions, for there was work to be got all the year round at three
dollars a day in America, and no military service to do.

"But the American Kaiser would not take everybody. Oh, no! He
himself had a great difficulty in getting accepted, and the venerable
man in uniform had to go out of the room several times to work the
telegraph on his behalf. The American Kaiser engaged him at last at
three dollars, he being young and strong. However, many able young
men backed out, afraid of the great distance; besides, those only who
had some money could be taken. There were some who sold their huts
and their land because it cost a lot of money to get to America; but
then, once there, you had three dollars a day, and if you were clever
you could find places where true gold could be picked up on the
ground. His father's house was getting over full. Two of his brothers
were married and had children. He promised to send money home from
America by post twice a year. His father sold an old cow, a pair of
piebald mountain ponies of his own raising, and a cleared plot of fair
pasture land on the sunny slope of a pine-clad pass to a Jew inn-keeper
in order to pay the people of the ship that took men to America to get
rich in a short time.

"He must have been a real adventurer at heart, for how many of the
greatest enterprises in the conquest of the earth had for their beginning
just such a bargaining away of the paternal cow for the mirage or true
gold far away! I have been telling you more or less in my own words
what I learned fragmentarily in the course of two or three years, during
which I seldom missed an opportunity of a friendly chat with him. He
told me this story of his adventure with many flashes of white teeth and
lively glances of black eyes, at first in a sort of anxious baby-talk, then,
as he acquired the language, with great fluency, but always with that
singing, soft, and at the same time vibrating intonation that instilled a
strangely penetrating power into the sound of the most familiar English
words, as if they had been the words of an unearthly language. And he
always would come to an end, with many emphatic shakes of his head,
upon that awful sensation of his heart melting within him directly he set
foot on board that ship. Afterwards there seemed to come for him a
period of blank ignorance, at any rate as to facts. No doubt he must
have been abominably sea-sick and abominably unhappy—this soft and
passionate adventurer, taken thus out of his knowledge, and feeling

bitterly as he lay in his emigrant bunk his utter loneliness; for his was a highly sensitive nature. The next thing we know of him for certain is that he had been hiding in Hammond's pig-pound by the side of the road to Norton six miles, as the crow flies, from the sea. Of these experiences he was unwilling to speak: they seemed to have seared into his soul a sombre sort of wonder and indignation. Through the rumours of the country-side, which lasted for a good many days after his arrival, we know that the fishermen of West Colebrook had been disturbed and startled by heavy knocks against the walls of weatherboard cottages, and by a voice crying piercingly strange words in the night. Several of them turned out even, but, no doubt, he had fled in sudden alarm at their rough angry tones hailing each other in the darkness. A sort of frenzy must have helped him up the steep Norton hill. It was he, no doubt, who early the following morning had been seen lying (in a swoon, I should say) on the roadside grass by the Brenzett carrier, who actually got down to have a nearer look, but drew back, intimidated by the perfect immobility, and by something queer in the aspect of that tramp, sleeping so still under the showers. As the day advanced, some children came dashing into school at Norton in such a fright that the schoolmistress went out and spoke indignantly to a 'horrid-looking man' on the road. He edged away, hanging his head, for a few steps, and then suddenly ran off with extraordinary fleetness. The driver of Mr. Bradley's milk-cart made no secret of it that he had lashed with his whip at a hairy sort of gipsy fellow who, jumping up at a turn of the road by the Vents, made a snatch at the pony's bridle. And he caught him a good one too, right over the face, he said, that made him drop down in the mud a jolly sight quicker than he had jumped up; but it was a good half-a-mile before he could stop the pony. Maybe that in his desperate endeavours to get help, and in his need to get in touch with some one, the poor devil had tried to stop the cart. Also three boys confessed afterwards to throwing stones at a funny tramp, knocking about all wet and muddy, and, it seemed, very drunk, in the narrow deep lane by the limekilns. All this was the talk of three villages for days; but we have Mrs. Finn's (the wife of Smith's wagoner) unimpeachable testimony that she saw him get over the low wall of Hammond's pig-pound and lurch straight at her, babbling aloud in a voice that was enough to make one die of fright. Having the baby with her in a perambulator, Mrs. Finn called out to him to go away, and as he persisted in coming nearer, she hit him courageously with her umbrella over the head and, without once looking back, ran like the wind with the perambulator as far as the first house in the village. She stopped then, out of breath, and spoke to old Lewis, hammering there at a heap of stones; and the old chap, taking off his immense black wire goggles, got up on his shaky legs to look where she pointed. Together they followed with their eyes the figure of the man running over a field;

they saw him fall down, pick himself up, and run on again, staggering and waving his long arms above his head, in the direction of the New Barns Farm. From that moment he is plainly in the toils of his obscure and touching destiny. There is no doubt after this of what happened to him. All is certain now: Mrs. Smith's intense terror; Amy Foster's stolid conviction held against the other's nervous attack, that the man 'meant no harm'; Smith's exasperation (on his return from Darnford Market) at finding the dog barking himself into a fit, the back-door locked, his wife in hysterics; and all for an unfortunate dirty tramp, supposed to be even then lurking in his stackyard. Was he? He would teach him to frighten women.

"Smith is notoriously hot-tempered, but the sight of some nondescript and miry creature sitting cross-legged amongst a lot of loose straw, and swinging itself to and fro like a bear in a cage, made him pause. Then this tramp stood up silently before him, one mass of mud and filth from head to foot. Smith, alone amongst his stacks with this apparition, in the stormy twilight ringing with the infuriated barking of the dog, felt the dread of an inexplicable strangeness. But when that being, parting with his black hands the long matted locks that hung before his face, as you part the two halves of a curtain, looked out at him with glistening, wild, black-and-white eyes, the weirdness of this silent encounter fairly staggered him. He had admitted since (for the story has been a legitimate subject of conversation about here for years) that he made more than one step backwards. Then a sudden burst of rapid, senseless speech persuaded him at once that he had to do with an escaped lunatic. In fact, that impression never wore off completely. Smith has not in his heart given up his secret conviction of the man's essential insanity to this very day.

"As the creature approached him, jabbering in a most discomposing manner, Smith (unaware that he was being addressed as 'gracious lord,' and adjured in God's name to afford food and shelter) kept on speaking firmly but gently to it, and retreating all the time into the other yard. At last, watching his chance, by a sudden charge he bundled him headlong into the wood-lodge, and instantly shot the bolt. Thereupon he wiped his brow, though the day was cold. He had done his duty to the community by shutting up a wandering and probably dangerous maniac. Smith isn't a hard man at all, but he had room in his brain only for that one idea of lunacy. He was not imaginative enough to ask himself whether the man might not be perishing with cold and hunger. Meantime, at first, the maniac made a great deal of noise in the lodge. Mrs. Smith was screaming upstairs, where she had locked herself in her bedroom; but Amy Foster sobbed piteously at the kitchen door, wringing her hands and muttering, 'Don't! don't!' I daresay Smith had a rough time of it that evening with one noise and another, and this insane, disturbing voice crying obstinately through the door only added to his irritation. He couldn't possibly have connected this troublesome lunatic with the sinking of a ship in Eastbay, of which there had been a rumour in the Darnford marketplace. And I daresay the man inside had been very near to insanity on that night. Before his excitement collapsed and he became unconscious he was throwing himself violently about in the dark, rolling on some dirty sacks, and biting his fists with rage, cold, hunger, amazement, and despair.

"He was a mountaineer of the eastern range of the Carpathians, and the vessel sunk the night before in Eastbay was the Hamburg emigrant-ship *Herzogin Sophia-Dorothea*, of appalling memory.

"A few months later we could read in the papers the accounts of the bogus 'Emigration Agencies' among the Slavic peasantry in the more remote provinces of Austria. The object of these scoundrels was to get hold of the poor ignorant people's homesteads, and they were in league with the local usurers. They exported their victims through Hamburg mostly. As to the ship, I had watched her out of this very window, reaching close-hauled under short canvas into the bay on a dark, threatening afternoon. She came to an anchor, correctly by the chart, off the Brenzett Coastguard station. I remember before the night fell looking out again at the outlines of her spars and rigging that stood out dark and pointed on a background of ragged, slaty clouds like another and a slighter spire to the left of the Brenzett church-tower. In the evening the wind rose. At midnight I could hear in my bed the terrific gusts and the sounds of a driving deluge.

"About that time the Coastguardmen thought they saw the lights of a steamer over the anchoring-ground. In a moment they vanished; but it is clear that another vessel of some sort had tried for shelter in the bay on that awful, blind night, had rammed the German ship amidships (a breach—as one of the divers told me afterwards—'that you could sail a Thames barge through'), and then had gone out either scatheless or damaged, who shall say; but had gone out, unknown, unseen, and fatal, to perish mysteriously at sea. Of her nothing ever came to light, and yet the hue and cry that was raised all over the world would have found her out if she had been in existence anywhere on the face of the waters.

"A completeness without a clue, and a stealthy silence as of a neatly executed crime, characterize this murderous disaster, which, as you may remember, had its gruesome celebrity. The wind would have prevented the loudest outcries from reaching the shore; there had been evidently no time for signals of distress. It was death without any sort of fuss. The Hamburg ship, filling all at once, capsized as she sank, and at daylight there was not even the end of a spar to be seen above water. She was missed, of course, and at first the Coastguardmen surmised that she had either dragged her anchor or parted her cable some time during the night, and had been blown out to sea. Then, after the tide turned, the wreck must have shifted a little and released some of the bodies, because a child—a little fair-haired child in a red frock—came ashore abreast of the Martello tower. By the afternoon you could see along three miles of beach dark figures with bare legs dashing in and out of the tumbling foam, and rough-looking men, women with hard faces, children, mostly fair-haired, were being carried, stiff and dripping, on stretchers, on wattles, on ladders, in a long procession past the door of the 'Ship Inn,' to be laid out in a row under the north wall of the Brenzett Church.

"Officially, the body of the little girl in the red frock is the first thing that came ashore from that ship. But I have patients amongst the seafaring population of West Colebrook, and, unofficially, I am informed that very early that morning two brothers, who went down to look after their cobble hauled up on the beach, found, a good way from Brenzett, an ordinary ship's hencoop lying high and dry on the shore, with eleven drowned ducks inside. Their families ate the birds, and the hencoop was split into firewood with a hatchet. It is possible that a man (supposing he happened to be on deck at the time of the accident) might have floated ashore on that hencoop. He might. I admit it is improbable, but there was the man—and for days, nay, for weeks—it didn't enter our heads that we had amongst us the only living soul that had escaped from that disaster. The man himself, even when he learned to speak intelligibly, could tell us very little. He remembered he had felt better (after the ship had anchored, I suppose), and that the darkness, the wind, and the rain took his breath away. This looks as if he had been on deck some time during that night. But we mustn't forget he had been taken out of his knowledge, that he had been sea-sick and battened down below for four days, that he had no general notion of a ship or of the sea, and therefore could have no definite idea of what was happening to him. The rain, the wind, the darkness he knew; he understood the bleating of the sheep, and he remembered the pain of his wretchedness and misery, his heartbroken astonishment that it was neither seen nor understood, his dismay at finding all the men angry and all the women fierce. He had approached them as a beggar, it is true, he said; but in his country, even if they gave nothing, they spoke gently to beggars. The children in his country were not taught to throw stones at those who asked for compassion. Smith's strategy overcame him completely. The wood-lodge presented the horrible aspect of a dungeon. What would be done to him next? . . . No wonder that Amy Foster appeared to his eyes with the aureole of an angel of light. The girl had not been able to sleep for thinking of the poor man, and in the morning, before the Smiths were up, she slipped out across the back yard. Holding the door of the wood-lodge ajar, she looked in and extended to him half a loaf of white bread—'such bread as the rich eat in my country,' he used to say.

"At this he got up slowly from amongst all sorts of rubbish, stiff, hungry, trembling, miserable, and doubtful. 'Can you eat this?' she asked in her soft and timid voice. He must have taken her for a 'gracious lady.' He devoured ferociously, and tears were falling on the crust. Suddenly he dropped the bread, seized her wrist, and imprinted a kiss on her hand. She was not frightened. Through his forlorn condition she had observed that he was good-looking. She shut the door and walked back slowly to the kitchen. Much later on, she told Mrs. Smith, who shuddered at the bare idea of being touched by that creature.

"Through this act of impulsive pity he was brought back again within the pale of human relations with his new surroundings. He never forgot it—never.

"That very same morning old Mr. Swaffer (Smith's nearest neighbour) came over to give his advice, and ended by carrying him off. He stood, unsteady on his legs, meek, and caked over in half-dried mud, while the two men talked around him in an incomprehensible tongue. Mrs. Smith had refused to come downstairs till the madman was off the premises; Amy Foster, far from within the dark kitchen, watched through the open back door; and he obeyed the signs that were made to him to the best of his ability. But Smith was full of mistrust. 'Mind, sir! It may be all his cunning,' he cried repeatedly in a tone of warning. When Mr. Swaffer started the mare, the deplorable being sitting humbly by his side, through weakness, nearly fell out over the back of the high two-wheeled cart. Swaffer took him straight home. And it is then that I come upon the scene.

"I was called in by the simple process of the old man beckoning to me with his forefinger over the gate of his house as I happened to be driving past. I got down, of course.

"'I've got something here,' he mumbled, leading the way to an outhouse at a little distance from his other farm-buildings.

"It was there that I saw him first, in a long low room taken upon the space of that sort of coach-house. It was bare and whitewashed, with a small square aperture glazed with one cracked, dusty pane at its further end. He was lying on his back upon a straw pallet; they had given him a couple of horse-blankets, and he seemed to have spent the remainder of his strength in the exertion of cleaning himself. He was almost speechless; his quick breathing under the blankets pulled up to his chin, his glittering, restless black eyes reminded me of a wild bird caught in a snare. While I was examining him, old Swaffer stood silently by the door, passing the tips of his fingers along his shaven upper lip. I gave some directions, promised to send a bottle of medicine, and naturally made some inquiries.

"'Smith caught him in the stackyard at New Barns,' said the old chap in his deliberate, unmoved manner, and as if the other had been indeed a sort of wild animal. 'That's how I came by him. Quite a curiosity, isn't he? Now tell me, doctor—you've been all over the world—don't you think that's a bit of a Hindu we've got hold of here.'

"I was greatly surprised. His long black hair scattered over the straw bolster contrasted with the olive pallor of his face. It occurred to me he might be a Basque. It didn't necessarily follow that he should understand Spanish; but I tried him with the few words I know, and also with some French. The whispered sounds I caught by bending my ear to his lips puzzled me utterly. That afternoon the young ladies from the Rectory (one of them read Goethe with a dictionary, and the other had struggled with Dante for years), coming to see Miss Swaffer, tried their German and Italian on him from the doorway. They retreated, just the least bit scared by the flood of passionate speech which, turning on his pallet, he let out at them. They admitted that the sound was pleasant, soft, musical—but, in conjunction with his looks perhaps, it was startling—so excitable, so utterly unlike anything one had ever heard. The village boys climbed up the bank to have a peep through the little square aperture. Everybody was wondering what Mr. Swaffer would do with him.

"He simply kept him.

"Swaffer would be called eccentric were he not so much respected. They will tell you that Mr. Swaffer sits up as late as ten o'clock at night to read books, and they will tell you also that he can write a cheque for two hundred pounds without thinking twice about it. He himself would tell you that the Swaffers had owned land between this and Darnford for these three hundred years. He must be eighty-five to-day, but he does not look a bit older than when I first came here. He is a great breeder of sheep, and deals extensively in cattle. He attends market days for miles around in every sort of weather, and drives sitting bowed low over the reins, his lank grey hair curling over the collar of his warm coat, and with a green plaid rug round his legs. The calmness of advanced age gives a solemnity to his manner. He is clean-shaved; his lips are thin and sensitive; something rigid and monarchal in the set of his features lends a certain elevation to the character of his face. He has been known to drive miles in the rain to see a new kind of rose in somebody's garden, or a monstrous cabbage grown by a cottager. He loves to hear tell of or to be shown something that he calls 'outlandish.' Perhaps it was just that outlandishness of the man which influenced old Swaffer. Perhaps it was only an inexplicable caprice. All I know is that at the end of three weeks I caught sight of Smith's lunatic digging in Swaffer's kitchen garden. They had found out he could use a spade. He dug barefooted.

"His black hair flowed over his shoulders. I suppose it was Swaffer who had given him the striped old cotton shirt; but he wore still the national brown cloth trousers (in which he had been washed ashore) fitting to the leg almost like tights; was belted with a broad leathern belt studded with little brass discs; and had never yet ventured into the village. The land he looked upon seemed to him kept neatly, like the grounds round a landowner's house; the size of the cart-horses struck him with astonishment; the roads resembled garden walks, and the aspect of the people, especially on Sundays, spoke of opulence. He wondered what made them so hardhearted and their children so bold. He got his food at the back door, carried it in both hands carefully to his outhouse, and, sitting alone on his pallet, would make the sign of the cross before he began. Beside the same pallet, kneeling in the early darkness of the short days, he recited aloud the Lord's Prayer before he slept. Whenever he saw old Swaffer he would bow with veneration from the waist, and stand erect while the old man, with his fingers over his upper lip, surveyed him silently. He bowed also to Miss Swaffer, who kept house frugally for her father—a broad-shouldered, big-boned woman of forty-five, with the pocket of her dress full of keys, and a grey, steady eye. She was Church—as people said (while her father was one of the trustees of the Baptist Chapel)—and wore a little steel cross at her waist. She dressed severely in black, in memory of one of the innumerable Bradleys of the neighbourhood, to whom she had been engaged some twenty-five years ago—a young farmer who broke his neck out hunting on the eve of the wedding day. She had the unmoved countenance of the deaf, spoke very seldom, and her lips, thin like her father's, astonished one sometimes by a mysteriously ironic curl.

"These were the people to whom he owed allegiance, and an overwhelming loneliness seemed to fall from the leaden sky of that winter without sunshine. All the faces were sad. He could talk to no one, and had no hope of ever understanding anybody. It was as if these had been the faces of people from the other world—dead people—he used to tell me years afterwards. Upon my word, I wonder he did not go mad. He didn't know where he was. Somewhere very far from his mountains—somewhere over the water. Was this America, he wondered?

"If it hadn't been for the steel cross at Miss Swaffer's belt he would not, he confessed, have known whether he was in a Christian country at all. He used to cast stealthy glances at it, and feel comforted. There was nothing here the same as in his country! The earth and the water were different; there were no images of the Redeemer by the roadside. The very grass was different, and the trees. All the trees but the three old Norway pines on the bit of lawn before Swaffer's house, and these reminded him of his country. He had been detected once, after dusk, with his forehead against the trunk of one of them, sobbing, and talking to himself. They had been like brothers to him at that time, he affirmed. Everything else was strange. Conceive you the kind of an existence overshadowed, oppressed, by the everyday material appearances, as if by the visions of a nightmare. At night, when he could not sleep, he kept on thinking of the girl who gave him the first piece of bread he had eaten in this foreign land. She had been neither fierce nor angry, nor frightened. Her face he remembered as the only comprehensible face amongst all these faces that were as closed, as mysterious, and as mute as the faces of the dead who are possessed of a knowledge beyond the comprehension of the living. I wonder whether the memory of her compassion prevented him from cutting his throat. But there! I suppose I am an old sentimentalist, and forget the instinctive love of life which it takes all the strength of an uncommon despair to overcome.

"He did the work which was given him with an intelligence which surprised old Swaffer. By-and-by it was discovered that he could help at the plowing, could milk the cows, feed the bullocks in the cattle-yard, and was of some use with the sheep. He began to pick up words, too, very fast; and suddenly, one fine morning in spring, he rescued from an untimely death a grand-child of old Swaffer.

"Swaffer's younger daughter is married to Willcox, a solicitor and the Town Clerk of Colebrook. Regularly twice a year they come to stay with the old man for a few days. Their only child, a little girl not three years old at the time, ran out of the house alone in her little white pinafore, and, toddling across the grass of a terraced garden, pitched herself over a low wall head first into the horse-pond in the yard below.

"Our man was out with the wagoner and the plough in the field nearest to the house, and as he was leading the team round to begin a fresh furrow, he saw, through the gap of the gate, what for anybody else would have been a mere flutter of something white. But he had straight-glancing, quick, far-reaching eyes, that only seemed to flinch and lose their amazing power before the immensity of the sea. He was barefooted, and looking as outlandish as the heart of Swaffer could desire. Leaving the horses on the turn, to the inexpressible disgust of the wagoner he bounded off, going over the ploughed ground in long leaps, and suddenly appeared before the mother, thrust the child into her arms, and strode away.

"The pond was not very deep; but still, if he had not had such good eyes, the child would have perished—miserably suffocated in the foot or so of sticky mud at the bottom. Old Swaffer walked out slowly into the field, waited till the plough came over to his side, had a good look at him, and without saying a word went back to the house. But from that time they laid out his meals on the kitchen table; and at first, Miss Swaffer, all in black and with an inscrutable face, would come and stand in the doorway of the living-room to see him make a big sign of the cross before he fell to. I believe that from that day, too, Swaffer began to pay him regular wages.

"I can't follow step by step his development. He cut his hair short, was seen in the village and along the road going to and fro to his work like any other man. Children ceased to shout after him. He became aware of social differences, but remained for a long time surprised at the bare poverty of the churches among so much wealth. He couldn't understand either why they were kept shut up on week days. There was nothing to steal in them. Was it to keep people from praying too often? The rectory took much notice of him about that time, and I believe the young ladies attempted to prepare the ground for his conversion. They could not, however, break him of his habit of crossing himself, but he went so far as to take off the string with a couple of brass medals the size of a sixpence, a tiny metal cross, and a square sort of scapulary which he wore round his neck. He hung them on the wall by the side of his bed, and he was still to be heard every evening reciting the Lord's Prayer, in incomprehensible words and in a slow, fervent tone, as he had heard his old father do at the head of all the kneeling family, big and little, on every evening of his life. And though he wore corduroys at work, and a slop-made pepper-and-salt suit on Sundays, strangers would turn round to look after him on the road. His foreignness had a peculiar and indelible stamp. At last people became used to see him. But they never became used to him. His rapid, skimming walk; his swarthy complexion; his hat cocked on the left ear; his habit, on warm evenings, of wearing his coat over one shoulder, like a hussar's dolman; his manner of leaping over the stiles, not as a feat of agility, but in the ordinary course of progression—all these peculiarities were, as one may say, so many causes of scorn and offence to the inhabitants of the village. *They* wouldn't in their dinner hour lie flat on their backs on the grass to stare at the sky. Neither did they go about the fields screaming dismal tunes. Many times have I heard his high-pitched voice from behind the ridge of some sloping sheep-walk, a voice light and soaring, like a lark's, but with a melancholy human note, over our fields that hear only the song of birds. And I should be startled myself. Ah! He was different: innocent of heart, and full of good will, which nobody wanted, this castaway, that, like a man transplanted into another planet, was separated by an immense space from his past and by an immense ignorance from his future. His quick, fervent utterance positively shocked everybody. 'An excitable devil,' they called him. One evening, in the tap-room of the Coach and Horses (having drunk some whisky), he upset them all by singing a love song of his country. They hooted him down, and he was pained; but Preble, the lame wheelwright, and Vincent, the fat blacksmith, and the other notables too, wanted to drink their evening beer in peace. On another occasion he tried to show them how to dance. The dust rose in clouds from the sanded floor; he leaped straight up amongst the deal tables, struck his heels together, squatted on one heel in front of old Preble, shooting out the other leg, uttered wild and exulting cries, jumped up to whirl on one foot, snapping his fingers above his head—and a strange carter who was having a drink in there began to swear, and cleared out with his half-pint in his hand into the bar. But when suddenly he sprang upon a table and continued to dance among the glasses, the landlord interfered. He didn't want any 'acrobat tricks in the taproom.' They laid their hands on him. Having had a glass or two, Mr. Swaffer's foreigner tried to expostulate: was ejected forcibly: got a black eye.

"I believe he felt the hostility of his human surroundings. But he was tough—tough in spirit, too, as well as in body. Only the memory of the sea frightened him, with that vague terror that is left by a bad dream. His home was far away; and he did not want now to go to America. I had often explained to him that there is no place on earth where true gold can be found lying ready and to be got for the trouble of the picking up. How then, he asked, could he ever return home with empty hands when there had been sold a cow, two ponies, and a bit of land to pay for his going? His eyes would fill with tears, and, averting them from the immense shimmer of the sea, he would throw himself face down on the grass. But sometimes, cocking his hat with a little conquering air, he would defy my wisdom. He had found his bit of true gold. That was Amy Foster's heart; which was 'a golden heart, and soft to people's misery,' he would say in the accents of overwhelming conviction.

"He was called Yanko. He had explained that this meant little John; but as he would also repeat very often that he was a mountaineer (some word sounding in the dialect of his country like Goorall) he got it for his surname. And this is the only trace of him that the succeeding ages may find in the marriage register of the parish. There it stands—Yanko Goorall—in the rector's handwriting. The crooked cross made by the castaway, a cross whose tracing no doubt seemed to him the most solemn part of the whole ceremony, is all that remains now to perpetuate the memory of his name.

"His courtship had lasted some time—ever since he got his precarious footing in the community. It began by his buying for Amy Foster a green satin ribbon in Darnford. This was what you did in his country. You bought a ribbon at a Jew's stall on a fair-day. I don't suppose the girl knew what to do with it, but he seemed to think that his honourable intentions could not be mistaken.

"It was only when he declared his purpose to get married that I fully understood how, for a hundred futile and inappreciable reasons, how—shall I say odious?—he was to all the countryside. Every old woman in the village was up in arms. Smith, coming upon him near the farm, promised to break his head for him if he found him about again. But he twisted his little black moustache with such a bellicose air and rolled such big, black fierce eyes at Smith that this promise came to nothing. Smith, however, told the girl that she must be mad to take up with a man who was surely wrong in his head. All the same, when she heard him in the gloaming whistle from beyond the orchard a couple of bars of a weird and mournful tune, she would drop whatever she had in her hand—she would leave Mrs. Smith in the middle of a sentence—and she would run out to his call. Mrs. Smith called her a shameless hussy. She answered nothing. She said nothing at all to anybody, and went on her way as if she had been deaf. She and I alone all in the land, I fancy, could see his very real beauty. He was very good-looking, and most graceful in his bearing, with that something wild as of a woodland creature in his aspect. Her mother moaned over her dismally whenever the girl came to see her on her day out. The father was surly, but pretended not to know; and Mrs. Finn once told her plainly that 'this man, my dear, will do you some harm some day yet.' And so it went on. They could be seen on the roads, she tramping stolidly in her finery—grey dress, black feather, stout boots, prominent white cotton gloves that caught your eye a hundred yards away; and he, his coat slung picturesquely over one shoulder, pacing by her side, gallant of bearing and casting tender glances upon the girl with the golden heart. I wonder whether he saw how plain she was. Perhaps among types so different from what he had ever seen, he had not the power to judge; or perhaps he was seduced by the divine quality of her pity.

"Yanko was in great trouble meantime. In his country you get an old man for an ambassador in marriage affairs. He did not know how to proceed. However, one day in the midst of sheep in a field (he was now Swaffer's under-shepherd with Foster) he took off his hat to the father and declared himself humbly. 'I daresay she's fool enough to marry you,' was all Foster said. 'And then,' he used to relate, 'he puts his hat on his head, looks black at me as if he wanted to cut my throat, whistles the dog, and off he goes, leaving me to do the work.' The Fosters, of course, didn't like to lose the wages the girl earned: Amy used to give all her money to her mother. But there was in Foster a very genuine aversion to that match. He contended that the fellow was very good with sheep, but was not fit for any girl to marry. For one thing, he used to go along the hedges muttering to himself like a dam' fool; and then, these foreigners behave very queerly to women sometimes. And perhaps he would want to carry her off somewhere—or run off himself. It was not safe. He preached it to his daughter that the fellow might ill-use her in some way. She made no answer. It was, they said in the village, as if the man had done something to her. People discussed the matter. It was quite an excitement, and the two went on 'walking out' together in the face of opposition. Then something unexpected happened.

"I don't know whether old Swaffer ever understood how much he was regarded in the light of a father by his foreign retainer. Anyway the relation was curiously feudal. So when Yanko asked formally for an interview—'and the Miss too' (he called the severe, deaf Miss Swaffer simply *Miss*)—it was to obtain their permission to marry. Swaffer heard him unmoved, dismissed him by a nod, and then shouted the intelligence into Miss Swaffer's best ear. She showed no surprise, and only remarked grimly, in a veiled blank voice, 'He certainly won't get any other girl to marry him.'

"It is Miss Swaffer who has all the credit of the munificence: but in a very few days it came out that Mr. Swaffer had presented Yanko with a cottage (the cottage you've seen this morning) and something like an acre of ground—had made it over to him in absolute property. Willcox expedited the deed, and I remember him telling me he had a great pleasure in making it ready. It recited: 'In consideration of saving the life of my beloved grandchild, Bertha Willcox.'

"Of course, after that no power on earth could prevent them from getting married.

"Her infatuation endured. People saw her going out to meet him in the evening. She stared with unblinking, fascinated eyes up the road where he was expected to appear, walking freely, with a swing from the hip, and humming one of the love-tunes of his country. When the boy was born, he got elevated at the 'Coach and Horses,' essayed again a song and a dance, and was again ejected. People expressed their commiseration for a woman married to that Jack-in-the-box. He didn't care. There was a man now (he told me boastfully) to whom he could sing and talk in the language of his country, and show how to dance by-and-by.

"But I don't know. To me he appeared to have grown less springy of step, heavier in body, less keen of eye. Imagination, no doubt; but it seems to me now as if the net of fate had been drawn closer round him already.

"One day I met him on the footpath over the Talfourd Hill. He told me that 'women were funny.' I had heard already of domestic differences. People were saying that Amy Foster was beginning to find out what sort of man she had married. He looked upon the sea with indifferent, unseeing eyes. His wife had snatched the child out of his arms one day as he sat on the doorstep crooning to it a song such as the mothers sing to babies in his mountains. She seemed to think he was doing it some harm. Women are funny. And she had objected to him praying aloud in the evening. Why? He expected the boy to repeat the prayer aloud after him by-and-by, as he used to do after his old father when he was a child—in his own country. And I discovered he longed for their boy to grow up so that he could have a man to talk with in that language that to our ears sounded so disturbing, so passionate, and so bizarre. Why his wife should dislike the idea he couldn't tell. But that would pass, he said. And tilting his head knowingly, he tapped his breastbone to indicate that she had a good heart: not hard, not fierce, open to compassion, charitable to the poor!

"I walked away thoughtfully; I wondered whether his difference, his strangeness, were not penetrating with repulsion that dull nature they had begun by irresistibly attracting. I wondered. . . ."

The Doctor came to the window and looked out at the frigid splendour of the sea, immense in the haze, as if enclosing all the earth with all the hearts lost among the passions of love and fear.

"Physiologically, now," he said, turning away abruptly, "it was possible. It was possible."

He remained silent. Then went on—

"At all events, the next time I saw him he was ill—lung trouble. He was tough, but I daresay he was not acclimatized as well as I had supposed. It was a bad winter; and, of course, these mountaineers do get fits of home sickness; and a state of depression would make him vulnerable. He was lying half dressed on a couch downstairs.

"A table covered with a dark oilcloth took up all the middle of the little room. There was a wicker cradle on the floor, a kettle spouting steam on the hob, and some child's linen lay drying on the fender. The room was warm, but the door opens right into the garden, as you noticed perhaps.

"He was very feverish, and kept on muttering to himself. She sat on a chair and looked at him fixedly across the table with her brown, blurred eyes. 'Why don't you have him upstairs?' I asked. With a start and a confused stammer she said, 'Oh! ah! I couldn't sit with him upstairs, Sir.'

"I gave her certain directions; and going outside, I said again that he ought to be in bed upstairs. She wrung her hands. 'I couldn't. I couldn't. He keeps on saying something—I don't know what.' With the memory of all the talk against the man that had been dinned into her ears, I looked at her narrowly. I looked into her shortsighted eyes, at her dumb eyes that once in her life had seen an enticing shape, but seemed, staring at me, to see nothing at all now. But I saw she was uneasy.

"'What's the matter with him?' she asked in a sort of vacant trepidation. 'He doesn't look very ill. I never did see anybody look like this before. . . .'

"'Do you think,' I asked indignantly, 'he is shamming?'

"'I can't help it, sir,' she said stolidly. And suddenly she clapped her hands and looked right and left. 'And there's the baby. I am so frightened. He wanted me just now to give him the baby. I can't understand what he says to it.'

"'Can't you ask a neighbour to come in tonight?' I asked.

"'Please, sir, nobody seems to care to come,' she muttered, dully resigned all at once.

"I impressed upon her the necessity of the greatest care, and then had to go. There was a good deal of sickness that winter. 'Oh, I hope he won't talk!' she exclaimed softly just as I was going away.

"I don't know how it is I did not see—but I didn't. And yet, turning in my trap, I saw her lingering before the door, very still, and as if meditating a flight up the miry road.

"Towards the night his fever increased.

"He tossed, moaned, and now and then muttered a complaint. And she sat with the table between her and the couch, watching every movement and every sound, with the terror, the unreasonable terror, of that man she could not understand creeping over her. She had drawn the wicker cradle close to her feet. There was nothing in her now but the maternal instinct and that unaccountable fear.

"Suddenly coming to himself, parched, he demanded a drink of water. She did not move. She had not understood, though he may have thought he was speaking in English. He waited, looking at her, burning with fever, amazed at her silence and immobility, and then he shouted impatiently, 'Water! Give me water!'

"She jumped to her feet, snatched up the child, and stood still. He spoke to her, and his passionate remonstrances only increased her fear of that strange man. I believe he spoke to her for a long time, entreating, wondering, pleading, ordering, I suppose. She says she bore it as long as she could. And then a gust of rage came over him.

"He sat up and called out terribly one word—some word. Then he got up as though he hadn't been ill at all, she says. And as in fevered dismay, indignation, and wonder he tried to get to her round the table, she simply opened the door and ran out with the child in her arms. She heard him call twice after her down the road in a terrible voice—and fled. . . . Ah! but you should have seen stirring behind the dull, blurred glance of these eyes the spectre of the fear which had hunted her on that night three miles and a half to the door of Foster's cottage! I did the next day.

"And it was I who found him lying face down and his body in a puddle, just outside the little wicket-gate.

"I had been called out that night to an urgent case in the village, and on my way home at daybreak passed by the cottage. The door stood open. My man helped me to carry him in. We laid him on the couch. The lamp smoked, the fire was out, the chill of the stormy night oozed from the cheerless yellow paper on the wall. 'Amy!' I called aloud, and my voice seemed to lose itself in the emptiness of this tiny house as if I had cried in a desert. He opened his eyes. 'Gone!' he said distinctly. 'I had only asked for water—only for a little water. . . .'

"He was muddy. I covered him up and stood waiting in silence, catching a painfully gasped word now and then. They were no longer in his own language. The fever had left him, taking with it the heat of life. And with his panting breast and lustrous eyes he reminded me again of a wild creature under the net; of a bird caught in a snare. She had left him. She had left him—sick—helpless—thirsty. The spear of the hunter had entered his very soul. 'Why?' he cried in the penetrating and indignant voice of a man calling to a responsible Maker. A gust of wind and a swish of rain answered.

"And as I turned away to shut the door he pronounced the word 'Merciful!' and expired.

"Eventually I certified heart-failure as the immediate cause of death. His heart must have indeed failed him, or else he might have stood this night of storm and exposure, too. I closed his eyes and drove away. Not very far from the cottage I met Foster walking sturdily between the dripping hedges with his collie at his heels.

"'Do you know where your daughter is?' I asked.

"'Don't I!' he cried. 'I am going to talk to him a bit. Frightening a poor woman like this.'

"'He won't frighten her any more,' I said. 'He is dead.'

"He struck with his stick at the mud.

"'And there's the child.'

"Then, after thinking deeply for a while—'I don't know that it isn't for the best.'"

"That's what he said. And she says nothing at all now. Not a word of him. Never. Is his image as utterly gone from her mind as his lithe and striding figure, his caroling voice are gone from our fields? He is no longer before her eyes to excite her imagination into a passion of love or fear; and his memory seems to have vanished from her dull brain as a shadow passes away upon a white screen. She lives in the cottage and works for Miss Swaffer. She is Amy Foster for everybody, and the child is 'Amy Foster's boy.' She calls him Johnny—which means Little John.

"It is impossible to say whether this name recalls anything to her. Does she ever think of the past? I have seen her hanging over the boy's cot in a very passion of maternal tenderness. The little fellow was lying on his back, a little frightened at me, but very still, with his big black eyes, with his fluttered air of a bird in a snare. And looking at him I seemed to see again the other one—the father, cast out mysteriously by the sea to perish in the supreme disaster of loneliness and despair." the sea to perish in the supreme disaster of loneliness and despair."

Falk: A Reminiscence

Several of us, all more or less connected with the sea, were dining in a small river-hostelry not more than thirty miles from London, and less than twenty from that shallow and dangerous puddle to which our coasting men give the grandiose name of "German Ocean." And through the wide windows we had a view of the Thames; an enfilading view down the Lower Hope Reach. But the dinner was execrable, and all the feast was for the eyes.

That flavour of salt-water which for so many of us had been the very water of life permeated our talk. He who hath known the bitterness of the Ocean shall have its taste forever in his mouth. But one or two of us, pampered by the life of the land, complained of hunger. It was impossible to swallow any of that stuff. And indeed there was a strange mustiness in everything. The wooden dining-room stuck out over the mud of the shore like a lacustrine dwelling; the planks of the floor seemed rotten; a decrepit old waiter tottered pathetically to and fro before an antediluvian and worm-eaten sideboard; the chipped plates might have been disinterred from some kitchen midden near an inhabited lake; and the chops recalled times more ancient still. They brought forcibly to one's mind the night of ages when the primeval man, evolving the first rudiments of cookery from his dim consciousness, scorched lumps of flesh at a fire of sticks in the company of other good fellows; then, gorged and happy, sat him back among the gnawed bones to tell his artless tales of experience—the tales of hunger and hunt—and of women, perhaps!

But luckily the wine happened to be as old as the waiter. So, comparatively empty, but upon the whole fairly happy, we sat back and told our artless tales. We talked of the sea and all its works. The sea never changes, and its works for all the talk of men are wrapped in mystery. But we agreed that the times were changed. And we talked of old ships, of sea-accidents, of break-downs, dismastings; and of a man who brought his ship safe to Liverpool all the way from the River Platte under a jury rudder. We talked of wrecks, of short rations and of heroism—or at least of what the newspapers would have called heroism at sea—a manifestation of virtues quite different from the heroism of primitive times. And now and then falling silent all together we gazed at the sights of the river.

A P. & O. boat passed bound down. "One gets jolly good dinners on board these ships," remarked one of our band. A man with sharp eyes read out the name on her bows: *Arcadia.* "What a beautiful model of a ship!" murmured some of us. She was followed by a small cargo steamer, and the flag they hauled down aboard while we were looking showed her to be a Norwegian. She made an awful lot of smoke; and before it had quite blown away, a high-sided, short, wooden barque, in ballast and towed by a paddle-tug, appeared in front of the windows. All her hands were forward busy setting up the headgear; and aft a woman in a red hood, quite alone with the man at the wheel, paced the length of the poop back and forth, with the grey wool of some knitting work in her hands.

"German I should think," muttered one. "The skipper has his wife on board," remarked another; and the light of the crimson sunset all ablaze behind the London smoke, throwing a glow of Bengal light upon the barque's spars, faded away from the Hope Reach.

Then one of us, who had not spoken before, a man of over fifty, that had commanded ships for a quarter of a century, looking after the barque now gliding far away, all black on the lustre of the river, said:

This reminds me of an absurd episode in my life, now many years ago, when I got first the command of an iron barque, loading then in a certain Eastern seaport. It was also the capital of an Eastern kingdom, lying up a river as might be London lies up this old Thames of ours. No more need be said of the place; for this sort of thing might have happened anywhere where there are ships, skippers, tugboats, and orphan nieces of indescribable splendour. And the absurdity of the episode concerns only me, my enemy Falk, and my friend Hermann.

There seemed to be something like peculiar emphasis on the words "My friend Hermann," which caused one of us (for we had just been speaking of heroism at sea) to say idly and nonchalantly:

"And was this Hermann a hero?"

Not at all, said our grizzled friend. No hero at all. He was a Schiff-führer: Ship-conductor. That's how they call a Master Mariner in Germany. I prefer our way. The alliteration is good, and there is something in the nomenclature that gives to us as a body the sense of corporate existence: Apprentice, Mate, Master, in the ancient and honourable craft of the sea. As to my friend Hermann, he might have been a consummate master of the honourable craft, but he was called officially Schiff-führer, and had the simple, heavy appearance of a well-to-do farmer, combined with the good-natured shrewdness of a small shopkeeper. With his shaven chin, round limbs, and heavy eyelids he did not look like a toiler, and even less like an adventurer of the sea. Still, he toiled upon the seas, in his own way, much as a shopkeeper works behind his counter. And his ship was the means by which he maintained his growing family.

She was a heavy, strong, blunt-bowed affair, awakening the ideas of primitive solidity, like the wooden plough of our forefathers. And there were, about her, other suggestions of a rustic and homely nature. The extraordinary timber projections which I have seen in no other vessel made her square stern resemble the tail end of a miller's waggon. But the four stern ports of her cabin, glazed with six little greenish panes each, and framed in wooden sashes painted brown, might have been the windows of a cottage in the country. The tiny white curtains and the greenery of flower pots behind the glass completed the resemblance. On one or two occasions when passing under stern I had detected from my boat a round arm in the act of tilting a watering pot, and the bowed sleek head of a maiden whom I shall always call Hermann's niece, because as a matter of fact I've never heard her name, for all my intimacy with the family.

This, however, sprang up later on. Meantime in common with the rest of the shipping in that Eastern port, I was left in no doubt as to

Hermann's notions of hygienic clothing. Evidently he believed in wearing good stout flannel next his skin. On most days little frocks and pinafores could be seen drying in the mizzen rigging of his ship, or a tiny row of socks fluttering on the signal halyards; but once a fortnight the family washing was exhibited in force. It covered the poop entirely. The afternoon breeze would incite to a weird and flabby activity all that crowded mass of clothing, with its vague suggestions of drowned, mutilated and flattened humanity. Trunks without heads waved at you arms without hands; legs without feet kicked fantastically with collapsible flourishes; and there were long white garments that, taking the wind fairly through their neck openings edged with lace, became for a moment violently distended as by the passage of obese and invisible bodies. On these days you could make out that ship at a great distance by the multi-coloured grotesque riot going on abaft her mizzen mast.

She had her berth just ahead of me, and her name was *Diana*,— Diana not of Ephesus but of Bremen. This was proclaimed in white letters a foot long spaced widely across the stern (somewhat like the lettering of a shop-sign) under the cottage windows. This ridiculously unsuitable name struck one as an impertinence towards the memory of the most charming of goddesses; for, apart from the fact that the old craft was physically incapable of engaging in any sort of chase, there was a gang of four children belonging to her. They peeped over the rail at passing boats and occasionally dropped various objects into them. Thus, sometime before I knew Hermann to speak to, I received on my hat a horrid rag-doll belonging to Hermann's eldest daughter. However, these youngsters were upon the whole well behaved. They had fair heads, round eyes, round little knobby noses, and they resembled their father a good deal.

This *Diana* of Bremen was a most innocent old ship, and seemed to know nothing of the wicked sea, as there are on shore households that know nothing of the corrupt world. And the sentiments she suggested were unexceptionable and mainly of a domestic order. She was a home. All these dear children had learned to walk on her roomy quarter-deck. In such thoughts there is something pretty, even touching. Their teeth, I should judge, they had cut on the ends of her running gear. I have many times observed the baby Hermann (Nicholas) engaged in gnawing the whipping of the fore-royal brace. Nicholas' favourite place of residence was under the main fife-rail. Directly he was let loose he would crawl off there, and the first seaman who came along would bring him, carefully held aloft in tarry hands, back to the cabin door. I fancy there must have been a standing order to that effect. In the course of these transportations the baby, who was the only peppery person in the ship, tried to smite these stalwart young German sailors on the face.

Mrs. Hermann, an engaging, stout housewife, wore on board baggy blue dresses with white dots. When, as happened once or twice I caught her at an elegant little wash-tub rubbing hard on white collars, baby's socks, and Hermann's summer neckties, she would blush in girlish confusion, and raising her wet hands greet me from afar with many friendly nods. Her sleeves would be rolled up to the elbows, and the gold hoop of her wedding ring glittered among the soapsuds. Her voice was pleasant, she had a serene brow, smooth bands of very fair hair, and a good-humoured expression of the eyes. She was motherly and moderately talkative. When this simple matron smiled, youthful dimples broke out on her fresh broad cheeks. Hermann's niece on the other hand, an orphan and very silent, I never saw attempt a smile. This, however, was not gloom on her part but the restraint of youthful gravity.

They had carried her about with them for the last three years, to help with the children and be company for Mrs. Hermann, as Hermann mentioned once to me. It had been very necessary while they were all little, he had added in a vexed manner. It was her arm and her sleek head that I had glimpsed one morning, through the stern-windows of the cabin, hovering over the pots of fuchsias and mignonette; but the first time I beheld her full length I surrendered to her proportions. They fix her in my mind, as great beauty, great intelligence, quickness of wit or kindness of heart might have made some her other woman equally memorable.

With her it was form and size. It was her physical personality that had this imposing charm. She might have been witty, intelligent, and kind to an exceptional degree. I don't know, and this is not to the point. All I know is that she was built on a magnificent scale. Built is the only word. She was constructed, she was erected, as it were, with a regal lavishness. It staggered you to see this reckless expenditure of material upon a chit of a girl. She was youthful and also perfectly mature, as though she had been some fortunate immortal. She was heavy too, perhaps, but that's nothing. It only added to that notion of permanence. She was barely nineteen. But such shoulders! Such round arms! Such a shadowing forth of mighty limbs when with three long strides she pounced across the deck upon the overturned Nicholas—it's perfectly indescribable! She seemed a good, quiet girl, vigilant as to Lena's needs, Gustav's tumbles, the state of Carl's dear little nose— conscientious, hardworking, and all that. But what magnificent hair she had! Abundant, long, thick, of a tawny colour. It had the sheen of precious metals. She wore it plaited tightly into one single tress hanging girlishly down her back and its end reached down to her waist. The massiveness of it surprised you. On my word it reminded one of a club. Her face was big, comely, of an unruffled expression. She had a good complexion, and her blue eyes were so pale that she appeared to look at the world with the empty white candour of a statue. You could not call her good-looking. It was something much more impressive. The simplicity of her apparel, the opulence of her form, her imposing stature, and the extraordinary sense of vigorous life that seemed to emanate from her like a perfume exhaled by a flower, made her beautiful with a beauty of a rustic and olympian order. To watch her reaching up to the clothes-line with both arms raised high above her head, caused you to fall a musing in a strain of pagan piety. Excellent Mrs. Hermann's baggy cotton gowns had some sort of rudimentary frills at neck and bottom, but this girl's print frocks hadn't even a wrinkle; nothing but a few straight folds in the skirt falling to her feet, and these, when she stood still, had a severe and statuesque quality. She was inclined naturally to be still whether sitting or standing. However, I don't mean to say she was statuesque. She was too generously alive; but she could have stood for an allegoric statue of the Earth. I don't mean the worn-out earth of our possession, but a young Earth, a virginal planet undisturbed by the vision of a future teeming with the monstrous forms of life and death, clamorous with the cruel battles of hunger and thought.

The worthy Hermann himself was not very entertaining, though his English was fairly comprehensible. Mrs. Hermann, who always let off one speech at least at me in an hospitable, cordial tone (and in Platt-Deutsch I suppose) I could not understand. As to their niece, however satisfactory to look upon (and she inspired you somehow with a hopeful view as to the prospects of mankind) she was a modest and silent presence, mostly engaged in sewing, only now and then, as I observed, falling over that work into a state of maidenly meditation. Her aunt sat opposite her, sewing also, with her feet propped on a wooden footstool. On the other side of the deck Hermann and I would get a couple of chairs out of the cabin and settle down to a smoking match, accompanied at long intervals by the pacific exchange of a few words. I came nearly every evening. Hermann I would find in his shirt sleeves. As soon as he returned from the shore on board his ship he commenced operations by taking off his coat; then he put on his head an embroidered round cap with a tassel, and changed his boots for a pair of cloth slippers. Afterwards he smoked at the cabin-door, looking at his children with an air of civic virtue, till they got caught one after another and put to bed in various staterooms. Lastly, we would drink some beer in the cabin, which was furnished with a wooden table on cross legs, and with black straight-backed chairs—more like a farm kitchen than a ship's cuddy. The sea and all nautical affairs seemed very far removed from the hospitality of this exemplary family.

And I liked this because I had a rather worrying time on board my own ship. I had been appointed ex-officio by the British Consul to take charge of her after a man who had died suddenly, leaving for the guidance of his successor some suspiciously unreceipted bills, a few dry-dock estimates hinting at bribery, and a quantity of vouchers for three years' extravagant expenditure; all these mixed up together in a dusty old violin-case lined with ruby velvet. I found besides a large account-book, which, when opened, hopefully turned out to my infinite consternation to be filled with verses—page after page of rhymed doggerel of a jovial and improper character, written in the neatest minute hand I ever did see. In the same fiddle-case a photograph of my predecessor, taken lately in Saigon, represented in front of a garden view, and in company of a female in strange draperies, an elderly, squat, rugged man of stern aspect in a clumsy suit of black broadcloth, and with the hair brushed forward above the temples in a manner reminding one of a boar's tusks. Of a fiddle, however, the only trace on board was the case, its empty husk as it were; but of the two last freights the ship had indubitably earned of late, there were not even the husks left. It was impossible to say where all that money had gone to. It wasn't on board. It had not been remitted home; for a letter from the owners, preserved in a desk evidently by the merest accident, complained mildly enough that they had not been favoured by a scratch of the pen for the last eighteen months. There were next to no stores on board, not an inch of spare rope or a yard of canvas. The ship had been run bare, and I foresaw no end of difficulties before I could get her ready for sea.

As I was young then—not thirty yet—I took myself and my troubles very seriously. The old mate, who had acted as chief mourner at the captain's funeral, was not particularly pleased at my coming. But the fact is the fellow was not legally qualified for command, and the Consul was bound, if at all possible, to put a properly certificated man on board. As to the second mate, all I can say his name was Tottersen, or something like that. His practice was to wear on his head, in that tropical climate, a mangy fur cap. He was, without exception, the stupidest man I had ever seen on board ship. And he looked it too. He looked so confoundedly stupid that it was a matter of surprise for me when he answered to his name.

I drew no great comfort from their company, to say the least of it; while the prospect of making a long sea passage with those two fellows was depressing. And my other thoughts in solitude could not be of a gay complexion. The crew was sickly, the cargo was coming very slow; I foresaw I would have lots of trouble with the charterers, and doubted whether they would advance me enough money for the ship's expenses. Their attitude towards me was unfriendly. Altogether I was not getting on. I would discover at odd times (generally about midnight) that I was totally inexperienced, greatly ignorant of business, and hopelessly unfit for any sort of command; and when the steward had to be taken to the hospital ill with choleraic symptoms I felt bereaved of the only decent person at the after end of the ship. He was fully expected to recover, but in the meantime had to be replaced by some sort of servant. And on the recommendation of a certain Schomberg, the proprietor of the smaller of the two hotels in the place, I engaged a Chinaman. Schomberg, a brawny, hairy Alsatian, and an awful gossip, assured me that it was all right. "First-class boy that. Came in the *suite* of his Excellency Tseng the Commissioner—you know. His Excellency Tseng lodged with me here for three weeks."

He mouthed the Chinese Excellency at me with great unction, though the specimen of the "suite" did not seem very promising. At the time, however, I did not know what an untrustworthy humbug Schomberg was. The "boy" might have been forty or a hundred and forty for all you could tell—one of those Chinamen of the death's-head type of face and completely inscrutable. Before the end of the third day he had revealed himself as a confirmed opium-smoker, a gambler, a most audacious thief, and a first-class sprinter. When he departed at the top of his speed with thirty-two golden sovereigns of my own hard-earned savings it was the last straw. I had reserved that money in case my difficulties came to the worst. Now it was gone I felt as poor and naked as a fakir. I clung to my ship, for all the bother she caused me, but what I could not bear were the long lonely evenings in her cuddy, where the atmosphere, made smelly by a leaky lamp, was agitated by the snoring of the mate. That fellow shut himself up in his stuffy cabin punctually at eight, and made gross and revolting noises like a water-logged trump. It was odious not to be able to worry oneself in comfort on board one's own ship. Everything in this world, I reflected, even the command of a nice little barque, may be made a delusion and a snare for the unwary spirit of pride in man.

From such reflections I was glad to make any escape on board that Bremen *Diana*. There apparently no whisper of the world's iniquities had ever penetrated. And yet she lived upon the wide sea: and the sea tragic and comic, the sea with its horrors and its peculiar scandals, the sea peopled by men and ruled by iron necessity is indubitably a part of the world. But that patriarchal old tub, like some saintly retreat, echoed nothing of it. She was world proof. Her venerable innocence apparently had put a restraint on the roaring lusts of the sea. And yet I have known the sea too long to believe in its respect for decency. An elemental force is ruthlessly frank. It may, of course, have been Hermann's skilful seamanship, but to me it looked as if the allied oceans had refrained from smashing these high bulwarks, unshipping the lumpy rudder, frightening the children, and generally opening this family's eyes out of sheer reticence. It looked like reticence. The ruthless disclosure was in the end left for a man to make; a man strong and elemental enough and driven to unveil some secrets of the sea by the power of a simple and elemental desire.

This, however, occurred much later, and meantime I took sanctuary in that serene old ship early every evening. The only person on board that seemed to be in trouble was little Lena, and in due course I perceived that the health of the rag-doll was more than delicate. This object led a sort of "in extremis" existence in a wooden box placed against the starboard mooring-bitts, tended and nursed with the greatest sympathy and care by all the children, who greatly enjoyed pulling long faces and moving with hushed footsteps. Only the baby—Nicholas— looked on with a cold, ruffianly leer, as if he had belonged to another tribe altogether. Lena perpetually sorrowed over the box, and all of them were in deadly earnest. It was wonderful the way these children would work up their compassion for that bedraggled thing I wouldn't have touched with a pair of tongs. I suppose they were exercising and developing their racial sentimentalism by the means of that dummy. I was only surprised that Mrs. Hermann let Lena cherish and hug that bundle of rags to that extent, it was so disreputably and completely unclean. But Mrs. Hermann would raise her fine womanly eyes from her needlework to look on with amused sympathy, and did not seen to see it, somehow, that this object of affection was a disgrace to the ship's purity. Purity, not cleanliness, is the word. It was pushed so far that I seemed to detect in this too a sentimental excess, as if dirt had been removed in very love. It is impossible to give you an idea of such a meticulous neatness. It was as if every morning that ship had been arduously explored with—with toothbrushes. Her very bowsprit three times a week had its toilette made with a cake of soap and a piece of soft flannel. Arrayed—I *must* say arrayed—arrayed artlessly in dazzling white paint as to wood and dark green as to ironwork the simple-minded distribution of these colours evoked the images of simple-minded peace, of arcadian felicity; and the childish comedy of disease and sorrow struck me sometimes as an abominably real blot upon that ideal state.

I enjoyed it greatly, and on my part I brought a little mild excitement into it. Our intimacy arose from the pursuit of that thief. It was in the evening, and Hermann, who, contrary to his habits, had stayed on shore late that day, was extricating himself backwards out of a little gharry on the river bank, opposite his ship, when the hunt passed. Realising the situation as though he had eyes in his shoulder-blades, he joined us with a leap and took the lead. The Chinaman fled silent like a rapid shadow on the dust of an extremely oriental road. I followed. A long way in the rear my mate whooped like a savage. A young moon threw a bashful light on a plain like a monstrous waste ground: the architectural mass of a Buddhist temple far away projected itself in dead black on the sky. We lost the thief of course; but in my disappointment I had to admire Hermann's presence of mind. The velocity that stodgy man developed in the interests of a complete stranger earned my warm gratitude—there was something truly cordial in his exertions.

He seemed as vexed as myself at our failure, and would hardly listen to my thanks. He said it was "nothings," and invited me on the spot to come on board his ship and drink a glass of beer with him. We poked sceptically for a while amongst the bushes, peered without conviction into a ditch or two. There was not a sound: patches of slime glimmered feebly amongst the reeds. Slowly we trudged back, drooping under the thin sickle of the moon, and I heard him mutter to himself, "Himmel! Zwei und dreissig Pfund!" He was impressed by the figure of my loss. For a long time we had ceased to hear the mate's whoops and yells.

Then he said to me, "Everybody has his troubles," and as we went on remarked that he would never have known anything of mine hadn't he by an extraordinary chance been detained on shore by Captain Falk. He didn't like to stay late ashore—he added with a sigh. The something doleful in his tone I put to his sympathy with my misfortune, of course.

On board the *Diana* Mrs. Hermann's fine eyes expressed much interest and commiseration. We had found the two women sewing face to face under the open skylight in the strong glare of the lamp. Hermann walked in first, starting in the very doorway to pull off his coat, and encouraging me with loud, hospitable ejaculations: "Come in! This way! Come in, captain!" At once, coat in hand, he began to tell his wife all about it. Mrs. Hermann put the palms of her plump hands together; I smiled and bowed with a heavy heart: the niece got up from her sewing to bring Hermann's slippers and his embroidered calotte, which he assumed pontifically, talking (about me) all the time. Billows of white stuff lay between the chairs on the cabin floor; I caught the words "Zwei und dreissig Pfund" repeated several times, and presently came the beer, which seemed delicious to my throat, parched with running and the emotions of the chase.

I didn't get away till well past midnight, long after the women had retired. Hermann had been trading in the East for three years or more, carrying freights of rice and timber mostly. His ship was well known in all the ports from Vladivostok to Singapore. She was his own property. The profits had been moderate, but the trade answered well enough while the children were small yet. In another year or so he hoped he would be able to sell the old *Diana* to a firm in Japan for a fair price. He intended to return home, to Bremen, by mail boat, second class, with Mrs. Hermann and the children. He told me all this stolidly, with slow puffs at his pipe. I was sorry when knocking the ashes out he began to rub his eyes. I would have sat with him till morning. What had I to hurry on board my own ship for? To face the broken rifled drawer in my state-room. Ugh! The very thought made me feel unwell.

I became their daily guest, as you know. I think that Mrs. Hermann from the first looked upon me as a romantic person. I did not, of course, tear my hair *coram populo* over my loss, and she took it for lordly indifference. Afterwards, I daresay, I did tell them some of my adventures—such as they were—and they marvelled greatly at the extent of my experience. Hermann would translate what he thought the most striking passages. Getting up on his legs, and as if delivering a lecture on a phenomenon, he addressed himself, with gestures, to the two women, who would let their sewing sink slowly on their laps. Meantime I sat before a glass of Hermann's beer, trying to look modest. Mrs. Hermann would glance at me quickly, emit slight "Ach's!" The girl never made a sound. Never. But she too would sometimes raise her pale eyes to look at me in her unseeing gentle way. Her glance was by no means stupid; it beamed out soft and diffuse as the moon beams upon a landscape—quite differently from the scrutinising inspection of the stars. You were drowned in it, and imagined yourself to appear blurred. And yet this same glance when turned upon Christian Falk must have been as efficient as the searchlight of a battle-ship.

Falk was the other assiduous visitor on board, but from his behaviour he might have been coming to see the quarter-deck capstan. He certainly used to stare at it a good deal when keeping us company outside the cabin door, with one muscular arm thrown over the back of the chair, and his big shapely legs, in very tight white trousers, extended far out and ending in a pair of black shoes as roomy as punts. On arrival he would shake Hermann's hand with a mutter, bow to the women, and take up his careless and misanthropic attitude by our side. He departed abruptly, with a jump, going through the performance of grunts, handshakes, bow, as if in a panic. Sometimes, with a sort of discreet and convulsive effort, he approached the women and exchanged a few low words with them, half a dozen at most. On these occasions Hermann's usual stare became positively glassy and Mrs. Hermann's kind countenance would colour up. The girl herself never turned a hair.

Falk was a Dane or perhaps a Norwegian, I can't tell now. At all events he was a Scandinavian of some sort, and a bloated monopolist to boot. It is possible he was unacquainted with the word, but he had a clear perception of the thing itself. His tariff of charges for towing ships in and out was the most brutally inconsiderate document of the sort I had ever seen. He was the commander and owner of the only tug-boat on the river, a very trim white craft of 150 tons or more, as elegantly neat as a yacht, with a round wheel-house rising like a glazed turret high above her sharp bows, and with one slender varnished pole mast forward. I daresay there are yet a few shipmasters afloat who remember Falk and his tug very well. He extracted his pound and a half of flesh from each of us merchant-skippers with an inflexible sort of indifference which made him detested and even feared. Schomberg used to remark: "I won't talk about the fellow. I don't think he has six drinks from year's end to year's end in my place. But my advice is, gentlemen, don't you have anything to do with him, if you can help it."

This advice, apart from unavoidable business relations, was easy to follow because Falk intruded upon no one. It seems absurd to compare a tugboat skipper to a centaur: but he reminded me somehow of an engraving in a little book I had as a boy, which represented centaurs at a stream, and there was one, especially in the foreground, prancing bow and arrows in hand, with regular severe features and an immense curled wavy beard, flowing down his breast. Falk's face reminded me of that centaur. Besides, he was a composite creature. Not a man-horse, it is true, but a man-boat. He lived on board his tug, which was always dashing up and down the river from early morn till dewy eve.

In the last rays of the setting sun, you could pick out far away down the reach his beard borne high up on the white structure, foaming up stream to anchor for the night. There was the white-clad man's body, and the rich brown patch of the hair, and nothing below the waist but the 'thwart-ship white lines of the bridge-screens, that lead the eye to the sharp white lines of the bows cleaving the muddy water of the river.

Separated from his boat to me at least he seemed incomplete. The tug herself without his head and torso on the bridge looked mutilated as it were. But he left her very seldom. All the time I remained in harbour I saw him only twice on shore. On the first occasion it was at my charterers, where he came in misanthropically to get paid for towing out a French barque the day before. The second time I could hardly believe my eyes, for I beheld him reclining under his beard in a cane-bottomed chair in the billiard-room of Schomberg's hotel.

It was very funny to see Schomberg ignoring him pointedly. The artificiality of it contrasted strongly with Falk's natural unconcern. The big Alsatian talked loudly with his other customers, going from one little table to the other, and passing Falk's place of repose with his eyes fixed straight ahead. Falk sat there with an untouched glass at his elbow. He must have known by sight and name every white man in the room, but he never addressed a word to anybody. He acknowledged my presence by a drop of his eyelids, and that was all. Sprawling there in the chair, he would, now and again, draw the palms of both his hands down his face, giving at the same time a slight, almost imperceptible, shudder.

It was a habit he had, and of course I was perfectly familiar with it, since you could not remain an hour in his company without being made to wonder at such a movement breaking some long period of stillness. It was a passionate and inexplicable gesture. He used to make it at all sorts of times; as likely as not after he had been listening to little Lena's chatter about the suffering doll, for instance. The Hermann children always besieged him about his legs closely, though, in a gentle way, he shrank from them a little. He seemed, however, to feel a great affection for the whole family. For Hermann himself especially. He sought his company. In this case, for instance, he must have been waiting for him, because as soon as he appeared Falk rose hastily, and they went out together. Then Schomberg expounded in my hearing to three or four people his theory that Falk was after Captain Hermann's niece, and asserted confidently that nothing would come of it. It was the same last year when Captain Hermann was loading here, he said.

Naturally, I did not believe Schomberg, but I own that for a time I observed closely what went on. All I discovered was some impatience on Hermann's part. At the sight of Falk, stepping over the gangway, the excellent man would begin to mumble and chew between his teeth something that sounded like German swear-words. However, as I've said, I'm not familiar with the language, and Hermann's soft, round-eyed countenance remained unchanged. Staring stolidly ahead he greeted him with, "Wie gehts," or in English, "How are you?" with a throaty enunciation. The girl would look up for an instant and move her lips slightly: Mrs. Hermann let her hands rest on her lap to talk volubly to him for a minute or so in her pleasant voice before she went on with her sewing again. Falk would throw himself into a chair, stretch his big legs, as like as not draw his hands down his face passionately. As to myself, he was not pointedly impertinent: it was rather as though he could not be bothered with such trifles as my existence; and the truth is that being a monopolist he was under no necessity to be amiable. He was sure to get his own extortionate terms out of me for towage whether he frowned or smiled. As a matter of fact, he did neither: but before many days elapsed he managed to astonish me not a little and to set Schomberg's tongue clacking more than ever.

It came about in this way. There was a shallow bar at the mouth of the river which ought to have been kept down, but the authorities of the State were piously busy gilding afresh the great Buddhist Pagoda just then, and I suppose had no money to spare for dredging operations. I don't know how it may be now, but at the time I speak of that sandbank was a great nuisance to the shipping. One of its consequences was that vessels of a certain draught of water, like Hermann's or mine, could not complete their loading in the river. After taking in as much as possible of their cargo, they had to go outside to fill up. The whole procedure was an unmitigated bore. When you thought you had as much on board as your ship could carry safely over the bar, you went and gave notice to your agents. They, in their turn, notified Falk that so-and-so was ready to go out. Then Falk (ostensibly when it fitted in with his other work, but, if the truth were known, simply when his arbitrary spirit moved him), after ascertaining carefully in the office that there was enough money to meet his bill, would come along unsympathetically, glaring at you with his yellow eyes from the bridge, and would drag you out dishevelled as to rigging, lumbered as to the decks, with unfeeling haste, as if to execution. And he would force you too to take the end of his own wire hawser, for the use of which there was of course an extra charge. To your shouted remonstrances against that extortion this towering trunk with one hand on the engine-room telegraph only shook its bearded head above the splash, the racket, and the clouds of smoke in which the tug, backing and filling in the smother of churning paddle-wheels behaved like a ferocious and impatient creature. He had her manned by the cheekiest gang of lascars I ever did see, whom he allowed to bawl at you insolently, and, once fast, he plucked you out of your berth as if he did not care what he smashed. Eighteen miles down the river you had to go behind him, and then three more along the coast to where a group of uninhabited rocky islets enclosed a sheltered anchorage. There you would have to lie at single anchor with your naked spars showing to seaward over these barren fragments of land scattered upon a very intensely blue sea. There was nothing to look at besides but a bare coast, the muddy edge of the brown plain with the sinuosities of the river you had left, traced in dull green, and the Great Pagoda uprising lonely and massive with shining curves and pinnacles like the gorgeous and stony efflorescence of tropical rocks. You had nothing to do but to wait fretfully for the balance of your cargo, which was sent out of the river with the greatest irregularity. And it was open to you to console yourself with the thought that, after all, this stage of bother meant that your departure from these shores was indeed approaching at last.

We both had to go through that stage, Hermann and I, and there was a sort of tacit emulation between the ships as to which should be ready first. We kept on neck and neck almost to the finish, when I won the race by going personally to give notice in the forenoon; whereas Hermann, who was very slow in making up his mind to go ashore, did not get to the agents' office till late in the day. They told him there that my ship was first on turn for next morning, and I believe he told them he was in no hurry. It suited him better to go the day after.

That evening, on board the *Diana*, he sat with his plump knees well apart, staring and puffing at the curved mouthpiece of his pipe. Presently he spoke with some impatience to his niece about putting the children to bed. Mrs. Hermann, who was talking to Falk, stopped short and looked at her husband uneasily, but the girl got up at once and drove the children before her into the cabin. In a little while Mrs. Hermann had to leave us to quell what, from the sounds inside, must have been a dangerous mutiny. At this Hermann grumbled to himself. For half an hour longer Falk left alone with us fidgeted on his chair, sighed lightly, then at last, after drawing his hands down his face, got up, and as if renouncing the hope of making himself understood (he hadn't opened his mouth once) he said in English: "Well. . . . Good night, Captain Hermann." He stopped for a moment before my chair and looked down fixedly; I may even say he glared: and he went so far as to make a deep noise in his throat. There was in all this something so marked that for the first time in our limited intercourse of nods and grunts he excited in me something like interest. But next moment he disappointed me—for he strode away hastily without a nod even.

His manner was usually odd it is true, and I certainly did not pay much attention to it; but that sort of obscure intention, which seemed to lurk in his nonchalance like a wary old carp in a pond, had never before come so near the surface. He had distinctly aroused my expectations. I would have been unable to say what it was I expected, but at all events I did not expect the absurd developments he sprung upon me no later than the break of the very next day.

I remember only that there was, on that evening, enough point in his behaviour to make me, after he had fled, wonder audibly what he might mean. To this Hermann, crossing his legs with a swing and settling himself viciously away from me in his chair, said: "That fellow don't know himself what he means."

There might have been some insight in such a remark. I said nothing, and, still averted, he added: "When I was here last year he was just the same." An eruption of tobacco smoke enveloped his head as if his temper had exploded like gunpowder.

I had half a mind to ask him point blank whether he, at least, didn't know why Falk, a notoriously unsociable man, had taken to visiting his ship with such assiduity. After all, I reflected suddenly, it was a most remarkable thing. I wonder now what Hermann would have said. As it turned out he didn't let me ask. Forgetting all about Falk apparently, he started a monologue on his plans for the future: the selling of the ship, the going home; and falling into a reflective and calculating mood he mumbled between regular jets of smoke about the expense. The necessity of disbursing passage money for all his tribe seemed to disturb him in a manner that was the more striking because otherwise he gave no signs of a miserly disposition. And yet he fussed over the prospect of that voyage home in a mail boat like a sedentary grocer who has made up his mind to see the world. He was racially thrifty I suppose, and for him there must have been a great novelty in finding himself obliged to pay for travelling—for sea travelling which was the normal state of life for the family—from the very cradle for most of them. I could see he grudged prospectively every single shilling which must be spent so absurdly. It was rather funny. He would become doleful over it, and then again, with a fretful sigh, he would suppose there was nothing for it now but to take three second-class tickets—and there were the four children to pay for besides. A lot of money that to spend at once. A big lot of money.

I sat with him listening (not for the first time) to these heart-searchings till I grew thoroughly sleepy, and then I left him and turned in on board my ship. At daylight I was awakened by a yelping of shrill voices, accompanied by a great commotion in the water, and the short, bullying blasts of a steam-whistle. Falk with his tug had come for me.

I began to dress. It was remarkable that the answering noise on board my ship together with the patter of feet above my head ceased suddenly. But I heard more remote guttural cries which seemed to express surprise and annoyance. Then the voice of my mate reached me howling expostulations to somebody at a distance. Other voices joined, apparently indignant; a chorus of something that sounded like abuse replied. Now and then the steam-whistle screeched.

Altogether that unnecessary uproar was distracting, but down there in my cabin I took it calmly. In another moment, I thought, I should be going down that wretched river, and in another week at the most I should be totally quit of the odious place and all the odious people in it.

Greatly cheered by the idea, I seized the hair-brushes and looking at myself in the glass began to use them. Suddenly a hush fell upon the noise outside, and I heard (the ports of my cabin were thrown open)—I heard a deep calm voice, not on board my ship, however, hailing resolutely in English, but with a strong foreign twang, "Go ahead!"

There may be tides in the affairs of men which taken at the flood . . . and so on. Personally I am still on the look out for that important turn. I am, however, afraid that most of us are fated to flounder for ever in the dead water of a pool whose shores are arid indeed. But I know that there are often in men's affairs unexpectedly—even irrationally—illuminating moments when an otherwise insignificant sound, perhaps only some perfectly commonplace gesture, suffices to reveal to us all the unreason, all the fatuous unreason, of our complacency. "Go ahead" are not particularly striking words even when pronounced with a foreign accent; yet they petrified me in the very act of smiling at myself in the glass. And then, refusing to believe my ears, but already boiling with indignation, I ran out of the cabin and up on deck.

It was incredibly true. It was perfectly true. I had no eyes for anything but the *Diana*. It was she, then, was being taken away. She was already out of her berth and shooting athwart the river. "The way this loonatic plucked that ship out is a caution," said the awed voice of my mate close to my ear. "Hey! Hallo! Falk! Hermann! What's this infernal trick?" I yelled in a fury.

Nobody heard me. Falk certainly could not hear me. His tug was turning at full speed away under the other bank. The wire hawser between her and the *Diana*, stretched as taut as a harp-string, vibrated alarmingly.

The high black craft careened over to the awful strain. A loud crack came out of her, followed by the tearing and splintering of wood. "There!" said the awed voice in my ear. "He's carried away their towing chock." And then, with enthusiasm, "Oh! Look! Look! sir, Look! at them Dutchmen skipping out of the way on the forecastle. I hope to goodness he'll break a few of their shins before he's done with 'em."

I yelled my vain protests. The rays of the rising sun coursing level along the plain warmed my back, but I was hot enough with rage. I could not have believed that a simple towing operation could suggest so plainly the idea of abduction, of rape. Falk was simply running off with the *Diana*.

The white tug careered out into the middle of the river. The red floats of her paddle-wheels revolving with mad rapidity tore up the whole reach into foam. The *Diana* in mid-stream waltzed round with as much grace as an old barn, and flew after her ravisher. Through the ragged fog of smoke driving headlong upon the water I had a glimpse of Falk's square motionless shoulders under a white hat as big as a cart-wheel, of his red face, his yellow staring eyes, his great beard. Instead of keeping a lookout ahead, he was deliberately turning his back on the river to glare at his tow. The tall heavy craft, never so used before in her life, seemed to have lost her senses; she took a wild sheer against her helm, and for a moment came straight at us, menacing and clumsy, like a runaway mountain. She piled up a streaming, hissing, boiling wave half-way up her blunt stem, my crew let out one great howl,—and then we held our breaths. It was a near thing. But Falk had her! He had her in his clutch. I fancied I could hear the steel hawser ping as it surged across the *Diana's* forecastle, with the hands on board of her bolting away from it in all directions. It was a near thing. Hermann, with his hair rumpled, in a snuffy flannel shirt and a pair of mustard-coloured trousers, had rushed to help with the wheel. I saw his terrified round face; I saw his very teeth uncovered by a sort of ghastly fixed grin; and in a great leaping tumult of water between the two ships the *Diana* whisked past so close that I could have flung a hair-brush at his head, for, it seems, I had kept them in my hands all the time. Meanwhile Mrs. Hermann sat placidly on the skylight, with a woollen shawl on her shoulders. The excellent woman in response to my indignant gesticulations fluttered a handkerchief, nodding and smiling in the kindest way imaginable. The boys, only half-dressed, were jumping about the poop in great glee, displaying their gaudy braces; and Lena in a short scarlet petticoat, with peaked elbows and thin bare arms, nursed the rag-doll with devotion. The whole family passed before my sight as if dragged across a scene of unparalleled violence. The last I saw was Hermann's niece with the baby Hermann in her arms standing apart from the others. Magnificent in her close-fitting print frock she displayed something so commanding in the manifest perfection of her figure that the sun seemed to be rising for her alone. The flood of light brought out the opulence of her form and the vigour of her youth in a glorifying way. She went by perfectly motionless and as if lost in meditation; only the hem of her skirt stirred in the draught; the sun rays broke on her sleek tawny hair; that bald-headed ruffian, Nicholas, was whacking her on the shoulder. I saw his tiny fat arm rise and fall in a workmanlike manner. And then the four cottage windows of the *Diana* came into view retreating swiftly down the river. The sashes were up, and one of the white calico curtains was fluttered straight out like a streamer above the agitated water of the wake.

To be thus tricked out of one's turn was an unheard of occurrence. In my agent's office, where I went to complain at once, they protested with apologies they couldn't understand how the mistake arose: but Schomberg when I dropped in later to get some tiffin, though surprised to see me, was perfectly ready with an explanation. I found him seated at the end of a long narrow table, facing his wife—a scraggy little woman, with long ringlets and a blue tooth, who smiled abroad stupidly and looked frightened when you spoke to her. Between them a waggling punkah fanned twenty cane-bottomed chairs and two rows of shiny plates. Three Chinamen in white jackets loafed with napkins in their hands around that desolation. Schomberg's pet *table d'hôte* was not much of a success that day. He was feeding himself ferociously and seemed to overflow with bitterness.

He began by ordering in a brutal voice the chops to be brought back for me, and turning in his chair: "Mistake they told you? Not a bit of it! Don't you believe it for a moment, captain! Falk isn't a man to make mistakes unless on purpose." His firm conviction was that Falk had been trying all along to curry favour on the cheap with Hermann. "On the cheap—mind you! It doesn't cost him a cent to put that insult upon you, and Captain Hermann gets in a day ahead of your ship. Time's money! Eh? You are very friendly with Captain Hermann I believe, but a man is bound to be pleased at any little advantage he may get. Captain Hermann is a good business man, and there's no such thing as a friend in business. Is there?" He leaned forward and began to cast stealthy glances as usual. "But Falk is, and always was, a miserable fellow. I would despise him."

I muttered, grumpily, that I had no particular respect for Falk.

"I would despise him," he insisted, with an appearance of anxiety which would have amused me if I had not been fathoms deep in discontent. To a young man fairly conscientious and as well-meaning as only the young man can be, the current ill-usage of life comes with a peculiar cruelty. Youth that is fresh enough to believe in guilt, in innocence, and in itself, will always doubt whether it have not perchance deserved its fate. Sombre of mind and without appetite, I struggled with the chop while Mrs. Schomberg sat with her everlasting stupid grin and Schomberg's talk gathered way like a slide of rubbish.

"Let me tell you. It's all about that girl. I don't know what Captain Hermann expects, but if he asked me I could tell him something about Falk. He's a miserable fellow. That man is a perfect slave. That's what I call him. A slave. Last year I started this *table d'hôte*, and sent cards out—you know. You think he had one meal in the house? Give the thing a trial? Not once. He has got hold now of a Madras cook—a blamed fraud that I hunted out of my cookhouse with a rattan. He was not fit to cook for white men. No, not for the white men's dogs either; but, see, any damned native that can boil a pot of rice is good enough for Mr. Falk. Rice and a little fish he buys for a few cents from the fishing boats outside is what he lives on. You would hardly credit it— eh? A white man, too. . . ."

He wiped his lips, using the napkin with indignation, and looking at me. It flashed through my mind in the midst of my depression that if all the meat in the town was like these *table d'hôte* chops, Falk wasn't so far wrong. I was on the point of saying this, but Schomberg's stare was intimidating. "He's a vegetarian, perhaps," I murmured instead.

"He's a miser. A miserable miser," affirmed the hotel-keeper with great force. "The meat here is not so good as at home—of course. And dear too. But look at me. I only charge a dollar for the tiffin, and one dollar and fifty cents for the dinner. Show me anything cheaper. Why am I doing it? There's little profit in this game. Falk wouldn't look at it. I do it for the sake of a lot of young white fellows here that hadn't a place where they could get a decent meal and eat it decently in good company. There's first-rate company always at my table."

The convinced way he surveyed the empty chairs made me feel as if I had intruded upon a tiffin of ghostly Presences.

"A white man should eat like a white man, dash it all," he burst out impetuously. "Ought to eat meat, must eat meat. I manage to get meat for my patrons all the year round. Don't I? I am not catering for a dam' lot of coolies: Have another chop captain. . . . No? You, boy—take away!"

He threw himself back and waited grimly for the curry. The half-closed jalousies darkened the room pervaded by the smell of fresh whitewash: a swarm of flies buzzed and settled in turns, and poor Mrs. Schomberg's smile seemed to express the quintessence of all the imbecility that had ever spoken, had ever breathed, had ever been fed on infamous buffalo meat within these bare walls. Schomberg did not open his lips till he was ready to thrust therein a spoonful of greasy rice. He rolled his eyes ridiculously before he swallowed the hot stuff, and only then broke out afresh.

"It is the most degrading thing. They take the dish up to the wheelhouse for him with a cover on it, and he shuts both the doors before he begins to eat. Fact! Must be ashamed of himself. Ask the engineer. He can't do without an engineer—don't you see—and as no respectable man can be expected to put up with such a table, he allows them fifteen dollars a month extra mess money. I assure you it is so! You just ask Mr. Ferdinand da Costa. That's the engineer he has now. You may have seen him about my place, a delicate dark young man, with very fine eyes and a little moustache. He arrived here a year ago from Calcutta. Between you and me, I guess the money-lenders there must have been after him. He rushes here for a meal every chance he can get, for just please tell me what satisfaction is that for a well-educated young fellow to feed all alone in his cabin—like a wild beast? That's what Falk expects his engineers to put up with for fifteen dollars extra. And the rows on board every time a little smell of cooking gets about the deck! You wouldn't believe! The other day da Costa got the cook to fry a steak for him—a turtle steak it was too, not beef at all—and the fat caught or something. Young da Costa himself was telling me of it here in this room. 'Mr. Schomberg'—says he-'if I had let a cylinder cover blow off through the skylight by my negligence Captain Falk couldn't have been more savage. He frightened the cook so that he won't put anything on the fire for me now.' Poor da Costa had tears in his eyes. Only try to put yourself in his place, captain: a sensitive, gentlemanly young fellow. Is he expected to eat his food raw? But that's your Falk all over. Ask any one you like. I suppose the fifteen dollars extra he has to give keep on rankling—in there."

And Schomberg tapped his manly breast. I sat half stunned by his irrelevant babble. Suddenly he gripped my forearm in an impressive and cautious manner, as if to lead me into a very cavern of confidence.

"It's nothing but enviousness," he said in a lowered tone, which had a stimulating effect upon my wearied hearing. "I don't suppose there is one person in this town that he isn't envious of. I tell you he's dangerous. Even I myself am not safe from him. I know for certain he tried to poison. . . ."

"Oh, come now," I cried, revolted.

"But I know for certain. The people themselves came and told me of it. He went about saying everywhere I was a worse pest to this town than the cholera. He had been talking against me ever since I opened this hotel. And he poisoned Captain Hermann's mind too. Last time the *Diana* was loading here Captain Hermann used to come in every day for a drink or a cigar. This time he hasn't been here twice in a week. How do you account for that?"

He squeezed my arm till he extorted from me some sort of mumble.

"He makes ten times the money I do. I've another hotel to fight against, and there is no other tug on the river. I am not in his way, am I? He wouldn't be fit to run an hotel if he tried. But that's just his nature. He can't bear to think I am making a living. I only hope it makes him properly wretched. He's like that in everything. He would like to keep a decent table well enough. But no—for the sake of a few cents. Can't do it. It's too much for him. That's what I call being a slave to it. But he's mean enough to kick up a row when his nose gets tickled a bit. See that? That just paints him. Miserly and envious. You can't account for it any other way. Can you? I have been studying him these three years."

He was anxious I should assent to his theory. And indeed on thinking it over it would have been plausible enough if there hadn't been always the essential falseness of irresponsibility in Schomberg's chatter. However, I was not disposed to investigate the psychology of Falk. I was engaged just then in eating despondently a piece of stale Dutch cheese, being too much crushed to care what I swallowed myself, let along bothering my head about Falk's ideas of gastronomy. I could expect from their study no clue to his conduct in matters of business, which seemed to me totally unrestrained by morality or even by the commonest sort of decency. How insignificant and contemptible I must appear, for the fellow to dare treat me like this—I reflected suddenly, writhing in silent agony. And I consigned Falk and all his peculiarities to the devil with so much mental fervour as to forget Schomberg's existence, till he grabbed my arm urgently. "Well, you may think and think till every hair of your head falls off, captain; but you can't explain it in any other way."

For the sake of peace and quietness I admitted hurriedly that I couldn't: persuaded that now he would leave off. But the only result was to make his moist face shine with the pride of cunning. He removed his hand for a moment to scare a black mass of flies off the sugar-basin and caught hold of my arm again.

"To be sure. And in the same way everybody is aware he would like to get married. Only he can't. Let me quote you an instance. Well, two years ago a Miss Vanlo, a very ladylike girl, came from home to keep house for her brother, Fred, who had an engineering shop for small repairs by the water side. Suddenly Falk takes to going up to their bungalow after dinner, and sitting for hours in the verandah saying nothing. The poor girl couldn't tell for the life of her what to do with such a man, so she would keep on playing the piano and singing to him evening after evening till she was ready to drop. And it wasn't as if she had been a strong young woman either. She was thirty, and the climate had been playing the deuce with her. Then—don't you know—Fred had to sit up with them for propriety, and during whole weeks on end never got a single chance to get to bed before midnight. That was not pleasant for a tired man—was it? And besides Fred had worries then because his shop didn't pay and he was dropping money fast. He just longed to get away from here and try his luck somewhere else, but for the sake of his sister he hung on and on till he ran himself into debt over his ears—I can tell you. I, myself, could show a handful of his chits for meals and drinks in my drawer. I could never find out tho' where he found all the money at last. Can't be but he must have got something out of that brother of his, a coal merchant in Port Said. Anyhow he paid everybody before he left, but the girl nearly broke her heart. Disappointment, of course, and at her age, don't you know. . . . Mrs. Schomberg here was very friendly with her, and she could tell you. Awful despair. Fainting fits. It was a scandal. A notorious scandal. To that extent that old Mr. Siegers—not your present charterer, but Mr. Siegers the father, the old gentleman who retired from business on a fortune and got buried at sea going home, *he* had to interview Falk in his private office. He was a man who could speak like a Dutch Uncle, and, besides, Messrs. Siegers had been helping Falk with a good bit of money from the start. In fact you may say they made him as far as that goes. It so happened that just at the time he turned up here, their firm was chartering a lot of sailing ships every year, and it suited their business that there should be good towing facilities on the river. See? . . . Well—there's always an ear at the keyhole—isn't there? In fact," he lowered his tone confidentially, "in this case a good friend of mine; a man you can see here any evening; only they conversed rather low. Anyhow my friend's certain that Falk was trying to make all sorts of excuses, and old Mr. Siegers was coughing a lot. And yet Falk wanted all the time to be married too. Why! It's notorious the man has been longing for years to make a home for himself. Only he can't face the expense. When it comes to putting his hand in his pocket—it chokes him off. That's the truth and no other. I've always said so, and everybody agrees with me by this time. What do you think of that—eh?"

He appealed confidently to my indignation, but having a mind to annoy him I remarked, "that it seemed to me very pitiful—if true."

He bounced in his chair as if I had run a pin into him. I don't know what he might have said, only at that moment we heard through the half open door of the billiard-room the footsteps of two men entering from the verandah, a murmur of two voices; at the sharp tapping of a coin on a table Mrs. Schomberg half rose irresolutely. "Sit still," he hissed at her, and then, in an hospitable, jovial tone, contrasting amazingly with the angry glance that had made his wife sink in her chair, he cried very loud: "Tiffin still going on in here, gentlemen."

There was no answer, but the voices dropped suddenly. The head Chinaman went out. We heard the clink of ice in the glasses, pouring sounds, the shuffling of feet, the scraping of chairs. Schomberg, after wondering in a low mutter who the devil could be there at this time of the day, got up napkin in hand to peep through the doorway cautiously. He retreated rapidly on tip-toe, and whispering behind his hand informed me that it was Falk, Falk himself who was in there, and, what's more, he had Captain Hermann with him.

The return of the tug from the outer Roads was unexpected but possible, for Falk had taken away the *Diana* at half-past five, and it was now two o'clock. Schomberg wished me to observe that neither of these men would spend a dollar on a tiffin, which they must have wanted. But by the time I was ready to leave the dining-room Falk had gone. I heard the last of his big boots on the planks of the verandah. Hermann was sitting quite alone in the large, wooden room with the two lifeless billiard tables shrouded in striped covers, mopping his face diligently. He wore his best go-ashore clothes, a stiff collar, black coat, large white waistcoat, grey trousers. A white cotton sunshade with a cane handle reposed between his legs, his side whiskers were neatly brushed, his chin had been freshly shaved; and he only distantly resembled the dishevelled and terrified man in a snuffy night shirt and ignoble old trousers I had seen in the morning hanging on to the wheel of the *Diana*.

He gave a start at my entrance, and addressed me at once in some confusion, but with genuine eagerness. He was anxious to make it clear he had nothing to do with what he called the "tam pizness" of the morning. It was most inconvenient. He had reckoned upon another day up in town to settle his bills and sign certain papers. There were also some few stores to come, and sundry pieces of "my ironwork," as he called it quaintly, landed for repairs, had been left behind. Now he would have to hire a native boat to take all this out to the ship. It would cost five or six dollars perhaps. He had had no warning from Falk. Nothing. . . . He hit the table with his dumpy fist. . . . Der verfluchte Kerl came in the morning like a "tam' ropper," making a great noise, and took him away. His mate was not prepared, his ship was moored fast—he protested it was shameful to come upon a man in that way. Shameful! Yet such was the power Falk had on the river that when I suggested in a chilling tone that he might have simply refused to have his ship moved, Hermann was quite startled at the idea. I never realised so well before that this is an age of steam. The exclusive possession of a marine boiler had given Falk the whip-hand of us all. Hermann, recovering, put it to me appealingly that I knew very well how unsafe it was to contradict that fellow. At this I only smiled distantly.

"Der Kerl!" he cried. He was sorry he had not refused. He was indeed. The damage! The damage! What for all that damage! There was no occasion for damage. Did I know how much damage he had done? It gave me a certain satisfaction to tell him that I had heard his old waggon of a ship crack fore and aft as she went by. "You passed close enough to me," I added significantly.

He threw both his hands up to heaven at the recollection. One of them grasped by the middle the white parasol, and he resembled curiously a caricature of a shop-keeping citizen in one of his own

German comic papers. "Ach! That was dangerous," he cried. I was amused. But directly he added with an appearance of simplicity, "The side of your iron ship would have been crushed in like—like this matchbox."

"Would it?" I growled, much less amused now; but by the time I had decided that this remark was not meant for a dig at me he had worked himself into a high state of resentfulness against Falk. The inconvenience, the damage, the expense! Gottferdam! Devil take the fellow. Behind the bar Schomberg with a cigar in his teeth, pretended to be writing with a pencil on a large sheet of paper; and as Hermann's excitement increased it made me comfortingly aware of my own calmness and superiority. But it occurred to me while I listened to his revilings, that after all the good man had come up in the tug. There perhaps—since he must come to town—he had no option. But evidently he had had a drink with Falk, either accepted or offered. How was that? So I checked him by saying loftily that I hoped he would make Falk pay for every penny of the damage.

"That's it! That's it! Go for him," called out Schomberg from the bar, flinging his pencil down and rubbing his hands.

We ignored his noise. But Hermann's excitement suddenly went off the boil as when you remove a saucepan from the fire. I urged on his consideration that he had done now with Falk and Falk's confounded tug. He, Hermann, would not, perhaps, turn up again in this part of the world for years to come, since he was going to sell the *Diana* at the end of this very trip ("Go home passenger in a mail boat," he murmured mechanically). He was therefore safe from Falk's malice. All he had to do was to race off to his consignees and stop payment of the towage bill before Falk had the time to get in and lift the money.

Nothing could have been less in the spirit of my advice than the thoughtful way in which he set about to make his parasol stay propped against the edge of the table.

While I watched his concentrated efforts with astonishment he threw at me one or two perplexed, half-shy glances. Then he sat down. "That's all very well," he said reflectively.

It cannot be doubted that the man had been thrown off his balance by being hauled out of the harbour against his wish. His stolidity had been profoundly stirred, else he would never have made up his mind to ask me unexpectedly whether I had not remarked that Falk had been casting eyes upon his niece. "No more than myself," I answered with literal truth. The girl was of the sort one necessarily casts eyes at in a sense. She made no noise, but she filled most satisfactorily a good bit of space.

"But you, captain, are not the same kind of man," observed Hermann.

I was not, I am happy to say, in a position to deny this. "What about the lady?" I could not help asking. At this he gazed for a time into my face, earnestly, and made as if to change the subject. I heard him beginning to mutter something unexpected, about his children growing old enough to require schooling. He would have to leave them ashore with their grandmother when he took up that new command he expected to get in Germany.

This constant harping on his domestic arrangements was funny. I suppose it must have been like the prospect of a complete alteration in his life. An epoch. He was going, too, to part with the *Diana*! He had served in her for years. He had inherited her. From an uncle, if I remember rightly. And the future loomed big before him, occupying his thought exclusively with all its aspects as on the eve of a venturesome enterprise. He sat there frowning and biting his lip, and suddenly he began to fume and fret.

I discovered to my momentary amusement that he seemed to imagine I could, should or ought, have caused Falk in some way to pronounce himself. Such a hope was incomprehensible, but funny. Then the contact with all this foolishness irritated me. I said crossly that I had seen no symptoms, but if there were any—since he, Hermann, was so sure—then it was still worse. What pleasure Falk found in humbugging people in just that way I couldn't say. It was, however, my solemn duty to warn him. It had lately, I said, come to my knowledge that there was a man (not a very long time ago either) who had been taken in just like this.

All this passed in undertones, and at this point Schomberg, exasperated at our secrecy, went out of the room slamming the door with a crash that positively lifted us in our chairs. This, or else what I had said, huffed my Hermann, He supposed, with a contemptuous toss of his head towards the door which trembled yet, that I had got hold of some of that man's silly tales. It looked, indeed, as though his mind had been thoroughly poisoned against Schomberg. "His tales were—they were," he repeated, seeking for the word—"trash." They were trash, he reiterated, and moreover I was young yet . . .

This horrid aspersion (I regret I am no longer exposed to that sort of insult) made me huffy too. I felt ready in my own mind to back up every assertion of Schomberg's and on any subject. In a moment, devil only knows why, Hermann and I were looking at each other most inimically. He caught up his hat without more ado and I gave myself the pleasure of calling after him:

"Take my advice and make Falk pay for breaking up your ship. You aren't likely to get anything else out of him."

When I got on board my ship later on, the old mate, who was very full of the events of the morning, remarked:

"I saw the tug coming back from the outer Roads just before two P.M. " (He never by any chance used the words morning or afternoon.

Always P.M. or A.M., log-book style.) "Smart work that. Man's always in a state of hurry. He's a regular chucker-out, ain't he, sir? There's a few pubs I know of in the East-end of London that would be all the better for one of his sort around the bar." He chuckled at his joke. "A regular chucker-out. Now he has fired out that Dutchman head over heels, I suppose our turn's coming to-morrow morning."

We were all on deck at break of day (even the sick—poor devils— had crawled out) ready to cast off in the twinkling of an eye. Nothing came. Falk did not come. At last, when I began to think that probably something had gone wrong in his engine-room, we perceived the tug going by, full pelt, down the river, as if we hadn't existed. For a moment I entertained the wild notion that he was going to turn round in the next reach. Afterwards I watched his smoke appear above the plain, now here, now there, according to the windings of the river. It disappeared. Then without a word I went down to breakfast. I just simply went down to breakfast.

Not one of us uttered a sound till the mate, after imbibing—by means of suction out of a saucer—his second cup of tea, exclaimed: "Where the devil is the man gone to?"

"Courting!" I shouted, with such a fiendish laugh that the old chap didn't venture to open his lips any more.

I started to the office perfectly calm. Calm with excessive rage. Evidently they knew all about it already, and they treated me to a show of consternation. The manager, a soft-footed, immensely obese man, breathing short, got up to meet me, while all round the room the young clerks, bending over the papers on their desks, cast upward glances in my direction. The fat man, without waiting for my complaint, wheezing heavily and in a tone as if he himself were incredulous, conveyed to me the news that Falk—Captain Falk—had declined—had absolutely declined—to tow my ship—to have anything to do with my ship—this day or any other day. Never!

I did my best to preserve a cool appearance, but, all the same, I must have shown how much taken aback I was. We were talking in the middle of the room. Suddenly behind my back some ass blew his nose with great force, and at the same time another quill-driver jumped up and went out on the landing hastily. It occurred to me I was cutting a foolish figure there. I demanded angrily to see the principal in his private room.

The skin of Mr. Siegers' head showed dead white between the iron grey streaks of hair lying plastered cross-wise from ear to ear over the top of his skull in the manner of a bandage. His narrow sunken face was of an uniform and permanent terra-cotta colour, like a piece of pottery. He was sickly, thin, and short, with wrists like a boy of ten. But from that debile body there issued a bullying voice, tremendously loud, harsh and resonant, as if produced by some powerful mechanical contrivance in the nature of a fog-horn. I do not know what he did with it in the private life of his home, but in the larger sphere of business it presented the advantage of overcoming arguments without the slightest mental effort, by the mere volume of sound. We had had several passages of arms. It took me all I knew to guard the interests of my owners—whom, *nota bene*, I had never seen—while Siegers (who had made their acquaintance some years before, during a business tour in Australia) pretended to the knowledge of their innermost minds, and, in the character of "our very good friends," threw them perpetually at my head.

He looked at me with a jaundiced eye (there was no love lost between us), and declared at once that it was strange, very strange. His pronunciation of English was so extravagant that I can't even attempt to reproduce it. For instance, he said "Fferie strantch." Combined with the bellowing intonation it made the language of one's childhood sound weirdly startling, and even if considered purely as a kind of unmeaning noise it filled you with astonishment at first. "They had," he continued, "been acquainted with Captain Falk for very many years, and never had any reason. . . ."

"That's why I come to you, of course," I interrupted. "I've the right to know the meaning of this infernal nonsense." In the half light of the room, which was greenish, because of the tree-tops screening the window, I saw him writhe his meagre shoulders. It came into my head, as disconnected ideas will come at all sorts of times into one's head, that this, most likely, was the very room where, if the tale were true, Falk had been lectured by Mr. Siegers, the father. Mr. Siegers' (the son's) overwhelming voice, in brassy blasts, as though he had been trying to articulate his words through a trombone, was expressing his great regret at a conduct characterised by a very marked want of discretion . . . As I lived I was being lectured too! His deafening gibberish was difficult to follow, but it was *my* conduct—mine!—that . . . Damn! I wasn't going to stand this.

"What on earth are you driving at?" I asked in a passion. I put my hat on my head (he never offered a seat to anybody), and as he seemed for the moment struck dumb by my irreverence, I turned my back on him and marched out. His vocal arrangements blared after me a few threats of coming down on the ship for the demurrage of the lighters, and all the other expenses consequent upon the delays arising from my frivolity.

Once outside in the sunshine my head swam. It was no longer a question of mere delay. I perceived myself involved in hopeless and humiliating absurdities that were leading me to something very like a disaster. "Let us be calm," I muttered to myself, and ran into the shade of a leprous wall. From that short side-street I could see the broad main thoroughfare ruinous and gay, running away, away between stretches of decaying masonry, bamboo fences, ranges of arcades of brick and plaster, hovels of lath and mud, lofty temple gates of carved timber, huts of rotten mats—an immensely wide thoroughfare, loosely packed as far as the eye could reach with a barefooted and brown multitude paddling ankle deep in the dust. For a moment I felt myself about to go out of my mind with worry and desperation.

Some allowance must be made for the feelings of a young man new to responsibility. I thought of my crew. Half of them were ill, and I really began to think that some of them would end by dying on board if I couldn't get them out to sea soon. Obviously I should have to take my ship down the river, either working under canvas or dredging with the anchor down; operations which, in common with many modern sailors, I only knew theoretically. And I almost shrank from undertaking them shorthanded and without local knowledge of the river bed, which is so necessary for the confident handling of the ship. There were no pilots, no beacons, no buoys of any sort; but there was a very devil of a current for anybody to see, no end of shoal places, and at least two obviously awkward turns of the channel between me and the sea. But how dangerous these turns were I would not tell. I didn't even know what my ship was capable of! I had never handled her in my life. A misunderstanding between a man and his ship in a difficult river with no room to make it up, is bound to end in trouble for the man. On the other hand, it must be owned I had not much reason to count upon a general run of good luck. And suppose I had the misfortune to pile her up high and dry on some beastly shoal? That would have been the final undoing of that voyage. It was plain that if Falk refused to tow me out he would also refuse to pull me off. This meant—what? A day lost at the very best; but more likely a whole fortnight of frizzling on some pestilential mud-flat, of desperate work, of discharging cargo; more than likely it meant borrowing money at an exorbitant rate of interest—from the Siegers' gang too at that. They were a power in the port. And that elderly seaman of mine, Gambril, had looked pretty ghastly when I went forward to dose him with quinine that morning. *He* would certainly die—not to speak of two or three others that seemed nearly as bad, and of the rest of them just ready to catch any tropical disease going. Horror, ruin and everlasting remorse. And no help. None. I had fallen amongst a lot of unfriendly lunatics!

At any rate, if I must take my ship down myself it was my duty to procure if possible some local knowledge. But that was not easy. The only person I could think of for that service was a certain Johnson, formerly captain of a country ship, but now spliced to a country wife and gone utterly to the bad. I had only heard of him in the vaguest way, as living concealed in the thick of two hundred thousand natives, and only emerging into the light of day for the purpose of hunting up some brandy. I had a notion that if I could lay my hands on him I would sober him on board my ship and use him for a pilot. Better than nothing. Once a sailor always a sailor—and he had known the river for years. But in our Consulate (where I arrived dripping after a sharp walk) they could tell me nothing. The excellent young men on the staff, though willing to help me, belonged to a sphere of the white colony for which that sort of Johnson does not exist. Their suggestion was that I should hunt the man up myself with the help of the Consulate's constable—an ex-sergeant-major of a regiment of Hussars.

This man, whose usual duty apparently consisted in sitting behind a little table in an outer room of Consular offices, when ordered to assist me in my search for Johnson displayed lots of energy and a marvellous amount of local knowledge of a sort. But he did not conceal an immense and sceptical contempt for the whole business. We explored together on that afternoon an infinity of infamous grog shops, gambling dens, opium dens. We walked up narrow lanes where our gharry—a tiny box of a thing on wheels, attached to a jibbing Burmah pony—could by no means have passed. The constable seemed to be on terms of scornful intimacy with Maltese, with Eurasians, with Chinamen, with Klings, and with the sweepers attached to a temple, with whom he talked at the gate. We interviewed also through a grating in a mud wall closing a blind alley an immensely corpulent Italian, who, the ex-sergeant-major remarked to me perfunctorily, had "killed another man last year." Thereupon he addressed him as "Antonio" and "Old Buck," though that bloated carcase, apparently more than half filling the sort of cell wherein it sat, recalled rather a fat pig in a stye. Familiar and never unbending, the sergeant chucked—absolutely chucked—under the chin a horribly wrinkled and shrivelled old hag propped on a stick, who had volunteered some sort of information: and with the same stolid face he kept up an animated conversation with the groups of swathed brown women, who sat smoking cheroots on the door-steps of a long range of clay hovels. We got out of the gharry and clambered into dwellings airy like packing crates, or descended into places sinister like cellars. We got in, we drove on, we got out again for the sole purpose, as it seemed, of looking behind a heap of rubble. The sun declined; my companion was curt and sardonic in his answers, but it appears we were just missing Johnson all along. At last our conveyance stopped once more with a jerk, and the driver jumping down opened the door.

A black mudhole blocked the lane. A mound of garbage crowned with the dead body of a dog arrested us not. An empty Australian beef tin bounded cheerily before the toe of my boot. Suddenly we clambered through a gap in a prickly fence. . . .

It was a very clean native compound: and the big native woman, with bare brown legs as thick as bedposts, pursuing on all fours a silver dollar that came rolling out from somewhere, was Mrs. Johnson herself.

"Your man's at home," said the ex-sergeant, and stepped aside in complete and marked indifference to anything that might follow. Johnson—at home—stood with his back to a native house built on posts and with its walls made of mats. In his left hand he held a banana. Out of the right he dealt another dollar into space. The woman captured this one on the wing, and there and then plumped down on the ground to look at us with greater comfort.

My man was sallow of face, grizzled, unshaven, muddy on elbows and back; where the seams of his serge coat yawned you could see his white nakedness. The vestiges of a paper collar encircled his neck. He looked at us with a grave, swaying surprise. "Where do you come from?" he asked. My heart sank. How could I have been stupid enough to waste energy and time for this?

But having already gone so far I approached a little nearer and declared the purpose of my visit. He would have to come at once with me, sleep on board my ship, and to-morrow, with the first of the ebb, he would give me his assistance in getting my ship down to the sea, without steam. A six-hundred-ton barque, drawing nine feet aft. I proposed to give him eighteen dollars for his local knowledge; and all the time I was speaking he kept on considering attentively the various aspects of the banana, holding first one side up to his eye, then the other.

"You've forgotten to apologise," he said at last with extreme precision. "Not being a gentleman yourself, you don't know apparently when you intrude upon a gentleman. I am one. I wish you to understand that when I am in funds I don't work, and now . . ."

I would have pronounced him perfectly sober hadn't he paused in great concern to try and brush a hole off the knee of his trousers.

"I have money—and friends. Every gentleman has. Perhaps you would like to know my friend? His name is Falk. You could borrow some money. Try to remember. F-A-L-K, Falk." Abruptly his tone changed. "A noble heart," he said muzzily.

"Has Falk been giving you some money?" I asked, appalled by the detailed finish of the dark plot.

"Lent me, my good man, not given me. Lent," he corrected suavely. "Met me taking the air last evening, and being as usual anxious to oblige—Hadn't you better go to the devil out of my compound?"

And upon this, without other warning, he let fly with the banana which missed my head, and took the constable just under the left eye. He rushed at the miserable Johnson, stammering with fury. They fell. . . . But why dwell on the wretchedness, the breathlessness, the degradation, the senselessness, the weariness, the ridicule and humiliation and—and—the perspiration, of these moments? I dragged the ex-hussar off. He was like a wild beast. It seems he had been greatly annoyed at losing his free afternoon on my account. The garden of his bungalow required his personal attention, and at the slight blow of the banana the brute in him had broken loose. We left Johnson on his back, still black in the face, but beginning to kick feebly. Meantime, the big woman had remained sitting on the ground, apparently paralysed with extreme terror.

For half an hour we jolted inside our rolling box, side by side, in profound silence. The ex-sergeant was busy staunching the blood of a long scratch on his cheek. "I hope you're satisfied," he said suddenly. "That's what comes of all that tomfool business. If you hadn't quarrelled with that tugboat skipper over some girl or other, all this wouldn't have happened."

"You heard *that* story?" I said.

"Of course I heard. And I shouldn't wonder if the Consul-General himself doesn't come to hear of it. How am I to go before him to-morrow with that thing on my cheek—I want to know. Its *you* who ought to have got this!"

After that, till the gharry stopped and he jumped out without leave-taking, he swore to himself steadily, horribly; muttering great, purposeful, trooper oaths, to which the worst a sailor can do is like the prattle of a child. For my part I had just the strength to crawl into Schomberg's coffee-room, where I wrote at a little table a note to the mate instructing him to get everything ready for dropping down the river next day. I couldn't face my ship. Well! she had a clever sort of skipper and no mistake—poor thing! What a horrid mess! I took my head between my hands. At times the obviousness of my innocence would reduce me to despair. What had I done? If I had done something to bring about the situation I should at least have learned not to do it again. But I felt guiltless to the point of imbecility. The room was empty yet; only Schomberg prowled round me goggle-eyed and with a sort of awed respectful curiosity. No doubt he had set the story going himself; but he was a good-hearted chap, and I am really persuaded he participated in all my troubles. He did what he could for me. He ranged aside the heavy match-stand, set a chair straight, pushed a spittoon slightly with his foot—as you show small attentions to a friend under a great sorrow—sighed, and at last, unable to hold his tongue:

"Well! I warned you, captain. That's what comes of running your head against Mr. Falk. Man'll stick at nothing."

I sat without stirring, and after surveying me with a sort of commiseration in his eyes he burst out in a hoarse whisper: "But for a fine lump of a girl, she's a fine lump of a girl." He made a loud smacking noise with his thick lips. "The finest lump of a girl that I ever . . ." he was going on with great unction, but for some reason or other broke off. I fancied myself throwing something at his head. "I don't blame you, captain. Hang me if I do," he said with a patronising air.

"Thank you," I said resignedly. It was no use fighting against this false fate. I don't know even if I was sure myself where the truth of the matter began. The conviction that it would end disastrously had been driven into me by all the successive shocks my sense of security had received. I began to ascribe an extraordinary potency to agents in themselves powerless. It was as if Schomberg's baseless gossip had the power to bring about the thing itself or the abstract enmity of Falk could put my ship ashore.

I have already explained how fatal this last would have been. For my further action, my youth, my inexperience, my very real concern for the health of my crew must be my excuse. The action itself, when it came, was purely impulsive. It was set in movement quite undiplomatically and simply by Falk's appearance in the doorway.

The room was full by then and buzzing with voices. I had been looked at with curiosity by every one, but how am I to describe the sensation produced by the appearance of Falk himself blocking the doorway? The tension of expectation could be measured by the profundity of the silence that fell upon the very click of the billiard balls. As to Schomberg, he looked extremely frightened; he hated mortally any sort of row (*fracas* he called it) in his establishment. *Fracas* was bad for business, he affirmed; but, in truth, this specimen of portly, middle-aged manhood was of a timid disposition. I don't know what, considering my presence in the place, they all hoped would come of it. A sort of stag fight, perhaps. Or they may have supposed Falk had come in only to annihilate me completely. As a matter of fact, Falk had come in because Hermann had asked him to inquire after the precious white cotton parasol which, in the worry and excitement of the previous day, he had forgotten at the table where we had held our little discussion.

It was this that gave me my opportunity. I don't think I would have gone to seek Falk out. No. I don't think so. There are limits. But there was an opportunity and I seized it—I have already tried to explain why. Now I will merely state that, in my opinion, to get his sickly crew into the sea air and secure a quick despatch for his ship a skipper would be justified in going to any length, short of absolute crime. He should put his pride in his pocket; he may accept confidences; explain his innocence as if it were a sin; he may take advantage of misconceptions, of desires and of weaknesses; he ought to conceal his horror and other emotions, and, if the fate of a human being, and that human being a magnificent young girl, is strangely involved—why, he should contemplate that fate (whatever it might seem to be) without turning a hair. And all these things I have done; the explaining, the listening, the pretending—even to the discretion—and nobody, not even Hermann's niece, I believe, need throw stones at me now. Schomberg at all events needn't, since from first to last, I am happy to say, there was not the slightest "*fracas.*"

Overcoming a nervous contraction of the windpipe, I had managed to exclaim "Captain Falk!" His start of surprise was perfectly genuine, but afterwards he neither smiled nor scowled. He simply waited. Then, when I had said, "I must have a talk with you," and had pointed to a chair at my table, he moved up to me, though he didn't sit down. Schomberg, however, with a long tumbler in his hand, was making towards us prudently, and I discovered then the only sign of weakness in Falk. He had for Schomberg a repulsion resembling that sort of physical fear some people experience at the sight of a toad. Perhaps to a man so essentially and silently concentrated upon himself (though he could talk well enough, as I was to find out presently) the other's irrepressible loquacity, embracing every human being within range of the tongue, might have appeared unnatural, disgusting, and monstrous. He suddenly gave signs of restiveness—positively like a horse about to rear, and, muttering hurriedly as if in great pain, "No. I can't stand that fellow," seemed ready to bolt. This weakness of his gave me the advantage at the very start. "Verandah," I suggested, as if rendering him a service, and walked him out by the arm. We stumbled over a few chairs; we had the feeling of open space before us, and felt the fresh breath of the river—fresh, but tainted. The Chinese theatres across the water made, in the sparsely twinkling masses of gloom an Eastern town presents at night, blazing centres of light, and of a distant and howling uproar. I felt him become suddenly tractable again like an animal, like a good-tempered horse when the object that scares him is removed. Yes. I felt in the darkness there how tractable he was, without my conviction of his inflexibility—tenacity, rather, perhaps—being in the least weakened. His very arm abandoning itself to my grasp was as hard as marble—like a limb of iron. But I heard a tumultuous scuffling of boot-soles within. The unspeakable idiots inside were crowding to the windows, climbing over each other's backs behind the blinds, billiard cues and all. Somebody broke a window pane, and with the sound of falling glass, so suggestive of riot and devastation, Schomberg reeled out after us in a state of funk which had prevented his parting with his brandy and soda. He must have trembled like an aspen leaf. The piece of ice in the long tumbler he held in his hand tinkled with an effect of chattering teeth. "I beg you, gentlemen," he expostulated thickly. "Come! Really, now, I must insist . . ."

How proud I am of my presence of mind! "Hallo," I said instantly in a loud and naive tone, "somebody's breaking your windows, Schomberg. Would you please tell one of your boys to bring out here a pack of cards and a couple of lights? And two long drinks. Will you?"

To receive an order soothed him at once. It was business. "Certainly," he said in an immensely relieved tone. The night was rainy, with wandering gusts of wind, and while we waited for the candles Falk said, as if to justify his panic, "I don't interfere in anybody's business. I don't give any occasion for talk. I am a respectable man. But this fellow is always making out something wrong, and can never rest till he gets somebody to believe him."

This was the first of my knowledge of Falk. This desire of respectability, of being like everybody else, was the only recognition he vouchsafed to the organisation of mankind. For the rest he might have been the member of a herd, not of a society. Self-preservation was his only concern. Not selfishness, but mere self-preservation. Selfishness presupposes consciousness, choice, the presence of other men; but his instinct acted as though he were the last of mankind nursing that law like the only spark of a sacred fire. I don't mean to say that living naked in a cavern would have satisfied him. Obviously he was the creature of the conditions to which he was born. No doubt self-preservation meant also the preservation of these conditions. But essentially it meant something much more simple, natural, and powerful. How shall I express it? It meant the preservation of the five senses of his body—let us say—taking it in its narrowest as well as in its widest meaning. I think you will admit before long the justice of this judgment. However, as we stood there together in the dark verandah I had judged nothing as yet—and I had no desire to judge—which is an idle practice anyhow. The light was long in coming.

"Of course," I said in a tone of mutual understanding, "it isn't exactly a game of cards I want with you."

I saw him draw his hands down his face—the vague stir of the passionate and meaningless gesture; but he waited in silent patience. It was only when the lights had been brought out that he opened his lips. I understood his mumble to mean that "he didn't know any game."

"Like this Schomberg and all the other fools will have to keep off," I said tearing open the pack. "Have you heard that we are universally supposed to be quarrelling about a girl? You know who—of course. I am really ashamed to ask, but is it possible that you do me the honour to think me dangerous?"

As I said these words I felt how absurd it was and also I felt flattered—for, really, what else could it be? His answer, spoken in his usual dispassionate undertone, made it clear that it was so, but not precisely as flattering as I supposed. He thought me dangerous with Hermann, more than with the girl herself; but, as to quarrelling, I saw at once how inappropriate the word was. We had no quarrel. Natural forces are not quarrelsome. You can't quarrel with the wind that inconveniences and humiliates you by blowing off your hat in a street full of people. He had no quarrel with me. Neither would a boulder, falling on my head, have had. He fell upon me in accordance with the law by which he was moved—not of gravitation, like a detached stone, but of self-preservation. Of course this is giving it a rather wide interpretation. Strictly speaking, he had existed and could have existed without being married. Yet he told me that he had found it more and more difficult to live alone. Yes. He told me this in his low, careless voice, to such a pitch of confidence had we arrived at the end of half an hour.

It took me just about that time to convince him that I had never dreamed of marrying Hermann's niece. Could any necessity have been more extravagant? And the difficulty was the greater because he was so hard hit that he couldn't imagine anybody being able to remain in a state of indifference. Any man with eyes in his head, he seemed to think, could not help coveting so much bodily magnificence. This profound belief was conveyed by the manner he listened sitting sideways to the table and playing absently with a few cards I had dealt to him at random. And the more I saw into him the more I saw of him. The wind swayed the lights so that his sunburnt face, whiskered to the eyes, seemed to successively flicker crimson at me and to go out. I saw the extraordinary breadth of the high cheek-bones, the perpendicular style of the features, the massive forehead, steep like a cliff, denuded at the top, largely uncovered at the temples. The fact is I had never before seen him without his hat; but now, as if my fervour had made him hot, he had taken it off and laid it gently on the floor. Something peculiar in the shape and setting of his yellow eyes gave them the provoking silent intensity which characterised his glance. But the face was thin, furrowed, worn; I discovered that through the bush of his hair, as you may detect the gnarled shape of a tree trunk lost in a dense undergrowth. These overgrown cheeks were sunken. It was an anchorite's bony head fitted with a Capuchin's beard and adjusted to a herculean body. I don't mean athletic. Hercules, I take it, was not an athlete. He was a strong man, susceptible to female charms, and not afraid of dirt. And thus with Falk, who was a strong man. He was extremely strong, just as the girl (since I must think of them together) was magnificently attractive by the masterful power of flesh and blood, expressed in shape, in size, in attitude—that is by a straight appeal to the senses. His mind meantime, preoccupied with respectability, quailed before Schomberg's tongue and seemed absolutely impervious to my protestations; and I went so far as to protest that I would just as soon think of marrying my mother's (dear old lady!) faithful female cook as Hermann's niece. Sooner, I protested, in my desperation, much sooner; but it did not appear that he saw anything outrageous in the proposition, and in his sceptical immobility he seemed to nurse the argument that at all events the cook was very, very far away. It must be said that, just before, I had gone wrong by appealing to the evidence of my manner whenever I called on board the *Diana*. I had never attempted to approach the girl, or to speak to her, or even to look at her in any marked way. Nothing could be clearer. But, as his own idea of—

let us say—courting, seemed to consist precisely in sitting silently for hours in the vicinity of the beloved object, that line of argument inspired him with distrust. Staring down his extended legs he let out a grunt—as much as to say, "That's all very fine, but you can't throw dust in *my* eyes."

At last I was exasperated into saying, "Why don't you put the matter at rest by talking to Hermann?" and I added sneeringly: "You don't expect me perhaps to speak for you?"

To this he said, very loud for him, "Would you?"

And for the first time he lifted his head to look at me with wonder and incredulity. He lifted his head so sharply that there could be no mistake. I had touched a spring. I saw the whole extent of my opportunity, and could hardly believe in it.

"Why. Speak to . . . Well, of course," I proceeded very slowly, watching him with great attention, for, on my word, I feared a joke. "Not, perhaps, to the young lady herself. I can't speak German, you know. But . . ."

He interrupted me with the earnest assurance that Hermann had the highest opinion of me; and at once I felt the need for the greatest possible diplomacy at this juncture. So I demurred just enough to draw him on. Falk sat up, but except for a very noticeable enlargement of the pupils, till the irises of his eyes were reduced to two narrow yellow rings, his face, I should judge, was incapable of expressing excitement. "Oh, yes! Hermann did have the greatest . . ."

"Take up your cards. Here's Schomberg peeping at us through the blind!" I said.

We went through the motions of what might have been a game of écarté. Presently the intolerable scandalmonger withdrew, probably to inform the people in the billiard-room that we two were gambling on the verandah like mad.

We were not gambling, but it was a game; a game in which I felt I held the winning cards. The stake, roughly speaking, was the success of the voyage—for me; and he, I apprehended, had nothing to lose. Our intimacy matured rapidly, and before many words had been exchanged I perceived that the excellent Hermann had been making use of me. That simple and astute Teuton had been, it seems, holding me up to Falk in the light of a rival. I was young enough to be shocked at so much duplicity. "Did he tell you that in so many words?" I asked with indignation.

Hermann had not. He had given hints only; and of course it had not taken very much to alarm Falk; but, instead of declaring himself, he had taken steps to remove the family from under my influence. He was perfectly straightforward about it—as straightforward as a tile falling on your head. There was no duplicity in that man; and when I congratulated him on the perfection of his arrangements—even to the bribing of the wretched Johnson against me—he had a genuine movement of protest. Never bribed. He knew the man wouldn't work as long as he had a few cents in his pocket to get drunk on, and, naturally (he said—"*naturally*") he let him have a dollar or two. He was himself a sailor, he said, and anticipated the view another sailor, like myself, was bound to take. On the other hand, he was sure that I should have to come to grief. He hadn't been knocking about for the last seven years up and down that river for nothing. It would have been no disgrace to me—but he asserted confidently I would have had my ship very awkwardly ashore at a spot two miles below the Great Pagoda. . . .

And with all that he had no ill-will. That was evident. This was a crisis in which his only object had been to gain time—I fancy. And presently he mentioned that he had written for some jewellery, real good jewellery—had written to Hong-Kong for it. It would arrive in a day or two.

"Well, then," I said cheerily, "everything is all right. All you've got to do is to present it to the lady together with your heart, and live happy ever after."

Upon the whole he seemed to accept that view as far as the girl was concerned, but his eyelids drooped. There was still something in the way. For one thing Hermann disliked him so much. As to me, on the contrary, it seemed as though he could not praise me enough. Mrs. Hermann too. He didn't know why they disliked him so. It made everything most difficult.

I listened impassive, feeling more and more diplomatic. His speech was not transparently clear. He was one of those men who seem to live, feel, suffer in a sort of mental twilight. But as to being fascinated by the girl and possessed by the desire of home life with her—it was as clear as daylight. So much being at stake, he was afraid of putting it to the hazard of declaration. Besides, there was something else. And with Hermann being so set against him . . .

"I see," I said thoughtfully, while my heart beat fast with the excitement of my diplomacy. "I don't mind sounding Hermann. In fact, to show you how mistaken you were, I am ready to do all I can for you in that way."

A light sigh escaped him. He drew his hands down his face, and it emerged, bony, unchanged of expression, as if all the tissues had been ossified. All the passion was in those big brown hands. He was satisfied. Then there was that other matter. If there were anybody on earth it was I who could persuade Hermann to take a reasonable view! I had a knowledge of the world and lots of experience. Hermann admitted this himself. And then I was a sailor too. Falk thought that a sailor would be able to understand certain things best. . . .

He talked as if the Hermanns had been living all their life in a rural hamlet, and I alone had been capable, with my practice in life, of a large and indulgent view of certain occurrences. That was what my diplomacy was leading me to. I began suddenly to dislike it.

"I say, Falk," I asked quite brusquely, "you haven't already a wife put away somewhere?"

The pain and disgust of his denial were very striking. Couldn't I understand that he was as respectable as any white man hereabouts; earning his living honestly. He was suffering from my suspicion, and the low undertone of his voice made his protestations sound very pathetic. For a moment he shamed me, but, my diplomacy notwithstanding, I seemed to develop a conscience, as if in very truth it were in my power to decide the success of this matrimonial enterprise. By pretending hard enough we come to believe anything—anything to our advantage. And I had been pretending very hard, because I meant yet to be towed safely down the river. But through conscience or stupidity, I couldn't help alluding to the Vanlo affair. "You acted rather badly there. Didn't you?" was what I ventured actually to say—for the logic of our conduct is always at the mercy of obscure and unforeseen impulses.

His dilated pupils swerved from my face, glancing at the window with a sort of scared fury. We heard behind the blinds the continuous and sudden clicking of ivory, a jovial murmur of many voices, and Schomberg's deep manly laugh.

"That confounded old woman of a hotel-keeper then would never, never let it rest!" Falk exclaimed. "Well, yes! It had happened two years ago." When it came to the point he owned he couldn't make up his mind to trust Fred Vanlo—no sailor, a bit of a fool too. He could not trust him, but, to stop his row, he had lent him enough money to pay all his debts before he left. I was greatly surprised to hear this. Then Falk could not be such a miser after all. So much the better for the girl. For a time he sat silent; then he picked up a card, and while looking at it he said:

"You need not think of anything bad. It was an accident. I've been unfortunate once."

"Then in heaven's name say nothing about it."

As soon as these words were out of my mouth I fancied I had said something immoral. He shook his head negatively. It had to be told. He considered it proper that the relations of the lady should know. No doubt—I thought to myself—had Miss Vanlo not been thirty and damaged by the climate he would have found it possible to entrust Fred Vanlo with this confidence. And then the figure of Hermann's niece appeared before my mind's eye, with the wealth of her opulent form, her rich youth, her lavish strength. With that powerful and immaculate vitality, her girlish form must have shouted aloud of life to that man, whereas poor Miss Vanlo could only sing sentimental songs to the strumming of a piano.

"And that Hermann hates me, I know it!" he cried in his undertone, with a sudden recrudescence of anxiety. "I must tell them. It is proper that they should know. You would say so yourself."

He then murmured an utterly mysterious allusion to the necessity for peculiar domestic arrangements. Though my curiosity was excited I did not want to hear any of his confidences. I feared he might give me a piece of information that would make my assumed *rôle* of match-maker odious—however unreal it was. I was aware that he could have the girl for the asking; and keeping down a desire to laugh in his face, I expressed a confident belief in my ability to argue away Hermann's dislike for him. "I am sure I can make it all right," I said. He looked very pleased.

And when we rose not a word had been said about towage! Not a word! The game was won and the honour was safe. Oh! blessed white cotton umbrella! We shook hands, and I was holding myself with difficulty from breaking into a step dance of joy when he came back, striding all the length of the verandah, and said doubtfully:

"I say, captain, I have your word? You—you—won't turn round?"

Heavens! The fright he gave me. Behind his tone of doubt there was something desperate and menacing. The infatuated ass. But I was equal to the situation.

"My dear Falk," I said, beginning to lie with a glibness and effrontery that amazed me even at the time—"confidence for confidence." (He had made no confidences.) "I will tell you that I am already engaged to an extremely charming girl at home, and so you understand. . . ."

He caught my hand and wrung it in a crushing grip.

"Pardon me. I feel it every day more difficult to live alone . . ."

"On rice and fish," I interrupted smartly, giggling with the sheer nervousness of a danger escaped.

He dropped my hand as if it had become suddenly red hot. A moment of profound silence ensued, as though something extraordinary had happened.

"I promise you to obtain Hermann's consent," I faltered out at last, and it seemed to me that he could not help seeing through that humbugging promise. "If there's anything else to get over I shall endeavour to stand by you," I conceded further, feeling somehow defeated and over-borne; "but you must do your best yourself."

"I have been unfortunate once," he muttered unemotionally, and turning his back on me he went away, thumping slowly the plank floor as if his feet had been shod with iron.

Next morning, however, he was lively enough as man-boat, a combination of splashing and shouting; of the insolent commotion below with the steady overbearing glare of the silent head-piece above. He turned us out most unnecessarily at an ungodly hour, but it was nearly eleven in the morning before he brought me up a cable's length from Hermann's ship. And he did it very badly too, in a hurry, and nearly contriving to miss altogether the patch of good holding ground, because, forsooth, he had caught sight of Hermann's niece on the poop. And so did I; and probably as soon as he had seen her himself. I saw the modest, sleek glory of the tawny head, and the full, grey shape of the girlish print frock she filled so perfectly, so satisfactorily, with the seduction of unfaltering curves—a very nymph of Diana the Huntress. And *Diana* the ship sat, high-walled and as solid as an institution, on the smooth level of the water, the most uninspiring and respectable craft upon the seas, useful and ugly, devoted to the support of domestic virtues like any grocer's shop on shore. At once Falk steamed away; for there was some work for him to do. He would return in the evening.

He ranged close by us, passing out dead slow, without a hail. The beat of the paddle-wheels reverberating amongst the stony islets, as if from the ruined walls of a vast arena, filled the anchorage confusedly with the clapping sounds of a mighty and leisurely applause. Abreast of Hermann's ship he stopped the engines; and a profound silence reigned over the rocks, the shore and the sea, for the time it took him to raise his hat aloft before the nymph of the grey print frock. I had snatched up my binoculars, and I can answer for it she didn't stir a limb, standing by the rail shapely and erect, with one of her hands grasping a rope at the height of her head, while the way of the tug carried slowly past her the lingering and profound homage of the man. There was for me an enormous significance in the scene, the sense of having witnessed a solemn declaration. The die was cast. After such a manifestation he couldn't back out. And I reflected that it was nothing whatever to me now. With a rush of black smoke belching suddenly out of the funnel, and a mad swirl of paddle-wheels provoking a burst of weird and precipitated clapping, the tug shot out of the desolate arena. The rocky islets lay on the sea like the heaps of a cyclopean ruin on a plain; the centipedes and scorpions lurked under the stones; there was not a single blade of grass in sight anywhere, not a single lizard sunning himself on a boulder by the shore. When I looked again at Hermann's ship the girl had disappeared. I could not detect the smallest dot of a bird on the immense sky, and the flatness of the land continued the flatness of the sea to the naked line of the horizon.

This is the setting now inseparably connected with my knowledge of Falk's misfortune. My diplomacy had brought me there, and now I had only to wait the time for taking up the *rôle* of an ambassador. My diplomacy was a success; my ship was safe; old Gambril would probably live; a feeble sound of a tapping hammer came intermittently from the *Diana*. During the afternoon I looked at times at the old homely ship, the faithful nurse of Hermann's progeny, or yawned towards the distant temple of Buddha, like a lonely hillock on the plain, where shaven priests cherish the thoughts of that Annihilation which is the worthy reward of us all. Unfortunate! He had been unfortunate once. Well, that was not so bad as life goes. And what the devil could be the nature of that misfortune? I remembered that I had known a man before who had declared himself to have fallen, years ago, a victim to misfortune; but this misfortune, whose effects appeared permanent (he looked desperately hard up) when considered dispassionately, seemed indistinguishable from a breach of trust. Could it be something of that nature? Apart, however, from the utter improbability that he would offer to talk of it even to his future uncle-in-law, I had a strange feeling that Falk's physique unfitted him for that sort of delinquency. As the person of Hermann's niece exhaled the profound physical charm of feminine form, so her adorer's big frame embodied to my senses the hard, straight masculinity that would conceivably kill but would not condescend to cheat. The thing was obvious. I might just as well have suspected the girl of a curvature of the spine. And I perceived that the sun was about to set.

The smoke of Falk's tug hove in sight, far away at the mouth of the river. It was time for me to assume the character of an ambassador, and the negotiation would not be difficult except in the matter of keeping my countenance. It was all too extravagantly nonsensical, and I conceived that it would be best to compose for myself a grave demeanour. I practised this in my boat as I went along, but the bashfulness that came secretly upon me the moment I stepped on the deck of the Diana is inexplicable. As soon as we had exchanged greetings Hermann asked me eagerly if I knew whether Falk had found his white parasol.

"He's going to bring it to you himself directly," I said with great solemnity. "Meantime I am charged with an important message for which he begs your favourable consideration. He is in love with your niece. . . ."

"*Ach So!*" he hissed with an animosity that made my assumed gravity change into the most genuine concern. What meant this tone? And I hurried on.

"He wishes, with your consent of course, to ask her to marry him at once—before you leave here, that is. He would speak to the Consul."

Hermann sat down and smoked violently. Five minutes passed in that furious meditation, and then, taking the long pipe out of his mouth, he burst into a hot diatribe against Falk—against his cupidity, his stupidity (a fellow that can hardly be got to say "yes" or "no" to the simplest question)—against his outrageous treatment of the shipping in port (because he saw they were at his mercy)—and against his manner of walking, which to his (Hermann's) mind showed a conceit positively unbearable. The damage to the old *Diana* was not forgotten, of course, and there was nothing of any nature said or done by Falk (even to the last offer of refreshment in the hotel) that did not seem to have been a cause of offence. "Had the cheek" to drag him (Hermann) into that coffee-room; as though a drink from him could make up for forty-seven dollars and fifty cents of damage in the cost of wood alone—not counting two days' work for the carpenter. Of course he would not stand in the girl's way. He was going home to Germany. There were plenty of poor girls walking about in Germany.

"He's very much in love," was all I found to say.

"Yes," he cried. "And it is time too after making himself and me talked about ashore the last voyage I was here, and then now again; coming on board every evening unsettling the girl's mind, and saying nothing. What sort of conduct is that?"

The seven thousand dollars the fellow was always talking about did not, in his opinion, justify such behaviour. Moreover, nobody had seen them. He (Hermann) seriously doubted if there were seven thousand cents, and the tug, no doubt, was mortgaged up to the top of the funnel to the firm of Siegers. But let that pass. He wouldn't stand in the girl's way. Her head was so turned that she had become no good to them of late. Quite unable even to put the children to bed without her aunt. It was bad for the children; they got unruly; and yesterday he actually had to give Gustav a thrashing.

For that, too, Falk was made responsible apparently. And looking at my Hermann's heavy, puffy, good-natured face, I knew he would not exert himself till greatly exasperated, and, therefore, would thrash very hard, and being fat would resent the necessity. How Falk had managed to turn the girl's head was more difficult to understand. I supposed Hermann would know. And then hadn't there been Miss Vanlo? It could not be his silvery tongue, or the subtle seduction of his manner; he had no more of what is called "manner" than an animal—which, however, on the other hand, is never, and can never be called vulgar. Therefore it must have been his bodily appearance, exhibiting a virility of nature as exaggerated as his beard, and resembling a sort of constant ruthlessness. It was seen in the very manner he lolled in the chair. He meant no offence, but his intercourse was characterised by that sort of frank disregard of susceptibilities a man of seven foot six, living in a world of dwarfs, would naturally assume, without in the least wishing to be unkind. But amongst men of his own stature, or nearly, this frank use of his advantages, in such matters as the awful towage bills for instance, caused much impotent gnashing of teeth. When attentively considered it seemed appalling at times. He was a strange beast. But maybe women liked it. Seen in that light he was well worth taming, and I suppose every woman at the bottom of her heart considers herself as a tamer of strange beasts. But Hermann arose with precipitation to carry the news to his wife. I had barely the time, as he made for the cabin door, to grab him by the seat of his inexpressibles. I begged him to wait till Falk in person had spoken with him. There remained some small matter to talk over, as I understood.

He sat down again at once, full of suspicion.

"What matter?" he said surlily. "I have had enough of his nonsense. There's no matter at all, as he knows very well; the girl has nothing in the world. She came to us in one thin dress when my brother died, and I have a growing family."

"It can't be anything of that kind," I opined. "He's desperately enamoured of your niece. I don't know why he did not say so before. Upon my word, I believe it is because he was afraid to lose, perhaps, the felicity of sitting near her on your quarter deck."

I intimated my conviction that his love was so great as to be in a sense cowardly. The effects of a great passion are unaccountable. It has been known to make a man timid. But Hermann looked at me as if I had foolishly raved; and the twilight was dying out rapidly.

"You don't believe in passion, do you, Hermann?" I said cheerily. "The passion of fear will make a cornered rat courageous. Falk's in a corner. He will take her off your hands in one thin frock just as she came to you. And after ten years' service it isn't a bad bargain," I added.

Far from taking offence, he resumed his air of civic virtue. The sudden night came upon him while he stared placidly along the deck, bringing in contact with his thick lips, and taking away again after a jet of smoke, the curved mouthpiece fitted to the stem of his pipe. The night came upon him and buried in haste his whiskers, his globular eyes, his puffy pale face, his fat knees and the vast flat slippers on his fatherly feet. Only his short arms in respectable white shirt-sleeves remained very visible, propped up like the flippers of a seal reposing on the strand.

"Falk wouldn't settle anything about repairs. Told me to find out first how much wood I should require and he would see," he remarked; and after he had spat peacefully in the dusk we heard over the water the beat of the tug's floats. There is, on a calm night, nothing more suggestive of fierce and headlong haste than the rapid sound made by the paddle-wheels of a boat threshing her way through a quiet sea; and the approach of Falk towards his fate seemed to be urged by an impatient and passionate desire. The engines must have been driven to the very utmost of their revolutions. We heard them slow down at last, and, vaguely, the white hull of the tug appeared moving against the black islets, whilst a slow and rhythmical clapping as of thousands of hands rose on all sides. It ceased all at once, just before Falk brought her up. A single brusque splash was followed by the long drawn rumbling of iron links running through the hawse pipe. Then a solemn silence fell upon the Roadstead.

"He will soon be here," I murmured, and after that we waited for him without a word. Meantime, raising my eyes, I beheld the glitter of a lofty sky above the *Diana's* mastheads. The multitude of stars gathered into clusters, in rows, in lines, in masses, in groups, shone all together, unanimously—and the few isolated ones, blazing by themselves in the midst of dark patches, seemed to be of a superior kind and of an inextinguishable nature. But long striding footsteps were heard hastening along the deck; the high bulwarks of the Diana made a deeper darkness. We rose from our chairs quickly, and Falk, appearing before us, all in white, stood still.

Nobody spoke at first, as though we had been covered with confusion. His arrival was fiery, but his white bulk, of indefinite shape and without features, made him loom up like a man of snow.

"The captain here has been telling me . . ." Hermann began in a homely and amicable voice; and Falk had a low, nervous laugh. His cool, negligent undertone had no inflexions, but the strength of a powerful emotion made him ramble in his speech. He had always desired a home. It was difficult to live alone, though he was not answerable. He was domestic; there had been difficulties; but since he had seen Hermann's niece he found that it had become at last impossible to live by himself. "I mean—impossible," he repeated with no sort of emphasis and only with the slightest of pauses, but the word fell into my mind with the force of a new idea.

"I have not said anything to her yet," Hermann observed quietly. And Falk dismissed this by a "That's all right. Certainly. Very proper." There was a necessity for perfect frankness—in marrying, especially. Hermann seemed attentive, but he seized the first opportunity to ask us into the cabin. "And by-the-by, Falk," he said innocently, as we passed in, "the timber came to no less than forty-seven dollars and fifty cents."

Falk, uncovering his head, lingered in the passage. "Some other time," he said; and Hermann nudged me angrily—I don't know why. The girl alone in the cabin sat sewing at some distance from the table. Falk stopped short in the doorway. Without a word, without a sign, without the slightest inclination of his bony head, by the silent intensity of his look alone, he seemed to lay his herculean frame at her feet. Her hands sank slowly on her lap, and raising her clear eyes, she let her soft, beaming glance enfold him from head to foot like a slow and pale caress. He was very hot when he sat down; she, with bowed head, went on with her sewing; her neck was very white under the light of the lamp; but Falk, hiding his face in the palms of his hands, shuddered faintly. He drew them down, even to his beard, and his uncovered eyes astonished me by their tense and irrational expression—as though he had just swallowed a heavy gulp of alcohol. It passed away while he was binding us to secrecy. Not that he cared, but he did not like to be spoken about; and I looked at the girl's marvellous, at her wonderful, at her regal hair, plaited tight into that one astonishing and maidenly tress.

Whenever she moved her well-shaped head it would stir stiffly to and fro on her back. The thin cotton sleeve fitted the irreproachable roundness of her arm like a skin; and her very dress, stretched on her bust, seemed to palpitate like a living tissue with the strength of vitality animating her body. How good her complexion was, the outline of her soft cheek and the small convoluted conch of her rosy ear! To pull her needle she kept the little finger apart from the others; it seemed a waste of power to see her sewing—eternally sewing—with that industrious and precise movement of her arm, going on eternally upon all the oceans, under all the skies, in innumerable harbours. And suddenly I heard Falk's voice declare that he could not marry a woman unless she knew of something in his life that had happened ten years ago. It was an accident. An unfortunate accident. It would affect the domestic arrangements of their home, but, once told, it need not be alluded to again for the rest of their lives. "I should want my wife to feel for me," he said. "It has made me unhappy." And how could he keep the knowledge of it to himself—he asked us—perhaps through years and years of companionship? What sort of companionship would that be? He had thought it over. A wife must know. Then why not at once? He counted on Hermann's kindness for presenting the affair in the best possible light. And Hermann's countenance, mystified before, became very sour. He stole an inquisitive glance at me. I shook my head blankly. Some people thought, Falk went on, that such an experience changed a man for the rest of his life. He couldn't say. It was hard, awful, and not to be forgotten, but he did not think himself a worse man than before. Only he talked in his sleep now, he believed. . . . At last I began to think he had accidentally killed some one; perhaps a friend— his own father maybe; when he went on to say that probably we were aware he never touched meat. Throughout he spoke English, of course of my account.

He swayed forward heavily.

The girl, with her hands raised before her pale eyes, was threading her needle. He glanced at her, and his mighty trunk overshadowed the table, bringing nearer to us the breadth of his shoulders, the thickness of his neck, and that incongruous, anchorite head, burnt in the desert, hollowed and lean as if by excesses of vigils and fasting. His beard flowed imposingly downwards, out of sight, between the two brown hands gripping the edge of the table, and his persistent glance made sombre by the wide dilations of the pupils, fascinated.

"Imagine to yourselves," he said in his ordinary voice, "that I have eaten man."

I could only ejaculate a faint "Ah!" of complete enlightenment. But Hermann, dazed by the excessive shock, actually murmured, "Himmel! What for?"

"It was my terrible misfortune to do so," said Falk in a measured undertone. The girl, unconscious, sewed on. Mrs. Hermann was absent in one of the state-rooms, sitting up with Lena, who was feverish; but Hermann suddenly put both his hands up with a jerk. The embroidered calotte fell, and, in the twinkling of an eye, he had rumpled his hair all ends up in a most extravagant manner. In this state he strove to speak; with every effort his eyes seemed to start further out of their sockets; his head looked like a mop. He choked, gasped, swallowed, and managed to shriek out the one word, "Beast!"

From that moment till Falk went out of the cabin the girl, with her hands folded on the work lying in her lap, never took her eyes off him. His own, in the blindness of his heart, darted all over the cabin, only seeking to avoid the sight of Hermann's raving. It was ridiculous, and was made almost terrible by the stillness of every other person present. It was contemptible, and was made appalling by the man's over-mastering horror of this awful sincerity, coming to him suddenly, with the confession of such a fact. He walked with great strides; he gasped. He wanted to know from Falk how dared he to come and tell him this? Did he think himself a proper person to be sitting in this cabin where his wife and children lived? Tell his niece! Expected him to tell his niece! His own brother's daughter! Shameless! Did I ever hear tell of such impudence?—he appealed to me. "This man here ought to have gone and hidden himself out of sight instead of . . ."

"But it's a great misfortune for me. But it's a great misfortune for me," Falk would ejaculate from time to time.

However, Hermann kept on running frequently against the corners of the table. At last he lost a slipper, and crossing his arms on his breast, walked up with one stocking foot very close to Falk, in order to ask him whether he did think there was anywhere on earth a woman abandoned enough to mate with such a monster. "Did he? Did he? Did he?" I tried to restrain him. He tore himself out of my hands; he found his slipper, and, endeavouring to put it on, stormed standing on one leg—and Falk, with a face unmoved and averted eyes, grasped all his mighty beard in one vast palm.

"Was it right then for me to die myself?" he asked thoughtfully. I laid my hand on his shoulder.

"Go away," I whispered imperiously, without any clear reason for this advice, except that I wished to put an end to Hermann's odious noise. "Go away."

He looked searchingly for a moment at Hermann before he made a move. I left the cabin too to see him out of the ship. But he hung about the quarter-deck.

"It is my misfortune," he said in a steady voice.

"You were stupid to blurt it out in such a manner. After all, we don't hear such confidences every day."

"What does the man mean?" he mused in deep undertones.

"Somebody had to die—but why me?"

He remained still for a time in the dark—silent; almost invisible. All at once he pinned my elbows to my sides. I felt utterly powerless in his grip, and his voice, whispering in my ear, vibrated.

"It's worse than hunger. Captain, do you know what that means? And I could kill then—or be killed. I wish the crowbar had smashed my skull ten years ago. And I've got to live now. Without her. Do you understand? Perhaps many years. But how? What can be done? If I had allowed myself to look at her once I would have carried her off before that man in my hands—like this."

I felt myself snatched off the deck, then suddenly dropped—and I staggered backwards, feeling bewildered and bruised. What a man! All was still; he was gone. I heard Hermann's voice declaiming in the cabin, and I went in.

I could not at first make out a single word, but Mrs. Hermann, who, attracted by the noise, had come in some time before, with an expression of surprise and mild disapproval, depicted broadly on her face, was giving now all the signs of profound, helpless agitation. Her husband shot a string of guttural words at her, and instantly putting out one hand to the bulkhead as if to save herself from falling, she clutched the loose bosom of her dress with the other. He harangued the two women extraordinarily, with much of his shirt hanging out of his waist-belt, stamping his foot, turning from one to the other, sometimes throwing both his arms together, straight up above his rumpled hair, and keeping them in that position while he uttered a passage of loud denunciation; at others folding them tight across his breast—and then he hissed with indignation, elevating his shoulders and protruding his head. The girl was crying.

She had not changed her attitude. From her steady eyes that, following Falk in his retreat, had remained fixed wistfully on the cabin door, the tears fell rapid, thick, on her hands, on the work in her lap, warm and gentle like a shower in spring. She wept without grimacing, without noise—very touching, very quiet, with something more of pity than of pain in her face, as one weeps in compassion rather than in grief—and Hermann, before her, declaimed. I caught several times the word "Mensch," man; and also "Fressen," which last I looked up afterwards in my dictionary. It means "Devour." Hermann seemed to be requesting an answer of some sort from her; his whole body swayed. She remained mute and perfectly still; at last his agitation gained her; she put the palms of her hands together, her full lips parted, no sound came. His voice scolded shrilly, his arms went like a windmill— suddenly he shook a thick fist at her. She burst out into loud sobs. He seemed stupefied.

Mrs. Hermann rushed forward babbling rapidly. The two women fell on each other's necks, and, with an arm round her niece's waist, she led her away. Her own eyes were simply streaming, her face was flooded. She shook her head back at me negatively, I wonder why to this day. The girl's head dropped heavily on her shoulder. They disappeared.

Then Hermann sat down and stared at the cabin floor.

"We don't know all the circumstances," I ventured to break the silence. He retorted tartly that he didn't want to know of any. According to his ideas no circumstances could excuse a crime—and certainly not such a crime. This was the opinion generally received. The duty of a human being was to starve. Falk therefore was a beast, an animal; base, low, vile, despicable, shameless, and deceitful. He had been deceiving him since last year. He was, however, inclined to think that Falk must have gone mad quite recently; for no sane person, without necessity, uselessly, for no earthly reason, and regardless of another's self-respect and peace of mind, would own to having devoured human flesh. "Why tell?" he cried. "Who was asking him?" It showed Falk's brutality because after all he had selfishly caused him (Hermann) much pain. He would have preferred not to know that such an unclean creature had been in the habit of caressing his children. He hoped I would say nothing of all this ashore, though. He wouldn't like it to get about that he had been intimate with an eater of men—a common cannibal. As to the scene he had made (which I judged quite unnecessary) he was not going to inconvenience and restrain himself for a fellow that went about courting and upsetting girls' heads, while he knew all the time that no decent housewifely girl could think of marrying him. At least he (Hermann) could not conceive how any girl could. Fancy Lena! . . . No, it was impossible. The thoughts that would come into their heads every time they sat down to a meal. Horrible! Horrible!

"You are too squeamish, Hermann," I said.

He seemed to think it was eminently proper to be squeamish if the word meant disgust at Falk's conduct; and turning up his eyes sentimentally he drew my attention to the horrible fate of the victims— the victims of that Falk. I said that I knew nothing about them. He seemed surprised. Could not anybody imagine without knowing? He— for instance—felt he would like to avenge them. But what if—said I— there had not been any? They might have died as it were, naturally—of starvation. He shuddered. But to be eaten—after death! To be devoured! He gave another deep shudder, and asked suddenly, "Do you think it is true?"

His indignation and his personality together would have been enough to spoil the reality of the most authentic thing. When I looked at him I doubted the story—but the remembrance of Falk's words, looks, gestures, invested it not only with an air of reality but with the absolute truth of primitive passion.

"It is true just as much as you are able to make it; and exactly in the way you like to make it. For my part, when I hear you clamouring about it, I don't believe it is true at all."

And I left him pondering. The men in my boat lying at the foot of *Diana's* side ladder told me that the captain of the tug had gone away in his gig some time ago.

I let my fellows pull an easy stroke; because of the heavy dew the clear sparkle of the stars seemed to fall on me cold and wetting. There was a sense of lurking gruesome horror somewhere in my mind, and it was mingled with clear and grotesque images. Schomberg's gastronomic tittle-tattle was responsible for these; and I half hoped I should never see Falk again. But the first thing my anchor-watchman told me was that the captain of the tug was on board. He had sent his boat away and was now waiting for me in the cuddy.

He was lying full length on the stern settee, his face buried in the cushions. I had expected to see it discomposed, contorted, despairing. It was nothing of the kind; it was just as I had seen it twenty times, steady and glaring from the bridge of the tug. It was immovably set and hungry, dominated like the whole man by the singleness of one instinct.

He wanted to live. He had always wanted to live. So we all do— but in us the instinct serves a complex conception, and in him this instinct existed alone. There is in such simple development a gigantic force, and like the pathos of a child's naive and uncontrolled desire. He wanted that girl, and the utmost that can be said for him was that he wanted that particular girl alone. I think I saw then the obscure beginning, the seed germinating in the soil of an unconscious need, the first shoot of that tree bearing now for a mature mankind the flower and the fruit, the infinite gradation in shades and in flavour of our discriminating love. He was a child. He was as frank as a child too. He was hungry for the girl, terribly hungry, as he had been terribly hungry for food.

Don't be shocked if I declare that in my belief it was the same need, the same pain, the same torture. We are in his case allowed to contemplate the foundation of all the emotions—that one joy which is to live, and the one sadness at the root of the innumerable torments. It was made plain by the way he talked. He had never suffered so. It was gnawing, it was fire; it was there, like this! And after pointing below his breastbone, he made a hard wringing motion with his hands. And I assure you that, seen as I saw it with my bodily eyes, it was anything but laughable. And again, as he was presently to tell me (alluding to an early incident of the disastrous voyage when some damaged meat had been flung overboard), he said that a time soon came when his heart ached (that was the expression he used), and he was ready to tear his hair out at the thought of all that rotten beef thrown away.

I had heard all this; I witnessed his physical struggles, seeing the working of the rack and hearing the true voice of pain. I witnessed it all patiently, because the moment I came into the cuddy he had called upon me to stand by him—and this, it seems, I had diplomatically promised.

His agitation was impressive and alarming in the little cabin, like the floundering of a great whale driven into a shallow cove in a coast. He stood up; he flung himself down headlong; he tried to tear the cushion with his teeth; and again hugging it fiercely to his face he let himself fall on the couch. The whole ship seemed to feel the shock of his despair; and I contemplated with wonder the lofty forehead, the noble touch of time on the uncovered temples, the unchanged hungry character of the face—so strangely ascetic and so incapable of portraying emotion.

What should he do? He had lived by being near her. He had sat—in the evening—I knew?-all his life! She sewed. Her head was bent—so. Her head—like this—and her arms. Ah! Had I seen? Like this.

He dropped on a stool, bowed his powerful neck whose nape was red, and with his hands stitched the air, ludicrous, sublimely imbecile and comprehensible.

And now he couldn't have her? No! That was too much. After thinking too that . . . What had he done? What was my advice? Take her by force? No? Mustn't he? Who was there then to kill him? For the first time I saw one of his features move; a fighting teeth-baring curl of the lip. . . . "Not Hermann, perhaps." He lost himself in thought as though he had fallen out of the world.

I may note that the idea of suicide apparently did not enter his head for a single moment. It occurred to me to ask:

"Where was it that this shipwreck of yours took place?"

"Down south," he said vaguely with a start.

"You are not down south now," I said. "Violence won't do. They would take her away from you in no time. And what was the name of the ship?"

"*Borgmester Dahl*," he said. "It was no shipwreck."

He seemed to be waking up by degrees from that trance, and waking up calmed.

"Not a shipwreck? What was it?"

"Break down," he answered, looking more like himself every moment. By this only I learned that it was a steamer. I had till then supposed they had been starving in boats or on a raft—or perhaps on a barren rock.

"She did not sink then?" I asked in surprise. He nodded. "We sighted the southern ice," he pronounced dreamily.

"And you alone survived?"

He sat down. "Yes. It was a terrible misfortune for me. Everything went wrong. All the men went wrong. I survived."

Remembering the things one reads of it was difficult to realise the true meaning of his answers. I ought to have seen at once—but I did not; so difficult is it for our minds, remembering so much, instructed so much, informed of so much, to get in touch with the real actuality at our elbow. And with my head full of preconceived notions as to how a case of "cannibalism and suffering at sea" should be managed I said— "You were then so lucky in the drawing of lots?"

"Drawing of lots?" he said. "What lots? Do you think I would have allowed my life to go for the drawing of lots?"

Not if he could help if, I perceived, no matter what other life went.

"It was a great misfortune. Terrible. Awful," he said. "Many heads went wrong, but the best men would live."

"The toughest, you mean," I said. He considered the word. Perhaps it was strange to him, though his English was so good.

"Yes," he asserted at last. "The best. It was everybody for himself at last and the ship open to all."

Thus from question to question I got the whole story. I fancy it was the only way I could that night have stood by him. Outwardly at least he was himself again; the first sign of it was the return of that incongruous trick he had of drawing both his hands down his face—and it had its meaning now, with that slight shudder of the frame and the passionate anguish of these hands uncovering a hungry immovable face, the wide pupils of the intent, silent, fascinating eyes.

It was an iron steamer of a most respectable origin. The burgomaster of Falk's native town had built her. She was the first steamer ever launched there. The burgomaster's daughter had christened her. Country people drove in carts from miles around to see her. He told me all this. He got the berth as what we should call a chief mate. He seemed to think it had been a feather in his cap; and, in his own corner of the world, this lover of life was of good parentage.

The burgomaster had advanced ideas in the ship-owning line. At that time not every one would have known enough to think of despatching a cargo steamer to the Pacific. But he loaded her with pitch-pine deals and sent her off to hunt for her luck. Wellington was to be the first port, I fancy. It doesn't matter, because in latitude 44 d south and somewhere halfway between Good Hope and New Zealand the tail shaft broke and the propeller dropped off.

They were steaming then with a fresh gale on the quarter and all their canvas set, to help the engines. But by itself the sail power was not enough to keep way on her. When the propeller went the ship broached-to at once, and the masts got whipped overboard.

The disadvantage of being dismasted consisted in this, that they had nothing to hoist flags on to make themselves visible at a distance. In the course of the first few days several ships failed to sight them; and the gale was drifting them out of the usual track. The voyage had been, from the first, neither very successful nor very harmonious. There had been quarrels on board. The captain was a clever, melancholic man, who had no unusual grip on his crew. The ship had been amply provisioned for the passage, but, somehow or other, several barrels of meat were found spoiled on opening, and had been thrown overboard soon after leaving home, as a sanitary measure. Afterwards the crew of the *Borgmester Dahl* thought of that rotten carrion with tears of regret, covetousness and despair.

She drove south. To begin with, there had been an appearance of organisation, but soon the bonds of discipline became relaxed. A sombre idleness succeeded. They looked with sullen eyes at the horizon. The gales increased: she lay in the trough, the seas made a clean breach over her. On one frightful night, when they expected their hulk to turn over with them every moment, a heavy sea broke on board, deluged the store-rooms and spoiled the best part of the remaining provisions. It seems the hatch had not been properly secured. This instance of neglect is characteristic of utter discouragement. Falk tried to inspire some energy into his captain, but failed. From that time he retired more into himself, always trying to do his utmost in the situation. It grew worse. Gale succeeded gale, with black mountains of water hurling themselves on the *Borgmester Dahl*. Some of the men never left their bunks; many became quarrelsome. The chief engineer, an old man, refused to speak at all to anybody. Others shut themselves up in their berths to cry. On calm days the inert steamer rolled on a leaden sea under a murky sky, or showed, in sunshine, the squalor of sea waifs, the dried white salt, the rust, the jagged broken places. Then the gales came again. They kept body and soul together on short rations. Once, an English ship, scudding in a storm, tried to stand by them, heaving-to pluckily under their lee. The seas swept her decks; the men in oilskins clinging to her rigging looked at them, and they made desperate signs over their shattered bulwarks. Suddenly her main-topsail went, yard and all, in a terrific squall; she had to bear up under bare poles, and disappeared.

Other ships had spoken them before, but at first they had refused to be taken off, expecting the assistance of some steamer. There were very few steamers in those latitudes then; and when they desired to leave this dead and drifting carcase, no ship came in sight. They had drifted south out of men's knowledge. They failed to attract the attention of a lonely whaler, and very soon the edge of the polar ice-cap rose from the sea and closed the southern horizon like a wall. One morning they were alarmed by finding themselves floating amongst detached pieces of ice. But the fear of sinking passed away like their vigour, like their hopes; the shocks of the floes knocking against the ship's side could not rouse them from their apathy: and the *Borgmester Dahl* drifted out again unharmed into open water. They hardly noticed the change.

The funnel had gone overboard in one of the heavy rolls; two of their three boats had disappeared, washed away in bad weather, and the davits swung to and fro, unsecured, with chafed rope's ends waggling to the roll. Nothing was done on board, and Falk told me how he had often listened to the water washing about the dark engine-room where the engines, stilled for ever, were decaying slowly into a mass of rust, as the stilled heart decays within the lifeless body. At first, after the loss of the motive power, the tiller had been thoroughly secured by lashings. But in course of time these had rotted, chafed, rusted, parting one by one: and the rudder, freed, banged heavily to and fro night and day, sending dull shocks through the whole frame of the vessel. This was dangerous. Nobody cared enough to lift a little finger. He told me that even now sometimes waking up at night, he fancied he could hear the dull vibrating thuds. The pintles carried away, and it dropped off at last.

The final catastrophe came with the sending off of their one remaining boat. It was Falk who had managed to preserve her intact, and now it was agreed that some of the hands should sail away into the track of the shipping to procure assistance. She was provisioned with all the food they could spare for the six who were to go. They waited for a fine day. It was long in coming. At last one morning they lowered her into the water.

Directly, in that demoralised crowd, trouble broke out. Two men who had no business there had jumped into the boat under the pretence of unhooking the tackles, while some sort of squabble arose on the deck amongst these weak, tottering spectres of a ship's company. The captain, who had been for days living secluded and unapproachable in the chart-room, came to the rail. He ordered the two men to come up on board and menaced them with his revolver. They pretended to obey, but suddenly cutting the boat's painter, gave a shove against the ship's side and made ready to hoist the sail.

"Shoot, sir! Shoot them down!" cried Falk—"and I will jump overboard to regain the boat." But the captain, after taking aim with an irresolute arm, turned suddenly away.

A howl of rage arose. Falk dashed into his cabin for his own pistol. When he returned it was too late. Two more men had leaped into the water, but the fellows in the boat beat them off with the oars, hoisted the boat's lug and sailed away. They were never heard of again.

Consternation and despair possessed the remaining ship's company, till the apathy of utter hopelessness re-asserted its sway. That day a fireman committed suicide, running up on deck with his throat cut from ear to ear, to the horror of all hands. He was thrown overboard. The captain had locked himself in the chart-room, and Falk, knocking vainly for admittance, heard him reciting over and over again the names of his wife and children, not as if calling upon them or commending them to God, but in a mechanical voice like an exercise of memory. Next day the doors of the chart-room were swinging open to the roll of the ship, and the captain had disappeared. He must during the night have jumped into the sea. Falk locked both the doors and kept the keys.

The organised life of the ship had come to an end. The solidarity of the men had gone. They became indifferent to each other. It was Falk who took in hand the distribution of such food as remained. They boiled their boots for soup to eke out the rations, which only made their hunger more intolerable. Sometimes whispers of hate were heard passing between the languid skeletons that drifted endlessly to and fro, north and south, east and west, upon that carcase of a ship.

And in this lies the grotesque horror of this sombre story. The last extremity of sailors, overtaking a small boat or a frail craft, seems easier to bear, because of the direct danger of the seas. The confined space, the close contact, the imminent menace of the waves, seem to draw men together, in spite of madness, suffering and despair. But there was a ship—safe, convenient, roomy: a ship with beds, bedding, knives, forks, comfortable cabins, glass and china, and a complete cook's galley, pervaded, ruled and possessed by the pitiless spectre of starvation. The lamp oil had been drunk, the wicks cut up for food, the candles eaten. At night she floated dark in all her recesses, and full of fears. One day Falk came upon a man gnawing a splinter of pine wood. Suddenly he threw the piece of wood away, tottered to the rail, and fell over. Falk, too late to prevent the act, saw him claw the ship's side desperately before he went down. Next day another man did the same thing, after uttering horrible imprecations. But this one somehow managed to get hold of the broken rudder chains and hung on there, silently. Falk set about trying to save him, and all the time the man, holding with both hands, looked at him anxiously with his sunken eyes. Then, just as Falk was ready to put his hand on him, the man let go his hold and sank like a stone. Falk reflected on these sights. His heart revolted against the horror of death, and he said to himself that he would struggle for every precious minute of his life.

One afternoon—as the survivors lay about on the after deck—the carpenter, a tall man with a black beard, spoke of the last sacrifice. There was nothing eatable left on board. Nobody said a word to this; but that company separated quickly, these listless feeble spectres slunk off one by one to hide in fear of each other. Falk and the carpenter remained on deck together. Falk liked the big carpenter. He had been the best man of the lot, helpful and ready as long as there was anything to do, the longest hopeful, and had preserved to the last some vigour and decision of mind.

They did not speak to each other. Henceforth no voices were to be heard conversing sadly on board that ship. After a time the carpenter tottered away forward; but later on, Falk going to drink at the fresh-water pump, had the inspiration to turn his head. The carpenter had stolen upon him from behind, and, summoning all his strength, was aiming with a crowbar a blow at the back of his skull.

Dodging just in time, Falk made his escape and ran into his cabin. While he was loading his revolver there, he heard the sound of heavy blows struck upon the bridge. The locks of the chartroom doors were slight, they flew open, and the carpenter, possessing himself of the captain's revolver, fired a shot of defiance.

Falk was about to go on deck and have it out at once, when he remarked that one of the ports of his cabin commanded the approaches to the freshwater pump. Instead of going out he remained in and secured the door. "The best man shall survive," he said to himself—and the other, he reasoned, must at some time or other come there to drink. These starving men would drink often to cheat the pangs of their hunger. But the carpenter too must have noticed the position of the port. They were the two best men in the ship, and the game was with them. All the rest of the day Falk saw no one and heard no sound. At night he strained his eyes. It was dark—he heard a rustling noise once, but he was certain that no one could have come near the pump. It was to the left of his deck port, and he could not have failed to see a man, for the night was clear and starry. He saw nothing; towards morning another faint noise made him suspicious. Deliberately and quietly he unlocked his door. He had not slept, and had not given way to the horror of the situation. He wanted to live.

But during the night the carpenter, without at all trying to approach the pump, had managed to creep quietly along the starboard bulwark, and, unseen, had crouched down right under Falk's deck port. When daylight came he rose up suddenly, looked in, and putting his arm through the round brass framed opening, fired at Falk within a foot. He missed—and Falk, instead of attempting to seize the arm holding the weapon, opened his door unexpectedly, and with the muzzle of his long revolver nearly touching the other's side, shot him dead.

The best man had survived. Both of them had at the beginning just strength enough to stand on their feet, and both had displayed pitiless resolution, endurance, cunning and courage—all the qualities of classic heroism. At once Falk threw overboard the captain's revolver. He was a born monopolist. Then after the report of the two shots, followed by a profound silence, there crept out into the cold, cruel dawn of Antarctic regions, from various hiding-places, over the deck of that dismantled corpse of a ship floating on a grey sea ruled by iron necessity and with a heart of ice—there crept into view one by one, cautious, slow, eager, glaring, and unclean, a band of hungry and livid skeletons. Falk faced them, the possessor of the only fire-arm on board, and the second best man—the carpenter—was lying dead between him and them.

"He was eaten, of course," I said.

He bent his head slowly, shuddered a little, drawing his hands over his face, and said, "I had never any quarrel with that man. But there were our lives between him and me."

Why continue the story of that ship, that story before which, with its fresh-water pump like a spring of death, its man with the weapon, the sea ruled by iron necessity, its spectral band swayed by terror and hope, its mute and unhearing heaven?-the fable of the *Flying Dutchman* with its convention of crime and its sentimental retribution fades like a graceful wreath, like a wisp of white mist. What is there to say that every one of us cannot guess for himself? I believe Falk began by going through the ship, revolver in hand, to annex all the matches. Those starving wretches had plenty of matches! He had no mind to have the ship set on fire under his feet, either from hate or from despair. He lived in the open, camping on the bridge, commanding all the after deck and the only approach to the pump. He lived! Some of the others lived too—concealed, anxious, coming out one by one from their hiding-places at the seductive sound of a shot. And he was not selfish. They shared, but only three of them all were alive when a whaler, returning from her cruising ground, nearly ran over the water-logged hull of the *Borgmester Dahl*, which, it seems, in the end had in some way sprung a leak in both her holds, but being loaded with deals could not sink.

"They all died," Falk said. "These three too, afterwards. But I would not die. All died, all! under this terrible misfortune. But was I too to throw away my life? Could I? Tell me, captain? I was alone there, quite alone, just like the others. Each man was alone. Was I to give up my revolver? Who to? Or was I to throw it into the sea? What would have been the good? Only the best man would survive. It was a great, terrible, and cruel misfortune."

He had survived! I saw him before me as though preserved for a witness to the mighty truth of an unerring and eternal principle. Great beads of perspiration stood on his forehead. And suddenly it struck the table with a heavy blow, as he fell forward throwing his hands out.

"And this is worse," he cried. "This is a worse pain! This is more terrible."

He made my heart thump with the profound conviction of his cries. And after he had left me alone I called up before my mental eye the image of the girl weeping silently, abundantly, patiently, and as if irresistibly. I thought of her tawny hair. I thought how, if unplaited, it would have covered her all round as low as the hips, like the hair of a siren. And she had bewitched him. Fancy a man who would guard his own life with the inflexibility of a pitiless and immovable fate, being brought to lament that once a crowbar had missed his skull! The sirens sing and lure to death, but this one had been weeping silently as if for the pity of his life. She was the tender and voiceless siren of this appalling navigator. He evidently wanted to live his whole conception of life. Nothing else would do. And she too was a servant of that life that, in the midst of death, cries aloud to our senses. She was eminently fitted to interpret for him its feminine side. And in her own way, and with her own profusion of sensuous charms, she also seemed to illustrate the eternal truth of an unerring principle. I don't know though what sort of principle Hermann illustrated when he turned up early on board my ship with a most perplexed air. It struck me, however, that he too would do his best to survive. He seemed greatly calmed on the subject of Falk, but still very full of it.

"What is it you said I was last night? You know," he asked after some preliminary talk. "Too—too—I don't know. A very funny word."

"Squeamish?" I suggested.

"Yes. What does it mean?"

"That you exaggerate things—to yourself. Without inquiry, and so on."

He seemed to turn it over in his mind. We went on talking. This Falk was the plague of his life. Upsetting everybody like this! Mrs. Hermann was unwell rather this morning. His niece was crying still. There was nobody to look after the children. He struck his umbrella on the deck. She would be like that for months. Fancy carrying all the way home, second class, a perfectly useless girl who is crying all the time. It was bad for Lena too, he observed; but on what grounds I could not guess. Perhaps of the bad example. That child was already sorrowing and crying enough over the rag doll. Nicholas was really the least sentimental person of the family.

"Why does she weep?" I asked.

"From pity," cried Hermann.

It was impossible to make out women. Mrs. Hermann was the only one he pretended to understand. She was very, very upset and doubtful.

"Doubtful about what?" I asked.

He averted his eyes and did not answer this. It was impossible to make them out. For instance, his niece was weeping for Falk. Now he (Hermann) would like to wring his neck—but then . . . He supposed he had too tender a heart. "Frankly," he asked at last, "what do you think of what we heard last night, captain?"

"In all these tales," I observed, "there is always a good deal of exaggeration."

And not letting him recover from his surprise I assured him that I knew all the details. He begged me not to repeat them. His heart was too tender. They made him feel unwell. Then, looking at his feet and speaking very slowly, he supposed that he need not see much of them after they were married. For, indeed, he could not bear the sight of Falk. On the other hand it was ridiculous to take home a girl with her head turned. A girl that weeps all the time and is of no help to her aunt.

"Now you will be able to do with one cabin only on your passage home," I said.

"Yes, I had thought of that," he said brightly, almost. "Yes! Himself, his wife, four children—one cabin might do. Whereas if his niece went . . ."

"And what does Mrs. Hermann say to it?" I inquired.

Mrs. Hermann did not know whether a man of that sort could make a girl happy—she had been greatly deceived in Captain Falk. She had been very upset last night.

Those good people did not seem to be able to retain an impression for a whole twelve hours. I assured him on my own personal knowledge that Falk possessed in himself all the qualities to make his niece's future prosperous. He said he was glad to hear this, and that he would tell his wife. Then the object of the visit came out. He wished me to help him to resume relations with Falk. His niece, he said, had expressed the hope I would do so in my kindness. He was evidently anxious that I should, for though he seemed to have forgotten nine-tenths of his last night's opinions and the whole of his indignation, yet he evidently feared to be sent to the right-about. "You told me he was very much in love," he concluded slyly, and leered in a sort of bucolic way.

As soon as he had left my ship I called Falk on board by signal—the tug still lying at the anchorage. He took the news with calm gravity, as though he had all along expected the stars to fight for him in their courses.

I saw them once more together, and only once—on the quarter-deck of the *Diana*. Hermann sat smoking with a shirt-sleeved elbow hooked over the back of his chair. Mrs. Hermann was sewing alone. As Falk stepped over the gangway, Hermann's niece, with a slight swish of the skirt and a swift friendly nod to me, glided past my chair.

They met in sunshine abreast of the mainmast. He held her hands and looked down at them, and she looked up at him with her candid and unseeing glance. It seemed to me they had come together as if attracted, drawn and guided to each other by a mysterious influence. They were a complete couple. In her grey frock, palpitating with life, generous of form, olympian and simple, she was indeed the siren to fascinate that dark navigator, this ruthless lover of the five senses. From afar I seemed to feel the masculine strength with which he grasped those hands she had extended to him with a womanly swiftness. Lena, a little pale, nursing her beloved lump of dirty rags, ran towards her big friend; and then in the drowsy silence of the good old ship Mrs. Hermann's voice rang out so changed that it made me spin round in my chair to see what was the matter.

"Lena, come here!" she screamed. And this good-natured matron gave me a wavering glance, dark and full of fearsome distrust. The child ran back, surprised to her knee. But the two, standing before each other in sunlight with clasped hands, had heard nothing, had seen nothing and no one. Three feet away from them in the shade a seaman sat on a spar, very busy splicing a strop, and dipping his fingers into a tar-pot, as if utterly unaware of their existence.

When I returned in command of another ship, some five years afterwards, Mr. and Mrs. Falk had left the place. I should not wonder if Schomberg's tongue had succeeded at last in scaring Falk away for good; and, indubitably, there was a tale still going about the town of a certain Falk, owner of a tug, who had won his wife at cards from the captain of an English ship.

Typhoon

I

Captain MacWhirr, of the steamer *Nan-Shan*, had a physiognomy that, in the order of material appearances, was the exact counterpart of his mind: it presented no marked characteristics of firmness or stupidity; it had no pronounced characteristics whatever; it was simply ordinary, irresponsive, and unruffled.

The only thing his aspect might have been said to suggest, at times, was bashfulness; because he would sit, in business offices ashore, sunburnt and smiling faintly, with downcast eyes. When he raised them, they were perceived to be direct in their glance and of blue color. His hair was fair and extremely fine, clasping from temple to temple the bald dome of his skull in a clamp as of fluffy silk. The hair of his face, on the contrary, carroty and flaming, resembled a growth of copper wire clipped short to the line of the lip; while, no matter how close he shaved, fiery metallic gleams passed, when he moved his head, over the surface of his cheeks. He was rather below the medium height, a bit round-shouldered, and so sturdy of limb that his clothes always looked a shade too tight for his arms and legs. As if unable to grasp what is due to the difference of latitudes, he wore a brown bowler hat, a complete suit of a brownish hue, and clumsy black boots. These harbor togs gave to his thick figure an air of stiff and uncouth smartness. A thin silver watch chain looped his waistcoat, and he never left his ship for the shore without clutching in his powerful, hairy fist an elegant umbrella of the very best quality, but generally unrolled. Young Jukes, the chief mate, attending his commander to the gangway, would sometimes venture to say, with the greatest gentleness, "Allow me, sir"—and possessing himself of the umbrella deferentially, would elevate the ferule, shake the folds, twirl a neat furl in a jiffy, and hand it back; going through the performance with a face of such portentous gravity, that Mr. Solomon Rout, the chief engineer, smoking his morning cigar over the skylight, would turn away his head in order to hide a smile. "Oh! aye! The blessed gamp. . . . Thank 'ee, Jukes, thank 'ee," would mutter Captain MacWhirr, heartily, without looking up.

Having just enough imagination to carry him through each successive day, and no more, he was tranquilly sure of himself; and from the very same cause he was not in the least conceited. It is your imaginative superior who is touchy, overbearing, and difficult to please; but every ship Captain MacWhirr commanded was the floating abode of harmony and peace. It was, in truth, as impossible for him to take a flight of fancy as it would be for a watchmaker to put together a chronometer with nothing except a two-pound hammer and a whipsaw in the way of tools. Yet the uninteresting lives of men so entirely given to the actuality of the bare existence have their mysterious side. It was impossible in Captain MacWhirr's case, for instance, to understand what under heaven could have induced that perfectly satisfactory son of a petty grocer in Belfast to run away to sea. And yet he had done that very thing at the age of fifteen. It was enough, when you thought it over, to give you the idea of an immense, potent, and invisible hand thrust into the ant-heap of the earth, laying hold of shoulders, knocking heads together, and setting the unconscious faces of the multitude towards inconceivable goals and in undreamt-of directions.

His father never really forgave him for this undutiful stupidity. "We could have got on without him," he used to say later on, "but there's the business. And he an only son, too!" His mother wept very much after his disappearance. As it had never occurred to him to leave word behind, he was mourned over for dead till, after eight months, his first letter arrived from Talcahuano. It was short, and contained the statement: "We had very fine weather on our passage out." But evidently, in the writer's mind, the only important intelligence was to the effect that his captain had, on the very day of writing, entered him regularly on the ship's articles as Ordinary Seaman. "Because I can do the work," he explained. The mother again wept copiously, while the remark, "Tom's an ass," expressed the emotions of the father. He was a corpulent man, with a gift for sly chaffing, which to the end of his life he exercised in his intercourse with his son, a little pityingly, as if upon a half-witted person.

MacWhirr's visits to his home were necessarily rare, and in the course of years he dispatched other letters to his parents, informing them of his successive promotions and of his movements upon the vast earth. In these missives could be found sentences like this: "The heat here is very great." Or: "On Christmas day at 4 P. M. we fell in with some icebergs." The old people ultimately became acquainted with a good many names of ships, and with the names of the skippers who commanded them—with the names of Scots and English shipowners— with the names of seas, oceans, straits, promontories—with outlandish names of lumber ports, of rice ports, of cotton ports—with the names of islands—with the name of their son's young woman. She was called Lucy. It did not suggest itself to him to mention whether he thought the name pretty. And then they died.

The great day of MacWhirr's marriage came in due course, following shortly upon the great day when he got his first command.

All these events had taken place many years before the morning when, in the chart-room of the steamer *Nan-Shan*, he stood confronted by the fall of a barometer he had no reason to distrust. The fall—taking into account the excellence of the instrument, the time of the year, and the ship's position on the terrestrial globe—was of a nature ominously prophetic; but the red face of the man betrayed no sort of inward disturbance. Omens were as nothing to him, and he was unable to discover the message of a prophecy till the fulfillment had brought it home to his very door. "That's a fall, and no mistake," he thought. "There must be some uncommonly dirty weather knocking about."

The *Nan-Shan* was on her way from the southward to the treaty port of Fu-chau, with some cargo in her lower holds, and two hundred Chinese coolies returning to their village homes in the province of Fo-kien, after a few years of work in various tropical colonies. The morning was fine, the oily sea heaved without a sparkle, and there was a queer white misty patch in the sky like a halo of the sun. The foredeck, packed with Chinamen, was full of somber clothing, yellow faces, and pigtails, sprinkled over with a good many naked shoulders, for there was no wind, and the heat was close. The coolies lounged, talked, smoked, or stared over the rail; some, drawing water over the side, sluiced each other; a few slept on hatches, while several small parties of six sat on their heels surrounding iron trays with plates of rice and tiny teacups; and every single Celestial of them was carrying with him all he had in the world—a wooden chest with a ringing lock and brass on the corners, containing the savings of his labors: some clothes of ceremony, sticks of incense, a little opium maybe, bits of nameless rubbish of conventional value, and a small hoard of silver dollars, toiled for in coal lighters, won in gambling houses or in petty trading, grubbed out of earth, sweated out in mines, on railway lines, in deadly jungles under heavy burdens—amassed patiently, guarded with care, cherished fiercely.

A cross swell had set in from the direction of Formosa Channel about ten o'clock, without disturbing these passengers much, because the *Nan-Shan*, with her flat bottom, rolling chocks on bilges, and great breadth of beam, had the reputation of an exceptionally steady ship in a seaway. Mr. Jukes, in moments of expansion on shore, would proclaim loudly that the "old girl was as good as she was pretty." It would never have occurred to Captain MacWhirr to express his favorable opinion so loud or in terms so fanciful.

She was a good ship, undoubtedly, and not old either. She had been built in Dumbarton less than three years before, to the order of a firm of merchants in Siam—Messrs. Sigg and Son. When she lay afloat, finished in every detail and ready to take up the work of her life, the builders contemplated her with pride.

"Sigg has asked us for a reliable skipper to take her out," remarked one of the partners; and the other, after reflecting for a while, said: "I think MacWhirr is ashore just at present." "Is he? Then wire him at once. He's the very man," declared the senior, without a moment's hesitation.

Next morning MacWhirr stood before them unperturbed, having travelled from London by the midnight express after a sudden but undemonstrative parting with his wife. She was the daughter of a superior couple who had seen better days.

"We had better be going together over the ship, Captain," said the senior partner; and the three men started to view the perfections of the *Nan-Shan* from stem to stern, and from her keelson to the trucks of her two stumpy pole-masts.

Captain MacWhirr had begun by taking off his coat, which he hung on the end of a steam windless embodying all the latest improvements.

"My uncle wrote of you favorably by yesterday's mail to our good friends—Messrs. Sigg, you know—and doubtless they'll continue you out there in command," said the junior partner. "You'll be able to boast of being in charge of the handiest boat of her size on the coast of China, Captain," he added.

"Have you? Thank 'ee," mumbled vaguely MacWhirr, to whom the view of a distant eventuality could appeal no more than the beauty of a wide landscape to a purblind tourist; and his eyes happening at the moment to be at rest upon the lock of the cabin door, he walked up to it, full of purpose, and began to rattle the handle vigorously, while he observed, in his low, earnest voice, "You can't trust the workmen nowadays. A brand-new lock, and it won't act at all. Stuck fast. See? See?"

As soon as they found themselves alone in their office across the yard: "You praised that fellow up to Sigg. What is it you see in him?" asked the nephew, with faint contempt.

"I admit he has nothing of your fancy skipper about him, if that's what you mean," said the elder man, curtly. "Is the foreman of the joiners on the *Nan-Shan* outside? . . . Come in, Bates. How is it that you let Tait's people put us off with a defective lock on the cabin door? The Captain could see directly he set eye on it. Have it replaced at once. The little straws, Bates . . . the little straws. . . ."

The lock was replaced accordingly, and a few days afterwards the *Nan-Shan* steamed out to the East, without MacWhirr having offered any further remark as to her fittings, or having been heard to utter a single word hinting at pride in his ship, gratitude for his appointment, or satisfaction at his prospects.

With a temperament neither loquacious nor taciturn he found very little occasion to talk. There were matters of duty, of course—directions, orders, and so on; but the past being to his mind done with, and the future not there yet, the more general actualities of the day required no comment—because facts can speak for themselves with overwhelming precision.

Old Mr. Sigg liked a man of few words, and one that "you could be sure would not try to improve upon his instructions." MacWhirr satisfying these requirements, was continued in command of the *Nan-Shan*, and applied himself to the careful navigation of his ship in the China seas. She had come out on a British register, but after some time Messrs. Sigg judged it expedient to transfer her to the Siamese flag.

At the news of the contemplated transfer Jukes grew restless, as if under a sense of personal affront. He went about grumbling to himself, and uttering short scornful laughs. "Fancy having a ridiculous Noah's Ark elephant in the ensign of one's ship," he said once at the engine-room door. "Dash me if I can stand it; I'll throw up the billet. Don't it make you sick, Mr. Rout?" The chief engineer only cleared his throat with the air of a man who knows the value of a good billet.

The first morning the new flag floated over the stern of the *Nan-Shan* Jukes stood looking at it bitterly from the bridge. He struggled with his feelings for a while, and then remarked, "Queer flag for a man to sail under, sir."

"What's the matter with the flag?" inquired Captain MacWhirr. "Seems all right to me." And he walked across to the end of the bridge to have a good look.

"Well, it looks queer to me," burst out Jukes, greatly exasperated, and flung off the bridge.

Captain MacWhirr was amazed at these manners. After a while he stepped quietly into the chart room, and opened his International Signal Code Book at the plate where the flags of all the nations are correctly figured in gaudy rows. He ran his finger over them, and when he came to Siam he contemplated with great attention the red field and the white elephant. Nothing could be more simple; but to make sure he brought the book out on the bridge for the purpose of comparing the colored drawing with the real thing at the flagstaff astern. When next Jukes, who was carrying on the duty that day with a sort of suppressed fierceness, happened on the bridge, his commander observed:

"There's nothing amiss with that flag."

"Isn't there?" mumbled Jukes, falling on his knees before a deck-locker and jerking therefrom viciously a spare lead line.

"No. I looked up the book. Length twice the breadth and the

elephant exactly in the middle. I thought the people ashore would know how to make the local flag. Stands to reason. You were wrong, Jukes. . . ."

"Well, sir," began Jukes, getting up excitedly, "all I can say—" He fumbled for the end of the coil of line with trembling hands.

"That's all right." Captain MacWhirr soothed him, sitting heavily on a little canvas folding stool he greatly affected. "All you have to do is to take care they don't hoist the elephant upside-down before they get quite used to it."

Jukes flung the new lead line over on the foredeck with a loud "Here you are, bosun—don't forget to wet it thoroughly," and turned with immense resolution towards his commander; but Captain MacWhirr spread his elbows on the bridge rail comfortably.

"Because it would be, I suppose, understood as a signal of distress," he went on. "What do you think? That elephant there, I take it, stands for something in the nature of the Union Jack in the flag. . . ."

"Does it!" yelled Jukes, so that every head on the *Nan-Shan*'s decks looked towards the bridge. Then he sighed, and with sudden resignation: "It would certainly be a dam' distressful sight," he said, meekly.

Later in the day he accosted the chief engineer with a confidential, "Here, let me tell you the old man's latest."

Mr. Solomon Rout (frequently alluded to as Long Sol, Old Sol, or Father Rout), from finding himself almost invariably the tallest man on board every ship he joined, had acquired the habit of a stooping, leisurely condescension. His hair was scant and sandy, his flat cheeks were pale, his bony wrists and long scholarly hands were pale, too, as though he had lived all his life in the shade.

He smiled from on high at Jukes, and went on smoking and glancing about quietly, in the manner of a kind uncle lending an ear to the tale of an excited schoolboy. Then, greatly amused but impassive, he asked:

"And did you throw up the billet?"

"No," cried Jukes, raising a weary, discouraged voice above the harsh buzz of the *Nan-Shan*'s friction winches. All of them were hard at work, snatching slings of cargo, high up, to the end of long derricks, only, as it seemed, to let them rip down recklessly by the run. The cargo chains groaned in the gins, clinked on coamings, rattled over the side; and the whole ship quivered, with her long gray flanks smoking in wreaths of steam. "No," cried Jukes, "I didn't. What's the good? I might just as well fling my resignation at this bulkhead. I don't believe you can make a man like that understand anything. He simply knocks me over."

At that moment Captain MacWhirr, back from the shore, crossed the deck, umbrella in hand, escorted by a mournful, self-possessed

Chinaman, walking behind in paper-soled silk shoes, and who also carried an umbrella.

The master of the *Nan-Shan*, speaking just audibly and gazing at his boots as his manner was, remarked that it would be necessary to call at Fu-chau this trip, and desired Mr. Rout to have steam up tomorrow afternoon at one o'clock sharp. He pushed back his hat to wipe his forehead, observing at the same time that he hated going ashore anyhow; while overtopping him Mr. Rout, without deigning a word, smoked austerely, nursing his right elbow in the palm of his left hand. Then Jukes was directed in the same subdued voice to keep the forward 'tween-deck clear of cargo. Two hundred coolies were going to be put down there. The Bun Hin Company were sending that lot home. Twenty-five bags of rice would be coming off in a sampan directly, for stores. All seven-years'-men they were, said Captain MacWhirr, with a camphor-wood chest to every man. The carpenter should be set to work nailing three-inch battens along the deck below, fore and aft, to keep these boxes from shifting in a seaway. Jukes had better look to it at once. "D'ye hear, Jukes?" This Chinaman here was coming with the ship as far as Fu-chau—a sort of interpreter he would be. Bun Hin's clerk he was, and wanted to have a look at the space. Jukes had better take him forward. "D'ye hear, Jukes?"

Jukes took care to punctuate these instructions in proper places with the obligatory "Yes, sir," ejaculated without enthusiasm. His brusque "Come along, John; make look see" set the Chinaman in motion at his heels.

"Wanchee look see, all same look see can do," said Jukes, who having no talent for foreign languages mangled the very pidgin-English cruelly. He pointed at the open hatch. "Catchee number one piecie place to sleep in. Eh?"

He was gruff, as became his racial superiority, but not unfriendly. The Chinaman, gazing sad and speechless into the darkness of the hatchway, seemed to stand at the head of a yawning grave.

"No catchee rain down there—savee?" pointed out Jukes. "Suppose all'ee same fine weather, one piecie coolie-man come topside," he pursued, warming up imaginatively. "Make so— Phooooo!" He expanded his chest and blew out his cheeks. "Savee, John? Breathe—fresh air. Good. Eh? Washee him piecie pants, chow-chow topside—see, John?"

With his mouth and hands he made exuberant motions of eating rice and washing clothes; and the Chinaman, who concealed his distrust of this pantomime under a collected demeanor tinged by a gentle and refined melancholy, glanced out of his almond eyes from Jukes to the hatch and back again. "Velly good," he murmured, in a disconsolate undertone, and hastened smoothly along the decks, dodging obstacles in his course. He disappeared, ducking low under a sling of ten dirty gunny bags full of some costly merchandise and exhaling a repulsive smell.

Captain MacWhirr meantime had gone on the bridge, and into the chart room, where a letter, commenced two days before, awaited termination. These long letters began with the words, "My darling wife," and the steward, between the scrubbing of the floors and the dusting of chronometer-boxes, snatched at every opportunity to read them. They interested him much more than they possibly could the woman for whose eye they were intended; and this for the reason that they related in minute detail each successive trip of the *Nan-Shan*.

Her master, faithful to facts, which alone his consciousness reflected, would set them down with painstaking care upon many pages. The house in a northern suburb to which these pages were addressed had a bit of garden before the bow-windows, a deep porch of good appearance, colored glass with imitation lead frame in the front door. He paid five-and-forty pounds a year for it, and did not think the rent too high, because Mrs. MacWhirr (a pretentious person with a scraggy neck and a disdainful manner) was admittedly ladylike, and in the neighborhood considered as "quite superior." The only secret of her life was her abject terror of the time when her husband would come home to stay for good. Under the same roof there dwelt also a daughter called Lydia and a son, Tom. These two were but slightly acquainted with their father. Mainly, they knew him as a rare but privileged visitor, who of an evening smoked his pipe in the dining room and slept in the house. The lanky girl, upon the whole, was rather ashamed of him; the boy was frankly and utterly indifferent in a straightforward, delightful, unaffected way manly boys have.

And Captain MacWhirr wrote home from the coast of China twelve times every year, desiring quaintly to be "remembered to the children," and subscribing himself "your loving husband," as calmly as if the words so long used by so many men were, apart from their shape, worn-out things, and of a faded meaning.

The China seas north and south are narrow seas. They are seas full of everyday, eloquent facts, such as islands, sand banks, reefs, swift and changeable currents—tangled facts that nevertheless speak to a seaman in clear and definite language. Their speech appealed to Captain MacWhirr's sense of realities so forcibly that he had given up his stateroom below and practically lived all his days on the bridge of his ship, often having his meals sent up, and sleeping at night in the chart room. And he indited there his home letters. Each of them, without exception, contained the phrase, "The weather has been very fine this trip," or some other form of a statement to that effect. And this statement, too, in its wonderful persistence, was of the same perfect accuracy as all the others they contained.

Mr. Rout likewise wrote letters; only no one on board knew how chatty he could be pen in hand, because the chief engineer had enough imagination to keep his desk locked. His wife relished his style greatly. They were a childless couple, and Mrs. Rout, a big, high-bosomed, jolly woman of forty, shared with Mr. Rout's toothless and venerable mother a little cottage near Teddington. She would run over her correspondence, at breakfast, with lively eyes, and scream out interesting passages in a joyous voice at the deaf old lady, prefacing each extract by the warning shout, "Solomon says!" She had the trick of firing off Solomon's utterances also upon strangers, astonishing them easily by the unfamiliar text and the unexpectedly jocular vein of these quotations. On the day the new curate called for the first time at the cottage, she found occasion to remark, "As Solomon says: 'the engineers that go down to the sea in ships behold the wonders of sailor nature'"; when a change in the visitor's countenance made her stop and stare.

"Solomon. . . . Oh! . . . Mrs. Rout," stuttered the young man, very red in the face, "I must say . . . I don't. . . ."

"He's my husband," she announced in a great shout, throwing herself back in the chair. Perceiving the joke, she laughed immoderately with a handkerchief to her eyes, while he sat wearing a forced smile, and, from his inexperience of jolly women, fully persuaded that she must be deplorably insane. They were excellent friends afterwards; for, absolving her from irreverent intention, he came to think she was a very worthy person indeed; and he learned in time to receive without flinching other scraps of Solomon's wisdom.

"For my part," Solomon was reported by his wife to have said once, "give me the dullest ass for a skipper before a rogue. There is a way to take a fool; but a rogue is smart and slippery." This was an airy generalization drawn from the particular case of Captain MacWhirr's honesty, which, in itself, had the heavy obviousness of a lump of clay. On the other hand, Mr. Jukes, unable to generalize, unmarried, and unengaged, was in the habit of opening his heart after another fashion to an old chum and former shipmate, actually serving as second officer on board an Atlantic liner.

First of all he would insist upon the advantages of the Eastern trade, hinting at its superiority to the Western ocean service. He extolled the sky, the seas, the ships, and the easy life of the Far East. The *Nan-Shan*, he affirmed, was second to none as a sea boat.

"We have no brass-bound uniforms, but then we are like brothers here," he wrote. "We all mess together and live like fighting cocks. . . . All the chaps of the black-squad are as decent as they make that kind, and old Sol, the Chief, is a dry stick. We are good friends. As to our old man, you could not find a quieter skipper. Sometimes you would think he hadn't sense enough to see anything wrong. And yet it isn't that. Can't be. He has been in command for a good few years now. He doesn't do anything actually foolish, and gets his ship along all right without worrying anybody. I believe he hasn't brains enough to enjoy kicking up a row. I don't take advantage of him. I would scorn it. Outside the routine of duty he doesn't seem to understand more than half of what you tell him. We get a laugh out of this at times; but it is dull, too, to be with a man like this—in the long run. Old Sol says he hasn't much conversation. Conversation! O Lord! He never talks. The other day I had been yarning under the bridge with one of the engineers, and he must have heard us. When I came up to take my watch, he steps out of the chart room and has a good look all round, peeps over at the sidelights, glances at the compass, squints upward at the stars. That's his regular performance. By and by he says: 'Was that you talking just now in the port alleyway?' 'Yes, sir.' 'With the third engineer?' 'Yes, sir.' He walks off to starboard, and sits under the dodger on a little campstool of his, and for half an hour perhaps he makes no sound, except that I heard him sneeze once. Then after a while I hear him getting up over there, and he strolls across to port, where I was. 'I can't understand what you can find to talk about,' says he. 'Two solid hours. I am not blaming you. I see people ashore at it all day long, and then in the evening they sit down and keep at it over the drinks. Must be saying the same things over and over again. I can't understand.'

"Did you ever hear anything like that? And he was so patient about it. It made me quite sorry for him. But he is exasperating, too, sometimes. Of course one would not do anything to vex him even if it were worth while. But it isn't. He's so jolly innocent that if you were to put your thumb to your nose and wave your fingers at him he would only wonder gravely to himself what got into you. He told me once quite simply that he found it very difficult to make out what made people always act so queerly. He's too dense to trouble about, and that's the truth."

Thus wrote Mr. Jukes to his chum in the Western ocean trade, out of the fullness of his heart and the liveliness of his fancy.

He had expressed his honest opinion. It was not worth while trying to impress a man of that sort. If the world had been full of such men, life would have probably appeared to Jukes an unentertaining and unprofitable business. He was not alone in his opinion. The sea itself, as if sharing Mr. Jukes' good-natured forbearance, had never put itself out to startle the silent man, who seldom looked up, and wandered innocently over the waters with the only visible purpose of getting food, raiment, and house-room for three people ashore. Dirty weather he had known, of course. He had been made wet, uncomfortable, tired in the usual way, felt at the time and presently forgotten. So that upon the whole he had been justified in reporting fine weather at home. But he had never been given a glimpse of immeasurable strength and of immoderate wrath, the wrath that passes exhausted but never appeased—the wrath and fury of the passionate sea. He knew it existed, as we know that crime and abominations exist; he had heard of it as a peaceable citizen in a town hears of battles, famines, and floods, and yet knows nothing of what these things mean—though, indeed, he may have been mixed up in a street row, have gone without his dinner once, or been soaked to the skin in a shower. Captain MacWhirr had sailed over the surface of the oceans as some men go skimming over the years of existence to sink gently into a placid grave, ignorant of life to the last, without ever having been made to see all it may contain of perfidy, of violence, and of terror. There are on sea and land such men thus fortunate—or thus disdained by destiny or by the sea.

II

Observing the steady fall of the barometer, Captain MacWhirr thought, "There's some dirty weather knocking about." This is precisely what he thought. He had had an experience of moderately dirty weather—the term dirty as applied to the weather implying only moderate discomfort to the seaman. Had he been informed by an indisputable authority that the end of the world was to be finally accomplished by a catastrophic disturbance of the atmosphere, he would have assimilated the information under the simple idea of dirty weather, and no other, because he had no experience of cataclysms, and belief does not necessarily imply comprehension. The wisdom of his country had pronounced by means of an Act of Parliament that before he could be considered as fit to take charge of a ship he should be able to answer certain simple questions on the subject of circular storms such as hurricanes, cyclones, typhoons; and apparently he had answered them, since he was now in command of the *Nan-Shan* in the China seas during the season of typhoons. But if he had answered he remembered nothing of it. He was, however, conscious of being made uncomfortable by the clammy heat. He came out on the bridge, and found no relief to this oppression. The air seemed thick. He gasped like a fish, and began to believe himself greatly out of sorts.

The *Nan-Shan* was plowing a vanishing furrow upon the circle of the sea that had the surface and the shimmer of an undulating piece of gray silk. The sun, pale and without rays, poured down leaden heat in a strangely indecisive light, and the Chinamen were lying prostrate about the decks. Their bloodless, pinched, yellow faces were like the faces of bilious invalids. Captain MacWhirr noticed two of them especially, stretched out on their backs below the bridge. As soon as they had closed their eyes they seemed dead. Three others, however, were quarrelling barbarously away forward; and one big fellow, half naked, with herculean shoulders, was hanging limply over a winch; another, sitting on the deck, his knees up and his head drooping sideways in a girlish attitude, was plaiting his pigtail with infinite languor depicted in his whole person and in the very movement of his fingers. The smoke struggled with difficulty out of the funnel, and instead of streaming away spread itself out like an infernal sort of cloud, smelling of sulphur and raining soot all over the decks.

"What the devil are you doing there, Mr. Jukes?" asked Captain MacWhirr.

This unusual form of address, though mumbled rather than spoken, caused the body of Mr. Jukes to start as though it had been prodded under the fifth rib. He had had a low bench brought on the bridge, and sitting on it, with a length of rope curled about his feet and a piece of canvas stretched over his knees, was pushing a sail-needle vigorously. He looked up, and his surprise gave to his eyes an expression of innocence and candor.

"I am only roping some of that new set of bags we made last trip for whipping up coals," he remonstrated, gently. "We shall want them for the next coaling, sir."

"What became of the others?"

"Why, worn out of course, sir."

Captain MacWhirr, after glaring down irresolutely at his chief mate, disclosed the gloomy and cynical conviction that more than half of them had been lost overboard, "if only the truth was known," and retired to the other end of the bridge. Jukes, exasperated by this unprovoked attack, broke the needle at the second stitch, and dropping his work got up and cursed the heat in a violent undertone.

The propeller thumped, the three Chinamen forward had given up squabbling very suddenly, and the one who had been plaiting his tail clasped his legs and stared dejectedly over his knees. The lurid sunshine cast faint and sickly shadows. The swell ran higher and swifter every moment, and the ship lurched heavily in the smooth, deep hollows of the sea.

"I wonder where that beastly swell comes from," said Jukes aloud, recovering himself after a stagger.

"Northeast," grunted the literal MacWhirr, from his side of the bridge. "There's some dirty weather knocking about. Go and look at the glass."

When Jukes came out of the chart-room, the cast of his countenance had changed to thoughtfulness and concern. He caught hold of the bridge rail and stared ahead.

The temperature in the engine room had gone up to a hundred and seventeen degrees. Irritated voices were ascending through the skylight and through the fiddle of the stokehold in a harsh and resonant uproar, mingled with angry clangs and scrapes of metal, as if men with limbs of iron and throats of bronze had been quarrelling down there. The second engineer was falling foul of the stokers for letting the steam go down. He was a man with arms like a blacksmith, and generally feared; but that afternoon the stokers were answering him back recklessly, and slammed the furnace doors with the fury of despair. Then the noise ceased suddenly, and the second engineer appeared, emerging out of the stokehold streaked with grime and soaking wet like a chimney-sweep coming out of a well. As soon as his head was clear of the fiddle he began to scold Jukes for not trimming properly the stokehold ventilators; and in answer Jukes made with his hands deprecatory soothing signs meaning: "No wind—can't be helped—you can see for yourself." But the other wouldn't hear reason. His teeth flashed angrily in his dirty face. He didn't mind, he said, the trouble of punching their blanked heads down there, blank his soul, but did the condemned sailors think you could keep steam up in the God-forsaken boilers simply by knocking the blanked stokers about? No, by George! You had to get some draught, too—may he be everlastingly blanked for a swab-headed deck hand if you didn't! And the chief, too, rampaging before the steam gauge and carrying on like a lunatic up and down the engine room ever since noon. What did Jukes think he was stuck up there for, if he couldn't get one of his decayed, good-for-nothing deck-cripples to turn the ventilators to the wind?

The relations of the "engine room" and the "deck" of the *Nan-Shan* were, as is known, of a brotherly nature; therefore Jukes leaned over and begged the other in a restrained tone not to make a disgusting ass of himself; the skipper was on the other side of the bridge. But the second declared mutinously that he didn't care a rap who was on the other side of the bridge, and Jukes, passing in a flash from lofty disapproval into a state of exaltation, invited him in unflattering terms to come up and twist the beastly things to please himself, and catch such wind as a donkey of his sort could find. The second rushed up to the fray. He flung himself at the port ventilator as though he meant to tear it out bodily and toss it overboard. All he did was to move the cowl round a few inches, with an enormous expenditure of force, and seemed spent in the effort. He leaned against the back of the wheelhouse, and Jukes walked up to him.

"Oh, Heavens!" ejaculated the engineer in a feeble voice. He lifted his eyes to the sky, and then let his glassy stare descend to meet the horizon that, tilting up to an angle of forty degrees, seemed to hang on a slant for a while and settled down slowly. "Heavens! Phew! What's up, anyhow?"

Jukes, straddling his long legs like a pair of compasses, put on an air of superiority. "We're going to catch it this time," he said. "The barometer is tumbling down like anything, Harry. And you trying to kick up that silly row. . . ."

The word "barometer" seemed to revive the second engineer's mad animosity. Collecting afresh all his energies, he directed Jukes in a low and brutal tone to shove the unmentionable instrument down his gory throat. Who cared for his crimson barometer? It was the steam—the steam—that was going down; and what between the firemen going faint and the chief going silly, it was worse than a dog's life for him; he didn't care a tinker's curse how soon the whole show was blown out of the water. He seemed on the point of having a cry, but after regaining his breath he muttered darkly, "I'll faint them," and dashed off. He stopped upon the fiddle long enough to shake his fist at the unnatural daylight, and dropped into the dark hole with a whoop.

When Jukes turned, his eyes fell upon the rounded back and the big red ears of Captain MacWhirr, who had come across. He did not look at his chief officer, but said at once, "That's a very violent man, that second engineer."

"Jolly good second, anyhow," grunted Jukes. "They can't keep up steam," he added, rapidly, and made a grab at the rail against the coming lurch.

Captain MacWhirr, unprepared, took a run and brought himself up with a jerk by an awning stanchion.

"A profane man," he said, obstinately. "If this goes on, I'll have to get rid of him the first chance."

"It's the heat," said Jukes. "The weather's awful. It would make a saint swear. Even up here I feel exactly as if I had my head tied up in a woolen blanket."

Captain MacWhirr looked up. "D'ye mean to say, Mr. Jukes, you ever had your head tied up in a blanket? What was that for?"

"It's a manner of speaking, sir," said Jukes, stolidly.

"Some of you fellows do go on! What's that about saints swearing? I wish you wouldn't talk so wild. What sort of saint would that be that would swear? No more saint than yourself, I expect. And what's a blanket got to do with it—or the weather either. . . . The heat does not make me swear—does it? It's filthy bad temper. That's what it is. And what's the good of your talking like this?"

Thus Captain MacWhirr expostulated against the use of images in speech, and at the end electrified Jukes by a contemptuous snort, followed by words of passion and resentment: "Damme! I'll fire him out of the ship if he don't look out."

And Jukes, incorrigible, thought: "Goodness me! Somebody's put a new inside to my old man. Here's temper, if you like. Of course it's the weather; what else? It would make an angel quarrelsome—let alone a saint."

All the Chinamen on deck appeared at their last gasp.

At its setting the sun had a diminished diameter and an expiring brown, rayless glow, as if millions of centuries elapsing since the morning had brought it near its end. A dense bank of cloud became visible to the northward; it had a sinister dark olive tint, and lay low and motionless upon the sea, resembling a solid obstacle in the path of the ship. She went floundering towards it like an exhausted creature driven to its death. The coppery twilight retired slowly, and the darkness brought out overhead a swarm of unsteady, big stars, that, as if blown upon, flickered exceedingly and seemed to hang very near the earth. At eight o'clock Jukes went into the chart room to write up the ship's log.

He copied neatly out of the rough-book the number of miles, the course of the ship, and in the column for "wind" scrawled the word "calm" from top to bottom of the eight hours since noon. He was exasperated by the continuous, monotonous rolling of the ship. The heavy inkstand would slide away in a manner that suggested perverse intelligence in dodging the pen. Having written in the large space under the head of "Remarks" "Heat very oppressive," he stuck the end of the penholder in his teeth, pipe fashion, and mopped his face carefully.

"Ship rolling heavily in a high cross swell," he began again, and commented to himself, "Heavily is no word for it." Then he wrote: "Sunset threatening, with a low bank of clouds to N. and E. Sky clear overhead."

Sprawling over the table with arrested pen, he glanced out of the door, and in that frame of his vision he saw all the stars flying upwards between the teakwood jambs on a black sky. The whole lot took flight together and disappeared, leaving only a blackness flecked with white flashes, for the sea was as black as the sky and speckled with foam afar. The stars that had flown to the roll came back on the return swing of the ship, rushing downwards in their glittering multitude, not of fiery points, but enlarged to tiny discs brilliant with a clear wet sheen.

Jukes watched the flying big stars for a moment, and then wrote: "8 P.M. Swell increasing. Ship laboring and taking water on her decks. Battened down the coolies for the night. Barometer still falling." He paused, and thought to himself, "Perhaps nothing whatever'll come of it." And then he closed resolutely his entries: "Every appearance of a typhoon coming on."

On going out he had to stand aside, and Captain MacWhirr strode over the doorstep without saying a word or making a sign.

"Shut the door, Mr. Jukes, will you?" he cried from within.

Jukes turned back to do so, muttering ironically: "Afraid to catch cold, I suppose." It was his watch below, but he yearned for communion with his kind; and he remarked cheerily to the second mate: "Doesn't look so bad, after all—does it?"

The second mate was marching to and fro on the bridge, tripping down with small steps one moment, and the next climbing with difficulty the shifting slope of the deck. At the sound of Jukes' voice he stood still, facing forward, but made no reply.

"Hallo! That's a heavy one," said Jukes, swaying to meet the long roll till his lowered hand touched the planks. This time the second mate made in his throat a noise of an unfriendly nature.

He was an oldish, shabby little fellow, with bad teeth and no hair on his face. He had been shipped in a hurry in Shanghai, that trip when the second officer brought from home had delayed the ship three hours in port by contriving (in some manner Captain MacWhirr could never understand) to fall overboard into an empty coal lighter lying alongside, and had to be sent ashore to the hospital with concussion of the brain and a broken limb or two.

Jukes was not discouraged by the unsympathetic sound. "The Chinamen must be having a lovely time of it down there," he said. "It's lucky for them the old girl has the easiest roll of any ship I've ever been in. There now! This one wasn't so bad."

"You wait," snarled the second mate.

With his sharp nose, red at the tip, and his thin pinched lips, he always looked as though he were raging inwardly; and he was concise in his speech to the point of rudeness. All his time off duty he spent in his cabin with the door shut, keeping so still in there that he was supposed to fall asleep as soon as he had disappeared; but the man who came in to wake him for his watch on deck would invariably find him with his eyes wide open, flat on his back in the bunk, and glaring irritably from a soiled pillow. He never wrote any letters, did not seem to hope for news from anywhere; and though he had been heard once to mention West Hartlepool, it was with extreme bitterness, and only in connection with the extortionate charges of a boardinghouse. He was one of those men who are picked up at need in the ports of the world. They are competent enough, appear hopelessly hard up, show no evidence of any sort of vice, and carry about them all the signs of manifest failure. They come aboard on an emergency, care for no ship afloat, live in their own atmosphere of casual connection amongst their shipmates who know nothing of them, and make up their minds to leave at inconvenient times. They clear out with no words of leave-taking in some God-forsaken port other men would fear to be stranded in, and go ashore in company of a shabby sea chest, corded like a treasure box, and with an air of shaking the ship's dust off their feet.

"You wait," he repeated, balanced in great swings with his back to Jukes, motionless and implacable.

"Do you mean to say we are going to catch it hot?" asked Jukes with boyish interest.

"Say? . . . I say nothing. You don't catch me," snapped the little second mate, with a mixture of pride, scorn, and cunning, as if Jukes' question had been a trap cleverly detected. "Oh, no! None of you here shall make a fool of me if I know it," he mumbled to himself.

Jukes reflected rapidly that this second mate was a mean little beast, and in his heart he wished poor Jack Allen had never smashed himself up in the coal lighter. The far-off blackness ahead of the ship was like another night seen through the starry night of the earth—the starless night of the immensities beyond the created universe, revealed in its appalling stillness through a low fissure in the glittering sphere of which the earth is the kernel.

"Whatever there might be about," said Jukes, "we are steaming straight into it."

"*You've* said it," caught up the second mate, always with his back to Jukes. "You've said it, mind—not I."

"Oh, go to Jericho!" said Jukes, frankly; and the other emitted a triumphant little chuckle.

"You've said it," he repeated.

"And what of that?"

"I've known some real good men get into trouble with their skippers for saying a dam' sight less," answered the second mate feverishly. "Oh, no! You don't catch me."

"You seem deucedly anxious not to give yourself away," said Jukes, completely soured by such absurdity. "I wouldn't be afraid to say what I think."

"Aye, to me! That's no great trick. I am nobody, and well I know it."

The ship, after a pause of comparative steadiness, started upon a series of rolls, one worse than the other, and for a time Jukes, preserving his equilibrium, was too busy to open his mouth. As soon as the violent swinging had quieted down somewhat, he said: "This is a bit too much of a good thing. Whether anything is coming or not I think she ought to be put head on to that swell. The old man is just gone in to lie down. Hang me if I don't speak to him."

But when he opened the door of the chart room he saw his captain reading a book. Captain MacWhirr was not lying down: he was standing up with one hand grasping the edge of the bookshelf and the other holding open before his face a thick volume. The lamp wriggled in the gimbals, the loosened books toppled from side to side on the shelf, the long barometer swung in jerky circles, the table altered its slant every moment. In the midst of all this stir and movement Captain MacWhirr, holding on, showed his eyes above the upper edge, and asked, "What's the matter?"

"Swell getting worse, sir."

"Noticed that in here," muttered Captain MacWhirr. "Anything wrong?"

Jukes, inwardly disconcerted by the seriousness of the eyes looking at him over the top of the book, produced an embarrassed grin.

"Rolling like old boots," he said, sheepishly.

"Aye! Very heavy—very heavy. What do you want?"

At this Jukes lost his footing and began to flounder. "I was thinking of our passengers," he said, in the manner of a man clutching at a straw.

"Passengers?" wondered the Captain, gravely. "What passengers?"

"Why, the Chinamen, sir," explained Jukes, very sick of this conversation.

"The Chinamen! Why don't you speak plainly? Couldn't tell what you meant. Never heard a lot of coolies spoken of as passengers before. Passengers, indeed! What's come to you?"

Captain MacWhirr, closing the book on his forefinger, lowered his arm and looked completely mystified. "Why are you thinking of the Chinamen, Mr. Jukes?" he inquired.

Jukes took a plunge, like a man driven to it. "She's rolling her decks full of water, sir. Thought you might put her head on perhaps— for a while. Till this goes down a bit—very soon, I dare say. Head to the eastward. I never knew a ship roll like this."

He held on in the doorway, and Captain MacWhirr, feeling his grip on the shelf inadequate, made up his mind to let go in a hurry, and fell heavily on the couch.

"Head to the eastward?" he said, struggling to sit up. "That's more than four points off her course."

"Yes, sir. Fifty degrees. . . . Would just bring her head far enough round to meet this. . . ."

Captain MacWhirr was now sitting up. He had not dropped the book, and he had not lost his place.

"To the eastward?" he repeated, with dawning astonishment. "To the . . . Where do you think we are bound to? You want me to haul a full-powered steamship four points off her course to make the Chinamen comfortable! Now, I've heard more than enough of mad things done in the world—but this. . . . If I didn't know you, Jukes, I would think you were in liquor. Steer four points off. . . . And what afterwards? Steer four points over the other way, I suppose, to make the course good. What put it into your head that I would start to tack a steamer as if she were a sailing-ship?"

"Jolly good thing she isn't," threw in Jukes, with bitter readiness. "She would have rolled every blessed stick out of her this afternoon."

"Aye! And you just would have had to stand and see them go," said Captain MacWhirr, showing a certain animation. "It's a dead calm, isn't it?"

"It is, sir. But there's something out of the common coming, for sure."

"Maybe. I suppose you have a notion I should be getting out of the way of that dirt," said Captain MacWhirr, speaking with the utmost simplicity of manner and tone, and fixing the oilcloth on the floor with a heavy stare. Thus he noticed neither Jukes' discomfiture nor the mixture of vexation and astonished respect on his face.

"Now, here's this book," he continued with deliberation, slapping his thigh with the closed volume. "I've been reading the chapter on the storms there."

This was true. He had been reading the chapter on the storms. When he had entered the chart room, it was with no intention of taking the book down. Some influence in the air—the same influence, probably, that caused the steward to bring without orders the Captain's sea-boots and oilskin coat up to the chart-room—had as it were guided his hand to the shelf; and without taking the time to sit down he had waded with a conscious effort into the terminology of the subject. He lost himself amongst advancing semi-circles, left- and right-hand quadrants, the curves of the tracks, the probable bearing of the center, the shifts of wind and the readings of barometer. He tried to bring all these things into a definite relation to himself, and ended by becoming contemptuously angry with such a lot of words, and with so much advice, all head-work and supposition, without a glimmer of certitude.

"It's the damnedest thing, Jukes," he said. "If a fellow was to believe all that's in there, he would be running most of his time all over the sea trying to get behind the weather."

Again he slapped his leg with the book; and Jukes opened his mouth, but said nothing.

"Running to get behind the weather! Do you understand that, Mr. Jukes? It's the maddest thing!" ejaculated Captain MacWhirr, with pauses, gazing at the floor profoundly. "You would think an old woman had been writing this. It passes me. If that thing means anything useful, then it means that I should at once alter the course away, away to the devil somewhere, and come booming down on Fu-chau from the northward at the tail of this dirty weather that's supposed to be knocking about in our way. From the north! Do you understand, Mr. Jukes? Three hundred extra miles to the distance, and a pretty coal bill to show. I couldn't bring myself to do that if every word in there was gospel truth, Mr. Jukes. Don't you expect me . . ."

And Jukes, silent, marveled at this display of feeling and loquacity.

"But the truth is that you don't know if the fellow is right, anyhow. How can you tell what a gale is made of till you get it? He isn't aboard here, is he? Very well. Here he says that the center of them things bears eight points off the wind; but we haven't got any wind, for all the barometer falling. Where's his center now?"

"We will get the wind presently," mumbled Jukes.

"Let it come, then," said Captain MacWhirr, with dignified indignation. "It's only to let you see, Mr. Jukes, that you don't find everything in books. All these rules for dodging breezes and circumventing the winds of heaven, Mr. Jukes, seem to me the maddest thing, when you come to look at it sensibly."

He raised his eyes, saw Jukes gazing at him dubiously, and tried to illustrate his meaning.

"About as queer as your extraordinary notion of dodging the ship head to sea, for I don't know how long, to make the Chinamen comfortable; whereas all we've got to do is to take them to Fu-chau, being timed to get there before noon on Friday. If the weather delays me—very well. There's your logbook to talk straight about the weather. But suppose I went swinging off my course and came in two days late, and they asked me: 'Where have you been all that time, Captain?' What could I say to that? 'Went around to dodge the bad weather,' I would say. 'It must've been damn' bad,' they would say. 'Don't know,' I would have to say; 'I've dodged clear of it.' See that, Jukes? I have been thinking it all out this afternoon."

He looked up again in his unseeing, unimaginative way. No one had ever heard him say so much at one time. Jukes, with his arms open in the doorway, was like a man invited to behold a miracle. Unbounded wonder was the intellectual meaning of his eye, while incredulity was seated in his whole countenance.

"A gale is a gale, Mr. Jukes," resumed the Captain, "and a full-powered steamship has got to face it. There's just so much dirty weather knocking about the world, and the proper thing is to go through it with none of what old Captain Wilson of the *Melita* calls 'storm strategy.' The other day ashore I heard him hold forth about it to a lot of shipmasters who came in and sat at a table next to mine. It seemed to me the greatest nonsense. He was telling them how he outmaneuvered, I think he said, a terrific gale, so that it never came nearer than fifty miles to him. A neat piece of headwork he called it. How he knew there was a terrific gale fifty miles off beats me altogether. It was like listening to a crazy man. I would have thought Captain Wilson was old enough to know better."

Captain MacWhirr ceased for a moment, then said, "It's your watch below, Mr. Jukes?"

Jukes came to himself with a start. "Yes, sir."

"Leave orders to call me at the slightest change," said the Captain. He reached up to put the book away, and tucked his legs upon the couch. "Shut the door so that it don't fly open, will you? I can't stand a door banging. They've put a lot of rubbishy locks into this ship, I must say."

Captain MacWhirr closed his eyes.

He did so to rest himself. He was tired, and he experienced that state of mental vacuity which comes at the end of an exhaustive discussion that has liberated some belief matured in the course of meditative years. He had indeed been making his confession of faith, had he only known it; and its effect was to make Jukes, on the other side of the door, stand scratching his head for a good while.

Captain MacWhirr opened his eyes.

He thought he must have been asleep. What was that loud noise? Wind? Why had he not been called? The lamp wriggled in its gimbals, the barometer swung in circles, the table altered its slant every moment; a pair of limp sea boots with collapsed tops went sliding past the couch. He put out his hand instantly, and captured one.

Jukes' face appeared in a crack of the door: only his face, very red, with staring eyes. The flame of the lamp leaped, a piece of paper flew up, a rush of air enveloped Captain MacWhirr. Beginning to draw on the boot, he directed an expectant gaze at Jukes' swollen, excited features.

"Came on like this," shouted Jukes, "five minutes ago . . . all of a sudden."

The head disappeared with a bang, and a heavy splash and patter of drops swept past the closed door as if a pail-full of melted lead had been flung against the house. A whistling could be heard now upon the deep vibrating noise outside. The stuffy chart room seemed as full of draughts as a shed. Captain MacWhirr collared the other sea boot on its violent passage along the floor. He was not flustered, but he could not find at once the opening for inserting his foot. The shoes he had flung off were scurrying from end to end of the cabin, gamboling playfully over each other like puppies. As soon as he stood up he kicked at them viciously, but without effect.

He threw himself into the attitude of a lunging fencer, to reach after his oilskin coat; and afterwards he staggered all over the confined space while he jerked himself into it. Very grave, straddling his legs far apart, and stretching his neck, he started to tie deliberately the strings of his sou'-wester under his chin, with thick fingers that trembled slightly. He went through all the movements of a woman putting on her bonnet before a glass, with a strained, listening attention, as though he had expected every moment to hear the shout of his name in the confused clamor that had suddenly beset his ship. Its increase filled his ears while he was getting ready to go out and confront whatever it might mean. It was tumultuous and very loud—made up of the rush of the wind, the crashes of the sea, with that prolonged deep vibration of the air, like the roll of an immense and remote drum beating the charge of the gale.

He stood for a moment in the light of the lamp, thick, clumsy, shapeless in his panoply of combat, vigilant and red-faced.

"There's a lot of weight in this," he muttered.

As soon as he attempted to open the door the wind caught it. Clinging to the handle, he was dragged out over the doorstep, and at once found himself engaged with the wind in a sort of personal scuffle whose object was the shutting of that door. At the last moment a tongue of air scurried in and licked out the flame of the lamp.

Ahead of the ship he perceived a great darkness lying upon a multitude of white flashes; on the starboard beam a few amazing stars drooped, dim and fitful, above an immense waste of broken seas, as if seen through a mad drift of smoke.

On the bridge a knot of men, indistinct and toiling, were making great efforts in the light of the wheelhouse windows that shone mistily on their heads and backs. Suddenly darkness closed upon one pane, then on another. The voices of the lost group reached him after the manner of men's voices in a gale, in shreds and fragments of forlorn shouting snatched past the ear. All at once Jukes appeared at his side, yelling, with his head down.

"Watch—put—in—wheelhouse—shutters—glass—afraid—blow in."

Jukes heard his commander upbraiding.

"This—come—anything—warning—call me."

He tried to explain, with the uproar pressing on his lips.

"Light air—remained—bridge—sudden—northeast—could turn—thought—you—sure—hear."

They had gained the shelter of the weather cloth, and could converse with raised voices, as people quarrel.

"I got the hands along to cover up all the ventilators. Good job I had remained on deck. I didn't think you would be asleep, and so . . . What did you say, sir? What?"

"Nothing," cried Captain MacWhirr. "I said—all right."

"By all the powers! We've got it this time," observed Jukes in a howl.

"You haven't altered her course?" inquired Captain MacWhirr, straining his voice.

"No, sir. Certainly not. Wind came out right ahead. And here comes the head sea."

A plunge of the ship ended in a shock as if she had landed her forefoot upon something solid. After a moment of stillness a lofty flight of sprays drove hard with the wind upon their faces.

"Keep her at it as long as we can," shouted Captain MacWhirr.

Before Jukes had squeezed the salt water out of his eyes all the stars had disappeared.

III

Jukes was as ready a man as any half-dozen young mates that may be caught by casting a net upon the waters; and though he had been somewhat taken aback by the startling viciousness of the first squall, he had pulled himself together on the instant, had called out the hands and had rushed them along to secure such openings about the deck as had not been already battened down earlier in the evening. Shouting in his fresh, stentorian voice, "Jump, boys, and bear a hand!" he led in the work, telling himself the while that he had "just expected this."

But at the same time he was growing aware that this was rather more than he had expected. From the first stir of the air felt on his cheek the gale seemed to take upon itself the accumulated impetus of an avalanche. Heavy sprays enveloped the *Nan-Shan* from stem to stern, and instantly in the midst of her regular rolling she began to jerk and plunge as though she had gone mad with fright.

Jukes thought, "This is no joke." While he was exchanging explanatory yells with his captain, a sudden lowering of the darkness came upon the night, falling before their vision like something palpable. It was as if the masked lights of the world had been turned down. Jukes was uncritically glad to have his captain at hand. It relieved him as though that man had, by simply coming on deck, taken most of the gale's weight upon his shoulders. Such is the prestige, the privilege, and the burden of command.

Captain MacWhirr could expect no relief of that sort from any one on earth. Such is the loneliness of command. He was trying to see, with that watchful manner of a seaman who stares into the wind's eye as if into the eye of an adversary, to penetrate the hidden intention and guess the aim and force of the thrust. The strong wind swept at him out of a vast obscurity; he felt under his feet the uneasiness of his ship, and he could not even discern the shadow of her shape. He wished it were not so; and very still he waited, feeling stricken by a blind man's helplessness.

To be silent was natural to him, dark or shine. Jukes, at his elbow, made himself heard yelling cheerily in the gusts, "We must have got the worst of it at once, sir." A faint burst of lightning quivered all round, as if flashed into a cavern—into a black and secret chamber of the sea, with a floor of foaming crests.

It unveiled for a sinister, fluttering moment a ragged mass of clouds hanging low, the lurch of the long outlines of the ship, the black figures of men caught on the bridge, heads forward, as if petrified in the act of butting. The darkness palpitated down upon all this, and then the real thing came at last.

It was something formidable and swift, like the sudden smashing of a vial of wrath. It seemed to explode all round the ship with an overpowering concussion and a rush of great waters, as if an immense dam had been blown up to windward. In an instant the men lost touch of each other. This is the disintegrating power of a great wind: it isolates one from one's kind. An earthquake, a landslip, an avalanche, overtake a man incidentally, as it were—without passion. A furious gale attacks him like a personal enemy, tries to grasp his limbs, fastens upon his mind, seeks to rout his very spirit out of him.

Jukes was driven away from his commander. He fancied himself whirled a great distance through the air. Everything disappeared—even, for a moment, his power of thinking; but his hand had found one of the rail stanchions. His distress was by no means alleviated by an inclination to disbelieve the reality of this experience. Though young, he had seen some bad weather, and had never doubted his ability to imagine the worst; but this was so much beyond his powers of fancy that it appeared incompatible with the existence of any ship whatever. He would have been incredulous about himself in the same way, perhaps, had he not been so harassed by the necessity of exerting a wrestling effort against a force trying to tear him away from his hold. Moreover, the conviction of not being utterly destroyed returned to him through the sensations of being half-drowned, bestially shaken, and partly choked.

It seemed to him he remained there precariously alone with the stanchion for a long, long time. The rain poured on him, flowed, drove in sheets. He breathed in gasps; and sometimes the water he swallowed was fresh and sometimes it was salt. For the most part he kept his eyes shut tight, as if suspecting his sight might be destroyed in the immense flurry of the elements. When he ventured to blink hastily, he derived some moral support from the green gleam of the starboard light shining feebly upon the flight of rain and sprays. He was actually looking at it when its ray fell upon the up-rearing sea which put it out. He saw the head of the wave topple over, adding the mite of its crash to the tremendous uproar raging around him, and almost at the same instant the stanchion was wrenched away from his embracing arms. After a crushing thump on his back he found himself suddenly afloat and borne upwards. His first irresistible notion was that the whole China Sea had climbed on the bridge. Then, more sanely, he concluded himself gone overboard. All the time he was being tossed, flung, and rolled in great volumes of water, he kept on repeating mentally, with the utmost precipitation, the words: "My God! My God! My God! My God!"

All at once, in a revolt of misery and despair, he formed the crazy resolution to get out of that. And he began to thresh about with his arms and legs. But as soon as he commenced his wretched struggles he discovered that he had become somehow mixed up with a face, an oilskin coat, somebody's boots. He clawed ferociously all these things in turn, lost them, found them again, lost them once more, and finally was himself caught in the firm clasp of a pair of stout arms. He returned the embrace closely round a thick solid body. He had found his captain.

They tumbled over and over, tightening their hug. Suddenly the water let them down with a brutal bang; and, stranded against the side of the wheelhouse, out of breath and bruised, they were left to stagger up in the wind and hold on where they could.

Jukes came out of it rather horrified, as though he had escaped some unparalleled outrage directed at his feelings. It weakened his faith in himself. He started shouting aimlessly to the man he could feel near him in that fiendish blackness, "Is it you, sir? Is it you, sir?" till his temples seemed ready to burst. And he heard in answer a voice, as if crying far away, as if screaming to him fretfully from a very great distance, the one word "Yes!" Other seas swept again over the bridge. He received them defenselessly right over his bare head, with both his hands engaged in holding.

The motion of the ship was extravagant. Her lurches had an appalling helplessness: she pitched as if taking a header into a void, and seemed to find a wall to hit every time. When she rolled she fell on her side headlong, and she would be righted back by such a demolishing blow that Jukes felt her reeling as a clubbed man reels before he collapses. The gale howled and scuffled about gigantically in the darkness, as though the entire world were one black gully. At certain moments the air streamed against the ship as if sucked through a tunnel with a concentrated solid force of impact that seemed to lift her clean out of the water and keep her up for an instant with only a quiver running through her from end to end. And then she would begin her tumbling again as if dropped back into a boiling cauldron. Jukes tried hard to compose his mind and judge things coolly.

The sea, flattened down in the heavier gusts, would uprise and overwhelm both ends of the *Nan-Shan* in snowy rushes of foam, expanding wide, beyond both rails, into the night. And on this dazzling sheet, spread under the blackness of the clouds and emitting a bluish glow, Captain MacWhirr could catch a desolate glimpse of a few tiny specks black as ebony, the tops of the hatches, the battened companions, the heads of the covered winches, the foot of a mast. This was all he could see of his ship. Her middle structure, covered by the bridge which bore him, his mate, the closed wheelhouse where a man was steering shut up with the fear of being swept overboard together with the whole thing in one great crash—her middle structure was like a half-tide rock awash upon a coast. It was like an outlying rock with the water boiling up, streaming over, pouring off, beating round—like a rock in the surf to which shipwrecked people cling before they let go— only it rose, it sank, it rolled continuously, without respite and rest, like a rock that should have miraculously struck adrift from a coast and gone wallowing upon the sea.

The *Nan-Shan* was being looted by the storm with a senseless, destructive fury: trysails torn out of the extra gaskets, double-lashed awnings blown away, bridge swept clean, weather cloths burst, rails twisted, light-screens smashed—and two of the boats had gone already. They had gone unheard and unseen, melting, as it were, in the shock and smother of the wave. It was only later, when upon the white flash of another high sea hurling itself amidships, Jukes had a vision of two pairs of davits leaping black and empty out of the solid blackness, with one overhauled fall flying and an iron-bound block capering in the air, that he became aware of what had happened within about three yards of his back.

He poked his head forward, groping for the ear of his commander. His lips touched it—big, fleshy, very wet. He cried in an agitated tone, "Our boats are going now, sir."

And again he heard that voice, forced and ringing feebly, but with a penetrating effect of quietness in the enormous discord of noises, as if sent out from some remote spot of peace beyond the black wastes of the gale; again he heard a man's voice—the frail and indomitable sound that can be made to carry an infinity of thought, resolution and purpose, that shall be pronouncing confident words on the last day, when heavens fall, and justice is done—again he heard it, and it was crying to him, as if from very, very far—"All right."

He thought he had not managed to make himself understood. "Our boats—I say boats—the boats, sir! Two gone!"

The same voice, within a foot of him and yet so remote, yelled sensibly, "Can't be helped."

Captain MacWhirr had never turned his face, but Jukes caught some more words on the wind.

"What can—expect—when hammering through—such—Bound to leave—something behind—stands to reason."

Watchfully Jukes listened for more. No more came. This was all Captain MacWhirr had to say; and Jukes could picture to himself rather than see the broad squat back before him. An impenetrable obscurity pressed down upon the ghostly glimmers of the sea. A dull conviction seized upon Jukes that there was nothing to be done.

If the steering-gear did not give way, if the immense volumes of water did not burst the deck in or smash one of the hatches, if the engines did not give up, if way could be kept on the ship against this terrific wind, and she did not bury herself in one of these awful seas, of whose white crests alone, topping high above her bows, he could now and then get a sickening glimpse—then there was a chance of her coming out of it. Something within him seemed to turn over, bringing uppermost the feeling that the *Nan-Shan* was lost.

"She's done for," he said to himself, with a surprising mental agitation, as though he had discovered an unexpected meaning in this thought. One of these things was bound to happen. Nothing could be prevented now, and nothing could be remedied. The men on board did not count, and the ship could not last. This weather was too impossible.

Jukes felt an arm thrown heavily over his shoulders; and to this overture he responded with great intelligence by catching hold of his captain round the waist.

They stood clasped thus in the blind night, bracing each other against the wind, cheek to cheek and lip to ear, in the manner of two hulks lashed stem to stern together.

And Jukes heard the voice of his commander hardly any louder than before, but nearer, as though, starting to march athwart the prodigious rush of the hurricane, it had approached him, bearing that strange effect of quietness like the serene glow of a halo.

"D'ye know where the hands got to?" it asked, vigorous and evanescent at the same time, overcoming the strength of the wind, and swept away from Jukes instantly.

Jukes didn't know. They were all on the bridge when the real force of the hurricane struck the ship. He had no idea where they had crawled to. Under the circumstances they were nowhere, for all the use that could be made of them. Somehow the Captain's wish to know distressed Jukes.

"Want the hands, sir?" he cried, apprehensively.

"Ought to know," asserted Captain MacWhirr. "Hold hard."

They held hard. An outburst of unchained fury, a vicious rush of the wind absolutely steadied the ship; she rocked only, quick and light like a child's cradle, for a terrific moment of suspense, while the whole atmosphere, as it seemed, streamed furiously past her, roaring away from the tenebrous earth.

It suffocated them, and with eyes shut they tightened their grasp. What from the magnitude of the shock might have been a column of water running upright in the dark, butted against the ship, broke short, and fell on her bridge, crushingly, from on high, with a dead burying weight.

A flying fragment of that collapse, a mere splash, enveloped them in one swirl from their feet over their heads, filling violently their ears, mouths and nostrils with salt water. It knocked out their legs, wrenched in haste at their arms, seethed away swiftly under their chins; and opening their eyes, they saw the piled-up masses of foam dashing to and fro amongst what looked like the fragments of a ship. She had given way as if driven straight in. Their panting hearts yielded, too, before the tremendous blow; and all at once she sprang up again to her desperate plunging, as if trying to scramble out from under the ruins.

The seas in the dark seemed to rush from all sides to keep her back where she might perish. There was hate in the way she was handled, and a ferocity in the blows that fell. She was like a living creature thrown to the rage of a mob: hustled terribly, struck at, borne up, flung down, leaped upon. Captain MacWhirr and Jukes kept hold of each other, deafened by the noise, gagged by the wind; and the great physical tumult beating about their bodies, brought, like an unbridled display of passion, a profound trouble to their souls. One of those wild and appalling shrieks that are heard at times passing mysteriously overhead in the steady roar of a hurricane, swooped, as if borne on wings, upon the ship, and Jukes tried to out-scream it.

"Will she live through this?"

The cry was wrenched out of his breast. It was as unintentional as the birth of a thought in the head, and he heard nothing of it himself. It all became extinct at once—thought, intention, effort—and of his cry the inaudible vibration added to the tempest waves of the air.

He expected nothing from it. Nothing at all. For indeed what answer could be made? But after a while he heard with amazement the frail and resisting voice in his ear, the dwarf sound, unconquered in the giant tumult.

"She may!"

It was a dull yell, more difficult to seize than a whisper. And presently the voice returned again, half submerged in the vast crashes, like a ship battling against the waves of an ocean.

"Let's hope so!" it cried—small, lonely and unmoved, a stranger to the visions of hope or fear; and it flickered into disconnected words: "Ship. . . . This. . . . Never—Anyhow . . . for the best." Jukes gave it up.

Then, as if it had come suddenly upon the one thing fit to withstand the power of a storm, it seemed to gain force and firmness for the last broken shouts:

"Keep on hammering . . . builders . . . good men. . . . And chance it . . . engines. . . . Rout . . . good man."

Captain MacWhirr removed his arm from Jukes' shoulders, and thereby ceased to exist for his mate, so dark it was; Jukes, after a tense stiffening of every muscle, would let himself go limp all over. The gnawing of profound discomfort existed side by side with an incredible disposition to somnolence, as though he had been buffeted and worried into drowsiness. The wind would get hold of his head and try to shake it off his shoulders; his clothes, full of water, were as heavy as lead, cold and dripping like an armor of melting ice: he shivered—it lasted a long time; and with his hands closed hard on his hold, he was letting himself sink slowly into the depths of bodily misery. His mind became concentrated upon himself in an aimless, idle way, and when something pushed lightly at the back of his knees he nearly, as the saying is, jumped out of his skin.

In the start forward he bumped the back of Captain MacWhirr, who didn't move; and then a hand gripped his thigh. A lull had come, a menacing lull of the wind, the holding of a stormy breath—and he felt himself pawed all over. It was the boatswain. Jukes recognized these hands, so thick and enormous that they seemed to belong to some new species of man.

The boatswain had arrived on the bridge, crawling on all fours against the wind, and had found the chief mate's legs with the top of his head. Immediately he crouched and began to explore Jukes' person upwards with prudent, apologetic touches, as became an inferior.

He was an ill-favored, undersized, gruff sailor of fifty, coarsely hairy, short-legged, long-armed, resembling an elderly ape. His strength was immense; and in his great lumpy paws, bulging like brown boxing gloves on the end of furry forearms, the heaviest objects were handled like playthings. Apart from the grizzled pelt on his chest, the menacing demeanor and the hoarse voice, he had none of the classical attributes of his rating. His good nature almost amounted to imbecility: the men did what they liked with him, and he had not an ounce of initiative in his character, which was easy-going and talkative. For these reasons Jukes disliked him; but Captain MacWhirr, to Jukes' scornful disgust, seemed to regard him as a first-rate petty officer.

He pulled himself up by Jukes' coat, taking that liberty with the greatest moderation, and only so far as it was forced upon him by the hurricane.

"What is it, bosun, what is it?" yelled Jukes, impatiently. What could that fraud of a bosun want on the bridge? The typhoon had got on Jukes' nerves. The husky bellowings of the other, though unintelligible, seemed to suggest a state of lively satisfaction. There could be no mistake. The old fool was pleased with something.

The boatswain's other hand had found some other body, for in a changed tone he began to inquire: "Is it you, sir? Is it you, sir?" The wind strangled his howls.

"Yes!" cried Captain MacWhirr.

IV

All that the boatswain, out of a superabundance of yells, could make clear to Captain MacWhirr was the bizarre intelligence that "All them Chinamen in the fore 'tween-deck have fetched away, sir."

Jukes to leeward could hear these two shouting within six inches of his face, as you may hear on a still night half a mile away two men conversing across a field. He heard Captain MacWhirr's exasperated "What? What?" and the strained pitch of the other's hoarseness. "In a lump . . . seen them myself. . . . Awful sight, sir . . . thought . . . tell you."

Jukes remained indifferent, as if rendered irresponsible by the force of the hurricane, which made the very thought of action utterly vain. Besides, being very young, he had found the occupation of keeping his heart completely steeled against the worst so engrossing that he had come to feel an overpowering dislike towards any other form of activity whatever. He was not scared; he knew this because, firmly believing he would never see another sunrise, he remained calm in that belief.

These are the moments of do-nothing heroics to which even good men surrender at times. Many officers of ships can no doubt recall a case in their experience when just such a trance of confounded stoicism would come all at once over a whole ship's company. Jukes, however, had no wide experience of men or storms. He conceived himself to be calm—inexorably calm; but as a matter of fact he was daunted; not abjectly, but only so far as a decent man may, without becoming loathsome to himself.

It was rather like a forced-on numbness of spirit. The long, long stress of a gale does it; the suspense of the interminably culminating catastrophe; and there is a bodily fatigue in the mere holding on to existence within the excessive tumult; a searching and insidious fatigue that penetrates deep into a man's breast to cast down and sadden his heart, which is incorrigible, and of all the gifts of the earth—even before life itself—aspires to peace.

Jukes was benumbed much more than he supposed. He held on— very wet, very cold, stiff in every limb; and in a momentary hallucination of swift visions (it is said that a drowning man thus reviews all his life) he beheld all sorts of memories altogether unconnected with his present situation. He remembered his father, for instance: a worthy business man, who at an unfortunate crisis in his affairs went quietly to bed and died forthwith in a state of resignation. Jukes did not recall these circumstances, of course, but remaining otherwise unconcerned he seemed to see distinctly the poor man's face; a certain game of nap played when quite a boy in Table Bay on board a ship, since lost with all hands; the thick eyebrows of his first skipper; and without any emotion, as he might years ago have walked listlessly into her room and found her sitting there with a book, he remembered his mother—dead, too, now—the resolute woman, left badly off, who had been very firm in his bringing up.

It could not have lasted more than a second, perhaps not so much. A heavy arm had fallen about his shoulders; Captain MacWhirr's voice was speaking his name into his ear.

"Jukes! Jukes!"

He detected the tone of deep concern. The wind had thrown its weight on the ship, trying to pin her down amongst the seas. They made a clean breach over her, as over a deep-swimming log; and the gathered weight of crashes menaced monstrously from afar. The breakers flung out of the night with a ghostly light on their crests—the light of sea-foam that in a ferocious, boiling-up pale flash showed upon the slender body of the ship the toppling rush, the downfall, and the seething mad scurry of each wave. Never for a moment could she shake herself clear of the water; Jukes, rigid, perceived in her motion the ominous sign of haphazard floundering. She was no longer struggling intelligently. It was the beginning of the end; and the note of busy concern in Captain MacWhirr's voice sickened him like an exhibition of blind and pernicious folly.

The spell of the storm had fallen upon Jukes. He was penetrated by it, absorbed by it; he was rooted in it with a rigor of dumb attention. Captain MacWhirr persisted in his cries, but the wind got between them like a solid wedge. He hung round Jukes' neck as heavy as a millstone, and suddenly the sides of their heads knocked together.

"Jukes! Mr. Jukes, I say!"

He had to answer that voice that would not be silenced. He answered in the customary manner: ". . . Yes, sir."

And directly, his heart, corrupted by the storm that breeds a craving for peace, rebelled against the tyranny of training and command.

Captain MacWhirr had his mate's head fixed firm in the crook of his elbow, and pressed it to his yelling lips mysteriously. Sometimes Jukes would break in, admonishing hastily: "Look out, sir!" or Captain MacWhirr would bawl an earnest exhortation to "Hold hard, there!" and the whole black universe seemed to reel together with the ship. They paused. She floated yet. And Captain MacWhirr would resume his shouts. ". . . Says . . . whole lot . . . fetched away. . . . Ought to see . . . what's the matter."

Directly the full force of the hurricane had struck the ship, every part of her deck became untenable; and the sailors, dazed and dismayed, took shelter in the port alleyway under the bridge. It had a door aft, which they shut; it was very black, cold, and dismal. At each heavy fling of the ship they would groan all together in the dark, and tons of water could be heard scuttling about as if trying to get at them from above. The boatswain had been keeping up a gruff talk, but a more unreasonable lot of men, he said afterwards, he had never been with. They were snug enough there, out of harm's way, and not wanted to do anything, either; and yet they did nothing but grumble and complain peevishly like so many sick kids. Finally, one of them said that if there had been at least some light to see each other's noses by, it wouldn't be so bad. It was making him crazy, he declared, to lie there in the dark waiting for the blamed hooker to sink.

"Why don't you step outside, then, and be done with it at once?" the boatswain turned on him.

This called up a shout of execration. The boatswain found himself overwhelmed with reproaches of all sorts. They seemed to take it ill that a lamp was not instantly created for them out of nothing. They would whine after a light to get drowned by—anyhow! And though the unreason of their revilings was patent—since no one could hope to reach the lamp room, which was forward—he became greatly distressed. He did not think it was decent of them to be nagging at him like this. He told them so, and was met by general contumely. He sought refuge, therefore, in an embittered silence. At the same time their grumbling and sighing and muttering worried him greatly, but by and by it occurred to him that there were six globe lamps hung in the 'tween-deck, and that there could be no harm in depriving the coolies of one of them.

The *Nan-Shan* had an athwartship coal bunker, which, being at times used as cargo space, communicated by an iron door with the fore 'tween-deck. It was empty then, and its manhole was the foremost one in the alleyway. The boatswain could get in, therefore, without coming out on deck at all; but to his great surprise he found he could induce no one to help him in taking off the manhole cover. He groped for it all the same, but one of the crew lying in his way refused to budge.

"Why, I only want to get you that blamed light you are crying for," he expostulated, almost pitifully.

Somebody told him to go and put his head in a bag. He regretted he could not recognize the voice, and that it was too dark to see, otherwise, as he said, he would have put a head on *that* son of a sea-cook, anyway, sink or swim. Nevertheless, he had made up his mind to show them he could get a light, if he were to die for it.

Through the violence of the ship's rolling, every movement was dangerous. To be lying down seemed labor enough. He nearly broke his neck dropping into the bunker. He fell on his back, and was sent shooting helplessly from side to side in the dangerous company of a heavy iron bar—a coal-trimmer's slice probably—left down there by somebody. This thing made him as nervous as though it had been a wild beast. He could not see it, the inside of the bunker coated with coal-dust being perfectly and impenetrably black; but he heard it sliding and clattering, and striking here and there, always in the neighborhood of his head. It seemed to make an extraordinary noise, too—to give heavy thumps as though it had been as big as a bridge girder. This was remarkable enough for him to notice while he was flung from port to starboard and back again, and clawing desperately the smooth sides of the bunker in the endeavor to stop himself. The door into the 'tween-deck not fitting quite true, he saw a thread of dim light at the bottom.

Being a sailor, and a still active man, he did not want much of a chance to regain his feet; and as luck would have it, in scrambling up he put his hand on the iron slice, picking it up as he rose. Otherwise he would have been afraid of the thing breaking his legs, or at least knocking him down again. At first he stood still. He felt unsafe in this darkness that seemed to make the ship's motion unfamiliar, unforeseen, and difficult to counteract. He felt so much shaken for a moment that he dared not move for fear of "taking charge again." He had no mind to get battered to pieces in that bunker.

He had struck his head twice; he was dazed a little. He seemed to hear yet so plainly the clatter and bangs of the iron slice flying about his ears that he tightened his grip to prove to himself he had it there safely in his hand. He was vaguely amazed at the plainness with which down there he could hear the gale raging. Its howls and shrieks seemed to take on, in the emptiness of the bunker, something of the human character, of human rage and pain—being not vast but infinitely poignant. And there were, with every roll, thumps, too—profound, ponderous thumps, as if a bulky object of five-ton weight or so had got play in the hold. But there was no such thing in the cargo. Something on deck? Impossible. Or alongside? Couldn't be.

He thought all this quickly, clearly, competently, like a seaman, and in the end remained puzzled. This noise, though, came deadened from outside, together with the washing and pouring of water on deck above his head. Was it the wind? Must be. It made down there a row like the shouting of a big lot of crazed men. And he discovered in himself a desire for a light, too—if only to get drowned by—and a nervous anxiety to get out of that bunker as quickly as possible.

He pulled back the bolt: the heavy iron plate turned on its hinges; and it was as though he had opened the door to the sounds of the tempest. A gust of hoarse yelling met him: the air was still; and the rushing of water overhead was covered by a tumult of strangled, throaty shrieks that produced an effect of desperate confusion. He straddled his legs the whole width of the doorway and stretched his neck. And at first he perceived only what he had come to seek: six small yellow flames swinging violently on the great body of the dusk.

It was stayed like the gallery of a mine, with a row of stanchions in the middle, and crossbeams overhead, penetrating into the gloom ahead—indefinitely. And to port there loomed, like the caving in of one of the sides, a bulky mass with a slanting outline. The whole place, with the shadows and the shapes, moved all the time. The boatswain glared: the ship lurched to starboard, and a great howl came from that mass that had the slant of fallen earth.

Pieces of wood whizzed past. Planks, he thought, inexpressibly startled, and flinging back his head. At his feet a man went sliding over, open-eyed, on his back, straining with uplifted arms for nothing: and another came bounding like a detached stone with his head between his legs and his hands clenched. His pigtail whipped in the air; he made a grab at the boatswain's legs, and from his opened hand a bright white disc rolled against the boatswain's foot. He recognized a silver dollar, and yelled at it with astonishment. With a precipitated sound of trampling and shuffling of bare feet, and with guttural cries, the mound of writhing bodies piled up to port detached itself from the ship's side and sliding, inert and struggling, shifted to starboard, with a dull, brutal thump. The cries ceased. The boatswain heard a long moan through the roar and whistling of the wind; he saw an inextricable confusion of heads and shoulders, naked soles kicking upwards, fists raised, tumbling backs, legs, pigtails, faces.

"Good Lord!" he cried, horrified, and banged-to the iron door upon this vision.

This was what he had come on the bridge to tell. He could not keep it to himself; and on board ship there is only one man to whom it is worth while to unburden yourself. On his passage back the hands in the alleyway swore at him for a fool. Why didn't he bring that lamp? What the devil did the coolies matter to anybody? And when he came out, the extremity of the ship made what went on inside of her appear of little moment.

At first he thought he had left the alleyway in the very moment of her sinking. The bridge ladders had been washed away, but an enormous sea filling the after-deck floated him up. After that he had to lie on his stomach for some time, holding to a ring-bolt, getting his breath now and then, and swallowing salt water. He struggled farther on his hands and knees, too frightened and distracted to turn back. In this way he reached the after-part of the wheelhouse. In that comparatively sheltered spot he found the second mate. The boatswain was pleasantly surprised—his impression being that everybody on deck must have been washed away a long time ago. He asked eagerly where the Captain was.

The second mate was lying low, like a malignant little animal under a hedge.

"Captain? Gone overboard, after getting us into this mess." The mate, too, for all he knew or cared. Another fool. Didn't matter. Everybody was going by and by.

The boatswain crawled out again into the strength of the wind; not because he much expected to find anybody, he said, but just to get away from "that man." He crawled out as outcasts go to face an inclement world. Hence his great joy at finding Jukes and the Captain. But what was going on in the 'tween-deck was to him a minor matter by that time. Besides, it was difficult to make yourself heard. But he managed to convey the idea that the Chinaman had broken adrift together with their boxes, and that he had come up on purpose to report this. As to the hands, they were all right. Then, appeased, he subsided on the deck in a sitting posture, hugging with his arms and legs the stand of the engine-room telegraph—an iron casting as thick as a post. When that went, why, he expected he would go, too. He gave no more thought to the coolies.

Captain MacWhirr had made Jukes understand that he wanted him to go down below—to see.

"What am I to do then, sir?" And the trembling of his whole wet body caused Jukes' voice to sound like bleating.

"See first . . . Bosun . . . says . . . adrift."

"That bosun is a confounded fool," howled Jukes, shakily.

The absurdity of the demand made upon him revolted Jukes. He was as unwilling to go as if the moment he had left the deck the ship were sure to sink.

"I must know . . . can't leave. . . ."

"They'll settle, sir."

"Fight . . . bosun says they fight. . . . Why? Can't have . . . fighting . . . board ship. . . . Much rather keep you here . . . case . . . I should . . . washed overboard myself. . . . Stop it . . . some way. You see and tell me . . . through engine-room tube. Don't want you . . . up here . . . too often. Dangerous . . . moving about . . . deck."

Jukes, held with his head in chancery, had to listen to what seemed horrible suggestions.

"Don't want . . . you get lost . . . so long . . . ship isn't. . . . Rout . . . Good man . . . Ship . . . may . . . through this . . . all right yet."

All at once Jukes understood he would have to go.

"Do you think she may?" he screamed.

But the wind devoured the reply, out of which Jukes heard only the one word, pronounced with great energy ". . . Always. . . ."

Captain MacWhirr released Jukes, and bending over the boatswain, yelled, "Get back with the mate." Jukes only knew that the arm was gone off his shoulders. He was dismissed with his orders—to do what? He was exasperated into letting go his hold carelessly, and on the instant was blown away. It seemed to him that nothing could stop him from being blown right over the stern. He flung himself down hastily, and the boatswain, who was following, fell on him.

"Don't you get up yet, sir," cried the boatswain. "No hurry!"

A sea swept over. Jukes understood the boatswain to splutter that the bridge ladders were gone. "I'll lower you down, sir, by your hands," he screamed. He shouted also something about the smokestack being as likely to go overboard as not. Jukes thought it very possible, and imagined the fires out, the ship helpless. . . . The boatswain by his side kept on yelling. "What? What is it?" Jukes cried distressfully; and the other repeated, "What would my old woman say if she saw me now?"

In the alleyway, where a lot of water had got in and splashed in the dark, the men were still as death, till Jukes stumbled against one of them and cursed him savagely for being in the way. Two or three voices then asked, eager and weak, "Any chance for us, sir?"

"What's the matter with you fools?" he said brutally. He felt as though he could throw himself down amongst them and never move any more. But they seemed cheered; and in the midst of obsequious warnings, "Look out! Mind that manhole lid, sir," they lowered him into the bunker. The boatswain tumbled down after him, and as soon as he had picked himself up he remarked, "She would say, 'Serve you right, you old fool, for going to sea.'"

The boatswain had some means, and made a point of alluding to them frequently. His wife—a fat woman—and two grown-up daughters kept a greengrocer's shop in the East End of London.

In the dark, Jukes, unsteady on his legs, listened to a faint thunderous patter. A deadened screaming went on steadily at his elbow, as it were; and from above the louder tumult of the storm descended upon these near sounds. His head swam. To him, too, in that bunker, the motion of the ship seemed novel and menacing, sapping his resolution as though he had never been afloat before.

He had half a mind to scramble out again; but the remembrance of Captain MacWhirr's voice made this impossible. His orders were to go and see. What was the good of it, he wanted to know. Enraged, he told himself he would see—of course. But the boatswain, staggering clumsily, warned him to be careful how he opened that door; there was a blamed fight going on. And Jukes, as if in great bodily pain, desired irritably to know what the devil they were fighting for.

"Dollars! Dollars, sir. All their rotten chests got burst open. Blamed money skipping all over the place, and they are tumbling after it head over heels—tearing and biting like anything. A regular little hell in there."

Jukes convulsively opened the door. The short boatswain peered under his arm.

One of the lamps had gone out, broken perhaps. Rancorous, guttural cries burst out loudly on their ears, and a strange panting sound, the working of all these straining breasts. A hard blow hit the side of the ship: water fell above with a stunning shock, and in the forefront of the gloom, where the air was reddish and thick, Jukes saw a head bang the deck violently, two thick calves waving on high, muscular arms twined round a naked body, a yellow-face, open-mouthed and with a set wild stare, look up and slide away. An empty chest clattered turning over; a man fell head first with a jump, as if lifted by a kick; and farther off, indistinct, others streamed like a mass of rolling stones down a bank, thumping the deck with their feet and flourishing their arms wildly. The hatchway ladder was loaded with coolies swarming on it like bees on a branch. They hung on the steps in a crawling, stirring cluster, beating madly with their fists the underside of the battened hatch, and the headlong rush of the water above was heard in the intervals of their yelling. The ship heeled over more, and they began to drop off: first one, then two, then all the rest went away together, falling straight off with a great cry.

Jukes was confounded. The boatswain, with gruff anxiety, begged him, "Don't you go in there, sir."

The whole place seemed to twist upon itself, jumping incessantly the while; and when the ship rose to a sea Jukes fancied that all these men would be shot upon him in a body. He backed out, swung the door to, and with trembling hands pushed at the bolt. . . .

As soon as his mate had gone Captain MacWhirr, left alone on the bridge, sidled and staggered as far as the wheelhouse. Its door being hinged forward, he had to fight the gale for admittance, and when at last he managed to enter, it was with an instantaneous clatter and a bang, as though he had been fired through the wood. He stood within, holding on to the handle.

The steering gear leaked steam, and in the confined space the glass of the binnacle made a shiny oval of light in a thin white fog. The wind howled, hummed, whistled, with sudden booming gusts that rattled the doors and shutters in the vicious patter of sprays. Two coils of lead line and a small canvas bag hung on a long lanyard, swung wide off, and came back clinging to the bulkheads. The gratings underfoot were nearly afloat; with every sweeping blow of a sea, water squirted violently through the cracks all round the door, and the man at the helm had flung down his cap, his coat, and stood propped against the gear casing in a striped cotton shirt open on his breast. The little brass wheel in his hands had the appearance of a bright and fragile toy. The cords of his neck stood hard and lean, a dark patch lay in the hollow of his throat, and his face was still and sunken as in death.

Captain MacWhirr wiped his eyes. The sea that had nearly taken him overboard had, to his great annoyance, washed his sou'-wester hat off his bald head. The fluffy, fair hair, soaked and darkened, resembled a mean skein of cotton threads festooned round his bare skull. His face, glistening with sea water, had been made crimson with the wind, with the sting of sprays. He looked as though he had come off sweating from before a furnace.

"You here?" he muttered, heavily.

The second mate had found his way into the wheelhouse some time before. He had fixed himself in a corner with his knees up, a fist pressed against each temple; and this attitude suggested rage, sorrow, resignation, surrender, with a sort of concentrated unforgiveness. He said mournfully and defiantly, "Well, it's my watch below now; ain't it?"

The steam gear clattered, stopped, clattered again; and the helmsman's eyeballs seemed to project out of a hungry face as if the compass card behind the binnacle glass had been meat. God knows how long he had been left there to steer, as if forgotten by all his shipmates. The bells had not been struck; there had been no reliefs; the ship's routine had gone down wind; but he was trying to keep her head north-northeast. The rudder might have been gone for all he knew, the fires out, the engines broken down, the ship ready to roll over like a corpse. He was anxious not to get muddled and lose control of her head, because the compass-card swung far both ways, wriggling on the pivot, and sometimes seemed to whirl right round. He suffered from mental stress. He was horribly afraid, also, of the wheelhouse going. Mountains of water kept on tumbling against it. When the ship took one of her desperate dives the corners of his lips twitched.

Captain MacWhirr looked up at the wheelhouse clock. Screwed to the bulk-head, it had a white face on which the black hands appeared to stand quite still. It was half-past one in the morning.

"Another day," he muttered to himself.

The second mate heard him, and lifting his head as one grieving amongst ruins, "You won't see it break," he exclaimed. His wrists and his knees could be seen to shake violently. "No, by God! You won't. . . ."

He took his face again between his fists.

The body of the helmsman had moved slightly, but his head didn't budge on his neck—like a stone head fixed to look one way from a column. During a roll that all but took his booted legs from under him, and in the very stagger to save himself, Captain MacWhirr said austerely, "Don't you pay any attention to what that man says." And then, with an indefinable change of tone very grave, he added, "He isn't on duty."

The sailor said nothing.

The hurricane boomed, shaking the little place, which seemed air-tight; and the light of the binnacle flickered all the time.

"You haven't been relieved," Captain MacWhirr went on, looking down. "I want you to stick to the helm, though, as long as you can. You've got the hang of her. Another man coming here might make a mess of it. Wouldn't do. No child's play. And the hands are probably busy with a job down below. . . . Think you can?"

The steering gear leaped into an abrupt short clatter, stopped smoldering like an ember; and the still man, with a motionless gaze, burst out, as if all the passion in him had gone into his lips: "By Heavens, sir! I can steer forever if nobody talks to me."

"Oh! aye! All right. . . ." The Captain lifted his eyes for the first time to the man, ". . . Hackett."

And he seemed to dismiss this matter from his mind. He stooped to the engine-room speaking-tube, blew in, and bent his head. Mr. Rout below answered, and at once Captain MacWhirr put his lips to the mouthpiece.

With the uproar of the gale around him he applied alternately his lips and his ear, and the engineer's voice mounted to him, harsh and as if out of the heat of an engagement. One of the stokers was disabled, the others had given in, the second engineer and the donkeyman were firing-up. The third engineer was standing by the steam valve. The engines were being tended by hand. How was it above?

"Bad enough. It mostly rests with you," said Captain MacWhirr. Was the mate down there yet? No? Well, he would be presently. Would

Mr. Rout let him talk through the speaking tube?—through the deck speaking tube, because he—the Captain—was going out again on the bridge directly. There was some trouble amongst the Chinamen. They were fighting, it seemed. Couldn't allow fighting anyhow. . . .

Mr. Rout had gone away, and Captain MacWhirr could feel against his ear the pulsation of the engines, like the beat of the ship's heart. Mr. Rout's voice down there shouted something distantly. The ship pitched headlong, the pulsation leaped with a hissing tumult, and stopped dead. Captain MacWhirr's face was impassive, and his eyes were fixed aimlessly on the crouching shape of the second mate. Again Mr. Rout's voice cried out in the depths, and the pulsating beats recommenced, with slow strokes—growing swifter.

Mr. Rout had returned to the tube. "It don't matter much what they do," he said, hastily; and then, with irritation, "She takes these dives as if she never meant to come up again."

"Awful sea," said the Captain's voice from above.

"Don't let me drive her under," barked Solomon Rout up the pipe.

"Dark and rain. Can't see what's coming," uttered the voice. "Must—keep—her—moving—enough to steer—and chance it," it went on to state distinctly.

"I am doing as much as I dare."

"We are—getting—smashed up—a good deal up here," proceeded the voice mildly. "Doing—fairly well—though. Of course, if the wheelhouse should go. . . ."

Mr. Rout, bending an attentive ear, muttered peevishly something under his breath.

But the deliberate voice up there became animated to ask: "Jukes turned up yet?" Then, after a short wait, "I wish he would bear a hand. I want him to be done and come up here in case of anything. To look after the ship. I am all alone. The second mate's lost. . . ."

"What?" shouted Mr. Rout into the engine-room, taking his head away. Then up the tube he cried, "Gone overboard?" and clapped his ear to.

"Lost his nerve," the voice from above continued in a matter-of-fact tone. "Damned awkward circumstance."

Mr. Rout, listening with bowed neck, opened his eyes wide at this. However, he heard something like the sounds of a scuffle and broken exclamations coming down to him. He strained his hearing; and all the time Beale, the third engineer, with his arms uplifted, held between the palms of his hands the rim of a little black wheel projecting at the side of a big copper pipe.

He seemed to be poising it above his head, as though it were a correct attitude in some sort of game.

To steady himself, he pressed his shoulder against the white bulkhead, one knee bent, and a sweat-rag tucked in his belt hanging on his hip. His smooth cheek was begrimed and flushed, and the coal dust on his eyelids, like the black penciling of a make-up, enhanced the liquid brilliance of the whites, giving to his youthful face something of a feminine, exotic and fascinating aspect. When the ship pitched he would with hasty movements of his hands screw hard at the little wheel.

"Gone crazy," began the Captain's voice suddenly in the tube. "Rushed at me. . . . Just now. Had to knock him down. . . . This minute. You heard, Mr. Rout?"

"The devil!" muttered Mr. Rout. "Look out, Beale!"

His shout rang out like the blast of a warning trumpet, between the iron walls of the engine-room. Painted white, they rose high into the dusk of the skylight, sloping like a roof; and the whole lofty space resembled the interior of a monument, divided by floors of iron grating, with lights flickering at different levels, and a mass of gloom lingering in the middle, within the columnar stir of machinery under the motionless swelling of the cylinders. A loud and wild resonance, made up of all the noises of the hurricane, dwelt in the still warmth of the air. There was in it the smell of hot metal, of oil, and a slight mist of steam. The blows of the sea seemed to traverse it in an unringing, stunning shock, from side to side.

Gleams, like pale long flames, trembled upon the polish of metal; from the flooring below the enormous crank-heads emerged in their turns with a flash of brass and steel—going over; while the connecting rods, big-jointed, like skeleton limbs, seemed to thrust them down and pull them up again with an irresistible precision. And deep in the half-light other rods dodged deliberately to and fro, crossheads nodded, discs of metal rubbed smoothly against each other, slow and gentle, in a commingling of shadows and gleams.

Sometimes all those powerful and unerring movements would slow down simultaneously, as if they had been the functions of a living organism, stricken suddenly by the blight of languor; and Mr. Rout's eyes would blaze darker in his long sallow face. He was fighting this fight in a pair of carpet slippers. A short shiny jacket barely covered his loins, and his white wrists protruded far out of the tight sleeves, as though the emergency had added to his stature, had lengthened his limbs, augmented his pallor, hollowed his eyes.

He moved, climbing high up, disappearing low down, with a restless, purposeful industry, and when he stood still, holding the guard rail in front of the starting gear, he would keep glancing to the right at the steam gauge, at the water gauge, fixed upon the white wall in the light of a swaying lamp. The mouths of two speaking-tubes gaped stupidly at his elbow, and the dial of the engine-room telegraph resembled a clock of large diameter, bearing on its face curt words instead of figures. The grouped letters stood out heavily black, around the pivot-head of the indicator, emphatically symbolic of loud exclamations: AHEAD, ASTERN, SLOW, HALF, STAND BY; and the fat black hand pointed downwards to the word FULL, which, thus singled out, captured the eye as a sharp cry secures attention.

The wood-encased bulk of the low-pressure cylinder, frowning portly from above, emitted a faint wheeze at every thrust, and except for that low hiss the engines worked their steel limbs headlong or slow with a silent, determined smoothness. And all this, the white walls, the moving steel, the floor plates under Solomon Rout's feet, the floors of iron grating above his head, the dusk and the gleams, uprose and sank continuously, with one accord, upon the harsh wash of the waves against the ship's side. The whole loftiness of the place, booming hollow to the great voice of the wind, swayed at the top like a tree, would go over bodily, as if borne down this way and that by the tremendous blasts.

"You've got to hurry up," shouted Mr. Rout, as soon as he saw Jukes appear in the stokehold doorway.

Jukes' glance was wandering and tipsy; his red face was puffy, as though he had overslept himself. He had had an arduous road, and had travelled over it with immense vivacity, the agitation of his mind corresponding to the exertions of his body. He had rushed up out of the bunker, stumbling in the dark alleyway amongst a lot of bewildered men who, trod upon, asked "What's up, sir?" in awed mutters all round him;—down the stokehold ladder, missing many iron rungs in his hurry, down into a place deep as a well, black as Tophet, tipping over back and forth like a seesaw. The water in the bilges thundered at each roll, and lumps of coal skipped to and fro, from end to end, rattling like an avalanche of pebbles on a slope of iron.

Somebody in there moaned with pain, and somebody else could be seen crouching over what seemed the prone body of a dead man; a lusty voice blasphemed; and the glow under each fire door was like a pool of flaming blood radiating quietly in a velvety blackness.

A gust of wind struck upon the nape of Jukes' neck and next moment he felt it streaming about his wet ankles. The stokehold ventilators hummed; in front of the six fire doors two wild figures, stripped to the waist, staggered and stooped, wrestling with two shovels.

"Hallo! Plenty of draught now," yelled the second engineer at once, as though he had been all the time looking out for Jukes. The donkeyman, a dapper little chap with a dazzling fair skin and a tiny, gingery moustache, worked in a sort of mute transport. They were keeping a full head of steam, and a profound rumbling, as of an empty furniture van trotting over a bridge, made a sustained bass to all the other noises of the place.

"Blowing off all the time," went on yelling the second. With a sound as of a hundred scoured saucepans, the orifice of a ventilator spat upon his shoulder a sudden gush of salt water, and he volleyed a stream of curses upon all things on earth including his own soul, ripping and raving, and all the time attending to his business. With a sharp clash of metal the ardent pale glare of the fire opened upon his bullet head, showing his spluttering lips, his insolent face, and with another clang closed like the white-hot wink of an iron eye.

"Where's the blooming ship? Can you tell me? Blast my eyes! Under water—or what? It's coming down here in tons. Are the condemned cowls gone to Hades? Hey? Don't you know anything—you jolly sailor-man you . . . ?"

Jukes, after a bewildered moment, had been helped by a roll to dart through; and as soon as his eyes took in the comparative vastness, peace and brilliance of the engine-room, the ship, setting her stern heavily in the water, sent him charging head down upon Mr. Rout.

The chief's arm, long like a tentacle, and straightening as if worked by a spring, went out to meet him, and deflected his rush into a spin towards the speaking-tubes. At the same time Mr. Rout repeated earnestly:

"You've got to hurry up, whatever it is."

Jukes yelled "Are you there, sir?" and listened. Nothing. Suddenly the roar of the wind fell straight into his ear, but presently a small voice shoved aside the shouting hurricane quietly.

"You, Jukes?—Well?"

Jukes was ready to talk: it was only time that seemed to be wanting. It was easy enough to account for everything. He could perfectly imagine the coolies battened down in the reeking 'tween-deck, lying sick and scared between the rows of chests. Then one of these chests—or perhaps several at once—breaking loose in a roll, knocking out others, sides splitting, lids flying open, and all these clumsy Chinamen rising up in a body to save their property. Afterwards every fling of the ship would hurl that tramping, yelling mob here and there, from side to side, in a whirl of smashed wood, torn clothing, rolling dollars. A struggle once started, they would be unable to stop themselves. Nothing could stop them now except main force. It was a disaster. He had seen it, and that was all he could say. Some of them must be dead, he believed. The rest would go on fighting. . . .

He sent up his words, tripping over each other, crowding the narrow tube. They mounted as if into a silence of an enlightened comprehension dwelling alone up there with a storm. And Jukes wanted to be dismissed from the face of that odious trouble intruding on the great need of the ship.

V

He waited. Before his eyes the engines turned with slow labor, that in the moment of going off into a mad fling would stop dead at Mr. Rout's shout, "Look out, Beale!" They paused in an intelligent immobility, stilled in mid-stroke, a heavy crank arrested on the cant, as if conscious of danger and the passage of time. Then, with a "Now, then!" from the chief, and the sound of a breath expelled through clenched teeth, they would accomplish the interrupted revolution and begin another.

There was the prudent sagacity of wisdom and the deliberation of enormous strength in their movements. This was their work—this patient coaxing of a distracted ship over the fury of the waves and into the very eye of the wind. At times Mr. Rout's chin would sink on his breast, and he watched them with knitted eyebrows as if lost in thought.

The voice that kept the hurricane out of Jukes' ear began: "Take the hands with you . . . ," and left off unexpectedly.

"What could I do with them, sir?"

A harsh, abrupt, imperious clang exploded suddenly. The three pairs of eyes flew up to the telegraph dial to see the hand jump from FULL to STOP, as if snatched by a devil. And then these three men in the engine-room had the intimate sensation of a check upon the ship, of a strange shrinking, as if she had gathered herself for a desperate leap.

"Stop her!" bellowed Mr. Rout.

Nobody—not even Captain MacWhirr, who alone on deck had caught sight of a white line of foam coming on at such a height that he couldn't believe his eyes—nobody was to know the steepness of that sea and the awful depth of the hollow the hurricane had scooped out behind the running wall of water.

It raced to meet the ship, and, with a pause, as of girding the loins, the *Nan-Shan* lifted her bows and leaped. The flames in all the lamps sank, darkening the engine-room. One went out. With a tearing crash and a swirling, raving tumult, tons of water fell upon the deck, as though the ship had darted under the foot of a cataract.

Down there they looked at each other, stunned.

"Swept from end to end, by God!" bawled Jukes.

She dipped into the hollow straight down, as if going over the edge of the world. The engine-room toppled forward menacingly, like the inside of a tower nodding in an earthquake. An awful racket, of iron things falling, came from the stokehold. She hung on this appalling slant long enough for Beale to drop on his hands and knees and begin to crawl as if he meant to fly on all fours out of the engine-room, and for Mr. Rout to turn his head slowly, rigid, cavernous, with the lower jaw dropping. Jukes had shut his eyes, and his face in a moment became hopelessly blank and gentle, like the face of a blind man.

At last she rose slowly, staggering, as if she had to lift a mountain with her bows.

Mr. Rout shut his mouth; Jukes blinked; and little Beale stood up hastily.

"Another one like this, and that's the last of her," cried the chief.

He and Jukes looked at each other, and the same thought came into their heads. The Captain! Everything must have been swept away. Steering gear gone—ship like a log. All over directly.

"Rush!" ejaculated Mr. Rout thickly, glaring with enlarged, doubtful eyes at Jukes, who answered him by an irresolute glance.

The clang of the telegraph gong soothed them instantly. The black hand dropped in a flash from STOP to FULL.

"Now then, Beale!" cried Mr. Rout.

The steam hissed low. The piston rods slid in and out. Jukes put his ear to the tube. The voice was ready for him. It said: "Pick up all the money. Bear a hand now. I'll want you up here." And that was all.

"Sir?" called up Jukes. There was no answer.

He staggered away like a defeated man from the field of battle. He had got, in some way or other, a cut above his left eyebrow—a cut to the bone. He was not aware of it in the least: quantities of the China Sea, large enough to break his neck for him, had gone over his head, had cleaned, washed, and salted that wound. It did not bleed, but only gaped red; and this gash over the eye, his disheveled hair, the disorder of his clothes, gave him the aspect of a man worsted in a fight with fists.

"Got to pick up the dollars." He appealed to Mr. Rout, smiling pitifully at random.

"What's that?" asked Mr. Rout, wildly. "Pick up . . . ? I don't care. . . ." Then, quivering in every muscle, but with an exaggeration of paternal tone, "Go away now, for God's sake. You deck people'll drive me silly. There's that second mate been going for the old man. Don't you know? You fellows are going wrong for want of something to do. . . ."

At these words Jukes discovered in himself the beginnings of anger. Want of something to do—indeed. . . . Full of hot scorn against the chief, he turned to go the way he had come. In the stokehold the plump donkeyman toiled with his shovel mutely, as if his tongue had been cut out; but the second was carrying on like a noisy, undaunted maniac, who had preserved his skill in the art of stoking under a marine boiler.

"Hallo, you wandering officer! Hey! Can't you get some of your slush-slingers to wind up a few of them ashes? I am getting choked with them here. Curse it! Hallo! Hey! Remember the articles: *Sailors and firemen to assist each other*. Hey! D'ye hear?"

Jukes was climbing out frantically, and the other, lifting up his face after him, howled, "Can't you speak? What are you poking about here for? What's your game, anyhow?"

A frenzy possessed Jukes. By the time he was back amongst the men in the darkness of the alleyway, he felt ready to wring all their necks at the slightest sign of hanging back. The very thought of it exasperated him. *He* couldn't hang back. They shouldn't.

The impetuosity with which he came amongst them carried them along. They had already been excited and startled at all his comings and goings—by the fierceness and rapidity of his movements; and more felt than seen in his rushes, he appeared formidable—busied with matters of life and death that brooked no delay. At his first word he heard them drop into the bunker one after another obediently, with heavy thumps.

They were not clear as to what would have to be done. "What is it? What is it?" they were asking each other. The boatswain tried to explain; the sounds of a great scuffle surprised them; and the mighty shocks, reverberating awfully in the black bunker, kept them in mind of their danger. When the boatswain threw open the door it seemed that an eddy of the hurricane, stealing through the iron sides of the ship, had set all these bodies whirling like dust: there came to them a confused uproar, a tempestuous tumult, a fierce mutter, gusts of screams dying away, and the tramping of feet mingling with the blows of the sea.

For a moment they glared amazed, blocking the doorway. Jukes pushed through them brutally. He said nothing, and simply darted in. Another lot of coolies on the ladder, struggling suicidally to break through the battened hatch to a swamped deck, fell off as before, and he disappeared under them like a man overtaken by a landslide.

The boatswain yelled excitedly: "Come along. Get the mate out. He'll be trampled to death. Come on."

They charged in, stamping on breasts, on fingers, on faces, catching their feet in heaps of clothing, kicking broken wood; but before they could get hold of him Jukes emerged waist deep in a multitude of clawing hands. In the instant he had been lost to view, all the buttons of his jacket had gone, its back had got split up to the collar, his waistcoat had been torn open. The central struggling mass of Chinamen went over to the roll, dark, indistinct, helpless, with a wild gleam of many eyes in the dim light of the lamps.

"Leave me alone—damn you. I am all right," screeched Jukes. "Drive them forward. Watch your chance when she pitches. Forward with 'em. Drive them against the bulkhead. Jam 'em up."

The rush of the sailors into the seething 'tween-deck was like a splash of cold water into a boiling cauldron. The commotion sank for a moment.

The bulk of Chinamen were locked in such a compact scrimmage that, linking their arms and aided by an appalling dive of the ship, the seamen sent it forward in one great shove, like a solid block. Behind their backs small clusters and loose bodies tumbled from side to side. The boatswain performed prodigious feats of strength. With his long arms open, and each great paw clutching at a stanchion, he stopped the rush of seven entwined Chinamen rolling like a boulder. His joints cracked; he said, "Ha!" and they flew apart. But the carpenter showed the greater intelligence. Without saying a word to anybody he went back into the alleyway, to fetch several coils of cargo gear he had seen there—chain and rope. With these life lines were rigged.

There was really no resistance. The struggle, however it began, had turned into a scramble of blind panic. If the coolies had started up after their scattered dollars they were by that time fighting only for their footing. They took each other by the throat merely to save themselves from being hurled about. Whoever got a hold anywhere would kick at the others who caught at his legs and hung on, till a roll sent them flying together across the deck.

The coming of the white devils was a terror. Had they come to kill? The individuals torn out of the ruck became very limp in the seamen's hands: some, dragged aside by the heels, were passive, like dead bodies, with open, fixed eyes. Here and there a coolie would fall on his knees as if begging for mercy; several, whom the excess of fear made unruly, were hit with hard fists between the eyes, and cowered; while those who were hurt submitted to rough handling, blinking rapidly without a plaint. Faces streamed with blood; there were raw places on the shaven heads, scratches, bruises, torn wounds, gashes. The broken porcelain out of the chests was mostly responsible for the latter. Here and there a Chinaman, wild-eyed, with his tail unplaited, nursed a bleeding sole.

They had been ranged closely, after having been shaken into submission, cuffed a little to allay excitement, addressed in gruff words of encouragement that sounded like promises of evil. They sat on the deck in ghastly, drooping rows, and at the end the carpenter, with two hands to help him, moved busily from place to place, setting taut and hitching the life lines. The boatswain, with one leg and one arm embracing a stanchion, struggled with a lamp pressed to his breast, trying to get a light, and growling all the time like an industrious gorilla. The figures of seamen stooped repeatedly, with the movements of gleaners, and everything was being flung into the bunker: clothing, smashed wood, broken china, and the dollars, too, gathered up in men's jackets. Now and then a sailor would stagger towards the doorway with his arms full of rubbish; and dolorous, slanting eyes followed his movements.

With every roll of the ship the long rows of sitting Celestials would sway forward brokenly, and her headlong dives knocked together the line of shaven polls from end to end. When the wash of water rolling on the deck died away for a moment, it seemed to Jukes, yet quivering from his exertions, that in his mad struggle down there he had overcome the wind somehow: that a silence had fallen upon the ship, a silence in which the sea struck thunderously at her sides.

Everything had been cleared out of the 'tween-deck—all the wreckage, as the men said. They stood erect and tottering above the level of heads and drooping shoulders. Here and there a coolie sobbed for his breath. Where the high light fell, Jukes could see the salient ribs of one, the yellow, wistful face of another; bowed necks; or would meet a dull stare directed at his face. He was amazed that there had been no corpses; but the lot of them seemed at their last gasp, and they appeared to him more pitiful than if they had been all dead.

Suddenly one of the coolies began to speak. The light came and went on his lean, straining face; he threw his head up like a baying hound. From the bunker came the sounds of knocking and the tinkle of some dollars rolling loose; he stretched out his arm, his mouth yawned black, and the incomprehensible guttural hooting sounds, that did not seem to belong to a human language, penetrated Jukes with a strange emotion as if a brute had tried to be eloquent.

Two more started mouthing what seemed to Jukes fierce denunciations; the others stirred with grunts and growls. Jukes ordered the hands out of the 'tween-decks hurriedly. He left last himself, backing through the door, while the grunts rose to a loud murmur and hands were extended after him as after a malefactor. The boatswain shot the bolt, and remarked uneasily, "Seems as if the wind had dropped, sir."

The seamen were glad to get back into the alleyway. Secretly each of them thought that at the last moment he could rush out on deck—and that was a comfort. There is something horribly repugnant in the idea of being drowned under a deck. Now they had done with the Chinamen, they again became conscious of the ship's position.

Jukes on coming out of the alleyway found himself up to the neck in the noisy water. He gained the bridge, and discovered he could detect obscure shapes as if his sight had become preternaturally acute. He saw faint outlines. They recalled not the familiar aspect of the *Nan-Shan*, but something remembered—an old dismantled steamer he had seen years ago rotting on a mudbank. She recalled that wreck.

There was no wind, not a breath, except the faint currents created by the lurches of the ship. The smoke tossed out of the funnel was settling down upon her deck. He breathed it as he passed forward. He felt the deliberate throb of the engines, and heard small sounds that seemed to have survived the great uproar: the knocking of broken fittings, the rapid tumbling of some piece of wreckage on the bridge. He perceived dimly the squat shape of his captain holding on to a twisted bridge rail, motionless and swaying as if rooted to the planks.

The unexpected stillness of the air oppressed Jukes.

"We have done it, sir," he gasped.

"Thought you would," said Captain MacWhirr.

"Did you?" murmured Jukes to himself.

"Wind fell all at once," went on the Captain.

Jukes burst out: "If you think it was an easy job—"

But his captain, clinging to the rail, paid no attention. "According to the books the worst is not over yet."

"If most of them hadn't been half dead with seasickness and fright, not one of us would have come out of that 'tween-deck alive," said Jukes.

"Had to do what's fair by them," mumbled MacWhirr, stolidly. "You don't find everything in books."

"Why, I believe they would have risen on us if I hadn't ordered the hands out of that pretty quick," continued Jukes with warmth.

After the whisper of their shouts, their ordinary tones, so distinct, rang out very loud to their ears in the amazing stillness of the air. It seemed to them they were talking in a dark and echoing vault.

Through a jagged aperture in the dome of clouds the light of a few stars fell upon the black sea, rising and falling confusedly. Sometimes the head of a watery cone would topple on board and mingle with the rolling flurry of foam on the swamped deck; and the *Nan-Shan* wallowed heavily at the bottom of a circular cistern of clouds. This ring of dense vapors, gyrating madly round the calm of the center, encompassed the ship like a motionless and unbroken wall of an aspect inconceivably sinister. Within, the sea, as if agitated by an internal commotion, leaped in peaked mounds that jostled each other, slapping heavily against her sides; and a low moaning sound, the infinite plaint of the storm's fury, came from beyond the limits of the menacing calm. Captain MacWhirr remained silent, and Jukes' ready ear caught suddenly the faint, long-drawn roar of some immense wave rushing unseen under that thick blackness, which made the appalling boundary of his vision.

"Of course," he started resentfully, "they thought we had caught at the chance to plunder them. Of course! You said—pick up the money. Easier said than done. They couldn't tell what was in our heads. We came in, smash—right into the middle of them. Had to do it by a rush."

"As long as it's done . . . ," mumbled the Captain, without attempting to look at Jukes. "Had to do what's fair."

"We shall find yet there's the devil to pay when this is over," said Jukes, feeling very sore. "Let them only recover a bit, and you'll see. They will fly at our throats, sir. Don't forget, sir, she isn't a British ship now. These brutes know it well, too. The damned Siamese flag."

"We are on board, all the same," remarked Captain MacWhirr.

"The trouble's not over yet," insisted Jukes, prophetically, reeling and catching on. "She's a wreck," he added, faintly.

"The trouble's not over yet," assented Captain MacWhirr, half aloud. . . . "Look out for her a minute."

"Are you going off the deck, sir?" asked Jukes, hurriedly, as if the storm were sure to pounce upon him as soon as he had been left alone with the ship.

He watched her, battered and solitary, laboring heavily in a wild scene of mountainous black waters lit by the gleams of distant worlds. She moved slowly, breathing into the still core of the hurricane the excess of her strength in a white cloud of steam—and the deep-toned vibration of the escape was like the defiant trumpeting of a living creature of the sea impatient for the renewal of the contest. It ceased suddenly. The still air moaned. Above Jukes' head a few stars shone into a pit of black vapors. The inky edge of the cloud-disc frowned upon the ship under the patch of glittering sky. The stars, too, seemed to look at her intently, as if for the last time, and the cluster of their splendor sat like a diadem on a lowering brow.

Captain MacWhirr had gone into the chart room. There was no light there; but he could feel the disorder of that place where he used to live tidily. His armchair was upset. The books had tumbled out on the floor: he scrunched a piece of glass under his boot. He groped for the matches, and found a box on a shelf with a deep ledge. He struck one, and puckering the corners of his eyes, held out the little flame towards the barometer whose glittering top of glass and metals nodded at him continuously.

It stood very low—incredibly low, so low that Captain MacWhirr grunted. The match went out, and hurriedly he extracted another, with thick, stiff fingers.

Again a little flame flared up before the nodding glass and metal of the top. His eyes looked at it, narrowed with attention, as if expecting an imperceptible sign. With his grave face he resembled a booted and misshapen pagan burning incense before the oracle of a joss. There was no mistake. It was the lowest reading he had ever seen in his life.

Captain MacWhirr emitted a low whistle. He forgot himself till the flame diminished to a blue spark, burnt his fingers and vanished. Perhaps something had gone wrong with the thing!

There was an aneroid glass screwed above the couch. He turned that way, struck another match, and discovered the white face of the other instrument looking at him from the bulkhead, meaningly, not to be gainsaid, as though the wisdom of men were made unerring by the indifference of matter. There was no room for doubt now. Captain MacWhirr pshawed at it, and threw the match down.

The worst was to come, then—and if the books were right this worst would be very bad. The experience of the last six hours had enlarged his conception of what heavy weather could be like. "It'll be terrific," he pronounced, mentally. He had not consciously looked at anything by the light of the matches except at the barometer; and yet somehow he had seen that his water bottle and the two tumblers had been flung out of their stand. It seemed to give him a more intimate knowledge of the tossing the ship had gone through. "I wouldn't have believed it," he thought. And his table had been cleared, too; his rulers, his pencils, the inkstand—all the things that had their safe appointed places—they were gone, as if a mischievous hand had plucked them out one by one and flung them on the wet floor. The hurricane had broken in upon the orderly arrangements of his privacy. This had never happened before, and the feeling of dismay reached the very seat of his composure. And the worst was to come yet! He was glad the trouble in the 'tween-deck had been discovered in time. If the ship had to go after all, then, at least, she wouldn't be going to the bottom with a lot of people in her fighting teeth and claw. That would have been odious. And in that feeling there was a humane intention and a vague sense of the fitness of things.

These instantaneous thoughts were yet in their essence heavy and slow, partaking of the nature of the man. He extended his hand to put back the matchbox in its corner of the shelf. There were always matches there—by his order. The steward had his instructions impressed upon him long before. "A box . . . just there, see? Not so very full . . . where I can put my hand on it, steward. Might want a light in a hurry. Can't tell on board ship *what* you might want in a hurry. Mind, now."

And of course on his side he would be careful to put it back in its place scrupulously. He did so now, but before he removed his hand it occurred to him that perhaps he would never have occasion to use that box any more. The vividness of the thought checked him and for an infinitesimal fraction of a second his fingers closed again on the small object as though it had been the symbol of all these little habits that chain us to the weary round of life. He released it at last, and letting himself fall on the settee, listened for the first sounds of returning wind.

Not yet. He heard only the wash of water, the heavy splashes, the dull shocks of the confused seas boarding his ship from all sides. She would never have a chance to clear her decks.

But the quietude of the air was startlingly tense and unsafe, like a slender hair holding a sword suspended over his head. By this awful pause the storm penetrated the defenses of the man and unsealed his lips. He spoke out in the solitude and the pitch darkness of the cabin, as if addressing another being awakened within his breast.

"I shouldn't like to lose her," he said half aloud.

He sat unseen, apart from the sea, from his ship, isolated, as if withdrawn from the very current of his own existence, where such freaks as talking to himself surely had no place. His palms reposed on his knees, he bowed his short neck and puffed heavily, surrendering to a strange sensation of weariness he was not enlightened enough to recognize for the fatigue of mental stress.

From where he sat he could reach the door of a washstand locker. There should have been a towel there. There was. Good. . . . He took it out, wiped his face, and afterwards went on rubbing his wet head. He toweled himself with energy in the dark, and then remained motionless with the towel on his knees. A moment passed, of a stillness so profound that no one could have guessed there was a man sitting in that cabin. Then a murmur arose.

"She may come out of it yet."

When Captain MacWhirr came out on deck, which he did brusquely, as though he had suddenly become conscious of having stayed away too long, the calm had lasted already more than fifteen minutes—long enough to make itself intolerable even to his imagination. Jukes, motionless on the forepart of the bridge, began to speak at once. His voice, blank and forced as though he were talking through hard-set teeth, seemed to flow away on all sides into the darkness, deepening again upon the sea.

"I had the wheel relieved. Hackett began to sing out that he was done. He's lying in there alongside the steering gear with a face like death. At first I couldn't get anybody to crawl out and relieve the poor devil. That bosun's worse than no good, I always said. Thought I would have had to go myself and haul out one of them by the neck."

"Ah, well," muttered the Captain. He stood watchful by Jukes' side.

"The second mate's in there, too, holding his head. Is he hurt, sir?"

"No—crazy," said Captain MacWhirr, curtly.

"Looks as if he had a tumble, though."

"I had to give him a push," explained the Captain.

Jukes gave an impatient sigh.

"It will come very sudden," said Captain MacWhirr, "and from over there, I fancy. God only knows though. These books are only good to muddle your head and make you jumpy. It will be bad, and there's an end. If we only can steam her round in time to meet it. . . ."

A minute passed. Some of the stars winked rapidly and vanished.

"You left them pretty safe?" began the Captain abruptly, as though the silence were unbearable.

"Are you thinking of the coolies, sir? I rigged lifelines all ways across that 'tween-deck."

"Did you? Good idea, Mr. Jukes."

"I didn't . . . think you cared to . . . know," said Jukes—the lurching of the ship cut his speech as though somebody had been jerking him around while he talked—"how I got on with . . . that infernal job. We did it. And it may not matter in the end."

"Had to do what's fair, for all—they are only Chinamen. Give them the same chance with ourselves—hang it all. She isn't lost yet. Bad enough to be shut up below in a gale—"

"That's what I thought when you gave me the job, sir," interjected Jukes, moodily.

"—without being battered to pieces," pursued Captain MacWhirr with rising vehemence. "Couldn't let that go on in my ship, if I knew she hadn't five minutes to live. Couldn't bear it, Mr. Jukes."

A hollow echoing noise, like that of a shout rolling in a rocky chasm, approached the ship and went away again. The last star, blurred, enlarged, as if returning to the fiery mist of its beginning, struggled with the colossal depth of blackness hanging over the ship—and went out.

"Now for it!" muttered Captain MacWhirr. "Mr. Jukes."

"Here, sir."

The two men were growing indistinct to each other.

"We must trust her to go through it and come out on the other side. That's plain and straight. There's no room for Captain Wilson's storm-strategy here."

"No, sir."

"She will be smothered and swept again for hours," mumbled the Captain. "There's not much left by this time above deck for the sea to take away—unless you or me."

"Both, sir," whispered Jukes, breathlessly.

"You are always meeting trouble halfway, Jukes," Captain MacWhirr remonstrated quaintly. "Though it's a fact that the second mate is no good. D'ye hear, Mr. Jukes? You would be left alone if. . . ."

Captain MacWhirr interrupted himself, and Jukes, glancing on all sides, remained silent.

"Don't you be put out by anything," the Captain continued, mumbling rather fast. "Keep her facing it. They may say what they like, but the heaviest seas run with the wind. Facing it—always facing it—that's the way to get through. You are a young sailor. Face it. That's enough for any man. Keep a cool head."

"Yes, sir," said Jukes, with a flutter of the heart.

In the next few seconds the Captain spoke to the engine-room and got an answer.

For some reason Jukes experienced an access of confidence, a sensation that came from outside like a warm breath, and made him feel equal to every demand. The distant muttering of the darkness stole into his ears. He noted it unmoved, out of that sudden belief in himself, as a man safe in a shirt of mail would watch a point.

The ship labored without intermission amongst the black hills of water, paying with this hard tumbling the price of her life. She rumbled in her depths, shaking a white plummet of steam into the night, and

Jukes' thought skimmed like a bird through the engine-room, where Mr. Rout—good man—was ready. When the rumbling ceased it seemed to him that there was a pause of every sound, a dead pause in which Captain MacWhirr's voice rang out startlingly.

"What's that? A puff of wind?"—it spoke much louder than Jukes had ever heard it before—"On the bow. That's right. She may come out of it yet."

The mutter of the winds drew near apace. In the forefront could be distinguished a drowsy waking plaint passing on, and far off the growth of a multiple clamor, marching and expanding. There was the throb as of many drums in it, a vicious rushing note, and like the chant of a tramping multitude.

Jukes could no longer see his captain distinctly. The darkness was absolutely piling itself upon the ship. At most he made out movements, a hint of elbows spread out, of a head thrown up.

Captain MacWhirr was trying to do up the top button of his oilskin coat with unwonted haste. The hurricane, with its power to madden the seas, to sink ships, to uproot trees, to overturn strong walls and dash the very birds of the air to the ground, had found this taciturn man in its path, and, doing its utmost, had managed to wring out a few words. Before the renewed wrath of winds swooped on his ship, Captain MacWhirr was moved to declare, in a tone of vexation, as it were: "I wouldn't like to lose her."

He was spared that annoyance.

VI

On a bright sunshiny day, with the breeze chasing her smoke far ahead, the *Nan-Shan* came into Fu-chau. Her arrival was at once noticed on shore, and the seamen in harbor said: "Look! Look at that steamer. What's that? Siamese—isn't she? Just look at her!"

She seemed, indeed, to have been used as a running target for the secondary batteries of a cruiser. A hail of minor shells could not have given her upper works a more broken, torn, and devastated aspect; and she had about her the worn, weary air of ships coming from the far ends of the world—and indeed with truth, for in her short passage she had been very far; sighting, verily, even the coast of the Great Beyond, whence no ship ever returns to give up her crew to the dust of the earth. She was incrusted and gray with salt to the trucks of her masts and to the top of her funnel; as though (as some facetious seaman said) "the crowd on board had fished her out somewhere from the bottom of the sea and brought her in here for salvage." And further, excited by the felicity of his own wit, he offered to give five pounds for her—"as she stands."

Before she had been quite an hour at rest, a meager little man, with a red-tipped nose and a face cast in an angry mold, landed from a sampan on the quay of the Foreign Concession, and incontinently turned to shake his fist at her.

A tall individual, with legs much too thin for a rotund stomach, and with watery eyes, strolled up and remarked, "Just left her—eh? Quick work."

He wore a soiled suit of blue flannel with a pair of dirty cricketing shoes; a dingy gray moustache drooped from his lip, and daylight could be seen in two places between the rim and the crown of his hat.

"Hallo! what are you doing here?" asked the ex-second-mate of the *Nan-Shan*, shaking hands hurriedly.

"Standing by for a job—chance worth taking—got a quiet hint," explained the man with the broken hat, in jerky, apathetic wheezes.

The second shook his fist again at the *Nan-Shan*. "There's a fellow there that ain't fit to have the command of a scow," he declared, quivering with passion, while the other looked about listlessly.

"Is there?"

But he caught sight on the quay of a heavy seaman's chest, painted brown under a fringed sailcloth cover, and lashed with new manila line. He eyed it with awakened interest.

"I would talk and raise trouble if it wasn't for that damned Siamese flag. Nobody to go to—or I would make it hot for him. The fraud! Told his chief engineer—that's another fraud for you—I had lost my nerve. The greatest lot of ignorant fools that ever sailed the seas. No! You can't think. . . ."

"Got your money all right?" inquired his seedy acquaintance suddenly.

"Yes. Paid me off on board," raged the second mate. "'Get your breakfast on shore,' says he."

"Mean skunk!" commented the tall man, vaguely, and passed his tongue on his lips. "What about having a drink of some sort?"

"He struck me," hissed the second mate.

"No! Struck! You don't say?" The man in blue began to bustle about sympathetically. "Can't possibly talk here. I want to know all about it. Struck—eh? Let's get a fellow to carry your chest. I know a quiet place where they have some bottled beer. . . ."

Mr. Jukes, who had been scanning the shore through a pair of glasses, informed the chief engineer afterwards that "our late second mate hasn't been long in finding a friend. A chap looking uncommonly like a bummer. I saw them walk away together from the quay."

The hammering and banging of the needful repairs did not disturb Captain MacWhirr. The steward found in the letter he wrote, in a tidy chart room, passages of such absorbing interest that twice he was nearly caught in the act. But Mrs. MacWhirr, in the drawing room of the forty-pound house, stifled a yawn—perhaps out of self-respect—for she was alone.

She reclined in a plush-bottomed and gilt hammock-chair near a tiled fireplace, with Japanese fans on the mantel and a glow of coals in the grate. Lifting her hands, she glanced wearily here and there into the many pages. It was not her fault they were so prosy, so completely uninteresting—from "My darling wife" at the beginning, to "Your loving husband" at the end. She couldn't be really expected to understand all these ship affairs. She was glad, of course, to hear from him, but she had never asked herself why, precisely.

". . . They are called typhoons . . . The mate did not seem to like it . . . Not in books . . . Couldn't think of letting it go on. . . ."

The paper rustled sharply. ". . . . A calm that lasted more than twenty minutes," she read perfunctorily; and the next words her thoughtless eyes caught, on the top of another page, were: "see you and the children again. . . ." She had a movement of impatience. He was always thinking of coming home. He had never had such a good salary before. What was the matter now?

It did not occur to her to turn back overleaf to look. She would have found it recorded there that between 4 and 6 A. M. on December 25th, Captain MacWhirr did actually think that his ship could not possibly live another hour in such a sea, and that he would never see his wife and children again. Nobody was to know this (his letters got mislaid so quickly)—nobody whatever but the steward, who had been greatly impressed by that disclosure. So much so, that he tried to give the cook some idea of the "narrow squeak we all had" by saying solemnly, "The old man himself had a dam' poor opinion of our chance."

"How do you know?" asked, contemptuously, the cook, an old soldier. "He hasn't told you, maybe?"

"Well, he did give me a hint to that effect," the steward brazened it out.

"Get along with you! He will be coming to tell me next," jeered the old cook, over his shoulder.

Mrs. MacWhirr glanced farther, on the alert. ". . . Do what's fair. . . Miserable objects. . . . Only three, with a broken leg each, and one . . . Thought had better keep the matter quiet . . . hope to have done the fair thing. . . ."

She let fall her hands. No: there was nothing more about coming home. Must have been merely expressing a pious wish. Mrs. MacWhirr's mind was set at ease, and a black marble clock, priced by the local jeweler at £3 18s. 6d., had a discreet stealthy tick.

The door flew open, and a girl in the long-legged, short-frocked period of existence, flung into the room. A lot of colorless, rather lanky hair was scattered over her shoulders. Seeing her mother, she stood still, and directed her pale prying eyes upon the letter.

"From father," murmured Mrs. MacWhirr. "What have you done with your ribbon?"

The girl put her hands up to her head and pouted.

"He's well," continued Mrs. MacWhirr languidly. "At least I think so. He never says." She had a little laugh. The girl's face expressed a wandering indifference, and Mrs. MacWhirr surveyed her with fond pride.

"Go and get your hat," she said after a while. "I am going out to do some shopping. There is a sale at Linom's."

"Oh, how jolly!" uttered the child, impressively, in unexpectedly grave vibrating tones, and bounded out of the room.

It was a fine afternoon, with a gray sky and dry sidewalks. Outside the draper's Mrs. MacWhirr smiled upon a woman in a black mantle of generous proportions armored in jet and crowned with flowers blooming falsely above a bilious matronly countenance. They broke into a swift little babble of greetings and exclamations both together, very hurried, as if the street were ready to yawn open and swallow all that pleasure before it could be expressed.

Behind them the high glass doors were kept on the swing. People couldn't pass, men stood aside waiting patiently, and Lydia was absorbed in poking the end of her parasol between the stone flags. Mrs. MacWhirr talked rapidly.

"Thank you very much. He's not coming home yet. Of course it's very sad to have him away, but it's such a comfort to know he keeps so well." Mrs. MacWhirr drew breath. "The climate there agrees with him," she added, beamingly, as if poor MacWhirr had been away touring in China for the sake of his health.

Neither was the chief engineer coming home yet. Mr. Rout knew too well the value of a good billet.

"Solomon says wonders will never cease," cried Mrs. Rout joyously at the old lady in her armchair by the fire. Mr. Rout's mother moved slightly, her withered hands lying in black half-mittens on her lap.

The eyes of the engineer's wife fairly danced on the paper. "That captain of the ship he is in—a rather simple man, you remember, mother?—has done something rather clever, Solomon says."

"Yes, my dear," said the old woman meekly, sitting with bowed silvery head, and that air of inward stillness characteristic of very old people who seem lost in watching the last flickers of life. "I think I remember."

Solomon Rout, Old Sol, Father Sol, the Chief, "Rout, good man"—Mr. Rout, the condescending and paternal friend of youth, had been the baby of her many children—all dead by this time. And she remembered him best as a boy of ten—long before he went away to serve his apprenticeship in some great engineering works in the North.

She had seen so little of him since, she had gone through so many years, that she had now to retrace her steps very far back to recognize him plainly in the mist of time. Sometimes it seemed that her daughter-in-law was talking of some strange man.

Mrs. Rout, junior, was disappointed. "H'm. H'm." She turned the page. "How provoking! He doesn't say what it is. Says I couldn't understand how much there was in it. Fancy! What could it be so very clever? What a wretched man not to tell us!"

She read on without further remark soberly, and at last sat looking into the fire. The chief wrote just a word or two of the typhoon; but something had moved him to express an increased longing for the companionship of the jolly woman. "If it hadn't been that mother must be looked after, I would send you your passage money today. You could set up a small house out here. I would have a chance to see you sometimes then. We are not growing younger. . . ."

"He's well, mother," sighed Mrs. Rout, rousing herself.

"He always was a strong healthy boy," said the old woman, placidly.

But Mr. Jukes' account was really animated and very full. His friend in the Western Ocean trade imparted it freely to the other officers of his liner. "A chap I know writes to me about an extraordinary affair that happened on board his ship in that typhoon— you know—that we read of in the papers two months ago. It's the funniest thing! Just see for yourself what he says. I'll show you his letter."

There were phrases in it calculated to give the impression of light-hearted, indomitable resolution. Jukes had written them in good faith, for he felt thus when he wrote. He described with lurid effect the scenes in the 'tween-deck. ". . . It struck me in a flash that those confounded Chinamen couldn't tell we weren't a desperate kind of robbers. 'T isn't good to part the Chinaman from his money if he is the stronger party. We need have been desperate indeed to go thieving in such weather, but what could these beggars know of us? So, without thinking of it twice, I got the hands away in a jiffy. Our work was done—that the old man had set his heart on. We cleared out without staying to inquire how they felt. I am convinced that if they had not been so unmercifully shaken, and afraid—each individual one of them —to stand up, we would have been torn to pieces. Oh! It was pretty complete, I can tell you; and you may run to and fro across the Pond to the end of time before you find yourself with such a job on your hands."

After this he alluded professionally to the damage done to the ship, and went on thus:

"It was when the weather quieted down that the situation became confoundedly delicate. It wasn't made any better by us having been lately transferred to the Siamese flag; though the skipper can't see that it makes any difference—'as long as *we* are on board'—he says. There are feelings that this man simply hasn't got—and there's an end of it. You might just as well try to make a bedpost understand. But apart from this it is an infernally lonely state for a ship to be going about the China seas with no proper consuls, not even a gunboat of her own anywhere, nor a body to go to in case of some trouble.

"My notion was to keep these Johnnies under hatches for another fifteen hours or so; as we weren't much farther than that from Fu-chau. We would find there, most likely, some sort of a man-of-war, and once under her guns we were safe enough; for surely any skipper of a man-of-war—English, French or Dutch—would see white men through as far as row on board goes. We could get rid of them and their money afterwards by delivering them to their Mandarin or Taotai, or whatever they call these chaps in goggles you see being carried about in sedan chairs through their stinking streets.

"The old man wouldn't see it somehow. He wanted to keep the matter quiet. He got that notion into his head, and a steam windlass couldn't drag it out of him. He wanted as little fuss made as possible, for the sake of the ship's name and for the sake of the owners—'for the sake of all concerned,' says he, looking at me very hard. It made me angry hot. Of course you couldn't keep a thing like that quiet; but the chests had been secured in the usual manner and were safe enough for any earthly gale, while this had been an altogether fiendish business I couldn't give you even an idea of.

"Meantime, I could hardly keep on my feet. None of us had a spell of any sort for nearly thirty hours, and there the old man sat rubbing his chin, rubbing the top of his head, and so bothered he didn't even think of pulling his long boots off.

"'I hope, sir,' says I, 'you won't be letting them out on deck before we make ready for them in some shape or other.' Not, mind you, that I felt very sanguine about controlling these beggars if they meant to take charge. A trouble with a cargo of Chinamen is no child's play. I was dam' tired, too. 'I wish,' said I, 'you would let us throw the whole lot of these dollars down to them and leave them to fight it out amongst themselves, while we get a rest.'

"'Now you talk wild, Jukes,' says he, looking up in his slow way that makes you ache all over, somehow. 'We must plan out something that would be fair to all parties.'

"I had no end of work on hand, as you may imagine, so I set the hands going, and then I thought I would turn in a bit. I hadn't been asleep in my bunk ten minutes when in rushes the steward and begins to pull at my leg.

"'For God's sake, Mr. Jukes, come out! Come on deck quick, sir. Oh, do come out!'

"The fellow scared all the sense out of me. I didn't know what had happened: another hurricane—or what. Could hear no wind.

"'The Captain's letting them out. Oh, he is letting them out! Jump on deck, sir, and save us. The chief engineer has just run below for his revolver.'

"That's what I understood the fool to say. However, Father Rout swears he went in there only to get a clean pocket handkerchief. Anyhow, I made one jump into my trousers and flew on deck aft. There was certainly a good deal of noise going on forward of the bridge. Four of the hands with the bosun were at work abaft. I passed up to them some of the rifles all the ships on the China coast carry in the cabin, and led them on the bridge. On the way I ran against Old Sol, looking startled and sucking at an unlighted cigar.

"'Come along,' I shouted to him.

"We charged, the seven of us, up to the chart room. All was over. There stood the old man with his sea boots still drawn up to the hips and in shirtsleeves—got warm thinking it out, I suppose. Bun Hin's dandy clerk at his elbow, as dirty as a sweep, was still green in the face. I could see directly I was in for something.

"'What the devil are these monkey tricks, Mr. Jukes?' asks the old man, as angry as ever he could be. I tell you frankly it made me lose my tongue. 'For God's sake, Mr. Jukes,' says he, 'do take away these rifles from the men. Somebody's sure to get hurt before long if you don't. Damme, if this ship isn't worse than Bedlam! Look sharp now. I want you up here to help me and Bun Hin's Chinaman to count that money. You wouldn't mind lending a hand, too, Mr. Rout, now you are here. The more of us the better.'

"He had settled it all in his mind while I was having a snooze. Had we been an English ship, or only going to land our cargo of coolies in an English port, like Hong Kong, for instance, there would have been no end of inquiries and bother, claims for damages and so on. But these Chinamen know their officials better than we do.

"The hatches had been taken off already, and they were all on deck after a night and a day down below. It made you feel queer to see so many gaunt, wild faces together. The beggars stared about at the sky, at the sea, at the ship, as though they had expected the whole thing to have been blown to pieces. And no wonder! They had had a doing that would have shaken the soul out of a white man. But then they say a Chinaman has no soul. He has, though, something about him that is deuced tough. There was a fellow (amongst others of the badly hurt) who had had his eye all but knocked out. It stood out of his head the size of half a hen's egg. This would have laid out a white man on his back for a month; and yet there was that chap elbowing here and there in the crowd and talking to the others as if nothing had been the matter. They made a great hubbub amongst themselves, and whenever the old man showed his bald head on the foreside of the bridge, they would all leave off jawing and look at him from below.

"It seems that after he had done his thinking he made that Bun Hin's fellow go down and explain to them the only way they could get their money back. He told me afterwards that, all the coolies having worked in the same place and for the same length of time, he reckoned he would be doing the fair thing by them as near as possible if he shared all the cash we had picked up equally among the lot. You couldn't tell one man's dollars from another's, he said, and if you asked each man how much money he brought on board he was afraid they would lie, and he would find himself a long way short. I think he was right there. As to giving up the money to any Chinese official he could scare up in Fu-chau, he said he might just as well put the lot in his own pocket at once for all the good it would be to them. I suppose they thought so, too.

"We finished the distribution before dark. It was rather a sight: the sea running high, the ship a wreck to look at, these Chinamen staggering up on the bridge one by one for their share, and the old man still booted, and in his shirt-sleeves, busy paying out at the chart-room door, perspiring like anything, and now and then coming down sharp on myself or Father Rout about one thing or another not quite to his mind. He took the share of those who were disabled himself to them on the No. 2 hatch. There were three dollars left over, and these went to the three most damaged coolies, one to each. We turned-to afterwards, and shoveled out on deck heaps of wet rags, all sorts of fragments of things without shape, and that you couldn't give a name to, and let them settle the ownership themselves.

"This certainly is coming as near as can be to keeping the thing quiet for the benefit of all concerned. What's your opinion, you pampered mailboat swell? The old chief says that this was plainly the only thing that could be done. The skipper remarked to me the other day, 'There are things you find nothing about in books.' I think that he got out of it very well for such a stupid man."

The End of the Tether

I

For a long time after the course of the steamer *Sofala* had been altered for the land, the low swampy coast had retained its appearance of a mere smudge of darkness beyond a belt of glitter. The sunrays seemed to fall violently upon the calm sea—seemed to shatter themselves upon an adamantine surface into sparkling dust, into a dazzling vapor of light that blinded the eye and wearied the brain with its unsteady brightness.

Captain Whalley did not look at it. When his Serang, approaching the roomy cane arm-chair which he filled capably, had informed him in a low voice that the course was to be altered, he had risen at once and had remained on his feet, face forward, while the head of his ship swung through a quarter of a circle. He had not uttered a single word, not even the word to steady the helm. It was the Serang, an elderly, alert, little Malay, with a very dark skin, who murmured the order to the helmsman. And then slowly Captain Whalley sat down again in the arm-chair on the bridge and fixed his eyes on the deck between his feet.

He could not hope to see anything new upon this lane of the sea. He had been on these coasts for the last three years. From Low Cape to Malantan the distance was fifty miles, six hours' steaming for the old ship with the tide, or seven against. Then you steered straight for the land, and by-and-by three palms would appear on the sky, tall and slim, and with their disheveled heads in a bunch, as if in confidential criticism of the dark mangroves. The *Sofala* would be headed towards the sombre strip of the coast, which at a given moment, as the ship closed with it obliquely, would show several clean shining fractures— the brimful estuary of a river. Then on through a brown liquid, three parts water and one part black earth, on and on between the low shores, three parts black earth and one part brackish water, the *Sofala* would plow her way upstream, as she had done once every month for these seven years or more, long before he was aware of her existence, long before he had ever thought of having anything to do with her and her invariable voyages. The old ship ought to have known the road better than her men, who had not been kept so long at it without a change; better than the faithful Serang, whom he had brought over from his last ship to keep the captain's watch; better than he himself, who had been her captain for the last three years only. She could always be depended upon to make her courses. Her compasses were never out. She was no trouble at all to take about, as if her great age had given her knowledge, wisdom, and steadiness. She made her landfalls to a degree of the bearing, and almost to a minute of her allowed time. At any moment, as he sat on the bridge without looking up, or lay sleepless in his bed, simply by reckoning the days and the hours he could tell where he was—the precise spot of the beat. He knew it well, too, this monotonous huckster's round, up and down the Straits; he knew its order and its sights and its people. Malacca to begin with, in at daylight and out at dusk, to cross over with a rigid phosphorescent wake this highway of the Far East. Darkness and gleams on the water, clear stars on a black sky, perhaps the lights of a home steamer keeping her unswerving course in the middle, or maybe the elusive shadow of a native craft with her mat sails flitting by silently—and the low land on the other side in sight at daylight. At noon the three palms of the next place of call, up a sluggish river. The only white man residing there was a retired young sailor, with whom he had become friendly in the course of many voyages. Sixty miles farther on there was another place of call, a deep bay with only a couple of houses on the beach. And so on, in and out, picking up coastwise cargo here and there, and finishing with a hundred miles' steady steaming through the maze of an archipelago of small islands up to a large native town at the end of the beat. There was a three days' rest for the old ship before he started her again in inverse order, seeing the same shores from another bearing, hearing the same voices in the same places, back again to the *Sofala*'s port of registry on the great highway to the East, where he would take up a berth nearly opposite the big stone pile of the harbour office till it was time to start again on the old round of 1,600 miles and thirty days. Not a very enterprising life, this, for Captain Whalley, Henry Whalley, otherwise Dare-devil Harry Whalley, of the *Condor*, a famous clipper in her day. No. Not a very enterprising life for a man who had served famous firms, who had sailed famous ships (more than one or two of them his own); who had made famous passages, had been the pioneer of new routes and new trades; who had steered across the unsurveyed tracts of the South Seas, and had seen the sun rise on uncharted islands. Fifty years at sea, and forty out in the East ("a pretty thorough apprenticeship," he used to remark smilingly), had made him honorably known to a generation of shipowners and merchants in all the ports from Bombay clear over to where the East merges into the West upon the coast of the two Americas. His fame remained writ, not very large but plain enough, on the Admiralty charts. Was there not somewhere between Australia and China a Whalley Island and a Condor Reef? On that dangerous coral formation the celebrated clipper had hung stranded for three days, her captain and crew throwing her cargo overboard with one hand and with the other, as it were, keeping off her a flotilla of savage war-canoes. At that time neither the island nor the reef had any official existence. Later the officers of her Majesty's steam-vessel *Fusilier*, despatched to make a survey of the route, recognized in the adoption of these two names the enterprise of the man and the solidity of the ship. Besides, as anyone who cares may see, the *General Directory* vol. ii. p. 410, begins the description of the "Malotu or Whalley Passage" with the words: "This advantageous route, first discovered in 1850 by Captain Whalley in the ship *Condor*," etc., and ends by recommending it warmly to sailing vessels leaving the China ports for the south in the months from December to April inclusive.

This was the clearest gain he had out of life. Nothing could rob him of this kind of fame. The piercing of the Isthmus of Suez, like the breaking of a dam, had let in upon the East a flood of new ships, new men, new methods of trade. It had changed the face of the Eastern seas and the very spirit of their life; so that his early experiences meant nothing whatever to the new generation of seamen.

In those bygone days he had handled many thousands of pounds of his employers' money and of his own; he had attended faithfully, as by law a shipmaster is expected to do, to the conflicting interests of owners, charterers, and underwriters. He had never lost a ship or consented to a shady transaction; and he had lasted well, outlasting in the end the conditions that had gone to the making of his name. He had buried his wife (in the Gulf of Petchili), had married off his daughter to the man of her unlucky choice, and had lost more than an ample competence in the crash of the notorious Travancore and Deccan Banking Corporation, whose downfall had shaken the East like an earthquake. And he was sixty-five years old.

II

His age sat lightly enough on him; and of his ruin he was not ashamed. He had not been alone to believe in the stability of the Banking Corporation. Men whose judgment in matters of finance was as expert as his seamanship had commended the prudence of his investments, and had themselves lost much money in the great failure. The only difference between him and them was that he had lost his all. And yet not his all. There had remained to him from his lost fortune a very pretty little barque, *Fair Maid*, which he had bought to occupy his leisure of a retired sailor—"to play with," as he expressed it himself.

He had formally declared himself tired of the sea the year preceding his daughter's marriage. But after the young couple had gone to settle in Melbourne he found out that he could not make himself happy on shore. He was too much of a merchant sea-captain for mere yachting to satisfy him. He wanted the illusion of affairs; and his acquisition of the *Fair Maid* preserved the continuity of his life. He introduced her to his acquaintances in various ports as "my last command." When he grew too old to be trusted with a ship, he would lay her up and go ashore to be buried, leaving directions in his will to have the barque towed out and scuttled decently in deep water on the day of the funeral. His daughter would not grudge him the satisfaction of knowing that no stranger would handle his last command after him. With the fortune he was able to leave her, the value of a 500-ton barque was neither here nor there. All this would be said with a jocular twinkle in his eye: the vigourous old man had too much vitality for the sentimentalism of regret; and a little wistfully withal, because he was at home in life, taking a genuine pleasure in its feelings and its possessions; in the dignity of his reputation and his wealth, in his love for his daughter, and in his satisfaction with the ship—the plaything of his lonely leisure.

He had the cabin arranged in accordance with his simple ideal of comfort at sea. A big bookcase (he was a great reader) occupied one side of his stateroom; the portrait of his late wife, a flat bituminous oil-painting representing the profile and one long black ringlet of a young woman, faced his bed-place. Three chronometers ticked him to sleep and greeted him on waking with the tiny competition of their beats. He rose at five every day. The officer of the morning watch, drinking his early cup of coffee aft by the wheel, would hear through the wide orifice of the copper ventilators all the splashings, blowings, and splutterings of his captain's toilet. These noises would be followed by a sustained deep murmur of the Lord's Prayer recited in a loud earnest voice. Five minutes afterwards the head and shoulders of Captain Whalley emerged out of the companion-hatchway. Invariably he paused for a while on the stairs, looking all round at the horizon; upwards at the trim of the sails; inhaling deep draughts of the fresh air. Only then he would step out on the poop, acknowledging the hand raised to the peak of the cap with a majestic and benign "Good morning to you." He walked the deck till eight scrupulously. Sometimes, not above twice a year, he had to use a thick cudgel-like stick on account of a stiffness in the hip—a slight touch of rheumatism, he supposed. Otherwise he knew nothing of the ills of the flesh. At the ringing of the breakfast bell he went below to feed his canaries, wind up the chronometers, and take the head of the table. From there he had before his eyes the big carbon photographs of his daughter, her husband, and two fat-legged babies—his grandchildren—set in black frames into the maple-wood bulkheads of the cuddy. After breakfast he dusted the glass over these portraits himself with a cloth, and brushed the oil painting of his wife with a plummet kept suspended from a small brass hook by the side of the heavy gold frame. Then with the door of his state-room shut, he would sit down on the couch under the portrait to read a chapter out of a thick pocket Bible—her Bible. But on some days he only sat there for half an hour with his finger between the leaves and the closed book resting on his knees. Perhaps he had remembered suddenly how fond of boat-sailing she used to be.

She had been a real shipmate and a true woman, too. It was like an article of faith with him that there never had been, and never could be, a brighter, cheerier home anywhere afloat or ashore than his home under the poop-deck of the *Condor*, with the big main cabin all white and gold, garlanded as if for a perpetual festival with an unfading wreath. She had decorated the center of every panel with a cluster of home flowers. It took her a twelvemonth to go round the cuddy with this labor of love. To him it had remained a marvel of painting, the highest achievement of taste and skill; and as to old Swinburne, his mate, every time he came down to his meals he stood transfixed with admiration before the progress of the work. You could almost smell these roses, he declared, sniffing the faint flavour of turpentine which at that time pervaded the saloon, and (as he confessed afterwards) made him somewhat less hearty than usual in tackling his food. But there was nothing of the sort to interfere with his enjoyment of her singing. "Mrs. Whalley is a regular out-and-out nightingale, sir," he would pronounce with a judicial air after listening profoundly over the skylight to the very end of the piece. In fine weather, in the second dog-watch, the two men could hear her trills and roulades going on to the accompaniment of the piano in the cabin. On the very day they got engaged he had written to London for the instrument; but they had been married for over a year before it reached them, coming out round the Cape. The big case made part of the first direct general cargo landed in Hongkong harbour—an event that to the men who walked the busy quays of to-day seemed as hazily remote as the dark ages of history. But Captain Whalley could in a half-hour of solitude live again all his life, with its romance, its idyl, and its sorrow. He had to close her eyes himself. She went away from under the ensign like a sailor's wife, a sailor herself at heart. He had read the service over her, out of her own prayer-book, without a break in his voice. When he raised his eyes he could see old Swinburne facing him with his cap pressed to his breast, and his rugged, weather-beaten, impassive face streaming with drops of water like a lump of chipped red granite in a shower. It was all very well for that old sea-dog to cry. He had to read on to the end; but after the splash he did not remember much of what happened for the next few days. An elderly sailor of the crew, deft at needlework, put together a mourning frock for the child out of one of her black skirts.

He was not likely to forget; but you cannot dam up life like a sluggish stream. It will break out and flow over a man's troubles, it will close upon a sorrow like the sea upon a dead body, no matter how much love has gone to the bottom. And the world is not bad. People had been very kind to him; especially Mrs. Gardner, the wife of the senior partner in Gardner, Patteson, & Co., the owners of the *Condor*. It was she who volunteered to look after the little one, and in due course took her to England (something of a journey in those days, even by the overland mail route) with her own girls to finish her education. It was ten years before he saw her again.

As a little child she had never been frightened of bad weather; she would beg to be taken up on deck in the bosom of his oilskin coat to watch the big seas hurling themselves upon the *Condor*. The swirl and crash of the waves seemed to fill her small soul with a breathless delight. "A good boy spoiled," he used to say of her in joke. He had named her Ivy because of the sound of the word, and obscurely fascinated by a vague association of ideas. She had twined herself tightly round his heart, and he intended her to cling close to her father as to a tower of strength; forgetting while she was little, that in the nature of things she would probably elect to cling to someone else. But he loved life well enough for even that event to give him a certain satisfaction, apart from his more intimate feeling of loss.

After he had purchased the *Fair Maid* to occupy his loneliness, he hastened to accept a rather unprofitable freight to Australia simply for the opportunity of seeing his daughter in her own home. What made him dissatisfied there was not to see that she clung now to somebody else, but that the prop she had selected seemed on closer examination "a rather poor stick"—even in the matter of health. He disliked his son-in-law's studied civility perhaps more than his method of handling the sum of money he had given Ivy at her marriage. But of his apprehensions he said nothing. Only on the day of his departure, with the hall-door open all ready, holding her hands and looking steadily into her eyes, he had said, "You know, my dear, all I have is for you and the chicks. Mind you write to me openly." She had answered him by an almost imperceptible movement of her head. She resembled her mother in the colour of her eyes, and in character—and also in this, that she understood him without many words.

Sure enough she had to write; and some of these letters made Captain Whalley lift his white eye-brows. For the rest he considered he was reaping the true reward of his life by being thus able to produce on demand whatever was needed. He had not enjoyed himself so much in a way since his wife had died. Characteristically enough his son-in-law's punctuality in failure caused him at a distance to feel a sort of kindness towards the man. The fellow was so perpetually being jammed on a lee shore that to charge it all to his reckless navigation would be manifestly unfair. No, no! He knew well what that meant. It was bad luck. His own had been simply marvelous, but he had seen in his life too many good men—seamen and others—go under with the sheer weight of bad luck not to recognize the fatal signs. For all that, he was cogitating on the best way of tying up very strictly every penny he had to leave, when with a preliminary rumble of rumors (whose first sound reached him in Shanghai as it happened), the shock of the big failure came; and, after passing through the phases of stupor, of incredulity, of indignation, he had to accept the fact that he had nothing to speak of to leave.

Upon that, as if he had only waited for this catastrophe, the unlucky man, away there in Melbourne, gave up his unprofitable game, and sat down—in an invalid's bath-chair at that too. "He will never walk again," wrote the wife. For the first time in his life Captain Whalley was a bit staggered.

The *Fair Maid* had to go to work in bitter earnest now. It was no longer a matter of preserving alive the memory of Dare-devil Harry Whalley in the Eastern Seas, or of keeping an old man in pocket-money and clothes, with, perhaps, a bill for a few hundred first-class cigars thrown in at the end of the year. He would have to buckle-to, and keep her going hard on a scant allowance of gilt for the ginger-bread scrolls at her stem and stern.

This necessity opened his eyes to the fundamental changes of the world. Of his past only the familiar names remained, here and there, but the things and the men, as he had known them, were gone. The name of Gardner, Patteson, & Co. was still displayed on the walls of warehouses by the waterside, on the brass plates and window-panes in the business quarters of more than one Eastern port, but there was no longer a Gardner or a Patteson in the firm. There was no longer for Captain Whalley an arm-chair and a welcome in the private office, with a bit of business ready to be put in the way of an old friend, for the sake of bygone services. The husbands of the Gardner girls sat behind the desks in that room where, long after he had left the employ, he had kept his right of entrance in the old man's time. Their ships now had yellow funnels with black tops, and a time-table of appointed routes like a confounded service of tramways. The winds of December and June were all one to them; their captains (excellent young men he doubted not) were, to be sure, familiar with Whalley Island, because of late years the Government had established a white fixed light on the north end (with a red danger sector over the Condor Reef), but most of them would have been extremely surprised to hear that a flesh-and-blood Whalley still existed—an old man going about the world trying to pick up a cargo here and there for his little barque.

And everywhere it was the same. Departed the men who would have nodded appreciatively at the mention of his name, and would have thought themselves bound in honor to do something for Dare-devil Harry Whalley. Departed the opportunities which he would have known how to seize; and gone with them the white-winged flock of clippers that lived in the boisterous uncertain life of the winds, skimming big fortunes out of the foam of the sea. In a world that pared down the profits to an irreducible minimum, in a world that was able to count its disengaged tonnage twice over every day, and in which lean charters were snapped up by cable three months in advance, there were no chances of fortune for an individual wandering haphazard with a little barque—hardly indeed any room to exist.

He found it more difficult from year to year. He suffered greatly from the smallness of remittances he was able to send his daughter. Meantime he had given up good cigars, and even in the matter of inferior cheroots limited himself to six a day. He never told her of his difficulties, and she never enlarged upon her struggle to live. Their confidence in each other needed no explanations, and their perfect understanding endured without protestations of gratitude or regret. He would have been shocked if she had taken it into her head to thank him in so many words, but he found it perfectly natural that she should tell him she needed two hundred pounds.

He had come in with the *Fair Maid* in ballast to look for a freight in the *Sofala*'s port of registry, and her letter met him there. Its tenor was that it was no use mincing matters. Her only resource was in opening a boarding-house, for which the prospects, she judged, were good. Good enough, at any rate, to make her tell him frankly that with two hundred pounds she could make a start. He had torn the envelope open, hastily, on deck, where it was handed to him by the ship-chandler's runner, who had brought his mail at the moment of anchoring. For the second time in his life he was appalled, and remained stock-still at the cabin door with the paper trembling between his fingers. Open a boarding-house! Two hundred pounds for a start! The only resource! And he did not know where to lay his hands on two hundred pence.

All that night Captain Whalley walked the poop of his anchored ship, as though he had been about to close with the land in thick weather, and uncertain of his position after a run of many gray days without a sight of sun, moon, or stars. The black night twinkled with the guiding lights of seamen and the steady straight lines of lights on shore; and all around the *Fair Maid* the riding lights of ships cast trembling trails upon the water of the roadstead. Captain Whalley saw not a gleam anywhere till the dawn broke and he found out that his clothing was soaked through with the heavy dew.

His ship was awake. He stopped short, stroked his wet beard, and descended the poop ladder backwards, with tired feet. At the sight of him the chief officer, lounging about sleepily on the quarterdeck, remained open-mouthed in the middle of a great early-morning yawn.

"Good morning to you," pronounced Captain Whalley solemnly, passing into the cabin. But he checked himself in the doorway, and without looking back, "By the bye," he said, "there should be an empty wooden case put away in the lazarette. It has not been broken up—has it?"

The mate shut his mouth, and then asked as if dazed, "What empty case, sir?"

"A big flat packing-case belonging to that painting in my room. Let it be taken up on deck and tell the carpenter to look it over. I may want to use it before long."

The chief officer did not stir a limb till he had heard the door of the captain's stateroom slam within the cuddy. Then he beckoned aft the second mate with his forefinger to tell him that there was something "in the wind."

When the bell rang Captain Whalley's authoritative voice boomed out through a closed door, "Sit down and don't wait for me." And his impressed officers took their places, exchanging looks and whispers across the table. What! No breakfast? And after apparently knocking about all night on deck, too! Clearly, there was something in the wind. In the skylight above their heads, bowed earnestly over the plates, three wire cages rocked and rattled to the restless jumping of the hungry canaries; and they could detect the sounds of their "old man's" deliberate movements within his state-room. Captain Whalley was methodically winding up the chronometers, dusting the portrait of his late wife, getting a clean white shirt out of the drawers, making himself ready in his punctilious unhurried manner to go ashore. He could not have swallowed a single mouthful of food that morning. He had made up his mind to sell the *Fair Maid.*

III

Just at that time the Japanese were casting far and wide for ships of European build, and he had no difficulty in finding a purchaser, a speculator who drove a hard bargain, but paid cash down for the *Fair Maid*, with a view to a profitable resale. Thus it came about that Captain Whalley found himself on a certain afternoon descending the steps of one of the most important post-offices of the East with a slip of bluish paper in his hand. This was the receipt of a registered letter enclosing a draft for two hundred pounds, and addressed to Melbourne. Captain Whalley pushed the paper into his waistcoat-pocket, took his stick from under his arm, and walked down the street.

It was a recently opened and untidy thoroughfare with rudimentary side-walks and a soft layer of dust cushioning the whole width of the road. One end touched the slummy street of Chinese shops near the harbour, the other drove straight on, without houses, for a couple of miles, through patches of jungle-like vegetation, to the yard gates of the new Consolidated Docks Company. The crude frontages of the new Government buildings alternated with the blank fencing of vacant plots, and the view of the sky seemed to give an added spaciousness to the broad vista. It was empty and shunned by natives after business hours, as though they had expected to see one of the tigers from the neighborhood of the New Waterworks on the hill coming at a loping canter down the middle to get a Chinese shopkeeper for supper. Captain Whalley was not dwarfed by the solitude of the grandly planned street. He had too fine a presence for that. He was only a lonely figure walking purposefully, with a great white beard like a pilgrim, and with a thick stick that resembled a weapon. On one side the new Courts of Justice had a low and unadorned portico of squat columns half concealed by a few old trees left in the approach. On the other the pavilion wings of the new Colonial Treasury came out to the line of the street. But Captain Whalley, who had now no ship and no home, remembered in passing that on that very site when he first came out from England there had stood a fishing village, a few mat huts erected on piles between a muddy tidal creek and a miry pathway that went writhing into a tangled wilderness without any docks or waterworks.

No ship—no home. And his poor Ivy away there had no home either. A boarding-house is no sort of home though it may get you a living. His feelings were horribly rasped by the idea of the boarding-house. In his rank of life he had that truly aristocratic temperament characterized by a scorn of vulgar gentility and by prejudiced views as to the derogatory nature of certain occupations. For his own part he had always preferred sailing merchant ships (which is a straightforward occupation) to buying and selling merchandise of which the essence is to get the better of somebody in a bargain—an undignified trial of wits at best. His father had been Colonel Whalley (retired) of the H. E. I. Company's service, with very slender means besides his pension, but with distinguished connections. He could remember as a boy how frequently waiters at the inns, country tradesmen and small people of that sort, used to "My lord" the old warrior on the strength of his appearance.

Captain Whalley himself (he would have entered the Navy if his father had not died before he was fourteen) had something of a grand air which would have suited an old and glorious admiral; but he became lost like a straw in the eddy of a brook amongst the swarm of brown and yellow humanity filling a thoroughfare, that by contrast with the vast and empty avenue he had left seemed as narrow as a lane and absolutely riotous with life. The walls of the houses were blue; the shops of the Chinamen yawned like cavernous lairs; heaps of nondescript merchandise overflowed the gloom of the long range of arcades, and the fiery serenity of sunset took the middle of the street from end to end with a glow like the reflection of a fire. It fell on the bright colours and the dark faces of the bare-footed crowd, on the pallid yellow backs of the half-naked jostling coolies, on the accouterments of a tall Sikh trooper with a parted beard and fierce moustaches on sentry before the gate of the police compound. Looming very big above the heads in a red haze of dust, the tightly packed car of the cable tramway navigated cautiously up the human stream, with the incessant blare of its horn, in the manner of a steamer groping in a fog.

Captain Whalley emerged like a diver on the other side, and in the desert shade between the walls of closed warehouses removed his hat to cool his brow. A certain disrepute attached to the calling of a landlady of a boarding-house. These women were said to be rapacious, unscrupulous, untruthful; and though he contemned no class of his fellow-creatures—God forbid!—these were suspicions to which it was unseemly that a Whalley should lay herself open. He had not expostulated with her, however. He was confident she shared his feelings; he was sorry for her; he trusted her judgment; he considered it a merciful dispensation that he could help her once more—but in his aristocratic heart of hearts he would have found it more easy to reconcile himself to the idea of her turning seamstress. Vaguely he remembered reading years ago a touching piece called the "Song of the Shirt." It was all very well making songs about poor women. The granddaughter of Colonel Whalley, the landlady of a boarding-house! Pooh! He replaced his hat, dived into two pockets, and stopping a moment to apply a flaring match to the end of a cheap cheroot, blew an embittered cloud of smoke at a world that could hold such surprises.

Of one thing he was certain—that she was the own child of a clever mother. Now he had got over the wrench of parting with his ship, he perceived clearly that such a step had been unavoidable. Perhaps he had been growing aware of it all along with an unconfessed knowledge. But she, far away there, must have had an intuitive perception of it, with the pluck to face that truth and the courage to speak out—all the qualities which had made her mother a woman of such excellent counsel.

It would have had to come to that in the end! It was fortunate she had forced his hand. In another year or two it would have been an utterly barren sale. To keep the ship going he had been involving himself deeper every year. He was defenseless before the insidious work of adversity, to whose more open assaults he could present a firm front; like a cliff that stands unmoved the open battering of the sea, with a lofty ignorance of the treacherous backwash undermining its base. As it was, every liability satisfied, her request answered, and owing no man a penny, there remained to him from the proceeds a sum of five hundred pounds put away safely. In addition he had upon his person some forty odd dollars—enough to pay his hotel bill, providing he did not linger too long in the modest bedroom where he had taken refuge.

Scantily furnished, and with a waxed floor, it opened into one of the side-verandahs. The straggling building of bricks, as airy as a bird-cage, resounded with the incessant flapping of rattan screens worried by the wind between the whitewashed square pillars of the sea-front. The rooms were lofty, a ripple of sunshine flowed over the ceilings; and the periodical invasions of tourists from some passenger steamer in the harbour flitted through the wind-swept dusk of the apartments with the tumult of their unfamiliar voices and impermanent presences, like relays of migratory shades condemned to speed headlong round the earth without leaving a trace. The babble of their irruptions ebbed out as suddenly as it had arisen; the draughty corridors and the long chairs of the verandahs knew their sight-seeing hurry or their prostrate repose no more; and Captain Whalley, substantial and dignified, left well nigh alone in the vast hotel by each light-hearted skurry, felt more and more like a stranded tourist with no aim in view, like a forlorn traveler without a home. In the solitude of his room he smoked thoughtfully, gazing at the two sea-chests which held all that he could call his own in this world. A thick roll of charts in a sheath of sailcloth leaned in a corner; the flat packing-case containing the portrait in oils and the three carbon photographs had been pushed under the bed. He was tired of discussing terms, of assisting at surveys, of all the routine of the business. What to the other parties was merely the sale of a ship was to him a momentous event involving a radically new view of existence. He knew that after this ship there would be no other; and the hopes of his youth, the exercise of his abilities, every feeling and achievement of his manhood, had been indissolubly connected with ships. He had served ships; he had owned ships; and even the years of his actual retirement from the sea had been made bearable by the idea that he had only to stretch out his hand full of money to get a ship. He had been at liberty to feel as though he were the owner of all the ships in the world. The selling of this one was weary work; but when she passed from him at last, when he signed the last receipt, it was as though all the ships had gone out of the world together, leaving him on the shore of inaccessible oceans with seven hundred pounds in his hands.

Striding firmly, without haste, along the quay, Captain Whalley averted his glances from the familiar roadstead. Two generations of seamen born since his first day at sea stood between him and all these ships at the anchorage. His own was sold, and he had been asking himself, What next?

From the feeling of loneliness, of inward emptiness—and of loss, too, as if his very soul had been taken out of him forcibly—there had sprung at first a desire to start right off and join his daughter. "Here are the last pence," he would say to her; "take them, my dear. And here's your old father: you must take him too."

His soul recoiled, as if afraid of what lay hidden at the bottom of this impulse. Give up! Never! When one is thoroughly weary all sorts of nonsense come into one's head. A pretty gift it would have been for a poor woman—this seven hundred pounds with the incumbrance of a hale old fellow more than likely to last for years and years to come. Was he not as fit to die in harness as any of the youngsters in charge of these anchored ships out yonder? He was as solid now as ever he had been. But as to who would give him work to do, that was another matter. Were he, with his appearance and antecedents, to go about looking for a junior's berth, people, he was afraid, would not take him seriously; or else if he succeeded in impressing them, he would maybe obtain their pity, which would be like stripping yourself naked to be kicked. He was not anxious to give himself away for less than nothing. He had no use for anybody's pity. On the other hand, a command—the only thing he could try for with due regard for common decency—was not likely to be lying in wait for him at the corner of the next street. Commands don't go a-begging nowadays. Ever since he had come ashore to carry out the business of the sale he had kept his ears open, but had heard no hint of one being vacant in the port. And even if there had been one, his successful past itself stood in his way. He had been his own employer too long. The only credential he could produce was the testimony of his whole life. What better recommendation could anyone require? But vaguely he felt that the unique document would be looked upon as an archaic curiosity of the Eastern waters, a screed traced in obsolete words—in a half-forgotten language.

IV

Revolving these thoughts, he strolled on near the railings of the quay, broad-chested, without a stoop, as though his big shoulders had never felt the burden of the loads that must be carried between the cradle and the grave. No single betraying fold or line of care disfigured the reposeful modeling of his face. It was full and untanned; and the upper part emerged, massively quiet, out of the downward flow of silvery hair, with the striking delicacy of its clear complexion and the powerful width of the forehead. The first cast of his glance fell on you candid and swift, like a boy's; but because of the ragged snowy thatch of the eyebrows the affability of his attention acquired the character of a dark and searching scrutiny. With age he had put on flesh a little, had increased his girth like an old tree presenting no symptoms of decay; and even the opulent, lustrous ripple of white hairs upon his chest seemed an attribute of unquenchable vitality and vigour.

Once rather proud of his great bodily strength, and even of his personal appearance, conscious of his worth, and firm in his rectitude, there had remained to him, like the heritage of departed prosperity, the tranquil bearing of a man who had proved himself fit in every sort of way for the life of his choice. He strode on squarely under the projecting brim of an ancient Panama hat. It had a low crown, a crease through its whole diameter, a narrow black ribbon. Imperishable and a little discoloured, this headgear made it easy to pick him out from afar on thronged wharves and in the busy streets. He had never adopted the comparatively modern fashion of pipeclayed cork helmets. He disliked the form; and he hoped he could manage to keep a cool head to the end of his life without all these contrivances for hygienic ventilation. His hair was cropped close, his linen always of immaculate whiteness; a suit of thin gray flannel, worn threadbare but scrupulously brushed, floated about his burly limbs, adding to his bulk by the looseness of its cut. The years had mellowed the good-humoured, imperturbable audacity of his prime into a temper carelessly serene; and the leisurely tapping of his iron-shod stick accompanied his footfalls with a self-confident sound on the flagstones. It was impossible to connect such a fine presence and this unruffled aspect with the belittling troubles of poverty; the man's whole existence appeared to pass before you, facile and large, in the freedom of means as ample as the clothing of his body.

The irrational dread of having to break into his five hundred pounds for personal expenses in the hotel disturbed the steady poise of his mind. There was no time to lose. The bill was running up. He nourished the hope that this five hundred would perhaps be the means, if everything else failed, of obtaining some work which, keeping his body and soul together (not a matter of great outlay), would enable him to be of use to his daughter. To his mind it was her own money which he employed, as it were, in backing her father and solely for her benefit. Once at work, he would help her with the greater part of his earnings; he was good for many years yet, and this boarding-house business, he argued to himself, whatever the prospects, could not be much of a gold-mine from the first start. But what work? He was ready to lay hold of anything in an honest way so that it came quickly to his hand; because the five hundred pounds must be preserved intact for eventual use. That was the great point. With the entire five hundred one felt a substance at one's back; but it seemed to him that should he let it dwindle to four-fifty or even four-eighty, all the efficiency would be gone out of the money, as though there were some magic power in the round figure. But what sort of work?

Confronted by that haunting question as by an uneasy ghost, for whom he had no exorcising formula, Captain Whalley stopped short on the apex of a small bridge spanning steeply the bed of a canalized creek with granite shores. Moored between the square blocks a sea-going Malay prau floated half hidden under the arch of masonry, with her spars lowered down, without a sound of life on board, and covered from stem to stern with a ridge of palm-leaf mats. He had left behind him the overheated pavements bordered by the stone frontages that, like the sheer face of cliffs, followed the sweep of the quays; and an unconfined spaciousness of orderly and sylvan aspect opened before him its wide plots of rolled grass, like pieces of green carpet smoothly pegged out, its long ranges of trees lined up in colossal porticos of dark shafts roofed with a vault of branches.

Some of these avenues ended at the sea. It was a terraced shore; and beyond, upon the level expanse, profound and glistening like the gaze of a dark-blue eye, an oblique band of stippled purple lengthened itself indefinitely through the gap between a couple of verdant twin islets. The masts and spars of a few ships far away, hull down in the outer roads, sprang straight from the water in a fine maze of rosy lines penciled on the clear shadow of the eastern board. Captain Whalley gave them a long glance. The ship, once his own, was anchored out there. It was staggering to think that it was open to him no longer to take a boat at the jetty and get himself pulled off to her when the evening came. To no ship. Perhaps never more. Before the sale was concluded, and till the purchase-money had been paid, he had spent daily some time on board the *Fair Maid*. The money had been paid this very morning, and now, all at once, there was positively no ship that he could go on board of when he liked; no ship that would need his presence in order to do her work—to live. It seemed an incredible state of affairs, something too bizarre to last. And the sea was full of craft of all sorts. There was that prau lying so still swathed in her shroud of sewn palm-leaves—she, too, had her indispensable man. They lived through each other, this Malay he had never seen, and this high-sterned thing of no size that seemed to be resting after a long journey. And of all the ships in sight, near and far, each was provided with a man, the man without whom the finest ship is a dead thing, a floating and purposeless log.

After his one glance at the roadstead he went on, since there was nothing to turn back for, and the time must be got through somehow. The avenues of big trees ran straight over the Esplanade, cutting each other at diverse angles, columnar below and luxuriant above. The interlaced boughs high up there seemed to slumber; not a leaf stirred overhead: and the reedy cast-iron lamp-posts in the middle of the road, gilt like scepters, diminished in a long perspective, with their globes of white porcelain atop, resembling a barbarous decoration of ostriches' eggs displayed in a row. The flaming sky kindled a tiny crimson spark upon the glistening surface of each glassy shell.

With his chin sunk a little, his hands behind his back, and the end of his stick marking the gravel with a faint wavering line at his heels, Captain Whalley reflected that if a ship without a man was like a body without a soul, a sailor without a ship was of not much more account in this world than an aimless log adrift upon the sea. The log might be sound enough by itself, tough of fibre, and hard to destroy—but what of that! And a sudden sense of irremediable idleness weighted his feet like a great fatigue.

A succession of open carriages came bowling along the newly opened sea-road. You could see across the wide grass-plots the discs of vibration made by the spokes. The bright domes of the parasols swayed lightly outwards like full-blown blossoms on the rim of a vase; and the quiet sheet of dark-blue water, crossed by a bar of purple, made a background for the spinning wheels and the high action of the horses, whilst the turbaned heads of the Indian servants elevated above the line of the sea horizon glided rapidly on the paler blue of the sky. In an open space near the little bridge each turn-out trotted smartly in a wide curve away from the sunset; then pulling up sharp, entered the main alley in a long slow-moving file with the great red stillness of the sky at the back. The trunks of mighty trees stood all touched with red on the same side, the air seemed aflame under the high foliage, the very ground under the hoofs of the horses was red. The wheels turned solemnly; one after another the sunshades drooped, folding their colours like gorgeous flowers shutting their petals at the end of the day.

In the whole half-mile of human beings no voice uttered a distinct word, only a faint thudding noise went on mingled with slight jingling sounds, and the motionless heads and shoulders of men and women sitting in couples emerged stolidly above the lowered hoods—as if wooden. But one carriage and pair coming late did not join the line.

It fled along in a noiseless roll; but on entering the avenue one of the dark bays snorted, arching his neck and shying against the steel-tipped pole; a flake of foam fell from the bit upon the point of a satiny shoulder, and the dusky face of the coachman leaned forward at once over the hands taking a fresh grip of the reins. It was a long dark-green landau, having a dignified and buoyant motion between the sharply curved C-springs, and a sort of strictly official majesty in its supreme elegance. It seemed more roomy than is usual, its horses seemed slightly bigger, the appointments a shade more perfect, the servants perched somewhat higher on the box. The dresses of three women— two young and pretty, and one, handsome, large, of mature age— seemed to fill completely the shallow body of the carriage. The fourth face was that of a man, heavy lidded, distinguished and sallow, with a sombre, thick, iron-gray imperial and moustaches, which somehow had the air of solid appendages. His Excellency—

The rapid motion of that one equipage made all the others appear utterly inferior, blighted, and reduced to crawl painfully at a snail's pace. The landau distanced the whole file in a sort of sustained rush; the features of the occupant whirling out of sight left behind an impression of fixed stares and impassive vacancy; and after it had vanished in full flight as it were, notwithstanding the long line of vehicles hugging the curb at a walk, the whole lofty vista of the avenue seemed to lie open and emptied of life in the enlarged impression of an august solitude.

Captain Whalley had lifted his head to look, and his mind, disturbed in its meditation, turned with wonder (as men's minds will do) to matters of no importance. It struck him that it was to this port, where he had just sold his last ship, that he had come with the very first he had ever owned, and with his head full of a plan for opening a new trade with a distant part of the Archipelago. The then governor had given him no end of encouragement. No Excellency he—this Mr. Denham—this governor with his jacket off; a man who tended night and day, so to speak, the growing prosperity of the settlement with the self-forgetful devotion of a nurse for a child she loves; a lone bachelor who lived as in a camp with the few servants and his three dogs in what was called then the Government Bungalow: a low-roofed structure on the half-cleared slope of a hill, with a new flagstaff in front and a police orderly on the verandah. He remembered toiling up that hill under a heavy sun for his audience; the unfurnished aspect of the cool shaded room; the long table covered at one end with piles of papers, and with two guns, a brass telescope, a small bottle of oil with a feather stuck in the neck at the other—and the flattering attention given to him by the man in power. It was an undertaking full of risk he had come to expound, but a twenty minutes' talk in the Government Bungalow on the hill had made it go smoothly from the start. And as he was retiring Mr. Denham, already seated before the papers, called out after him, "Next month the *Dido* starts for a cruise that way, and I shall request her captain officially to give you a look in and see how you get on." The *Dido* was one of the smart frigates on the China station—and five-and-thirty years make a big slice of time. Five-and-thirty years ago an enterprise like his had for the colony enough importance to be looked after by a Queen's ship. A big slice of time. Individuals were of some account then. Men like himself; men, too, like poor Evans, for instance, with his red face, his coal-black whiskers, and his restless eyes, who had set up the first patent slip for repairing small ships, on the edge of the forest, in a lonely bay three miles up the coast. Mr. Denham had encouraged that enterprise, too, and yet somehow poor Evans had ended by dying at home deucedly hard up. His son, they said, was squeezing oil out of cocoa-nuts for a living on some God-forsaken islet of the Indian Ocean; but it was from that patent slip in a lonely wooded bay that had sprung the workshops of the Consolidated Docks Company, with its three graving basins carved out of solid rock, its wharves, its jetties, its electric-light plant, its steam-power houses— with its gigantic sheer-legs, fit to lift the heaviest weight ever carried afloat, and whose head could be seen like the top of a queer white monument peeping over bushy points of land and sandy promontories, as you approached the New Harbour from the west.

There had been a time when men counted: there were not so many carriages in the colony then, though Mr. Denham, he fancied, had a buggy. And Captain Whalley seemed to be swept out of the great avenue by the swirl of a mental backwash. He remembered muddy shores, a harbour without quays, the one solitary wooden pier (but that was a public work) jutting out crookedly, the first coal-sheds erected on Monkey Point, that caught fire mysteriously and smoldered for days, so that amazed ships came into a roadstead full of sulphurous fog, and the sun hung blood-red at midday. He remembered the things, the faces, and something more besides—like the faint flavour of a cup quaffed to the bottom, like a subtle sparkle of the air that was not to be found in the atmosphere of to-day.

In this evocation, swift and full of detail like a flash of magnesium light into the niches of a dark memorial hall, Captain Whalley contemplated things once important, the efforts of small men, the growth of a great place, but now robbed of all consequence by the greatness of accomplished facts, by hopes greater still; and they gave him for a moment such an almost physical grip upon time, such a comprehension of our unchangeable feelings, that he stopped short, struck the ground with his stick, and ejaculated mentally, "What the devil am I doing here!" He seemed lost in a sort of surprise; but he heard his name called out in wheezy tones once, twice—and turned on his heels slowly.

He beheld then, waddling towards him autocratically, a man of an old-fashioned and gouty aspect, with hair as white as his own, but with shaved, florid cheeks, wearing a necktie—almost a neckcloth—whose stiff ends projected far beyond his chin; with round legs, round arms, a round body, a round face—generally producing the effect of his short figure having been distended by means of an air-pump as much as the seams of his clothing would stand. This was the Master-Attendant of the port. A master-attendant is a superior sort of harbour-master; a person, out in the East, of some consequence in his sphere; a Government official, a magistrate for the waters of the port, and possessed of vast but ill-defined disciplinary authority over seamen of all classes. This particular Master-Attendant was reported to consider it miserably inadequate, on the ground that it did not include the power of life and death. This was a jocular exaggeration. Captain Eliott was fairly satisfied with his position, and nursed no inconsiderable sense of such power as he had. His conceited and tyrannical disposition did not allow him to let it dwindle in his hands for want of use. The uproarious, choleric frankness of his comments on people's character and conduct caused him to be feared at bottom. Though in conversation many pretended not to mind him in the least, others would only smile sourly at the mention of his name, and there were even some who dared to pronounce him "a meddlesome old ruffian." But for almost all of them one of Captain Eliott's outbreaks was nearly as distasteful to face as a chance of annihilation.

V

As soon as he had come up quite close he said, mouthing in a growl—

"What's this I hear, Whalley? Is it true you're selling the *Fair Maid?*"

Captain Whalley, looking away, said the thing was done—money had been paid that morning; and the other expressed at once his approbation of such an extremely sensible proceeding. He had got out of his trap to stretch his legs, he explained, on his way home to dinner. Sir Frederick looked well at the end of his time. Didn't he?

Captain Whalley could not say; had only noticed the carriage going past.

The Master-Attendant, plunging his hands into the pockets of an alpaca jacket inappropriately short and tight for a man of his age and appearance, strutted with a slight limp, and with his head reaching only to the shoulder of Captain Whalley, who walked easily, staring straight before him. They had been good comrades years ago, almost intimates. At the time when Whalley commanded the renowned *Condor*, Eliott had charge of the nearly as famous *Ringdove* for the same owners; and when the appointment of Master-Attendant was created, Whalley would have been the only other serious candidate. But Captain Whalley, then in the prime of life, was resolved to serve no one but his own auspicious Fortune. Far away, tending his hot irons, he was glad to hear the other had been successful. There was a worldly suppleness in bluff Ned Eliott that would serve him well in that sort of official appointment. And they were so dissimilar at bottom that as they came slowly to the end of the avenue before the Cathedral, it had never come into Whalley's head that he might have been in that man's place— provided for to the end of his days.

The sacred edifice, standing in solemn isolation amongst the converging avenues of enormous trees, as if to put grave thoughts of heaven into the hours of ease, presented a closed Gothic portal to the light and glory of the west. The glass of the rosace above the ogive glowed like fiery coal in the deep carvings of a wheel of stone. The two men faced about.

"I'll tell you what they ought to do next, Whalley," growled Captain Eliott suddenly.

"Well?"

"They ought to send a real live lord out here when Sir Frederick's time is up. Eh?"

Captain Whalley perfunctorily did not see why a lord of the right sort should not do as well as anyone else. But this was not the other's point of view.

"No, no. Place runs itself. Nothing can stop it now. Good enough for a lord," he growled in short sentences. "Look at the changes in our own time. We need a lord here now. They have got a lord in Bombay."

He dined once or twice every year at the Government House—a many-windowed, arcaded palace upon a hill laid out in roads and gardens. And lately he had been taking about a duke in his Master-Attendant's steam-launch to visit the harbour improvements. Before that he had "most obligingly" gone out in person to pick out a good berth for the ducal yacht. Afterwards he had an invitation to lunch on board. The duchess herself lunched with them. A big woman with a red face. Complexion quite sunburnt. He should think ruined. Very gracious manners. They were going on to Japan. . . .

He ejaculated these details for Captain Whalley's edification, pausing to blow out his cheeks as if with a pent-up sense of importance, and repeatedly protruding his thick lips till the blunt crimson end of his nose seemed to dip into the milk of his moustache. The place ran itself;

it was fit for any lord; it gave no trouble except in its Marine department—in its Marine department, he repeated twice, and after a heavy snort began to relate how the other day her Majesty's Consul-General in French Cochin-China had cabled to him—in his official capacity—asking for a qualified man to be sent over to take charge of a Glasgow ship whose master had died in Saigon.

"I sent word of it to the officers' quarters in the Sailors' Home," he continued, while the limp in his gait seemed to grow more accentuated with the increasing irritation of his voice. "Place's full of them. Twice as many men as there are berths going in the local trade. All hungry for an easy job. Twice as many—and—What d'you think, Whalley? . . ."

He stopped short; his hands clenched and thrust deeply downwards, seemed ready to burst the pockets of his jacket. A slight sigh escaped Captain Whalley.

"Hey? You would think they would be falling over each other. Not a bit of it. Frightened to go home. Nice and warm out here to lie about a verandah waiting for a job. I sit and wait in my office. Nobody. What did they suppose? That I was going to sit there like a dummy with the Consul-General's cable before me? Not likely. So I looked up a list of them I keep by me and sent word for Hamilton—the worst loafer of them all—and just made him go. Threatened to instruct the steward of the Sailors' Home to have him turned out neck and crop. He did not think the berth was good enough—if you—please. 'I've your little records by me,' said I. 'You came ashore here eighteen months ago, and you haven't done six months' work since. You are in debt for your board now at the Home, and I suppose you reckon the Marine Office will pay in the end. Eh? So it shall; but if you don't take this chance, away you go to England, assisted passage, by the first homeward steamer that comes along. You are no better than a pauper. We don't want any white paupers here.' I scared him. But look at the trouble all this gave me."

"You would not have had any trouble," Captain Whalley said almost involuntarily, "if you had sent for me."

Captain Eliott was immensely amused; he shook with laughter as he walked. But suddenly he stopped laughing. A vague recollection had crossed his mind. Hadn't he heard it said at the time of the Travancore and Deccan smash that poor Whalley had been cleaned out completely? "Fellow's hard up, by heavens!" he thought; and at once he cast a sidelong upward glance at his companion. But Captain Whalley was smiling austerely straight before him, with a carriage of the head inconceivable in a penniless man—and he became reassured. Impossible. Could not have lost everything. That ship had been only a hobby of his. And the reflection that a man who had confessed to receiving that very morning a presumably large sum of money was not likely to spring upon him a demand for a small loan put him entirely at his ease again. There had come a long pause in their talk, however, and not knowing how to begin again, he growled out soberly, "We old fellows ought to take a rest now."

"The best thing for some of us would be to die at the oar," Captain Whalley said, negligently.

"Come, now. Aren't you a bit tired by this time of the whole show?" muttered the other, sullenly.

"Are you?"

Captain Eliott was. Infernally tired. He only hung on to his berth so long in order to get his pension on the highest scale before he went home. It would be no better than poverty, anyhow; still, it was the only thing between him and the workhouse. And he had a family. Three girls, as Whalley knew. He gave "Harry, old boy," to understand that these three girls were a source of the greatest anxiety and worry to him. Enough to drive a man distracted.

"Why? What have they been doing now?" asked Captain Whalley with a sort of amused absent-mindedness.

"Doing! Doing nothing. That's just it. Lawn-tennis and silly novels from morning to night. . . ."

If one of them at least had been a boy. But all three! And, as ill-luck would have it, there did not seem to be any decent young fellows left in the world. When he looked around in the club he saw only a lot of conceited popinjays too selfish to think of making a good woman happy. Extreme indigence stared him in the face with all that crowd to keep at home. He had cherished the idea of building himself a little house in the country—in Surrey—to end his days in, but he was afraid it was out of the question . . . and his staring eyes rolled upwards with such a pathetic anxiety that Captain Whalley charitably nodded down at him, restraining a sort of sickening desire to laugh.

"You must know what it is yourself, Harry. Girls are the very devil for worry and anxiety."

"Ay! But mine is doing well," Captain Whalley pronounced slowly, staring to the end of the avenue.

The Master-Attendant was glad to hear this. Uncommonly glad. He remembered her well. A pretty girl she was.

Captain Whalley, stepping out carelessly, assented as if in a dream: "She was pretty."

The procession of carriages was breaking up.

One after another they left the file to go off at a trot, animating the vast avenue with their scattered life and movement; but soon the aspect of dignified solitude returned and took possession of the straight wide road. A syce in white stood at the head of a Burmah pony harnessed to a varnished two-wheel cart; and the whole thing waiting by the curb seemed no bigger than a child's toy forgotten under the soaring trees. Captain Eliott waddled up to it and made as if to clamber in, but refrained; and keeping one hand resting easily on the shaft, he changed the conversation from his pension, his daughters, and his poverty back again to the only other topic in the world—the Marine Office, the men and the ships of the port.

He proceeded to give instances of what was expected of him; and his thick voice drowsed in the still air like the obstinate droning of an enormous bumble-bee. Captain Whalley did not know what was the force or the weakness that prevented him from saying good-night and walking away. It was as though he had been too tired to make the effort. How queer. More queer than any of Ned's instances. Or was it that overpowering sense of idleness alone that made him stand there and listen to these stories? Nothing very real had ever troubled Ned Eliott; and gradually he seemed to detect deep in, as if wrapped up in the gross wheezy rumble, something of the clear hearty voice of the young captain of the *Ringdove*. He wondered if he, too, had changed to the same extent; and it seemed to him that the voice of his old chum had not changed so very much—that the man was the same. Not a bad fellow the pleasant, jolly Ned Eliott, friendly, well up to his business— and always a bit of a humbug. He remembered how he used to amuse his poor wife. She could read him like an open book. When the *Condor* and the *Ringdove* happened to be in port together, she would frequently ask him to bring Captain Eliott to dinner. They had not met often since those old days. Not once in five years, perhaps. He regarded from under his white eyebrows this man he could not bring himself to take into his confidence at this juncture; and the other went on with his intimate outpourings, and as remote from his hearer as though he had been talking on a hill-top a mile away.

He was in a bit of a quandary now as to the steamer *Sofala*. Ultimately every hitch in the port came into his hands to undo. They would miss him when he was gone in another eighteen months, and most likely some retired naval officer had been pitchforked into the appointment—a man that would understand nothing and care less. That steamer was a coasting craft having a steady trade connection as far north as Tenasserim; but the trouble was she could get no captain to take her on her regular trip. Nobody would go in her. He really had no power, of course, to order a man to take a job. It was all very well to stretch a point on the demand of a consul-general, but. . . .

"What's the matter with the ship?" Captain Whalley interrupted in measured tones.

"Nothing's the matter. Sound old steamer. Her owner has been in my office this afternoon tearing his hair."

"Is he a white man?" asked Whalley in an interested voice.

"He calls himself a white man," answered the Master-Attendant scornfully; "but if so, it's just skin-deep and no more. I told him that to his face too."

"But who is he, then?"

"He's the chief engineer of her. See *that*, Harry?"

"I see," Captain Whalley said thoughtfully. "The engineer. I see."

How the fellow came to be a shipowner at the same time was quite a tale. He came out third in a home ship nearly fifteen years ago, Captain Eliott remembered, and got paid off after a bad sort of row both with his skipper and his chief. Anyway, they seemed jolly glad to get rid of him at all costs. Clearly a mutinous sort of chap. Well, he remained out here, a perfect nuisance, everlastingly shipped and unshipped, unable to keep a berth very long; pretty nigh went through every engine-room afloat belonging to the colony. Then suddenly, "What do you think happened, Harry?"

Captain Whalley, who seemed lost in a mental effort as of doing a sum in his head, gave a slight start. He really couldn't imagine. The Master-Attendant's voice vibrated dully with hoarse emphasis. The man actually had the luck to win the second prize in the Manilla lottery. All these engineers and officers of ships took tickets in that gamble. It seemed to be a perfect mania with them all.

Everybody expected now that he would take himself off home with his money, and go to the devil in his own way. Not at all. The *Sofala*, judged too small and not quite modern enough for the sort of trade she was in, could be got for a moderate price from her owners, who had ordered a new steamer from Europe. He rushed in and bought her. This man had never given any signs of that sort of mental intoxication the mere fact of getting hold of a large sum of money may produce—not till he got a ship of his own; but then he went off his balance all at once: came bouncing into the Marine Office on some transfer business, with his hat hanging over his left eye and switching a little cane in his hand, and told each one of the clerks separately that "Nobody could put him out now. It was his turn. There was no one over him on earth, and there never would be either." He swaggered and strutted between the desks, talking at the top of his voice, and trembling like a leaf all the while, so that the current business of the office was suspended for the time he was in there, and everybody in the big room stood open-mouthed looking at his antics. Afterwards he could be seen during the hottest hours of the day with his face as red as fire rushing along up and down the quays to look at his ship from different points of view: he seemed inclined to stop every stranger he came across just to let them know "that there would be no longer anyone over him; he had bought a ship; nobody on earth could put him out of his engine-room now."

Good bargain as she was, the price of the *Sofala* took up pretty near all the lottery-money. He had left himself no capital to work with. That did not matter so much, for these were the halcyon days of steam coasting trade, before some of the home shipping firms had thought of establishing local fleets to feed their main lines. These, when once organized, took the biggest slices out of that cake, of course; and by and by a squad of confounded German tramps turned up east of Suez Canal and swept up all the crumbs. They prowled on the cheap to and fro along the coast and between the islands, like a lot of sharks in the water ready to snap up anything you let drop. And then the high old times were over for good; for years the *Sofala* had made no more, he judged, than a fair living. Captain Eliott looked upon it as his duty in every way to assist an English ship to hold her own; and it stood to reason that if for want of a captain the *Sofala* began to miss her trips she would very soon lose her trade. There was the quandary. The man was too impracticable. "Too much of a beggar on horseback from the first," he explained. "Seemed to grow worse as the time went on. In the last three years he's run through eleven skippers; he had tried every single man here, outside of the regular lines. I had warned him before that this would not do. And now, of course, no one will look at the *Sofala*. I had one or two men up at my office and talked to them; but, as they said to me, what was the good of taking the berth to lead a regular dog's life for a month and then get the sack at the end of the first trip? The fellow, of course, told me it was all nonsense; there has been a plot hatching for years against him. And now it had come. All the horrid sailors in the port had conspired to bring him to his knees, because he was an engineer." Captain Eliott emitted a throaty chuckle.

"And the fact is, that if he misses a couple more trips he need never trouble himself to start again. He won't find any cargo in his old trade. There's too much competition nowadays for people to keep their stuff lying about for a ship that does not turn up when she's expected. It's a bad lookout for him. He swears he will shut himself on board and starve to death in his cabin rather than sell her—even if he could find a buyer. And that's not likely in the least. Not even the Japs would give her insured value for her. It isn't like selling sailing-ships. Steamers *do* get out of date, besides getting old."

"He must have laid by a good bit of money though," observed Captain Whalley, quietly.

The Harbour-master puffed out his purple cheeks to an amazing size.

"Not a stiver, Harry. Not—a—single—sti-ver."

He waited; but as Captain Whalley, stroking his beard slowly, looked down on the ground without a word, he tapped him on the forearm, tiptoed, and said in a hoarse whisper—

"The Manila lottery has been eating him up."

He frowned a little, nodding in tiny affirmative jerks. They all were going in for it; a third of the wages paid to ships' officers ("in my port," he snorted) went to Manila. It was a mania. That fellow Massy had been bitten by it like the rest of them from the first; but after winning once he seemed to have persuaded himself he had only to try again to get another big prize. He had taken dozens and scores of tickets for every drawing since. What with this vice and his ignorance of affairs, ever since he had improvidently bought that steamer he had been more or less short of money.

This, in Captain Eliott's opinion, gave an opening for a sensible sailor-man with a few pounds to step in and save that fool from the consequences of his folly. It was his craze to quarrel with his captains. He had had some really good men, too, who would have been too glad to stay if he would only let them. But no. He seemed to think he was no owner unless he was kicking somebody out in the morning and having a row with the new man in the evening. What was wanted for him was a master with a couple of hundred or so to take an interest in the ship on proper conditions. You don't discharge a man for no fault, only because of the fun of telling him to pack up his traps and go ashore, when you know that in that case you are bound to buy back his share. On the other hand, a fellow with an interest in the ship is not likely to throw up his job in a huff about a trifle. He had told Massy that. He had said: "'This won't do, Mr. Massy. We are getting very sick of you here in the Marine Office. What you must do now is to try whether you could get a sailor to join you as partner. That seems to be the only way.' And that was sound advice, Harry."

Captain Whalley, leaning on his stick, was perfectly still all over, and his hand, arrested in the act of stroking, grasped his whole beard. And what did the fellow say to that?

The fellow had the audacity to fly out at the Master-Attendant. He had received the advice in a most impudent manner. "I didn't come here to be laughed at," he had shrieked. "I appeal to you as an Englishman and a shipowner brought to the verge of ruin by an illegal conspiracy of your beggarly sailors, and all you condescend to do for me is to tell me to go and get a partner!" . . . The fellow had presumed to stamp with rage on the floor of the private office. Where was he going to get a partner? Was he being taken for a fool? Not a single one of that contemptible lot ashore at the "Home" had twopence in his pocket to bless himself with. The very native curs in the bazaar knew that much. . . . "And it's true enough, Harry," rumbled Captain Eliott judicially. "They are much more likely one and all to owe money to the Chinamen in Denham Road for the clothes on their backs. 'Well,' said I, 'you make too much noise over it for my taste, Mr. Massy. Good morning.' He banged the door after him; he dared to bang my door, confound his cheek!"

The head of the Marine department was out of breath with indignation; then recollecting himself as it were, "I'll end by being late to dinner—yarning with you here. . . . wife doesn't like it."

He clambered ponderously into the trap; leaned out sideways, and only then wondered wheezily what on earth Captain Whalley could have been doing with himself of late. They had had no sight of each other for years and years till the other day when he had seen him unexpectedly in the office.

What on earth. . . .

Captain Whalley seemed to be smiling to himself in his white beard.

"The earth is big," he said vaguely.

The other, as if to test the statement, stared all round from his driving-seat. The Esplanade was very quiet; only from afar, from very far, a long way from the sea-shore, across the stretches of grass, through the long ranges of trees, came faintly the toot—toot—toot of the cable car beginning to roll before the empty peristyle of the Public Library on its three-mile journey to the New Harbour Docks.

"Doesn't seem to be so much room on it," growled the Master-Attendant, "since these Germans came along shouldering us at every turn. It was not so in our time."

He fell into deep thought, breathing stertorously, as though he had been taking a nap open-eyed. Perhaps he, too, on his side, had detected in the silent pilgrim-like figure, standing there by the wheel, like an arrested wayfarer, the buried lineaments of the features belonging to the young captain of the *Condor*. Good fellow—Harry Whalley—never very talkative. You never knew what he was up to—a bit too off-hand with people of consequence, and apt to take a wrong view of a fellow's actions. Fact was he had a too good opinion of himself. He would have liked to tell him to get in and drive him home to dinner. But one never knew. Wife would not like it.

"And it's funny to think, Harry," he went on in a big, subdued drone, "that of all the people on it there seems only you and I left to remember this part of the world as it used to be. . . ."

He was ready to indulge in the sweetness of a sentimental mood had it not struck him suddenly that Captain Whalley, unstirring and without a word, seemed to be awaiting something—perhaps expecting. . . . He gathered the reins at once and burst out in bluff hearty growls—

"Ha! My dear boy. The men we have known—the ships we've sailed—ay! and the things we've done. . . ."

The pony plunged—the syce skipped out of the way. Captain Whalley raised his arm.

"Good-bye."

VI

The sun had set. And when, after drilling a deep hole with his stick, he moved from that spot the night had massed its army of shadows under the trees. They filled the eastern ends of the avenue as if only waiting the signal for a general advance upon the open spaces of the world; they were gathering low between the deep stone-faced banks of the canal. The Malay prau, half concealed under the arch of the bridge, had not altered its position a quarter of an inch. For a long time Captain Whalley stared down over the parapet, till at last the floating immobility of that beshrouded thing seemed to grow upon him into something inexplicable and alarming. The twilight abandoned the zenith; its reflected gleams left the world below, and the water of the canal seemed to turn into pitch. Captain Whalley crossed it.

The turning to the right, which was his way to his hotel, was only a very few steps farther. He stopped again (all the houses of the sea-front were shut up, the quayside was deserted, but for one or two figures of natives walking in the distance) and began to reckon the amount of his bill. So many days in the hotel at so many dollars a day. To count the days he used his fingers: plunging one hand into his pocket, he jingled a few silver coins. All right for three days more; and then, unless something turned up, he must break into the five hundred—Ivy's money—invested in her father. It seemed to him that the first meal coming out of that reserve would choke him—for certain. Reason was of no use. It was a matter of feeling. His feelings had never played him false.

He did not turn to the right. He walked on, as if there still had been a ship in the roadstead to which he could get himself pulled off in the evening. Far away, beyond the houses, on the slope of an indigo promontory closing the view of the quays, the slim column of a factory-chimney smoked quietly straight up into the clear air. A Chinaman, curled down in the stern of one of the half-dozen sampans floating off the end of the jetty, caught sight of a beckoning hand. He jumped up, rolled his pigtail round his head swiftly, tucked in two rapid movements his wide dark trousers high up his yellow thighs, and by a single, noiseless, finlike stir of the oars, sheered the sampan alongside the steps with the ease and precision of a swimming fish.

"*Sofala*," articulated Captain Whalley from above; and the Chinaman, a new emigrant probably, stared upwards with a tense attention as if waiting to see the queer word fall visibly from the white man's lips. "*Sofala*," Captain Whalley repeated; and suddenly his heart failed him. He paused. The shores, the islets, the high ground, the low points, were dark: the horizon had grown sombre; and across the eastern sweep of the shore the white obelisk, marking the landing-place of the telegraph-cable, stood like a pale ghost on the beach before the dark spread of uneven roofs, intermingled with palms, of the native town. Captain Whalley began again:

"*Sofala*. Savee *So-fa-la*, John?"

This time the Chinaman made out that bizarre sound, and grunted his assent uncouthly, low down in his bare throat. With the first yellow twinkle of a star that appeared like the head of a pin stabbed deep into the smooth, pale, shimmering fabric of the sky, the edge of a keen chill seemed to cleave through the warm air of the earth. At the moment of stepping into the sampan to go and try for the command of the *Sofala* Captain Whalley shivered a little.

When on his return he landed on the quay again, Venus, like a choice jewel set low on the hem of the sky, cast a faint gold trail behind him upon the roadstead, as level as a floor made of one dark and polished stone. The lofty vaults of the avenues were black—all black overhead—and the porcelain globes on the lamp-posts resembled egg-shaped pearls, gigantic and luminous, displayed in a row whose farther end seemed to sink in the distance, down to the level of his knees. He put his hands behind his back. He would now consider calmly the discretion of it before saying the final word to-morrow. His feet scrunched the gravel loudly—the discretion of it. It would have been easier to appraise had there been a workable alternative. The honesty of it was indubitable: he meant well by the fellow; and periodically his shadow leaped up intense by his side on the trunks of the trees, to lengthen itself, oblique and dim, far over the grass—repeating his stride.

The discretion of it. Was there a choice? He seemed already to have lost something of himself; to have given up to a hungry specter something of his truth and dignity in order to live. But his life was necessary. Let poverty do its worst in exacting its toll of humiliation. It was certain that Ned Eliott had rendered him, without knowing it, a service for which it would have been impossible to ask. He hoped Ned would not think there had been something underhand in his action. He supposed that now when he heard of it he would understand—or perhaps he would only think Whalley an eccentric old fool. What would have been the good of telling him—any more than of blurting the whole tale to that man Massy? Five hundred pounds ready to invest. Let him make the best of that. Let him wonder. You want a captain—I want a ship. That's enough. B-r-r-r. What a disagreeable impression that empty, dark, echoing steamer had made upon him. . . .

A laid-up steamer was a dead thing and no mistake; a sailing-ship somehow seems always ready to spring into life with the breath of the incorruptible heaven; but a steamer, thought Captain Whalley, with her fires out, without the warm whiffs from below meeting you on her decks, without the hiss of steam, the clangs of iron in her breast—lies there as cold and still and pulseless as a corpse.

In the solitude of the avenue, all black above and lighted below, Captain Whalley, considering the discretion of his course, met, as it were incidentally, the thought of death. He pushed it aside with dislike and contempt. He almost laughed at it; and in the unquenchable vitality of his age only thought with a kind of exultation how little he needed to keep body and soul together. Not a bad investment for the poor woman

this solid carcass of her father. And for the rest—in case of anything—
the agreement should be clear: the whole five hundred to be paid back
to her integrally within three months. Integrally. Every penny. He was
not to lose any of her money whatever else had to go—a little dignity—
some of his self-respect. He had never before allowed anybody to
remain under any sort of false impression as to himself. Well, let that
go—for her sake. After all, he had never *said* anything misleading—
and Captain Whalley felt himself corrupt to the marrow of his bones.
He laughed a little with the intimate scorn of his worldly prudence.
Clearly, with a fellow of that sort, and in the peculiar relation they were
to stand to each other, it would not have done to blurt out everything.
He did not like the fellow. He did not like his spells of fawning
loquacity and bursts of resentfulness. In the end—a poor devil. He
would not have liked to stand in his shoes. Men were not evil, after all.
He did not like his sleek hair, his queer way of standing at right angles,
with his nose in the air, and glancing along his shoulder at you. No. On
the whole, men were not bad—they were only silly or unhappy.

Captain Whalley had finished considering the discretion of that
step—and there was the whole long night before him. In the full light
his long beard would glisten like a silver breastplate covering his heart;
in the spaces between the lamps his burly figure passed less distinct,
loomed very big, wandering, and mysterious. No; there was not much
real harm in men: and all the time a shadow marched with him, slanting
on his left hand—which in the East is a presage of evil.

* * * * *

"Can you make out the clump of palms yet, Serang?" asked
Captain Whalley from his chair on the bridge of the *Sofala* approaching
the bar of Batu Beru.

"No, Tuan. By and by see." The old Malay, in a blue dungaree suit,
planted on his bony dark feet under the bridge awning, put his hands
behind his back and stared ahead out of the innumerable wrinkles at the
corners of his eyes.

Captain Whalley sat still, without lifting his head to look for
himself. Three years—thirty-six times. He had made these palms thirty-
six times from the southward. They would come into view at the proper
time. Thank God, the old ship made her courses and distances trip after
trip, as correct as clockwork. At last he murmured again—

"In sight yet?"

"The sun makes a very great glare, Tuan."

"Watch well, Serang."

"Ya, Tuan."

A white man had ascended the ladder from the deck noiselessly,
and had listened quietly to this short colloquy. Then he stepped out on

the bridge and began to walk from end to end, holding up the long cherrywood stem of a pipe. His black hair lay plastered in long lanky wisps across the bald summit of his head; he had a furrowed brow, a yellow complexion, and a thick shapeless nose. A scanty growth of whisker did not conceal the contour of his jaw. His aspect was of brooding care; and sucking at a curved black mouthpiece, he presented such a heavy overhanging profile that even the Serang could not help reflecting sometimes upon the extreme unloveliness of some white men.

Captain Whalley seemed to brace himself up in his chair, but gave no recognition whatever to his presence. The other puffed jets of smoke; then suddenly—

"I could never understand that new mania of yours of having this Malay here for your shadow, partner."

Captain Whalley got up from the chair in all his imposing stature and walked across to the binnacle, holding such an unswerving course that the other had to back away hurriedly, and remained as if intimidated, with the pipe trembling in his hand. "Walk over me now," he muttered in a sort of astounded and discomfited whisper. Then slowly and distinctly he said—

"I—am—not—dirt." And then added defiantly, "As you seem to think."

The Serang jerked out—

"See the palms now, Tuan."

Captain Whalley strode forward to the rail; but his eyes, instead of going straight to the point, with the assured keen glance of a sailor, wandered irresolutely in space, as though he, the discoverer of new routes, had lost his way upon this narrow sea.

Another white man, the mate, came up on the bridge. He was tall, young, lean, with a moustache like a trooper, and something malicious in the eye. He took up a position beside the engineer. Captain Whalley, with his back to them, inquired—

"What's on the log?"

"Eighty-five," answered the mate quickly, and nudged the engineer with his elbow.

Captain Whalley's muscular hands squeezed the iron rail with an extraordinary force; his eyes glared with an enormous effort; he knitted his eyebrows, the perspiration fell from under his hat,—and in a faint voice he murmured, "Steady her, Serang—when she is on the proper bearing."

The silent Malay stepped back, waited a little, and lifted his arm warningly to the helmsman. The wheel revolved rapidly to meet the swing of the ship. Again the made nudged the engineer. But Massy turned upon him.

"Mr. Sterne," he said violently, "let me tell you—as a shipowner—

that you are no better than a confounded fool."

VII

Sterne went down smirking and apparently not at all disconcerted, but the engineer Massy remained on the bridge, moving about with uneasy self-assertion. Everybody on board was his inferior—everyone without exception. He paid their wages and found them in their food. They ate more of his bread and pocketed more of his money than they were worth; and they had no care in the world, while he alone had to meet all the difficulties of shipowning. When he contemplated his position in all its menacing entirety, it seemed to him that he had been for years the prey of a band of parasites: and for years he had scowled at everybody connected with the *Sofala* except, perhaps, at the Chinese firemen who served to get her along. Their use was manifest: they were an indispensable part of the machinery of which he was the master.

When he passed along his decks he shouldered those he came across brutally; but the Malay deck hands had learned to dodge out of his way. He had to bring himself to tolerate them because of the necessary manual labor of the ship which must be done. He had to struggle and plan and scheme to keep the *Sofala* afloat—and what did he get for it? Not even enough respect. They could not have given him enough of that if all their thoughts and all their actions had been directed to that end. The vanity of possession, the vainglory of power, had passed away by this time, and there remained only the material embarrassments, the fear of losing that position which had turned out not worth having, and an anxiety of thought which no abject subservience of men could repay.

He walked up and down. The bridge was his own after all. He had paid for it; and with the stem of the pipe in his hand he would stop short at times as if to listen with a profound and concentrated attention to the deadened beat of the engines (his own engines) and the slight grinding of the steering chains upon the continuous low wash of water alongside. But for these sounds, the ship might have been lying as still as if moored to a bank, and as silent as if abandoned by every living soul; only the coast, the low coast of mud and mangroves with the three palms in a bunch at the back, grew slowly more distinct in its long straight line; without a single feature to arrest attention. The native passengers of the *Sofala* lay about on mats under the awnings; the smoke of her funnel seemed the only sign of her life and connected with her gliding motion in a mysterious manner.

Captain Whalley on his feet, with a pair of binoculars in his hand and the little Malay Serang at his elbow, like an old giant attended by a wizened pigmy, was taking her over the shallow water of the bar.

This submarine ridge of mud, scoured by the stream out of the soft bottom of the river and heaped up far out on the hard bottom of the sea, was difficult to get over. The alluvial coast having no distinguishing marks, the bearings of the crossing-place had to be taken from the shape of the mountains inland. The guidance of a form flattened and uneven at the top like a grinder tooth, and of another smooth, saddle-backed summit, had to be searched for within the great unclouded glare that seemed to shift and float like a dry fiery mist, filling the air, ascending from the water, shrouding the distances, scorching to the eye. In this veil of light the near edge of the shore alone stood out almost coal-black with an opaque and motionless solidity. Thirty miles away the serrated range of the interior stretched across the horizon, its outlines and shades of blue, faint and tremulous like a background painted on airy gossamer on the quivering fabric of an impalpable curtain let down to the plain of alluvial soil; and the openings of the estuary appeared, shining white, like bits of silver let into the square pieces snipped clean and sharp out of the body of the land bordered with mangroves.

On the forepart of the bridge the giant and the pigmy muttered to each other frequently in quiet tones. Behind them Massy stood sideways with an expression of disdain and suspense on his face. His globular eyes were perfectly motionless, and he seemed to have forgotten the long pipe he held in his hand.

On the fore-deck below the bridge, steeply roofed with the white slopes of the awnings, a young lascar seaman had clambered outside the rail. He adjusted quickly a broad band of sail canvas under his armpits, and throwing his chest against it, leaned out far over the water. The sleeves of his thin cotton shirt, cut off close to the shoulder, bared his brown arm of full rounded form and with a satiny skin like a woman's. He swung it rigidly with the rotary and menacing action of a slinger: the 14-lb. weight hurtled circling in the air, then suddenly flew ahead as far as the curve of the bow. The wet thin line swished like scratched silk running through the dark fingers of the man, and the plunge of the lead close to the ship's side made a vanishing silvery scar upon the golden glitter; then after an interval the voice of the young Malay uplifted and long-drawn declared the depth of the water in his own language.

"Tiga stengah," he cried after each splash and pause, gathering the line busily for another cast. "Tiga stengah," which means three fathom and a half. For a mile or so from seaward there was a uniform depth of water right up to the bar. "Half-three. Half-three. Half-three,"—and his modulated cry, returned leisurely and monotonous, like the repeated call of a bird, seemed to float away in sunshine and disappear in the spacious silence of the empty sea and of a lifeless shore lying open, north and south, east and west, without the stir of a single cloud-shadow or the whisper of any other voice.

The owner-engineer of the *Sofala* remained very still behind the two seamen of different race, creed, and colour; the European with the time-defying vigour of his old frame, the little Malay, old, too, but slight and shrunken like a withered brown leaf blown by a chance wind under the mighty shadow of the other. Very busy looking forward at the land, they had not a glance to spare; and Massy, glaring at them from behind, seemed to resent their attention to their duty like a personal slight upon himself.

This was unreasonable; but he had lived in his own world of unreasonable resentments for many years. At last, passing his moist palm over the rare lanky wisps of coarse hair on the top of his yellow head, he began to talk slowly.

"A leadsman, you want! I suppose that's your correct mail-boat style. Haven't you enough judgment to tell where you are by looking at the land? Why, before I had been a twelvemonth in the trade I was up to that trick—and I am only an engineer. I can point to you from here where the bar is, and I could tell you besides that you are as likely as not to stick her in the mud in about five minutes from now; only you would call it interfering, I suppose. And there's that written agreement of ours, that says I mustn't interfere."

His voice stopped. Captain Whalley, without relaxing the set severity of his features, moved his lips to ask in a quick mumble—

"How near, Serang?"

"Very near now, Tuan," the Malay muttered, rapidly.

"Dead slow," said the Captain aloud in a firm tone.

The Serang snatched at the handle of the telegraph. A gong clanged down below. Massy with a scornful snigger walked off and put his head down the engineroom skylight.

"You may expect some rare fooling with the engines, Jack," he bellowed. The space into which he stared was deep and full of gloom; and the gray gleams of steel down there seemed cool after the intense glare of the sea around the ship. The air, however, came up clammy and hot on his face. A short hoot on which it would have been impossible to put any sort of interpretation came from the bottom cavernously. This was the way in which the second engineer answered his chief.

He was a middle-aged man with an inattentive manner, and apparently wrapped up in such a taciturn concern for his engines that he seemed to have lost the use of speech. When addressed directly his only answer would be a grunt or a hoot, according to the distance. For all the years he had been in the *Sofala* he had never been known to exchange as much as a frank Good-morning with any of his shipmates. He did not seem aware that men came and went in the world; he did not seem to see them at all. Indeed he never recognized his shipmates on shore. At table (the four white men of the *Sofala* messed together) he sat looking into his plate dispassionately, but at the end of the meal would jump up and bolt down below as if a sudden thought had impelled him to rush and see whether somebody had not stolen the engines while he dined. In port at the end of the trip he went ashore regularly, but no one knew where he spent his evenings or in what manner. The local coasting fleet had preserved a wild and incoherent tale of his infatuation for the wife of a sergeant in an Irish infantry regiment. The regiment, however, had done its turn of garrison duty there ages before, and was gone somewhere to the other side of the earth, out of men's knowledge. Twice or perhaps three times in the course of the year he would take too much to drink. On these occasions he would return on board at an earlier hour than usual; run across the deck balancing himself with his spread arms like a tight-rope walker; and locking the door of his cabin, he would converse and argue with himself the livelong night in an amazing variety of tones; storm, sneer, and whine with an inexhaustible persistence. Massy in his berth next door, raising himself on his elbow, would discover that his second had remembered the name of every white man that had passed through the *Sofala* for years and years back. He remembered the names of men that had died, that had gone home, that had gone to America: he remembered in his cups the names of men whose connection with the ship had been so short that Massy had almost forgotten its circumstances and could barely recall their faces. The inebriated voice on the other side of the bulkhead commented upon them all with an extraordinary and ingenious venom of scandalous inventions. It seems they had all offended him in some way, and in return he had found them all out. He muttered darkly; he laughed sardonically; he crushed them one after another; but of his chief, Massy, he babbled with an envious and naïve admiration. Clever scoundrel! Don't meet the likes of him every day. Just look at him. Ha! Great! Ship of his own. Wouldn't catch *him* going wrong. No fear—the beast! And Massy, after listening with a gratified smile to these artless tributes to his greatness, would begin to shout, thumping at the bulkhead with both fists—

"Shut up, you lunatic! Won't you let me go to sleep, you fool!"

But a half smile of pride lingered on his lips; outside the solitary lascar told off for night duty in harbour, perhaps a youth fresh from a forest village, would stand motionless in the shadows of the deck listening to the endless drunken gabble. His heart would be thumping with breathless awe of white men: the arbitrary and obstinate men who pursue inflexibly their incomprehensible purposes,—beings with weird intonations in the voice, moved by unaccountable feelings, actuated by inscrutable motives.

VIII

For a while after his second's answering hoot Massy hung over the engine-room gloomily. Captain Whalley, who, by the power of five hundred pounds, had kept his command for three years, might have been suspected of never having seen that coast before. He seemed unable to put down his glasses, as though they had been glued under his contracted eyebrows. This settled frown gave to his face an air of invincible and just severity; but his raised elbow trembled slightly, and the perspiration poured from under his hat as if a second sun had suddenly blazed up at the zenith by the side of the ardent still globe already there, in whose blinding white heat the earth whirled and shone like a mote of dust.

From time to time, still holding up his glasses, he raised his other hand to wipe his streaming face. The drops rolled down his cheeks, fell like rain upon the white hairs of his beard, and brusquely, as if guided by an uncontrollable and anxious impulse, his arm reached out to the stand of the engine-room telegraph.

The gong clanged down below. The balanced vibration of the dead-slow speed ceased together with every sound and tremor in the ship, as if the great stillness that reigned upon the coast had stolen in through her sides of iron and taken possession of her innermost recesses. The illusion of perfect immobility seemed to fall upon her from the luminous blue dome without a stain arching over a flat sea without a stir. The faint breeze she had made for herself expired, as if all at once the air had become too thick to budge; even the slight hiss of the water on her stem died out. The narrow, long hull, carrying its way without a ripple, seemed to approach the shoal water of the bar by stealth. The plunge of the lead with the mournful, mechanical cry of the lascar came at longer and longer intervals; and the men on her bridge seemed to hold their breath. The Malay at the helm looked fixedly at the compass card, the Captain and the Serang stared at the coast.

Massy had left the skylight, and, walking flat-footed, had returned softly to the very spot on the bridge he had occupied before. A slow, lingering grin exposed his set of big white teeth: they gleamed evenly in the shade of the awning like the keyboard of a piano in a dusky room.

At last, pretending to talk to himself in excessive astonishment, he said not very loud—

"Stop the engines now. What next, I wonder?"

He waited, stooping from the shoulders, his head bowed, his glance oblique. Then raising his voice a shade—

"If I dared make an absurd remark I would say that you haven't the stomach to. . . ."

But a yelling spirit of excitement, like some frantic soul wandering unsuspected in the vast stillness of the coast, had seized upon the body of the lascar at the lead. The languid monotony of his sing-song changed to a swift, sharp clamor. The weight flew after a single whirr, the line whistled, splash followed splash in haste. The water had shoaled, and the man, instead of the drowsy tale of fathoms, was calling out the soundings in feet.

"Fifteen feet. Fifteen, fifteen! Fourteen, fourteen. . . ."

Captain Whalley lowered the arm holding the glasses. It descended slowly as if by its own weight; no other part of his towering body stirred; and the swift cries with their eager warning note passed him by as though he had been deaf.

Massy, very still, and turning an attentive ear, had fastened his eyes upon the silvery, close-cropped back of the steady old head. The ship herself seemed to be arrested but for the gradual decrease of depth under her keel.

"Thirteen feet . . . Thirteen! Twelve!" cried the leadsman anxiously below the bridge. And suddenly the barefooted Serang stepped away noiselessly to steal a glance over the side.

Narrow of shoulder, in a suit of faded blue cotton, an old gray felt hat rammed down on his head, with a hollow in the nape of his dark neck, and with his slender limbs, he appeared from the back no bigger than a boy of fourteen. There was a childlike impulsiveness in the curiosity with which he watched the spread of the voluminous, yellowish convolutions rolling up from below to the surface of the blue water like massive clouds driving slowly upwards on the unfathomable sky. He was not startled at the sight in the least. It was not doubt, but the certitude that the keel of the *Sofala* must be stirring the mud now, which made him peep over the side.

His peering eyes, set aslant in a face of the Chinese type, a little old face, immovable, as if carved in old brown oak, had informed him long before that the ship was not headed at the bar properly. Paid off from the *Fair Maid*, together with the rest of the crew, after the completion of the sale, he had hung, in his faded blue suit and floppy gray hat, about the doors of the Harbour Office, till one day, seeing Captain Whalley coming along to get a crew for the *Sofala*, he had put himself quietly in the way, with his bare feet in the dust and an upward mute glance. The eyes of his old commander had fallen on him favourably—it must have been an auspicious day—and in less than half an hour the white men in the "Ofiss" had written his name on a document as Serang of the fire-ship *Sofala*. Since that time he had repeatedly looked at that estuary, upon that coast, from this bridge and from this side of the bar. The record of the visual world fell through his eyes upon his unspeculating mind as on a sensitized plate through the lens of a camera. His knowledge was absolute and precise;

nevertheless, had he been asked his opinion, and especially if questioned in the downright, alarming manner of white men, he would have displayed the hesitation of ignorance. He was certain of his facts—but such a certitude counted for little against the doubt what answer would be pleasing. Fifty years ago, in a jungle village, and before he was a day old, his father (who died without ever seeing a white face) had had his nativity cast by a man of skill and wisdom in astrology, because in the arrangement of the stars may be read the last word of human destiny. His destiny had been to thrive by the favour of various white men on the sea. He had swept the decks of ships, had tended their helms, had minded their stores, had risen at last to be a Serang; and his placid mind had remained as incapable of penetrating the simplest motives of those he served as they themselves were incapable of detecting through the crust of the earth the secret nature of its heart, which may be fire or may be stone. But he had no doubt whatever that the *Sofala* was out of the proper track for crossing the bar at Batu Beru.

It was a slight error. The ship could not have been more than twice her own length too far to the northward; and a white man at a loss for a cause (since it was impossible to suspect Captain Whalley of blundering ignorance, of want of skill, or of neglect) would have been inclined to doubt the testimony of his senses. It was some such feeling that kept Massy motionless, with his teeth laid bare by an anxious grin. Not so the Serang. He was not troubled by any intellectual mistrust of his senses. If his captain chose to stir the mud it was well. He had known in his life white men indulge in outbreaks equally strange. He was only genuinely interested to see what would come of it. At last, apparently satisfied, he stepped back from the rail.

He had made no sound: Captain Whalley, however, seemed to have observed the movements of his Serang. Holding his head rigidly, he asked with a mere stir of his lips—

"Going ahead still, Serang?"

"Still going a little, Tuan," answered the Malay. Then added casually, "She is over."

The lead confirmed his words; the depth of water increased at every cast, and the soul of excitement departed suddenly from the lascar swung in the canvas belt over the *Sofala*'s side. Captain Whalley ordered the lead in, set the engines ahead without haste, and averting his eyes from the coast directed the Serang to keep a course for the middle of the entrance.

Massy brought the palm of his hand with a loud smack against his thigh.

"You grazed on the bar. Just look astern and see if you didn't. Look at the track she left. You can see it plainly. Upon my soul, I thought you would! What made you do that? What on earth made you do that? I believe you are trying to scare me."

He talked slowly, as it were circumspectly, keeping his prominent black eyes on his captain. There was also a slight plaintive note in his rising choler, for, primarily, it was the clear sense of a wrong suffered undeservedly that made him hate the man who, for a beggarly five hundred pounds, claimed a sixth part of the profits under the three years' agreement. Whenever his resentment got the better of the awe the person of Captain Whalley inspired he would positively whimper with fury.

"You don't know what to invent to plague my life out of me. I would not have thought that a man of your sort would condescend. . . ."

He paused, half hopefully, half timidly, whenever Captain Whalley made the slightest movement in the deck-chair, as though expecting to be conciliated by a soft speech or else rushed upon and hunted off the bridge.

"I am puzzled," he went on again, with the watchful unsmiling baring of his big teeth. "I don't know what to think. I do believe you are trying to frighten me. You very nearly planted her on the bar for at least twelve hours, besides getting the engines choked with mud. Ships can't afford to lose twelve hours on a trip nowadays—as you ought to know very well, and do know very well to be sure, only. . . ."

His slow volubility, the sideways cranings of his neck, the black glances out of the very corners of his eyes, left Captain Whalley unmoved. He looked at the deck with a severe frown. Massy waited for some little time, then began to threaten plaintively.

"You think you've got me bound hand and foot in that agreement. You think you can torment me in any way you please. Ah! But remember it has another six weeks to run yet. There's time for me to dismiss you before the three years are out. You will do yet something that will give me the chance to dismiss you, and make you wait a twelvemonth for your money before you can take yourself off and pull out your five hundred, and leave me without a penny to get the new boilers for her. You gloat over that idea—don't you? I do believe you sit here gloating. It's as if I had sold my soul for five hundred pounds to be everlastingly damned in the end. . . ."

He paused, without apparent exasperation, then continued evenly—

". . . With the boilers worn out and the survey hanging over my head, Captain Whalley—Captain Whalley, I say, what do you do with your money? You must have stacks of money somewhere—a man like you must. It stands to reason. I am not a fool, you know, Captain Whalley—partner."

Again he paused, as though he had done for good. He passed his tongue over his lips, gave a backward glance at the Serang conning the ship with quiet whispers and slight signs of the hand. The wash of the propeller sent a swift ripple, crested with dark froth, upon a long flat spit of black slime. The *Sofala* had entered the river; the trail she had stirred up over the bar was a mile astern of her now, out of sight, had disappeared utterly; and the smooth, empty sea along the coast was left behind in the glittering desolation of sunshine. On each side of her, low down, the growth of sombre twisted mangroves covered the semi-liquid banks; and Massy continued in his old tone, with an abrupt start, as if his speech had been ground out of him, like the tune of a music-box, by turning a handle.

"Though if anybody ever got the best of me, it is you. I don't mind saying this. I've said it—there! What more can you want? Isn't that enough for your pride, Captain Whalley. You got over me from the first. It's all of a piece, when I look back at it. You allowed me to insert that clause about intemperance without saying anything, only looking very sick when I made a point of it going in black on white. How could I tell what was wrong about you? There's generally something wrong somewhere. And, lo and behold! when you come on board it turns out that you've been in the habit of drinking nothing but water for years and years."

His dogmatic reproachful whine stopped. He brooded profoundly, after the manner of crafty and unintelligent men. It seemed inconceivable that Captain Whalley should not laugh at the expression of disgust that overspread the heavy, yellow countenance. But Captain Whalley never raised his eyes—sitting in his arm-chair, outraged, dignified, and motionless.

"Much good it was to me," Massy remonstrated monotonously, "to insert a clause for dismissal for intemperance against a man who drinks nothing but water. And you looked so upset, too, when I read my draft in the lawyer's office that morning, Captain Whalley,—you looked so crestfallen, that I made sure I had gone home on your weak spot. A shipowner can't be too careful as to the sort of skipper he gets. You must have been laughing at me in your sleeve all the blessed time. . . . Eh? What are you going to say?"

Captain Whalley had only shuffled his feet slightly. A dull animosity became apparent in Massy's sideways stare.

"But recollect that there are other grounds of dismissal. There's habitual carelessness, amounting to incompetence—there's gross and persistent neglect of duty. I am not quite as big a fool as you try to make me out to be. You have been careless of late—leaving everything to that Serang. Why! I've seen you letting that old fool of a Malay take bearings for you, as if you were too big to attend to your work yourself. And what do you call that silly touch-and-go manner in which you took the ship over the bar just now? You expect me to put up with that?"

Leaning on his elbow against the ladder abaft the bridge, Sterne, the mate, tried to hear, blinking the while from the distance at the second engineer, who had come up for a moment, and stood in the engine-room companion. Wiping his hands on a bunch of cotton waste, he looked about with indifference to the right and left at the river banks slipping astern of the *Sofala* steadily.

Massy turned full at the chair. The character of his whine became again threatening.

"Take care. I may yet dismiss you and freeze to your money for a year. I may. . . ."

But before the silent, rigid immobility of the man whose money had come in the nick of time to save him from utter ruin, his voice died out in his throat.

"Not that I want you to go," he resumed after a silence, and in an absurdly insinuating tone. "I want nothing better than to be friends and renew the agreement, if you will consent to find another couple of hundred to help with the new boilers, Captain Whalley. I've told you before. She must have new boilers; you know it as well as I do. Have you thought this over?"

He waited. The slender stem of the pipe with its bulky lump of a bowl at the end hung down from his thick lips. It had gone out. Suddenly he took it from between his teeth and wrung his hands slightly.

"Don't you believe me?" He thrust the pipe bowl into the pocket of his shiny black jacket.

"It's like dealing with the devil," he said. "Why don't you speak? At first you were so high and mighty with me I hardly dared to creep about my own deck. Now I can't get a word from you. You don't seem to see me at all. What does it mean? Upon my soul, you terrify me with this deaf and dumb trick. What's going on in that head of yours? What are you plotting against me there so hard that you can't say a word? You will never make me believe that you—you—don't know where to lay your hands on a couple of hundred. You have made me curse the day I was born. . . ."

"Mr. Massy," said Captain Whalley, suddenly, without stirring.

The engineer started violently.

"If that is so I can only beg you to forgive me."

"Starboard," muttered the Serang to the helmsman; and the *Sofala* began to swing round the bend into the second reach.

"Ough!" Massy shuddered. "You make my blood run cold. What made you come here? What made you come aboard that evening all of a sudden, with your high talk and your money—tempting me? I always wondered what was your motive? You fastened yourself on me to have easy times and grow fat on my life blood, I tell you. Was that it? I believe you are the greatest miser in the world, or else why. . . ."

"No. I am only poor," interrupted Captain Whalley, stonily.

"Steady," murmured the Serang. Massy turned away with his chin on his shoulder.

"I don't believe it," he said in his dogmatic tone. Captain Whalley made no movement. "There you sit like a gorged vulture—exactly like a vulture."

He embraced the middle of the reach and both the banks in one blank, unseeing, circular glance, and left the bridge slowly.

IX

On turning to descend Massy perceived the head of Sterne the mate loitering, with his sly confident smile, his red moustaches and blinking eyes, at the foot of the ladder.

Sterne had been a junior in one of the larger shipping concerns before joining the *Sofala*. He had thrown up his berth, he said, "on general principles." The promotion in the employ was very slow, he complained, and he thought it was time for him to try and get on a bit in the world. It seemed as though nobody would ever die or leave the firm; they all stuck fast in their berths till they got mildewed; he was tired of waiting; and he feared that when a vacancy did occur the best servants were by no means sure of being treated fairly. Besides, the captain he had to serve under—Captain Provost—was an unaccountable sort of man and had taken a dislike to him for some reason or other. For doing rather more than his bare duty as likely as not. When he had done anything wrong he could take a talking to, like a man; but he expected to be treated like a man, too, and not to be addressed invariably as though he were a dog. He had asked Captain Provost plump and plain to tell him where he was at fault, and Captain Provost, in a most scornful way, had told him that he was a perfect officer, and that if he disliked the way he was being spoken to there was the gangway—he could take himself off ashore at once. But everybody knew what sort of man Captain Provost was. It was no use appealing to the office. Captain Provost had too much influence in the employ. All the same, they had to give him a good character. He made bold to say there was nothing in the world against him, and, as he had happened to hear that the mate of the *Sofala* had been taken to the hospital that morning with a sunstroke, he thought there would be no harm in seeing whether he would not do. . . .

He had come to Captain Whalley freshly shaved, red-faced, thin-flanked, throwing out his lean chest; and had recited his little tale with an open and manly assurance. Now and then his eyelids quivered slightly, his hand would steal up to the end of the flaming moustache; his eyebrows were straight, furry, of a chestnut colour, and the directness of his gaze seemed to tremble on the verge of impudence. Captain Whalley had engaged him temporarily; then, the other man having been ordered home by the doctors, Sterne had remained for the next trip, and then the next. He had now attained permanency, and the performance of his duties was marked by an air of serious, single-minded application. Directly he was spoken to, he began to smile attentively, with a great deference expressed in his whole attitude; but there was in the rapid winking which went on all the time something quizzical, as though he had possessed the secret of some universal joke cheating all creation and impenetrable to other mortals.

Grave and smiling he watched Massy come down step by step; when the chief engineer had reached the deck he swung about, and they found themselves face to face. Matched as to height and utterly dissimilar, they confronted each other as if there had been something between them—something else than the bright strip of sunlight that, falling through the wide lacing of two awnings, cut crosswise the narrow planking of the deck and separated their feet as it were a stream; something profound and subtle and incalculable, like an unexpressed understanding, a secret mistrust, or some sort of fear.

At last Sterne, blinking his deep-set eyes and sticking forward his scraped, clean-cut chin, as crimson as the rest of his face, murmured—

"You've seen? He grazed! You've seen?"

Massy, contemptuous, and without raising his yellow, fleshy countenance, replied in the same pitch—

"Maybe. But if it had been you we would have been stuck fast in the mud."

"Pardon me, Mr. Massy. I beg to deny it. Of course a shipowner may say what he jolly well pleases on his own deck. That's all right; but I beg to. . . ."

"Get out of my way!"

The other had a slight start, the impulse of suppressed indignation perhaps, but held his ground. Massy's downward glance wandered right and left, as though the deck all round Sterne had been bestrewn with eggs that must not be broken, and he had looked irritably for places where he could set his feet in flight. In the end he, too, did not move, though there was plenty of room to pass on.

"I heard you say up there," went on the mate—"and a very just remark it was, too—that there's always something wrong. . . ."

"Eavesdropping is what's wrong with *you*, Mr. Sterne."

"Now, if you would only listen to me for a moment, Mr. Massy, sir, I could. . . ."

"You are a sneak," interrupted Massy in a great hurry, and even managed to get so far as to repeat, "a common sneak," before the mate had broken in argumentatively—

"Now, sir, what is it you want? You want. . . ."

"I want—I want," stammered Massy, infuriated and astonished—"I want. How do you know that I want anything? How dare you? . . . What do you mean? . . . What are you after—you. . . ."

"Promotion." Sterne silenced him with candid bravado. The engineer's round soft cheeks quivered still, but he said quietly enough—

"You are only worrying my head off," and Sterne met him with a confident little smile.

"A chap in business I know (well up in the world he is now) used to tell me that this was the proper way. 'Always push on to the front,' he would say. 'Keep yourself well before your boss. Interfere whenever you get a chance. Show him what you know. Worry him into seeing you.' That was his advice. Now I know no other boss than you here. You are the owner, and no one else counts for *that* much in my eyes. See, Mr. Massy? I want to get on. I make no secret of it that I am one of the sort that means to get on. These are the men to make use of, sir. You haven't arrived at the top of the tree, sir, without finding that out— I dare say."

"Worry your boss in order to get on," repeated Massy, as if awestruck by the irreverent originality of the idea. "I shouldn't wonder if this was just what the Blue Anchor people kicked you out of their employ for. Is that what you call getting on? You shall get on in the same way here if you aren't careful—I can promise you."

At this Sterne hung his head, thoughtful, perplexed, winking hard at the deck. All his attempts to enter into confidential relations with his owner had led of late to nothing better than these dark threats of dismissal; and a threat of dismissal would check him at once into a hesitating silence as though he were not sure that the proper time for defying it had come. On this occasion he seemed to have lost his tongue for a moment, and Massy, getting in motion, heavily passed him by with an abortive attempt at shouldering. Sterne defeated it by stepping aside. He turned then swiftly, opening his mouth very wide as if to shout something after the engineer, but seemed to think better of it.

Always—as he was ready to confess—on the lookout for an opening to get on, it had become an instinct with him to watch the conduct of his immediate superiors for something "that one could lay hold of." It was his belief that no skipper in the world would keep his command for a day if only the owners could be "made to know." This romantic and naïve theory had led him into trouble more than once, but he remained incorrigible; and his character was so instinctively disloyal that whenever he joined a ship the intention of ousting his commander out of the berth and taking his place was always present at the back of his head, as a matter of course. It filled the leisure of his waking hours with the reveries of careful plans and compromising discoveries—the dreams of his sleep with images of lucky turns and favourable accidents. Skippers had been known to sicken and die at sea, than which nothing could be better to give a smart mate a chance of showing what he's made of. They also would tumble overboard sometimes: he had heard of one or two such cases. Others again. . . . But, as it were constitutionally, he was faithful to the belief that the conduct of no single one of them would stand the test of careful watching by a man who "knew what's what" and who kept his eyes "skinned pretty well" all the time.

After he had gained a permanent footing on board the *Sofala* he allowed his perennial hope to rise high. To begin with, it was a great advantage to have an old man for captain: the sort of man besides who in the nature of things was likely to give up the job before long from one cause or another. Sterne was greatly chagrined, however, to notice that he did not seem anyway near being past his work yet. Still, these old men go to pieces all at once sometimes. Then there was the owner-engineer close at hand to be impressed by his zeal and steadiness. Sterne never for a moment doubted the obvious nature of his own merits (he was really an excellent officer); only, nowadays, professional merit alone does not take a man along fast enough. A chap must have some push in him, and must keep his wits at work, too, to help him forward. He made up his mind to inherit the charge of this steamer if it was to be done at all; not indeed estimating the command of the *Sofala* as a very great catch, but for the reason that, out East especially, to make a start is everything, and one command leads to another.

He began by promising himself to behave with great circumspection; Massy's sombre and fantastic humours intimidated him as being outside one's usual sea experience; but he was quite intelligent enough to realize almost from the first that he was there in the presence of an exceptional situation. His peculiar prying imagination penetrated it quickly; the feeling that there was in it an element which eluded his grasp exasperated his impatience to get on. And so one trip came to an end, then another, and he had begun his third before he saw an opening by which he could step in with any sort of effect. It had all been very queer and very obscure; something had been going on near him, as if separated by a chasm from the common life and the working routine of the ship, which was exactly like the life and the routine of any other coasting steamer of that class.

Then one day he made his discovery.

It came to him after all these weeks of watchful observation and puzzled surmises, suddenly, like the long-sought solution of a riddle that suggests itself to the mind in a flash. Not with the same authority, however. Great heavens! Could it be that? And after remaining thunderstruck for a few seconds he tried to shake it off with self-contumely, as though it had been the product of an unhealthy bias towards the Incredible, the Inexplicable, the Unheard-of—the Mad!

This—the illuminating moment—had occurred the trip before, on the return passage. They had just left a place of call on the mainland called Pangu; they were steaming straight out of a bay. To the east a massive headland closed the view, with the tilted edges of the rocky strata showing through its ragged clothing of rank bushes and thorny creepers. The wind had begun to sing in the rigging; the sea along the coast, green and as if swollen a little above the line of the horizon, seemed to pour itself over, time after time, with a slow and thundering fall, into the shadow of the leeward cape; and across the wide opening the nearest of a group of small islands stood enveloped in the hazy yellow light of a breezy sunrise; still farther out the hummocky tops of other islets peeped out motionless above the water of the channels between, scoured tumultuously by the breeze.

The usual track of the *Sofala* both going and returning on every trip led her for a few miles along this reef-infested region. She followed a broad lane of water, dropping astern, one after another, these crumbs of the earth's crust resembling a squadron of dismasted hulks run in disorder upon a foul ground of rocks and shoals. Some of these fragments of land appeared, indeed, no bigger than a stranded ship; others, quite flat, lay awash like anchored rafts, like ponderous, black rafts of stone; several, heavily timbered and round at the base, emerged in squat domes of deep green foliage that shuddered darkly all over to the flying touch of cloud shadows driven by the sudden gusts of the squally season. The thunderstorms of the coast broke frequently over that cluster; it turned then shadowy in its whole extent; it turned more dark, and as if more still in the play of fire; as if more impenetrably silent in the peals of thunder; its blurred shapes vanished—dissolving utterly at times in the thick rain—to reappear clear-cut and black in the stormy light against the gray sheet of the cloud—scattered on the slaty round table of the sea. Unscathed by storms, resisting the work of years, unfretted by the strife of the world, there it lay unchanged as on that day, four hundred years ago, when first beheld by Western eyes from the deck of a high-pooped caravel.

It was one of these secluded spots that may be found on the busy sea, as on land you come sometimes upon the clustered houses of a hamlet untouched by men's restlessness, untouched by their need, by their thought, and as if forgotten by time itself. The lives of uncounted generations had passed it by, and the multitudes of seafowl, urging their way from all the points of the horizon to sleep on the outer rocks of the group, unrolled the converging evolutions of their flight in long, sombre streamers upon the glow of the sky. The palpitating cloud of their wings soared and stooped over the pinnacles of the rocks, over the rocks slender like spires, squat like martello towers; over the pyramidal heaps like fallen ruins, over the lines of bald boulders showing like a wall of stones battered to pieces and scorched by lightning—with the sleepy, clear glimmer of water in every breach. The noise of their continuous and violent screaming filled the air.

This great noise would meet the *Sofala* coming up from Batu Beru; it would meet her on quiet evenings, a pitiless and savage clamour enfeebled by distance, the clamour of seabirds settling to rest, and struggling for a footing at the end of the day. No one noticed it especially on board; it was the voice of their ship's unerring landfall, ending the steady stretch of a hundred miles. She had made good her course, she had run her distance till the punctual islets began to emerge one by one, the points of rocks, the hummocks of earth . . . and the cloud of birds hovered—the restless cloud emitting a strident and cruel uproar, the sound of the familiar scene, the living part of the broken land beneath, of the outspread sea, and of the high sky without a flaw.

But when the *Sofala* happened to close with the land after sunset she would find everything very still there under the mantle of the night. All would be still, dumb, almost invisible—but for the blotting out of the low constellations occulted in turns behind the vague masses of the islets whose true outlines eluded the eye amongst the dark spaces of the heaven: and the ship's three lights, resembling three stars—the red and the green with the white above—her three lights, like three companion stars wandering on the earth, held their unswerving course for the passage at the southern end of the group. Sometimes there were human eyes open to watch them come nearer, traveling smoothly in the sombre void; the eyes of a naked fisherman in his canoe floating over a reef. He thought drowsily: "Ha! The fire-ship that once in every moon goes in and comes out of Pangu Bay." More he did not know of her. And just as he had detected the faint rhythm of the propeller beating the calm water a mile and a half away, the time would come for the *Sofala* to alter her course, the lights would swing off him their triple beam—and disappear.

A few miserable, half-naked families, a sort of outcast tribe of long-haired, lean, and wild-eyed people, strove for their living in this lonely wilderness of islets, lying like an abandoned outwork of the land at the gates of the bay. Within the knots and loops of the rocks the water rested more transparent than crystal under their crooked and leaky canoes, scooped out of the trunk of a tree: the forms of the bottom undulated slightly to the dip of a paddle; and the men seemed to hang in the air, they seemed to hang enclosed within the fibres of a dark, sodden log, fishing patiently in a strange, unsteady, pellucid, green air above the shoals.

Their bodies stalked brown and emaciated as if dried up in the sunshine; their lives ran out silently; the homes where they were born, went to rest, and died—flimsy sheds of rushes and coarse grass eked out with a few ragged mats—were hidden out of sight from the open sea. No glow of their household fires ever kindled for a seaman a red spark upon the blind night of the group: and the calms of the coast, the flaming long calms of the equator, the unbreathing, concentrated calms like the deep introspection of a passionate nature, brooded awfully for days and weeks together over the unchangeable inheritance of their children; till at last the stones, hot like live embers, scorched the naked sole, till the water clung warm, and sickly, and as if thickened, about the legs of lean men with girded loins, wading thigh-deep in the pale blaze of the shallows. And it would happen now and then that the *Sofala*, through some delay in one of the ports of call, would heave in sight making for Pangu bay as late as noonday.

Only a blurring cloud at first, the thin mist of her smoke would arise mysteriously from an empty point on the clear line of sea and sky. The taciturn fishermen within the reefs would extend their lean arms toward the offing; and the brown figures stooping on the tiny beaches, the brown figures of men, women, and children grubbing in the sand in search of turtles' eggs, would rise up, crooked elbow aloft and hand over the eyes, to watch this monthly apparition glide straight on, swerve off—and go by. Their ears caught the panting of that ship; their eyes followed her till she passed between the two capes of the mainland going at full speed as though she hoped to make her way unchecked into the very bosom of the earth.

On such days the luminous sea would give no sign of the dangers lurking on both sides of her path. Everything remained still, crushed by the overwhelming power of the light; and the whole group, opaque in the sunshine,—the rocks resembling pinnacles, the rocks resembling spires, the rocks resembling ruins; the forms of islets resembling beehives, resembling mole-hills, the islets recalling the shapes of haystacks, the contours of ivy-clad towers,—would stand reflected together upside down in the unwrinkled water, like carved toys of ebony disposed on the silvered plate-glass of a mirror.

The first touch of blowing weather would envelop the whole at once in the spume of the windward breakers, as if in a sudden cloudlike burst of steam; and the clear water seemed fairly to boil in all the passages. The provoked sea outlined exactly in a design of angry foam the wide base of the group; the submerged level of broken waste and refuse left over from the building of the coast near by, projecting its dangerous spurs, all awash, far into the channel, and bristling with wicked long spits often a mile long: with deadly spits made of froth and stones.

And even nothing more than a brisk breeze—as on that morning, the voyage before, when the *Sofala* left Pangu Bay early, and Mr. Sterne's discovery was to blossom out like a flower of incredible and evil aspect from the tiny seed of instinctive suspicion—even such a breeze had enough strength to tear the placid mask from the face of the sea. To Sterne, gazing with indifference, it had been like a revelation to behold for the first time the dangers marked by the hissing livid patches on the water as distinctly as on the engraved paper of a chart. It came into his mind that this was the sort of day most favourable for a stranger attempting the passage: a clear day, just windy enough for the sea to break on every ledge, buoying, as it were, the channel plainly to the sight; whereas during a calm you had nothing to depend on but the compass and the practiced judgment of your eye. And yet the successive captains of the *Sofala* had had to take her through at night more than once. Nowadays you could not afford to throw away six or seven hours of a steamer's time. That you couldn't. But then use is everything, and with proper care. . . . The channel was broad and safe enough; the main point was to hit upon the entrance correctly in the dark—for if a man got himself involved in that stretch of broken water over yonder he would never get out with a whole ship—if he ever got out at all.

This was Sterne's last train of thought independent of the great discovery. He had just seen to the securing of the anchor, and had remained forward idling away a moment or two. The captain was in charge on the bridge. With a slight yawn he had turned away from his survey of the sea and had leaned his shoulders against the fish davit.

These, properly speaking, were the very last moments of ease he was to know on board the *Sofala*. All the instants that came after were to be pregnant with purpose and intolerable with perplexity. No more idle, random thoughts; the discovery would put them on the rack, till sometimes he wished to goodness he had been fool enough not to make it at all. And yet, if his chance to get on rested on the discovery of "something wrong," he could not have hoped for a greater stroke of luck.

X

The knowledge was too disturbing, really. There was "something wrong" with a vengeance, and the moral certitude of it was at first simply frightful to contemplate. Sterne had been looking aft in a mood so idle, that for once he was thinking no harm of anyone. His captain on the bridge presented himself naturally to his sight. How insignificant, how casual was the thought that had started the train of discovery—like an accidental spark that suffices to ignite the charge of a tremendous mine!

Caught under by the breeze, the awnings of the foredeck bellied upwards and collapsed slowly, and above their heavy flapping the gray stuff of Captain Whalley's roomy coat fluttered incessantly around his arms and trunk. He faced the wind in full light, with his great silvery beard blown forcibly against his chest; the eyebrows overhung heavily the shadows whence his glance appeared to be staring ahead piercingly. Sterne could just detect the twin gleam of the whites shifting under the shaggy arches of the brow. At short range these eyes, for all the man's affable manner, seemed to look you through and through. Sterne never could defend himself from that feeling when he had occasion to speak with his captain. He did not like it. What a big heavy man he appeared up there, with that little shrimp of a Serang in close attendance—as was usual in this extraordinary steamer! Confounded absurd custom that. He resented it. Surely the old fellow could have looked after his ship without that loafing native at his elbow. Sterne wriggled his shoulders with disgust. What was it? Indolence or what?

That old skipper must have been growing lazy for years. They all grew lazy out East here (Sterne was very conscious of his own unimpaired activity); they got slack all over. But he towered very erect on the bridge; and quite low by his side, as you see a small child looking over the edge of a table, the battered soft hat and the brown face of the Serang peeped over the white canvas screen of the rail.

No doubt the Malay was standing back, nearer to the wheel; but the great disparity of size in close association amused Sterne like the observation of a bizarre fact in nature. They were as queer fish out of the sea as any in it.

He saw Captain Whalley turn his head quickly to speak to his Serang; the wind whipped the whole white mass of the beard sideways. He would be directing the chap to look at the compass for him, or what not. Of course. Too much trouble to step over and see for himself. Sterne's scorn for that bodily indolence which overtakes white men in the East increased on reflection. Some of them would be utterly lost if they hadn't all these natives at their beck and call; they grew perfectly shameless about it, too. He was not of that sort, thank God! It wasn't in him to make himself dependent for his work on any shriveled-up little Malay like that. As if one could ever trust a silly native for anything in the world! But that fine old man thought differently, it seems. There they were together, never far apart; a pair of them, recalling to the mind an old whale attended by a little pilot-fish.

The fancifulness of the comparison made him smile. A whale with an inseparable pilot-fish! That's what the old man looked like; for it could not be said he looked like a shark, though Mr. Massy had called him that very name. But Mr. Massy did not mind what he said in his savage fits. Sterne smiled to himself—and gradually the ideas evoked by the sound, by the imagined shape of the word pilot-fish; the ideas of aid, of guidance needed and received, came uppermost in his mind: the word pilot awakened the idea of trust, of dependence, the idea of the welcome, clear-eyed help brought to the seaman groping for the land in the dark: groping blindly in fogs: feeling his way in the thick weather of the gales that, filling the air with a salt mist blown up from the sea, contract the range of sight on all sides to a shrunken horizon that seems within reach of the hand.

A pilot sees better than a stranger, because his local knowledge, like a sharper vision, completes the shapes of things hurriedly glimpsed; penetrates the veils of mist spread over the land by the storms of the sea; defines with certitude the outlines of a coast lying under the pall of fog, the forms of landmarks half buried in a starless night as in a shallow grave. He recognizes because he already knows. It is not to his far-reaching eye but to his more extensive knowledge that the pilot looks for certitude; for this certitude of the ship's position on which may depend a man's good fame and the peace of his conscience, the justification of the trust deposited in his hands, with his own life, too, which is seldom wholly his to throw away, and the humble lives of others rooted in distant affections, perhaps, and made as weighty as the lives of kings by the burden of the awaiting mystery. The pilot's knowledge brings relief and certitude to the commander of a ship; the Serang, however, in his fanciful suggestion of a pilot-fish attending a whale, could not in any way be credited with a superior knowledge. Why should he have it? These two men had come on that run together—the white and the brown—on the same day: and of course a white man would learn more in a week than the best native would in a month. He was made to stick to the skipper as though he were of some use—as the pilot-fish, they say, is to the whale. But how—it was very marked—how? A pilot-fish—a pilot—a . . . But if not superior knowledge then. . . .

Sterne's discovery was made. It was repugnant to his imagination, shocking to his ideas of honesty, shocking to his conception of mankind. This enormity affected one's outlook on what was possible in this world: it was as if for instance the sun had turned blue, throwing a new and sinister light on men and nature. Really in the first moment he had felt sickish, as though he had got a blow below the belt: for a second the very colour of the sea seemed changed—appeared queer to his wandering eye; and he had a passing, unsteady sensation in all his limbs as though the earth had started turning the other way.

A very natural incredulity succeeding this sense of upheaval brought a measure of relief. He had gasped; it was over. But afterwards during all that day sudden paroxysms of wonder would come over him in the midst of his occupations. He would stop and shake his head. The revolt of his incredulity had passed away almost as quick as the first emotion of discovery, and for the next twenty-four hours he had no sleep. That would never do. At meal-times (he took the foot of the table set up for the white men on the bridge) he could not help losing himself in a fascinated contemplation of Captain Whalley opposite. He watched the deliberate upward movements of the arm; the old man put his food to his lips as though he never expected to find any taste in his daily bread, as though he did not know anything about it. He fed himself like a somnambulist. "It's an awful sight," thought Sterne; and he watched the long period of mournful, silent immobility, with a big brown hand lying loosely closed by the side of the plate, till he noticed the two engineers to the right and left looking at him in astonishment. He would close his mouth in a hurry then, and lowering his eyes, wink rapidly at his plate. It was awful to see the old chap sitting there; it was even awful to think that with three words he could blow him up sky-high. All he had to do was to raise his voice and pronounce a single short sentence, and yet that simple act seemed as impossible to attempt as moving the sun out of its place in the sky. The old chap could eat in his terrific mechanical way; but Sterne, from mental excitement, could not—not that evening, at any rate.

He had had ample time since to get accustomed to the strain of the meal-hours. He would never have believed it. But then use is everything; only the very potency of his success prevented anything resembling elation. He felt like a man who, in his legitimate search for a loaded gun to help him on his way through the world, chances to come upon a torpedo—upon a live torpedo with a shattering charge in its head and a pressure of many atmospheres in its tail. It is the sort of weapon to make its possessor careworn and nervous. He had no mind to be blown up himself; and he could not get rid of the notion that the explosion was bound to damage him, too, in some way.

This vague apprehension had restrained him at first. He was able now to eat and sleep with that fearful weapon by his side, with the conviction of its power always in mind. It had not been arrived at by any reflective process; but once the idea had entered his head, the conviction had followed overwhelmingly in a multitude of observed little facts to which before he had given only a languid attention. The abrupt and faltering intonations of the deep voice; the taciturnity put on like an armour; the deliberate, as if guarded, movements; the long immobilities, as if the man he watched had been afraid to disturb the very air: every familiar gesture, every word uttered in his hearing, every sigh overheard, had acquired a special significance, a confirmatory import.

Every day that passed over the *Sofala* appeared to Sterne simply crammed full with proofs—with incontrovertible proofs. At night, when off duty, he would steal out of his cabin in pyjamas (for more proofs) and stand a full hour, perhaps, on his bare feet below the bridge, as absolutely motionless as the awning stanchion in its deck socket near by. On the stretches of easy navigation it is not usual for a coasting captain to remain on deck all the time of his watch. The Serang keeps it for him as a matter of custom; in open water, on a straight course, he is usually trusted to look after the ship by himself. But this old man seemed incapable of remaining quietly down below. No doubt he could not sleep. And no wonder. This was also a proof. Suddenly in the silence of the ship panting upon the still, dark sea, Sterne would hear a low voice above him exclaiming nervously—

"Serang!"

"Tuan!"

"You are watching the compass well?"

"Yes, I am watching, Tuan."

"The ship is making her course?"

"She is, Tuan. Very straight."

"It is well; and remember, Serang, that the order is, that you are to mind the helmsmen and keep a lookout with care, the same as if I were not on deck."

Then, when the Serang had made his answer, the low tones on the bridge would cease, and everything round Sterne seemed to become more still and more profoundly silent. Slightly chilled and with his back aching a little from long immobility, he would steal away to his room on the port side of the deck. He had long since parted with the last vestige of incredulity; of the original emotions, set into a tumult by the discovery, some trace of the first awe alone remained. Not the awe of the man himself—he could blow him up sky-high with six words—rather it was an awestruck indignation at the reckless perversity of avarice (what else could it be?), at the mad and sombre resolution that for the sake of a few dollars more seemed to set at nought the common rule of conscience and pretended to struggle against the very decree of Providence.

You could not find another man like this one in the whole round world—thank God. There was something devilishly dauntless in the character of such a deception which made you pause.

Other considerations occurring to his prudence had kept him tongue-tied from day to day. It seemed to him now that it would yet have been easier to speak out in the first hour of discovery. He almost regretted not having made a row at once. But then the very monstrosity of the disclosure . . . Why! He could hardly face it himself, let alone pointing it out to somebody else. Moreover, with a desperado of that sort one never knew. The object was not to get him out (that was as well as done already), but to step into his place. Bizarre as the thought seemed, he might have shown fight. A fellow up to working such a fraud would have enough cheek for anything; a fellow that, as it were, stood up against God Almighty Himself. He was a horrid marvel—that's what he was: he was perfectly capable of brazening out the affair scandalously till he got him (Sterne) kicked out of the ship and everlastingly damaged his prospects in this part of the East. Yet if you want to get on something must be risked. At times Sterne thought he had been unduly timid of taking action in the past; and what was worse, it had come to this, that in the present he did not seem to know what action to take.

Massy's savage moroseness was too disconcerting. It was an incalculable factor of the situation. You could not tell what there was behind that insulting ferocity. How could one trust such a temper? It did not put Sterne in bodily fear for himself, but it frightened him exceedingly as to his prospects.

Though of course inclined to credit himself with exceptional powers of observation, he had by now lived too long with his discovery. He had gone on looking at nothing else, till at last one day it occurred to him that the thing was so obvious that no one could miss seeing it. There were four white men in all on board the *Sofala*. Jack, the second engineer, was too dull to notice anything that took place out of his engine-room. Remained Massy—the owner—the interested person—nearly going mad with worry. Sterne had heard and seen more than enough on board to know what ailed him; but his exasperation seemed to make him deaf to cautious overtures. If he had only known it, there was the very thing he wanted. But how could you bargain with a man of that sort? It was like going into a tiger's den with a piece of raw meat in your hand. He was as likely as not to rend you for your pains. In fact, he was always threatening to do that very thing; and the urgency of the case, combined with the impossibility of handling it with safety, made Sterne in his watches below toss and mutter open-eyed in his bunk, for hours, as though he had been burning with fever.

Occurrences like the crossing of the bar just now were extremely alarming to his prospects. He did not want to be left behind by some swift catastrophe. Massy being on the bridge, the old man had to brace himself up, and make a show, he supposed. But it was getting very bad with him, very bad indeed, now. Even Massy had been emboldened to find fault this time; Sterne, listening at the foot of the ladder, had heard the other's whimpering and artless denunciations. Luckily the beast was very stupid and could not see the why of all this. However, small blame to him; it took a clever man to hit upon the cause. Nevertheless, it was high time to do something. The old man's game could not be kept up for many days more.

"I may yet lose my life at this fooling—let alone my chance," Sterne mumbled angrily to himself, after the stooping back of the chief engineer had disappeared round the corner of the skylight. Yes, no doubt—he thought; but to blurt out his knowledge would not advance his prospects. On the contrary, it would blast them utterly as likely as not. He dreaded another failure. He had a vague consciousness of not being much liked by his fellows in this part of the world; inexplicably enough, for he had done nothing to them. Envy, he supposed. People were always down on a clever chap who made no bones about his determination to get on. To do your duty and count on the gratitude of that brute Massy would be sheer folly. He was a bad lot. Unmanly! A vicious man! Bad! Bad! A brute! A brute without a spark of anything human about him; without so much as simple curiosity even, or else surely he would have responded in some way to all these hints he had been given. . . . Such insensibility was almost mysterious. Massy's state of exasperation seemed to Sterne to have made him stupid beyond the ordinary silliness of shipowners.

Sterne, meditating on the embarrassments of that stupidity, forgot himself completely. His stony, unwinking stare was fixed on the planks of the deck.

The slight quiver agitating the whole fabric of the ship was more perceptible in the silent river, shaded and still like a forest path. The *Sofala*, gliding with an even motion, had passed beyond the coast-belt of mud and mangroves. The shores rose higher, in firm sloping banks, and the forest of big trees came down to the brink. Where the earth had been crumbled by the floods it showed a steep brown cut, denuding a mass of roots intertwined as if wrestling underground; and in the air, the interlaced boughs, bound and loaded with creepers, carried on the struggle for life, mingled their foliage in one solid wall of leaves, with here and there the shape of an enormous dark pillar soaring, or a ragged opening, as if torn by the flight of a cannon-ball, disclosing the impenetrable gloom within, the secular inviolable shade of the virgin forest. The thump of the engines reverberated regularly like the strokes of a metronome beating the measure of the vast silence, the shadow of the western wall had fallen across the river, and the smoke pouring backwards from the funnel eddied down behind the ship, spread a thin dusky veil over the sombre water, which, checked by the flood-tide, seemed to lie stagnant in the whole straight length of the reaches.

Sterne's body, as if rooted on the spot, trembled slightly from top to toe with the internal vibration of the ship; from under his feet came sometimes a sudden clang of iron, the noisy burst of a shout below; to the right the leaves of the tree-tops caught the rays of the low sun, and seemed to shine with a golden green light of their own shimmering around the highest boughs which stood out black against a smooth blue sky that seemed to droop over the bed of the river like the roof of a tent. The passengers for Batu Beru, kneeling on the planks, were engaged in rolling their bedding of mats busily; they tied up bundles, they snapped the locks of wooden chests. A pockmarked peddler of small wares threw his head back to drain into his throat the last drops out of an earthenware bottle before putting it away in a roll of blankets. Knots of traveling traders standing about the deck conversed in low tones; the followers of a small Rajah from down the coast, broad-faced, simple young fellows in white drawers and round white cotton caps with their coloured sarongs twisted across their bronze shoulders, squatted on their hams on the hatch, chewing betel with bright red mouths as if they had been tasting blood. Their spears, lying piled up together within the circle of their bare toes, resembled a casual bundle of dry bamboos; a thin, livid Chinaman, with a bulky package wrapped up in leaves already thrust under his arm, gazed ahead eagerly; a wandering Kling rubbed his teeth with a bit of wood, pouring over the side a bright stream of water out of his lips; the fat Rajah dozed in a shabby deck-chair—and at the turn of every bend the two walls of leaves reappeared running parallel along the banks, with their impenetrable solidity fading at the top to a vaporous mistiness of countless slender twigs growing free, of young delicate branches shooting from the topmost limbs of hoary trunks, of feathery heads of climbers like delicate silver sprays standing up without a quiver. There was not a sign of a clearing anywhere; not a trace of human habitation, except when in one place, on the bare end of a low point under an isolated group of slender tree-ferns, the jagged, tangled remnants of an old hut on piles appeared with that peculiar aspect of ruined bamboo walls that look as if smashed with a club. Farther on, half hidden under the drooping bushes, a canoe containing a man and a woman together with a dozen green cocoanuts in a heap, rocked helplessly after the *Sofala* had passed, like a navigating contrivance of venturesome insects, of traveling ants; while two glassy folds of water streaming away from each bow of the steamer across the whole width of the river ran with her up stream smoothly, fretting their outer ends into a brown whispering tumble of froth against the miry foot of each bank.

"I must," thought Sterne, "bring that brute Massy to his bearings. It's getting too absurd in the end. Here's the old man up there buried in his chair—he may just as well be in his grave for all the use he'll ever be in the world—and the Serang's in charge. Because that's what he is. In charge. In the place that's mine by rights. I must bring that savage brute to his bearings. I'll do it at once, too. . . ."

When the mate made an abrupt start, a little brown, half-naked boy, with large black eyes, and the string of a written charm round his neck, became panic-struck at once. He dropped the banana he had been munching, and ran to the knee of a grave dark Arab in flowing robes, sitting like a Biblical figure, incongruously, on a yellow tin trunk corded with a rope of twisted rattan. The father, unmoved, put out his hand to pat the little shaven poll protectingly.

XI

Sterne crossed the deck upon the track of the chief engineer. Jack, the second, retreating backwards down the engine-room ladder, and still wiping his hands, treated him to an incomprehensible grin of white teeth out of his grimy hard face; Massy was nowhere to be seen. Sterne scratched at the door softly, then, putting his lips to the rose of the ventilator, said—

"I must speak to you, Mr. Massy. Just give me a minute or two."

"I am busy. Go away from my door."

"But pray, Mr. Massy. . . ."

"You go away. D'you hear? Take yourself off altogether—to the other end of the ship—quite away. . . ." The voice inside dropped low. "To the devil."

Sterne paused: then very quietly—

"It's rather pressing. When do you think you will be at liberty, sir?"

The answer to this was an exasperated "Never"; and at once Sterne, with a very firm expression of face, turned the handle.

Mr. Massy's stateroom—a narrow, one-berth cabin—smelt strongly of soap, and presented to view a swept, dusted, unadorned neatness, not so much bare as barren, not so much severe as starved and lacking in humanity, like the ward of a public hospital, or rather (owing to the small size) like the clean retreat of a desperately poor but exemplary person. Not a single photograph frame ornamented the bulkheads; not a single article of clothing, not as much as a spare cap, hung from the brass hooks. All the inside was painted in one plain tint of pale blue; two big sea-chests in sailcloth covers and with iron padlocks fitted exactly in the space under the bunk. One glance was enough to embrace all the strip of scrubbed planks within the four unconcealed corners. The absence of the usual settee was striking; the teak-wood top of the washing-stand seemed hermetically closed, and so was the lid of the writing-desk, which protruded from the partition at the foot of the bed-place, containing a mattress as thin as a pancake under a threadbare blanket with a faded red stripe, and a folded mosquito-net against the nights spent in harbour. There was not a scrap of paper anywhere in sight, no boots on the floor, no litter of any sort, not a speck of dust anywhere; no traces of pipe-ash even, which, in a heavy smoker, was morally revolting, like a manifestation of extreme hypocrisy; and the bottom of the old wooden arm-chair (the only seat there), polished with much use, shone as if its shabbiness had been waxed. The screen of leaves on the bank, passing as if unrolled endlessly in the round opening of the port, sent a wavering network of light and shade into the place.

Sterne, holding the door open with one hand, had thrust in his head and shoulders. At this amazing intrusion Massy, who was doing absolutely nothing, jumped up speechless.

"Don't call names," murmured Sterne, hurriedly. "I won't be called names. I think of nothing but your good, Mr. Massy."

A pause as of extreme astonishment followed. They both seemed to have lost their tongues. Then the mate went on with a discreet glibness:

"You simply couldn't conceive what's going on on board your ship. It wouldn't enter your head for a moment. You are too good—too—too upright, Mr. Massy, to suspect anybody of such a. . . . It's enough to make your hair stand on end."

He watched for the effect: Massy seemed dazed, uncomprehending. He only passed the palm of his hand on the coal-black wisps plastered across the top of his head. In a tone suddenly changed to confidential audacity Sterne hastened on:

"Remember that there's only six weeks left to run. . . ." The other was looking at him stonily . . . "So anyhow you shall require a captain for the ship before long."

Then only, as if that suggestion had scarified his flesh in the manner of red-hot iron, Massy gave a start and seemed ready to shriek. He contained himself by a great effort.

"Require—a—captain," he repeated with scathing slowness. "Who requires a captain? You dare to tell me that I need any of you humbugging sailors to run my ship. You and your likes have been fattening on me for years. It would have hurt me less to throw my money overboard. Pam—pe—red us—e—less f-f-f-frauds. The old ship knows as much as the best of you." He snapped his teeth audibly and growled through them. "The silly law requires a captain."

Sterne had taken heart of grace meantime.

"And the silly insurance people, too, as well," he said lightly. "But never mind that. What I want to ask is: Why shouldn't *I* do, sir? I don't say but you could take a steamer about the world as well as any of us sailors. I don't pretend to tell *you* that it is a very great trick. . . ." He emitted a short, hollow guffaw, familiarly. . . . "I didn't make the law—but there it is; and I am an active young fellow; I quite hold with your ideas; I know your ways by this time, Mr. Massy. I wouldn't try to give myself airs like that—that—er lazy specimen of an old man up there."

He put a marked emphasis on the last sentence, to lead Massy away from the track in case . . . but he did not doubt of now holding his success. The chief engineer seemed nonplused, like a slow man invited to catch hold of a whirligig of some sort.

"What you want, sir, is a chap with no nonsense about him, who would be content to be your sailing-master. Quite right, too. Well, I am fit for the work as much as that Serang. Because that's what it amounts to. Do you know, sir, that a dam' Malay like a monkey is in charge of your ship—and no one else? Just listen to his feet pit-patting above us on the bridge—real officer in charge. He's taking her up the river while the great man is wallowing in the chair—perhaps asleep; and if he is, that would not make it much worse either—take my word for it."

He tried to thrust himself farther in. Massy, with lowered forehead, one hand grasping the back of the arm-chair, did not budge.

"You think, sir, that the man has got you tight in his agreement. . . ." Massy raised a heavy snarling face at this. . . . "Well, sir, one can't help hearing of it on board. It's no secret. And it has been the talk on shore for years; fellows have been making bets about it. No, sir! It's *you* who have got him at your mercy. You will say that you can't dismiss him for indolence. Difficult to prove in court, and so on. Why, yes. But if you say the word, sir, I can tell you something about his indolence that will give you the clear right to fire him out on the spot and put me in charge for the rest of this very trip—yes, sir, before we leave Batu Beru—and make him pay a dollar a day for his keep till we get back, if you like. Now, what do you think of that? Come, sir. Say the word. It's really well worth your while, and I am quite ready to take your bare word. A definite statement from you would be as good as a bond."

His eyes began to shine. He insisted. A simple statement—and he thought to himself that he would manage somehow to stick in his berth as long as it suited him. He would make himself indispensable; the ship had a bad name in her port; it would be easy to scare the fellows off. Massy would have to keep him.

"A definite statement from me would be enough," Massy repeated, slowly.

"Yes, sir. It would." Sterne stuck out his chin cheerily and blinked at close quarters with that unconscious impudence which had the power to enrage Massy beyond anything.

The engineer spoke very distinctly:

"Listen well to me, then, Mr. Sterne: I wouldn't—d'ye hear?—I wouldn't promise you the value of two pence for anything *you* can tell me."

He struck Sterne's arm away with a smart blow, and catching hold of the handle pulled the door to. The terrific slam darkened the cabin instantaneously to his eyes as if after the flash of an explosion. At once he dropped into the chair. "Oh, no! You don't!" he whispered faintly.

The ship had in that place to shave the bank so close that the gigantic wall of leaves came gliding like a shutter against the port; the darkness of the primeval forest seemed to flow into that bare cabin with the odour of rotting leaves, of sodden soil—the strong muddy smell of the living earth steaming uncovered after the passing of a deluge. The bushes swished loudly alongside; above there was a series of crackling sounds, with a sharp rain of small broken branches falling on the bridge; a creeper with a great rustle snapped on the head of a boat davit, and a long, luxuriant green twig actually whipped in and out of the open port, leaving behind a few torn leaves that remained suddenly at rest on Mr. Massy's blanket. Then, the ship sheering out in the stream, the light began to return, but did not augment beyond a subdued clearness: for the sun was very low already, and the river, wending its sinuous course through a multitude of secular trees as if at the bottom of a precipitous gorge, had been already invaded by a deepening gloom—the swift precursor of the night.

"Oh, no, you don't!" murmured the engineer again. His lips trembled almost imperceptibly; his hands, too, a little: and to calm himself he opened the writing-desk, spread out a sheet of thin grayish paper covered with a mass of printed figures and began to scan them attentively for the twentieth time this trip at least.

With his elbows propped, his head between his hands, he seemed to lose himself in the study of an abstruse problem in mathematics. It was the list of the winning numbers from the last drawing of the great lottery which had been the one inspiring fact of so many years of his existence. The conception of a life deprived of that periodical sheet of paper had slipped away from him entirely, as another man, according to his nature, would not have been able to conceive a world without fresh air, without activity, or without affection. A great pile of flimsy sheets had been growing for years in his desk, while the *Sofala*, driven by the faithful Jack, wore out her boilers in tramping up and down the Straits, from cape to cape, from river to river, from bay to bay; accumulating by that hard labour of an overworked, starved ship the blackened mass of these documents. Massy kept them under lock and key like a treasure. There was in them, as in the experience of life, the fascination of hope, the excitement of a half-penetrated mystery, the longing of a half-satisfied desire.

For days together, on a trip, he would shut himself up in his berth with them: the thump of the toiling engines pulsated in his ear; and he would weary his brain poring over the rows of disconnected figures, bewildering by their senseless sequence, resembling the hazards of destiny itself. He nourished a conviction that there must be some logic lurking somewhere in the results of chance. He thought he had seen its very form. His head swam; his limbs ached; he puffed at his pipe mechanically; a contemplative stupor would soothe the fretfulness of his temper, like the passive bodily quietude procured by a drug, while the intellect remains tensely on the stretch. Nine, nine, nought, four, two. He made a note. The next winning number of the great prize was forty-seven thousand and five. These numbers of course would have to be avoided in the future when writing to Manila for the tickets. He mumbled, pencil in hand . . . "and five. Hm . . . hm." He wetted his finger: the papers rustled. Ha! But what's this? Three years ago, in the September drawing, it was number nine, nought, four, two that took the first prize. Most remarkable. There was a hint there of a definite rule! He was afraid of missing some recondite principle in the overwhelming wealth of his material. What could it be? and for half an hour he would remain dead still, bent low over the desk, without twitching a muscle. At his back the whole berth would be thick with a heavy body of smoke, as if a bomb had burst in there, unnoticed, unheard.

At last he would lock up the desk with the decision of unshaken confidence, jump and go out. He would walk swiftly back and forth on that part of the foredeck which was kept clear of the lumber and of the bodies of the native passengers. They were a great nuisance, but they were also a source of profit that could not be disdained. He needed every penny of profit the *Sofala* could make. Little enough it was, in all conscience! The incertitude of chance gave him no concern, since he had somehow arrived at the conviction that, in the course of years, every number was bound to have his winning turn. It was simply a matter of time and of taking as many tickets as he could afford for every drawing. He generally took rather more; all the earnings of the ship went that way, and also the wages he allowed himself as chief engineer. It was the wages he paid to others that he begrudged with a reasoned and at the same time a passionate regret. He scowled at the lascars with their deck brooms, at the quartermasters rubbing the brass rails with greasy rags; he was eager to shake his fist and roar abuse in bad Malay at the poor carpenter—a timid, sickly, opium-fuddled Chinaman, in loose blue drawers for all costume, who invariably dropped his tools and fled below, with streaming tail and shaking all over, before the fury of that "devil." But it was when he raised up his eyes to the bridge where one of these sailor frauds was always planted by law in charge of his ship that he felt almost dizzy with rage. He abominated them all; it was an old feud, from the time he first went to sea, an unlicked cub with a great opinion of himself, in the engine-room. The slights that had been put upon him. The persecutions he had suffered at the hands of skippers—of absolute nobodies in a steamship after all. And now that he had risen to be a shipowner they were still a plague to him: he had absolutely to pay away precious money to the conceited useless loafers:—As if a fully qualified engineer—who was the owner as well—were not fit to be trusted with the whole charge of a ship. Well! he made it pretty warm for them; but it was a poor consolation. He had come in time to hate the ship, too, for the repairs she required, for the coal-bills he had to pay, for the poor beggarly freights she earned. He would clench his hand as he walked and hit the rail a sudden blow, viciously, as though she could be made to feel pain. And yet he could not do without her; he needed her; he must hang on to her tooth and nail to keep his head above water till the expected flood of fortune came sweeping up and landed him safely on the high shore of his ambition.

It was now to do nothing, nothing whatever, and have plenty of money to do it on. He had tasted of power, the highest form of it his limited experience was aware of—the power of shipowning. What a deception! Vanity of vanities! He wondered at his folly. He had thrown away the substance for the shadow. Of the gratification of wealth he did not know enough to excite his imagination with any visions of luxury. How could he—the child of a drunken boiler-maker—going straight from the workshop into the engine-room of a north-country collier! But the notion of the absolute idleness of wealth he could very well conceive. He reveled in it, to forget his present troubles; he imagined himself walking about the streets of Hull (he knew their gutters well as a boy) with his pockets full of sovereigns. He would buy himself a house; his married sisters, their husbands, his old workshop chums, would render him infinite homage. There would be nothing to think of. His word would be law. He had been out of work for a long time before he won his prize, and he remembered how Carlo Mariani (commonly known as Paunchy Charley), the Maltese hotel-keeper at the slummy end of Denham Street, had cringed joyfully before him in the evening, when the news had come. Poor Charley, though he made his living by ministering to various abject vices, gave credit for their food to many a piece of white wreckage. He was naïvely overjoyed at the idea of his old bills being paid, and he reckoned confidently on a spell of festivities in the cavernous grog-shop downstairs. Massy remembered the curious, respectful looks of the "trashy" white men in the place. His heart had swelled within him. Massy had left Charley's infamous den directly he had realized the possibilities open to him, with his nose in the air. Afterwards the memory of these adulations was a great sadness.

This was the true power of money—and no trouble with it, nor any thinking required either. He thought with difficulty and felt vividly; to his blunt brain the problems offered by any ordered scheme of life seemed in their cruel toughness to have been put in his way by the obvious malevolence of men. As a shipowner everyone had conspired to make him a nobody. How could he have been such a fool as to purchase that accursed ship? He had been abominably swindled; there was no end to this swindling; and as the difficulties of his improvident ambition gathered thicker round him, he really came to hate everybody he had ever come in contact with. A temper naturally irritable and an amazing sensitiveness to the claims of his own personality had ended by making of life for him a sort of inferno—a place where his lost soul had been given up to the torment of savage brooding.

But he had never hated anyone so much as that old man who had turned up one evening to save him from an utter disaster,—from the conspiracy of the wretched sailors. He seemed to have fallen on board from the sky. His footsteps echoed on the empty steamer, and the strange deep-toned voice on deck repeating interrogatively the words, "Mr. Massy, Mr. Massy there?" had been startling like a wonder. And coming up from the depths of the cold engine-room, where he had been pottering dismally with a candle amongst the enormous shadows, thrown on all sides by the skeleton limbs of machinery, Massy had been struck dumb by astonishment in the presence of that imposing old man with a beard like a silver plate, towering in the dusk rendered lurid by the expiring flames of sunset.

"Want to see me on business? What business? I am doing no business. Can't you see that this ship is laid up?" Massy had turned at bay before the pursuing irony of his disaster. Afterwards he could not believe his ears. What was that old fellow getting at? Things don't happen that way. It was a dream. He would presently wake up and find the man vanished like a shape of mist. The gravity, the dignity, the firm and courteous tone of that athletic old stranger impressed Massy. He was almost afraid. But it was no dream. Five hundred pounds are no dream. At once he became suspicious. What did it mean? Of course it was an offer to catch hold of for dear life. But what could there be behind?

Before they had parted, after appointing a meeting in a solicitor's office early on the morrow, Massy was asking himself, What is his motive? He spent the night in hammering out the clauses of the agreement—a unique instrument of its sort whose tenor got bruited abroad somehow and became the talk and wonder of the port.

Massy's object had been to secure for himself as many ways as possible of getting rid of his partner without being called upon at once to pay back his share. Captain Whalley's efforts were directed to making the money secure. Was it not Ivy's money—a part of her fortune whose only other asset was the time-defying body of her old father? Sure of his forbearance in the strength of his love for her, he accepted, with stately serenity, Massy's stupidly cunning paragraphs against his incompetence, his dishonesty, his drunkenness, for the sake of other stringent stipulations. At the end of three years he was at liberty to withdraw from the partnership, taking his money with him. Provision was made for forming a fund to pay him off. But if he left the *Sofala* before the term, from whatever cause (barring death), Massy was to have a whole year for paying. "Illness?" the lawyer had suggested: a young man fresh from Europe and not overburdened with business, who was rather amused. Massy began to whine unctuously, "How could he be expected? . . ."

"Let that go," Captain Whalley had said with a superb confidence in his body. "Acts of God," he added. In the midst of life we are in death, but he trusted his Maker with a still greater fearlessness—his Maker who knew his thoughts, his human affections, and his motives. His Creator knew what use he was making of his health—how much he wanted it. . . . "I trust my first illness will be my last. I've never been ill that I can remember," he had remarked. "Let it go."

But at this early stage he had already awakened Massy's hostility by refusing to make it six hundred instead of five. "I cannot do that," was all he had said, simply, but with so much decision that Massy desisted at once from pressing the point, but had thought to himself, "Can't! Old curmudgeon. *Won't!* He must have lots of money, but he would like to get hold of a soft berth and the sixth part of my profits for nothing if he only could."

And during these years Massy's dislike grew under the restraint of something resembling fear. The simplicity of that man appeared dangerous. Of late he had changed, however, had appeared less formidable and with a lessened vigour of life, as though he had received a secret wound. But still he remained incomprehensible in his simplicity, fearlessness, and rectitude. And when Massy learned that he meant to leave him at the end of the time, to leave him confronted with the problem of boilers, his dislike blazed up secretly into hate.

It had made him so clear-eyed that for a long time now Mr. Sterne could have told him nothing he did not know. He had much ado in trying to terrorize that mean sneak into silence; he wanted to deal alone with the situation; and—incredible as it might have appeared to Mr. Sterne—he had not yet given up the desire and the hope of inducing that hated old man to stay. Why! there was nothing else to do, unless he were to abandon his chances of fortune. But now, suddenly, since the crossing of the bar at Batu Beru things seemed to be coming rapidly to a point. It disquieted him so much that the study of the winning numbers failed to soothe his agitation: and the twilight in the cabin deepened, very sombre.

He put the list away, muttering once more, "Oh, no, my boy, you don't. Not if I know it." He did not mean the blinking, eavesdropping humbug to force his action. He took his head again into his hands; his immobility confined in the darkness of this shut-up little place seemed to make him a thing apart infinitely removed from the stir and the sounds of the deck.

He heard them: the passengers were beginning to jabber excitedly; somebody dragged a heavy box past his door. He heard Captain Whalley's voice above—

"Stations, Mr. Sterne." And the answer from somewhere on deck forward—

"Ay, ay, sir."

"We shall moor head up stream this time; the ebb has made."

"Head upstream, sir."

"You will see to it, Mr. Sterne."

The answer was covered by the autocratic clang on the engine-room gong. The propeller went on beating slowly: one, two, three; one, two three—with pauses as if hesitating on the turn. The gong clanged time after time, and the water churned this way and that by the blades was making a great noisy commotion alongside. Mr. Massy did not move. A shore-light on the other bank, a quarter of a mile across the river, drifted, no bigger than a tiny star, passing slowly athwart the circle of the port. Voices from Mr. Van Wyk's jetty answered the hails from the ship; ropes were thrown and missed and thrown again; the swaying flame of a torch carried in a large sampan coming to fetch away in state the Rajah from down the coast cast a sudden ruddy glare into his cabin, over his very person. Mr. Massy did not move. After a few last ponderous turns the engines stopped, and the prolonged clanging of the gong signified that the captain had done with them. A great number of boats and canoes of all sizes boarded the off-side of the *Sofala*. Then after a time the tumult of splashing, of cries, of shuffling feet, of packages dropped with a thump, the noise of the native passengers going away, subsided slowly. On the shore, a voice, cultivated, slightly authoritative, spoke very close alongside—

"Brought any mail for me this time?"

"Yes, Mr. Van Wyk." This was from Sterne, answering over the rail in a tone of respectful cordiality. "Shall I bring it up to you?"

But the voice asked again—

"Where's the captain?"

"Still on the bridge, I believe. He hasn't left his chair. Shall I. . . ."

The voice interrupted negligently.

"I will come on board."

"Mr. Van Wyk," Sterne suddenly broke out with an eager effort, "will you do me the favour. . . ."

The mate walked away quickly towards the gangway. A silence fell. Mr. Massy in the dark did not move.

He did not move even when he heard slow shuffling footsteps pass his cabin lazily. He contented himself to bellow out through the closed door—

"You—Jack!"

The footsteps came back without haste; the door handle rattled, and the second engineer appeared in the opening, shadowy in the sheen of the skylight at his back, with his face apparently as black as the rest of his figure.

"We have been very long coming up this time," Mr. Massy growled, without changing his attitude.

"What do you expect with half the boiler tubes plugged up for leaks?" The second defended himself loquaciously.

"None of your lip," said Massy.

"None of your rotten boilers—I say," retorted his faithful subordinate without animation, huskily.

"Go down there and carry a head of steam on them yourself—if you dare. I don't."

"You aren't worth your salt then," Massy said. The other made a faint noise which resembled a laugh but might have been a snarl.

"Better go slow than stop the ship altogether," he admonished his admired superior. Mr. Massy moved at last. He turned in his chair, and grinding his teeth—

"Dam' you and the ship! I wish she were at the bottom of the sea. Then you would have to starve."

The trusty second engineer closed the door gently.

Massy listened. Instead of passing on to the bathroom where he should have gone to clean himself, the second entered his cabin, which was next door. Mr. Massy jumped up and waited. Suddenly he heard the lock snap in there. He rushed out and gave a violent kick to the door.

"I believe you are locking yourself up to get drunk," he shouted.

A muffled answer came after a while.

"My own time."

"If you take to boozing on the trip I'll fire you out," Massy cried.

An obstinate silence followed that threat. Massy moved away, perplexed. On the bank two figures appeared, approaching the gangway. He heard a voice tinged with contempt—

"I would rather doubt your word. But I shall certainly speak to him of this."

The other voice, Sterne's, said with a sort of regretful formality—

"Thanks. That's all I want. I must do my duty."

Mr. Massy was surprised. A short, dapper figure leaped lightly on the deck and nearly bounded into him where he stood beyond the circle of light from the gangway lamp. When it had passed towards the bridge, after exchanging a hurried "Good evening," Massy said surlily to Sterne, who followed with slow steps—

"What is it you're making up to Mr. Van Wyk for, now?"

"Far from it, Mr. Massy. I am not good enough for Mr. Van Wyk. Neither are you, sir, in his opinion, I am afraid. Captain Whalley is, it seems. He's gone to ask him to dine up at the house this evening."

Then he murmured to himself darkly—

"I hope he will like it."

XII

Mr. Van Wyk, the white man of Batu Beru, an ex-naval officer who, for reasons best known to himself, had thrown away the promise of a brilliant career to become the pioneer of tobacco-planting on that remote part of the coast, had learned to like Captain Whalley. The appearance of the new skipper had attracted his attention. Nothing more unlike all the diverse types he had seen succeeding each other on the bridge of the *Sofala* could be imagined.

At that time Batu Beru was not what it has become since: the centre of a prosperous tobacco-growing district, a tropically suburban-looking little settlement of bungalows in one long street shaded with two rows of trees, embowered by the flowering and trim luxuriance of the gardens, with a three-mile-long carriage-road for the afternoon drives and a first-class Resident with a fat, cheery wife to lead the society of married estate-managers and unmarried young fellows in the service of the big companies.

All this prosperity was not yet; and Mr. Van Wyk prospered alone on the left bank on his deep clearing carved out of the forest, which came down above and below to the water's edge. His lonely bungalow faced across the river the houses of the Sultan: a restless and melancholy old ruler who had done with love and war, for whom life no longer held any savour (except of evil forebodings) and time never had any value. He was afraid of death, and hoped he would die before the white men were ready to take his country from him. He crossed the river frequently (with never less than ten boats crammed full of people), in the wistful hope of extracting some information on the subject from his own white man. There was a certain chair on the verandah he always took: the dignitaries of the court squatted on the rugs and skins between the furniture: the inferior people remained below on the grass-plot between the house and the river in rows three or four deep all along the front. Not seldom the visit began at daybreak. Mr. Van Wyk tolerated these inroads. He would nod out of his bedroom window, toothbrush or razor in hand, or pass through the throng of courtiers in his bathing robe. He appeared and disappeared humming a tune, polished his nails with attention, rubbed his shaved face with eau-de-Cologne, drank his early tea, went out to see his coolies at work; returned, looked through some papers on his desk, read a page or two in a book or sat before his cottage piano leaning back on the stool, his arms extended, fingers on the keys, his body swaying slightly from side to side. When absolutely forced to speak he gave evasive, vaguely soothing answers out of pure compassion: the same feeling perhaps made him so lavishly hospitable with the aerated drinks that more than once he left himself without soda-water for a whole week. That old man had granted him as much land as he cared to have cleared: it was neither more nor less than a fortune.

Whether it was fortune or seclusion from his kind that Mr. Van Wyk sought, he could not have pitched upon a better place. Even the mail-boats of the subsidized company calling on the veriest clusters of palm-thatched hovels along the coast steamed past the mouth of Batu Beru river far away in the offing. The contract was old: perhaps in a few years' time, when it had expired, Batu Beru would be included in the service; meantime all Mr. Van Dyk's mail was addressed to Malacca, whence his agent sent it across once a month by the *Sofala*. It followed that whenever Massy had run short of money (through taking too many lottery tickets), or got into a difficulty about a skipper, Mr. Van Wyk was deprived of his letter and newspapers. In so far he had a personal interest in the fortunes of the *Sofala*. Though he considered himself a hermit (and for no passing whim evidently, since he had stood eight years of it already), he liked to know what went on in the world.

Handy on the verandah upon a walnut étagère (it had come last year by the *Sofala*—everything came by the *Sofala)* there lay, piled up under bronze weights, a pile of *The Times* weekly edition, the large sheets of the *Rotterdam Courant*, the *Graphic* in its world-wide green wrappers, an illustrated Dutch publication without a cover, the numbers of a German magazine with covers of the "Bismarck malade" colour. There were also parcels of new music—though the piano (it had come years ago by the *Sofala)* in the damp atmosphere of the forests was generally out of tune. It was vexing to be cut off from everything for sixty days at a stretch sometimes, without any means of knowing what was the matter. And when the *Sofala* reappeared Mr. Van Wyk would descend the steps of the verandah and stroll over the grass-plot in front of his house, down to the water-side, with a frown on his white brow.

"You've been laid up after an accident, I presume."

He addressed the bridge, but before anybody could answer Massy was sure to have already scrambled ashore over the rail and pushed in, squeezing the palms of his hands together, bowing his sleek head as if gummed all over the top with black threads and tapes. And he would be so enraged at the necessity of having to offer such an explanation that his moaning would be positively pitiful, while all the time he tried to compose his big lips into a smile.

"No, Mr. Van Wyk. You would not believe it. I couldn't get one of those wretches to take the ship out. Not a single one of the lazy beasts could be induced, and the law, you know, Mr. Van Wyk. . . ."

He moaned at great length apologetically; the words conspiracy, plot, envy, came out prominently, whined with greater energy. Mr. Van Wyk, examining with a faint grimace his polished finger-nails, would say, "H'm. Very unfortunate," and turn his back on him.

Fastidious, clever, slightly skeptical, accustomed to the best society (he had held a much-envied shore appointment at the Ministry of Marine for a year preceding his retreat from his profession and from Europe), he possessed a latent warmth of feeling and a capacity for sympathy which were concealed by a sort of haughty, arbitrary indifference of manner arising from his early training; and by a something an enemy might have called foppish, in his aspect—like a distorted echo of past elegance. He managed to keep an almost military discipline amongst the coolies of the estate he had dragged into the light of day out of the tangle and shadows of the jungle; and the white shirt he put on every evening with its stiff glossy front and high collar looked as if he had meant to preserve the decent ceremony of evening-dress, but had wound a thick crimson sash above his hips as a concession to the wilderness, once his adversary, now his vanquished companion. Moreover, it was a hygienic precaution. Worn wide open in front, a short jacket of some airy silken stuff floated from his shoulders. His fluffy, fair hair, thin at the top, curled slightly at the sides; a carefully arranged moustache, an ungarnished forehead, the gleam of low patent shoes peeping under the wide bottom of trousers cut straight from the same stuff as the gossamer coat, completed a figure recalling, with its sash, a pirate chief of romance, and at the same time the elegance of a slightly bald dandy indulging, in seclusion, a taste for unorthodox costume.

It was his evening get-up. The proper time for the *Sofala* to arrive at Batu Beru was an hour before sunset, and he looked picturesque, and somehow quite correct, too, walking at the water's edge on the background of grass slope crowned with a low, long bungalow with an immensely steep roof of palm thatch, and clad to the eaves in flowering creepers. While the *Sofala* was being made fast he strolled in the shade of the few trees left near the landing-place, waiting till he could go on board. Her white men were not of his kind. The old Sultan (though his wistful invasions were a nuisance) was really much more acceptable to his fastidious taste. But still they were white; the periodical visits of the ship made a break in the well-filled sameness of the days without disturbing his privacy. Moreover, they were necessary from a business point of view; and through a strain of preciseness in his nature he was irritated when she failed to appear at the appointed time.

The cause of the irregularity was too absurd, and Massy, in his opinion, was a contemptible idiot. The first time the *Sofala* reappeared under the new agreement swinging out of the bend below, after he had almost given up all hope of ever seeing her again, he felt so angry that he did not go down at once to the landing-place. His servants had come running to him with the news, and he had dragged a chair close against the front rail of the verandah, spread his elbows out, rested his chin on his hands, and went on glaring at her fixedly while she was being made fast opposite his house. He could make out easily all the white faces on board. Who on earth was that kind of patriarch they had got there on the bridge now?

At last he sprang up and walked down the gravel path. It was a fact that the very gravel for his paths had been imported by the *Sofala*. Exasperated out of his quiet superciliousness, without looking at anyone right or left, he accosted Massy straightway in so determined a manner that the engineer, taken aback, began to stammer unintelligibly. Nothing could be heard but the words: "Mr. Van Wyk . . . Indeed, Mr. Van Wyk. . . . For the future, Mr. Van Wyk"—and by the suffusion of blood Massy's vast bilious face acquired an unnatural orange tint, out of which the disconcerted coal-black eyes shone in an extraordinary manner.

"Nonsense. I am tired of this. I wonder you have the impudence to come alongside my jetty as if I had it made for your convenience alone."

Massy tried to protest earnestly. Mr. Van Wyk was very angry. He had a good mind to ask that German firm—those people in Malacca— what was their name?—boats with green funnels. They would be only too glad of the opening to put one of their small steamers on the run.

Yes; Schnitzler, Jacob Schnitzler, would in a moment. Yes. He had decided to write without delay.

In his agitation Massy caught up his falling pipe.

"You don't mean it, sir!" he shrieked.

"You shouldn't mismanage your business in this ridiculous manner."

Mr. Van Wyk turned on his heel. The other three whites on the bridge had not stirred during the scene. Massy walked hastily from side to side, puffed out his cheeks, suffocated.

"Stuck-up Dutchman!"

And he moaned out feverishly a long tale of griefs. The efforts he had made for all these years to please that man. This was the return you got for it, eh? Pretty. Write to Schnitzler—let in the green-funnel boats—get an old Hamburg Jew to ruin him. No, really he could laugh. . . . He laughed sobbingly. . . . Ha! ha! ha! And make him carry the letter in his own ship presumably.

He stumbled across a grating and swore. He would not hesitate to fling the Dutchman's correspondence overboard—the whole confounded bundle. He had never, never made any charge for that accommodation. But Captain Whalley, his new partner, would not let him probably; besides, it would be only putting off the evil day. For his own part he would make a hole in the water rather than look on tamely at the green funnels overrunning his trade.

He raved aloud. The China boys hung back with the dishes at the foot of the ladder. He yelled from the bridge down at the deck, "Aren't we going to have any chow this evening at all?" then turned violently to Captain Whalley, who waited, grave and patient, at the head of the table, smoothing his beard in silence now and then with a forbearing gesture.

"You don't seem to care what happens to me. Don't you see that this affects your interests as much as mine? It's no joking matter."

He took the foot of the table growling between his teeth.

"Unless you have a few thousands put away somewhere. I haven't."

Mr. Van Wyk dined in his thoroughly lit-up bungalow, putting a point of splendor in the night of his clearing above the dark bank of the river. Afterwards he sat down to his piano, and in a pause he became aware of slow footsteps passing on the path along the front. A plank or two creaked under a heavy tread; he swung half round on the music-stool, listening with his finger-tips at rest on the keyboard. His little terrier barked violently, backing in from the verandah. A deep voice apologized gravely for "this intrusion." He walked out quickly.

At the head of the steps the patriarchal figure, who was the new captain of the *Sofala* apparently (he had seen a round dozen of them, but not one of that sort), towered without advancing. The little dog barked unceasingly, till a flick of Mr. Van Wyk's handkerchief made him spring aside into silence. Captain Whalley, opening the matter, was met by a punctiliously polite but determined opposition.

They carried on their discussion standing where they had come face to face. Mr. Van Wyk observed his visitor with attention. Then at last, as if forced out of his reserve—

"I am surprised that you should intercede for such a confounded fool."

This outbreak was almost complimentary, as if its meaning had been, "That such a man as you should intercede!" Captain Whalley let it pass by without flinching. One would have thought he had heard nothing. He simply went on to state that he was personally interested in putting things straight between them. Personally. . . .

But Mr. Van Wyk, really carried away by his disgust with Massy, became very incisive—

"Indeed—if I am to be frank with you—his whole character does not seem to me particularly estimable or trustworthy . . ."

Captain Whalley, always straight, seemed to grow an inch taller and broader, as if the girth of his chest had suddenly expanded under his beard.

"My dear sir, you don't think I came here to discuss a man with whom I am—I am—h'm—closely associated."

A sort of solemn silence lasted for a moment. He was not used to asking favours, but the importance he attached to this affair had made him willing to try. . . . Mr. Van Wyk, favourably impressed, and suddenly mollified by a desire to laugh, interrupted—

"That's all right if you make it a personal matter; but you can do no less than sit down and smoke a cigar with me."

A slight pause, then Captain Whalley stepped forward heavily. As to the regularity of the service, for the future he made himself responsible for it; and his name was Whalley—perhaps to a sailor (he was speaking to a sailor, was he not?) not altogether unfamiliar. There was a lighthouse now, on an island. Maybe Mr. Van Wyk himself. . . .

"Oh, yes. Oh, indeed." Mr. Van Wyk caught on at once. He indicated a chair. How very interesting. For his own part he had seen some service in the last Acheen War, but had never been so far East. Whalley Island? Of course. Now that was very interesting. What changes his guest must have seen since.

"I can look further back even—on a whole half-century."

Captain Whalley expanded a bit. The flavour of a good cigar (it was a weakness) had gone straight to his heart, also the civility of that young man. There was something in that accidental contact of which he had been starved in his years of struggle.

The front wall retreating made a square recess furnished like a room. A lamp with a milky glass shade, suspended below the slope of the high roof at the end of a slender brass chain, threw a bright round of light upon a little table bearing an open book and an ivory paper-knife. And, in the translucent shadows beyond, other tables could be seen, a number of easy-chairs of various shapes, with a great profusion of skin rugs strewn on the teakwood planking all over the verandah. The flowering creepers scented the air. Their foliage clipped out between the uprights made as if several frames of thick, unstirring leaves reflecting the lamplight in a green glow. Through the opening at his elbow Captain Whalley could see the gangway lantern of the *Sofala* burning dim by the shore, the shadowy masses of the town beyond the open lustrous darkness of the river, and, as if hung along the straight edge of the projecting eaves, a narrow black strip of the night sky full of stars—resplendent. The famous cigar in hand he had a moment of complacency.

"A trifle. Somebody must lead the way. I just showed that the thing could be done; but you men brought up to the use of steam cannot conceive the vast importance of my bit of venturesomeness to the Eastern trade of the time. Why, that new route reduced the average time of a southern passage by eleven days for more than half the year. Eleven days! It's on record. But the remarkable thing—speaking to a sailor—I should say was. . . ."

He talked well, without egotism, professionally. The powerful voice, produced without effort, filled the bungalow even into the empty rooms with a deep and limpid resonance, seemed to make a stillness outside; and Mr. Van Wyk was surprised by the serene quality of its tone, like the perfection of manly gentleness. Nursing one small foot, in a silk sock and a patent leather shoe, on his knee, he was immensely entertained. It was as if nobody could talk like this now, and the over-shadowed eyes, the flowing white beard, the big frame, the serenity, the whole temper of the man, were an amazing survival from the prehistoric times of the world coming up to him out of the sea.

Captain Whalley had been also the pioneer of the early trade in the Gulf of Petchili. He even found occasion to mention that he had buried his "dear wife" there six-and-twenty years ago. Mr. Van Wyk, impassive, could not help speculating in his mind swiftly as to the sort of woman that would mate with such a man. Did they make an adventurous and well-matched pair? No. Very possible she had been small, frail, no doubt very feminine—or most likely commonplace with domestic instincts, utterly insignificant. But Captain Whalley was no garrulous bore, and shaking his head as if to dissipate the momentary gloom that had settled on his handsome old face, he alluded conversationally to Mr. Van Wyk's solitude.

Mr. Van Wyk affirmed that sometimes he had more company than he wanted. He mentioned smilingly some of the peculiarities of his intercourse with "My Sultan." He made his visits in force. Those people damaged his grass-plot in front (it was not easy to obtain some approach to a lawn in the tropics) and the other day had broken down some rare bushes he had planted over there. And Captain Whalley remembered immediately that, in 'forty-seven, the then Sultan, "this man's grandfather," had been notorious as a great protector of the piratical fleets of praus from farther East. They had a safe refuge in the river at Batu Beru. He financed more especially a Balinini chief called Haji Daman. Captain Whalley, nodding significantly his bushy white eyebrows, had very good reason to know something of that. The world had progressed since that time.

Mr. Van Wyk demurred with unexpected acrimony. Progressed in what? he wanted to know.

Why, in knowledge of truth, in decency, in justice, in order—in honesty, too, since men harmed each other mostly from ignorance. It was, Captain Whalley concluded quaintly, more pleasant to live in.

Mr. Van Wyk whimsically would not admit that Mr. Massy, for instance, was more pleasant naturally than the Balinini pirates.

The river had not gained much by the change. They were in their way every bit as honest. Massy was less ferocious than Haji Daman no doubt, but. . . .

"And what about you, my good sir?" Captain Whalley laughed a deep soft laugh. "*You* are an improvement, surely."

He continued in a vein of pleasantry. A good cigar was better than a knock on the head—the sort of welcome he would have found on this river forty or fifty years ago. Then leaning forward slightly, he became earnestly serious. It seems as if, outside their own sea-gypsy tribes, these rovers had hated all mankind with an incomprehensible, bloodthirsty hatred. Meantime their depredations had been stopped, and what was the consequence? The new generation was orderly, peaceable, settled in prosperous villages. He could speak from personal knowledge. And even the few survivors of that time—old men now—had changed so much, that it would have been unkind to remember against them that they had ever slit a throat in their lives. He had one especially in his mind's eye: a dignified, venerable headman of a certain large coast village about sixty miles sou'west of Tampasuk. It did one's heart good to see him—to hear that man speak. He might have been a ferocious savage once. What men wanted was to be checked by superior intelligence, by superior knowledge, by superior force, too—yes, by force held in trust from God and sanctified by its use in accordance with His declared will. Captain Whalley believed a disposition for good existed in every man, even if the world were not a very happy place as a whole. In the wisdom of men he had not so much confidence. The disposition had to be helped up pretty sharply sometimes, he admitted. They might be silly, wrongheaded, unhappy; but naturally evil—no. There was at bottom a complete harmlessness at least. . . .

"Is there?" Mr. Van Wyk snapped acrimoniously.

Captain Whalley laughed at the interjection, in the good humour of large, tolerating certitude. He could look back at half a century, he pointed out. The smoke oozed placidly through the white hairs hiding his kindly lips.

"At all events," he resumed after a pause, "I am glad that they've had no time to do you much harm as yet."

This allusion to his comparative youthfulness did not offend Mr. Van Wyk, who got up and wriggled his shoulders with an enigmatic half-smile. They walked out together amicably into the starry night towards the river-side. Their footsteps resounded unequally on the dark path. At the shore end of the gangway the lantern, hung low to the handrail, threw a vivid light on the white legs and the big black feet of Mr. Massy waiting about anxiously. From the waist upwards he remained shadowy, with a row of buttons gleaming up to the vague outline of his chin.

"You may thank Captain Whalley for this," Mr. Van Wyk said, curtly, to him before turning away.

The lamps on the verandah flung three long squares of light between the uprights far over the grass. A bat flitted before his face like a circling flake of velvety blackness. Along the jasmine hedge the night air seemed heavy with the fall of perfumed dew; flowerbeds bordered the path; the clipped bushes uprose in dark, rounded clumps here and there before the house; the dense foliage of creepers filtered the sheen of the lamplight within in a soft glow all along the front; and everything near and far stood still in a great immobility, in a great sweetness.

Mr. Van Wyk (a few years before he had had occasion to imagine himself treated more badly than anybody alive had ever been by a woman) felt for Captain Whalley's optimistic views the disdain of a man who had once been credulous himself. His disgust with the world (the woman for a time had filled it for him completely) had taken the form of activity in retirement, because, though capable of great depth of feeling, he was energetic and essentially practical. But there was in that uncommon old sailor, drifting on the outskirts of his busy solitude, something that fascinated his skepticism. His very simplicity (amusing enough) was like a delicate refinement of an upright character. The striking dignity of manner could be nothing else, in a man reduced to such a humble position, but the expression of something essentially noble in the character. With all his trust in mankind he was no fool; the serenity of his temper at the end of so many years, since it could not obviously have been appeased by success, wore an air of profound wisdom. Mr. Van Wyk was amused at it sometimes. Even the very physical traits of the old captain of the *Sofala*, his powerful frame, his reposeful mien, his intelligent, handsome face, the big limbs, the benign courtesy, the touch of rugged severity in the shaggy eyebrows, made up a seductive personality. Mr. Van Wyk disliked littleness of every kind, but there was nothing small about that man, and in the exemplary regularity of many trips an intimacy had grown up between them, a warm feeling at bottom under a kindly stateliness of forms agreeable to his fastidiousness.

They kept their respective opinions on all worldly matters. His other convictions Captain Whalley never intruded. The difference of their ages was like another bond between them. Once, when twitted with the uncharitableness of his youth, Mr. Van Wyk, running his eye over the vast proportions of his interlocutor, retorted in friendly banter—

"Oh. You'll come to my way of thinking yet. You'll have plenty of time. Don't call yourself old: you look good for a round hundred."

But he could not help his stinging incisiveness, and though moderating it by an almost affectionate smile, he added—

"And by then you will probably consent to die from sheer disgust."

Captain Whalley, smiling, too, shook his head. "God forbid!"

He thought that perhaps on the whole he deserved something better than to die in such sentiments. The time of course would have to come, and he trusted to his Maker to provide a manner of going out of which he need not be ashamed. For the rest he hoped he would live to a hundred if need be; other men had been known; it would be no miracle. He expected no miracles.

The pronounced, argumentative tone caused Mr. Van Wyk to raise his head and look at him steadily. Captain Whalley was gazing fixedly with a rapt expression, as though he had seen his Creator's favourable decree written in mysterious characters on the wall. He kept perfectly motionless for a few seconds, then got his vast bulk on to his feet so impetuously that Mr. Van Wyk was startled.

He struck first a heavy blow on his inflated chest: and, throwing out horizontally a big arm that remained steady, extended in the air like the limb of a tree on a windless day—

"Not a pain or an ache there. Can you see this shake in the least?"

His voice was low, in an awing, confident contrast with the headlong emphasis of his movements. He sat down abruptly.

"This isn't to boast of it, you know. I am nothing," he said in his effortless strong voice, that seemed to come out as naturally as a river flows. He picked up the stump of the cigar he had laid aside, and added peacefully, with a slight nod, "As it happens, my life is necessary; it isn't my own, it isn't—God knows."

He did not say much for the rest of the evening, but several times Mr. Van Wyk detected a faint smile of assurance flitting under the heavy moustache.

Later on Captain Whalley would now and then consent to dine "at the house." He could even be induced to drink a glass of wine. "Don't think I am afraid of it, my good sir," he explained. "There was a very good reason why I should give it up."

On another occasion, leaning back at ease, he remarked, "You have treated me most—most humanely, my dear Mr. Van Wyk, from the very first."

"You'll admit there was some merit," Mr. Van Wyk hinted slyly. "An associate of that excellent Massy. . . . Well, well, my dear captain, I won't say a word against him."

"It would be no use your saying anything against him," Captain Whalley affirmed a little moodily. "As I've told you before, my life— my work, is necessary, not for myself alone. I can't choose. . . ." He paused, turned the glass before him right round. . . . "I have an only child—a daughter."

The ample downward sweep of his arm over the table seemed to suggest a small girl at a vast distance. "I hope to see her once more before I die. Meantime it's enough to know that she has me sound and solid, thank God. You can't understand how one feels. Bone of my bone, flesh of my flesh; the very image of my poor wife. Well, she . . ."

Again he paused, then pronounced stoically the words, "She has a hard struggle."

And his head fell on his breast, his eyebrows remained knitted, as by an effort of meditation. But generally his mind seemed steeped in the serenity of boundless trust in a higher power. Mr. Van Wyk wondered sometimes how much of it was due to the splendid vitality of the man, to the bodily vigour which seems to impart something of its force to the soul. But he had learned to like him very much.

XIII

This was the reason why Mr. Sterne's confidential communication, delivered hurriedly on the shore alongside the dark silent ship, had disturbed his equanimity. It was the most incomprehensible and unexpected thing that could happen; and the perturbation of his spirit was so great that, forgetting all about his letters, he ran rapidly up the bridge ladder.

The portable table was being put together for dinner to the left of the wheel by two pig-tailed "boys," who as usual snarled at each other over the job, while another, a doleful, burly, very yellow Chinaman, resembling Mr. Massy, waited apathetically with the cloth over his arm and a pile of thick dinner-plates against his chest. A common cabin lamp with its globe missing, brought up from below, had been hooked to the wooden framework of the awning; the side-screens had been lowered all round; Captain Whalley filling the depths of the wicker-chair, seemed to sit benumbed in a canvas tent crudely lighted, and used for the storing of nautical objects; a shabby steering-wheel, a battered brass binnacle on a stout mahogany stand, two dingy life-buoys, an old cork fender lying in a corner, dilapidated deck-lockers with loops of thin rope instead of door-handles.

He shook off the appearance of numbness to return Mr. Van Wyk's unusually brisk greeting, but relapsed directly afterwards. To accept a pressing invitation to dinner "up at the house" cost him another very visible physical effort. Mr. Van Wyk, perplexed, folded his arms, and leaning back against the rail, with his little, black, shiny feet well out, examined him covertly.

"I've noticed of late that you are not quite yourself, old friend."

He put an affectionate gentleness into the last two words. The real intimacy of their intercourse had never been so vividly expressed before.

"Tut, tut, tut!"

The wicker-chair creaked heavily.

"Irritable," commented Mr. Van Wyk to himself; and aloud, "I'll expect to see you in half an hour, then," he said, negligently, moving off.

"In half an hour," Captain Whalley's rigid silvery head repeated behind him as if out of a trance.

Amidships, below, two voices, close against the engine-room, could be heard answering each other—one angry and slow, the other alert.

"I tell you the beast has locked himself in to get drunk."

"Can't help it now, Mr. Massy. After all, a man has a right to shut himself up in his cabin in his own time."

"Not to get drunk."

"I heard him swear that the worry with the boilers was enough to drive any man to drink," Sterne said, maliciously.

Massy hissed out something about bursting the door in. Mr. Van Wyk, to avoid them, crossed in the dark to the other side of the deserted deck. The planking of the little wharf rattled faintly under his hasty feet.

"Mr. Van Wyk! Mr. Van Wyk!"

He walked on: somebody was running on the path. "You've forgotten to get your mail."

Sterne, holding a bundle of papers in his hand, caught up with him.

"Oh, thanks."

But, as the other continued at his elbow, Mr. Van Wyk stopped short. The overhanging eaves, descending low upon the lighted front of the bungalow, threw their black straight-edged shadow into the great body of the night on that side. Everything was very still. A tinkle of cutlery and a slight jingle of glasses were heard. Mr. Van Wyk's servants were laying the table for two on the verandah.

"I'm afraid you give me no credit whatever for my good intentions in the matter I've spoken to you about," said Sterne.

"I simply don't understand you."

"Captain Whalley is a very audacious man, but he will understand that his game is up. That's all that anybody need ever know of it from me. Believe me, I am very considerate in this, but duty is duty. I don't want to make a fuss. All I ask you, as his friend, is to tell him from me that the game's up. That will be sufficient."

Mr. Van Wyk felt a loathsome dismay at this queer privilege of friendship. He would not demean himself by asking for the slightest explanation; to drive the other away with contumely he did not think prudent—as yet, at any rate. So much assurance staggered him. Who could tell what there could be in it? he thought His regard for Captain Whalley had the tenacity of a disinterested sentiment, and his practical instinct coming to his aid, he concealed his scorn.

"I gather, then, that this is something grave."

"Very grave," Sterne assented, solemnly, delighted at having produced an effect at last. He was ready to add some effusive protestations of regret at the "unavoidable necessity," but Mr. Van Wyk cut him short—very civilly, however.

Once on the verandah Mr. Van Wyk put his hands in his pockets, and, straddling his legs, stared down at a black panther skin lying on the floor before a rocking-chair. "It looks as if the fellow had not the pluck to play his own precious game openly," he thought.

This was true enough. In the face of Massy's last rebuff Sterne dared not declare his knowledge. His object was simply to get charge of the steamer and keep it for some time. Massy would never forgive him for forcing himself on; but if Captain Whalley left the ship of his own accord, the command would devolve upon him for the rest of the trip; so he hit upon the brilliant idea of scaring the old man away. A vague menace, a mere hint, would be enough in such a brazen case; and, with a strange admixture of compassion, he thought that Batu Beru was a very good place for throwing up the sponge. The skipper could go ashore quietly, and stay with that Dutchman of his. Weren't these two as thick as thieves together? And on reflection he seemed to see that there was a way to work the whole thing through that great friend of the old man's. This was another brilliant idea. He had an inborn preference for circuitous methods. In this particular case he desired to remain in the background as much as possible, to avoid exasperating Massy needlessly. No fuss! Let it all happen naturally.

Mr. Van Wyk all through the dinner was conscious of a sense of isolation that invades sometimes the closeness of human intercourse. Captain Whalley failed lamentably and obviously in his attempts to eat something. He seemed overcome by a strange absentmindedness. His hand would hover irresolutely, as if left without guidance by a preoccupied mind. Mr. Van Wyk had heard him coming up from a long way off in the profound stillness of the river-side, and had noticed the irresolute character of the footfalls. The toe of his boot had struck the bottom stair as though he had come along mooning with his head in the air right up to the steps of the verandah. Had the captain of the *Sofala* been another sort of man he would have suspected the work of age there. But one glance at him was enough. Time—after, indeed, marking him for its own—had given him up to his usefulness, in which his simple faith would see a proof of Divine mercy. "How could I contrive to warn him?" Mr. Van Wyk wondered, as if Captain Whalley had been miles and miles away, out of sight and earshot of all evil. He was sickened by an immense disgust of Sterne. Even to mention his threat to a man like Whalley would be positively indecent. There was something more vile and insulting in its hint than in a definite charge of crime—the debasing taint of blackmailing. "What could anyone bring against him?" he asked himself. This was a limpid personality. "And for what object?" The Power that man trusted had thought fit to leave him nothing on earth that envy could lay hold of, except a bare crust of bread.

"Won't you try some of this?" he asked, pushing a dish slightly. Suddenly it occurred to Mr. Van Wyk that Sterne might possibly be coveting the command of the *Sofala*. His cynicism was quite startled by what looked like a proof that no man may count himself safe from his kind unless in the very abyss of misery. An intrigue of that sort was hardly worth troubling about, he judged; but still, with such a fool as Massy to deal with, Whalley ought to and must be warned.

At this moment Captain Whalley, bolt upright, the deep cavities of the eyes overhung by a bushy frown, and one large brown hand resting on each side of his empty plate, spoke across the table-cloth abruptly—

"Mr. Van Wyk, you've always treated me with the most humane consideration."

"My dear captain, you make too much of the simple fact that I am not a savage." Mr. Van Wyk, utterly revolted by the thought of Sterne's obscure attempt, raised his voice incisively, as if the mate had been hiding somewhere within earshot. "Any consideration I have been able to show was no more than the rightful due of a character I've learned to regard by this time with an esteem that nothing can shake."

A slight ring of glass made him lift his eyes from the slice of pineapple he was cutting into small pieces on his plate. In changing his position Captain Whalley had contrived to upset an empty tumbler.

Without looking that way, leaning sideways on his elbow, his other hand shading his brow, he groped shakily for it, then desisted. Van Wyk stared blankly, as if something momentous had happened all at once. He did not know why he should feel so startled; but he forgot Sterne utterly for the moment.

"Why, what's the matter?"

And Captain Whalley, half-averted, in a deadened, agitated voice, muttered—

"Esteem!"

"And I may add something more," Mr. Van Wyk, very steady-eyed, pronounced slowly.

"Hold! Enough!" Captain Whalley did not change his attitude or raise his voice. "Say no more! I can make you no return. I am too poor even for that now. Your esteem is worth having. You are not a man that would stoop to deceive the poorest sort of devil on earth, or make a ship unseaworthy every time he takes her to sea."

Mr. Van Wyk, leaning forward, his face gone pink all over, with the starched table-napkin over his knees, was inclined to mistrust his senses, his power of comprehension, the sanity of his guest.

"Where? Why? In the name of God!—what's this? What ship? I don't understand who. . . ."

"Then, in the name of God, it is I! A ship's unseaworthy when her captain can't see. I am going blind."

Mr. Van Wyk made a slight movement, and sat very still afterwards for a few seconds; then, with the thought of Sterne's "The game's up," he ducked under the table to pick up the napkin which had slipped off his knees. This was the game that was up. And at the same time the muffled voice of Captain Whalley passed over him—

"I've deceived them all. Nobody knows."

He emerged flushed to the eyes. Captain Whalley, motionless under the full blaze of the lamp, shaded his face with his hand.

"And you had that courage?"

"Call it by what name you like. But you are a humane man—a—a—gentleman, Mr. Van Wyk. You may have asked me what I had done with my conscience."

He seemed to muse, profoundly silent, very still in his mournful pose.

"I began to tamper with it in my pride. You begin to see a lot of things when you are going blind. I could not be frank with an old chum even. I was not frank with Massy—no, not altogether. I knew he took me for a wealthy sailor fool, and I let him. I wanted to keep up my importance—because there was poor Ivy away there—my daughter. What did I want to trade on his misery for? I did trade on it—for her. And now, what mercy could I expect from him? He would trade on mine if he knew it. He would hunt the old fraud out, and stick to the money for a year. Ivy's money. And I haven't kept a penny for myself. How am I going to live for a year? A year! In a year there will be no sun in the sky for her father."

His deep voice came out, awfully veiled, as though he had been overwhelmed by the earth of a landslide and talking of the thoughts that haunt the dead in their graves. A cold shudder ran down Mr. Van Wyk's back.

"And how long is it since you have . . . ?" he began.

"It was a long time before I could bring myself to believe in this—this—visitation." Captain Whalley spoke with gloomy patience from under his hand.

He had not thought he had deserved it. He had begun by deceiving himself from day to day, from week to week. He had the Serang at hand there—an old servant. It came on gradually, and when he could no longer deceive himself. . . .

His voice died out almost.

"Rather than give her up I set myself to deceive you all."

"It's incredible," whispered Mr. Van Wyk. Captain Whalley's appalling murmur flowed on.

"Not even the sign of God's anger could make me forget her. How could I forsake my child, feeling my vigour all the time—the blood warm within me? Warm as yours. It seems to me that, like the blinded Samson, I would find the strength to shake down a temple upon my head. She's a struggling woman—my own child that we used to pray over together, my poor wife and I. Do you remember that day I as well as told you that I believed God would let me live to a hundred for her sake? What sin is there in loving your child? Do you see it? I was ready for her sake to live for ever. I half believed I would. I've been praying for death since. Ha! Presumptuous man—you wanted to live. . . ."

A tremendous, shuddering upheaval of that big frame, shaken by a gasping sob, set the glasses jingling all over the table, seemed to make the whole house tremble to the roof-tree. And Mr. Van Wyk, whose feeling of outraged love had been translated into a form of struggle with nature, understood very well that, for that man whose whole life had been conditioned by action, there could exist no other expression for all the emotions; that, to voluntarily cease venturing, doing, enduring, for his child's sake, would have been exactly like plucking his warm love for her out of his living heart. Something too monstrous, too impossible, even to conceive.

Captain Whalley had not changed his attitude, that seemed to express something of shame, sorrow, and defiance.

"I have even deceived you. If it had not been for that word 'esteem.' These are not the words for me. I would have lied to you. Haven't I lied to you? Weren't you going to trust your property on board this very trip?"

"I have a floating yearly policy," Mr. Van Wyk said almost unwittingly, and was amazed at the sudden cropping up of a commercial detail.

"The ship is unseaworthy, I tell you. The policy would be invalid if it were known. . . ."

"We shall share the guilt, then."

"Nothing could make mine less," said Captain Whalley.

He had not dared to consult a doctor; the man would have perhaps asked who he was, what he was doing; Massy might have heard something. He had lived on without any help, human or divine. The very prayers stuck in his throat. What was there to pray for? and death seemed as far as ever. Once he got into his cabin he dared not come out again; when he sat down he dared not get up; he dared not raise his eyes to anybody's face; he felt reluctant to look upon the sea or up to the sky. The world was fading before his great fear of giving himself away. The old ship was his last friend; he was not afraid of her; he knew every inch of her deck; but at her, too, he hardly dared to look, for fear of finding he could see less than the day before. A great incertitude enveloped him. The horizon was gone; the sky mingled darkly with the sea. Who was this figure standing over yonder? what was this thing lying down there? And a frightful doubt of the reality of what he could see made even the remnant of sight that remained to him an added torment, a pitfall always open for his miserable pretense. He was afraid to stumble inexcusably over something—to say a fatal Yes or No to a question. The hand of God was upon him, but it could not tear him away from his child. And, as if in a nightmare of humiliation, every featureless man seemed an enemy.

He let his hand fall heavily on the table. Mr. Van Wyk, arms down, chin on breast, with a gleam of white teeth pressing on the lower lip, meditated on Sterne's "The game's up."

"The Serang of course does not know."

"Nobody," said Captain Whalley, with assurance.

"Ah, yes. Nobody. Very well. Can you keep it up to the end of the trip? That is the last under the agreement with Massy."

Captain Whalley got up and stood erect, very stately, with the great white beard lying like a silver breastplate over the awful secret of his heart. Yes; that was the only hope there was for him of ever seeing her again, of securing the money, the last he could do for her, before he crept away somewhere—useless, a burden, a reproach to himself. His voice faltered.

"Think of it! Never see her any more: the only human being besides myself now on earth that can remember my wife. She's just like her mother. Lucky the poor woman is where there are no tears shed over those they loved on earth and that remain to pray not to be led into temptation—because, I suppose, the blessed know the secret of grace in God's dealings with His created children."

He swayed a little, said with austere dignity—

"I don't. I know only the child He has given me."

And he began to walk. Mr. Van Wyk, jumping up, saw the full meaning of the rigid head, the hesitating feet, the vaguely extended hand. His heart was beating fast; he moved a chair aside, and instinctively advanced as if to offer his arm. But Captain Whalley passed him by, making for the stairs quite straight.

"He could not see me at all out of his line," Van Wyk thought, with a sort of awe. Then going to the head of the stairs, he asked a little tremulously—

"What is it like—like a mist—like. . . ." Captain Whalley, half-way down, stopped, and turned round undismayed to answer:

"It is as if the light were ebbing out of the world. Have you ever watched the ebbing sea on an open stretch of sands withdrawing farther and farther away from you? It is like this—only there will be no flood to follow. Never. It is as if the sun were growing smaller, the stars going out one by one. There can't be many left that I can see by this. But I haven't had the courage to look of late. . . ." He must have been able to make out Mr. Van Wyk, because he checked him by an authoritative gesture and a stoical—

"I can get about alone yet."

It was as if he had taken his line, and would accept no help from men, after having been cast out, like a presumptuous Titan, from his heaven. Mr. Van Wyk, arrested, seemed to count the footsteps right out of earshot. He walked between the tables, tapping smartly with his heels, took up a paper-knife, dropped it after a vague glance along the blade; then happening upon the piano, struck a few chords, standing up before the keyboard with an attentive poise of the head like a piano-tuner; closing it, he pivoted on his heels brusquely, avoided the little terrier sleeping trustfully on crossed forepaws, came upon the stairs next, and, as though he had lost his balance on the top step, ran down headlong out of the house. His servants, beginning to clear the table, heard him mutter to himself (evil words no doubt) down there, and then after a pause go away with a strolling gait in the direction of the wharf.

The bulwarks of the *Sofala* lying alongside the bank made a low, black wall on the undulating contour of the shore. Two masts and a funnel uprose from behind it with a great rake, as if about to fall: a solid, square elevation in the middle bore the ghostly shapes of white boats, the curves of davits, lines of rail and stanchions, all confused and mingling darkly everywhere; but low down, amidships, a single lighted port stared out on the night, perfectly round, like a small, full moon, whose yellow beam caught a patch of wet mud, the edge of trodden grass, two turns of heavy cable wound round the foot of a thick wooden post in the ground.

Mr. Van Wyk, peering alongside, heard a muzzy boastful voice apparently jeering at a person called Prendergast. It mouthed abuse thickly, choked; then pronounced very distinctly the word "Murphy," and chuckled. Glass tinkled tremulously. All these sounds came from the lighted port. Mr. Van Wyk hesitated, stooped; it was impossible to look through unless he went down into the mud.

"Sterne," he said, half aloud.

The drunken voice within said gladly:

"Sterne—of course. Look at him blink. Look at him! Sterne, Whalley, Massy. Massy, Whalley, Sterne. But Massy's the best. You can't come over him. He would just love to see you starve."

Mr. Van Wyk moved away, made out farther forward a shadowy head stuck out from under the awnings as if on the watch, and spoke quietly in Malay, "Is the mate asleep?"

"No. Here, at your service."

In a moment Sterne appeared, walking as noiselessly as a cat on the wharf.

"It's so jolly dark, and I had no idea you would be down to-night."

"What's this horrible raving?" asked Mr. Van Wyk, as if to explain the cause of a shudder than ran over him audibly.

"Jack's broken out on a drunk. That's our second. It's his way. He will be right enough by to-morrow afternoon, only Mr. Massy will keep on worrying up and down the deck. We had better get away."

He muttered suggestively of a talk "up at the house." He had long desired to effect an entrance there, but Mr. Van Wyk nonchalantly demurred: it would not, he feared, be quite prudent, perhaps; and the opaque black shadow under one of the two big trees left at the landing-place swallowed them up, impenetrably dense by the side of the wide river that seemed to spin into threads of glitter the light of a few big stars dropped here and there upon its outspread and flowing stillness.

"The situation is grave beyond doubt," Mr. Van Wyk said. Ghost-like in their white clothes they could not distinguish each others' features, and their feet made no sound on the soft earth. A sort of purring was heard. Mr. Sterne felt gratified by such a beginning.

"I thought, Mr. Van Wyk, a gentleman of your sort would see at once how awkwardly I was situated."

"Yes, very. Obviously his health is bad. Perhaps he's breaking up. I see, and he himself is well aware—I assume I am speaking to a man of sense—he is well aware that his legs are giving out."

"His legs—ah!" Mr. Sterne was disconcerted, and then turned sulky. "You may call it his legs if you like; what I want to know is whether he intends to clear out quietly. That's a good one, too! His legs! Pooh!"

"Why, yes. Only look at the way he walks." Mr. Van Wyk took him up in a perfectly cool and undoubting tone. "The question, however, is whether your sense of duty does not carry you too far from your true interest. After all, I, too, could do something to serve you. You know who I am."

"Everybody along the Straits has heard of you, sir."

Mr. Van Wyk presumed that this meant something favourable.

Sterne had a soft laugh at this pleasantry. He should think so! To the opening statement, that the partnership agreement was to expire at the end of this very trip, he gave an attentive assent. He was aware. One heard of nothing else on board all the blessed day long. As to Massy, it was no secret that he was in a jolly deep hole with these worn-out boilers. He would have to borrow somewhere a couple of hundred first of all to pay off the captain; and then he would have to raise money on mortgage upon the ship for the new boilers—that is, if he could find a lender at all. At best it meant loss of time, a break in the trade, short earnings for the year—and there was always the danger of having his connection filched away from him by the Germans. It was whispered about that he had already tried two firms. Neither would have anything to do with him. Ship too old, and the man too well known in the place. . . . Mr. Sterne's final rapid winking remained buried in the deep darkness sibilating with his whispers.

"Supposing, then, he got the loan," Mr. Van Wyk resumed in a deliberate undertone, "on your own showing he's more than likely to get a mortgagee's man thrust upon him as captain. For my part, I know that I would make that very stipulation myself if I had to find the money. And as a matter of fact I am thinking of doing so. It would be worth my while in many ways. Do you see how this would bear on the case under discussion?"

"Thank you, sir. I am sure you couldn't get anybody that would care more for your interests."

"Well, it suits my interest that Captain Whalley should finish his time. I shall probably take a passage with you down the Straits. If that can be done, I'll be on the spot when all these changes take place, and in a position to look after *your* interests."

"Mr. Van Wyk, I want nothing better. I am sure I am infinitely. . . ."

"I take it, then, that this may be done without any trouble."

"Well, sir, what risk there is can't be helped; but (speaking to you as my employer now) the thing is more safe than it looks. If anybody had told me of it I wouldn't have believed it, but I have been looking on myself. That old Serang has been trained up to the game. There's nothing the matter with his—his—limbs, sir. He's got used to doing things himself in a remarkable way. And let me tell you, sir, that Captain Whalley, poor man, is by no means useless. Fact. Let me explain to you, sir. He stiffens up that old monkey of a Malay, who knows well enough what to do. Why, he must have kept captain's watches in all sorts of country ships off and on for the last five-and-twenty years. These natives, sir, as long as they have a white man close at the back, will go on doing the right thing most surprisingly well—even if left quite to themselves. Only the white man must be of the sort to put starch into them, and the captain is just the one for that. Why, sir, he has drilled him so well that now he needs hardly speak at all. I have seen that little wrinkled ape made to take the ship out of Pangu Bay on a blowy morning and on all through the islands; take her out first-rate, sir, dodging under the old man's elbow, and in such quiet style that you could not have told for the life of you which of the two was doing the work up there. That's where our poor friend would be still of use to the ship even if—if—he could no longer lift a foot, sir. Providing the Serang does not know that there's anything wrong."

"He doesn't."

"Naturally not. Quite beyond his apprehension. They aren't capable of finding out anything about us, sir."

"You seem to be a shrewd man," said Mr. Van Wyk in a choked mutter, as though he were feeling sick.

"You'll find me a good enough servant, sir."

Mr. Sterne hoped now for a handshake at least, but unexpectedly, with a "What's this? Better not to be seen together," Mr. Van Wyk's white shape wavered, and instantly seemed to melt away in the black air under the roof of boughs. The mate was startled. Yes. There was that faint thumping clatter.

He stole out silently from under the shade. The lighted port-hole shone from afar. His head swam with the intoxication of sudden success. What a thing it was to have a gentleman to deal with! He crept aboard, and there was something weird in the shadowy stretch of empty decks, echoing with shouts and blows proceeding from a darker part amidships. Mr. Massy was raging before the door of the berth: the drunken voice within flowed on undisturbed in the violent racket of kicks.

"Shut up! Put your light out and turn in, you confounded swilling pig—you! D'you hear me, you beast?"

The kicking stopped, and in the pause the muzzy oracular voice announced from within—

"Ah! Massy, now—that's another thing. Massy's deep."

"Who's that aft there? You, Sterne? He'll drink himself into a fit of horrors." The chief engineer appeared vague and big at the corner of the engine-room.

"He will be good enough for duty to-morrow. I would let him be, Mr. Massy."

Sterne slipped away into his berth, and at once had to sit down. His head swam with exultation. He got into his bunk as if in a dream. A feeling of profound peace, of pacific joy, came over him. On deck all was quiet.

Mr. Massy, with his ear against the door of Jack's cabin, listened critically to a deep, stertorous breathing within. This was a dead-drunk sleep. The bout was over: tranquilized on that score, he, too went in, and with slow wriggles got out of his old tweed jacket. It was a garment with many pockets, which he used to put on at odd times of the day, being subject to sudden chilly fits, and when he felt warmed he would take it off and hang it about anywhere all over the ship. It would be seen swinging on belaying-pins, thrown over the heads of winches, suspended on people's very door-handles for that matter. Was he not the owner? But his favourite place was a hook on a wooden awning stanchion on the bridge, almost against the binnacle. He had even in the early days more than one tussle on that point with Captain Whalley, who desired the bridge to be kept tidy. He had been overawed then. Of late, though, he had been able to defy his partner with impunity. Captain Whalley never seemed to notice anything now. As to the Malays, in their awe of that scowling man not one of the crew would dream of laying a hand on the thing, no matter where or what it swung from.

With an unexpectedness which made Mr. Massy jump and drop the coat at his feet, there came from the next berth the crash and thud of a headlong, jingling, clattering fall. The faithful Jack must have dropped to sleep suddenly as he sat at his revels, and now had gone over chair and all, breaking, as it seemed by the sound, every single glass and bottle in the place. After the terrific smash all was still for a time in there, as though he had killed himself outright on the spot. Mr. Massy held his breath. At last a sleepy, uneasy groaning sigh was exhaled slowly on the other side of the bulkhead.

"I hope to goodness he's too drunk to wake up now," muttered Mr. Massy.

The sound of a softly knowing laugh nearly drove him to despair. He swore violently under his breath. The fool would keep him awake all night now for certain. He cursed his luck. He wanted to forget his maddening troubles in sleep sometimes. He could detect no movements. Without apparently making the slightest attempt to get up, Jack went on sniggering to himself where he lay; then began to speak, where he had left off as it were—

"Massy! I love the dirty rascal. He would like to see his poor old Jack starve—but just you look where he has climbed to. . . ." He hiccoughed in a superior, leisurely manner. . . . "Shipowning it with the best. A lottery ticket you want. Ha! ha! I will give you lottery tickets, my boy. Let the old ship sink and the old chum starve—that's right. He don't go wrong—Massy don't. Not he. He's a genius—that man is. That's the way to win your money. Ship and chum must go."

"The silly fool has taken it to heart," muttered Massy to himself. And, listening with a softened expression of face for any slight sign of returning drowsiness, he was discouraged profoundly by a burst of laughter full of joyful irony.

"Would like to see her at the bottom of the sea! Oh, you clever, clever devil! Wish her sunk, eh? I should think you would, my boy; the damned old thing and all your troubles with her. Rake in the insurance money —turn your back on your old chum—all's well—gentleman again."

A grim stillness had come over Massy's face. Only his big black eyes rolled uneasily. The raving fool. And yet it was all true. Yes. Lottery tickets, too. All true. What? Beginning again? He wished he wouldn't. . . .

But it was even so. The imaginative drunkard on the other side of the bulkhead shook off the deathlike stillness that after his last words had fallen on the dark ship moored to a silent shore.

"Don't you dare to say anything against George Massy, Esquire. When he's tired of waiting he will do away with her. Look out! Down she goes—chum and all. He'll know how to. . . ."

The voice hesitated, weary, dreamy, lost, as if dying away in a vast open space.

". . . Find a trick that will work. He's up to it—never fear. . . ."

He must have been very drunk, for at last the heavy sleep gripped him with the suddenness of a magic spell, and the last word lengthened itself into an interminable, noisy, indrawn snore. And then even the snoring stopped, and all was still.

But it seemed as though Mr. Massy had suddenly come to doubt the efficacy of sleep as against a man's troubles; or perhaps he had found the relief he needed in the stillness of a calm contemplation that may contain the vivid thoughts of wealth, of a stroke of luck, of long idleness, and may bring before you the imagined form of every desire; for, turning about and throwing his arms over the edge of his bunk, he stood there with his feet on his favourite old coat, looking out through the round port into the night over the river. Sometimes a breath of wind would enter and touch his face, a cool breath charged with the damp, fresh feel from a vast body of water. A glimmer here and there was all he could see of it; and once he might after all suppose he had dozed off, since there appeared before his vision, unexpectedly and connected with no dream, a row of flaming and gigantic figures—three naught seven one two—making up a number such as you may see on a lottery ticket. And then all at once the port was no longer black: it was pearly gray, framing a shore crowded with houses, thatched roof beyond thatched roof, walls of mats and bamboo, gables of carved teak timber. Rows of dwellings raised on a forest of piles lined the steely bank of the river, brimful and still, with the tide at the turn. This was Batu Beru—and the day had come.

Mr. Massy shook himself, put on the tweed coat, and, shivering nervously as if from some great shock, made a note of the number. A fortunate, rare hint that. Yes; but to pursue fortune one wanted money—ready cash.

Then he went out and prepared to descend into the engine-room.

Several small jobs had to be seen to, and Jack was lying dead drunk on the floor of his cabin, with the door locked at that. His gorge rose at the thought of work. Ay! But if you wanted to do nothing you had to get first a good bit of money. A ship won't save you. True, all true. He was tired of waiting for some chance that would rid him at last of that ship that had turned out a curse on his life.

XIV

The deep, interminable hoot of the steam-whistle had, in its grave, vibrating note, something intolerable, which sent a slight shudder down Mr. Van Wyk's back. It was the early afternoon; the *Sofala* was leaving Batu Beru for Pangu, the next place of call. She swung in the stream, scantily attended by a few canoes, and, gliding on the broad river, became lost to view from the Van Wyk bungalow.

Its owner had not gone this time to see her off. Generally he came down to the wharf, exchanged a few words with the bridge while she cast off, and waved his hand to Captain Whalley at the last moment. This day he did not even go as far as the balustrade of the verandah. "He couldn't see me if I did," he said to himself. "I wonder whether he can make out the house at all." And this thought somehow made him feel more alone than he had ever felt for all these years. What was it? six or seven? Seven. A long time.

He sat on the verandah with a closed book on his knee, and, as it were, looked out upon his solitude, as if the fact of Captain Whalley's blindness had opened his eyes to his own. There were many sorts of heartaches and troubles, and there was no place where they could not find a man out. And he felt ashamed, as though he had for six years behaved like a peevish boy.

His thought followed the *Sofala* on her way. On the spur of the moment he had acted impulsively, turning to the thing most pressing. And what else could he have done? Later on he should see. It seemed necessary that he should come out into the world, for a time at least. He had money—something could be arranged; he would grudge no time, no trouble, no loss of his solitude. It weighed on him now—and Captain Whalley appeared to him as he had sat shading his eyes, as if, being deceived in the trust of his faith, he were beyond all the good and evil that can be wrought by the hands of men.

Mr. Van Wyk's thoughts followed the *Sofala* down the river, winding about through the belt of the coast forest, between the buttressed shafts of the big trees, through the mangrove strip, and over the bar. The ship crossed it easily in broad daylight, piloted, as it happened, by Mr. Sterne, who took the watch from four to six, and then went below to hug himself with delight at the prospect of being virtually employed by a rich man—like Mr. Van Wyk. He could not see how any hitch could occur now. He did not seem able to get over the feeling of being "fixed up at last." From six to eight, in the course of duty, the Serang looked alone after the ship. She had a clear road before her now till about three in the morning, when she would close with the Pangu group. At eight Mr. Sterne came out cheerily to take charge again till midnight. At ten he was still chirruping and humming to himself on the bridge, and about that time Mr. Van Wyk's thought abandoned the *Sofala*. Mr. Van Wyk had fallen asleep at last.

Massy, blocking the engine-room companion, jerked himself into his tweed jacket surlily, while the second waited with a scowl.

"Oh. You came out! You sot! Well, what have you got to say for yourself?"

He had been in charge of the engines till then. A sombre fury darkened his mind: a hot anger against the ship, against the facts of life, against the men for their cheating, against himself, too—because of an inward tremor of his heart.

An incomprehensible growl answered him.

"What? Can't you open your mouth now? You yelp out your infernal rot loud enough when you are drunk. What do you mean by abusing people in that way?—you old useless boozer, you!"

"Can't help it. Don't remember anything about it. You shouldn't listen."

"You dare to tell me! What do you mean by going on a drunk like this?"

"Don't ask me. Sick of the dam' boilers—you would be. Sick of life."

"I wish you were dead, then. You've made me sick of you. Don't you remember the uproar you made last night? You miserable old soaker!"

"No; I don't. Don't want to. Drink is drink."

"I wonder what prevents me from kicking you out. What do you want here?"

"Relieve you. You've been long enough down there, George."

"Don't you George me—you tippling old rascal, you! If I were to die to-morrow you would starve. Remember that. Say Mr. Massy."

"Mr. Massy," repeated the other, stolidly.

Disheveled, with dull blood-shot eyes, a snuffy, grimy shirt, greasy trousers, naked feet thrust into ragged slippers, he bolted in head down directly Massy had made way for him.

The chief engineer looked around. The deck was empty as far as the taffrail. All the native passengers had left in Batu Beru this time, and no others had joined. The dial of the patent log tinkled periodically in the dark at the end of the ship. It was a dead calm, and, under the clouded sky, through the still air that seemed to cling warm, with a seaweed smell, to her slim hull, on a sea of sombre gray and unwrinkled, the ship moved on an even keel, as if floating detached in empty space. But Mr. Massy slapped his forehead, tottered a little, caught hold of a belaying-pin at the foot of the mast.

"I shall go mad," he muttered, walking across the deck unsteadily. A shovel was scraping loose coal down below—a fire-door clanged. Sterne on the bridge began whistling a new tune.

Captain Whalley, sitting on the couch, awake and fully dressed, heard the door of his cabin open. He did not move in the least, waiting to recognize the voice, with an appalling strain of prudence.

A bulkhead lamp blazed on the white paint, the crimson plush, the brown varnish of mahogany tops. The white wood packing-case under the bed-place had remained unopened for three years now, as though Captain Whalley had felt that, after the *Fair Maid* was gone, there could be no abiding-place on earth for his affections. His hands rested on his knees; his handsome head with big eyebrows presented a rigid profile to the doorway. The expected voice spoke out at last.

"Once more, then. What am I to call you?"

Ha! Massy. Again. The weariness of it crushed his heart—and the pain of shame was almost more than he could bear without crying out.

"Well. Is it to be 'partner' still?"

"You don't know what you ask."

"I know what I want. . . ."

Massy stepped in and closed the door.

". . . And I am going to have a try for it with you once more."

His whine was half persuasive, half menacing.

"For it's no manner of use to tell me that you are poor. You don't spend anything on yourself, that's true enough; but there's another name for that. You think you are going to have what you want out of me for three years, and then cast me off without hearing what I think of you. You think I would have submitted to your airs if I had known you had only a beggarly five hundred pounds in the world. You ought to have told me."

"Perhaps," said Captain Whalley, bowing his head. "And yet it has saved you. . . . "Massy laughed scornfully. . . . "I have told you often enough since."

"And I don't believe you now. When I think how I let you lord it over my ship! Do you remember how you used to bullyrag me about my coat and *your* bridge? It was in his way. *His* bridge! 'And I won't be a party to this—and I couldn't think of doing that.' Honest man! And now it all comes out. 'I am poor, and I can't. I have only this five hundred in the world.'"

He contemplated the immobility of Captain Whalley, that seemed to present an inconquerable obstacle in his path. His face took a mournful cast.

"You are a hard man."

"Enough," said Captain Whalley, turning upon him. "You shall get nothing from me, because I have nothing of mine to give away now."

"Tell that to the marines!"

Mr. Massy, going out, looked back once; then the door closed, and Captain Whalley, alone, sat as still as before. He had nothing of his own—even his own past of honour, of truth, of just pride, was gone. All his spotless life had fallen into the abyss. He had said his last good-bye to it. But what belonged to *her*, that he meant to save. Only a little money. He would take it to her in his own hands—this last gift of a man that had lasted too long. And an immense and fierce impulse, the very passion of paternity, flamed up with all the unquenched vigour of his worthless life in a desire to see her face.

Just across the deck Massy had gone straight to his cabin, struck a light, and hunted up the note of the dreamed number whose figures had flamed up also with the fierceness of another passion. He must contrive somehow not to miss a drawing. That number meant something. But what expedient could he contrive to keep himself going?

"Wretched miser!" he mumbled.

If Mr. Sterne could at no time have told him anything new about his partner, he could have told Mr. Sterne that another use could be made of a man's affliction than just to kick him out, and thus defer the term of a difficult payment for a year. To keep the secret of the affliction and induce him to stay was a better move. If without means, he would be anxious to remain; and that settled the question of refunding him his share. He did not know exactly how much Captain Whalley was disabled; but if it so happened that he put the ship ashore somewhere for good and all, it was not the owner's fault—was it? He was not obliged to know that there was anything wrong. But probably nobody would raise such a point, and the ship was fully insured. He had had enough self-restraint to pay up the premiums. But this was not all. He could not believe Captain Whalley to be so confoundedly destitute as not to have some more money put away somewhere. If he, Massy, could get hold of it, that would pay for the boilers, and everything went on as before. And if she got lost in the end, so much the better. He hated her: he loathed the troubles that took his mind off the chances of fortune. He wished her at the bottom of the sea, and the insurance money in his pocket. And as, baffled, he left Captain Whalley's cabin, he enveloped in the same hatred the ship with the worn-out boilers and the man with the dimmed eyes.

And our conduct after all is so much a matter of outside suggestion, that had it not been for his Jack's drunken gabble he would have there and then had it out with this miserable man, who would neither help, nor stay, nor yet lose the ship. The old fraud! He longed to kick him out. But he restrained himself. Time enough for that—when he liked. There was a fearful new thought put into his head. Wasn't he up to it after all? How that beast Jack had raved! "Find a safe trick to get rid of her." Well, Jack was not so far wrong. A very clever trick had occurred to him. Aye! But what of the risk?

A feeling of pride—the pride of superiority to common prejudices—crept into his breast, made his heart beat fast, his mouth turn dry. Not everybody would dare; but he was Massy, and he was up to it!

Six bells were struck on deck. Eleven! He drank a glass of water, and sat down for ten minutes or so to calm himself. Then he got out of his chest a small bull's-eye lantern of his own and lit it.

Almost opposite his berth, across the narrow passage under the bridge, there was, in the iron deck-structure covering the stokehold fiddle and the boiler-space, a storeroom with iron sides, iron roof, iron-plated floor, too, on account of the heat below. All sorts of rubbish was shot there: it had a mound of scrap-iron in a corner; rows of empty oil-cans; sacks of cotton-waste, with a heap of charcoal, a deck-forge, fragments of an old hencoop, winch-covers all in rags, remnants of lamps, and a brown felt hat, discarded by a man dead now (of a fever on the Brazil coast), who had been once mate of the *Sofala*, had remained for years jammed forcibly behind a length of burst copper pipe, flung at some time or other out of the engine-room. A complete and imperious blackness pervaded that Capharnaum of forgotten things. A small shaft of light from Mr. Massy's bull's-eye fell slanting right through it.

His coat was unbuttoned; he shot the bolt of the door (there was no other opening), and, squatting before the scrap-heap, began to pack his pockets with pieces of iron. He packed them carefully, as if the rusty nuts, the broken bolts, the links of cargo chain, had been so much gold he had that one chance to carry away. He packed his side-pockets till they bulged, the breast pocket, the pockets inside. He turned over the pieces. Some he rejected. A small mist of powdered rust began to rise about his busy hands. Mr. Massy knew something of the scientific basis of his clever trick. If you want to deflect the magnetic needle of a ship's compass, soft iron is the best; likewise many small pieces in the pockets of a jacket would have more effect than a few large ones, because in that way you obtain a greater amount of surface for weight in your iron, and it's surface that tells.

He slipped out swiftly—two strides sufficed—and in his cabin he perceived that his hands were all red—red with rust. It disconcerted him, as though he had found them covered with blood: he looked himself over hastily. Why, his trousers, too! He had been rubbing his rusty palms on his legs.

He tore off the waistband button in his haste, brushed his coat, washed his hands. Then the air of guilt left him, and he sat down to wait.

He sat bolt upright and weighted with iron in his chair. He had a hard, lumpy bulk against each hip, felt the scrappy iron in his pockets touch his ribs at every breath, the downward drag of all these pounds hanging upon his shoulders. He looked very dull, too, sitting idle there, and his yellow face, with motionless black eyes, had something passive and sad in its quietness.

When he heard eight bells struck above his head, he rose and made ready to go out. His movements seemed aimless, his lower lip had dropped a little, his eyes roamed about the cabin, and the tremendous tension of his will had robbed them of every vestige of intelligence.

With the last stroke of the bell the Serang appeared noiselessly on the bridge to relieve the mate. Sterne overflowed with good nature, since he had nothing more to desire.

"Got your eyes well open yet, Serang? It's middling dark; I'll wait till you get your sight properly."

The old Malay murmured, looked up with his worn eyes, sidled away into the light of the binnacle, and, crossing his hands behind his back, fixed his eyes on the compass-card.

"You'll have to keep a good lookout ahead for land, about half-past three. It's fairly clear, though. You have looked in on the captain as you came along—eh? He knows the time? Well, then, I am off."

At the foot of the ladder he stood aside for the captain. He watched him go up with an even, certain tread, and remained thoughtful for a moment. "It's funny," he said to himself, "but you can never tell whether that man has seen you or not. He might have heard me breathe this time."

He was a wonderful man when all was said and done. They said he had had a name in his day. Mr. Sterne could well believe it; and he concluded serenely that Captain Whalley must be able to see people more or less —as himself just now, for instance—but not being certain of anybody, had to keep up that unnoticing silence of manner for fear of giving himself away. Mr. Sterne was a shrewd guesser.

This necessity of every moment brought home to Captain Whalley's heart the humiliation of his falsehood. He had drifted into it from paternal love, from incredulity, from boundless trust in divine justice meted out to men's feelings on this earth. He would give his poor Ivy the benefit of another month's work; perhaps the affliction was only temporary. Surely God would not rob his child of his power to help, and cast him naked into a night without end. He had caught at every hope; and when the evidence of his misfortune was stronger than hope, he tried not to believe the manifest thing.

In vain. In the steadily darkening universe a sinister clearness fell upon his ideas. In the illuminating moments of suffering he saw life, men, all things, the whole earth with all her burden of created nature, as he had never seen them before.

Sometimes he was seized with a sudden vertigo and an overwhelming terror; and then the image of his daughter appeared. Her, too, he had never seen so clearly before. Was it possible that he should ever be unable to do anything whatever for her? Nothing. And not see her any more? Never.

Why? The punishment was too great for a little presumption, for a little pride. And at last he came to cling to his deception with a fierce determination to carry it out to the end, to save her money intact, and behold her once more with his own eyes. Afterwards—what? The idea of suicide was revolting to the vigour of his manhood. He had prayed for death till the prayers had stuck in his throat. All the days of his life he had prayed, for daily bread, and not to be led into temptation, in a childlike humility of spirit. Did words mean anything? Whence did the gift of speech come? The violent beating of his heart reverberated in his head—seemed to shake his brain to pieces.

He sat down heavily in the deck-chair to keep the pretense of his watch. The night was dark. All the nights were dark now.

"Serang," he said, half aloud.

"Ada, Tuan. I am here."

"There are clouds on the sky?"

"There are, Tuan."

"Let her be steered straight. North."

"She is going north, Tuan."

The Serang stepped back. Captain Whalley recognized Massy's footfalls on the bridge.

The engineer walked over to port and returned, passing behind the chair several times. Captain Whalley detected an unusual character as of prudent care in this prowling. The near presence of that man brought with it always a recrudescence of moral suffering for Captain Whalley. It was not remorse. After all, he had done nothing but good to the poor devil. There was also a sense of danger—the necessity of a greater care.

Massy stopped and said—

"So you still say you must go?"

"I must indeed."

"And you couldn't at least leave the money for a term of years?"

"Impossible."

"Can't trust it with me without your care, eh?"

Captain Whalley remained silent. Massy sighed deeply over the back of the chair.

"It would just do to save me," he said in a tremulous voice.

"I've saved you once."

The chief engineer took off his coat with careful movements, and proceeded to feel for the brass hook screwed into the wooden stanchion. For this purpose he placed himself right in front of the binnacle, thus hiding completely the compass-card from the quartermaster at the wheel. "Tuan!" the lascar at last murmured softly, meaning to let the white man know that he could not see to steer.

Mr. Massy had accomplished his purpose. The coat was hanging from the nail, within six inches of the binnacle. And directly he had stepped aside the quartermaster, a middle-aged, pock-marked, Sumatra Malay, almost as dark as a negro, perceived with amazement that in that short time, in this smooth water, with no wind at all, the ship had gone swinging far out of her course. He had never known her get away like this before. With a slight grunt of astonishment he turned the wheel hastily to bring her head back north, which was the course. The grinding of the steering-chains, the chiding murmurs of the Serang, who had come over to the wheel, made a slight stir, which attracted Captain Whalley's anxious attention. He said, "Take better care." Then everything settled to the usual quiet on the bridge. Mr. Massy had disappeared.

But the iron in the pockets of the coat had done its work; and the *Sofala*, heading north by the compass made untrue by this simple device, was no longer making a safe course for Pangu Bay.

The hiss of water parted by her stem, the throb of her engines, all the sounds of her faithful and laborious life, went on uninterrupted in the great calm of the sea joining on all sides the motionless layer of cloud over the sky. A gentle stillness as vast as the world seemed to wait upon her path, enveloping her lovingly in a supreme caress. Mr. Massy thought there could be no better night for an arranged shipwreck.

Run up high and dry on one of the reefs east of Pangu—wait for daylight—hole in the bottom—out boats—Pangu Bay same evening. That's about it. As soon as she touched he would hasten on the bridge, get hold of the coat (nobody would notice in the dark), and shake it upside-down over the side, or even fling it into the sea. A detail. Who could guess? Coat been seen hanging there from that hook hundreds of times. Nevertheless, when he sat down on the lower step of the bridge-ladder his knees knocked together a little. The waiting part was the worst of it. At times he would begin to pant quickly, as though he had been running, and then breathe largely, swelling with the intimate sense of a mastered fate. Now and then he would hear the shuffle of the Serang's bare feet up there: quiet, low voices would exchange a few words, and lapse almost at once into silence. . . .

"Tell me directly you see any land, Serang."

"Yes, Tuan. Not yet."

"No, not yet," Captain Whalley would agree.

The ship had been the best friend of his decline. He had sent all the money he had made by and in the *Sofala* to his daughter. His thought lingered on the name. How often he and his wife had talked over the cot of the child in the big stern-cabin of the *Condor*; she would grow up, she would marry, she would love them, they would live near her and look at her happiness—it would go on without end. Well, his wife was dead, to the child he had given all he had to give; he wished he could come near her, see her, see her face once, live in the sound of her voice, that could make the darkness of the living grave ready for him supportable. He had been starved of love too long. He imagined her tenderness.

The Serang had been peering forward, and now and then glancing at the chair. He fidgeted restlessly, and suddenly burst out close to Captain Whalley—

"Tuan, do you see anything of the land?"

The alarmed voice brought Captain Whalley to his feet at once. He! See! And at the question, the curse of his blindness seemed to fall on him with a hundredfold force.

"What's the time?" he cried.

"Half-past three, Tuan."

"We are close. You *must* see. Look, I say. Look."

Mr. Massy, awakened by the sudden sound of talking from a short doze on the lowest step, wondered why he was there. Ah! A faintness came over him. It is one thing to sow the seed of an accident and another to see the monstrous fruit hanging over your head ready to fall in the sound of agitated voice. "There's no danger," he muttered thickly to himself.

The horror of incertitude had seized upon Captain Whalley, the miserable mistrust of men, of things—of the very earth. He had steered that very course thirty-six times by the same compass—if anything was certain in this world it was its absolute, unerring correctness. Then what had happened? Did the Serang lie? Why lie? Why? Was he going blind, too?

"Is there a mist? Look low on the water. Low down, I say."

"Tuan, there's no mist. See for yourself."

Captain Whalley steadied the trembling of his limbs by an effort. Should he stop the engines at once and give himself away? A gust of irresolution swayed all sorts of bizarre notions in his mind. The unusual had come, and he was not fit to deal with it. In this passage of inexpressible anguish he saw her face—the face of a young girl—with an amazing strength of illusion. No, he must not give himself away after having gone so far for her sake. "You steered the course? You made it? Speak the truth."

"Ya, Tuan. On the course now. Look."

Captain Whalley strode to the binnacle, which to him made such a dim spot of light in an infinity of shapeless shadow. By bending his face right down to the glass he had been able before. . . .

Having to stoop so low, he put out, instinctively, his arm to where he knew there was a stanchion to steady himself against. His hand closed on something that was not wood but cloth. The slight pull adding to the weight, the loop broke, and Mr. Massy's coat falling, struck the deck heavily with a dull thump, accompanied by a lot of clicks.

"What's this?"

Captain Whalley fell on his knees, with groping hands extended in a frank gesture of blindness. They trembled, these hands feeling for the truth. He saw it. Iron near the compass. Wrong course. Wreck her! His ship. Oh no. Not that.

"Jump and stop her!" he roared out in a voice not his own.

He ran himself—hands forward, a blind man, and while the clanging of the gong echoed still all over the ship, she seemed to butt full tilt into the side of a mountain.

It was low water along the north side of the strait. Mr. Massy had not reckoned on that. Instead of running aground for half her length, the *Sofala* butted the sheer ridge of a stone reef which would have been awash at high water. This made the shock absolutely terrific. Everybody in the ship that was standing was thrown down headlong: the shaken rigging made a great rattling to the very trucks. All the lights went out; several chain-guys, snapping, clattered against the funnel; there were crashes, pings of parted wire-rope, splintering sounds, loud cracks; the masthead lamp flew over the bows, and all the doors about the deck began to bang heavily. Then, after having hit, she rebounded, hit the second time the very same spot like a battering-ram. This completed the havoc: the funnel, with all the guys gone, fell over with a hollow sound of thunder, smashing the wheel to bits, crushing the frame of the awnings, breaking the lockers, filling the bridge with a mass of broken wood. Captain Whalley picked himself up and stood knee-deep in wreckage, torn, bleeding, knowing the nature of the danger he had escaped mostly by the sound, and holding Mr. Massy's coat in his arms.

By this time Sterne (he had been flung out of his bunk) had set the engines astern. They worked for a few turns, then a voice bawled out, "Get out of the damned engine-room, Jack!"—and they stopped; but the ship had gone clear of the reef and lay still, with a heavy cloud of steam issuing from the broken deck-pipes, and vanishing in wispy shapes into the night. Notwithstanding the suddenness of the disaster there was no shouting, as if the very violence of the shock had half-stunned the shadowy lot of people swaying here and there about her decks. The voice of the Serang pronounced distinctly above the confused murmurs—

"No bottom." He had heaved the lead.

Mr. Sterne cried out next in a strained pitch—

"Where the devil has she got to? Where are we?"

Captain Whalley replied in a calm bass—

"Amongst the reefs to the eastward."

"You know it, sir? Then she will never get out again."

"She will be sunk in five minutes. Boats, Sterne. Even one will save you all in this calm."

The Chinaman stokers went in a disorderly rush for the port boats. Nobody tried to check them. The Malays, after a moment of confusion, became quiet, and Mr. Sterne showed a good countenance. Captain Whalley had not moved. His thoughts were darker than this night in which he had lost his first ship.

"He made me lose a ship."

Another tall figure standing before him amongst the litter of the smash on the bridge whispered insanely—

"Say nothing of it."

Massy stumbled closer. Captain Whalley heard the chattering of his teeth.

"I have the coat."

"Throw it down and come along," urged the chattering voice. "B-b-b-b-boat!"

"You will get five years for this."

Mr. Massy had lost his voice. His speech was a mere dry rustling in his throat.

"Have mercy!"

"Had you any when you made me lose my ship? Mr. Massy, you shall get five years for this!"

"I wanted money! Money! My own money! I will give you some money. Take half of it. You love money yourself."

"There's a justice. . . ."

Massy made an awful effort, and in a strange, half choked utterance—

"You blind devil! It's you that drove me to it."

Captain Whalley, hugging the coat to his breast, made no sound. The light had ebbed for ever from the world—let everything go. But this man should not escape scot-free.

Sterne's voice commanded—

"Lower away!"

The blocks rattled.

"Now then," he cried, "over with you. This way. You, Jack, here. Mr. Massy! Mr. Massy! Captain! Quick, sir! Let's get—

"I shall go to prison for trying to cheat the insurance, but you'll get exposed; you, honest man, who has been cheating me. You are poor. Aren't you? You've nothing but the five hundred pounds. Well, you have nothing at all now. The ship's lost, and the insurance won't be paid."

Captain Whalley did not move. True! Ivy's money! Gone in this wreck. Again he had a flash of insight. He was indeed at the end of his tether.

Urgent voices cried out together alongside. Massy did not seem able to tear himself away from the bridge. He chattered and hissed despairingly—

"Give it up to me! Give it up!"

"No," said Captain Whalley; "I could not give it up. You had better go. Don't wait, man, if you want to live. She's settling down by the head fast. No; I shall keep it, but I shall stay on board."

Massy did not seem to understand; but the love of life, awakened suddenly, drove him away from the bridge.

Captain Whalley laid the coat down, and stumbled amongst the heaps of wreckage to the side.

"Is Mr. Massy in with you?" he called out into the night.

Sterne from the boat shouted—

"Yes; we've got him. Come along, sir. It's madness to stay longer."

Captain Whalley felt along the rail carefully, and, without a word, cast off the painter. They were expecting him still down there. They were waiting, till a voice suddenly exclaimed—

"We are adrift! Shove off!"

"Captain Whalley! Leap! . . . pull up a little . . . leap! You can swim."

In that old heart, in that vigorous body, there was, that nothing should be wanting, a horror of death that apparently could not be overcome by the horror of blindness. But after all, for Ivy he had carried his point, walking in his darkness to the very verge of a crime. God had not listened to his prayers. The light had finished ebbing out of the world; not a glimmer. It was a dark waste; but it was unseemly that a Whalley who had gone so far to carry a point should continue to live. He must pay the price.

"Leap as far as you can, sir; we will pick you up."

They did not hear him answer. But their shouting seemed to remind him of something. He groped his way back, and sought for Mr. Massy's coat. He could swim indeed; people sucked down by the whirlpool of a sinking ship do come up sometimes to the surface, and it was unseemly that a Whalley, who had made up his mind to die, should be beguiled by chance into a struggle. He would put all these pieces of iron into his own pockets.

They, looking from the boat, saw the *Sofala*, a black mass upon a black sea, lying still at an appalling cant. No sound came from her. Then, with a great bizarre shuffling noise, as if the boilers had broken through the bulkheads, and with a faint muffled detonation, where the ship had been there appeared for a moment something standing upright and narrow, like a rock out of the sea. Then that, too, disappeared.

When the *Sofala* failed to come back to Batu Beru at the proper time, Mr. Van Wyk understood at once that he would never see her any more. But he did not know what had happened till some months afterwards, when, in a native craft lent him by his Sultan, he had made his way to the *Sofala*'s port of registry, where already her existence and the official inquiry into her loss was beginning to be forgotten.

It had not been a very remarkable or interesting case, except for the fact that the captain had gone down with his sinking ship. It was the only life lost; and Mr. Van Wyk would not have been able to learn any details had it not been for Sterne, whom he met one day on the quay near the bridge over the creek, almost on the very spot where Captain Whalley, to preserve his daughter's five hundred pounds intact, had turned to get a sampan which would take him on board the *Sofala*.

From afar Mr. Van Wyk saw Sterne blink straight at him and raise his hand to his hat. They drew into the shade of a building (it was a bank), and the mate related how the boat with the crew got into Pangu Bay about six hours after the accident, and how they had lived for a fortnight in a state of destitution before they found an opportunity to get away from that beastly place. The inquiry had exonerated everybody from all blame. The loss of the ship was put down to an unusual set of the current. Indeed, it could not have been anything else: there was no other way to account for the ship being set seven miles to the eastward of her position during the middle watch.

"A piece of bad luck for me, sir."

Sterne passed his tongue on his lips, and glanced aside. "I lost the advantage of being employed by you, sir. I can never be sorry enough. But here it is: one man's poison, another man's meat. This could not have been handier for Mr. Massy if he had arranged that shipwreck himself. The most timely total loss I've ever heard of."

"What became of that Massy?" asked Mr. Van Wyk.

"He, sir? Ha! ha! He would keep on telling me that he meant to buy another ship; but as soon as he had the money in his pocket he cleared out for Manila by mail-boat early in the morning. I gave him chase right aboard, and he told me then he was going to make his fortune dead sure in Manila. I could go to the devil for all he cared. And yet he as good as promised to give me the command if I didn't talk too much."

"You never said anything. . . ." Mr. Van Wyk began.

"Not I, sir. Why should I? I mean to get on, but the dead aren't in my way," said Sterne. His eyelids were beating rapidly, then drooped for an instant. "Besides, sir, it would have been an awkward business. You made me hold my tongue just a bit too long."

"Do you know how it was that Captain Whalley remained on board? Did he really refuse to leave? Come now! Or was it perhaps an accidental . . . ?"

"Nothing!" Sterne interrupted with energy. "I tell you I yelled for

him to leap overboard. He simply *must* have cast off the painter of the
boat himself. We all yelled to him—that is, Jack and I. He wouldn't
even answer us. The ship was as silent as a grave to the last. Then the
boilers fetched away, and down she went. Accident! Not it! The game
was up, sir, I tell you."

This was all that Sterne had to say.

Mr. Van Wyk had been of course made the guest of the club for a
fortnight, and it was there that he met the lawyer in whose office had
been signed the agreement between Massy and Captain Whalley.

"Extraordinary old man," he said. "He came into my office from
nowhere in particular as you may say, with his five hundred pounds to
invest, and that engineer fellow following him anxiously. And now he
is gone out a little inexplicably, just as he came. I could never
understand him quite. There was no mystery at all about that Massy,
eh? I wonder whether Whalley refused to leave the ship. It would have
been foolish. He was blameless, as the court found."

Mr. Van Wyk had known him well, he said, and he could not
believe in suicide. Such an act would not have been in character with
what he knew of the man.

"It is my opinion, too," the lawyer agreed. The general theory was
that the captain had remained too long on board trying to save
something of importance. Perhaps the chart which would clear him, or
else something of value in his cabin. The painter of the boat had come
adrift of itself, it was supposed. However, strange to say, some little
time before that voyage poor Whalley had called in his office and had
left with him a sealed envelope addressed to his daughter, to be
forwarded to her in case of his death. Still it was nothing very unusual,
especially in a man of his age. Mr. Van Wyk shook his head. Captain
Whalley looked good for a hundred years.

"Perfectly true," assented the lawyer. "The old fellow looked as
though he had come into the world full grown and with that long beard.
I could never, somehow, imagine him either younger or older—don't
you know. There was a sense of physical power about that man, too.
And perhaps that was the secret of that something peculiar in his person
which struck everybody who came in contact with him. He looked
indestructible by any ordinary means that put an end to the rest of us.
His deliberate, stately courtesy of manner was full of significance. It
was as though he were certain of having plenty of time for everything.
Yes, there was something indestructible about him; and the way he
talked sometimes you might have thought he believed it himself. When
he called on me last with that letter he wanted me to take charge of, he
was not depressed at all. Perhaps a shade more deliberate in his talk and
manner. Not depressed in the least. Had he a presentiment, I wonder?
Perhaps! Still it seems a miserable end for such a striking figure."

"Oh yes! It was a miserable end," Mr. Van Wyk said, with so

much fervour that the lawyer looked up at him curiously; and afterwards, after parting with him, he remarked to an acquaintance—

"Queer person that Dutch tobacco-planter from Batu Beru. Know anything of him?"

"Heaps of money," answered the bank manager. "I hear he's going home by the next mail to form a company to take over his estates. Another tobacco district thrown open. He's wise, I think. These good times won't last for ever."

In the southern hemisphere Captain Whalley's daughter had no presentiment of evil when she opened the envelope addressed to her in the lawyer's handwriting. She had received it in the afternoon; all the boarders had gone out, her boys were at school, her husband sat upstairs in his big arm-chair with a book, thin-faced, wrapped up in rugs to the waist. The house was still, and the grayness of a cloudy day lay against the panes of the windows.

In a shabby dining-room, where a faint cold smell of dishes lingered all the year round, sitting at the end of a long table surrounded by many chairs pushed in with their backs close against the edge of the perpetually laid table-cloth, she read the opening sentence: "Most profound regret—painful duty—your father is no more—in accordance with his instructions—fatal casualty—consolation—no blame attached to his memory. . . ."

Her face was thin, her temples a little sunk under the smooth bands of black hair, her lips remained resolutely compressed, while her dark eyes grew larger, till at last, with a low cry, she stood up, and instantly stooped to pick up another envelope which had slipped off her knees on to the floor.

She tore it open, snatched out the enclosure. . . .

"My dearest child," it said, "I am writing this while I am able yet to write legibly. I am trying hard to save for you all the money that is left; I have only kept it to serve you better. It is yours. It shall not be lost; it shall not be touched. There's five hundred pounds. Of what I have earned I have kept nothing back till now. For the future, if I live, I must keep back some—a little—to bring me to you. I must come to you. I must see you once more.

"It is hard to believe that you will ever look on these lines. God seems to have forgotten me. I want to see you—and yet death would be a greater favour. If you ever read these words, I charge you to begin by thanking a God merciful at last, for I shall be dead then, and it will be well. My dear, I am at the end of my tether."

The next paragraph began with the words: "My sight is going. . . ."

She read no more that day. The hand holding up the paper to her eyes fell slowly, and her slender figure in a plain black dress walked rigidly to the window. Her eyes were dry: no cry of sorrow or whisper of thanks went up to heaven from her lips. Life had been too hard, for all the efforts of his love. It had silenced her emotions. But for the first time in all these years its sting had departed, the carking care of poverty, the meanness of a hard struggle for bread. Even the image of her husband and of her children seemed to glide away from her into the gray twilight; it was her father's face alone that she saw, as though he had come to see her, always quiet and big, as she had seen him last, but with something more august and tender in his aspect.

She slipped his folded letter between the two buttons of her plain black bodice, and leaning her forehead against a window-pane remained there till dusk, perfectly motionless, giving him all the time she could spare. Gone! Was it possible? My God, was it possible? The blow had come softened by the spaces of the earth, by the years of absence. There had been whole days when she had not thought of him at all—had no time. But she had loved him, she felt she had loved him, after all.

The Duel

A MILITARY TALE

I

Napoleon I, whose career had the quality of a duel against the whole of Europe, disliked duelling between the officers of his army. The great military emperor was not a swashbuckler, and had little respect for tradition.

Nevertheless, a story of duelling, which became a legend in the army, runs through the epic of imperial wars. To the surprise and admiration of their fellows, two officers, like insane artists trying to gild refined gold or paint the lily, pursued a private contest through the years of universal carnage. They were officers of cavalry, and their connection with the high-spirited but fanciful animal which carries men into battle seems particularly appropriate. It would be difficult to imagine for heroes of this legend two officers of infantry of the line, for example, whose fantasy is tamed by much walking exercise, and whose valour necessarily must be of a more plodding kind. As to gunners or engineers, whose heads are kept cool on a diet of mathematics, it is simply unthinkable.

The names of the two officers were Feraud and D'Hubert, and they were both lieutenants in a regiment of hussars, but not in the same regiment.

Feraud was doing regimental work, but Lieutenant D'Hubert had the good fortune to be attached to the person of the general commanding the division, as *officier d'ordonnance*. It was in

Strasbourg, and in this agreeable and important garrison they were enjoying greatly a short interval of peace. They were enjoying it, though both intensely warlike, because it was a sword-sharpening, firelock-cleaning peace, dear to a military heart and undamaging to military prestige, inasmuch that no one believed in its sincerity or duration.

Under those historical circumstances, so favourable to the proper appreciation of military leisure, Lieutenant D'Hubert, one fine afternoon, made his way along a quiet street of a cheerful suburb towards Lieutenant Feraud's quarters, which were in a private house with a garden at the back, belonging to an old maiden lady.

His knock at the door was answered instantly by a young maid in Alsatian costume. Her fresh complexion and her long eyelashes, lowered demurely at the sight of the tall officer, caused Lieutenant D'Hubert, who was accessible to esthetic impressions, to relax the cold, severe gravity of his face. At the same time he observed that the girl had over her arm a pair of hussar's breeches, blue with a red stripe.

"Lieutenant Feraud in?" he inquired, benevolently.

"Oh, no, sir! He went out at six this morning."

The pretty maid tried to close the door. Lieutenant D'Hubert, opposing this move with gentle firmness, stepped into the ante-room, jingling his spurs.

"Come, my dear! You don't mean to say he has not been home since six o'clock this morning?"

Saying these words, Lieutenant D'Hubert opened without ceremony the door of a room so comfortably and neatly ordered that only from internal evidence in the shape of boots, uniforms, and military accoutrements did he acquire the conviction that it was Lieutenant Feraud's room. And he saw also that Lieutenant Feraud was not at home. The truthful maid had followed him, and raised her candid eyes to his face.

"H'm!" said Lieutenant D'Hubert, greatly disappointed, for he had already visited all the haunts where a lieutenant of hussars could be found of a fine afternoon. "So he's out? And do you happen to know, my dear, why he went out at six this morning?"

"No," she answered, readily. "He came home late last night, and snored. I heard him when I got up at five. Then he dressed himself in his oldest uniform and went out. Service, I suppose."

"Service? Not a bit of it!" cried Lieutenant D'Hubert. "Learn, my angel, that he went out thus early to fight a duel with a civilian."

She heard this news without a quiver of her dark eyelashes. It was very obvious that the actions of Lieutenant Feraud were generally above criticism. She only looked up for a moment in mute surprise, and Lieutenant D'Hubert concluded from this absence of emotion that she must have seen Lieutenant Feraud since the morning. He looked around the room.

"Come!" he insisted, with confidential familiarity. "He's perhaps somewhere in the house now?"

She shook her head.

"So much the worse for him!" continued Lieutenant D'Hubert, in a tone of anxious conviction. "But he has been home this morning."

This time the pretty maid nodded slightly.

"He has!" cried Lieutenant D'Hubert. "And went out again? What for? Couldn't he keep quietly indoors! What a lunatic! My dear girl—"

Lieutenant D'Hubert's natural kindness of disposition and strong sense of comradeship helped his powers of observation. He changed his tone to a most insinuating softness, and, gazing at the hussar's breeches hanging over the arm of the girl, he appealed to the interest she took in Lieutenant Feraud's comfort and happiness. He was pressing and persuasive. He used his eyes, which were kind and fine, with excellent effect. His anxiety to get hold at once of Lieutenant Feraud, for Lieutenant Feraud's own good, seemed so genuine that at last it overcame the girl's unwillingness to speak. Unluckily she had not much to tell. Lieutenant Feraud had returned home shortly before ten, had walked straight into his room, and had thrown himself on his bed to resume his slumbers. She had heard him snore rather louder than before far into the afternoon. Then he got up, put on his best uniform, and went out. That was all she knew.

She raised her eyes, and Lieutenant D'Hubert stared into them incredulously.

"It's incredible. Gone parading the town in his best uniform! My dear child, don't you know he ran that civilian through this morning? Clean through, as you spit a hare."

The pretty maid heard the gruesome intelligence without any signs of distress. But she pressed her lips together thoughtfully.

"He isn't parading the town," she remarked in a low tone. "Far from it."

"The civilian's family is making an awful row," continued Lieutenant D'Hubert, pursuing his train of thought. "And the general is very angry. It's one of the best families in the town. Feraud ought to have kept close at least—"

"What will the general do to him?" inquired the girl, anxiously.

"He won't have his head cut off, to be sure," grumbled Lieutenant D'Hubert. "His conduct is positively indecent. He's making no end of trouble for himself by this sort of bravado."

"But he isn't parading the town," the maid insisted in a shy murmur.

"Why, yes! Now I think of it, I haven't seen him anywhere about. What on earth has he done with himself?"

"He's gone to pay a call," suggested the maid, after a moment of silence.

Lieutenant D'Hubert started.

"A call! Do you mean a call on a lady? The cheek of the man! And how do you know this, my dear?"

Without concealing her woman's scorn for the denseness of the masculine mind, the pretty maid reminded him that Lieutenant Feraud had arrayed himself in his best uniform before going out. He had also put on his newest dolman, she added, in a tone as if this conversation were getting on her nerves, and turned away brusquely.

Lieutenant D'Hubert, without questioning the accuracy of the deduction, did not see that it advanced him much on his official quest. For his quest after Lieutenant Feraud had an official character. He did not know any of the women this fellow, who had run a man through in the morning, was likely to visit in the afternoon. The two young men knew each other but slightly. He bit his gloved finger in perplexity.

"Call!" he exclaimed. "Call on the devil!"

The girl, with her back to him, and folding the hussars breeches on a chair, protested with a vexed little laugh:

"Oh, dear, no! On Madame de Lionne."

Lieutenant D'Hubert whistled softly. Madame de Lionne was the wife of a high official who had a well-known salon and some pretensions to sensibility and elegance. The husband was a civilian, and old; but the society of the *salon* was young and military. Lieutenant D'Hubert had whistled, not because the idea of pursuing Lieutenant Feraud into that very salon was disagreeable to him, but because, having arrived in Strasbourg only lately, he had not had the time as yet to get an introduction to Madame de Lionne. And what was that swashbuckler Feraud doing there, he wondered. He did not seem the sort of man who—

"Are you certain of what you say?" asked Lieutenant D'Hubert.

The girl was perfectly certain. Without turning round to look at him, she explained that the coachman of their next door neighbours knew the *maître-d'hôtel* of Madame de Lionne. In this way she had her information. And she was perfectly certain. In giving this assurance she sighed. Lieutenant Feraud called there nearly every afternoon, she added.

"Ah, bah!" exclaimed D'Hubert, ironically. His opinion of Madame de Lionne went down several degrees. Lieutenant Feraud did not seem to him specially worthy of attention on the part of a woman with a reputation for sensibility and elegance. But there was no saying. At bottom they were all alike—very practical rather than idealistic. Lieutenant D'Hubert, however, did not allow his mind to dwell on these considerations.

"By thunder!" he reflected aloud. "The general goes there sometimes. If he happens to find the fellow making eyes at the lady there will be the devil to pay! Our general is not a very accommodating person, I can tell you."

"Go quickly, then! Don't stand here now I've told you where he is!" cried the girl, colouring to the eyes.

"Thanks, my dear! I don't know what I would have done without you."

After manifesting his gratitude in an aggressive way, which at first was repulsed violently, and then submitted to with a sudden and still more repellent indifference, Lieutenant D'Hubert took his departure.

He clanked and jingled along the streets with a martial swagger. To run a comrade to earth in a drawing-room where he was not known did not trouble him in the least. A uniform is a passport. His position as *officier d'ordonnance* of the general added to his assurance. Moreover, now that he knew where to find Lieutenant Feraud, he had no option. It was a service matter.

Madame de Lionne's house had an excellent appearance. A man in livery, opening the door of a large drawing-room with a waxed floor, shouted his name and stood aside to let him pass. It was a reception day. The ladies wore big hats surcharged with a profusion of feathers; their bodies sheathed in clinging white gowns, from the armpits to the tips of the low satin shoes, looked sylph-like and cool in a great display of bare necks and arms. The men who talked with them, on the contrary, were arrayed heavily in multi-coloured garments with collars up to their ears and thick sashes round their waists. Lieutenant D'Hubert made his unabashed way across the room and, bowing low before a sylph-like form reclining on a couch, offered his apologies for this intrusion, which nothing could excuse but the extreme urgency of the service order he had to communicate to his comrade Feraud. He proposed to himself to return presently in a more regular manner and beg forgiveness for interrupting the interesting conversation . . .

A bare arm was extended towards him with gracious nonchalance even before he had finished speaking. He pressed the hand respectfully to his lips, and made the mental remark that it was bony. Madame de Lionne was a blonde, with too fine a skin and a long face.

"*C'est ça!*" she said, with an ethereal smile, disclosing a set of large teeth. "Come this evening to plead for your forgiveness."

"I will not fail, madame."

Meantime, Lieutenant Feraud, splendid in his new dolman and the extremely polished boots of his calling, sat on a chair within a foot of the couch, one hand resting on his thigh, the other twirling his moustache to a point. At a significant glance from D'Hubert he rose without alacrity, and followed him into the recess of a window.

"What is it you want with me?" he asked, with astonishing indifference. Lieutenant D'Hubert could not imagine that in the innocence of his heart and simplicity of his conscience Lieutenant

Feraud took a view of his duel in which neither remorse nor yet a rational apprehension of consequences had any place. Though he had no clear recollection how the quarrel had originated (it was begun in an establishment where beer and wine are drunk late at night), he had not the slightest doubt of being himself the outraged party. He had had two experienced friends for his seconds. Everything had been done according to the rules governing that sort of adventures. And a duel is obviously fought for the purpose of someone being at least hurt, if not killed outright. The civilian got hurt. That also was in order. Lieutenant Feraud was perfectly tranquil; but Lieutenant D'Hubert took it for affectation, and spoke with a certain vivacity.

"I am directed by the general to give you the order to go at once to your quarters, and remain there under close arrest."

It was now the turn of Lieutenant Feraud to be astonished. "What the devil are you telling me there?" he murmured, faintly, and fell into such profound wonder that he could only follow mechanically the motions of Lieutenant D'Hubert. The two officers, one tall, with an interesting face and a moustache the colour of ripe corn, the other, short and sturdy, with a hooked nose and a thick crop of black curly hair, approached the mistress of the house to take their leave. Madame de Lionne, a woman of eclectic taste, smiled upon these armed young men with impartial sensibility and an equal share of interest. Madame de Lionne took her delight in the infinite variety of the human species. All the other eyes in the drawing-room followed the departing officers; and when they had gone out one or two men, who had already heard of the duel, imparted the information to the sylph-like ladies, who received it with faint shrieks of humane concern.

Meantime, the two hussars walked side by side, Lieutenant Feraud trying to master the hidden reason of things which in this instance eluded the grasp of his intellect, Lieutenant D'Hubert feeling annoyed at the part he had to play, because the general's instructions were that he should see personally that Lieutenant Feraud carried out his orders to the letter, and at once.

"The chief seems to know this animal," he thought, eyeing his companion, whose round face, the round eyes, and even the twisted-up jet black little moustache seemed animated by a mental exasperation against the incomprehensible. And aloud he observed rather reproachfully, "The general is in a devilish fury with you!"

Lieutenant Feraud stopped short on the edge of the pavement, and cried in accents of unmistakable sincerity, "What on earth for?" The innocence of the fiery Gascon soul was depicted in the manner in which he seized his head in both hands as if to prevent it bursting with perplexity.

"For the duel," said Lieutenant D'Hubert, curtly. He was annoyed greatly by this sort of perverse fooling.

"The duel! The . . ."

Lieutenant Feraud passed from one paroxysm of astonishment into another. He dropped his hands and walked on slowly, trying to reconcile this information with the state of his own feelings. It was impossible. He burst out indignantly, "Was I to let that sauerkraut-eating civilian wipe his boots on the uniform of the 7th Hussars?"

Lieutenant D'Hubert could not remain altogether unmoved by that simple sentiment. This little fellow was a lunatic, he thought to himself, but there was something in what he said.

"Of course, I don't know how far you were justified," he began, soothingly. "And the general himself may not be exactly informed. Those people have been deafening him with their lamentations."

"Ah! the general is not exactly informed," mumbled Lieutenant Feraud, walking faster and faster as his choler at the injustice of his fate began to rise. "He is not exactly . . . And he orders me under close arrest, with God knows what afterwards!"

"Don't excite yourself like this," remonstrated the other. "Your adversary's people are very influential, you know, and it looks bad enough on the face of it. The general had to take notice of their complaint at once. I don't think he means to be over-severe with you. It's the best thing for you to be kept out of sight for a while."

"I am very much obliged to the general," muttered Lieutenant Feraud through his teeth. "And perhaps you would say I ought to be grateful to you, too, for the trouble you have taken to hunt me up in the drawing-room of a lady who—"

"Frankly," interrupted Lieutenant D'Hubert, with an innocent laugh, "I think you ought to be. I had no end of trouble to find out where you were. It wasn't exactly the place for you to disport yourself in under the circumstances. If the general had caught you there making eyes at the goddess of the temple . . . oh, my word! . . . He hates to be bothered with complaints against his officers, you know. And it looked uncommonly like sheer bravado."

The two officers had arrived now at the street door of Lieutenant Feraud's lodgings. The latter turned towards his companion. "Lieutenant D'Hubert," he said, "I have something to say to you, which can't be said very well in the street. You can't refuse to come up."

The pretty maid had opened the door. Lieutenant Feraud brushed past her brusquely, and she raised her scared and questioning eyes to Lieutenant D'Hubert, who could do nothing but shrug his shoulders slightly as he followed with marked reluctance.

In his room Lieutenant Feraud unhooked the clasp, flung his new dolman on the bed, and, folding his arms across his chest, turned to the other hussar.

"Do you imagine I am a man to submit tamely to injustice?" he inquired, in a boisterous voice.

"Oh, do be reasonable!" remonstrated Lieutenant D'Hubert.

"I am reasonable! I am perfectly reasonable!" retorted the other with ominous restraint. "I can't call the general to account for his behaviour, but you are going to answer me for yours."

"I can't listen to this nonsense," murmured Lieutenant D'Hubert, making a slightly contemptuous grimace.

"You call this nonsense? It seems to me a perfectly plain statement. Unless you don't understand French."

"What on earth do you mean?"

"I mean," screamed suddenly Lieutenant Feraud, "to cut off your ears to teach you to disturb me with the general's orders when I am talking to a lady!"

A profound silence followed this mad declaration; and through the open window Lieutenant D'Hubert heard the little birds singing sanely in the garden. He said, preserving his calm, "Why! If you take that tone, of course I shall hold myself at your disposition whenever you are at liberty to attend to this affair; but I don't think you will cut my ears off."

"I am going to attend to it at once," declared Lieutenant Feraud, with extreme truculence. "If you are thinking of displaying your airs and graces to-night in Madame de Lionne's *salon* you are very much mistaken."

"Really!" said Lieutenant D'Hubert, who was beginning to feel irritated, "you are an impracticable sort of fellow. The general's orders to me were to put you under arrest, not to carve you into small pieces. Good-morning!" And turning his back on the little Gascon, who, always sober in his potations, was as though born intoxicated with the sunshine of his vine-ripening country, the Northman, who could drink hard on occasion, but was born sober under the watery skies of Picardy, made for the door. Hearing, however, the unmistakable sound behind his back of a sword drawn from the scabbard, he had no option but to stop.

"Devil take this mad Southerner!" he thought, spinning round and surveying with composure the warlike posture of Lieutenant Feraud, with a bare sword in his hand.

"At once!—at once!" stuttered Feraud, beside himself.

"You had my answer," said the other, keeping his temper very well.

At first he had been only vexed, and somewhat amused; but now his face got clouded. He was asking himself seriously how he could manage to get away. It was impossible to run from a man with a sword, and as to fighting him, it seemed completely out of the question. He waited awhile, then said exactly what was in his heart.

"Drop this! I won't fight with you. I won't be made ridiculous."

"Ah, you won't?" hissed the Gascon. "I suppose you prefer to be made infamous. Do you hear what I say? . . . Infamous! Infamous! Infamous!" he shrieked, rising and falling on his toes and getting very red in the face.

Lieutenant D'Hubert, on the contrary, became very pale at the sound of the unsavoury word for a moment, then flushed pink to the roots of his fair hair. "But you can't go out to fight; you are under arrest, you lunatic!" he objected, with angry scorn.

"There's the garden: it's big enough to lay out your long carcass in," spluttered the other with such ardour that somehow the anger of the cooler man subsided.

"This is perfectly absurd," he said, glad enough to think he had found a way out of it for the moment. "We shall never get any of our comrades to serve as seconds. It's preposterous."

"Seconds! Damn the seconds! We don't want any seconds. Don't you worry about any seconds. I shall send word to your friends to come and bury you when I am done. And if you want any witnesses, I'll send word to the old girl to put her head out of a window at the back. Stay! There's the gardener. He'll do. He's as deaf as a post, but he has two eyes in his head. Come along! I will teach you, my staff officer, that the carrying about of a general's orders is not always child's play."

While thus discoursing he had unbuckled his empty scabbard. He sent it flying under the bed, and, lowering the point of the sword, brushed past the perplexed Lieutenant D'Hubert, exclaiming, "Follow me!" Directly he had flung open the door a faint shriek was heard and the pretty maid, who had been listening at the keyhole, staggered away, putting the backs of her hands over her eyes. Feraud did not seem to see her, but she ran after him and seized his left arm. He shook her off, and then she rushed towards Lieutenant D'Hubert and clawed at the sleeve of his uniform.

"Wretched man!" she sobbed. "Is this what you wanted to find him for?"

"Let me go," entreated Lieutenant D'Hubert, trying to disengage himself gently. "It's like being in a madhouse," he protested, with exasperation. "Do let me go! I won't do him any harm."

A fiendish laugh from Lieutenant Feraud commented that assurance. "Come along!" he shouted, with a stamp of his foot.

And Lieutenant D'Hubert did follow. He could do nothing else. Yet in vindication of his sanity it must be recorded that as he passed through the ante-room the notion of opening the street door and bolting out presented itself to this brave youth, only of course to be instantly dismissed, for he felt sure that the other would pursue him without shame or compunction. And the prospect of an officer of hussars being chased along the street by another officer of hussars with a naked sword could not be for a moment entertained. Therefore he followed into the garden. Behind them the girl tottered out, too. With ashy lips and wild, scared eyes, she surrendered herself to a dreadful curiosity. She had also the notion of rushing if need be between Lieutenant Feraud and death.

The deaf gardener, utterly unconscious of approaching footsteps, went on watering his flowers till Lieutenant Feraud thumped him on the back. Beholding suddenly an enraged man flourishing a big sabre, the old chap trembling in all his limbs dropped the watering-pot. At once Lieutenant Feraud kicked it away with great animosity, and, seizing the gardener by the throat, backed him against a tree. He held him there, shouting in his ear, "Stay here, and look on! You understand? You've got to look on! Don't dare budge from the spot!"

Lieutenant D'Hubert came slowly down the walk, unclasping his dolman with unconcealed disgust. Even then, with his hand already on the hilt of his sword, he hesitated to draw till a roar, "*En garde, fichtre!* What do you think you came here for?" and the rush of his adversary forced him to put himself as quickly as possible in a posture of defence.

The clash of arms filled that prim garden, which hitherto had known no more warlike sound than the click of clipping shears; and presently the upper part of an old lady's body was projected out of a window upstairs. She tossed her arms above her white cap, scolding in a cracked voice. The gardener remained glued to the tree, his toothless mouth open in idiotic astonishment, and a little farther up the path the pretty girl, as if spellbound to a small grass plot, ran a few steps this way and that, wringing her hands and muttering crazily. She did not rush between the combatants: the onslaughts of Lieutenant Feraud were so fierce that her heart failed her. Lieutenant D'Hubert, his faculties concentrated upon defence, needed all his skill and science of the sword to stop the rushes of his adversary. Twice already he had to break ground. It bothered him to feel his foothold made insecure by the round, dry gravel of the path rolling under the hard soles of his boots. This was most unsuitable ground, he thought, keeping a watchful, narrowed gaze, shaded by long eyelashes, upon the fiery stare of his thick-set adversary. This absurd affair would ruin his reputation of a sensible, well-behaved, promising young officer. It would damage, at any rate, his immediate prospects, and lose him the good-will of his general. These worldly preoccupations were no doubt misplaced in view of the solemnity of the moment. A duel, whether regarded as a ceremony in the cult of honour, or even when reduced in its moral essence to a form of manly sport, demands a perfect singleness of intention, a homicidal austerity of mood. On the other hand, this vivid concern for his future had not a bad effect inasmuch as it began to rouse the anger of Lieutenant D'Hubert. Some seventy seconds had elapsed since they had crossed blades, and Lieutenant D'Hubert had to break ground again in order to avoid impaling his reckless adversary like a beetle for a cabinet of specimens. The result was that misapprehending the motive, Lieutenant Feraud with a triumphant sort of snarl pressed his attack.

"This enraged animal will have me against the wall directly," thought Lieutenant D'Hubert. He imagined himself much closer to the house than he was, and he dared not turn his head; it seemed to him that he was keeping his adversary off with his eyes rather more than with his point. Lieutenant Feraud crouched and bounded with a fierce tigerish agility fit to trouble the stoutest heart. But what was more appalling than the fury of a wild beast, accomplishing in all innocence of heart a natural function, was the fixity of savage purpose man alone is capable of displaying. Lieutenant D'Hubert in the midst of his worldly preoccupations perceived it at last. It was an absurd and damaging affair to be drawn into, but whatever silly intention the fellow had started with, it was clear enough that by this time he meant to kill—nothing less. He meant it with an intensity of will utterly beyond the inferior faculties of a tiger.

As is the case with constitutionally brave men, the full view of the danger interested Lieutenant D'Hubert. And directly he got properly interested, the length of his arm and the coolness of his head told in his favour. It was the turn of Lieutenant Feraud to recoil, with a bloodcurdling grunt of baffled rage. He made a swift feint, and then rushed straight forward.

"Ah! you would, would you?" Lieutenant D'Hubert exclaimed, mentally. The combat had lasted nearly two minutes, time enough for any man to get embittered, apart from the merits of the quarrel. And all at once it was over. Trying to close breast to breast under his adversary's guard Lieutenant Feraud received a slash on his shortened arm. He did not feel it in the least, but it checked his rush, and his feet slipping on the gravel he fell backwards with great violence. The shock jarred his boiling brain into the perfect quietude of insensibility. Simultaneously with his fall the pretty servant-girl shrieked; but the old maiden lady at the window ceased her scolding, and began to cross herself piously.

Beholding his adversary stretched out perfectly still, his face to the sky, Lieutenant D'Hubert thought he had killed him outright. The impression of having slashed hard enough to cut his man clean in two abode with him for a while in an exaggerated memory of the right good-will he had put into the blow. He dropped on his knees hastily by the side of the prostrate body. Discovering that not even the arm was severed, a slight sense of disappointment mingled with the feeling of relief. The fellow deserved the worst. But truly he did not want the death of that sinner. The affair was ugly enough as it stood, and Lieutenant D'Hubert addressed himself at once to the task of stopping the bleeding. In this task it was his fate to be ridiculously impeded by the pretty maid. Rending the air with screams of horror, she attacked him from behind and, twining her fingers in his hair, tugged back at his head. Why she should choose to hinder him at this precise moment he could not in the least understand. He did not try. It was all like a very wicked and harassing dream. Twice to save himself from being pulled over he had to rise and fling her off. He did this stoically, without a word, kneeling down again at once to go on with his work. But the third time, his work being done, he seized her and held her arms pinned to her body. Her cap was half off, her face was red, her eyes blazed with crazy boldness. He looked mildly into them while she called him a wretch, a traitor, and a murderer many times in succession. This did not annoy him so much as the conviction that she had managed to scratch his face abundantly. Ridicule would be added to the scandal of the story. He imagined the adorned tale making its way through the garrison of the town, through the whole army on the frontier, with every possible distortion of motive and sentiment and circumstance, spreading a doubt upon the sanity of his conduct and the distinction of his taste even to the very ears of his honourable family. It was all very well for that fellow Feraud, who had no connections, no family to speak of, and no quality but courage, which, anyhow, was a matter of course, and possessed by every single trooper in the whole mass of French cavalry. Still holding down the arms of the girl in a strong grip, Lieutenant D'Hubert glanced over his shoulder. Lieutenant Feraud had opened his eyes. He did not move. Like a man just waking from a deep sleep he stared without any expression at the evening sky.

Lieutenant D'Hubert's urgent shouts to the old gardener produced no effect—not so much as to make him shut his toothless mouth. Then he remembered that the man was stone deaf. All that time the girl struggled, not with maidenly coyness, but like a pretty, dumb fury, kicking his shins now and then. He continued to hold her as if in a vice, his instinct telling him that were he to let her go she would fly at his eyes. But he was greatly humiliated by his position. At last she gave up. She was more exhausted than appeased, he feared. Nevertheless, he attempted to get out of this wicked dream by way of negotiation.

"Listen to me," he said, as calmly as he could. "Will you promise to run for a surgeon if I let you go?"

With real affliction he heard her declare that she would do nothing of the kind. On the contrary, her sobbed out intention was to remain in the garden, and fight tooth and nail for the protection of the vanquished man. This was shocking.

"My dear child!" he cried in despair, "is it possible that you think me capable of murdering a wounded adversary? Is it. . . . Be quiet, you little wild cat, you!"

They struggled. A thick, drowsy voice said behind him, "What are you after with that girl?"

Lieutenant Feraud had raised himself on his good arm. He was looking sleepily at his other arm, at the mess of blood on his uniform, at a small red pool on the ground, at his sabre lying a foot away on the path. Then he laid himself down gently again to think it all out, as far as a thundering headache would permit of mental operations.

Lieutenant D'Hubert released the girl who crouched at once by the side of the other lieutenant. The shades of night were falling on the little trim garden with this touching group, whence proceeded low murmurs of sorrow and compassion, with other feeble sounds of a different character, as if an imperfectly awake invalid were trying to swear. Lieutenant D'Hubert went away.

He passed through the silent house, and congratulated himself upon the dusk concealing his gory hands and scratched face from the passers-by. But this story could by no means be concealed. He dreaded the discredit and ridicule above everything, and was painfully aware of sneaking through the back streets in the manner of a murderer. Presently the sounds of a flute coming out of the open window of a lighted upstairs room in a modest house interrupted his dismal reflections. It was being played with a persevering virtuosity, and through the *fioritures* of the tune one could hear the regular thumping of the foot beating time on the floor.

Lieutenant D'Hubert shouted a name, which was that of an army surgeon whom he knew fairly well. The sounds of the flute ceased, and the musician appeared at the window, his instrument still in his hand, peering into the street.

"Who calls? You, D'Hubert? What brings you this way?"

He did not like to be disturbed at the hour when he was playing the flute. He was a man whose hair had turned grey already in the thankless task of tying up wounds on battlefields where others reaped advancement and glory.

"I want you to go at once and see Feraud. You know Lieutenant Feraud? He lives down the second street. It's but a step from here."

"What's the matter with him?"

"Wounded."

"Are you sure?"

"Sure!" cried D'Hubert. "I come from there."

"That's amusing," said the elderly surgeon. Amusing was his favourite word; but the expression of his face when he pronounced it never corresponded. He was a stolid man. "Come in," he added. "I'll get ready in a moment."

"Thanks! I will. I want to wash my hands in your room."

Lieutenant D'Hubert found the surgeon occupied in unscrewing his flute, and packing the pieces methodically in a case. He turned his head.

"Water there—in the corner. Your hands do want washing."

"I've stopped the bleeding," said Lieutenant D'Hubert. "But you had better make haste. It's rather more than ten minutes ago, you know."

The surgeon did not hurry his movements.

"What's the matter? Dressing came off? That's amusing. I've been at work in the hospital all day but I've been told this morning by somebody that he had come off without a scratch."

"Not the same duel probably," growled moodily Lieutenant D'Hubert, wiping his hands on a coarse towel.

"Not the same. . . . What? Another. It would take the very devil to make me go out twice in one day." The surgeon looked narrowly at Lieutenant D'Hubert. "How did you come by that scratched face? Both sides, too—and symmetrical. It's amusing."

"Very!" snarled Lieutenant D'Hubert. "And you will find his slashed arm amusing, too. It will keep both of you amused for quite a long time."

The doctor was mystified and impressed by the brusque bitterness of Lieutenant D'Hubert's tone. They left the house together, and in the street he was still more mystified by his conduct.

"Aren't you coming with me?" he asked.

"No," said Lieutenant D'Hubert. "You can find the house by yourself. The front door will be standing open very likely."

"All right. Where's his room?"

"Ground floor. But you had better go right through and look in the garden first."

This astonishing piece of information made the surgeon go off without further parley. Lieutenant D'Hubert regained his quarters nursing a hot and uneasy indignation. He dreaded the chaff of his comrades almost as much as the anger of his superiors. The truth was confoundedly grotesque and embarrassing, even putting aside the irregularity of the combat itself, which made it come abominably near a criminal offence. Like all men without much imagination, a faculty which helps the process of reflective thought, Lieutenant D'Hubert became frightfully harassed by the obvious aspects of his predicament. He was certainly glad that he had not killed Lieutenant Feraud outside all rules, and without the regular witnesses proper to such a transaction. Uncommonly glad. At the same time he felt as though he would have liked to wring his neck for him without ceremony.

He was still under the sway of these contradictory sentiments when the surgeon amateur of the flute came to see him. More than three days had elapsed. Lieutenant D'Hubert was no longer *officier d'ordonnance* to the general commanding the division. He had been sent back to his regiment. And he was resuming his connection with the soldiers' military family by being shut up in close confinement, not at his own quarters in town, but in a room in the barracks. Owing to the gravity of the incident, he was forbidden to see any one. He did not know what had happened, what was being said, or what was being thought. The arrival of the surgeon was a most unexpected thing to the worried captive. The amateur of the flute began by explaining that he was there only by a special favour of the colonel.

"I represented to him that it would be only fair to let you have some authentic news of your adversary," he continued. "You'll be glad to hear he's getting better fast."

Lieutenant D'Hubert's face exhibited no conventional signs of gladness. He continued to walk the floor of the dusty bare room.

"Take this chair, doctor," he mumbled.

The doctor sat down.

"This affair is variously appreciated—in town and in the army. In fact, the diversity of opinions is amusing."

"Is it!" mumbled Lieutenant D'Hubert, tramping steadily from wall to wall. But within himself he marvelled that there could be two opinions on the matter. The surgeon continued.

"Of course, as the real facts are not known—"

"I should have thought," interrupted D'Hubert, "that the fellow would have put you in possession of facts."

"He said something," admitted the other, "the first time I saw him. And, by the by, I did find him in the garden. The thump on the back of his head had made him a little incoherent then. Afterwards he was rather reticent than otherwise."

"Didn't think he would have the grace to be ashamed!" mumbled D'Hubert, resuming his pacing while the doctor murmured, "It's very amusing. Ashamed! Shame was not exactly his frame of mind. However, you may look at the matter otherwise."

"What are you talking about? What matter?" asked D'Hubert, with a sidelong look at the heavy-faced, grey-haired figure seated on a wooden chair.

"Whatever it is," said the surgeon a little impatiently, "I don't want to pronounce any opinion on your conduct—"

"By heavens, you had better not!" burst out D'Hubert.

"There!—there! Don't be so quick in flourishing the sword. It doesn't pay in the long run. Understand once for all that I would not carve any of you youngsters except with the tools of my trade. But my advice is good. If you go on like this you will make for yourself an ugly reputation."

"Go on like what?" demanded Lieutenant D'Hubert, stopping short, quite startled. "I!—I!—make for myself a reputation. . . . What do you imagine?"

"I told you I don't wish to judge of the rights and wrongs of this incident. It's not my business. Nevertheless—"

"What on earth has he been telling you?" interrupted Lieutenant D'Hubert, in a sort of awed scare.

"I told you already, that at first, when I picked him up in the garden, he was incoherent. Afterwards he was naturally reticent. But I gather at least that he could not help himself."

"He couldn't?" shouted Lieutenant D'Hubert in a great voice. Then, lowering his tone impressively, "And what about me? Could I help myself?"

The surgeon stood up. His thoughts were running upon the flute, his constant companion with a consoling voice. In the vicinity of field ambulances, after twenty-four hours' hard work, he had been known to trouble with its sweet sounds the horrible stillness of battlefields, given over to silence and the dead. The solacing hour of his daily life was approaching, and in peace time he held on to the minutes as a miser to his hoard.

"Of course!—of course!" he said, perfunctorily. "You would think so. It's amusing. However, being perfectly neutral and friendly to you both, I have consented to deliver his message to you. Say that I am humouring an invalid if you like. He wants you to know that this affair is by no means at an end. He intends to send you his seconds directly he has regained his strength—providing, of course, the army is not in the field at that time."

"He intends, does he? Why, certainly," spluttered Lieutenant D'Hubert in a passion.

The secret of his exasperation was not apparent to the visitor; but this passion confirmed the surgeon in the belief which was gaining ground outside that some very serious difference had arisen between these two young men, something serious enough to wear an air of mystery, some fact of the utmost gravity. To settle their urgent difference about that fact, those two young men had risked being broken and disgraced at the outset almost of their career. The surgeon feared that the forthcoming inquiry would fail to satisfy the public curiosity. They would not take the public into their confidence as to that something which had passed between them of a nature so outrageous as to make them face a charge of murder—neither more nor less. But what could it be?

The surgeon was not very curious by temperament; but that question haunting his mind caused him twice that evening to hold the instrument off his lips and sit silent for a whole minute—right in the middle of a tune—trying to form a plausible conjecture.

II

He succeeded in this object no better than the rest of the garrison and the whole of society. The two young officers, of no especial consequence till then, became distinguished by the universal curiosity as to the origin of their quarrel. Madame de Lionne's *salon* was the centre of ingenious surmises; that lady herself was for a time assailed by inquiries as being the last person known to have spoken to these unhappy and reckless young men before they went out together from her house to a savage encounter with swords, at dusk, in a private garden. She protested she had not observed anything unusual in their demeanour. Lieutenant Feraud had been visibly annoyed at being called away. That was natural enough; no man likes to be disturbed in a conversation with a lady famed for her elegance and sensibility. But in truth the subject bored Madame de Lionne, since her personality could by no stretch of reckless gossip be connected with this affair. And it irritated her to hear it advanced that there might have been some woman in the case. This irritation arose, not from her elegance or sensibility, but from a more instinctive side of her nature. It became so great at last that she peremptorily forbade the subject to be mentioned under her roof. Near her couch the prohibition was obeyed, but farther off in the *salon* the pall of the imposed silence continued to be lifted more or less. A personage with a long, pale face, resembling the countenance of a sheep, opined, shaking his head, that it was a quarrel of long standing envenomed by time. It was objected to him that the men themselves were too young for such a theory. They belonged also to different and distant parts of France. There were other physical impossibilities, too. A sub-commissary of the Intendence, an agreeable and cultivated bachelor in kerseymere breeches, Hessian boots, and a blue coat embroidered with silver lace, who affected to believe in the transmigration of souls, suggested that the two had met perhaps in some previous existence. The feud was in the forgotten past. It might have been something quite inconceivable in the present state of their being; but their souls remembered the animosity, and manifested an instinctive antagonism. He developed this theme jocularly. Yet the affair was so absurd from the worldly, the military, the honourable, or the prudential point of view, that this weird explanation seemed rather more reasonable than any other.

The two officers had confided nothing definite to any one. Humiliation at having been worsted arms in hand, and an uneasy feeling of having been involved in a scrape by the injustice of fate, kept Lieutenant Feraud savagely dumb. He mistrusted the sympathy of mankind. That would, of course, go to that dandified staff officer. Lying in bed, he raved aloud to the pretty maid who administered to his needs with devotion, and listened to his horrible imprecations with alarm. That Lieutenant D'Hubert should be made to "pay for it," seemed to her just and natural. Her principal care was that Lieutenant Feraud should not excite himself. He appeared so wholly admirable and fascinating to the humility of her heart that her only concern was to see him get well quickly, even if it were only to resume his visits to Madame de Lionne's *salon*.

Lieutenant D'Hubert kept silent for the immediate reason that there was no one, except a stupid young soldier servant, to speak to. Further, he was aware that the episode, so grave professionally, had its comic side. When reflecting upon it, he still felt that he would like to wring Lieutenant Feraud's neck for him. But this formula was figurative rather than precise, and expressed more a state of mind than an actual physical impulse. At the same time, there was in that young man a feeling of comradeship and kindness which made him unwilling to make the position of Lieutenant Feraud worse than it was. He did not want to talk at large about this wretched affair. At the inquiry he would have, of course, to speak the truth in self-defence. This prospect vexed him.

But no inquiry took place. The army took the field instead. Lieutenant D'Hubert, liberated without remark, took up his regimental duties; and Lieutenant Feraud, his arm just out of the sling, rode unquestioned with his squadron to complete his convalescence in the smoke of battlefields and the fresh air of night bivouacs. This bracing treatment suited him so well, that at the first rumour of an armistice being signed he could turn without misgivings to the thoughts of his private warfare.

This time it was to be regular warfare. He sent two friends to Lieutenant D'Hubert, whose regiment was stationed only a few miles away. Those friends had asked no questions of their principal. "I owe him one, that pretty staff officer," he had said, grimly, and they went away quite contentedly on their mission. Lieutenant D'Hubert had no difficulty in finding two friends equally discreet and devoted to their principal. "There's a crazy fellow to whom I must give a lesson," he had declared curtly; and they asked for no better reasons.

On these grounds an encounter with duelling-swords was arranged one early morning in a convenient field. At the third set-to Lieutenant D'Hubert found himself lying on his back on the dewy grass with a hole in his side. A serene sun rising over a landscape of meadows and woods hung on his left. A surgeon—not the flute player, but another— was bending over him, feeling around the wound.

"Narrow squeak. But it will be nothing," he pronounced.

Lieutenant D'Hubert heard these words with pleasure. One of his seconds, sitting on the wet grass, and sustaining his head on his lap, said, "The fortune of war, *mon pauvre vieux*. What will you have? You had better make it up like two good fellows. Do!"

"You don't know what you ask," murmured Lieutenant D'Hubert, in a feeble voice. "However, if he . . ."

In another part of the meadow the seconds of Lieutenant Feraud were urging him to go over and shake hands with his adversary.

"You have paid him off now—*que diable*. It's the proper thing to do. This D'Hubert is a decent fellow."

"I know the decency of these generals' pets," muttered Lieutenant Feraud through his teeth, and the sombre expression of his face discouraged further efforts at reconciliation. The seconds, bowing from a distance, took their men off the field. In the afternoon Lieutenant D'Hubert, very popular as a good comrade uniting great bravery with a frank and equable temper, had many visitors. It was remarked that Lieutenant Feraud did not, as is customary, show himself much abroad to receive the felicitations of his friends. They would not have failed him, because he, too, was liked for the exuberance of his southern nature and the simplicity of his character. In all the places where officers were in the habit of assembling at the end of the day the duel of the morning was talked over from every point of view. Though Lieutenant D'Hubert had got worsted this time, his sword play was commended. No one could deny that it was very close, very scientific. It was even whispered that if he got touched it was because he wished to spare his adversary. But by many the vigour and dash of Lieutenant Feraud's attack were pronounced irresistible.

The merits of the two officers as combatants were frankly discussed; but their attitude to each other after the duel was criticised lightly and with caution. It was irreconcilable, and that was to be regretted. But after all they knew best what the care of their honour dictated. It was not a matter for their comrades to pry into over-much. As to the origin of the quarrel, the general impression was that it dated from the time they were holding garrison in Strasbourg. The musical surgeon shook his head at that. It went much farther back, he thought.

"Why, of course! You must know the whole story," cried several voices, eager with curiosity. "What was it?"

He raised his eyes from his glass deliberately. "Even if I knew ever so well, you can't expect me to tell you, since both the principals choose to say nothing."

He got up and went out, leaving the sense of mystery behind him. He could not stay any longer, because the witching hour of flute-playing was drawing near.

After he had gone a very young officer observed solemnly, "Obviously, his lips are sealed!"

Nobody questioned the high correctness of that remark. Somehow it added to the impressiveness of the affair. Several older officers of both regiments, prompted by nothing but sheer kindness and love of harmony, proposed to form a Court of Honour, to which the two young men would leave the task of their reconciliation. Unfortunately they began by approaching Lieutenant Feraud, on the assumption that, having just scored heavily, he would be found placable and disposed to moderation.

The reasoning was sound enough. Nevertheless, the move turned out unfortunate. In that relaxation of moral fibre, which is brought about by the ease of soothed vanity, Lieutenant Feraud had condescended in the secret of his heart to review the case, and even had come to doubt not the justice of his cause, but the absolute sagacity of his conduct. This being so, he was disinclined to talk about it. The suggestion of the regimental wise men put him in a difficult position. He was disgusted at it, and this disgust, by a paradoxical logic, reawakened his animosity against Lieutenant D'Hubert. Was he to be pestered with this fellow for ever—the fellow who had an infernal knack of getting round people somehow? And yet it was difficult to refuse point blank that mediation sanctioned by the code of honour.

He met the difficulty by an attitude of grim reserve. He twisted his moustache and used vague words. His case was perfectly clear. He was not ashamed to state it before a proper Court of Honour, neither was he afraid to defend it on the ground. He did not see any reason to jump at the suggestion before ascertaining how his adversary was likely to take it.

Later in the day, his exasperation growing upon him, he was heard in a public place saying sardonically, "that it would be the very luckiest thing for Lieutenant D'Hubert, because the next time of meeting he need not hope to get off with the mere trifle of three weeks in bed."

This boastful phrase might have been prompted by the most profound Machiavellism. Southern natures often hide, under the outward impulsiveness of action and speech, a certain amount of astuteness.

Lieutenant Feraud, mistrusting the justice of men, by no means desired a Court of Honour; and the above words, according so well with his temperament, had also the merit of serving his turn. Whether meant so or not, they found their way in less than four-and-twenty hours into Lieutenant D'Hubert's bedroom. In consequence Lieutenant D'Hubert, sitting propped up with pillows, received the overtures made to him next day by the statement that the affair was of a nature which could not bear discussion.

The pale face of the wounded officer, his weak voice which he had yet to use cautiously, and the courteous dignity of his tone had a great effect on his hearers. Reported outside all this did more for deepening the mystery than the vapourings of Lieutenant Feraud. This last was greatly relieved at the issue. He began to enjoy the state of general wonder, and was pleased to add to it by assuming an attitude of fierce discretion.

The colonel of Lieutenant D'Hubert's regiment was a grey-haired, weather-beaten warrior, who took a simple view of his responsibilities. "I can't," he said to himself, "let the best of my subalterns get damaged like this for nothing. I must get to the bottom of this affair privately. He must speak out if the devil were in it. The colonel should be more than a father to these youngsters." And indeed he loved all his men with as much affection as a father of a large family can feel for every individual member of it. If human beings by an oversight of Providence came into the world as mere civilians, they were born again into a regiment as infants are born into a family, and it was that military birth alone which counted.

At the sight of Lieutenant D'Hubert standing before him very bleached and hollow-eyed the heart of the old warrior felt a pang of genuine compassion. All his affection for the regiment—that body of men which he held in his hand to launch forward and draw back, who ministered to his pride and commanded all his thoughts—seemed centred for a moment on the person of the most promising subaltern. He cleared his throat in a threatening manner, and frowned terribly. "You must understand," he began, "that I don't care a rap for the life of a single man in the regiment. I would send the eight hundred and forty-three of you men and horses galloping into the pit of perdition with no more compunction than I would kill a fly!"

"Yes, Colonel. You would be riding at our head," said Lieutenant D'Hubert with a wan smile.

The colonel, who felt the need of being very diplomatic, fairly roared at this. "I want you to know, Lieutenant D'Hubert, that I could stand aside and see you all riding to Hades if need be. I am a man to do even that if the good of the service and my duty to my country required it from me. But that's unthinkable, so don't you even hint at such a thing." He glared awfully, but his tone softened. "There's some milk yet about that moustache of yours, my boy. You don't know what a man like me is capable of. I would hide behind a haystack if . . . Don't grin at me, sir! How dare you? If this were not a private conversation I would . . . Look here! I am responsible for the proper expenditure of lives under my command for the glory of our country and the honour of the regiment. Do you understand that? Well, then, what the devil do you mean by letting yourself be spitted like this by that fellow of the 7th Hussars? It's simply disgraceful!"

Lieutenant D'Hubert felt vexed beyond measure. His shoulders moved slightly. He made no other answer. He could not ignore his responsibility.

The colonel veiled his glance and lowered his voice still more. "It's deplorable!" he murmured. And again he changed his tone. "Come!" he went on, persuasively, but with that note of authority which dwells in the throat of a good leader of men, "this affair must be settled. I desire to be told plainly what it is all about. I demand, as your best friend, to know."

The compelling power of authority, the persuasive influence of kindness, affected powerfully a man just risen from a bed of sickness. Lieutenant D'Hubert's hand, which grasped the knob of a stick, trembled slightly. But his northern temperament, sentimental yet cautious and clear-sighted, too, in its idealistic way, checked his impulse to make a clean breast of the whole deadly absurdity. According to the precept of transcendental wisdom, he turned his tongue seven times in his mouth before he spoke. He made then only a speech of thanks.

The colonel listened, interested at first, then looked mystified. At last he frowned. "You hesitate?—*mille tonnerres!* Haven't I told you that I will condescend to argue with you—as a friend?"

"Yes, Colonel!" answered Lieutenant D'Hubert, gently. "But I am afraid that after you have heard me out as a friend you will take action as my superior officer."

The attentive colonel snapped his jaws. "Well, what of that?" he said, frankly. "Is it so damnably disgraceful?"

"It is not," negatived Lieutenant D'Hubert, in a faint but firm voice.

"Of course, I shall act for the good of the service. Nothing can prevent me doing that. What do you think I want to be told for?"

"I know it is not from idle curiosity," protested Lieutenant D'Hubert. "I know you will act wisely. But what about the good fame of the regiment?"

"It cannot be affected by any youthful folly of a lieutenant," said the colonel, severely.

"No. It cannot be. But it can be by evil tongues. It will be said that a lieutenant of the 4th Hussars, afraid of meeting his adversary, is hiding behind his colonel. And that would be worse than hiding behind a haystack—for the good of the service. I cannot afford to do that, Colonel."

"Nobody would dare to say anything of the kind," began the colonel very fiercely, but ended the phrase on an uncertain note. The bravery of Lieutenant D'Hubert was well known. But the colonel was well aware that the duelling courage, the single combat courage, is rightly or wrongly supposed to be courage of a special sort. And it was eminently necessary that an officer of his regiment should possess every kind of courage—and prove it, too. The colonel stuck out his lower lip, and looked far away with a peculiar glazed stare. This was the expression of his perplexity—an expression practically unknown to his regiment; for perplexity is a sentiment which is incompatible with the rank of colonel of cavalry. The colonel himself was overcome by the unpleasant novelty of the sensation. As he was not accustomed to think except on professional matters connected with the welfare of men and horses, and the proper use thereof on the field of glory, his intellectual efforts degenerated into mere mental repetitions of profane language. "*Mille tonnerres! . . . Sacré nom de nom . . .*" he thought.

Lieutenant D'Hubert coughed painfully, and added in a weary voice: "There will be plenty of evil tongues to say that I've been cowed. And I am sure you will not expect me to pass that over. I may find myself suddenly with a dozen duels on my hands instead of this one affair."

The direct simplicity of this argument came home to the colonel's understanding. He looked at his subordinate fixedly. "Sit down, Lieutenant!" he said, gruffly. "This is the very devil of a . . . Sit down!"

"*Mon Colonel*," D'Hubert began again, "I am not afraid of evil tongues. There's a way of silencing them. But there's my peace of mind, too. I wouldn't be able to shake off the notion that I've ruined a brother officer. Whatever action you take, it is bound to go farther. The inquiry has been dropped—let it rest now. It would have been absolutely fatal to Feraud."

"Hey! What! Did he behave so badly?"

"Yes. It was pretty bad," muttered Lieutenant D'Hubert. Being still very weak, he felt a disposition to cry.

As the other man did not belong to his own regiment the colonel had no difficulty in believing this. He began to pace up and down the room. He was a good chief, a man capable of discreet sympathy. But he was human in other ways, too, and this became apparent because he was not capable of artifice.

"The very devil, Lieutenant," he blurted out, in the innocence of his heart, "is that I have declared my intention to get to the bottom of this affair. And when a colonel says something . . . you see . . ."

Lieutenant D'Hubert broke in earnestly: "Let me entreat you, Colonel, to be satisfied with taking my word of honour that I was put into a damnable position where I had no option; I had no choice whatever, consistent with my dignity as a man and an officer. . . . After all, Colonel, this fact is the very bottom of this affair. Here you've got it. The rest is mere detail. . . ."

The colonel stopped short. The reputation of Lieutenant D'Hubert for good sense and good temper weighed in the balance. A cool head, a warm heart, open as the day. Always correct in his behaviour. One had to trust him. The colonel repressed manfully an immense curiosity. "H'm! You affirm that as a man and an officer. . . . No option? Eh?"

"As an officer—an officer of the 4th Hussars, too," insisted Lieutenant D'Hubert, "I had not. And that is the bottom of the affair, Colonel."

"Yes. But still I don't see why, to one's colonel. . . . A colonel is a father—*que diable!*"

Lieutenant D'Hubert ought not to have been allowed out as yet. He was becoming aware of his physical insufficiency with humiliation and despair. But the morbid obstinacy of an invalid possessed him, and at the same time he felt with dismay his eyes filling with water. This trouble seemed too big to handle. A tear fell down the thin, pale cheek of Lieutenant D'Hubert.

The colonel turned his back on him hastily. You could have heard a pin drop. "This is some silly woman story—is it not?"

Saying these words the chief spun round to seize the truth, which is not a beautiful shape living in a well, but a shy bird best caught by stratagem. This was the last move of the colonel's diplomacy. He saw the truth shining unmistakably in the gesture of Lieutenant D'Hubert raising his weak arms and his eyes to heaven in supreme protest.

"Not a woman affair—eh?" growled the colonel, staring hard. "I don't ask you who or where. All I want to know is whether there is a woman in it?"

Lieutenant D'Hubert's arms dropped, and his weak voice was pathetically broken.

"Nothing of the kind, *mon Colonel.*"

"On your honour?" insisted the old warrior.

"On my honour."

"Very well," said the colonel, thoughtfully, and bit his lip. The arguments of Lieutenant D'Hubert, helped by his liking for the man, had convinced him. On the other hand, it was highly improper that his intervention, of which he had made no secret, should produce no visible effect. He kept Lieutenant D'Hubert a few minutes longer, and dismissed him kindly.

"Take a few days more in bed. Lieutenant. What the devil does the surgeon mean by reporting you fit for duty?"

On coming out of the colonel's quarters, Lieutenant D'Hubert said nothing to the friend who was waiting outside to take him home. He said nothing to anybody. Lieutenant D'Hubert made no confidences. But on the evening of that day the colonel, strolling under the elms growing near his quarters, in the company of his second in command, opened his lips.

"I've got to the bottom of this affair," he remarked. The Lieutenant-colonel, a dry, brown chip of a man with short side-whiskers, pricked up his ears at that without letting a sign of curiosity escape him.

"It's no trifle," added the colonel, oracularly. The other waited for a long while before he murmured:

"Indeed, sir!"

"No trifle," repeated the colonel, looking straight before him. "I've, however, forbidden D'Hubert either to send to or receive a challenge from Feraud for the next twelve months."

He had imagined this prohibition to save the prestige a colonel should have. The result of it was to give an official seal to the mystery surrounding this deadly quarrel. Lieutenant D'Hubert repelled by an impassive silence all attempts to worm the truth out of him. Lieutenant Feraud, secretly uneasy at first, regained his assurance as time went on. He disguised his ignorance of the meaning of the imposed truce by slight sardonic laughs, as though he were amused by what he intended to keep to himself. "But what will you do?" his chums used to ask him. He contented himself by replying "*Qui vivra verra*" with a little truculent air. And everybody admired his discretion.

Before the end of the truce Lieutenant D'Hubert got his troop. The promotion was well earned, but somehow no one seemed to expect the event. When Lieutenant Feraud heard of it at a gathering of officers, he muttered through his teeth, "Is that so?" At once he unhooked his sabre from a peg near the door, buckled it on carefully, and left the company without another word. He walked home with measured steps, struck a light with his flint and steel, and lit his tallow candle. Then snatching an unlucky glass tumbler off the mantelpiece he dashed it violently on the floor.

Now that D'Hubert was an officer of superior rank there could be no question of a duel. Neither of them could send or receive a challenge without rendering himself amenable to a court-martial. It was not to be thought of. Lieutenant Feraud, who for many days now had experienced no real desire to meet Lieutenant D'Hubert arms in hand, chafed again at the systematic injustice of fate. "Does he think he will escape me in that way?" he thought, indignantly. He saw in this promotion an intrigue, a conspiracy, a cowardly manœuvre. That colonel knew what he was doing. He had hastened to recommend his favourite for a step. It was outrageous that a man should be able to avoid the consequences of his acts in such a dark and tortuous manner.

Of a happy-go-lucky disposition, of a temperament more pugnacious than military, Lieutenant Feraud had been content to give and receive blows for sheer love of armed strife, and without much thought of advancement; but now an urgent desire to get on sprang up in his breast. This fighter by vocation resolved in his mind to seize showy occasions and to court the favourable opinion of his chiefs like a mere worldling. He knew he was as brave as any one, and never doubted his personal charm. Nevertheless, neither the bravery nor the charm seemed to work very swiftly. Lieutenant Feraud's engaging, careless truculence of a *beau sabreur* underwent a change. He began to make bitter allusions to "clever fellows who stick at nothing to get on." The army was full of them, he would say; you had only to look round. But all the time he had in view one person only, his adversary, D'Hubert. Once he confided to an appreciative friend: "You see, I don't know how to fawn on the right sort of people. It isn't in my character."

He did not get his step till a week after Austerlitz. The Light Cavalry of the Grand Army had its hands very full of interesting work for a little while. Directly the pressure of professional occupation had been eased Captain Feraud took measures to arrange a meeting without loss of time. "I know my bird," he observed, grimly. "If I don't look sharp he will take care to get himself promoted over the heads of a dozen better men than himself. He's got the knack for that sort of thing."

This duel was fought in Silesia. If not fought to a finish, it was, at any rate, fought to a standstill. The weapon was the cavalry sabre, and the skill, the science, the vigour, and the determination displayed by the adversaries compelled the admiration of the beholders. It became the subject of talk on both shores of the Danube, and as far as the garrisons of Gratz and Laybach. They crossed blades seven times. Both had many cuts which bled profusely. Both refused to have the combat stopped, time after time, with what appeared the most deadly animosity. This appearance was caused on the part of Captain D'Hubert by a rational desire to be done once for all with this worry; on the part of Captain Feraud by a tremendous exaltation of his pugnacious instincts and the incitement of wounded vanity. At last, dishevelled, their shirts in rags, covered with gore and hardly able to stand, they were led away forcibly by their marvelling and horrified seconds. Later on, besieged by comrades avid of details, these gentlemen declared that they could not have allowed that sort of hacking to go on indefinitely. Asked whether the quarrel was settled this time, they gave it out as their conviction that it was a difference which could only be settled by one of the parties remaining lifeless on the ground. The sensation spread from army corps to army corps, and penetrated at last to the smallest detachments of the troops cantoned between the Rhine and the Save. In the cafes in Vienna it was generally estimated, from details to hand, that the adversaries would be able to meet again in three weeks' time on the outside. Something really transcendent in the way of duelling was expected.

These expectations were brought to naught by the necessities of the service which separated the two officers. No official notice had been taken of their quarrel. It was now the property of the army, and not to be meddled with lightly. But the story of the duel, or rather their duelling propensities, must have stood somewhat in the way of their advancement, because they were still captains when they came together again during the war with Prussia. Detached north after Jena, with the army commanded by Marshal Bernadotte, Prince of Ponte Corvo, they entered Lübeck together.

It was only after the occupation of that town that Captain Feraud found leisure to consider his future conduct in view of the fact that

Captain D'Hubert had been given the position of third aide-de-camp to the marshal. He considered it a great part of a night, and in the morning summoned two sympathetic friends.

"I've been thinking it over calmly," he said, gazing at them with blood-shot, tired eyes. "I see that I must get rid of that intriguing personage. Here he's managed to sneak on to the personal staff of the marshal. It's a direct provocation to me. I can't tolerate a situation in which I am exposed any day to receive an order through him. And God knows what order, too! That sort of thing has happened once before— and that's once too often. He understands this perfectly, never fear. I can't tell you any more. Now you know what it is you have to do."

This encounter took place outside the town of Lübeck, on very open ground, selected with special care in deference to the general sentiment of the cavalry division belonging to the army corps, that this time the two officers should meet on horseback. After all, this duel was a cavalry affair, and to persist in fighting on foot would look like a slight on one's own arm of the service. The seconds, startled by the unusual nature of the suggestion, hastened to refer to their principals. Captain Feraud jumped at it with alacrity. For some obscure reason, depending, no doubt, on his psychology, he imagined himself invincible on horseback. All alone within the four walls of his room he rubbed his hands and muttered triumphantly, "Aha! my pretty staff officer, I've got you now."

Captain D'Hubert on his side, after staring hard for a considerable time at his friends, shrugged his shoulders slightly. This affair had hopelessly and unreasonably complicated his existence for him. One absurdity more or less in the development did not matter—all absurdity was distasteful to him; but, urbane as ever, he produced a faintly ironical smile, and said in his calm voice, "It certainly will do away to some extent with the monotony of the thing."

When left alone, he sat down at a table and took his head into his hands. He had not spared himself of late and the marshal had been working all his aides-decamp particularly hard. The last three weeks of campaigning in horrible weather had affected his health. When over-tired he suffered from a stitch in his wounded side, and that uncomfortable sensation always depressed him. "It's that brute's doing, too," he thought bitterly.

The day before he had received a letter from home, announcing that his only sister was going to be married. He reflected that from the time she was nineteen and he twenty-six, when he went away to garrison life in Strasbourg, he had had but two short glimpses of her. They had been great friends and confidants; and now she was going to be given away to a man whom he did not know—a very worthy fellow no doubt, but not half good enough for her. He would never see his old Léonie again. She had a capable little head, and plenty of tact; she would know how to manage the fellow, to be sure. He was easy in his mind about her happiness but he felt ousted from the first place in her thoughts which had been his ever since the girl could speak. A melancholy regret of the days of his childhood settled upon Captain D'Hubert, third aide-de-camp to the Prince of Ponte Corvo.

He threw aside the letter of congratulation he had begun to write as in duty bound, but without enthusiasm. He took a fresh piece of paper, and traced on it the words: "This is my last will and testament." Looking at these words he gave himself up to unpleasant reflection; a presentiment that he would never see the scenes of his childhood weighed down the equable spirits of Captain D'Hubert. He jumped up, pushing his chair back, yawned elaborately in sign that he didn't care anything for presentiments, and throwing himself on the bed went to sleep. During the night he shivered from time to time without waking up. In the morning he rode out of town between his two seconds, talking of indifferent things, and looking right and left with apparent detachment into the heavy morning mists shrouding the flat green fields bordered by hedges. He leaped a ditch, and saw the forms of many mounted men moving in the fog. "We are to fight before a gallery, it seems," he muttered to himself, bitterly.

His seconds were rather concerned at the state of the atmosphere, but presently a pale, sickly sun struggled out of the low vapours, and Captain D'Hubert made out, in the distance, three horsemen riding a little apart from the others. It was Captain Feraud and his seconds. He drew his sabre, and assured himself that it was properly fastened to his wrist. And now the seconds, who had been standing in close group with the heads of their horses together, separated at an easy canter, leaving a large, clear field between him and his adversary. Captain D'Hubert looked at the pale sun, at the dismal fields, and the imbecility of the impending fight filled him with desolation. From a distant part of the field a stentorian voice shouted commands at proper intervals: *Au pas— Au trot—Charrrgez!* . . . Presentiments of death don't come to a man for nothing, he thought at the very moment he put spurs to his horse.

And therefore he was more than surprised when, at the very first set-to, Captain Feraud laid himself open to a cut over the forehead, which blinding him with blood, ended the combat almost before it had fairly begun. It was impossible to go on. Captain D'Hubert, leaving his enemy swearing horribly and reeling in the saddle between his two appalled friends, leaped the ditch again into the road and trotted home with his two seconds, who seemed rather awestruck at the speedy issue of that encounter. In the evening Captain D'Hubert finished the congratulatory letter on his sister's marriage.

He finished it late. It was a long letter. Captain D'Hubert gave reins to his fancy. He told his sister that he would feel rather lonely after this great change in her life; but then the day would come for him, too, to get married. In fact, he was thinking already of the time when there would be no one left to fight with in Europe and the epoch of wars would be over. "I expect then," he wrote, "to be within measurable distance of a marshal's baton, and you will be an experienced married woman. You shall look out a wife for me. I will be, probably, bald by then, and a little *blasé*. I shall require a young girl, pretty of course, and with a large fortune, which should help me to close my glorious career in the splendour befitting my exalted rank." He ended with the information that he had just given a lesson to a worrying, quarrelsome fellow who imagined he had a grievance against him. "But if you, in the depths of your province," he continued, "ever hear it said that your brother is of a quarrelsome disposition, don't you believe it on any account. There is no saying what gossip from the army may reach your innocent ears. Whatever you hear you may rest assured that your ever-loving brother is not a duellist." Then Captain D'Hubert crumpled up the blank sheet of paper headed with the words "This is my last will and testament," and threw it in the fire with a great laugh at himself. He didn't care a snap for what that lunatic could do. He had suddenly acquired the conviction that his adversary was utterly powerless to affect his life in any sort of way; except, perhaps, in the way of putting a special excitement into the delightful, gay intervals between the campaigns.

From this on there were, however, to be no peaceful intervals in the career of Captain D'Hubert. He saw the fields of Eylau and Friedland, marched and countermarched in the snow, in the mud, in the dust of Polish plains, picking up distinction and advancement on all the roads of North-eastern Europe. Meantime, Captain Feraud, dispatched southwards with his regiment, made unsatisfactory war in Spain. It was only when the preparations for the Russian campaign began that he was ordered north again. He left the country of mantillas and oranges without regret.

The first signs of a not unbecoming baldness added to the lofty aspect of Colonel D'Hubert's forehead. This feature was no longer white and smooth as in the days of his youth; the kindly open glance of his blue eyes had grown a little hard as if from much peering through the smoke of battles. The ebony crop on Colonel Feraud's head, coarse and crinkly like a cap of horsehair, showed many silver threads about the temples. A detestable warfare of ambushes and inglorious surprises had not improved his temper. The beak-like curve of his nose was unpleasantly set off by a deep fold on each side of his mouth. The round orbits of his eyes radiated wrinkles. More than ever he recalled an irritable and staring bird—something like a cross between a parrot and an owl. He was still extremely outspoken in his dislike of "intriguing fellows." He seized every opportunity to state that he did not pick up his rank in the ante-rooms of marshals. The unlucky persons, civil or military, who, with an intention of being pleasant, begged Colonel Feraud to tell them how he came by that very apparent scar on the forehead, were astonished to find themselves snubbed in various ways, some of which were simply rude and others mysteriously sardonic. Young officers were warned kindly by their more experienced comrades not to stare openly at the colonel's scar. But indeed an officer need have been very young in his profession not to have heard the legendary tale of that duel originating in a mysterious, unforgivable offence.

III

The retreat from Moscow submerged all private feelings in a sea of disaster and misery. Colonels without regiments, D'Hubert and Feraud carried the musket in the ranks of the so-called sacred battalion—a battalion recruited from officers of all arms who had no longer any troops to lead.

In that battalion promoted colonels did duty as sergeants; the generals captained the companies; a marshal of France, Prince of the Empire, commanded the whole. All had provided themselves with muskets picked up on the road, and with cartridges taken from the dead. In the general destruction of the bonds of discipline and duty holding together the companies, the battalions, the regiments, the brigades, and divisions of an armed host, this body of men put its pride in preserving some semblance of order and formation. The only stragglers were those who fell out to give up to the frost their exhausted souls. They plodded on, and their passage did not disturb the mortal silence of the plains, shining with the livid light of snows under a sky the colour of ashes. Whirlwinds ran along the fields, broke against the dark column, enveloped it in a turmoil of flying icicles, and subsided, disclosing it creeping on its tragic way without the swing and rhythm of the military pace. It struggled onwards, the men exchanging neither words nor looks; whole ranks marched touching elbow, day after day and never raising their eyes from the ground, as if lost in despairing reflections. In the dumb, black forests of pines the cracking of overloaded branches was the only sound they heard. Often from daybreak to dusk no one spoke in the whole column. It was like a *macabre* march of struggling corpses towards a distant grave. Only an alarm of Cossacks could restore to their eyes a semblance of martial resolution. The battalion faced about and deployed, or formed square under the endless fluttering of snowflakes. A cloud of horsemen with fur caps on their heads, levelled long lances, and yelled "Hurrah! Hurrah!" around their menacing immobility whence, with muffled detonations, hundreds of dark red flames darted through the air thick with falling snow. In a very few moments the horsemen would disappear, as if carried off yelling in the gale, and the sacred battalion standing still, alone in the blizzard, heard only the howling of the wind, whose blasts searched their very hearts. Then, with a cry or two of "*Vive l'Empereur!*" it would resume its march, leaving behind a few lifeless bodies lying huddled up, tiny black specks on the white immensity of the snows.

Though often marching in the ranks, or skirmishing in the woods side by side, the two officers ignored each other; this not so much from inimical intention as from a very real indifference. All their store of moral energy was expended in resisting the terrific enmity of nature and the crushing sense of irretrievable disaster. To the last they counted among the most active, the least demoralized of the battalion; their vigorous vitality invested them both with the appearance of an heroic pair in the eyes of their comrades. And they never exchanged more than a casual word or two, except one day, when skirmishing in front of the battalion against a worrying attack of cavalry, they found themselves cut off in the woods by a small party of Cossacks. A score of fur-capped, hairy horsemen rode to and fro, brandishing their lances in ominous silence; but the two officers had no mind to lay down their arms, and Colonel Feraud suddenly spoke up in a hoarse, growling voice, bringing his firelock to the shoulder. "You take the nearest brute, Colonel D'Hubert; I'll settle the next one. I am a better shot than you are."

Colonel D'Hubert nodded over his levelled musket. Their shoulders were pressed against the trunk of a large tree; on their front enormous snowdrifts protected them from a direct charge. Two carefully aimed shots rang out in the frosty air, two Cossacks reeled in their saddles. The rest, not thinking the game good enough, closed round their wounded comrades and galloped away out of range. The two officers managed to rejoin their battalion halted for the night. During that afternoon they had leaned upon each other more than once, and towards the end, Colonel D'Hubert, whose long legs gave him an advantage in walking through soft snow, peremptorily took the musket of Colonel Feraud from him and carried it on his shoulder, using his own as a staff.

On the outskirts of a village half buried in the snow an old wooden barn burned with a clear and an immense flame. The sacred battalion of skeletons, muffled in rags, crowded greedily the windward side, stretching hundreds of numbed, bony hands to the blaze. Nobody had noted their approach. Before entering the circle of light playing on the sunken, glassy-eyed, starved faces, Colonel D'Hubert spoke in his turn:

"Here's your musket, Colonel Feraud. I can walk better than you."

Colonel Feraud nodded, and pushed on towards the warmth of the fierce flames. Colonel D'Hubert was more deliberate, but not the less bent on getting a place in the front rank. Those they shouldered aside tried to greet with a faint cheer the reappearance of the two indomitable companions in activity and endurance. Those manly qualities had never perhaps received a higher tribute than this feeble acclamation.

This is the faithful record of speeches exchanged during the retreat from Moscow by Colonels Feraud and D'Hubert. Colonel Feraud's taciturnity was the outcome of concentrated rage. Short, hairy, black faced, with layers of grime and the thick sprouting of a wiry beard, a frost-bitten hand wrapped up in filthy rags carried in a sling, he accused fate of unparalleled perfidy towards the sublime Man of Destiny. Colonel D'Hubert, his long moustaches pendent in icicles on each side of his cracked blue lips, his eyelids inflamed with the glare of snows, the principal part of his costume consisting of a sheepskin coat looted with difficulty from the frozen corpse of a camp follower found in an abandoned cart, took a more thoughtful view of events. His regularly handsome features, now reduced to mere bony lines and fleshless hollows, looked out of a woman's black velvet hood, over which was rammed forcibly a cocked hat picked up under the wheels of an empty army fourgon, which must have contained at one time some general officer's luggage. The sheepskin coat being short for a man of his inches ended very high up, and the skin of his legs, blue with the cold, showed through the tatters of his nether garments. This under the circumstances provoked neither jeers nor pity. No one cared how the next man felt or looked. Colonel D'Hubert himself, hardened to exposure, suffered mainly in his self-respect from the lamentable indecency of his costume. A thoughtless person may think that with a whole host of inanimate bodies bestrewing the path of retreat there could not have been much difficulty in supplying the deficiency. But to loot a pair of breeches from a frozen corpse is not so easy as it may appear to a mere theorist. It requires time and labour. You must remain behind while your companions march on. Colonel D'Hubert had his scruples as to falling out. Once he had stepped aside he could not be sure of ever rejoining his battalion; and the ghastly intimacy of a wrestling match with the frozen dead opposing the unyielding rigidity of iron to your violence was repugnant to the delicacy of his feelings. Luckily, one day, grubbing in a mound of snow between the huts of a village in the hope of finding there a frozen potato or some vegetable garbage he could put between his long and shaky teeth, Colonel D'Hubert uncovered a couple of mats of the sort Russian peasants use to line the sides of their carts with. These, beaten free of frozen snow, bent about his elegant person and fastened solidly round his waist, made a bell-shaped nether garment, a sort of stiff petticoat, which rendered Colonel D'Hubert a perfectly decent, but a much more noticeable figure than before.

Thus accoutred, he continued to retreat, never doubting of his personal escape, but full of other misgivings. The early buoyancy of his belief in the future was destroyed. If the road of glory led through such unforeseen passages, he asked himself—for he was reflective—whether the guide was altogether trustworthy. It was a patriotic sadness, not unmingled with some personal concern, and quite unlike the unreasoning indignation against men and things nursed by Colonel Feraud. Recruiting his strength in a little German town for three weeks, Colonel D'Hubert was surprised to discover within himself a love of repose. His returning vigour was strangely pacific in its aspirations. He meditated silently upon this bizarre change of mood. No doubt many of his brother officers of field rank went through the same moral experience. But these were not the times to talk of it. In one of his letters home Colonel D'Hubert wrote, "All your plans, my dear Léonie, for marrying me to the charming girl you have discovered in your neighbourhood, seem farther off than ever. Peace is not yet. Europe wants another lesson. It will be a hard task for us, but it shall be done, because the Emperor is invincible."

Thus wrote Colonel D'Hubert from Pomerania to his married sister Léonie, settled in the south of France. And so far the sentiments expressed would not have been disowned by Colonel Feraud, who wrote no letters to anybody, whose father had been in life an illiterate blacksmith, who had no sister or brother, and whom no one desired ardently to pair off for a life of peace with a charming young girl. But Colonel D'Hubert's letter contained also some philosophical generalities upon the uncertainty of all personal hopes, when bound up entirely with the prestigious fortune of one incomparably great it is true, yet still remaining but a man in his greatness. This view would have appeared rank heresy to Colonel Feraud. Some melancholy forebodings of a military kind, expressed cautiously, would have been pronounced as nothing short of high treason by Colonel Feraud. But Léonie, the sister of Colonel D'Hubert, read them with profound satisfaction, and, folding the letter thoughtfully, remarked to herself that "Armand was likely to prove eventually a sensible fellow." Since her marriage into a Southern family she had become a convinced believer in the return of the legitimate king. Hopeful and anxious she offered prayers night and morning, and burnt candles in churches for the safety and prosperity of her brother.

She had every reason to suppose that her prayers were heard. Colonel D'Hubert passed through Lutzen, Bautzen, and Leipsic losing no limb, and acquiring additional reputation. Adapting his conduct to the needs of that desperate time, he had never voiced his misgivings. He concealed them under a cheerful courtesy of such pleasant character that people were inclined to ask themselves with wonder whether Colonel D'Hubert was aware of any disasters. Not only his manners, but even his glances remained untroubled. The steady amenity of his blue eyes disconcerted all grumblers, and made despair itself pause.

This bearing was remarked favourably by the Emperor himself; for Colonel D'Hubert, attached now to the Major-General's staff, came on several occasions under the imperial eye. But it exasperated the higher strung nature of Colonel Feraud. Passing through Magdeburg on service, this last allowed himself, while seated gloomily at dinner with the *Commandant de Place*, to say of his life-long adversary: "This man does not love the Emperor," and his words were received by the other guests in profound silence. Colonel Feraud, troubled in his conscience at the atrocity of the aspersion, felt the need to back it up by a good argument. "I ought to know him," he cried, adding some oaths. "One studies one's adversary. I have met him on the ground half a dozen times, as all the army knows. What more do you want? If that isn't opportunity enough for any fool to size up his man, may the devil take me if I can tell what is." And he looked around the table, obstinate and sombre.

Later on in Paris, while extremely busy reorganizing his regiment, Colonel Feraud learned that Colonel D'Hubert had been made a general. He glared at his informant incredulously, then folded his arms and turned away muttering, "Nothing surprises me on the part of that man."

And aloud he added, speaking over his shoulder, "You would oblige me greatly by telling General D'Hubert at the first opportunity that his advancement saves him for a time from a pretty hot encounter. I was only waiting for him to turn up here."

The other officer remonstrated.

"Could you think of it, Colonel Feraud, at this time, when every life should be consecrated to the glory and safety of France?"

But the strain of unhappiness caused by military reverses had spoiled Colonel Feraud's character. Like many other men, he was rendered wicked by misfortune.

"I cannot consider General D'Hubert's existence of any account either for the glory or safety of France," he snapped viciously. "You don't pretend, perhaps, to know him better than I do—I who have met him half a dozen times on the ground—do you?"

His interlocutor, a young man, was silenced. Colonel Feraud walked up and down the room.

"This is not the time to mince matters," he said. "I can't believe that that man ever loved the Emperor. He picked up his general's stars under the boots of Marshal Berthier. Very well. I'll get mine in another fashion, and then we shall settle this business which has been dragging on too long."

General D'Hubert, informed indirectly of Colonel Feraud's attitude, made a gesture as if to put aside an importunate person. His thoughts were solicited by graver cares. He had had no time to go and see his family. His sister, whose royalist hopes were rising higher every day, though proud of her brother, regretted his recent advancement in a measure, because it put on him a prominent mark of the usurper's favour, which later on could have an adverse influence upon his career. He wrote to her that no one but an inveterate enemy could say he had got his promotion by favour. As to his career, he assured her that he looked no farther forward into the future than the next battlefield.

Beginning the campaign of France in this dogged spirit, General D'Hubert was wounded on the second day of the battle under Laon. While being carried off the field he heard that Colonel Feraud, promoted this moment to general, had been sent to replace him at the head of his brigade. He cursed his luck impulsively, not being able at the first glance to discern all the advantages of a nasty wound. And yet it was by this heroic method that Providence was shaping his future. Travelling slowly south to his sister's country home under the care of a trusty old servant, General D'Hubert was spared the humiliating contacts and the perplexities of conduct which assailed the men of Napoleonic empire at the moment of its downfall. Lying in his bed, with the windows of his room open wide to the sunshine of Provence, he perceived the undisguised aspect of the blessing conveyed by that jagged fragment of a Prussian shell, which, killing his horse and ripping open his thigh, saved him from an active conflict with his conscience. After the last fourteen years spent sword in hand in the saddle, and with the sense of his duty done to the very end, General D'Hubert found resignation an easy virtue. His sister was delighted with his reasonableness. "I leave myself altogether in your hands, my dear Léonie," he had said to her.

He was still laid up when, the credit of his brother-in-law's family being exerted on his behalf, he received from the royal government not only the confirmation of his rank, but the assurance of being retained on the active list. To this was added an unlimited convalescent leave. The unfavourable opinion entertained of him in Bonapartist circles, though it rested on nothing more solid than the unsupported pronouncement of General Feraud, was directly responsible for General D'Hubert's retention on the active list. As to General Feraud, his rank was confirmed, too. It was more than he dared to expect; but Marshal Soult, then Minister of War to the restored king, was partial to officers who had served in Spain. Only not even the marshal's protection could secure for him active employment. He remained irreconcilable, idle, and sinister. He sought in obscure restaurants the company of other half-pay officers who cherished dingy but glorious old tricolour cockades in their breast-pockets, and buttoned with the forbidden eagle buttons their shabby uniforms, declaring themselves too poor to afford the expense of the prescribed change.

The triumphant return from Elba, an historical fact as marvellous and incredible as the exploits of some mythological demi-god, found

General D'Hubert still quite unable to sit a horse. Neither could he walk very well. These disabilities, which Madame Léonie accounted most lucky, helped to keep her brother out of all possible mischief. His frame of mind at that time, she noted with dismay, became very far from reasonable. This general officer, still menaced by the loss of a limb, was discovered one night in the stables of the chateau by a groom, who, seeing a light, raised an alarm of thieves. His crutch was lying half-buried in the straw of the litter, and the general was hopping on one leg in a loose box around a snorting horse he was trying to saddle. Such were the effects of imperial magic upon a calm temperament and a pondered mind. Beset in the light of stable lanterns, by the tears, entreaties, indignation, remonstrances and reproaches of his family, he got out of the difficult situation by fainting away there and then in the arms of his nearest relatives, and was carried off to bed. Before he got out of it again, the second reign of Napoleon, the Hundred Days of feverish agitation and supreme effort, passed away like a terrifying dream. The tragic year 1815, begun in the trouble and unrest of consciences, was ending in vengeful proscriptions.

How General Feraud escaped the clutches of the Special Commission and the last offices of a firing squad he never knew himself. It was partly due to the subordinate position he was assigned during the Hundred Days. The Emperor had never given him active command, but had kept him busy at the cavalry depot in Paris, mounting and dispatching hastily drilled troopers into the field. Considering this task as unworthy of his abilities, he had discharged it with no offensively noticeable zeal; but for the greater part he was saved from the excesses of Royalist reaction by the interference of General D'Hubert.

This last, still on convalescent leave, but able now to travel, had been dispatched by his sister to Paris to present himself to his legitimate sovereign. As no one in the capital could possibly know anything of the episode in the stable he was received there with distinction. Military to the very bottom of his soul, the prospect of rising in his profession consoled him from finding himself the butt of Bonapartist malevolence, which pursued him with a persistence he could not account for. All the rancour of that embittered and persecuted party pointed to him as the man who had *never* loved the Emperor—a sort of monster essentially worse than a mere betrayer.

General D'Hubert shrugged his shoulders without anger at this ferocious prejudice. Rejected by his old friends, and mistrusting profoundly the advances of Royalist society, the young and handsome general (he was barely forty) adopted a manner of cold, punctilious courtesy, which at the merest shadow of an intended slight passed easily into harsh haughtiness. Thus prepared, General D'Hubert went about his affairs in Paris feeling inwardly very happy with the peculiar uplifting happiness of a man very much in love. The charming girl looked out by his sister had come upon the scene, and had conquered him in the thorough manner in which a young girl by merely existing in his sight can make a man of forty her own. They were going to be married as soon as General D'Hubert had obtained his official nomination to a promised command.

One afternoon, sitting on the *terrasse* of the *Café Tortoni*, General D'Hubert learned from the conversation of two strangers occupying a table near his own, that General Feraud, included in the batch of superior officers arrested after the second return of the king, was in danger of passing before the Special Commission. Living all his spare moments, as is frequently the case with expectant lovers, a day in advance of reality, and in a state of bestarred hallucination, it required nothing less than the name of his perpetual antagonist pronounced in a loud voice to call the youngest of Napoleon's generals away from the mental contemplation of his betrothed. He looked round. The strangers wore civilian clothes. Lean and weather-beaten, lolling back in their chairs, they scowled at people with moody and defiant abstraction from under their hats pulled low over their eyes. It was not difficult to recognize them for two of the compulsorily retired officers of the Old Guard. As from bravado or carelessness they chose to speak in loud tones, General D'Hubert, who saw no reason why he should change his seat, heard every word. They did not seem to be the personal friends of General Feraud. His name came up amongst others. Hearing it repeated, General D'Hubert's tender anticipations of a domestic future adorned with a woman's grace were traversed by the harsh regret of his warlike past, of that one long, intoxicating clash of arms, unique in the magnitude of its glory and disaster—the marvellous work and the special possession of his own generation. He felt an irrational tenderness towards his old adversary and appreciated emotionally the murderous absurdity their encounter had introduced into his life. It was like an additional pinch of spice in a hot dish. He remembered the flavour with sudden melancholy. He would never taste it again. It was all over. "I fancy it was being left lying in the garden that had exasperated him so against me from the first," he thought, indulgently.

The two strangers at the next table had fallen silent after the third mention of General Feraud's name. Presently the elder of the two, speaking again in a bitter tone, affirmed that General Feraud's account was settled. And why? Simply because he was not like some bigwigs who loved only themselves. The Royalists knew they could never make anything of him. He loved *The Other* too well.

The Other was the Man of St. Helena. The two officers nodded and touched glasses before they drank to an impossible return. Then the same who had spoken before, remarked with a sardonic laugh, "His adversary showed more cleverness."

"What adversary?" asked the younger, as if puzzled.

"Don't you know? They were two hussars. At each promotion they fought a duel. Haven't you heard of the duel going on ever since 1801?"

The other had heard of the duel, of course. Now he understood the allusion. General Baron D'Hubert would be able now to enjoy his fat king's favour in peace.

"Much good may it do to him," mumbled the elder. "They were both brave men. I never saw this D'Hubert—a sort of intriguing dandy, I am told. But I can well believe what I've heard Feraud say of him— that he *never* loved the Emperor."

They rose and went away.

General D'Hubert experienced the horror of a somnambulist who wakes up from a complacent dream of activity to find himself walking on a quagmire. A profound disgust of the ground on which he was making his way overcame him. Even the image of the charming girl was swept from his view in the flood of moral distress. Everything he had ever been or hoped to be would taste of bitter ignominy unless he could manage to save General Feraud from the fate which threatened so many braves. Under the impulse of this almost morbid need to attend to the safety of his adversary, General D'Hubert worked so well with hands and feet (as the French saying is), that in less than twenty-four hours he found means of obtaining an extraordinary private audience from the Minister of Police.

General Baron D'Hubert was shown in suddenly without preliminaries. In the dusk of the Minister's cabinet, behind the forms of writing-desk, chairs, and tables, between two bunches of wax candles blazing in sconces, he beheld a figure in a gorgeous coat posturing before a tall mirror. The old *conventionnel* Fouché, Senator of the Empire, traitor to every man, to every principle and motive of human conduct. Duke of Otranto, and the wily artizan of the second Restoration, was trying the fit of a court suit in which his young and accomplished *fiancée* had declared her intention to have his portrait painted on porcelain. It was a caprice, a charming fancy which the first Minister of Police of the second Restoration was anxious to gratify. For that man, often compared in wiliness of conduct to a fox, but whose ethical side could be worthily symbolized by nothing less emphatic than a skunk, was as much possessed by his love as General D'Hubert himself.

Startled to be discovered thus by the blunder of a servant, he met this little vexation with the characteristic impudence which had served his turn so well in the endless intrigues of his self-seeking career. Without altering his attitude a hair's-breadth, one leg in a silk stocking advanced, his head twisted over his left shoulder, he called out calmly, "This way, General. Pray approach. Well? I am all attention."

While General D'Hubert, ill at ease as if one of his own little weaknesses had been exposed, presented his request as shortly as possible, the Duke of Otranto went on feeling the fit of his collar, settling the lapels before the glass, and buckling his back in an effort to behold the set of the gold embroidered coat-skirts behind. His still face, his attentive eyes, could not have expressed a more complete interest in those matters if he had been alone.

"Exclude from the operations of the Special Court a certain Feraud, Gabriel Florian, General of brigade of the promotion of 1814?" he repeated, in a slightly wondering tone, and then turned away from the glass. "Why exclude *him* precisely?"

"I am surprised that your Excellency, so competent in the evaluation of men of his time, should have thought worth while to have that name put down on the list."

"A rabid Bonapartist!"

"So is every grenadier and every trooper of the army, as your Excellency well knows. And the individuality of General Feraud can have no more weight than that of any casual grenadier. He is a man of no mental grasp, of no capacity whatever. It is inconceivable that he should ever have any influence."

"He has a well-hung tongue, though," interjected Fouché.

"Noisy, I admit, but not dangerous."

"I will not dispute with you. I know next to nothing of him. Hardly his name, in fact."

"And yet your Excellency has the presidency of the Commission charged by the king to point out those who were to be tried," said General D'Hubert, with an emphasis which did not miss the minister's ear.

"Yes, General," he said, walking away into the dark part of the vast room, and throwing himself into a deep armchair that swallowed him up, all but the soft gleam of gold embroideries and the pallid patch of the face—"yes, General. Take this chair there."

General D'Hubert sat down.

"Yes, General," continued the arch-master in the arts of intrigue and betrayals, whose duplicity, as if at times intolerable to his self-knowledge, found relief in bursts of cynical openness. "I did hurry on the formation of the proscribing Commission, and I took its presidency. And do you know why? Simply from fear that if I did not take it quickly into my hands my own name would head the list of the proscribed. Such are the times in which we live. But I am minister of the king yet, and I ask you plainly why I should take the name of this obscure Feraud off the list? You wonder how his name got there! Is it possible that you should know men so little? My dear General, at the very first sitting of the Commission names poured on us like rain off the roof of the Tuileries. Names! We had our choice of thousands. How do you know that the name of this Feraud, whose life or death don't matter to France, does not keep out some other name?"

The voice out of the armchair stopped. Opposite General D'Hubert sat still, shadowy and silent. Only his sabre clinked slightly. The voice in the armchair began again. "And we must try to satisfy the exigencies of the Allied Sovereigns, too. The Prince de Talleyrand told me only yesterday that Nesselrode had informed him officially of His Majesty the Emperor Alexander's dissatisfaction at the small number of examples the Government of the king intends to make—especially amongst military men. I tell you this confidentially."

"Upon my word!" broke out General D'Hubert, speaking through his teeth, "if your Excellency deigns to favour me with any more confidential information I don't know what I will do. It's enough to break one's sword over one's knee, and fling the pieces. . . ."

"What government you imagined yourself to be serving?" interrupted the minister, sharply.

After a short pause the crestfallen voice of General D'Hubert answered, "The Government of France."

"That's paying your conscience off with mere words, General. The truth is that you are serving a government of returned exiles, of men who have been without country for twenty years. Of men also who have just got over a very bad and humiliating fright. . . . Have no illusions on that score."

The Duke of Otranto ceased. He had relieved himself, and had attained his object of stripping some self-respect off that man who had inconveniently discovered him posturing in a gold-embroidered court costume before a mirror. But they were a hot-headed lot in the army; it occurred to him that it would be inconvenient if a well-disposed general officer, received in audience on the recommendation of one of the Princes, were to do something rashly scandalous directly after a private interview with the minister. In a changed tone he put a question to the point: "Your relation—this Feraud?"

"No. No relation at all."

"Intimate friend?"

"Intimate . . . yes. There is between us an intimate connection of a nature which makes it a point of honour with me to try . . ."

The minister rang a bell without waiting for the end of the phrase. When the servant had gone out, after bringing in a pair of heavy silver candelabra for the writing-desk, the Duke of Otranto rose, his breast glistening all over with gold in the strong light, and taking a piece of paper out of a drawer, held it in his hand ostentatiously while he said with persuasive gentleness: "You must not speak of breaking your sword across your knee, General. Perhaps you would never get another. The Emperor will not return this time. . . . *Diable d'homme!* There was just a moment, here in Paris, soon after Waterloo, when he frightened me. It looked as though he were ready to begin all over again. Luckily one never does begin all over again, really. You must not think of breaking your sword, General."

General D'Hubert, looking on the ground, moved slightly his hand in a hopeless gesture of renunciation. The Minister of Police turned his eyes away from him, and scanned deliberately the paper he had been holding up all the time.

"There are only twenty general officers selected to be made an example of. Twenty. A round number. And let's see, Feraud. . . . Ah, he's there. Gabriel Florian. *Parfaitement.* That's your man. Well, there will be only nineteen examples made now."

General D'Hubert stood up feeling as though he had gone through an infectious illness. "I must beg your Excellency to keep my interference a profound secret. I attach the greatest importance to his never learning . . ."

"Who is going to inform him, I should like to know?" said Fouché, raising his eyes curiously to General D'Hubert's tense, set face. "Take one of these pens, and run it through the name yourself. This is the only list in existence. If you are careful to take up enough ink no one will be able to tell what was the name struck out. But, *par exemple*, I am not responsible for what Clarke will do with him afterwards. If he persists in being rabid he will be ordered by the Minister of War to reside in some provincial town under the supervision of the police."

A few days later General D'Hubert was saying to his sister, after the first greetings had been got over: "Ah, my dear Léonie! it seemed to me I couldn't get away from Paris quick enough."

"Effect of love," she suggested, with a malicious smile.

"And horror," added General D'Hubert, with profound seriousness. "I have nearly died there of . . . of nausea."

His face was contracted with disgust. And as his sister looked at him attentively he continued, "I have had to see Fouché. I have had an audience. I have been in his cabinet. There remains with one, who had the misfortune to breathe the air of the same room with that man, a sense of diminished dignity, an uneasy feeling of being not so clean, after all, as one hoped one was. . . . But you can't understand."

She nodded quickly several times. She understood very well, on the contrary. She knew her brother thoroughly, and liked him as he was. Moreover, the scorn and loathing of mankind were the lot of the *Jacobin* Fouché, who, exploiting for his own advantage every weakness, every virtue, every generous illusion of mankind, made dupes of his whole generation, and died obscurely as Duke of Otranto.

"My dear Armand," she said, compassionately, "what could you want from that man?"

"Nothing less than a life," answered General D'Hubert. "And I've got it. It had to be done. But I feel yet as if I could never forgive the necessity to the man I had to save."

General Feraud, totally unable (as is the case with most of us) to comprehend what was happening to him, received the Minister of War's order to proceed at once to a small town of Central France with feelings whose natural expression consisted in a fierce rolling of the eye and savage grinding of the teeth. The passing away of the state of war, the only condition of society he had ever known, the horrible view of a world at peace, frightened him. He went away to his little town firmly convinced that this could not last. There he was informed of his retirement from the army, and that his pension (calculated on the scale of a colonel's rank) was made dependent on the correctness of his conduct, and on the good reports of the police. No longer in the army! He felt suddenly strange to the earth, like a disembodied spirit. It was impossible to exist. But at first he reacted from sheer incredulity. This could not be. He waited for thunder, earthquakes, natural cataclysms; but nothing happened. The leaden weight of an irremediable idleness descended upon General Feraud, who having no resources within himself sank into a state of awe-inspiring hebetude. He haunted the streets of the little town, gazing before him with lack-lustre eyes, disregarding the hats raised on his passage; and people, nudging each other as he went by, whispered, "That's poor General Feraud. His heart is broken. Behold how he loved the Emperor."

The other living wreckage of Napoleonic tempest clustered round General Feraud with infinite respect. He, himself, imagined his soul to be crushed by grief. He suffered from quickly succeeding impulses to weep, to howl, to bite his fists till blood came, to spend days on his bed with his head thrust under the pillow; but these arose from sheer ennui, from the anguish of an immense, indescribable, inconceivable boredom. His mental inability to grasp the hopeless nature of his case as a whole saved him from suicide. He never even thought of it once. He thought of nothing. But his appetite abandoned him, and the difficulty he experienced to express the overwhelming nature of his feelings (the most furious swearing could do no justice to it) induced gradually a habit of silence—a sort of death to a southern temperament.

Great, therefore, was the sensation amongst the *anciens militaires* frequenting a certain little café; full of flies when one stuffy afternoon "that poor General Feraud" let out suddenly a volley of formidable curses.

He had been sitting quietly in his own privileged corner looking through the Paris gazettes with just as much interest as a condemned man on the eve of execution could be expected to show in the news of the day. A cluster of martial, bronzed faces, amongst which there was one lacking an eye, and another the tip of a nose frost-bitten in Russia, surrounded him anxiously.

"What's the matter, General?"

General Feraud sat erect, holding the folded newspaper at arm's length in order to make out the small print better. He read to himself, over again, fragments of the intelligence which had caused, what may be called, his resurrection.

"We are informed that General D'Hubert, till now on sick leave in the south, is to be called to the command of the Fifth Cavalry brigade in . . ."

He dropped the paper stonily. . . . "Called to the command" . . . and suddenly gave his forehead a mighty slap. "I had almost forgotten him," he muttered, in a conscience-stricken tone.

A deep-chested veteran shouted across the café: "'Some new villainy of the Government, General?"

"The villainies of these scoundrels," thundered General Feraud, " are innumerable. One more one less!" . . . He lowered his tone. "But I will set good order to one of them at least."

He looked all round the faces. "There's a pomaded, curled staff officer, the darling of some of the marshals who sold their father for a handful of English gold. He will find out presently that I am alive yet," he declared, in a dogmatic tone. "However, this is a private affair. An old affair of honour. Bah! Our honour does not matter. Here we are driven off with a split ear like a lot of cast troop horses—good only for a knacker's yard. But it would be like striking a blow for the Emperor. . . . Messieurs, I shall require the assistance of two of you."

Every man moved forward. General Feraud, deeply touched by this demonstration, called with visible emotion upon the one-eyed veteran cuirassier and the officer of the Chasseurs à Cheval who had left the tip of his nose in Russia. He excused his choice to the others.

"A cavalry affair this—you know."

He was answered with a varied chorus of *"Parfaitement, mon Général. . . . C'est juste. . . . Parbleu, c'est connu. . . ."* Everybody was satisfied. The three left the café together, followed by cries of "Bonne chance."

Outside they linked arms, the general in the middle. The three rusty cocked hats worn *en bataille* with a sinister forward slant barred the narrow street nearly right across. The overheated little town of grey stones and red tiles was drowsing away its provincial afternoon under a blue sky. The loud blows of a cooper hooping a cask reverberated regularly between the houses. The general dragged his left foot a little in the shade of the walls.

"This damned winter of 1813 has got into my bones for good. Never mind. We must take pistols, that's all. A little lumbago. We must have pistols. He's game for my bag. My eyes are as keen as ever. You should have seen me in Russia picking off the dodging Cossacks with a beastly old infantry musket. I have a natural gift for firearms."

In this strain General Feraud ran on, holding up his head, with owlish eyes and rapacious beak. A mere fighter all his life, a cavalry man, a *sabreur*, he conceived war with the utmost simplicity, as, in the main, a massed lot of personal contests, a sort of gregarious duelling. And here he had in hand a war of his own. He revived. The shadow of peace passed away from him like the shadow of death. It was the marvellous resurrection of the named Feraud, Gabriel Florian, *engage volontaire* of 1793, General of 1814, buried without ceremony by means of a service order signed by the War Minister of the Second Restoration.

IV

No man succeeds in everything he undertakes. In that sense we are all failures. The great point is not to fail in ordering and sustaining the effort of our life. In this matter vanity is what leads us astray. It hurries us into situations from which we must come out damaged; whereas pride is our safeguard, by the reserve it imposes on the choice of our endeavour as much as by the virtue of its sustaining power.

General D'Hubert was proud and reserved. He had not been damaged by his casual love affairs, successful or otherwise. In his war-scarred body his heart at forty remained unscratched. Entering with reserve into his sister's matrimonial plans, he had felt himself falling irremediably in love as one falls off a roof. He was too proud to be frightened. Indeed, the sensation was too delightful to be alarming.

The experience of a man of forty is a much more serious thing than the inexperience of a youth of twenty, for it is not helped out by the rashness of hot blood. The girl was mysterious, as young girls are by the mere effect of their guarded ingenuity; and to him the mysteriousness of that young girl appeared exceptional and fascinating. But there was nothing mysterious about the arrangements of the match which Madame Léonie had promoted. There was nothing peculiar, either. It was a very appropriate match, commending itself extremely to the young lady's mother (the father was dead) and tolerable to the young lady's uncle—an old *émigré* lately returned from Germany, and pervading, cane in hand, a lean ghost of the *ancien régime*, the garden walks of the young lady's ancestral home.

General D'Hubert was not the man to be satisfied merely with the woman and the fortune—when it came to the point. His pride (and pride aims always at true success) would be satisfied with nothing short of love. But as true pride excludes vanity, he could not imagine any reason why this mysterious creature with deep and brilliant eyes of a violet colour should have any feeling for him warmer than indifference. The young lady (her name was Adèle) baffled every attempt at a clear understanding on that point. It is true that the attempts were clumsy and made timidly, because by then General D'Hubert had become acutely aware of the number of his years, of his wounds, of his many moral imperfections, of his secret unworthiness—and had incidentally learned by experience the meaning of the word funk. As far as he could make out she seemed to imply that, with an unbounded confidence in her mother's affection and sagacity, she felt no unsurmountable dislike for the person of General D'Hubert; and that this was quite sufficient for a well-brought-up young lady to begin married life upon. This view hurt and tormented the pride of General D'Hubert. And yet he asked himself, with a sort of sweet despair, what more could he expect? She had a quiet and luminous forehead. Her violet eyes laughed while the lines of her lips and chin remained composed in admirable gravity. All this was set off by such a glorious mass of fair hair, by a complexion so marvellous, by such a grace of expression, that General D'Hubert really never found the opportunity to examine with sufficient detachment the lofty exigencies of his pride. In fact, he became shy of that line of inquiry since it had led once or twice to a crisis of solitary passion in which it was borne upon him that he loved her enough to kill her rather than lose her. From such passages, not unknown to men of forty, he would come out broken, exhausted, remorseful, a little dismayed. He derived, however, considerable comfort from the quietist practice of sitting now and then half the night by an open window and meditating upon the wonder of her existence, like a believer lost in the mystic contemplation of his faith.

It must not be supposed that all these variations of his inward state were made manifest to the world. General D'Hubert found no difficulty in appearing wreathed in smiles. Because, in fact, he was very happy. He followed the established rules of his condition, sending over flowers (from his sister's garden and hot-houses) early every morning, and a little later following himself to lunch with his intended, her mother, and her *émigré* uncle. The middle of the day was spent in strolling or sitting in the shade. A watchful deference, trembling on the verge of tenderness was the note of their intercourse on his side—with a playful turn of the phrase concealing the profound trouble of his whole being caused by her inaccessible nearness. Late in the afternoon General D'Hubert walked home between the fields of vines, sometimes intensely miserable, sometimes supremely happy, sometimes pensively sad; but always feeling a special intensity of existence, that elation common to artists, poets, and lovers—to men haunted by a great passion, a noble thought, or a new vision of plastic beauty.

The outward world at that time did not exist with any special distinctness for General D'Hubert. One evening, however, crossing a ridge from which he could see both houses, General D'Hubert became aware of two figures far down the road. The day had been divine. The festal decoration of the inflamed sky lent a gentle glow to the sober tints of the southern land. The grey rocks, the brown fields, the purple, undulating distances harmonized in luminous accord, exhaled already the scents of the evening. The two figures down the road presented themselves like two rigid and wooden silhouettes all black on the ribbon of white dust. General D'Hubert made out the long, straight, military *capotes* buttoned closely right up to the black stocks, the cocked hats, the lean, carven, brown countenances—old soldiers— *vieilles moustaches!* The taller of the two had a black patch over one eye; the other's hard, dry countenance presented some bizarre, disquieting peculiarity, which on nearer approach proved to be the absence of the tip of the nose. Lifting their hands with one movement to salute the slightly lame civilian walking with a thick stick, they inquired for the house where the General Baron D'Hubert lived, and what was the best way to get speech with him quietly.

"If you think this quiet enough," said General D'Hubert, looking round at the vine-fields, framed in purple lines, and dominated by the nest of grey and drab walls of a village clustering around the top of a conical hill, so that the blunt church tower seemed but the shape of a crowning rock—"if you think this spot quiet enough, you can speak to him at once. And I beg you, comrades, to speak openly, with perfect confidence."

They stepped back at this, and raised again their hands to their hats with marked ceremoniousness. Then the one with the chipped nose, speaking for both, remarked that the matter was confidential enough, and to be arranged discreetly. Their general quarters were established in that village over there, where the infernal clodhoppers—damn their false, Royalist hearts!—looked remarkably cross-eyed at three unassuming military men. For the present he should only ask for the name of General D'Hubert's friends.

"What friends?" said the astonished General D'Hubert, completely off the track. "I am staying with my brother-in-law over there."

"Well, he will do for one," said the chipped veteran.

"We're the friends of General Feraud," interjected the other, who had kept silent till then, only glowering with his one eye at the man who had *never* loved the Emperor. That was something to look at. For even the gold-laced Judases who had sold him to the English, the marshals and princes, had loved him at some time or other. But this man had *never* loved the Emperor. General Feraud had said so distinctly.

General D'Hubert felt an inward blow in his chest. For an infinitesimal fraction of a second it was as if the spinning of the earth had become perceptible with an awful, slight rustle in the eternal stillness of space. But this noise of blood in his ears passed off at once. Involuntarily he murmured, "Feraud! I had forgotten his existence."

"He's existing at present, very uncomfortably, it is true, in the infamous inn of that nest of savages up there," said the one-eyed cuirassier, drily. "We arrived in your parts an hour ago on post horses. He's awaiting our return with impatience. There is hurry, you know. The General has broken the ministerial order to obtain from you the satisfaction he's entitled to by the laws of honour, and naturally he's anxious to have it all over before the *gendarmerie* gets on his scent."

The other elucidated the idea a little further. "Get back on the quiet—you understand? Phitt. No one the wiser. We have broken out, too. Your friend the king would be glad to cut off our scurvy pittances at the first chance. It's a risk. But honour before everything."

General D'Hubert had recovered his powers of speech. "So you come here like this along the road to invite me to a throat-cutting match with that—that . . ." A laughing sort of rage took possession of him. "Ha! ha! ha! ha!"

His fists on his hips, he roared without restraint, while they stood before him lank and straight, as though they had been shot up with a snap through a trap door in the ground. Only four-and-twenty months ago the masters of Europe, they had already the air of antique ghosts, they seemed less substantial in their faded coats than their own narrow shadows falling so black across the white road: the military and grotesque shadows of twenty years of war and conquests. They had an outlandish appearance of two imperturbable bonzes of the religion of the sword. And General D'Hubert, also one of the ex-masters of Europe, laughed at these serious phantoms standing in his way.

Said one, indicating the laughing General with a jerk of the head: "A merry companion, that."

"There are some of us that haven't smiled from the day *The Other* went away," remarked his comrade.

A violent impulse to set upon and beat those unsubstantial wraiths to the ground frightened General D'Hubert. He ceased laughing suddenly. His desire now was to get rid of them, to get them away from his sight quickly before he lost control of himself. He wondered at the fury he felt rising in his breast. But he had no time to look into that peculiarity just then.

"I understand your wish to be done with me as quickly as possible. Don't let us waste time in empty ceremonies. Do you see that wood there at the foot of that slope? Yes, the wood of pines. Let us meet there to-morrow at sunrise. I will bring with me my sword or my pistols, or both if you like."

The seconds of General Feraud looked at each other.

"Pistols, General," said the cuirassier.

"So be it. Au revoir—to-morrow morning. Till then let me advise you to keep close if you don't want the *gendarmerie* making inquiries about you before it gets dark. Strangers are rare in this part of the country."

They saluted in silence. General D'Hubert, turning his back on their retreating forms, stood still in the middle of the road for a long time, biting his lower lip and looking on the ground. Then he began to walk straight before him, thus retracing his steps till he found himself before the park gate of his intended's house. Dusk had fallen. Motionless he stared through the bars at the front of the house, gleaming clear beyond the thickets and trees. Footsteps scrunched on the gravel, and presently a tall stooping shape emerged from the lateral alley following the inner side of the park wall.

Le Chevalier de Valmassigue, uncle of the adorable Adèle, ex-brigadier in the army of the Princes, bookbinder in Altona, afterwards shoemaker (with a great reputation for elegance in the fit of ladies' shoes) in another small German town, wore silk stockings on his lean shanks, low shoes with silver buckles, a brocaded waistcoat. A long-skirted coat, *à la française*, covered loosely his thin, bowed back. A small three-cornered hat rested on a lot of powdered hair, tied in a queue.

"*Monsieur le Chevalier*," called General D'Hubert, softly.

"What? You here again, *mon ami*? Have you forgotten something?"

"By heavens! that's just it. I have forgotten something. I am come to tell you of it. No—outside. Behind this wall. It's too ghastly a thing to be let in at all where she lives."

The Chevalier came out at once with that benevolent resignation some old people display towards the fugue of youth. Older by a quarter of a century than General D'Hubert, he looked upon him in the secret of his heart as a rather troublesome youngster in love. He had heard his enigmatical words very well, but attached no undue importance to what a mere man of forty so hard hit was likely to do or say. The turn of mind of the generation of Frenchmen grown up during the years of his exile was almost unintelligible to him. Their sentiments appeared to him unduly violent, lacking fineness and measure, their language needlessly exaggerated. He joined calmly the General on the road, and they made a few steps in silence, the General trying to master his agitation, and get proper control of his voice.

"It is perfectly true; I forgot something. I forgot till half an hour ago that I had an urgent affair of honour on my hands. It's incredible, but it is so!"

All was still for a moment. Then in the profound evening silence of the countryside the clear, aged voice of the Chevalier was heard trembling slightly: "Monsieur! That's an indignity."

It was his first thought. The girl born during his exile, the posthumous daughter of his poor brother murdered by a band of Jacobins, had grown since his return very dear to his old heart, which had been starving on mere memories of affection for so many years. "It is an inconceivable thing, I say! A man settles such affairs before he thinks of asking for a young girl's hand. Why! If you had forgotten for ten days longer, you would have been married before your memory returned to you. In my time men did not forget such things—nor yet what is due to the feelings of an innocent young woman. If I did not respect them myself, I would qualify your conduct in a way which you would not like."

General D'Hubert relieved himself frankly by a groan. "Don't let that consideration prevent you. You run no risk of offending her mortally."

But the old man paid no attention to this lover's nonsense. It's doubtful whether he even heard. "What is it?" he asked. "What's the nature of . . . ?" "Call it a youthful folly, *Monsieur le Chevalier*. An inconceivable, incredible result of . . ." He stopped short. "He will never believe the story," he thought. "He will only think I am taking him for a fool, and get offended." General D'Hubert spoke up again: "Yes, originating in youthful folly, it has become . . ."

The Chevalier interrupted: "Well, then it must be arranged."

"Arranged?"

"Yes, no matter at what cost to your *amour propre*. You should have remembered you were engaged. You forgot that, too, I suppose. And then you go and forget your quarrel. It's the most hopeless exhibition of levity I ever heard of."

"Good heavens, Monsieur! You don't imagine I have been picking up this quarrel last time I was in Paris, or anything of the sort, do you?"

"Eh! What matters the precise date of your insane conduct," exclaimed the Chevalier, testily. "The principal thing is to arrange it."

Noticing General D'Hubert getting restive and trying to place a word, the old *émigré* raised his hand, and added with dignity, "I've been a soldier, too. I would never dare suggest a doubtful step to the man whose name my niece is to bear. I tell you that *entre galants hommes* an affair can always be arranged."

"But *saperiotte, Monsieur le Chevalier*, it's fifteen or sixteen years ago. I was a lieutenant of hussars then."

The old Chevalier seemed confounded by the vehemently despairing tone of this information. "You were a lieutenant of hussars sixteen years ago," he mumbled in a dazed manner.

"Why, yes! You did not suppose I was made a general in my cradle like a royal prince."

In the deepening purple twilight of the fields spread with vine leaves, backed by a low band of sombre crimson in the west, the voice of the old ex-officer in the army of the Princes sounded collected, punctiliously civil.

"Do I dream? Is this a pleasantry? Or am I to understand that you have been hatching an affair of honour for sixteen years?"

"It has clung to me for that length of time. That is my precise meaning. The quarrel itself is not to be explained easily. We met on the ground several times during that time, of course."

"What manners! What horrible perversion of manliness! Nothing can account for such inhumanity but the sanguinary madness of the Revolution which has tainted a whole generation," mused the returned *émigré* in a low tone. "Who's your adversary?" he asked a little louder.

"My adversary? His name is Feraud."

Shadowy in his *tricorne* and old-fashioned clothes, like a bowed, thin ghost of the *ancien régime*, the Chevalier voiced a ghostly memory. "I can remember the feud about little Sophie Derval, between Monsieur de Brissac, Captain in the Bodyguards, and d'Anjorrant (not the pock-marked one, the other—the Beau d'Anjorrant, as they called him). They met three times in eighteen months in a most gallant manner. It was the fault of that little Sophie, too, who *would* keep on playing . . ."

"This is nothing of the kind," interrupted General D'Hubert. He laughed a little sardonically. "Not at all so simple," he added. "Nor yet half so reasonable," he finished, inaudibly, between his teeth, and ground them with rage.

After this sound nothing troubled the silence for a long time, till the Chevalier asked, without animation: "What is he—this Feraud?"

"Lieutenant of hussars, too—I mean, he's a general. A Gascon. Son of a blacksmith, I believe."

"There! I thought so. That Bonaparte had a special predilection for the *canaille*. I don't mean this for you, D'Hubert. You are one of us, though you have served this usurper, who . . ."

"Let's leave him out of this," broke in General D'Hubert.

The Chevalier shrugged his peaked shoulders. "Feraud of sorts. Offspring of a blacksmith and some village troll. See what comes of mixing yourself up with that sort of people."

"You have made shoes yourself, Chevalier."

"Yes. But I am not the son of a shoemaker. Neither are you, Monsieur D'Hubert. You and I have something that your Bonaparte's princes, dukes, and marshals have not, because there's no power on earth that could give it to them," retorted the *émigré*, with the rising animation of a man who has got hold of a hopeful argument. "Those people don't exist—all these Ferauds. Feraud! What is Feraud? A *va-nu-pieds* disguised into a general by a Corsican adventurer masquerading as an emperor. There is no earthly reason for a D'Hubert to *s'encanailler* by a duel with a person of that sort. You can make your excuses to him perfectly well. And if the *manant* takes into his head to decline them, you may simply refuse to meet him."

"You say I may do that?"

"I do. With the clearest conscience."

"*Monsieur le Chevalier*! To what do you think you have returned from your emigration?"

This was said in such a startling tone that the old man raised sharply his bowed head, glimmering silvery white under the points of the little *tricorne*. For a time he made no sound.

"God knows!" he said at last, pointing with a slow and grave gesture at a tall roadside cross mounted on a block of stone, and stretching its arms of forged iron all black against the darkening red band in the sky—"God knows! If it were not for this emblem, which I remember seeing on this spot as a child, I would wonder to what we who remained faithful to God and our king have returned. The very voices of the people have changed."

"Yes, it is a changed France," said General D'Hubert. He seemed to have regained his calm. His tone was slightly ironic. "Therefore I cannot take your advice. Besides, how is one to refuse to be bitten by a dog that means to bite? It's impracticable. Take my word for it— Feraud isn't a man to be stayed by apologies or refusals. But there are other ways. I could, for instance, send a messenger with a word to the brigadier of the *gendarmerie* in Senlac. He and his two friends are liable to arrest on my simple order. It would make some talk in the army, both the organized and the disbanded—especially the disbanded. All *canaille*! All once upon a time the companions in arms of Armand D'Hubert. But what need a D'Hubert care what people that don't exist may think? Or, better still, I might get my brother-in-law to send for the mayor of the village and give him a hint. No more would be needed to get the three 'brigands' set upon with flails and pitchforks and hunted into some nice, deep, wet ditch—and nobody the wiser! It has been done only ten miles from here to three poor devils of the disbanded Red Lancers of the Guard going to their homes. What says your conscience, *Chevalier*? Can a D'Hubert do that thing to three men who do not exist?"

A few stars had come out on the blue obscurity, clear as crystal, of the sky. The dry, thin voice of the Chevalier spoke harshly: "Why are you telling me all this?"

The General seized the withered old hand with a strong grip. "Because I owe you my fullest confidence. Who could tell Adèle but you? You understand why I dare not trust my brother-in-law nor yet my own sister. *Chevalier*! I have been so near doing these things that I tremble yet. You don't know how terrible this duel appears to me. And there's no escape from it."

He murmured after a pause, "It's a fatality," dropped the Chevalier's passive hand, and said in his ordinary conversational voice, "I shall have to go without seconds. If it is my lot to remain on the ground, you at least will know all that can be made known of this affair."

The shadowy ghost of the *ancien régime* seemed to have become more bowed during the conversation. "How am I to keep an indifferent face this evening before these two women?" he groaned. "General! I find it very difficult to forgive you."

General D'Hubert made no answer.

"Is your cause good, at least?"

"I am innocent."

This time he seized the Chevalier's ghostly arm above the elbow, and gave it a mighty squeeze. "I must kill him!" he hissed, and opening his hand strode away down the road.

The delicate attentions of his adoring sister had secured for the General perfect liberty of movement in the house where he was a guest. He had even his own entrance through a small door in one corner of the orangery. Thus he was not exposed that evening to the necessity of dissembling his agitation before the calm ignorance of the other inmates. He was glad of it. It seemed to him that if he had to open his lips he would break out into horrible and aimless imprecations, start breaking furniture, smashing china and glass. From the moment he opened the private door and while ascending the twenty-eight steps of a winding staircase, giving access to the corridor on which his room opened, he went through a horrible and humiliating scene in which an infuriated madman with blood-shot eyes and a foaming mouth played inconceivable havoc with everything inanimate that may be found in a well-appointed dining-room. When he opened the door of his apartment the fit was over, and his bodily fatigue was so great that he had to catch at the backs of the chairs while crossing the room to reach a low and broad divan on which he let himself fall heavily. His moral prostration was still greater. That brutality of feeling which he had known only when charging the enemy, sabre in hand, amazed this man of forty, who did not recognize in it the instinctive fury of his menaced passion. But in his mental and bodily exhaustion this passion got cleared, distilled, refined into a sentiment of melancholy despair at having, perhaps, to die before he had taught this beautiful girl to love him.

That night, General D'Hubert stretched out on his back with his hands over his eyes, or lying on his breast with his face buried in a cushion, made the full pilgrimage of emotions. Nauseating disgust at the absurdity of the situation, doubt of his own fitness to conduct his existence, and mistrust of his best sentiments (for what the devil did he want to go to Fouché for?)—he knew them all in turn. "I am an idiot, neither more nor less," he thought—"A sensitive idiot. Because I overheard two men talking in a café. . . . I am an idiot afraid of lies— whereas in life it is only truth that matters."

Several times he got up and, walking in his socks in order not to be heard by anybody downstairs, drank all the water he could find in the dark. And he tasted the torments of jealousy, too. She would marry somebody else. His very soul writhed. The tenacity of that Feraud, the awful persistence of that imbecile brute, came to him with the tremendous force of a relentless destiny. General D'Hubert trembled as he put down the empty water ewer. "He will have me," he thought. General D'Hubert was tasting every emotion that life has to give. He had in his dry mouth the faint sickly flavour of fear, not the excusable fear before a young girl's candid and amused glance, but the fear of death and the honourable man's fear of cowardice.

But if true courage consists in going out to meet an odious danger from which our body, soul, and heart recoil together, General D'Hubert had the opportunity to practise it for the first time in his life. He had charged exultingly at batteries and at infantry squares, and ridden with messages through a hail of bullets without thinking anything about it. His business now was to sneak out unheard, at break of day, to an obscure and revolting death. General D'Hubert never hesitated. He carried two pistols in a leather bag which he slung over his shoulder. Before he had crossed the garden his mouth was dry again. He picked two oranges. It was only after shutting the gate after him that he felt a slight faintness.

He staggered on, disregarding it, and after going a few yards regained the command of his legs. In the colourless and pellucid dawn the wood of pines detached its columns of trunks and its dark green canopy very clearly against the rocks of the grey hillside. He kept his eyes fixed on it steadily, and sucked at an orange as he walked. That temperamental good-humoured coolness in the face of danger which had made him an officer liked by his men and appreciated by his superiors was gradually asserting itself. It was like going into battle. Arriving at the edge of the wood he sat down on a boulder, holding the other orange in his hand, and reproached himself for coming so ridiculously early on the ground. Before very long, however, he heard the swishing of bushes, footsteps on the hard ground, and the sounds of a disjointed, loud conversation. A voice somewhere behind him said boastfully, "He's game for my bag."

He thought to himself, "Here they are. What's this about game? Are they talking of me?" And becoming aware of the other orange in his hand, he thought further, "These are very good oranges. Léonie's own tree. I may just as well eat this orange now instead of flinging it away."

Emerging from a wilderness of rocks and bushes, General Feraud and his seconds discovered General D'Hubert engaged in peeling the orange. They stood still, waiting till he looked up. Then the seconds raised their hats, while General Feraud, putting his hands behind his back, walked aside a little way.

"I am compelled to ask one of you, messieurs, to act for me. I have brought no friends. Will you?"

The one-eyed cuirassier said judicially, "That cannot be refused."

The other veteran remarked, "It's awkward all the same."

"Owing to the state of the people's minds in this part of the country there was no one I could trust safely with the object of your presence here," explained General D'Hubert, urbanely.

They saluted, looked round, and remarked both together:

"Poor ground."

"It's unfit."

"Why bother about ground, measurements, and so on? Let us simplify matters. Load the two pairs of pistols. I will take those of General Feraud, and let him take mine. Or, better still, let us take a mixed pair. One of each pair. Then let us go into the wood and shoot at sight, while you remain outside. We did not come here for ceremonies, but for war—war to the death. Any ground is good enough for that. If I fall, you must leave me where I lie and clear out. It wouldn't be healthy for you to be found hanging about here after that."

It appeared after a short parley that General Feraud was willing to accept these conditions. While the seconds were loading the pistols, he could be heard whistling, and was seen to rub his hands with perfect contentment. He flung off his coat briskly, and General D'Hubert took off his own and folded it carefully on a stone.

"Suppose you take your principal to the other side of the wood and let him enter exactly in ten minutes from now," suggested General D'Hubert, calmly, but feeling as if he were giving directions for his own execution. This, however, was his last moment of weakness. "Wait. Let us compare watches first."

He pulled out his own. The officer with the chipped nose went over to borrow the watch of General Feraud. They bent their heads over them for a time.

"That's it. At four minutes to six by yours. Seven to by mine."

It was the cuirassier who remained by the side of General D'Hubert, keeping his one eye fixed immovably on the white face of the watch he held in the palm of his hand. He opened his mouth, waiting for the beat of the last second long before he snapped out the word, "*Avancez.*"

General D'Hubert moved on, passing from the glaring sunshine of the Provencal morning into the cool and aromatic shade of the pines. The ground was clear between the reddish trunks, whose multitude, leaning at slightly different angles, confused his eye at first. It was like going into battle. The commanding quality of confidence in himself woke up in his breast. He was all to his affair. The problem was how to kill the adversary. Nothing short of that would free him from this imbecile nightmare. "It's no use wounding that brute," thought General D'Hubert. He was known as a resourceful officer. His comrades years ago used also to call him The Strategist. And it was a fact that he could think in the presence of the enemy. Whereas Feraud had been always a mere fighter—but a dead shot, unluckily.

"I must draw his fire at the greatest possible range," said General D'Hubert to himself.

At that moment he saw something white moving far off between the trees—the shirt of his adversary. He stepped out at once between the trunks, exposing himself freely; then, quick as lightning, leaped back. It had been a risky move but it succeeded in its object. Almost simultaneously with the pop of a shot a small piece of bark chipped off by the bullet stung his ear painfully.

General Feraud, with one shot expended, was getting cautious. Peeping round the tree, General D'Hubert could not see him at all. This ignorance of the foe's whereabouts carried with it a sense of insecurity. General D'Hubert felt himself abominably exposed on his flank and rear. Again something white fluttered in his sight. Ha! The enemy was still on his front, then. He had feared a turning movement. But apparently General Feraud was not thinking of it. General D'Hubert saw him pass without special haste from one tree to another in the straight line of approach. With great firmness of mind General D'Hubert stayed his hand. Too far yet. He knew he was no marksman. His must be a waiting game—to kill.

Wishing to take advantage of the greater thickness of the trunk, he sank down to the ground. Extended at full length, head on to his enemy, he had his person completely protected. Exposing himself would not do now, because the other was too near by this time. A conviction that Feraud would presently do something rash was like balm to General D'Hubert's soul. But to keep his chin raised off the ground was irksome, and not much use either. He peeped round, exposing a fraction of his head with dread, but really with little risk. His enemy, as a matter of fact, did not expect to see anything of him so far down as that. General D'Hubert caught a fleeting view of General Feraud shifting trees again with deliberate caution. "He despises my shooting," he thought, displaying that insight into the mind of his antagonist which is of such great help in winning battles. He was confirmed in his tactics of immobility. "If I could only watch my rear as well as my front!" he thought anxiously, longing for the impossible.

It required some force of character to lay his pistols down; but, on a sudden impulse, General D'Hubert did this very gently—one on each side of him. In the army he had been looked upon as a bit of a dandy because he used to shave and put on a clean shirt on the days of battle. As a matter of fact, he had always been very careful of his personal appearance. In a man of nearly forty, in love with a young and charming girl, this praiseworthy self-respect may run to such little weaknesses as, for instance, being provided with an elegant little leather folding-case containing a small ivory comb, and fitted with a piece of looking-glass on the outside. General D'Hubert, his hands being free, felt in his breeches' pockets for that implement of innocent vanity excusable in the possessor of long, silky moustaches. He drew it out, and then with the utmost coolness and promptitude turned himself over on his back. In this new attitude, his head a little raised, holding the little looking-glass just clear of his tree, he squinted into it with his left eye, while the right kept a direct watch on the rear of his position. Thus was proved Napoleon's saying, that "for a French soldier, the word impossible does not exist." He had the right tree nearly filling the field of his little mirror.

"If he moves from behind it," he reflected with satisfaction, "I am bound to see his legs. But in any case he can't come upon me unawares."

And sure enough he saw the boots of General Feraud flash in and out, eclipsing for an instant everything else reflected in the little mirror. He shifted its position accordingly. But having to form his judgment of the change from that indirect view he did not realize that now his feet and a portion of his legs were in plain sight of General Feraud.

General Feraud had been getting gradually impressed by the amazing cleverness with which his enemy was keeping cover. He had spotted the right tree with bloodthirsty precision. He was absolutely certain of it. And yet he had not been able to glimpse as much as the tip of an ear. As he had been looking for it at the height of about five feet ten inches from the ground it was no great wonder—but it seemed very wonderful to General Feraud.

The first view of these feet and legs determined a rush of blood to his head. He literally staggered behind his tree, and had to steady himself against it with his hand. The other was lying on the ground, then! On the ground! Perfectly still, too! Exposed! What could it mean? . . . The notion that he had knocked over his adversary at the first shot entered then General Feraud's head. Once there it grew with every second of attentive gazing, overshadowing every other supposition— irresistible, triumphant, ferocious.

"What an ass I was to think I could have missed him," he muttered to himself. "He was exposed *en plein*—the fool!—for quite a couple of seconds."

General Feraud gazed at the motionless limbs, the last vestiges of surprise fading before an unbounded admiration of his own deadly skill with the pistol.

"Turned up his toes! By the god of war, that was a shot!" he exulted mentally. "Got it through the head, no doubt, just where I aimed, staggered behind that tree, rolled over on his back, and died."

And he stared! He stared, forgetting to move, almost awed, almost sorry. But for nothing in the world would he have had it undone. Such a shot!—such a shot! Rolled over on his back and died!

For it was this helpless position, lying on the back, that shouted its direct evidence at General Feraud! It never occurred to him that it might have been deliberately assumed by a living man. It was inconceivable. It was beyond the range of sane supposition. There was no possibility to guess the reason for it. And it must be said, too, that General D'Hubert's turned-up feet looked thoroughly dead. General Feraud expanded his lungs for a stentorian shout to his seconds, but, from what he felt to be an excessive scrupulousness, refrained for a while.

"I will just go and see first whether he breathes yet," he mumbled to himself, leaving carelessly the shelter of his tree. This move was immediately perceived by the resourceful General D'Hubert. He concluded it to be another shift, but when he lost the boots out of the field of the mirror he became uneasy. General Feraud had only stepped a little out of the line, but his adversary could not possibly have supposed him walking up with perfect unconcern. General D'Hubert, beginning to wonder at what had become of the other, was taken unawares so completely that the first warning of danger consisted in the long, early-morning shadow of his enemy falling aslant on his outstretched legs. He had not even heard a footfall on the soft ground between the trees!

It was too much even for his coolness. He jumped up thoughtlessly, leaving the pistols on the ground. The irresistible instinct of an average man (unless totally paralyzed by discomfiture) would have been to stoop for his weapons, exposing himself to the risk of being shot down in that position. Instinct, of course, is irreflective. It is its very definition. But it may be an inquiry worth pursuing whether in reflective mankind the mechanical promptings of instinct are not affected by the customary mode of thought. In his young days, Armand D'Hubert, the reflective, promising officer, had emitted the opinion that in warfare one should "never cast back on the lines of a mistake." This idea, defended and developed in many discussions, had settled into one of the stock notions of his brain, had become a part of his mental individuality. Whether it had gone so inconceivably deep as to affect the dictates of his instinct, or simply because, as he himself declared afterwards, he was "too scared to remember the confounded pistols," the fact is that General D'Hubert never attempted to stoop for them. Instead of going back on his mistake, he seized the rough trunk with both hands, and swung himself behind it with such impetuosity that, going right round in the very flash and report of the pistol-shot, he reappeared on the other side of the tree face to face with General Feraud. This last, completely unstrung by such a show of agility on the part of a dead man, was trembling yet. A very faint mist of smoke hung before his face which had an extraordinary aspect, as if the lower jaw had come unhinged.

"Not missed!" he croaked, hoarsely, from the depths of a dry throat.

This sinister sound loosened the spell that had fallen on General D'Hubert's senses. "Yes, missed—*à bout portant*," he heard himself saying, almost before he had recovered the full command of his faculties. The revulsion of feeling was accompanied by a gust of homicidal fury, resuming in its violence the accumulated resentment of a lifetime. For years General D'Hubert had been exasperated and humiliated by an atrocious absurdity imposed upon him by this man's savage caprice. Besides, General D'Hubert had been in this last instance too unwilling to confront death for the reaction of his anguish not to take the shape of a desire to kill. "And I have my two shots to fire yet," he added, pitilessly.

General Feraud snapped-to his teeth, and his face assumed an irate, undaunted expression. "Go on!" he said, grimly.

These would have been his last words if General D'Hubert had been holding the pistols in his hands. But the pistols were lying on the ground at the foot of a pine. General D'Hubert had the second of leisure necessary to remember that he had dreaded death not as a man, but as a lover; not as a danger, but as a rival; not as a foe to life, but as an obstacle to marriage. And behold! there was the rival defeated!—utterly defeated, crushed, done for!

He picked up the weapons mechanically, and, instead of firing them into General Feraud's breast, he gave expression to the thoughts uppermost in his mind, "You will fight no more duels now."

His tone of leisurely, ineffable satisfaction was too much for General Feraud's stoicism. "Don't dawdle, then, damn you for a cold-blooded staff-coxcomb!" he roared out, suddenly, out of an impassive face held erect on a rigidly still body.

General D'Hubert uncocked the pistols carefully. This proceeding was observed with mixed feelings by the other general. "You missed me twice," the victor said, coolly, shifting both pistols to one hand; "the last time within a foot or so. By every rule of single combat your life belongs to me. That does not mean that I want to take it now."

"I have no use for your forbearance," muttered General Feraud, gloomily.

"Allow me to point out that this is no concern of mine," said General D'Hubert, whose every word was dictated by a consummate delicacy of feeling. In anger he could have killed that man, but in cold blood he recoiled from humiliating by a show of generosity this unreasonable being—a fellow-soldier of the *Grande Armée*, a companion in the wonders and terrors of the great military epic. "You don't set up the pretension of dictating to me what I am to do with what's my own."

General Feraud looked startled, and the other continued, "You've forced me on a point of honour to keep my life at your disposal, as it were, for fifteen years. Very well. Now that the matter is decided to my advantage, I am going to do what I like with your life on the same principle. You shall keep it at my disposal as long as I choose. Neither more nor less. You are on your honour till I say the word."

"I am! But, *sacrebleu!* This is an absurd position for a General of the Empire to be placed in!" cried General Feraud, in accents of profound and dismayed conviction. "It amounts to sitting all the rest of my life with a loaded pistol in a drawer waiting for your word. It's— it's idiotic; I shall be an object of—of—derision."

"Absurd?—idiotic? Do you think so?" queried General D'Hubert with sly gravity. "Perhaps. But I don't see how that can be helped. However, I am not likely to talk at large of this adventure. Nobody need ever know anything about it. Just as no one to this day, I believe, knows the origin of our quarrel. . . . Not a word more," he added, hastily. "I can't really discuss this question with a man who, as far as I am concerned, does not exist."

When the two duellists came out into the open, General Feraud walking a little behind, and rather with the air of walking in a trance, the two seconds hurried towards them, each from his station at the edge of the wood. General D'Hubert addressed them, speaking loud and distinctly, "Messieurs, I make it a point of declaring to you solemnly, in the presence of General Feraud, that our difference is at last settled for good. You may inform all the world of that fact."

"A reconciliation, after all!" they exclaimed together.

"Reconciliation? Not that exactly. It is something much more binding. Is it not so, General?"

General Feraud only lowered his head in sign of assent. The two veterans looked at each other. Later in the day, when they found themselves alone out of their moody friend's earshot, the cuirassier remarked suddenly, "Generally speaking, I can see with my one eye as far as most people; but this beats me. He won't say anything."

"In this affair of honour I understand there has been from first to last always something that no one in the army could quite make out," declared the chasseur with the imperfect nose. "In mystery it began, in mystery it went on, in mystery it is to end, apparently."

General D'Hubert walked home with long, hasty strides, by no means uplifted by a sense of triumph. He had conquered, yet it did not seem to him that he had gained very much by his conquest. The night before he had grudged the risk of his life which appeared to him magnificent, worthy of preservation as an opportunity to win a girl's love. He had known moments when, by a marvellous illusion, this love seemed to be already his, and his threatened life a still more magnificent opportunity of devotion. Now that his life was safe it had suddenly lost its special magnificence. It had acquired instead a specially alarming aspect as a snare for the exposure of unworthiness.

As to the marvellous illusion of conquered love that had visited him for a moment in the agitated watches of the night, which might have been his last on earth, he comprehended now its true nature. It had been merely a paroxysm of delirious conceit. Thus to this man, sobered by the victorious issue of a duel, life appeared robbed of its charm, simply because it was no longer menaced.

Approaching the house from the back, through the orchard and the kitchen garden, he could not notice the agitation which reigned in front. He never met a single soul. Only while walking softly along the corridor, he became aware that the house was awake and more noisy than usual. Names of servants were being called out down below in a confused noise of coming and going. With some concern he noticed that the door of his own room stood ajar, though the shutters had not been opened yet. He had hoped that his early excursion would have passed unperceived. He expected to find some servant just gone in; but the sunshine filtering through the usual cracks enabled him to see lying on the low divan something bulky, which had the appearance of two women clasped in each other's arms. Tearful and desolate murmurs issued mysteriously from that appearance. General D'Hubert pulled open the nearest pair of shutters violently. One of the women then jumped up. It was his sister. She stood for a moment with her hair hanging down and her arms raised straight up above her head, and then flung herself with a stifled cry into his arms. He returned her embrace, trying at the same time to disengage himself from it. The other woman had not risen. She seemed, on the contrary, to cling closer to the divan, hiding her face in the cushions. Her hair was also loose; it was admirably fair. General D'Hubert recognized it with staggering emotion. Mademoiselle de Valmassigue! Adèle! In distress!

He became greatly alarmed, and got rid of his sister's hug definitely. Madame Léonie then extended her shapely bare arm out of her *peignoir*, pointing dramatically at the divan. "This poor, terrified child has rushed here from home, on foot, two miles—running all the way."

"What on earth has happened?" asked General D'Hubert in a low, agitated voice.

But Madame Léonie was speaking loudly. "She rang the great bell at the gate and roused all the household—we were all asleep yet. You may imagine what a terrible shock. . . . Adèle, my dear child, sit up."

General D'Hubert's expression was not that of a man who "imagines" with facility. He did, however, fish out of the chaos of surmises the notion that his prospective mother-in-law had died suddenly, but only to dismiss it at once. He could not conceive the nature of the event or the catastrophe which would induce Mademoiselle de Valmassigue, living in a house full of servants, to bring the news over the fields herself, two miles, running all the way.

"But why are you in this room?" he whispered, full of awe.

"Of course, I ran up to see, and this child . . . I did not notice it . . . she followed me. It's that absurd Chevalier," went on Madame Léonie, looking towards the divan. . . . "Her hair is all come down. You may imagine she did not stop to call her maid to dress it before she started . . . Adèle, my dear, sit up. . . . He blurted it all out to her at half-past five in the morning. She woke up early and opened her shutters to breathe the fresh air, and saw him sitting collapsed on a garden bench at the end of the great alley. At that hour—you may imagine! And the evening before he had declared himself indisposed. She hurried on some clothes and flew down to him. One would be anxious for less. He loves her, but not very intelligently. He had been up all night, fully dressed, the poor old man, perfectly exhausted. He wasn't in a state to invent a plausible story. . . . What a confidant you chose there! My husband was furious. He said, 'We can't interfere now.' So we sat down to wait. It was awful. And this poor child running with her hair loose over here publicly! She has been seen by some people in the fields. She has roused the whole household, too. It's awkward for her. Luckily you are to be married next week. . . . Adèle, sit up. He has come home on his own legs. . . . We expected to see you coming on a stretcher, perhaps— what do I know? Go and see if the carriage is ready. I must take this child home at once. It isn't proper for her to stay here a minute longer."

General D'Hubert did not move. It was as though he had heard nothing. Madame Léonie changed her mind. "I will go and see myself," she cried. "I want also my cloak.—Adèle——" she began, but did not add "sit up." She went out saying, in a very loud and cheerful tone: "I leave the door open."

General D'Hubert made a movement towards the divan, but then Adèle sat up, and that checked him dead. He thought, "I haven't washed this morning. I must look like an old tramp. There's earth on the back of my coat and pine-needles in my hair." It occurred to him that the situation required a good deal of circumspection on his part.

"I am greatly concerned, mademoiselle," he began, vaguely, and abandoned that line. She was sitting up on the divan with her cheeks unusually pink and her hair, brilliantly fair, falling all over her shoulders—which was a very novel sight to the general. He walked away up the room, and looking out of the window for safety said, "I fear you must think I behaved like a madman," in accents of sincere despair. Then he spun round, and noticed that she had followed him with her eyes. They were not cast down on meeting his glance. And the expression of her face was novel to him also. It was, one might have said, reversed. Those eyes looked at him with grave thoughtfulness, while the exquisite lines of her mouth seemed to suggest a restrained smile. This change made her transcendental beauty much less mysterious, much more accessible to a man's comprehension. An amazing ease of mind came to the general—and even some ease of manner. He walked down the room with as much pleasurable excitement as he would have found in walking up to a battery vomiting death, fire, and smoke; then stood looking down with smiling eyes at the girl whose marriage with him (next week) had been so carefully arranged by the wise, the good, the admirable Léonie.

"Ah! mademoiselle," he said, in a tone of courtly regret, "if only I could be certain that you did not come here this morning, two miles, running all the way, merely from affection for your mother!"

He waited for an answer imperturbable but inwardly elated. It came in a demure murmur, eyelashes lowered with fascinating effect. "You must not be *méchant* as well as mad."

And then General D'Hubert made an aggressive movement towards the divan which nothing could check. That piece of furniture was not exactly in the line of the open door. But Madame Léonie, coming back wrapped up in a light cloak and carrying a lace shawl on her arm for Adèle to hide her incriminating hair under, had a swift impression of her brother getting up from his knees.

"Come along, my dear child," she cried from the doorway.

The General, now himself again in the fullest sense, showed the readiness of a resourceful cavalry officer and the peremptoriness of a leader of men. "You don't expect her to walk to the carriage," he said, indignantly. "She isn't fit. I shall carry her downstairs."

This he did slowly, followed by his awed and respectful sister; but he rushed back like a whirlwind to wash off all the signs of the night of anguish and the morning of war, and to put on the festive garments of a conqueror before hurrying over to the other house. Had it not been for that, General D'Hubert felt capable of mounting a horse and pursuing his late adversary in order simply to embrace him from excess of happiness. "I owe it all to this stupid brute," he thought. "He has made plain in a morning what might have taken me years to find out—for I am a timid fool. No self-confidence whatever. Perfect coward. And the Chevalier! Delightful old man!" General D'Hubert longed to embrace him also.

The Chevalier was in bed. For several days he was very unwell. The men of the Empire and the post-revolution young ladies were too much for him. He got up the day before the wedding, and, being curious by nature, took his niece aside for a quiet talk. He advised her to find out from her husband the true story of the affair of honour, whose claim, so imperative and so persistent, had led her to within an ace of tragedy. "It is right that his wife should be told. And next month or so will be your time to learn from him anything you want to know, my dear child."

Later on, when the married couple came on a visit to the mother of the bride, Madame la Géneralé D'Hubert communicated to her beloved old uncle the true story she had obtained without any difficulty from her husband.

The Chevalier listened with deep attention to the end, took a pinch of snuff, flicked the grains of tobacco from the frilled front of his shirt, and asked, calmly, "And that's all it was?"

"Yes, uncle," replied Madame la Générale, opening her pretty eyes very wide. "Isn't it funny? *C'est insense*—to think what men are capable of!"

"H'm!" commented the old *émigré*. "It depends what sort of men. That Bonaparte's soldiers were savages. It is *insensé*. As a wife, my dear, you must believe implicitly what your husband says."

But to Léonie's husband the Chevalier confided his true opinion. "If that's the tale the fellow made up for his wife, and during the honeymoon, too, you may depend on it that no one will ever know now the secret of this affair."

Considerably later still, General D'Hubert judged the time come, and the opportunity propitious to write a letter to General Feraud. This letter began by disclaiming all animosity. "I've never," wrote the General Baron D'Hubert, "wished for your death during all the time of our deplorable quarrel. Allow me," he continued, "to give you back in all form your forfeited life. It is proper that we two, who have been partners in so much military glory, should be friendly to each other publicly."

The same letter contained also an item of domestic information. It was in reference to this last that General Feraud answered from a little village on the banks of the Garonne, in the following words:

"If one of your boy's names had been Napoleon—or Joseph—or even Joachim, I could congratulate you on the event with a better heart. As you have thought proper to give him the names of Charles Henri Armand, I am confirmed in my conviction that you never loved the Emperor. The thought of that sublime hero chained to a rock in the middle of a savage ocean makes life of so little value that I would receive with positive joy your instructions to blow my brains out. From suicide I consider myself in honour debarred. But I keep a loaded pistol in my drawer."

Madame la Générale D'Hubert lifted up her hands in despair after perusing that answer.

"You see? He won't be reconciled," said her husband. "He must never, by any chance, be allowed to guess where the money comes from. It wouldn't do. He couldn't bear it."

"You are a *brave homme*, Armand," said Madame la Générale, appreciatively.

"My dear, I had the right to blow his brains out; but as I didn't, we can't let him starve. He has lost his pension and he is utterly incapable of doing anything in the world for himself. We must take care of him, secretly, to the end of his days. Don't I owe him the most ecstatic moment of my life? . . . Ha! ha! ha! Over the fields, two miles, running all the way! I couldn't believe my ears! . . . But for his stupid ferocity, it would have taken me years to find you out. It's extraordinary how in one way or another this man has managed to fasten himself on my deeper feelings."

The Secret Sharer

I

On my right hand there were lines of fishing stakes resembling a mysterious system of half-submerged bamboo fences, incomprehensible in its division of the domain of tropical fishes, and crazy of aspect as if abandoned forever by some nomad tribe of fishermen now gone to the other end of the ocean; for there was no sign of human habitation as far as the eye could reach. To the left a group of barren islets, suggesting ruins of stone walls, towers, and blockhouses, had its foundations set in a blue sea that itself looked solid, so still and stable did it lie below my feet; even the track of light from the westering sun shone smoothly, without that animated glitter which tells of an imperceptible ripple. And when I turned my head to take a parting glance at the tug which had just left us anchored outside the bar, I saw the straight line of the flat shore joined to the stable sea, edge to edge, with a perfect and unmarked closeness, in one leveled floor half brown, half blue under the enormous dome of the sky. Corresponding in their insignificance to the islets of the sea, two small clumps of trees, one on each side of the only fault in the impeccable joint, marked the mouth of the river Meinam we had just left on the first preparatory stage of our homeward journey; and, far back on the inland level, a larger and loftier mass, the grove surrounding the great Paknam pagoda, was the only thing on which the eye could rest from the vain task of exploring the monotonous sweep of the horizon. Here and there gleams as of a few scattered pieces of silver marked the windings of the great river; and on the nearest of them, just within the bar, the tug steaming right into the land became lost to my sight, hull and funnel and masts, as though the impassive earth had swallowed her up without an effort, without a tremor. My eye followed the light cloud of her smoke, now here, now there, above the plain, according to the devious curves of the stream, but always fainter and farther away, till I lost it at last behind the miter-shaped hill of the great pagoda. And then I was left alone with my ship, anchored at the head of the Gulf of Siam.

She floated at the starting point of a long journey, very still in an immense stillness, the shadows of her spars flung far to the eastward by the setting sun. At that moment I was alone on her decks. There was not a sound in her—and around us nothing moved, nothing lived, not a canoe on the water, not a bird in the air, not a cloud in the sky. In this breathless pause at the threshold of a long passage we seemed to be measuring our fitness for a long and arduous enterprise, the appointed task of both our existences to be carried out, far from all human eyes, with only sky and sea for spectators and for judges.

There must have been some glare in the air to interfere with one's sight, because it was only just before the sun left us that my roaming eyes made out beyond the highest ridges of the principal islet of the group something which did away with the solemnity of perfect solitude. The tide of darkness flowed on swiftly; and with tropical suddenness a swarm of stars came out above the shadowy earth, while I lingered yet, my hand resting lightly on my ship's rail as if on the shoulder of a trusted friend. But, with all that multitude of celestial bodies staring down at one, the comfort of quiet communion with her was gone for good. And there were also disturbing sounds by this time—voices, footsteps forward; the steward flitted along the main-deck, a busily ministering spirit; a hand bell tinkled urgently under the poop deck. . . .

I found my two officers waiting for me near the supper table, in the lighted cuddy. We sat down at once, and as I helped the chief mate, I said:

"Are you aware that there is a ship anchored inside the islands? I saw her mastheads above the ridge as the sun went down."

He raised sharply his simple face, overcharged by a terrible growth of whisker, and emitted his usual ejaculations: "Bless my soul, sir! You don't say so!"

My second mate was a round-cheeked, silent young man, grave beyond his years, I thought; but as our eyes happened to meet I detected a slight quiver on his lips. I looked down at once. It was not my part to encourage sneering on board my ship. It must be said, too, that I knew very little of my officers. In consequence of certain events of no particular significance, except to myself, I had been appointed to the command only a fortnight before. Neither did I know much of the hands forward. All these people had been together for eighteen months or so, and my position was that of the only stranger on board. I mention this because it has some bearing on what is to follow. But what I felt most was my being a stranger to the ship; and if all the truth must be told, I was somewhat of a stranger to myself. The youngest man on board (barring the second mate), and untried as yet by a position of the fullest responsibility, I was willing to take the adequacy of the others for granted. They had simply to be equal to their tasks; but I wondered how far I should turn out faithful to that ideal conception of one's own personality every man sets up for himself secretly.

Meantime the chief mate, with an almost visible effect of collaboration on the part of his round eyes and frightful whiskers, was trying to evolve a theory of the anchored ship. His dominant trait was to take all things into earnest consideration. He was of a painstaking turn of mind. As he used to say, he "liked to account to himself" for practically everything that came in his way, down to a miserable scorpion he had found in his cabin a week before. The why and the wherefore of that scorpion—how it got on board and came to select his room rather than the pantry (which was a dark place and more what a scorpion would be partial to), and how on earth it managed to drown itself in the inkwell of his writing desk—had exercised him infinitely. The ship within the islands was much more easily accounted for; and just as we were about to rise from table he made his pronouncement. She was, he doubted not, a ship from home lately arrived. Probably she drew too much water to cross the bar except at the top of spring tides. Therefore she went into that natural harbor to wait for a few days in preference to remaining in an open roadstead.

"That's so," confirmed the second mate, suddenly, in his slightly hoarse voice. "She draws over twenty feet. She's the Liverpool ship *Sephora* with a cargo of coal. Hundred and twenty-three days from Cardiff."

We looked at him in surprise.

"The tugboat skipper told me when he came on board for your letters, sir," explained the young man. "He expects to take her up the river the day after tomorrow."

After thus overwhelming us with the extent of his information he slipped out of the cabin. The mate observed regretfully that he "could not account for that young fellow's whims." What prevented him telling us all about it at once, he wanted to know.

I detained him as he was making a move. For the last two days the crew had had plenty of hard work, and the night before they had very little sleep. I felt painfully that I—a stranger—was doing something unusual when I directed him to let all hands turn in without setting an anchor watch. I proposed to keep on deck myself till one o'clock or thereabouts. I would get the second mate to relieve me at that hour.

"He will turn out the cook and the steward at four," I concluded, "and then give you a call. Of course at the slightest sign of any sort of wind we'll have the hands up and make a start at once."

He concealed his astonishment. "Very well, sir." Outside the cuddy he put his head in the second mate's door to inform him of my unheard-of caprice to take a five hours' anchor watch on myself. I heard the other raise his voice incredulously—"What? The Captain himself?" Then a few more murmurs, a door closed, then another. A few moments later I went on deck.

My strangeness, which had made me sleepless, had prompted that unconventional arrangement, as if I had expected in those solitary hours of the night to get on terms with the ship of which I knew nothing, manned by men of whom I knew very little more. Fast alongside a wharf, littered like any ship in port with a tangle of unrelated things, invaded by unrelated shore people, I had hardly seen her yet properly. Now, as she lay cleared for sea, the stretch of her main-deck seemed to me very find under the stars. Very fine, very roomy for her size, and very inviting. I descended the poop and paced the waist, my mind picturing to myself the coming passage through the Malay Archipelago, down the Indian Ocean, and up the Atlantic. All its phases were familiar enough to me, every characteristic, all the alternatives which were likely to face me on the high seas—everything! . . . except the novel responsibility of command. But I took heart from the reasonable thought that the ship was like other ships, the men like other men, and that the sea was not likely to keep any special surprises expressly for my discomfiture.

Arrived at that comforting conclusion, I bethought myself of a cigar and went below to get it. All was still down there. Everybody at the after end of the ship was sleeping profoundly. I came out again on the quarter-deck, agreeably at ease in my sleeping suit on that warm breathless night, barefooted, a glowing cigar in my teeth, and, going forward, I was met by the profound silence of the fore end of the ship. Only as I passed the door of the forecastle, I heard a deep, quiet, trustful sigh of some sleeper inside. And suddenly I rejoiced in the great security of the sea as compared with the unrest of the land, in my choice of that untempted life presenting no disquieting problems, invested with an elementary moral beauty by the absolute straightforwardness of its appeal and by the singleness of its purpose.

The riding light in the fore-rigging burned with a clear, untroubled, as if symbolic, flame, confident and bright in the mysterious shades of the night. Passing on my way aft along the other side of the ship, I observed that the rope side ladder, put over, no doubt, for the master of the tug when he came to fetch away our letters, had not been hauled in as it should have been. I became annoyed at this, for exactitude in some small matters is the very soul of discipline. Then I reflected that I had myself peremptorily dismissed my officers from duty, and by my own act had prevented the anchor watch being formally set and things properly attended to. I asked myself whether it was wise ever to interfere with the established routine of duties even from the kindest of motives. My action might have made me appear eccentric. Goodness only knew how that absurdly whiskered mate would "account" for my conduct, and what the whole ship thought of that informality of their new captain. I was vexed with myself.

Not from compunction certainly, but, as it were mechanically, I proceeded to get the ladder in myself. Now a side ladder of that sort is a light affair and comes in easily, yet my vigorous tug, which should have brought it flying on board, merely recoiled upon my body in a totally unexpected jerk. What the devil! . . . I was so astounded by the immovableness of that ladder that I remained stock-still, trying to account for it to myself like that imbecile mate of mine. In the end, of course, I put my head over the rail.

The side of the ship made an opaque belt of shadow on the darkling glassy shimmer of the sea. But I saw at once something elongated and pale floating very close to the ladder. Before I could form a guess a faint flash of phosphorescent light, which seemed to issue suddenly from the naked body of a man, flickered in the sleeping water with the elusive, silent play of summer lightning in a night sky. With a gasp I saw revealed to my stare a pair of feet, the long legs, a broad livid back immersed right up to the neck in a greenish cadaverous glow. One hand, awash, clutched the bottom rung of the ladder. He was complete but for the head. A headless corpse! The cigar dropped out of my gaping mouth with a tiny plop and a short hiss quite audible in the absolute stillness of all things under heaven. At that I suppose he raised up his face, a dimly pale oval in the shadow of the ship's side. But even then I could only barely make out down there the shape of his black-haired head. However, it was enough for the horrid, frost-bound sensation which had gripped me about the chest to pass off. The moment of vain exclamations was past, too. I only climbed on the spare spar and leaned over the rail as far as I could, to bring my eyes nearer to that mystery floating alongside.

As he hung by the ladder, like a resting swimmer, the sea lightning played about his limbs at every stir; and he appeared in it ghastly, silvery, fishlike. He remained as mute as a fish, too. He made no motion to get out of the water, either. It was inconceivable that he should not attempt to come on board, and strangely troubling to suspect that perhaps he did not want to. And my first words were prompted by just that troubled incertitude.

"What's the matter?" I asked in my ordinary tone, speaking down to the face upturned exactly under mine.

"Cramp," it answered, no louder. Then slightly anxious, "I say, no need to call anyone."

"I was not going to," I said.

"Are you alone on deck?"

"Yes."

I had somehow the impression that he was on the point of letting go the ladder to swim away beyond my ken—mysterious as he came. But, for the moment, this being appearing as if he had risen from the bottom of the sea (it was certainly the nearest land to the ship) wanted only to know the time. I told him. And he, down there, tentatively:

"I suppose your captain's turned in?"

"I am sure he isn't," I said.

He seemed to struggle with himself, for I heard something like the low, bitter murmur of doubt. "What's the good?" His next words came out with a hesitating effort.

"Look here, my man. Could you call him out quietly?"

I thought the time Had come to declare myself.

"I am the captain."

I heard a "By Jove!" whispered at the level of the water. The phosphorescence flashed in the swirl of the water all about his limbs, his other hand seized the ladder.

"My name's Leggatt."

The voice was calm and resolute. A good voice. The self-possession of that man had somehow induced a corresponding state in myself. It was very quietly that I remarked:

"You must be a good swimmer."

"Yes. I've been in the water practically since nine o'clock. The question for me now is whether I am to let go this ladder and go on swimming till I sink from exhaustion, or—to come on board here."

I felt this was no mere formula of desperate speech, but a real alternative in the view of a strong soul. I should have gathered from this that he was young; indeed, it is only the young who are ever confronted by such clear issues. But at the time it was pure intuition on my part. A mysterious communication was established already between us two—in the face of that silent, darkened tropical sea. I was young, too; young enough to make no comment. The man in the water began suddenly to climb up the ladder, and I hastened away from the rail to fetch some clothes.

Before entering the cabin I stood still, listening in the lobby at the foot of the stairs. A faint snore came through the closed door of the chief mate's room. The second mate's door was on the hook, but the darkness in there was absolutely soundless. He, too, was young and could sleep like a stone. Remained the steward, but he was not likely to wake up before he was called. I got a sleeping suit out of my room and, coming back on deck, saw the naked man from the sea sitting on the main hatch, glimmering white in the darkness, his elbows on his knees and his head in his hands. In a moment he had concealed his damp body in a sleeping suit of the same gray-stripe pattern as the one I was wearing and followed me like my double on the poop. Together we moved right aft, barefooted, silent.

"What is it?" I asked in a deadened voice, taking the lighted lamp out of the binnacle, and raising it to his face.

"An ugly business."

He had rather regular features; a good mouth; light eyes under somewhat heavy, dark eyebrows; a smooth, square forehead; no growth on his cheeks; a small, brown mustache, and a well-shaped, round chin. His expression was concentrated, meditative, under the inspecting light of the lamp I held up to his face; such as a man thinking hard in solitude might wear. My sleeping suit was just right for his size. A well-knit young fellow of twenty-five at most. He caught his lower lip with the edge of white, even teeth.

"Yes," I said, replacing the lamp in the binnacle. The warm, heavy tropical night closed upon his head again.

"There's a ship over there," he murmured.

"Yes, I know. The *Sephora*. Did you know of us?"

"Hadn't the slightest idea. I am the mate of her—" He paused and corrected himself. "I should say I *was*."

"Aha! Something wrong?"

"Yes. Very wrong indeed. I've killed a man."

"What do you mean? Just now?"

"No, on the passage. Weeks ago. Thirty-nine south. When I say a man—"

"Fit of temper," I suggested, confidently.

The shadowy, dark head, like mine, seemed to nod imperceptibly above the ghostly gray of my sleeping suit. It was, in the night, as though I had been faced by my own reflection in the depths of a somber and immense mirror.

"A pretty thing to have to own up to for a Conway boy," murmured my double, distinctly.

"You're a Conway boy?"

"I am," he said, as if startled. Then, slowly . . . "Perhaps you too—"

It was so; but being a couple of years older I had left before he joined. After a quick interchange of dates a silence fell; and I thought suddenly of my absurd mate with his terrific whiskers and the "Bless my soul—you don't say so" type of intellect. My double gave me an inkling of his thoughts by saying:

"My father's a parson in Norfolk. Do you see me before a judge and jury on that charge? For myself I can't see the necessity. There are fellows that an angel from heaven—And I am not that. He was one of those creatures that are just simmering all the time with a silly sort of wickedness. Miserable devils that have no business to live at all. He wouldn't do his duty and wouldn't let anybody else do theirs. But what's the good of talking! You know well enough the sort of ill-conditioned snarling cur—"

He appealed to me as if our experiences had been as identical as our clothes. And I knew well enough the pestiferous danger of such a character where there are no means of legal repression. And I knew well enough also that my double there was no homicidal ruffian. I did not think of asking him for details, and he told me the story roughly in brusque, disconnected sentences. I needed no more. I saw it all going on as though I were myself inside that other sleeping suit.

"It happened while we were setting a reefed foresail, at dusk.

Reefed foresail! You understand the sort of weather. The only sail we had left to keep the ship running; so you may guess what it had been like for days. Anxious sort of job, that. He gave me some of his cursed insolence at the sheet. I tell you I was overdone with this terrific weather that seemed to have no end to it. Terrific, I tell you—and a deep ship. I believe the fellow himself was half crazed with funk. It was no time for gentlemanly reproof, so I turned round and felled him like an ox. He up and at me. We closed just as an awful sea made for the ship. All hands saw it coming and took to the rigging, but I had him by the throat, and went on shaking him like a rat, the men above us yelling, 'Look out! look out!' Then a crash as if the sky had fallen on my head. They say that for over ten minutes hardly anything was to be seen of the ship—just the three masts and a bit of the forecastle head and of the poop all awash driving along in a smother of foam. It was a miracle that they found us, jammed together behind the forebits. It's clear that I meant business, because I was holding him by the throat still when they picked us up. He was black in the face. It was too much for them. It seems they rushed us aft together, gripped as we were, screaming 'Murder!' like a lot of lunatics, and broke into the cuddy. And the ship running for her life, touch and go all the time, any minute her last in a sea fit to turn your hair gray only a-looking at it. I understand that the skipper, too, started raving like the rest of them. The man had been deprived of sleep for more than a week, and to have this sprung on him at the height of a furious gale nearly drove him out of his mind. I wonder they didn't fling me overboard after getting the carcass of their precious shipmate out of my fingers. They had rather a job to separate us, I've been told. A sufficiently fierce story to make an old judge and a respectable jury sit up a bit. The first thing I heard when I came to myself was the maddening howling of that endless gale, and on that the voice of the old man. He was hanging on to my bunk, staring into my face out of his sou'wester.

"'Mr. Leggatt, you have killed a man. You can act no longer as chief mate of this ship.'"

His care to subdue his voice made it sound monotonous. He rested a hand on the end of the skylight to steady himself with, and all that time did not stir a limb, so far as I could see. "Nice little tale for a quiet tea party," he concluded in the same tone.

One of my hands, too, rested on the end of the skylight; neither did I stir a limb, so far as I knew. We stood less than a foot from each other. It occurred to me that if old "Bless my soul—you don't say so" were to put his head up the companion and catch sight of us, he would think he was seeing double, or imagine himself come upon a scene of weird witchcraft; the strange captain having a quiet confabulation by the wheel with his own gray ghost. I became very much concerned to prevent anything of the sort. I heard the other's soothing undertone.

"My father's a parson in Norfolk," it said. Evidently he had forgotten he had told me this important fact before. Truly a nice little tale.

"You had better slip down into my stateroom now," I said, moving off stealthily. My double followed my movements; our bare feet made no sound; I let him in, closed the door with care, and, after giving a call to the second mate, returned on deck for my relief.

"Not much sign of any wind yet," I remarked when he approached.

"No, sir. Not much," he assented, sleepily, in his hoarse voice, with just enough deference, no more, and barely suppressing a yawn.

"Well, that's all you have to look out for. You have got your orders."

"Yes, sir."

I paced a turn or two on the poop and saw him take up his position face forward with his elbow in the ratlines of the mizzen rigging before I went below. The mate's faint snoring was still going on peacefully. The cuddy lamp was burning over the table on which stood a vase with flowers, a polite attention from the ship's provision merchant—the last flowers we should see for the next three months at the very least. Two bunches of bananas hung from the beam symmetrically, one on each side of the rudder casing. Everything was as before in the ship—except that two of her captain's sleeping suits were simultaneously in use, one motionless in the cuddy, the other keeping very still in the captain's stateroom.

It must be explained here that my cabin had the form of the capital letter L, the door being within the angle and opening into the short part of the letter. A couch was to the left, the bed place to the right; my writing desk and the chronometers' table faced the door. But anyone opening it, unless he stepped right inside, had no view of what I call the long (or vertical) part of the letter. It contained some lockers surmounted by a bookcase; and a few clothes, a thick jacket or two, caps, oilskin coat, and such like, hung on hooks. There was at the bottom of that part a door opening into my bathroom, which could be entered also directly from the saloon. But that way was never used.

The mysterious arrival had discovered the advantage of this particular shape. Entering my room, lighted strongly by a big bulkhead lamp swung on gimbals above my writing desk, I did not see him anywhere till he stepped out quietly from behind the coats hung in the recessed part.

"I heard somebody moving about, and went in there at once," he whispered.

I, too, spoke under my breath.

"Nobody is likely to come in here without knocking and getting permission."

He nodded. His face was thin and the sunburn faded, as though he had been ill. And no wonder. He had been, I heard presently, kept under arrest in his cabin for nearly seven weeks. But there was nothing sickly in his eyes or in his expression. He was not a bit like me, really; yet, as we stood leaning over my bed place, whispering side by side, with our dark heads together and our backs to the door, anybody bold enough to open it stealthily would have been treated to the uncanny sight of a double captain busy talking in whispers with his other self.

"But all this doesn't tell me how you came to hang on to our side ladder," I inquired, in the hardly audible murmurs we used, after he had told me something more of the proceedings on board the *Sephora* once the bad weather was over.

"When we sighted Java Head I had had time to think all those matters out several times over. I had six weeks of doing nothing else, and with only an hour or so every evening for a tramp on the quarter-deck."

He whispered, his arms folded on the side of my bed place, staring through the open port. And I could imagine perfectly the manner of this thinking out—a stubborn if not a steadfast operation; something of which I should have been perfectly incapable.

"I reckoned it would be dark before we closed with the land," he continued, so low that I had to strain my hearing near as we were to each other, shoulder touching shoulder almost. "So I asked to speak to the old man. He always seemed very sick when he came to see me—as if he could not look me in the face. You know, that foresail saved the ship. She was too deep to have run long under bare poles. And it was I that managed to set it for him. Anyway, he came. When I had him in my cabin—he stood by the door looking at me as if I had the halter round my neck already—I asked him right away to leave my cabin door unlocked at night while the ship was going through Sunda Straits. There would be the Java coast within two or three miles, off Angier Point. I wanted nothing more. I've had a prize for swimming my second year in the Conway."

"I can believe it," I breathed out.

"God only knows why they locked me in every night. To see some of their faces you'd have thought they were afraid I'd go about at night strangling people. Am I a murdering brute? Do I look it? By Jove! If I had been he wouldn't have trusted himself like that into my room. You'll say I might have chucked him aside and bolted out, there and then—it was dark already. Well, no. And for the same reason I wouldn't think of trying to smash the door. There would have been a rush to stop me at the noise, and I did not mean to get into a confounded scrimmage. Somebody else might have got killed—for I would not have broken out only to get chucked back, and I did not want any more of that work. He refused, looking more sick than ever. He was afraid of the men, and also of that old second mate of his who had been sailing with him for years—a gray-headed old humbug; and his steward, too, had been with him devil knows how long—seventeen years or more—a dogmatic sort of loafer who hated me like poison, just because I was the chief mate. No chief mate ever made more than one voyage in the *Sephora*, you know. Those two old chaps ran the ship. Devil only knows what the skipper wasn't afraid of (all his nerve went to pieces altogether in that hellish spell of bad weather we had)—of what the law would do to him—of his wife, perhaps. Oh, yes! she's on board. Though I don't think she would have meddled. She would have been only too glad to have me out of the ship in any way. The 'brand of Cain' business, don't you see. That's all right. I was ready enough to go off wandering on the face of the earth—and that was price enough to pay for an Abel of that sort. Anyhow, he wouldn't listen to me. 'This thing must take its course. I represent the law here.' He was shaking like a leaf. 'So you won't?' 'No!' 'Then I hope you will be able to sleep on that,' I said, and turned my back on him. 'I wonder that you can,' cries he, and locks the door.

"Well after that, I couldn't. Not very well. That was three weeks ago. We have had a slow passage through the Java Sea; drifted about Carimata for ten days. When we anchored here they thought, I suppose, it was all right. The nearest land (and that's five miles) is the ship's destination; the consul would soon set about catching me; and there would have been no object in bolding to these islets there. I don't suppose there's a drop of water on them. I don't know how it was, but tonight that steward, after bringing me my supper, went out to let me eat it, and left the door unlocked. And I ate it—all there was, too. After I had finished I strolled out on the quarter-deck. I don't know that I meant to do anything. A breath of fresh air was all I wanted, I believe. Then a sudden temptation came over me. I kicked off my slippers and was in the water before I had made up my mind fairly. Somebody heard the splash and they raised an awful hullabaloo. 'He's gone! Lower the boats! He's committed suicide! No, he's swimming.' Certainly I was swimming. It's not so easy for a swimmer like me to commit suicide by drowning. I landed on the nearest islet before the boat left the ship's side. I heard them pulling about in the dark, hailing, and so on, but after a bit they gave up. Everything quieted down and the anchorage became still as death. I sat down on a stone and began to think. I felt certain they would start searching for me at daylight. There was no place to hide on those stony things—and if there had been, what would have been the good? But now I was clear of that ship, I was not going back. So after a while I took off all my clothes, tied them up in a bundle with a stone inside, and dropped them in the deep water on the outer side of that islet. That was suicide enough for me. Let them think what they liked, but I didn't mean to drown myself. I meant to swim till I sank— but that's not the same thing. I struck out for another of these little islands, and it was from that one that I first saw your riding light. Something to swim for. I went on easily, and on the way I came upon a flat rock a foot or two above water. In the daytime, I dare say, you might make it out with a glass from your poop. I scrambled up on it and rested myself for a bit. Then I made another start. That last spell must have been over a mile."

His whisper was getting fainter and fainter, and all the time he stared straight out through the porthole, in which there was not even a star to be seen. I had not interrupted him. There was something that made comment impossible in his narrative, or perhaps in himself; a sort of feeling, a quality, which I can't find a name for. And when he ceased, all I found was a futile whisper: "So you swam for our light?"

"Yes—straight for it. It was something to swim for. I couldn't see any stars low down because the coast was in the way, and I couldn't see the land, either. The water was like glass. One might have been swimming in a confounded thousand-feet deep cistern with no place for scrambling out anywhere; but what I didn't like was the notion of swimming round and round like a crazed bullock before I gave out; and as I didn't mean to go back . . . No. Do you see me being hauled back, stark naked, off one of these little islands by the scruff of the neck and fighting like a wild beast? Somebody would have got killed for certain, and I did not want any of that. So I went on. Then your ladder—"

"Why didn't you hail the ship?" I asked, a little louder.

He touched my shoulder lightly. Lazy footsteps came right over our heads and stopped. The second mate had crossed from the other side of the poop and might have been hanging over the rail for all we knew.

"He couldn't hear us talking—could he?" My double breathed into my very ear, anxiously.

His anxiety was in answer, a sufficient answer, to the question I had put to him. An answer containing all the difficulty of that situation. I closed the porthole quietly, to make sure. A louder word might have been overheard.

"Who's that?" he whispered then.

"My second mate. But I don't know much more of the fellow than you do."

And I told him a little about myself. I had been appointed to take charge while I least expected anything of the sort, not quite a fortnight ago. I didn't know either the ship or the people. Hadn't had the time in port to look about me or size anybody up. And as to the crew, all they knew was that I was appointed to take the ship home. For the rest, I was almost as much of a stranger on board as himself, I said. And at the moment I felt it most acutely. I felt that it would take very little to make me a suspect person in the eyes of the ship's company.

He had turned about meantime; and we, the two strangers in the ship, faced each other in identical attitudes.

"Your ladder—" he murmured, after a silence. "Who'd have thought of finding a ladder hanging over at night in a ship anchored out here! I felt just then a very unpleasant faintness. After the life I've been leading for nine weeks, anybody would have got out of condition. I wasn't capable of swimming round as far as your rudder chains. And, lo and behold! there was a ladder to get hold of. After I gripped it I said to myself, 'What's the good?' When I saw a man's head looking over I thought I would swim away presently and leave him shouting—in whatever language it was. I didn't mind being looked at. I—I liked it. And then you speaking to me so quietly—as if you had expected me— made me hold on a little longer. It had been a confounded lonely time—I don't mean while swimming. I was glad to talk a little to somebody that didn't belong to the *Sephora*. As to asking for the captain, that was a mere impulse. It could have been no use, with all the ship knowing about me and the other people pretty certain to be round here in the morning. I don't know—I wanted to be seen, to talk with somebody, before I went on. I don't know what I would have said. . . . 'Fine night, isn't it?' or something of the sort."

"Do you think they will be round here presently?" I asked with some incredulity.

"Quite likely," he said, faintly.

"He looked extremely haggard all of a sudden. His head rolled on his shoulders.

"H'm. We shall see then. Meantime get into that bed," I whispered. "Want help? There."

It was a rather high bed place with a set of drawers underneath. This amazing swimmer really needed the lift I gave him by seizing his leg. He tumbled in, rolled over on his back, and flung one arm across his eyes. And then, with his face nearly hidden, he must have looked exactly as I used to look in that bed. I gazed upon my other self for a while before drawing across carefully the two green serge curtains which ran on a brass rod. I thought for a moment of pinning them together for greater safety, but I sat down on the couch, and once there I felt unwilling to rise and hunt for a pin. I would do it in a moment. I was extremely tired, in a peculiarly intimate way, by the strain of stealthiness, by the effort of whispering and the general secrecy of this excitement. It was three o'clock by now and I had been on my feet since nine, but I was not sleepy; I could not have gone to sleep. I sat there, fagged out, looking at the curtains, trying to clear my mind of the confused sensation of being in two places at once, and greatly bothered by an exasperating knocking in my head. It was a relief to discover suddenly that it was not in my head at all, but on the outside of the door. Before I could collect myself the words "Come in" were out of my mouth, and the steward entered with a tray, bringing in my morning coffee. I had slept, after all, and I was so frightened that I shouted, "This way! I am here, steward," as though he had been miles away. He put down the tray on the table next the couch and only then said, very quietly, "I can see you are here, sir." I felt him give me a keen look, but I dared not meet his eyes just then. He must have wondered why I had drawn the curtains of my bed before going to sleep on the couch. He went out, hooking the door open as usual.

I heard the crew washing decks above me. I knew I would have been told at once if there had been any wind. Calm, I thought, and I was doubly vexed. Indeed, I felt dual more than ever. The steward reappeared suddenly in the doorway. I jumped up from the couch so quickly that he gave a start.

"What do you want here?"

"Close your port, sir—they are washing decks."

"It is closed," I said, reddening.

"Very well, sir." But he did not move from the doorway and returned my stare in an extraordinary, equivocal manner for a time. Then his eyes wavered, all his expression changed, and in a voice unusually gentle, almost coaxingly:

"May I come in to take the empty cup away, sir?"

"Of course!" I turned my back on him while he popped in and out. Then I unhooked and closed the door and even pushed the bolt. This sort of thing could not go on very long. The cabin was as hot as an oven, too. I took a peep at my double, and discovered that he had not moved, his arm was still over his eyes; but his chest heaved; his hair was wet; his chin glistened with perspiration. I reached over him and opened the port.

"I must show myself on deck," I reflected.

Of course, theoretically, I could do what I liked, with no one to say nay to me within the whole circle of the horizon; but to lock my cabin door and take the key away I did not dare. Directly I put my head out of the companion I saw the group of my two officers, the second mate barefooted, the chief mate in long India-rubber boots, near the break of the poop, and the steward halfway down the poop ladder talking to them eagerly. He happened to catch sight of me and dived, the second ran down on the main-deck shouting some order or other, and the chief mate came to meet me, touching his cap.

There was a sort of curiosity in his eye that I did not like. I don't know whether the steward had told them that I was "queer" only, or downright drunk, but I know the man meant to have a good look at me. I watched him coming with a smile which, as he got into point-blank range, took effect and froze his very whiskers. I did not give him time to open his lips.

"Square the yards by lifts and braces before the hands go to breakfast."

It was the first particular order I had given on board that ship; and I stayed on deck to see it executed, too. I had felt the need of asserting myself without loss of time. That sneering young cub got taken down a peg or two on that occasion, and I also seized the opportunity of having a good look at the face of every foremast man as they filed past me to go to the after braces. At breakfast time, eating nothing myself, I presided with such frigid dignity that the two mates were only too glad to escape from the cabin as soon as decency permitted; and all the time the dual working of my mind distracted me almost to the point of insanity. I was constantly watching myself, my secret self, as dependent on my actions as my own personality, sleeping in that bed, behind that door which faced me as I sat at the head of the table. It was very much like being mad, only it was worse because one was aware of it.

I had to shake him for a solid minute, but when at last he opened his eyes it was in the full possession of his senses, with an inquiring look.

"All's well so far," I whispered. "Now you must vanish into the bathroom."

He did so, as noiseless as a ghost, and then I rang for the steward, and facing him boldly, directed him to tidy up my stateroom while I was having my bath—"and be quick about it." As my tone admitted of no excuses, he said, "Yes, sir," and ran off to fetch his dustpan and brushes. I took a bath and did most of my dressing, splashing, and whistling softly for the steward's edification, while the secret sharer of my life stood drawn up bolt upright in that little space, his face looking very sunken in daylight, his eyelids lowered under the stern, dark line of his eyebrows drawn together by a slight frown.

When I left him there to go back to my room the steward was finishing dusting. I sent for the mate and engaged him in some insignificant conversation. It was, as it were, trifling with the terrific character of his whiskers; but my object was to give him an opportunity for a good look at my cabin. And then I could at last shut, with a clear conscience, the door of my stateroom and get my double back into the recessed part. There was nothing else for it. He had to sit still on a small folding stool, half smothered by the heavy coats hanging there. We listened to the steward going into the bathroom out of the saloon, filling the water bottles there, scrubbing the bath, setting things to rights, whisk, bang, clatter—out again into the saloon—turn the key—click. Such was my scheme for keeping my second self invisible. Nothing better could be contrived under the circumstances. And there we sat; I at my writing desk ready to appear busy with some papers, he behind me out of sight of the door. It would not have been prudent to talk in daytime; and I could not have stood the excitement of that queer sense of whispering to myself. Now and then, glancing over my shoulder, I saw him far back there, sitting rigidly on the low stool, his bare feet close together, his arms folded, his head hanging on his breast—and perfectly still. Anybody would have taken him for me.

I was fascinated by it myself. Every moment I had to glance over my shoulder. I was looking at him when a voice outside the door said:

"Beg pardon, sir."

"Well! . . . I kept my eyes on him, and so when the voice outside the door announced, "There's a ship's boat coming our way, sir," I saw him give a start—the first movement he had made for hours. But he did not raise his bowed head.

"All right. Get the ladder over."

I hesitated. Should I whisper something to him? But what? His immobility seemed to have been never disturbed. What could I tell him he did not know already? . . . Finally I went on deck.

II

The skipper of the *Sephora* had a thin red whisker all round his face, and the sort of complexion that goes with hair of that color; also the particular, rather smeary shade of blue in the eyes. He was not exactly a showy figure; his shoulders were high, his stature but middling—one leg slightly more bandy than the other. He shook hands, looking vaguely around. A spiritless tenacity was his main characteristic, I judged. I behaved with a politeness which seemed to disconcert him. Perhaps he was shy. He mumbled to me as if he were ashamed of what he was saying; gave his name (it was something like Archbold—but at this distance of years I hardly am sure), his ship's name, and a few other particulars of that sort, in the manner of a criminal making a reluctant and doleful confession. He had had terrible weather on the passage out—terrible—terrible—wife aboard, too.

By this time we were seated in the cabin and the steward brought in a tray with a bottle and glasses. "Thanks! No." Never took liquor. Would have some water, though. He drank two tumblerfuls. Terrible thirsty work. Ever since daylight had been exploring the islands round his ship.

"What was that for—fun?" I asked, with an appearance of polite interest.

"No!" He sighed. "Painful duty."

As he persisted in his mumbling and I wanted my double to hear every word, I hit upon the notion of informing him that I regretted to say I was hard of hearing.

"Such a young man, too!" he nodded, keeping his smeary blue, unintelligent eyes fastened upon me. "What was the cause of it—some disease?" he inquired, without the least sympathy and as if he thought that, if so, I'd got no more than I deserved.

"Yes; disease," I admitted in a cheerful tone which seemed to shock him. But my point was gained, because he had to raise his voice to give me his tale. It is not worth while to record his version. It was just over two months since all this had happened, and he had thought so much about it that he seemed completely muddled as to its bearings, but still immensely impressed.

"What would you think of such a thing happening on board your own ship? I've had the *Sephora* for these fifteen years. I am a well-known shipmaster."

He was densely distressed—and perhaps I should have sympathized with him if I had been able to detach my mental vision from the unsuspected sharer of my cabin as though he were my second self. There he was on the other side of the bulkhead, four or five feet from us, no more, as we sat in the saloon. I looked politely at Captain Archbold (if that was his name), but it was the other I saw, in a gray sleeping suit, seated on a low stool, his bare feet close together, his arms folded, and every word said between us falling into the ears of his dark head bowed on his chest.

"I have been at sea now, man and boy, for seven-and-thirty years, and I've never heard of such a thing happening in an English ship. And that it should be my ship. Wife on board, too."

I was hardly listening to him.

"Don't you think," I said, "that the heavy sea which, you told me, came aboard just then might have killed the man? I have seen the sheer weight of a sea kill a man very neatly, by simply breaking his neck."

"Good God!" he uttered, impressively, fixing his smeary blue eyes on me. "The sea! No man killed by the sea ever looked like that." He seemed positively scandalized at my suggestion. And as I gazed at him certainly not prepared for anything original on his part, he advanced his head close to mine and thrust his tongue out at me so suddenly that I couldn't help starting back.

After scoring over my calmness in this graphic way he nodded wisely. If I had seen the sight, he assured me, I would never forget it as long as I lived. The weather was too bad to give the corpse a proper sea burial. So next day at dawn they took it up on the poop, covering its face with a bit of bunting; he read a short prayer, and then, just as it was, in its oilskins and long boots, they launched it amongst those mountainous seas that seemed ready every moment to swallow up the ship herself and the terrified lives on board of her.

"That reefed foresail saved you," I threw in.

"Under God—it did," he exclaimed fervently. "It was by a special mercy, I firmly believe, that it stood some of those hurricane squalls."

"It was the setting of that sail which—" I began.

"God's own hand in it," he interrupted me. "Nothing less could have done it. I don't mind telling you that I hardly dared give the order. It seemed impossible that we could touch anything without losing it, and then our last hope would have been gone."

The terror of that gale was on him yet. I let him go on for a bit, then said, casually—as if returning to a minor subject:

"You were very anxious to give up your mate to the shore people, I believe?"

He was. To the law. His obscure tenacity on that point had in it something incomprehensible and a little awful; something, as it were, mystical, quite apart from his anxiety that he should not be suspected of "countenancing any doings of that sort." Seven-and-thirty virtuous years at sea, of which over twenty of immaculate command, and the last fifteen in the *Sephora*, seemed to have laid him under some pitiless obligation.

"And you know," he went on, groping shame-facedly amongst his feelings, "I did not engage that young fellow. His people had some interest with my owners. I was in a way forced to take him on. He looked very smart, very gentlemanly, and all that. But do you know—I never liked him, somehow. I am a plain man. You see, he wasn't exactly the sort for the chief mate of a ship like the *Sephora*."

I had become so connected in thoughts and impressions with the secret sharer of my cabin that I felt as if I, personally, were being given to understand that I, too, was not the sort that would have done for the chief mate of a ship like the *Sephora*. I had no doubt of it in my mind.

"Not at all the style of man. You understand," he insisted, superfluously, looking hard at me.

I smiled urbanely. He seemed at a loss for a while.

"I suppose I must report a suicide."

"Beg pardon?"

"Suicide! That's what I'll have to write to my owners directly I get in."

"Unless you manage to recover him before tomorrow," I assented, dispassionately. . . . "I mean, alive."

He mumbled something which I really did not catch, and I turned my ear to him in a puzzled manner. He fairly bawled:

"The land—I say, the mainland is at least seven miles off my anchorage."

"About that."

My lack of excitement, of curiosity, of surprise, of any sort of pronounced interest, began to arouse his distrust. But except for the felicitous pretense of deafness I had not tried to pretend anything. I had felt utterly incapable of playing the part of ignorance properly, and therefore was afraid to try. It is also certain that he had brought some ready-made suspicions with him, and that he viewed my politeness as a strange and unnatural phenomenon. And yet how else could I have received him? Not heartily! That was impossible for psychological reasons, which I need not state here. My only object was to keep off his inquiries. Surlily? Yes, but surliness might have provoked a point-blank question. From its novelty to him and from its nature, punctilious courtesy was the manner best calculated to restrain the man. But there was the danger of his breaking through my defense bluntly. I could not, I think, have met him by a direct lie, also for psychological (not moral) reasons. If he had only known how afraid I was of his putting my feeling of identity with the other to the test! But, strangely enough—(I thought of it only afterwards)—I believe that he was not a little disconcerted by the reverse side of that weird situation, by something in me that reminded him of the man he was seeking—suggested a mysterious similitude to the young fellow he had distrusted and disliked from the first.

However that might have been, the silence was not very prolonged. He took another oblique step.

"I reckon I had no more than a two-mile pull to your ship. Not a bit more."

"And quite enough, too, in this awful heat," I said.

Another pause full of mistrust followed. Necessity, they say, is mother of invention, but fear, too, is not barren of ingenious suggestions. And I was afraid he would ask me point-blank for news of my other self.

"Nice little saloon, isn't it?" I remarked, as if noticing for the first time the way his eyes roamed from one closed door to the other. "And very well fitted out, too. Here, for instance," I continued, reaching over the back of my seat negligently and flinging the door open, "is my bathroom."

He made an eager movement, but hardly gave it a glance. I got up, shut the door of the bathroom, and invited him to have a look round, as if I were very proud of my accommodation. He had to rise and be shown round, but he went through the business without any raptures whatever.

"And now we'll have a look at my stateroom," I declared, in a voice as loud as I dared to make it, crossing the cabin to the starboard side with purposely heavy steps.

He followed me in and gazed around. My intelligent double had vanished. I played my part.

"Very convenient—isn't it?"

"Very nice. Very comf . . ." He didn't finish and went out brusquely as if to escape from some unrighteous wiles of mine. But it was not to be. I had been too frightened not to feel vengeful; I felt I had him on the run, and I meant to keep him on the run. My polite insistence must have had something menacing in it, because he gave in suddenly. And I did not let him off a single item; mate's room, pantry, storerooms, the very sail locker which was also under the poop—he had to look into them all. When at last I showed him out on the quarter-deck he drew a long, spiritless sigh, and mumbled dismally that he must really be going back to his ship now. I desired my mate, who had joined us, to see to the captain's boat.

The man of whiskers gave a blast on the whistle which he used to wear hanging round his neck, and yelled, "*Sephora's* away!" My double down there in my cabin must have heard, and certainly could not feel more relieved than I. Four fellows came running out from somewhere forward and went over the side, while my own men, appearing on deck too, lined the rail. I escorted my visitor to the gangway ceremoniously, and nearly overdid it. He was a tenacious beast. On the very ladder he lingered, and in that unique, guiltily conscientious manner of sticking to the point:

"I say . . . you . . . you don't think that—"

I covered his voice loudly:

"Certainly not . . . . I am delighted. Good-by."

I had an idea of what he meant to say, and just saved myself by the privilege of defective hearing. He was too shaken generally to insist, but my mate, close witness of that parting, looked mystified and his face took on a thoughtful cast. As I did not want to appear as if I wished to avoid all communication with my officers, he had the opportunity to address me.

"Seems a very nice man. His boat's crew told our chaps a very extraordinary story, if what I am told by the steward is true. I suppose you had it from the captain, sir?"

"Yes. I had a story from the captain."

"A very horrible affair—isn't it, sir?"

"It is."

"Beats all these tales we hear about murders in Yankee ships."

"I don't think it beats them. I don't think it resembles them in the least."

"Bless my soul—you don't say so! But of course I've no acquaintance whatever with American ships, not I so I couldn't go against your knowledge. It's horrible enough for me. . . . But the queerest part is that those fellows seemed to have some idea the man was hidden aboard here. They had really. Did you ever hear of such a thing?"

"Preposterous—isn't it?"

We were walking to and fro athwart the quarter-deck. No one of the crew forward could be seen (the day was Sunday), and the mate pursued:

"There was some little dispute about it. Our chaps took offense. 'As if we would harbor a thing like that,' they said. 'Wouldn't you like to look for him in our coal-hole?' Quite a tiff. But they made it up in the end. I suppose he did drown himself. Don't you, sir?"

"I don't suppose anything."

"You have no doubt in the matter, sir?"

"None whatever."

I left him suddenly. I felt I was producing a bad impression, but with my double down there it was most trying to be on deck. And it was almost as trying to be below. Altogether a nerve-trying situation. But on the whole I felt less torn in two when I was with him. There was no one in the whole ship whom I dared take into my confidence. Since the hands had got to know his story, it would have been impossible to pass him off for anyone else, and an accidental discovery was to be dreaded now more than ever. . . .

The steward being engaged in laying the table for dinner, we could talk only with our eyes when I first went down. Later in the afternoon we had a cautious try at whispering. The Sunday quietness of the ship was against us; the stillness of air and water around her was against us; the elements, the men were against us—everything was against us in our secret partnership; time itself—for this could not go on forever. The very trust in Providence was, I suppose, denied to his guilt. Shall I confess that this thought cast me down very much? And as to the chapter of accidents which counts for so much in the book of success, I could only hope that it was closed. For what favorable accident could be expected?

"Did you hear everything?" were my first words as soon as we took up our position side by side, leaning over my bed place.

He had. And the proof of it was his earnest whisper, "The man told you he hardly dared to give the order."

I understood the reference to be to that saving foresail.

"Yes. He was afraid of it being lost in the setting."

"I assure you he never gave the order. He may think he did, but he never gave it. He stood there with me on the break of the poop after the main topsail blew away, and whimpered about our last hope—positively whimpered about it and nothing else—and the night coming on! To hear one's skipper go on like that in such weather was enough to drive any fellow out of his mind. It worked me up into a sort of desperation. I just took it into my own hands and went away from him, boiling, and—But what's the use telling you? *You* know! . . . Do you think that if I had not been pretty fierce with them I should have got the men to do anything? Not It! The bo's'n perhaps? Perhaps! It wasn't a heavy sea—it was a sea gone mad! I suppose the end of the world will be something like that; and a man may have the heart to see it coming once and be done with it—but to have to face it day after day—I don't blame anybody. I was precious little better than the rest. Only—I was an officer of that old coal wagon, anyhow—"

"I quite understand," I conveyed that sincere assurance into his ear. He was out of breath with whispering; I could hear him pant slightly. It was all very simple. The same strung-up force which had given twenty-four men a chance, at least, for their lives, had, in a sort of recoil, crushed an unworthy mutinous existence.

But I had no leisure to weigh the merits of the matter—footsteps in the saloon, a heavy knock. "There's enough wind to get under way with, sir." Here was the call of a new claim upon my thoughts and even upon my feelings.

"Turn the hands up," I cried through the door. "I'll be on deck directly."

I was going out to make the acquaintance of my ship. Before I left the cabin our eyes met—the eyes of the only two strangers on board. I pointed to the recessed part where the little campstool awaited him and laid my finger on my lips. He made a gesture—somewhat vague—a little mysterious, accompanied by a faint smile, as if of regret.

This is not the place to enlarge upon the sensations of a man who feels for the first time a ship move under his feet to his own independent word. In my case they were not unalloyed. I was not wholly alone with my command; for there was that stranger in my cabin. Or rather, I was not completely and wholly with her. Part of me was absent. That mental feeling of being in two places at once affected me physically as if the mood of secrecy had penetrated my very soul. Before an hour had elapsed since the ship had begun to move, having occasion to ask the mate (he stood by my side) to take a compass bearing of the pagoda, I caught myself reaching up to his ear in whispers. I say I caught myself, but enough had escaped to startle the man. I can't describe it otherwise than by saying that he shied. A grave, preoccupied manner, as though he were in possession of some perplexing intelligence, did not leave him henceforth. A little later I moved away from the rail to look at the compass with such a stealthy gait that the helmsman noticed it—and I could not help noticing the unusual roundness of his eyes. These are trifling instances, though it's to no commander's advantage to be suspected of ludicrous eccentricities. But I was also more seriously affected. There are to a seaman certain words, gestures, that should in given conditions come as naturally, as instinctively as the winking of a menaced eye. A certain order should spring on to his lips without thinking; a certain sign should get itself made, so to speak, without reflection. But all unconscious alertness had abandoned me. I had to make an effort of will to recall myself back (from the cabin) to the conditions of the moment. I felt that I was appearing an irresolute commander to those people who were watching me more or less critically.

And, besides, there were the scares. On the second day out, for instance, coming off the deck in the afternoon (I had straw slippers on my bare feet) I stopped at the open pantry door and spoke to the steward. He was doing something there with his back to me. At the sound of my voice he nearly jumped out of his skin, as the saying is, and incidentally broke a cup.

"What on earth's the matter with you?" I asked, astonished.

He was extremely confused. "Beg your pardon, sir. I made sure you were in your cabin."

"You see I wasn't."

"No, sir. I could have sworn I had heard you moving in there not a moment ago. It's most extraordinary . . . very sorry, sir."

I passed on with an inward shudder. I was so identified with my secret double that I did not even mention the fact in those scanty, fearful whispers we exchanged. I suppose he had made some slight noise of some kind or other. It would have been miraculous if he hadn't at one time or another. And yet, haggard as he appeared, he looked always perfectly self-controlled, more than calm—almost invulnerable. On my suggestion he remained almost entirely in the bathroom, which, upon the whole, was the safest place. There could be really no shadow of an excuse for anyone ever wanting to go in there, once the steward had done with it. It was a very tiny place. Sometimes he reclined on the floor, his legs bent, his head sustained on one elbow. At others I would find him on the campstool, sitting in his gray sleeping suit and with his cropped dark hair like a patient, unmoved convict. At night I would smuggle him into my bed place, and we would whisper together, with the regular footfalls of the officer of the watch passing and repassing over our heads. It was an infinitely miserable time. It was lucky that some tins of fine preserves were stowed in a locker in my stateroom; hard bread I could always get hold of; and so he lived on stewed chicken, paté de foie gras, asparagus, cooked oysters, sardines—on all sorts of abominable sham delicacies out of tins. My early-morning coffee he always drank; and it was all I dared do for him in that respect.

Every day there was the horrible maneuvering to go through so that my room and then the bathroom should be done in the usual way. I came to hate the sight of the steward, to abhor the voice of that harmless man. I felt that it was he who would bring on the disaster of discovery. It hung like a sword over our heads.

The fourth day out, I think (we were then working down the east side of the Gulf of Siam, tack for tack, in light winds and smooth water)—the fourth day, I say, of this miserable juggling with the unavoidable, as we sat at our evening meal, that man, whose slightest movement I dreaded, after putting down the dishes ran up on deck busily. This could not be dangerous. Presently he came down again; and then it appeared that he had remembered a coat of mine which I had thrown over a rail to dry after having been wetted in a shower which had passed over the ship in the afternoon. Sitting stolidly at the head of the table I became terrified at the sight of the garment on his arm. Of course he made for my door. There was no time to lose.

"Steward," I thundered. My nerves were so shaken that I could not govern my voice and conceal my agitation. This was the sort of thing that made my terrifically whiskered mate tap his forehead with his forefinger. I had detected him using that gesture while talking on deck with a confidential air to the carpenter. It was too far to hear a word, but I had no doubt that this pantomime could only refer to the strange new captain.

"Yes, sir," the pale-faced steward turned resignedly to me. It was this maddening course of being shouted at, checked without rhyme or reason, arbitrarily chased out of my cabin, suddenly called into it, sent flying out of his pantry on incomprehensible errands, that accounted for the growing wretchedness of his expression.

"Where are you going with that coat?"

"To your room, sir."

"Is there another shower coming?"

"I'm sure I don't know, sir. Shall I go up again and see, sir?"

"No! never mind."

My object was attained, as of course my other self in there would have heard everything that passed. During this interlude my two officers never raised their eyes off their respective plates; but the lip of that confounded cub, the second mate, quivered visibly.

I expected the steward to hook my coat on and come out at once. He was very slow about it; but I dominated my nervousness sufficiently not to shout after him. Suddenly I became aware (it could be heard plainly enough) that the fellow for some reason or other was opening the door of the bathroom. It was the end. The place was literally not big enough to swing a cat in. My voice died in my throat and I went stony all over. I expected to hear a yell of surprise and terror, and made a movement, but had not the strength to get on my legs. Everything remained still. Had my second self taken the poor wretch by the throat? I don't know what I could have done next moment if I had not seen the steward come out of my room, close the door, and then stand quietly by the sideboard.

"Saved," I thought. "But, no! Lost! Gone! He was gone!"

I laid my knife and fork down and leaned back in my chair. My head swam. After a while, when sufficiently recovered to speak in a steady voice, I instructed my mate to put the ship round at eight o'clock himself.

"I won't come on deck," I went on. "I think I'll turn in, and unless the wind shifts I don't want to be disturbed before midnight. I feel a bit seedy."

"You did look middling bad a little while ago," the chief mate remarked without showing any great concern.

They both went out, and I stared at the steward clearing the table. There was nothing to be read on that wretched man's face. But why did he avoid my eyes, I asked myself. Then I thought I should like to hear the sound of his voice.

"Steward!"

"Sir!" Startled as usual.

"Where did you hang up that coat?"

"In the bathroom, sir." The usual anxious tone. "It's not quite dry yet, sir."

For some time longer I sat in the cuddy. Had my double vanished as he had come? But of his coming there was an explanation, whereas his disappearance would be inexplicable. . . . I went slowly into my dark room, shut the door, lighted the lamp, and for a time dared not turn round. When at last I did I saw him standing bolt-upright in the narrow recessed part. It would not be true to say I had a shock, but an irresistible doubt of his bodily existence flitted through my mind. Can it be, I asked myself, that he is not visible to other eyes than mine? It was like being haunted. Motionless, with a grave face, he raised his hands slightly at me in a gesture which meant clearly, "Heavens! what a narrow escape!" Narrow indeed. I think I had come creeping quietly as near insanity as any man who has not actually gone over the border. That gesture restrained me, so to speak.

The mate with the terrific whiskers was now putting the ship on the other tack. In the moment of profound silence which follows upon the hands going to their stations I heard on the poop his raised voice: "Hard alee!" and the distant shout of the order repeated on the main-deck. The sails, in that light breeze, made but a faint fluttering noise. It ceased. The ship was coming round slowly: I held my breath in the renewed stillness of expectation; one wouldn't have thought that there was a single living soul on her decks. A sudden brisk shout, "Mainsail haul!" broke the spell, and in the noisy cries and rush overhead of the men running away with the main brace we two, down in my cabin, came together in our usual position by the bed place.

He did not wait for my question. "I heard him fumbling here and just managed to squat myself down in the bath," he whispered to me. "The fellow only opened the door and put his arm in to hang the coat up. All the same—"

"I never thought of that," I whispered back, even more appalled than before at the closeness of the shave, and marveling at that something unyielding in his character which was carrying him through so finely. There was no agitation in his whisper. Whoever was being driven distracted, it was not he. He was sane. And the proof of his sanity was continued when he took up the whispering again.

"It would never do for me to come to life again."

It was something that a ghost might have said. But what he was alluding to was his old captain's reluctant admission of the theory of suicide. It would obviously serve his turn—if I had understood at all the view which seemed to govern the unalterable purpose of his action.

"You must maroon me as soon as ever you can get amongst these islands off the Cambodje shore," he went on.

"Maroon you! We are not living in a boy's adventure tale," I protested. His scornful whispering took me up.

"We aren't indeed! There's nothing of a boy's tale in this. But there's nothing else for it. I want no more. You don't suppose I am afraid of what can be done to me? Prison or gallows or whatever they may please. But you don't see me coming back to explain such things to an old fellow in a wig and twelve respectable tradesmen, do you? What can they know whether I am guilty or not—or of *what* I am guilty, either? That's my affair. What does the Bible say? 'Driven off the face of the earth.' Very well, I am off the face of the earth now. As I came at night so I shall go."

"Impossible!" I murmured. "You can't."

"Can't? . . . Not naked like a soul on the Day of Judgment. I shall freeze on to this sleeping suit. The Last Day is not yet—and . . . you have understood thoroughly. Didn't you?"

I felt suddenly ashamed of myself. I may say truly that I understood—and my hesitation in letting that man swim away from my ship's side had been a mere sham sentiment, a sort of cowardice.

"It can't be done now till next night," I breathed out. "The ship is on the off-shore tack and the wind may fail us."

"As long as I know that you understand," he whispered. "But of course you do. It's a great satisfaction to have got somebody to understand. You seem to have been there on purpose." And in the same whisper, as if we two whenever we talked had to say things to each other which were not fit for the world to hear, he added, "It's very wonderful."

We remained side by side talking in our secret way—but sometimes silent or just exchanging a whispered word or two at long intervals. And as usual he stared through the port. A breath of wind came now and again into our faces. The ship might have been moored in dock, so gently and on an even keel she slipped through the water, that did not murmur even at our passage, shadowy and silent like a phantom sea.

At midnight I went on deck, and to my mate's great surprise put the ship round on the other tack. His terrible whiskers flitted round me in silent criticism. I certainly should not have done it if it had been only a question of getting out of that sleepy gulf as quickly as possible. I believe he told the second mate, who relieved him, that it was a great want of judgment. The other only yawned. That intolerable cub shuffled about so sleepily and lolled against the rails in such a slack, improper fashion that I came down on him sharply.

"Aren't you properly awake yet?"

"Yes, sir! I am awake."

"Well, then, be good enough to hold yourself as if you were. And keep a lookout. If there's any current we'll be closing with some islands before daylight."

The east side of the gulf is fringed with islands, some solitary, others in groups. One the blue background of the high coast they seem to float on silvery patches of calm water, arid and gray, or dark green and rounded like clumps of evergreen bushes, with the larger ones, a mile or two long, showing the outlines of ridges, ribs of gray rock under the dark mantle of matted leafage. Unknown to trade, to travel, almost to geography, the manner of life they harbor is an unsolved secret. There must be villages—settlements of fishermen at least—on the largest of them, and some communication with the world is probably kept up by native craft. But all that forenoon, as we headed for them, fanned along by the faintest of breezes, I saw no sign of man or canoe in the field of the telescope I kept on pointing at the scattered group.

At noon I have no orders for a change of course, and the mate's whiskers became much concerned and seemed to be offering themselves unduly to my notice. At last I said:

"I am going to stand right in. Quite in—as far as I can take her."

The stare of extreme surprise imparted an air of ferocity also to his eyes, and he looked truly terrific for a moment.

"We're not doing well in the middle of the gulf," I continued, casually. "I am going to look for the land breezes tonight."

"Bless my soul! Do you mean, sir, in the dark amongst the lot of all them islands and reefs and shoals?"

"Well—if there are any regular land breezes at all on this coast one must get close inshore to find them, mustn't one?"

"Bless my soul!" he exclaimed again under his breath. All that afternoon he wore a dreamy, contemplative appearance which in him was a mark of perplexity. After dinner I went into my stateroom as if I meant to take some rest. There we two bent our dark heads over a half-unrolled chart lying on my bed.

"There," I said. "It's got to be Koh-ring. I've been looking at it ever since sunrise. It has got two hills and a low point. It must be inhabited. And on the coast opposite there is what looks like the mouth of a biggish river—with some towns, no doubt, not far up. It's the best chance for you that I can see."

"Anything. Koh-ring let it be."

He looked thoughtfully at the chart as if surveying chances and distances from a lofty height—and following with his eyes his own figure wandering on the blank land of Cochin-China, and then passing off that piece of paper clean out of sight into uncharted regions. And it was as if the ship had two captains to plan her course for her. I had been so worried and restless running up and down that I had not had the patience to dress that day. I had remained in my sleeping suit, with straw slippers and a soft floppy hat. The closeness of the heat in the gulf had been most oppressive, and the crew were used to seeing me wandering in that airy attire.

"She will clear the south point as she heads now," I whispered into his ear. "Goodness only knows when, though, but certainly after dark. I'll edge her in to half a mile, as far as I may be able to judge in the dark—"

"Be careful," he murmured, warningly—and I realized suddenly that all my future, the only future for which I was fit, would perhaps go irretrievably to pieces in any mishap to my first command.

I could not stop a moment longer in the room. I motioned him to get out of sight and made my way on the poop. That unplayful cub had the watch. I walked up and down for a while thinking things out, then beckoned him over.

"Send a couple of hands to open the two quarter-deck ports," I said, mildly.

He actually had the impudence, or else so forgot himself in his wonder at such an incomprehensible order, as to repeat:

"Open the quarter-deck ports! What for, sir?"

"The only reason you need concern yourself about is because I tell you to do so. Have them open wide and fastened properly."

He reddened and went off, but I believe made some jeering remark to the carpenter as to the sensible practice of ventilating a ship's quarter-deck. I know he popped into the mate's cabin to impart the fact to him because the whiskers came on deck, as it were by chance, and stole glances at me from below—for signs of lunacy or drunkenness, I suppose.

A little before supper, feeling more restless than ever, I rejoined, for a moment, my second self. And to find him sitting so quietly was surprising, like something against nature, inhuman.

I developed my plan in a hurried whisper.

"I shall stand in as close as I dare and then put her round. I will presently find means to smuggle you out of here into the sail locker, which communicates with the lobby. But there is an opening, a sort of square for hauling the sails out, which gives straight on the quarter-deck and which is never closed in fine weather, so as to give air to the sails. When the ship's way is deadened in stays and all the hands are aft at the main braces you will have a clear road to slip out and get overboard through the open quarter-deck port. I've had them both fastened up. Use a rope's end to lower yourself into the water so as to avoid a splash—you know. It could be heard and cause some beastly complication."

He kept silent for a while, then whispered, "I understand."

"I won't be there to see you go," I began with an effort. "The rest .

. . I only hope I have understood, too."

"You have. From first to last"—and for the first time there seemed to be a faltering, something strained in his whisper. He caught hold of my arm, but the ringing of the supper bell made me start. He didn't though; he only released his grip.

After supper I didn't come below again till well past eight o'clock. The faint, steady breeze was loaded with dew; and the wet, darkened sails held all there was of propelling power in it. The night, clear and starry, sparkled darkly, and the opaque, lightless patches shifting slowly against the low stars were the drifting islets. On the port bow there was a big one more distant and shadowily imposing by the great space of sky it eclipsed.

On opening the door I had a back view of my very own self looking at a chart. He had come out of the recess and was standing near the table.

"Quite dark enough," I whispered.

He stepped back and leaned against my bed with a level, quiet glance. I sat on the couch. We had nothing to say to each other. Over our heads the officer of the watch moved here and there. Then I heard him move quickly. I knew what that meant. He was making for the companion; and presently his voice was outside my door.

"We are drawing in pretty fast, sir. Land looks rather close."

"Very well," I answered. "I am coming on deck directly."

I waited till he was gone out of the cuddy, then rose. My double moved too. The time had come to exchange our last whispers, for neither of us was ever to hear each other's natural voice.

"Look here!" I opened a drawer and took out three sovereigns. "Take this anyhow. I've got six and I'd give you the lot, only I must keep a little money to buy some fruit and vegetables for the crew from native boats as we go through Sunda Straits."

He shook his head.

"Take it," I urged him, whispering desperately. "No one can tell what—"

He smiled and slapped meaningly the only pocket of the sleeping jacket. It was not safe, certainly. But I produced a large old silk handkerchief of mine, and tying the three pieces of gold in a corner, pressed it on him. He was touched, I supposed, because he took it at last and tied it quickly round his waist under the jacket, on his bare skin.

Our eyes met; several seconds elapsed, till, our glances still mingled, I extended my hand and turned the lamp out. Then I passed through the cuddy, leaving the door of my room wide open. . . . "Steward!"

He was still lingering in the pantry in the greatness of his zeal, giving a rub-up to a plated cruet stand the last thing before going to bed. Being careful not to wake up the mate, whose room was opposite, I spoke in an undertone.

He looked round anxiously. "Sir!"

"Can you get me a little hot water from the galley?"

"I am afraid, sir, the galley fire's been out for some time now."

"Go and see."

He flew up the stairs.

"Now," I whispered, loudly, into the saloon—too loudly, perhaps, but I was afraid I couldn't make a sound. He was by my side in an instant—the double captain slipped past the stairs—through a tiny dark passage . . . a sliding door. We were in the sail locker, scrambling on our knees over the sails. A sudden thought struck me. I saw myself wandering barefooted, bareheaded, the sun beating on my dark poll. I snatched off my floppy hat and tried hurriedly in the dark to ram it on my other self. He dodged and fended off silently. I wonder what he thought had come to me before he understood and suddenly desisted. Our hands met gropingly, lingered united in a steady, motionless clasp for a second. . . . No word was breathed by either of us when they separated.

I was standing quietly by the pantry door when the steward returned.

"Sorry, sir. Kettle barely warm. Shall I light the spirit lamp?"

"Never mind."

I came out on deck slowly. It was now a matter of conscience to shave the land as close as possible—for now he must go overboard whenever the ship was put in stays. Must! There could be no going back for him. After a moment I walked over to leeward and my heart flew into my mouth at the nearness of the land on the bow. Under any other circumstances I would not have held on a minute longer. The second mate had followed me anxiously.

I looked on till I felt I could command my voice.

"She will weather," I said then in a quiet tone.

"Are you going to try that, sir?" he stammered out incredulously.

I took no notice of him and raised my tone just enough to be heard by the helmsman.

"Keep her good full."

"Good full, sir."

The wind fanned my cheek, the sails slept, the world was silent. The strain of watching the dark loom of the land grow bigger and denser was too much for me. I had shut my eyes—because the ship must go closer. She must! The stillness was intolerable. Were we standing still?

When I opened my eyes the second view started my heart with a thump. The black southern hill of Koh-ring seemed to hang right over the ship like a towering fragment of everlasting night. On that enormous mass of blackness there was not a gleam to be seen, not a sound to be heard. It was gliding irresistibly towards us and yet seemed already within reach of the hand. I saw the vague figures of the watch grouped in the waist, gazing in awed silence.

"Are you going on, sir?" inquired an unsteady voice at my elbow.

I ignored it. I had to go on.

"Keep her full. Don't check her way. That won't do now," I said warningly.

"I can't see the sails very well," the helmsman answered me, in strange, quavering tones.

Was she close enough? Already she was, I won't say in the shadow of the land, but in the very blackness of it, already swallowed up as it were, gone too close to be recalled, gone from me altogether.

"Give the mate a call," I said to the young man who stood at my elbow as still as death. "And turn all hands up."

My tone had a borrowed loudness reverberated from the height of the land. Several voices cried out together: "We are all on deck, sir."

Then stillness again, with the great shadow gliding closer, towering higher, without a light, without a sound. Such a hush had fallen on the ship that she might have been a bark of the dead floating in slowly under the very gate of Erebus.

"My God! Where are we?"

It was the mate moaning at my elbow. He was thunderstruck, and as it were deprived of the moral support of his whiskers. He clapped his hands and absolutely cried out, "Lost!"

"Be quiet," I said, sternly.

He lowered his tone, but I saw the shadowy gesture of his despair. "What are we doing here?"

"Looking for the land wind."

He made as if to tear his hair, and addressed me recklessly.

"She will never get out. You have done it, sir. I knew it'd end in something like this. She will never weather, and you are too close now to stay. She'll drift ashore before she's round. O my God!"

I caught his arm as he was raising it to batter his poor devoted head, and shook it violently.

"She's ashore already," he wailed, trying to tear himself away.

"Is she? . . . Keep good full there!"

"Good full, sir," cried the helmsman in a frightened, thin, childlike voice.

I hadn't let go the mate's arm and went on shaking it. "Ready about, do you hear? You go forward"—shake—"and stop there"—shake—"and hold your noise"—shake—"and see these head-sheets properly overhauled"—shake, shake—shake.

And all the time I dared not look towards the land lest my heart should fail me. I released my grip at last and he ran forward as if fleeing for dear life.

I wondered what my double there in the sail locker thought of this commotion. He was able to hear everything—and perhaps he was able to understand why, on my conscience, it had to be thus close—no less. My first order "Hard alee!" re-echoed ominously under the towering shadow of Koh-ring as if I had shouted in a mountain gorge. And then I watched the land intently. In that smooth water and light wind it was impossible to feel the ship coming-to. No! I could not feel her. And my second self was making now ready to ship out and lower himself overboard. Perhaps he was gone already . . . ?

The great black mass brooding over our very mastheads began to pivot away from the ship's side silently. And now I forgot the secret stranger ready to depart, and remembered only that I was a total stranger to the ship. I did not know her. Would she do it? How was she to be handled?

I swung the mainyard and waited helplessly. She was perhaps stopped, and her very fate hung in the balance, with the black mass of Koh-ring like the gate of the everlasting night towering over her taffrail. What would she do now? Had she way on her yet? I stepped to the side swiftly, and on the shadowy water I could see nothing except a faint phosphorescent flash revealing the glassy smoothness of the sleeping surface. It was impossible to tell—and I had not learned yet the feel of my ship. Was she moving? What I needed was something easily seen, a piece of paper, which I could throw overboard and watch. I had nothing on me. To run down for it I didn't dare. There was no time. All at once my strained, yearning stare distinguished a white object floating within a yard of the ship's side. White on the black water. A phosphorescent flash passed under it. What was that thing? . . . I recognized my own floppy hat. It must have fallen off his head . . . and he didn't bother. Now I had what I wanted—the saving mark for my eyes. But I hardly thought of my other self, now gone from the ship, to be hidden forever from all friendly faces, to be a fugitive and a vagabond on the earth, with no brand of the curse on his sane forehead to stay a slaying hand . . . too proud to explain.

And I watched the hat—the expression of my sudden pity for his mere flesh. It had been meant to save his homeless head from the dangers of the sun. And now—behold—it was saving the ship, by serving me for a mark to help out the ignorance of my strangeness. Ha! It was drifting forward, warning me just in time that the ship had gathered sternway.

"Shift the helm," I said in a low voice to the seaman standing still like a statue.

The man's eyes glistened wildly in the binnacle light as he jumped round to the other side and spun round the wheel.

I walked to the break of the poop. On the over-shadowed deck all hands stood by the forebraces waiting for my order. The stars ahead seemed to be gliding from right to left. And all was so still in the world that I heard the quiet remark, "She's round," passed in a tone of intense relief between two seamen.

"Let go and haul."

The foreyards ran round with a great noise, amidst cheery cries. And now the frightful whiskers made themselves heard giving various orders. Already the ship was drawing ahead. And I was alone with her. Nothing! no one in the world should stand now between us, throwing a shadow on the way of silent knowledge and mute affection, the perfect communion of a seaman with his first command.

Walking to the taffrail, I was in time to make out, on the very edge of a darkness thrown by a towering black mass like the very gateway of Erebus—yes, I was in time to catch an evanescent glimpse of my white hat left behind to mark the spot where the secret sharer of my cabin and of my thoughts, as though he were my second self, had lowered himself into the water to take his punishment: a free man, a proud swimmer striking out for a new destiny.

The Shadow-Line

> —*D'autre fois, calme plat, grand miroir*
> *De mon désespoir.*
> —BAUDELAIRE

PART ONE

I

Only the young have such moments. I don't mean the very young. No. The very young have, properly speaking, no moments. It is the privilege of early youth to live in advance of its days in all the beautiful continuity of hope which knows no pauses and no introspection.

One closes behind one the little gate of mere boyishness—and enters an enchanted garden. Its very shades glow with promise. Every turn of the path has its seduction. And it isn't because it is an undiscovered country. One knows well enough that all mankind had streamed that way. It is the charm of universal experience from which one expects an uncommon or personal sensation—a bit of one's own.

One goes on recognizing the landmarks of the predecessors, excited, amused, taking the hard luck and the good luck together—the kicks and the half-pence, as the saying is—the picturesque common lot that holds so many possibilities for the deserving or perhaps for the lucky. Yes. One goes on. And the time, too, goes on—till one perceives ahead a shadow-line warning one that the region of early youth, too, must be left behind.

This is the period of life in which such moments of which I have spoken are likely to come. What moments? Why, the moments of boredom, of weariness, of dissatisfaction. Rash moments. I mean moments when the still young are inclined to commit rash actions, such as getting married suddenly or else throwing up a job for no reason.

This is not a marriage story. It wasn't so bad as that with me. My action, rash as it was, had more the character of divorce—almost of desertion. For no reason on which a sensible person could put a finger I threw up my job—chucked my berth—left the ship of which the worst that could be said was that she was a steamship and therefore, perhaps, not entitled to that blind loyalty which. . . . However, it's no use trying to put a gloss on what even at the time I myself half suspected to be a caprice.

It was in an Eastern port. She was an Eastern ship, inasmuch as then she belonged to that port. She traded among dark islands on a blue reef-scarred sea, with the Red Ensign over the taffrail and at her masthead a house-flag, also red, but with a green border and with a white crescent in it. For an Arab owned her, and a Syed at that. Hence the green border on the flag. He was the head of a great House of Straits Arabs, but as loyal a subject of the complex British Empire as you could find east of the Suez Canal. World politics did not trouble him at all, but he had a great occult power amongst his own people.

It was all one to us who owned the ship. He had to employ white men in the shipping part of his business, and many of those he so employed had never set eyes on him from the first to the last day. I myself saw him but once, quite accidentally on a wharf—an old, dark little man blind in one eye, in a snowy robe and yellow slippers. He was having his hand severely kissed by a crowd of Malay pilgrims to whom he had done some favour, in the way of food and money. His alms-giving, I have heard, was most extensive, covering almost the whole Archipelago. For isn't it said that "The charitable man is the friend of Allah"?

Excellent (and picturesque) Arab owner, about whom one needed not to trouble one's head, a most excellent Scottish ship—for she was that from the keep up—excellent sea-boat, easy to keep clean, most handy in every way, and if it had not been for her internal propulsion, worthy of any man's love, I cherish to this day a profound respect for her memory. As to the kind of trade she was engaged in and the character of my shipmates, I could not have been happier if I had had the life and the men made to my order by a benevolent Enchanter.

And suddenly I left all this. I left it in that, to us, inconsequential manner in which a bird flies away from a comfortable branch. It was as though all unknowing I had heard a whisper or seen something. Well—perhaps! One day I was perfectly right and the next everything was gone—glamour, flavour, interest, contentment—everything. It was one of these moments, you know. The green sickness of late youth descended on me and carried me off. Carried me off that ship, I mean.

We were only four white men on board, with a large crew of Kalashes and two Malay petty officers. The Captain stared hard as if wondering what ailed me. But he was a sailor, and he, too, had been young at one time. Presently a smile came to lurk under his thick iron-gray moustache, and he observed that, of course, if I felt I must go he couldn't keep me by main force. And it was arranged that I should be paid off the next morning. As I was going out of his cabin he added suddenly, in a peculiar wistful tone, that he hoped I would find what I was so anxious to go and look for. A soft, cryptic utterance which seemed to reach deeper than any diamond-hard tool could have done. I do believe he understood my case.

But the second engineer attacked me differently. He was a sturdy young Scot, with a smooth face and light eyes. His honest red countenance emerged out of the engine-room companion and then the whole robust man, with shirt sleeves turned up, wiping slowly the massive fore-arms with a lump of cotton-waste. And his light eyes expressed bitter distaste, as though our friendship had turned to ashes. He said weightily: "Oh! Aye! I've been thinking it was about time for you to run away home and get married to some silly girl."

It was tacitly understood in the port that John Nieven was a fierce misogynist; and the absurd character of the sally convinced me that he meant to be nasty—very nasty—had meant to say the most crushing thing he could think of. My laugh sounded deprecatory. Nobody but a friend could be so angry as that. I became a little crestfallen. Our chief engineer also took a characteristic view of my action, but in a kindlier spirit.

He was young, too, but very thin, and with a mist of fluffy brown beard all round his haggard face. All day long, at sea or in harbour, he could be seen walking hastily up and down the after-deck, wearing an intense, spiritually rapt expression, which was caused by a perpetual consciousness of unpleasant physical sensations in his internal economy. For he was a confirmed dyspeptic. His view of my case was very simple. He said it was nothing but deranged liver. Of course! He suggested I should stay for another trip and meantime dose myself with a certain patent medicine in which his own belief was absolute. "I'll tell you what I'll do. I'll buy you two bottles, out of my own pocket. There. I can't say fairer than that, can I?"

I believe he would have perpetrated the atrocity (or generosity) at the merest sign of weakening on my part. By that time, however, I was more discontented, disgusted, and dogged than ever. The past eighteen months, so full of new and varied experience, appeared a dreary, prosaic waste of days. I felt—how shall I express it?—that there was no truth to be got out of them.

What truth? I should have been hard put to it to explain. Probably, if pressed, I would have burst into tears simply. I was young enough for that.

Next day the Captain and I transacted our business in the Harbour Office. It was a lofty, big, cool, white room, where the screened light of day glowed serenely. Everybody in it—the officials, the public—were in white. Only the heavy polished desks gleamed darkly in a central avenue, and some papers lying on them were blue. Enormous punkahs sent from on high a gentle draught through that immaculate interior and upon our perspiring heads.

The official behind the desk we approached grinned amiably and kept it up till, in answer to his perfunctory question, "Sign off and on again?" my Captain answered, "No! Signing off for good." And then his grin vanished in sudden solemnity. He did not look at me again till he handed me my papers with a sorrowful expression, as if they had been my passports for Hades.

While I was putting them away he murmured some question to the Captain, and I heard the latter answer good-humouredly:

"No. He leaves us to go home."

"Oh!" the other exclaimed, nodding mournfully over my sad condition.

I didn't know him outside the official building, but he leaned forward the desk to shake hands with me, compassionately, as one would with some poor devil going out to be hanged; and I am afraid I performed my part ungraciously, in the hardened manner of an impenitent criminal.

No homeward-bound mail-boat was due for three or four days. Being now a man without a ship, and having for a time broken my connection with the sea—become, in fact, a mere potential passenger— it would have been more appropriate perhaps if I had gone to stay at an hotel. There it was, too, within a stone's throw of the Harbour Office, low, but somehow palatial, displaying its white, pillared pavilions surrounded by trim grass plots. I would have felt a passenger indeed in there! I gave it a hostile glance and directed my steps toward the Officers' Sailors' Home.

I walked in the sunshine, disregarding it, and in the shade of the big trees on the esplanade without enjoying it. The heat of the tropical East descended through the leafy boughs, enveloping my thinly-clad body, clinging to my rebellious discontent, as if to rob it of its freedom.

The Officers' Home was a large bungalow with a wide verandah and a curiously suburban-looking little garden of bushes and a few trees between it and the street. That institution partook somewhat of the character of a residential club, but with a slightly Governmental flavour about it, because it was administered by the Harbour Office. Its manager was officially styled Chief Steward. He was an unhappy, wizened little man, who if put into a jockey's rig would have looked the part to perfection. But it was obvious that at some time or other in his life, in some capacity or other, he had been connected with the sea. Possibly in the comprehensive capacity of a failure.

I should have thought his employment a very easy one, but he used to affirm for some reason or other that his job would be the death of him some day. It was rather mysterious. Perhaps everything naturally was too much trouble for him. He certainly seemed to hate having people in the house.

On entering it I thought he must be feeling pleased. It was as still as a tomb. I could see no one in the living rooms; and the verandah, too, was empty, except for a man at the far end dozing prone in a long chair. At the noise of my footsteps he opened one horribly fish-like eye. He was a stranger to me. I retreated from there, and crossing the dining room—a very bare apartment with a motionless punkah hanging over the centre table—I knocked at a door labelled in black letters: "Chief Steward."

The answer to my knock being a vexed and doleful plaint: "Oh, dear! Oh, dear! What is it now?" I went in at once.

It was a strange room to find in the tropics. Twilight and stuffiness reigned in there. The fellow had hung enormously ample, dusty, cheap lace curtains over his windows, which were shut. Piles of cardboard boxes, such as milliners and dressmakers use in Europe, cumbered the corners; and by some means he had procured for himself the sort of furniture that might have come out of a respectable parlour in the East End of London—a horsehair sofa, arm-chairs of the same. I glimpsed grimy antimacassars scattered over that horrid upholstery, which was awe-inspiring, insomuch that one could not guess what mysterious accident, need, or fancy had collected it there. Its owner had taken off his tunic, and in white trousers and a thin, short-sleeved singlet prowled behind the chair-backs nursing his meagre elbows.

An exclamation of dismay escaped him when he heard that I had come for a stay; but he could not deny that there were plenty of vacant rooms.

"Very well. Can you give me the one I had before?"

He emitted a faint moan from behind a pile of cardboard boxes on the table, which might have contained gloves or handkerchiefs or neckties. I wonder what the fellow did keep in them? There was a smell of decaying coral, or Oriental dust of zoological specimens in that den of his. I could only see the top of his head and his unhappy eyes levelled at me over the barrier.

"It's only for a couple of days," I said, intending to cheer him up.

"Perhaps you would like to pay in advance?" he suggested eagerly.

"Certainly not!" I burst out directly I could speak. "Never heard of such a thing! This is the most infernal cheek. . . ."

He had seized his head in both hands—a gesture of despair which checked my indignation.

"Oh, dear! Oh, dear! Don't fly out like this. I am asking everybody."

"I don't believe it," I said bluntly.

"Well, I am going to. And if you gentlemen all agreed to pay in advance I could make Hamilton pay up, too. He's always turning up ashore dead broke, and even when he has some money he won't settle his bills. I don't know what to do with him. He swears at me and tells me I can't chuck a white man out into the street here. So if you only would. . . ."

I was amazed. Incredulous, too. I suspected the fellow of gratuitous impertinence. I told him with marked emphasis that I would see him and Hamilton hanged first, and requested him to conduct me to my room with no more of his nonsense. He produced then a key from somewhere and led the way out of his lair, giving me a vicious sidelong look in passing.

"Any one I know staying here?" I asked him before he left my room.

He had recovered his usual pained impatient tone, and said that Captain Giles was there, back from a Solo Sea trip. Two other guests were staying also. He paused. And, of course, Hamilton, he added.

"Oh, yes! Hamilton," I said, and the miserable creature took himself off with a final groan.

His impudence still rankled when I came into the dining room at tiffin time. He was there on duty overlooking the Chinamen servants. The tiffin was laid on one end only of the long table, and the punkah was stirring the hot air lazily—mostly above a barren waste of polished wood.

We were four around the cloth. The dozing stranger from the chair was one. Both his eyes were partly opened now, but they did not seem to see anything. He was supine. The dignified person next him, with short side whiskers and a carefully scraped chin, was, of course, Hamilton. I have never seen any one so full of dignity for the station in life Providence had been pleased to place him in. I had been told that he regarded me as a rank outsider. He raised not only his eyes, but his eyebrows as well, at the sound I made pulling back my chair.

Captain Giles was at the head of the table. I exchanged a few words of greeting with him and sat down on his left. Stout and pale, with a great shiny dome of a bald forehead and prominent brown eyes, he might have been anything but a seaman. You would not have been surprised to learn that he was an architect. To me (I know how absurd it is) to me he looked like a churchwarden. He had the appearance of a man from whom you would expect sound advice, moral sentiments, with perhaps a platitude or two thrown in on occasion, not from a desire to dazzle, but from honest conviction.

Though very well known and appreciated in the shipping world, he had no regular employment. He did not want it. He had his own peculiar position. He was an expert. An expert in—how shall I say it?—in intricate navigation. He was supposed to know more about remote and imperfectly charted parts of the Archipelago than any man living. His brain must have been a perfect warehouse of reefs, positions, bearings, images of headlands, shapes of obscure coasts, aspects of innumerable islands, desert and otherwise. Any ship, for instance, bound on a trip to Palawan or somewhere that way would have Captain Giles on board, either in temporary command or "to assist the master." It was said that he had a retaining fee from a wealthy firm of Chinese steamship owners, in view of such services. Besides, he was always ready to relieve any man who wished to take a spell ashore for a time. No owner was ever known to object to an arrangement of that sort. For it seemed to be the established opinion at the port that Captain Giles was as good as the best, if not a little better. But in Hamilton's view he was an "outsider." I believe that for Hamilton the generalization "outsider" covered the whole lot of us; though I suppose that he made some distinctions in his mind.

I didn't try to make conversation with Captain Giles, whom I had not seen more than twice in my life. But, of course, he knew who I was. After a while, inclining his big shiny head my way, he addressed me first in his friendly fashion. He presumed from seeing me there, he said, that I had come ashore for a couple of days' leave.

He was a low-voiced man. I spoke a little louder, saying that: No—I had left the ship for good.

"A free man for a bit," was his comment.

"I suppose I may call myself that—since eleven o'clock," I said.

Hamilton had stopped eating at the sound of our voices. He laid down his knife and fork gently, got up, and muttering something about "this infernal heat cutting one's appetite," went out of the room. Almost immediately we heard him leave the house down the verandah steps.

On this Captain Giles remarked easily that the fellow had no doubt gone off to look after my old job. The Chief Steward, who had been leaning against the wall, brought his face of an unhappy goat nearer to the table and addressed us dolefully. His object was to unburden himself of his eternal grievance against Hamilton. The man kept him in hot water with the Harbour Office as to the state of his accounts. He wished to goodness he would get my job, though in truth what would it be? Temporary relief at best.

I said: "You needn't worry. He won't get my job. My successor is on board already."

He was surprised, and I believe his face fell a little at the news.

Captain Giles gave a soft laugh. We got up and went out on the verandah, leaving the supine stranger to be dealt with by the Chinamen. The last thing I saw they had put a plate with a slice of pine-apple on it before him and stood back to watch what would happen. But the experiment seemed a failure. He sat insensible.

It was imparted to me in a low voice by Captain Giles that this was an officer of some Rajah's yacht which had come into our port to be dry-docked. Must have been "seeing life" last night, he added, wrinkling his nose in an intimate, confidential way which pleased me vastly. For Captain Giles had prestige. He was credited with wonderful adventures and with some mysterious tragedy in his life. And no man had a word to say against him. He continued:

"I remember him first coming ashore here some years ago. Seems only the other day. He was a nice boy. Oh! these nice boys!"

I could not help laughing aloud. He looked startled, then joined in the laugh. "No! No! I didn't mean that," he cried. "What I meant is that some of them do go soft mighty quick out here."

Jocularly I suggested the beastly heat as the first cause. But Captain Giles disclosed himself possessed of a deeper philosophy. Things out East were made easy for white men. That was all right. The difficulty was to go on keeping white, and some of these nice boys did not know how. He gave me a searching look, and in a benevolent, heavy-uncle manner asked point blank:

"Why did you throw up your berth?"

I became angry all of a sudden; for you can understand how exasperating such a question was to a man who didn't know. I said to myself that I ought to shut up that moralist; and to him aloud I said with challenging politeness:

"Why . . . ? Do you disapprove?"

He was too disconcerted to do more than mutter confusedly: "I! . . . In a general way . . ." and then gave me up. But he retired in good order, under the cover of a heavily humorous remark that he, too, was getting soft, and that this was his time for taking his little siesta—when he was on shore. "Very bad habit. Very bad habit."

There was a simplicity in the man which would have disarmed a touchiness even more youthful than mine. So when next day at tiffin he bent his head toward me and said that he had met my late Captain last evening, adding in an undertone: "He's very sorry you left. He had never had a mate that suited him so well," I answered him earnestly, without any affectation, that I certainly hadn't been so comfortable in any ship or with any commander in all my sea-going days.

"Well—then," he murmured.

"Haven't you heard, Captain Giles, that I intend to go home?"

"Yes," he said benevolently. "I have heard that sort of thing so often before."

"What of that?" I cried. I thought he was the most dull, unimaginative man I had ever met. I don't know what more I would have said, but the much-belated Hamilton came in just then and took his usual seat. So I dropped into a mumble.

"Anyhow, you shall see it done this time."

Hamilton, beautifully shaved, gave Captain Giles a curt nod, but didn't even condescend to raise his eyebrows at me; and when he spoke it was only to tell the Chief Steward that the food on his plate wasn't fit to be set before a gentleman. The individual addressed seemed much too unhappy to groan. He cast his eyes up to the punkah and that was all.

Captain Giles and I got up from the table, and the stranger next to Hamilton followed our example, manœuvring himself to his feet with difficulty. He, poor fellow, not because he was hungry but I verily believe only to recover his self-respect, had tried to put some of that unworthy food into his mouth. But after dropping his fork twice and generally making a failure of it, he had sat still with an air of intense mortification combined with a ghastly glazed stare. Both Giles and I had avoided looking his way at table.

On the verandah he stopped short on purpose to address to us anxiously a long remark which I failed to understand completely. It sounded like some horrible unknown language. But when Captain Giles, after only an instant for reflection, assured him with homely friendliness, "Aye, to be sure. You are right there," he appeared very much gratified indeed, and went away (pretty straight, too) to seek a distant long chair.

"What was he trying to say?" I asked with disgust.

"I don't know. Mustn't be down too much on a fellow. He's feeling pretty wretched, you may be sure; and to-morrow he'll feel worse yet."

Judging by the man's appearance it seemed impossible. I wondered what sort of complicated debauch had reduced him to that unspeakable condition. Captain Giles' benevolence was spoiled by a curious air of complacency which I disliked. I said with a little laugh:

"Well, he will have you to look after him."

He made a deprecatory gesture, sat down, and took up a paper. I did the same. The papers were old and uninteresting, filled up mostly with dreary stereotyped descriptions of Queen Victoria's first jubilee celebrations. Probably we should have quickly fallen into a tropical afternoon doze if it had not been for Hamilton's voice raised in the dining room. He was finishing his tiffin there. The big double doors stood wide open permanently, and he could not have had any idea how near to the doorway our chairs were placed. He was heard in a loud, supercilious tone answering some statement ventured by the Chief Steward.

"I am not going to be rushed into anything. They will be glad enough to get a gentleman I imagine. There is no hurry."

A loud whispering from the Steward succeeded and then again Hamilton was heard with even intenser scorn.

"What? That young ass who fancies himself for having been chief mate with Kent so long? . . . Preposterous."

Giles and I looked at each other. Kent being the name of my late commander, Captain Giles' whisper, "He's talking of you," seemed to me sheer waste of breath. The Chief Steward must have stuck to his point, whatever it was, because Hamilton was heard again more supercilious if possible, and also very emphatic:

"Rubbish, my good man! One doesn't *compete* with a rank outsider like that. There's plenty of time."

Then there were pushing of chairs, footsteps in the next room, and plaintive expostulations from the Steward, who was pursuing Hamilton, even out of doors through the main entrance.

"That's a very insulting sort of man," remarked Captain Giles— superfluously, I thought. "Very insulting. You haven't offended him in some way, have you?"

"Never spoke to him in my life," I said grumpily. "Can't imagine what he means by competing. He has been trying for my job after I left—and didn't get it. But that isn't exactly competition."

Captain Giles balanced his big benevolent head thoughtfully. "He didn't get it," he repeated very slowly. "No, not likely either, with Kent. Kent is no end sorry you left him. He gives you the name of a good seaman, too."

I flung away the paper I was still holding. I sat up, I slapped the table with my open palm. I wanted to know why he would keep harping on that, my absolutely private affair. It was exasperating, really.

Captain Giles silenced me by the perfect equanimity of his gaze. "Nothing to be annoyed about," he murmured reasonably, with an evident desire to soothe the childish irritation he had aroused. And he was really a man of an appearance so inoffensive that I tried to explain myself as much as I could. I told him that I did not want to hear any more about what was past and gone. It had been very nice while it lasted, but now it was done with I preferred not to talk about it or even think about it. I had made up my mind to go home.

He listened to the whole tirade in a particular lending-the-ear attitude, as if trying to detect a false note in it somewhere; then straightened himself up and appeared to ponder sagaciously over the matter.

"Yes. You told me you meant to go home. Anything in view there?"

Instead of telling him that it was none of his business I said sullenly:

"Nothing that I know of."

I had indeed considered that rather blank side of the situation I had created for myself by leaving suddenly my very satisfactory employment. And I was not very pleased with it. I had it on the tip of my tongue to say that common sense had nothing to do with my action, and that therefore it didn't deserve the interest Captain Giles seemed to be taking in it. But he was puffing at a short wooden pipe now, and looked so guileless, dense, and commonplace, that it seemed hardly worth while to puzzle him either with truth or sarcasm.

He blew a cloud of smoke, then surprised me by a very abrupt: "Paid your passage money yet?"

Overcome by the shameless pertinacity of a man to whom it was rather difficult to be rude, I replied with exaggerated meekness that I had not done so yet. I thought there would be plenty of time to do that to-morrow.

And I was about to turn away, withdrawing my privacy from his fatuous, objectless attempts to test what sort of stuff it was made of, when he laid down his pipe in an extremely significant manner, you know, as if a critical moment had come, and leaned sideways over the table between us.

"Oh! You haven't yet!" He dropped his voice mysteriously. "Well, then I think you ought to know that there's something going on here."

I had never in my life felt more detached from all earthly goings on. Freed from the sea for a time, I preserved the sailor's consciousness of complete independence from all land affairs. How could they concern me? I gazed at Captain Giles' animation with scorn rather than with curiosity.

To his obviously preparatory question whether our Steward had spoken to me that day I said he hadn't. And what's more he would have had precious little encouragement if he had tried to. I didn't want the fellow to speak to me at all.

Unrebuked by my petulance, Captain Giles, with an air of immense sagacity, began to tell me a minute tale about a Harbour Office peon. It was absolutely pointless. A peon was seen walking that morning on the verandah with a letter in his hand. It was in an official envelope. As the habit of these fellows is, he had shown it to the first white man he came across. That man was our friend in the arm-chair. He, as I knew, was not in a state to interest himself in any sublunary matters. He could only wave the peon away. The peon then wandered on along the verandah and came upon Captain Giles, who was there by an extraordinary chance. . . .

At this point he stopped with a profound look. The letter, he continued, was addressed to the Chief Steward. Now what could Captain Ellis, the Master Attendant, want to write to the Steward for? The fellow went every morning, anyhow, to the Harbour Office with his report, for orders or what not. He hadn't been back more than an hour before there was an office peon chasing him with a note. Now what was that for?

And he began to speculate. It was not for this—and it could not be for that. As to that other thing it was unthinkable.

The fatuousness of all this made me stare. If the man had not been somehow a sympathetic personality I would have resented it like an insult. As it was, I felt only sorry for him. Something remarkably earnest in his gaze prevented me from laughing in his face. Neither did I yawn at him. I just stared.

His tone became a shade more mysterious. Directly the fellow (meaning the Steward) got that note he rushed for his hat and bolted out of the house. But it wasn't because the note called him to the Harbour Office. He didn't go there. He was not absent long enough for that. He came darting back in no time, flung his hat away, and raced about the dining room moaning and slapping his forehead. All these exciting facts and manifestations had been observed by Captain Giles. He had, it seems, been meditating upon them ever since.

I began to pity him profoundly. And in a tone which I tried to make as little sarcastic as possible I said that I was glad he had found something to occupy his morning hours.

With his disarming simplicity he made me observe, as if it were a matter of some consequence, how strange it was that he should have spent the morning indoors at all. He generally was out before tiffin, visiting various offices, seeing his friends in the harbour, and so on. He had felt out of sorts somewhat on rising. Nothing much. Just enough to make him feel lazy.

All this with a sustained, holding stare which, in conjunction with the general inanity of the discourse, conveyed the impression of mild, dreary lunacy. And when he hitched his chair a little and dropped his voice to the low note of mystery, it flashed upon me that high professional reputation was not necessarily a guarantee of sound mind.

It never occurred to me then that I didn't know in what soundness of mind exactly consisted and what a delicate and, upon the whole, unimportant matter it was. With some idea of not hurting his feelings I blinked at him in an interested manner. But when he proceeded to ask me mysteriously whether I remembered what had passed just now between that Steward of ours and "that man Hamilton," I only grunted sourly assent and turned away my head.

"Aye. But do you remember every word?" he insisted tactfully.

"I don't know. It's none of my business," I snapped out, consigning, moreover, the Steward and Hamilton aloud to eternal perdition.

I meant to be very energetic and final, but Captain Giles continued to gaze at me thoughtfully. Nothing could stop him. He went on to point out that my personality was involved in that conversation. When I tried to preserve the semblance of unconcern he became positively cruel. I heard what the man had said? Yes? What did I think of it then?—he wanted to know.

Captain Giles' appearance excluding the suspicion of mere sly malice, I came to the conclusion that he was simply the most tactless idiot on earth. I almost despised myself for the weakness of attempting to enlighten his common understanding. I started to explain that I did not think anything whatever. Hamilton was not worth a thought. What such an offensive loafer . . . "Aye! that he is," interjected Captain Giles . . . thought or said was below any decent man's contempt, and I did not propose to take the slightest notice of it.

This attitude seemed to me so simple and obvious that I was really astonished at Giles giving no sign of assent. Such perfect stupidity was almost interesting.

"What would you like me to do?" I asked, laughing. "I can't start a row with him because of the opinion he has formed of me. Of course, I've heard of the contemptuous way he alludes to me. But he doesn't intrude his contempt on my notice. He has never expressed it in my hearing. For even just now he didn't know we could hear him. I should only make myself ridiculous."

That hopeless Giles went on puffing at his pipe moodily. All at once his face cleared, and he spoke.

"You missed my point."

"Have I? I am very glad to hear it," I said.

With increasing animation he stated again that I had missed his point. Entirely. And in a tone of growing self-conscious complacency he told me that few things escaped his attention, and he was rather used to think them out, and generally from his experience of life and men arrived at the right conclusion.

This bit of self-praise, of course, fitted excellently the laborious inanity of the whole conversation. The whole thing strengthened in me that obscure feeling of life being but a waste of days, which, half-unconsciously, had driven me out of a comfortable berth, away from men I liked, to flee from the menace of emptiness . . . and to find inanity at the first turn. Here was a man of recognized character and achievement disclosed as an absurd and dreary chatterer. And it was probably like this everywhere—from east to west, from the bottom to the top of the social scale.

A great discouragement fell on me. A spiritual drowsiness. Giles' voice was going on complacently; the very voice of the universal hollow conceit. And I was no longer angry with it. There was nothing original, nothing new, startling, informing, to expect from the world; no opportunities to find out something about oneself, no wisdom to acquire, no fun to enjoy. Everything was stupid and overrated, even as

Captain Giles was. So be it.

The name of Hamilton suddenly caught my ear and roused me up.

"I thought we had done with him," I said, with the greatest possible distaste.

"Yes. But considering what we happened to hear just now I think you ought to do it."

"Ought to do it?" I sat up bewildered. "Do what?"

Captain Giles confronted me very much surprised.

"Why! Do what I have been advising you to try. You go and ask the Steward what was there in that letter from the Harbour Office. Ask him straight out."

I remained speechless for a time. Here was something unexpected and original enough to be altogether incomprehensible. I murmured, astounded:

"But I thought it was Hamilton that you . . ."

"Exactly. Don't you let him. You do what I tell you. You tackle that Steward. You'll make him jump, I bet," insisted Captain Giles, waving his smouldering pipe impressively at me. Then he took three rapid puffs at it.

His aspect of triumphant acuteness was indescribable. Yet the man remained a strangely sympathetic creature. Benevolence radiated from him ridiculously, mildly, impressively. It was irritating, too. But I pointed out coldly, as one who deals with the incomprehensible, that I didn't see any reason to expose myself to a snub from the fellow. He was a very unsatisfactory steward and a miserable wretch besides, but I would just as soon think of tweaking his nose.

"Tweaking his nose," said Captain Giles in a scandalized tone. "Much use it would be to you."

That remark was so irrelevant that one could make no answer to it. But the sense of the absurdity was beginning at last to exercise its well-known fascination. I felt I must not let the man talk to me any more. I got up, observing curtly that he was too much for me—that I couldn't make him out.

Before I had time to move away he spoke again in a changed tone of obstinacy and puffing nervously at his pipe.

"Well—he's a—no account cuss—anyhow. You just—ask him. That's all."

That new manner impressed me—or rather made me pause. But sanity asserting its sway at once I left the verandah after giving him a mirthless smile. In a few strides I found myself in the dining room, now cleared and empty. But during that short time various thoughts occurred to me, such as: that Giles had been making fun of me, expecting some amusement at my expense; that I probably looked silly and gullible; that I knew very little of life. . . .

The door facing me across the dining room flew open to my

extreme surprise. It was the door inscribed with the word "Steward" and the man himself ran out of his stuffy, Philistinish lair in his absurd, hunted-animal manner, making for the garden door.

To this day I don't know what made me call after him. "I say! Wait a minute." Perhaps it was the sidelong glance he gave me; or possibly I was yet under the influence of Captain Giles' mysterious earnestness. Well, it was an impulse of some sort; an effect of that force somewhere within our lives which shapes them this way or that. For if these words had not escaped from my lips (my will had nothing to do with that) my existence would, to be sure, have been still a seaman's existence, but directed on now to me utterly inconceivable lines.

No. My will had nothing to do with it. Indeed, no sooner had I made that fateful noise than I became extremely sorry for it. Had the man stopped and faced me I would have had to retire in disorder. For I had no notion to carry out Captain Giles' idiotic joke, either at my own expense or at the expense of the Steward.

But here the old human instinct of the chase came into play. He pretended to be deaf, and I, without thinking a second about it, dashed along my own side of the dining table and cut him off at the very door.

"Why can't you answer when you are spoken to?" I asked roughly.

He leaned against the lintel of the door. He looked extremely wretched. Human nature is, I fear, not very nice right through. There are ugly spots in it. I found myself growing angry, and that, I believe, only because my quarry looked so woe-begone. Miserable beggar!

I went for him without more ado. "I understand there was an official communication to the Home from the Harbour Office this morning. Is that so?"

Instead of telling me to mind my own business, as he might have done, he began to whine with an undertone of impudence. He couldn't see me anywhere this morning. He couldn't be expected to run all over the town after me.

"Who wants you to?" I cried. And then my eyes became opened to the inwardness of things and speeches the triviality of which had been so baffling and tiresome.

I told him I wanted to know what was in that letter. My sternness of tone and behaviour was only half assumed. Curiosity can be a very fierce sentiment—at times.

He took refuge in a silly, muttering sulkiness. It was nothing to me, he mumbled. I had told him I was going home. And since I was going home he didn't see why he should. . . .

That was the line of his argument, and it was irrelevant enough to be almost insulting. Insulting to one's intelligence, I mean.

In that twilight region between youth and maturity, in which I had my being then, one is peculiarly sensitive to that kind of insult. I am afraid my behaviour to the Steward became very rough indeed. But it wasn't in him to face out anything or anybody. Drug habit or solitary tippling, perhaps. And when I forgot myself so far as to swear at him he broke down and began to shriek.

I don't mean to say that he made a great outcry. It was a cynical shrieking confession, only faint—piteously faint. It wasn't very coherent either, but sufficiently so to strike me dumb at first. I turned my eyes from him in righteous indignation, and perceived Captain Giles in the verandah doorway surveying quietly the scene, his own handiwork, if I may express it in that way. His smouldering black pipe was very noticeable in his big, paternal fist. So, too, was the glitter of his heavy gold watch-chain across the breast of his white tunic. He exhaled an atmosphere of virtuous sagacity serene enough for any innocent soul to fly to confidently. I flew to him.

"You would never believe it," I cried. "It was a notification that a master is wanted for some ship. There's a command apparently going about and this fellow puts the thing in his pocket."

The Steward screamed out in accents of loud despair: "You will be the death of me!"

The mighty slap he gave his wretched forehead was very loud, too. But when I turned to look at him he was no longer there. He had rushed away somewhere out of sight. This sudden disappearance made me laugh.

This was the end of the incident—for me. Captain Giles, however, staring at the place where the Steward had been, began to haul at his gorgeous gold chain till at last the watch came up from the deep pocket like solid truth from a well. Solemnly he lowered it down again and only then said:

"Just three o'clock. You will be in time—if you don't lose any, that is."

"In time for what?" I asked.

"Good Lord! For the Harbour Office. This must be looked into."

Strictly speaking, he was right. But I've never had much taste for investigation, for showing people up and all that no doubt ethically meritorious kind of work. And my view of the episode was purely ethical. If any one had to be the death of the Steward I didn't see why it shouldn't be Captain Giles himself, a man of age and standing, and a permanent resident. Whereas, I in comparison, felt myself a mere bird of passage in that port. In fact, it might have been said that I had already broken off my connection. I muttered that I didn't think—it was nothing to me. . . .

"Nothing!" repeated Captain Giles, giving some signs of quiet, deliberate indignation. "Kent warned me you were a peculiar young fellow. You will tell me next that a command is nothing to you—and after all the trouble I've taken, too!"

"The trouble!" I murmured, uncomprehending. What trouble? All I could remember was being mystified and bored by his conversation for a solid hour after tiffin. And he called that taking a lot of trouble.

He was looking at me with a self-complacency which would have been odious in any other man. All at once, as if a page of a book had been turned over disclosing a word which made plain all that had gone before, I perceived that this matter had also another than an ethical aspect.

And still I did not move. Captain Giles lost his patience a little. With an angry puff at his pipe he turned his back on my hesitation.

But it was not hesitation on my part. I had been, if I may express myself so, put out of gear mentally. But as soon as I had convinced myself that this stale, unprofitable world of my discontent contained such a thing as a command to be seized, I recovered my powers of locomotion.

It's a good step from the Officers' Home to the Harbour Office; but with the magic word "Command" in my head I found myself suddenly on the quay as if transported there in the twinkling of an eye, before a portal of dressed white stone above a flight of shallow white steps.

All this seemed to glide toward me swiftly. The whole great roadstead to the right was just a mere flicker of blue, and the dim cool hall swallowed me up out of the heat and glare of which I had not been aware till the very moment I passed in from it.

The broad inner staircase insinuated itself under my feet somehow. Command is a strong magic. The first human beings I perceived distinctly since I had parted with the indignant back of Captain Giles were the crew of the harbour steam-launch lounging on the spacious landing about the curtained archway of the shipping office.

It was there that my buoyancy abandoned me. The atmosphere of officialdom would kill anything that breathes the air of human endeavour, would extinguish hope and fear alike in the supremacy of paper and ink. I passed heavily under the curtain which the Malay coxswain of the harbour launch raised for me. There was nobody in the office except the clerks, writing in two industrious rows. But the head Shipping-Master hopped down from his elevation and hurried along on the thick mats to meet me in the broad central passage.

He had a Scottish name, but his complexion was of a rich olive hue, his short beard was jet black, and his eyes, also black, had a languishing expression. He asked confidentially:

"You want to see Him?"

All lightness of spirit and body having departed from me at the touch of officialdom, I looked at the scribe without animation and asked in my turn wearily:

"What do you think? Is it any use?"

"My goodness! He has asked for you twice today."

This emphatic He was the supreme authority, the Marine Superintendent, the Harbour-Master—a very great person in the eyes of every single quill-driver in the room. But that was nothing to the opinion he had of his own greatness.

Captain Ellis looked upon himself as a sort of divine (pagan) emanation, the deputy-Neptune for the circumambient seas. If he did not actually rule the waves, he pretended to rule the fate of the mortals whose lives were cast upon the waters.

This uplifting illusion made him inquisitorial and peremptory. And as his temperament was choleric there were fellows who were actually afraid of him. He was redoubtable, not in virtue of his office, but because of his unwarrantable assumptions. I had never had anything to do with him before.

I said: "Oh! He has asked for me twice. Then perhaps I had better go in."

"You must! You must!"

The Shipping-Master led the way with a mincing gait around the whole system of desks to a tall and important-looking door, which he opened with a deferential action of the arm.

He stepped right in (but without letting go of the handle) and, after gazing reverently down the room for a while, beckoned me in by a silent jerk of the head. Then he slipped out at once and shut the door after me most delicately.

Three lofty windows gave on the harbour. There was nothing in them but the dark-blue sparkling sea and the paler luminous blue of the sky. My eye caught in the depths and distances of these blue tones the white speck of some big ship just arrived and about to anchor in the outer roadstead. A ship from home—after perhaps ninety days at sea. There is something touching about a ship coming in from sea and folding her white wings for a rest.

The next thing I saw was the top-knot of silver hair surmounting Captain Ellis' smooth red face, which would have been apoplectic if it hadn't had such a fresh appearance.

Our deputy-Neptune had no beard on his chin, and there was no trident to be seen standing in a corner anywhere, like an umbrella. But his hand was holding a pen—the official pen, far mightier than the sword in making or marring the fortune of simple toiling men. He was looking over his shoulder at my advance.

When I had come well within range he saluted me by a nerve-shattering: "Where have you been all this time?"

As it was no concern of his I did not take the slightest notice of the shot. I said simply that I had heard there was a master needed for some vessel, and being a sailing-ship man I thought I would apply. . . .

He interrupted me. "Why! Hang it! *You* are the right man for that job—if there had been twenty others after it. But no fear of that. They are all afraid to catch hold. That's what's the matter."

He was very irritated. I said innocently: "Are they, sir. I wonder why?"

"Why!" he fumed. "Afraid of the sails. Afraid of a white crew. Too much trouble. Too much work. Too long out here. Easy life and deck-chairs more their mark. Here I sit with the Consul-General's cable before me, and the only man fit for the job not to be found anywhere. I began to think you were funking it, too. . . ."

"I haven't been long getting to the office," I remarked calmly.

"You have a good name out here, though," he growled savagely without looking at me.

"I am very glad to hear it from you, sir," I said.

"Yes. But you are not on the spot when you are wanted. You know you weren't. That steward of yours wouldn't dare to neglect a message from this office. Where the devil did you hide yourself for the best part of the day?"

I only smiled kindly down on him, and he seemed to recollect himself, and asked me to take a seat. He explained that the master of a British ship having died in Bangkok the Consul-General had cabled to him a request for a competent man to be sent out to take command.

Apparently, in his mind, I was the man from the first, though for the looks of the thing the notification addressed to the Sailors' Home was general. An agreement had already been prepared. He gave it to me to read, and when I handed it back to him with the remark that I accepted its terms, the deputy-Neptune signed it, stamped it with his own exalted hand, folded it in four (it was a sheet of blue foolscap) and presented it to me—a gift of extraordinary potency, for, as I put it in my pocket, my head swam a little.

"This is your appointment to the command," he said with a certain gravity. "An official appointment binding the owners to conditions which you have accepted. Now—when will you be ready to go?"

I said I would be ready that very day if necessary. He caught me at my word with great alacrity. The steamer Melita was leaving for Bangkok that evening about seven. He would request her captain officially to give me a passage and wait for me till ten o'clock.

Then he rose from his office chair, and I got up, too. My head swam, there was no doubt about it, and I felt a certain heaviness of limbs as if they had grown bigger since I had sat down on that chair. I made my bow.

A subtle change in Captain Ellis' manner became perceptible as though he had laid aside the trident of deputy-Neptune. In reality, it was only his official pen that he had dropped on getting up.

II

He shook hands with me: "Well, there you are, on your own, appointed officially under my responsibility."

He was actually walking with me to the door. What a distance off it seemed! I moved like a man in bonds. But we reached it at last. I opened it with the sensation of dealing with mere dream-stuff, and then at the last moment the fellowship of seamen asserted itself, stronger than the difference of age and station. It asserted itself in Captain Ellis' voice.

"Good-bye—and good luck to you," he said so heartily that I could only give him a grateful glance. Then I turned and went out, never to see him again in my life. I had not made three steps into the outer office when I heard behind my back a gruff, loud, authoritative voice, the voice of our deputy-Neptune.

It was addressing the head Shipping-Master who, having let me in, had, apparently, remained hovering in the middle distance ever since.

"Mr. R., let the harbour launch have steam up to take the captain here on board the Melita at half-past nine to-night."

I was amazed at the startled alacrity of R's "Yes, sir." He ran before me out on the landing. My new dignity sat yet so lightly on me that I was not aware that it was I, the Captain, the object of this last graciousness. It seemed as if all of a sudden a pair of wings had grown on my shoulders. I merely skimmed along the polished floor.

But R. was impressed.

"I say!" he exclaimed on the landing, while the Malay crew of the steam-launch standing by looked stonily at the man for whom they were going to be kept on duty so late, away from their gambling, from their girls, or their pure domestic joys. "I say! His own launch. What have you done to him?"

His stare was full of respectful curiosity. I was quite confounded.

"Was it for me? I hadn't the slightest notion," I stammered out.

He nodded many times. "Yes. And the last person who had it before you was a Duke. So, there!"

I think he expected me to faint on the spot. But I was in too much of a hurry for emotional displays. My feelings were already in such a whirl that this staggering information did not seem to make the slightest difference. It merely fell into the seething cauldron of my brain, and I carried it off with me after a short but effusive passage of leave-taking with R.

The favour of the great throws an aureole round the fortunate object of its selection. That excellent man enquired whether he could do anything for me. He had known me only by sight, and he was well aware he would never see me again; I was, in common with the other seamen of the port, merely a subject for official writing, filling up of forms with all the artificial superiority of a man of pen and ink to the men who grapple with realities outside the consecrated walls of official buildings. What ghosts we must have been to him! Mere symbols to juggle with in books and heavy registers, without brains and muscles and perplexities; something hardly useful and decidedly inferior.

And he—the office hours being over—wanted to know if he could be of any use to me!

I ought—properly speaking—I ought to have been moved to tears. But I did not even think of it. It was merely another miraculous manifestation of that day of miracles. I parted from him as if he were a mere symbol. I floated down the staircase. I floated out of the official and imposing portal. I went on floating along.

I use that word rather than the word "flew," because I have a distinct impression that, though uplifted by my aroused youth, my movements were deliberate enough. To that mixed white, brown, and yellow portion of mankind, out abroad on their own affairs, I presented the appearance of a man walking rather sedately. And nothing in the way of abstraction could have equalled my deep detachment from the forms and colours of this world. It was, as it were, final.

And yet, suddenly, I recognized Hamilton. I recognized him without effort, without a shock, without a start. There he was, strolling toward the Harbour Office with his stiff, arrogant dignity. His red face made him noticeable at a distance. It flamed, over there, on the shady side of the street.

He had perceived me, too. Something (unconscious exuberance of spirits perhaps) moved me to wave my hand to him elaborately. This lapse from good taste happened before I was aware that I was capable of it.

The impact of my impudence stopped him short, much as a bullet might have done. I verily believe he staggered, though as far as I could see he didn't actually fall. I had gone past in a moment and did not turn my head. I had forgotten his existence.

The next ten minutes might have been ten seconds or ten centuries for all my consciousness had to do with it. People might have been falling dead around me, houses crumbling, guns firing, I wouldn't have known. I was thinking: "By Jove! I have got it." *It* being the command. It had come about in a way utterly unforeseen in my modest day-dreams.

I perceived that my imagination had been running in conventional channels and that my hopes had always been drab stuff. I had envisaged a command as a result of a slow course of promotion in the employ of some highly respectable firm. The reward of faithful service. Well, faithful service was all right. One would naturally give that for one's own sake, for the sake of the ship, for the love of the life of one's choice; not for the sake of the reward.

There is something distasteful in the notion of a reward.

And now here I had my command, absolutely in my pocket, in a way undeniable indeed, but most unexpected; beyond my imaginings, outside all reasonable expectations, and even notwithstanding the existence of some sort of obscure intrigue to keep it away from me. It is true that the intrigue was feeble, but it helped the feeling of wonder—as if I had been specially destined for that ship I did not know, by some power higher than the prosaic agencies of the commercial world.

A strange sense of exultation began to creep into me. If I had worked for that command ten years or more there would have been nothing of the kind. I was a little frightened.

"Let us be calm," I said to myself.

Outside the door of the Officers' Home the wretched Steward seemed to be waiting for me. There was a broad flight of a few steps, and he ran to and fro on the top of it as if chained there. A distressed cur. He looked as though his throat were too dry for him to bark.

I regret to say I stopped before going in. There had been a revolution in my moral nature. He waited open-mouthed, breathless, while I looked at him for half a minute.

"And you thought you could keep me out of it," I said scathingly.

"You said you were going home," he squeaked miserably. "You said so. You said so."

"I wonder what Captain Ellis will have to say to that excuse," I uttered slowly with a sinister meaning.

His lower jaw had been trembling all the time and his voice was like the bleating of a sick goat. "You have given me away? You have done for me?"

Neither his distress nor yet the sheer absurdity of it was able to disarm me. It was the first instance of harm being attempted to be done to me—at any rate, the first I had ever found out. And I was still young enough, still too much on this side of the shadow line, not to be surprised and indignant at such things.

I gazed at him inflexibly. Let the beggar suffer. He slapped his forehead and I passed in, pursued, into the dining room, by his screech: "I always said you'd be the death of me."

This clamour not only overtook me, but went ahead as it were on to the verandah and brought out Captain Giles.

He stood before me in the doorway in all the commonplace solidity of his wisdom. The gold chain glittered on his breast. He clutched a smouldering pipe.

I extended my hand to him warmly and he seemed surprised, but did respond heartily enough in the end, with a faint smile of superior knowledge which cut my thanks short as if with a knife. I don't think that more than one word came out. And even for that one, judging by the temperature of my face, I had blushed as if for a bad action. Assuming a detached tone, I wondered how on earth he had managed to spot the little underhand game that had been going on.

He murmured complacently that there were but few things done in the town that he could not see the inside of. And as to this house, he had been using it off and on for nearly ten years. Nothing that went on in it could escape his great experience. It had been no trouble to him. No trouble at all.

Then in his quiet, thick tone he wanted to know if I had complained formally of the Steward's action.

I said that I hadn't—though, indeed, it was not for want of opportunity. Captain Ellis had gone for me bald-headed in a most ridiculous fashion for being out of the way when wanted.

"Funny old gentleman," interjected Captain Giles. "What did you say to that?"

"I said simply that I came along the very moment I heard of his message. Nothing more. I didn't want to hurt the Steward. I would scorn to harm such an object. No. I made no complaint, but I believe he thinks I've done so. Let him think. He's got a fright he won't forget in a hurry, for Captain Ellis would kick him out into the middle of Asia. . . ."

"Wait a moment," said Captain Giles, leaving me suddenly. I sat down feeling very tired, mostly in my head. Before I could start a train of thought he stood again before me, murmuring the excuse that he had to go and put the fellow's mind at ease.

I looked up with surprise. But in reality I was indifferent. He explained that he had found the Steward lying face downward on the horsehair sofa. He was all right now.

"He would not have died of fright," I said contemptuously.

"No. But he might have taken an overdose out of one of them little bottles he keeps in his room," Captain Giles argued seriously. "The confounded fool has tried to poison himself once—a few years ago."

"Really," I said without emotion. "He doesn't seem very fit to live, anyhow."

"As to that, it may be said of a good many."

"Don't exaggerate like this!" I protested, laughing irritably. "But I wonder what this part of the world would do if you were to leave off looking after it, Captain Giles? Here you have got me a command and saved the Steward's life in one afternoon. Though why you should have taken all that interest in either of us is more than I can understand."

Captain Giles remained silent for a minute. Then gravely:

"He's not a bad steward really. He can find a good cook, at any rate. And, what's more, he can keep him when found. I remember the cooks we had here before his time! . . ."

I must have made a movement of impatience, because he

interrupted himself with an apology for keeping me yarning there, while no doubt I needed all my time to get ready.

What I really needed was to be alone for a bit. I seized this opening hastily. My bedroom was a quiet refuge in an apparently uninhabited wing of the building. Having absolutely nothing to do (for I had not unpacked my things), I sat down on the bed and abandoned myself to the influences of the hour. To the unexpected influences. . . .

And first I wondered at my state of mind. Why was I not more surprised? Why? Here I was, invested with a command in the twinkling of an eye, not in the common course of human affairs, but more as if by enchantment. I ought to have been lost in astonishment. But I wasn't. I was very much like people in fairy tales. Nothing ever astonishes them. When a fully appointed gala coach is produced out of a pumpkin to take her to a ball, Cinderella does not exclaim. She gets in quietly and drives away to her high fortune.

Captain Ellis (a fierce sort of fairy) had produced a command out of a drawer almost as unexpectedly as in a fairy tale. But a command is an abstract idea, and it seemed a sort of "lesser marvel" till it flashed upon me that it involved the concrete existence of a ship.

A ship! My ship! She was mine, more absolutely mine for possession and care than anything in the world; an object of responsibility and devotion. She was there waiting for me, spell-bound, unable to move, to live, to get out into the world (till I came), like an enchanted princess. Her call had come to me as if from the clouds. I had never suspected her existence. I didn't know how she looked, I had barely heard her name, and yet we were indissolubly united for a certain portion of our future, to sink or swim together!

A sudden passion of anxious impatience rushed through my veins, gave me such a sense of the intensity of existence as I have never felt before or since. I discovered how much of a seaman I was, in heart, in mind, and, as it were, physically—a man exclusively of sea and ships; the sea the only world that counted, and the ships, the test of manliness, of temperament, of courage and fidelity—and of love.

I had an exquisite moment. It was unique also. Jumping up from my seat, I paced up and down my room for a long time. But when I came downstairs I behaved with sufficient composure. I only couldn't eat anything at dinner.

Having declared my intention not to drive but to walk down to the quay, I must render the wretched Steward justice that he bestirred himself to find me some coolies for the luggage. They departed, carrying all my worldly possessions (except a little money I had in my pocket) slung from a long pole. Captain Giles volunteered to walk down with me.

We followed the sombre, shaded alley across the Esplanade. It was moderately cool there under the trees. Captain Giles remarked, with a sudden laugh: "I know who's jolly thankful at having seen the last of you."

I guessed that he meant the Steward. The fellow had borne himself to me in a sulkily frightened manner at the last. I expressed my wonder that he should have tried to do me a bad turn for no reason at all.

"Don't you see that what he wanted was to get rid of our friend Hamilton by dodging him in front of you for that job? That would have removed him for good. See?"

"Heavens!" I exclaimed, feeling humiliated somehow. "Can it be possible? What a fool he must be! That overbearing, impudent loafer! Why! He couldn't. . . . And yet he's nearly done it, I believe; for the Harbour Office was bound to send somebody."

"Aye. A fool like our Steward can be dangerous sometimes," declared Captain Giles sententiously. "Just because he is a fool," he added, imparting further instruction in his complacent low tones. "For," he continued in the manner of a set demonstration, "no sensible person would risk being kicked out of the only berth between himself and starvation just to get rid of a simple annoyance—a small worry. Would he now?"

"Well, no," I conceded, restraining a desire to laugh at that something mysteriously earnest in delivering the conclusions of his wisdom as though it were the product of prohibited operations. "But that fellow looks as if he were rather crazy. He must be."

"As to that, I believe everybody in the world is a little mad," he announced quietly.

"You make no exceptions?" I inquired, just to hear his manner.

"Why! Kent says that even of you."

"Does he?" I retorted, extremely embittered all at once against my former captain. "There's nothing of that in the written character from him which I've got in my pocket. Has he given you any instances of my lunacy?"

Captain Giles explained in a conciliating tone that it had been only a friendly remark in reference to my abrupt leaving the ship for no apparent reason.

I muttered grumpily: "Oh! leaving his ship," and mended my pace. He kept up by my side in the deep gloom of the avenue as if it were his conscientious duty to see me out of the colony as an undesirable character. He panted a little, which was rather pathetic in a way. But I was not moved. On the contrary. His discomfort gave me a sort of malicious pleasure.

Presently I relented, slowed down, and said:

"What I really wanted was to get a fresh grip. I felt it was time. Is that so very mad?"

He made no answer. We were issuing from the avenue. On the bridge over the canal a dark, irresolute figure seemed to be awaiting something or somebody.

It was a Malay policeman, barefooted, in his blue uniform. The silver band on his little round cap shone dimly in the light of the street lamp. He peered in our direction timidly.

Before we could come up to him he turned about and walked in front of us in the direction of the jetty. The distance was some hundred yards; and then I found my coolies squatting on their heels. They had kept the pole on their shoulders, and all my worldly goods, still tied to the pole, were resting on the ground between them. As far as the eye could reach along the quay there was not another soul abroad except the police peon, who saluted us.

It seems he had detained the coolies as suspicious characters, and had forbidden them the jetty. But at a sign from me he took off the embargo with alacrity. The two patient fellows, rising together with a faint grunt, trotted off along the planks, and I prepared to take my leave of Captain Giles, who stood there with an air as though his mission were drawing to a close. It could not be denied that he had done it all. And while I hesitated about an appropriate sentence he made himself heard:

"I expect you'll have your hands pretty full of tangled-up business."

I asked him what made him think so; and he answered that it was his general experience of the world. Ship a long time away from her port, owners inaccessible by cable, and the only man who could explain matters dead and buried.

"And you yourself new to the business in a way," he concluded in a sort of unanswerable tone.

"Don't insist," I said. "I know it only too well. I only wish you could impart to me some small portion of your experience before I go. As it can't be done in ten minutes I had better not begin to ask you. There's that harbour launch waiting for me, too. But I won't feel really at peace till I have that ship of mine out in the Indian Ocean."

He remarked casually that from Bangkok to the Indian Ocean was a pretty long step. And this murmur, like a dim flash from a dark lantern, showed me for a moment the broad belt of islands and reefs between that unknown ship, which was mine, and the freedom of the great waters of the globe.

But I felt no apprehension. I was familiar enough with the Archipelago by that time. Extreme patience and extreme care would see me through the region of broken land, of faint airs, and of dead water to where I would feel at last my command swing on the great swell and list over to the great breath of regular winds, that would give her the feeling of a large, more intense life. The road would be long. All roads are long that lead toward one's heart's desire. But this road my mind's eye could see on a chart, professionally, with all its complications and difficulties, yet simple enough in a way. One is a seaman or one is not. And I had no doubt of being one.

The only part I was a stranger to was the Gulf of Siam. And I mentioned this to Captain Giles. Not that I was concerned very much. It belonged to the same region the nature of which I knew, into whose very soul I seemed to have looked during the last months of that existence with which I had broken now, suddenly, as one parts with some enchanting company.

"The gulf . . . Ay! A funny piece of water—that," said Captain Giles.

Funny, in this connection, was a vague word. The whole thing sounded like an opinion uttered by a cautious person mindful of actions for slander.

I didn't inquire as to the nature of that funniness. There was really no time. But at the very last he volunteered a warning.

"Whatever you do keep to the east side of it. The west side is dangerous at this time of the year. Don't let anything tempt you over. You'll find nothing but trouble there."

Though I could hardly imagine what could tempt me to involve my ship amongst the currents and reefs of the Malay shore, I thanked him for the advice.

He gripped my extended arm warmly, and the end of our acquaintance came suddenly in the words: "Good-night."

That was all he said: "Good-night." Nothing more. I don't know what I intended to say, but surprise made me swallow it, whatever it was. I choked slightly, and then exclaimed with a sort of nervous haste: "Oh! Good-night, Captain Giles, good-night."

His movements were always deliberate, but his back had receded some distance along the deserted quay before I collected myself enough to follow his example and made a half turn in the direction of the jetty.

Only my movements were not deliberate. I hurried down to the steps, and leaped into the launch. Before I had fairly landed in her stern-sheets the slim little craft darted away from the jetty with a sudden swirl of her propeller and the hard, rapid puffing of the exhaust in her vaguely gleaming brass funnel amidships.

The misty churning at her stern was the only sound in the world. The shore lay plunged in the silence of the deeper slumber. I watched the town recede still and soundless in the hot night, till the abrupt hail, "Steam-launch, ahoy!" made me spin round face forward. We were close to a white ghostly steamer. Lights shone on her decks, in her portholes. And the same voice shouted from her:

"Is that our passenger?"

"It is," I yelled.

Her crew had been obviously on the jump. I could hear them running about. The modern spirit of haste was loudly vocal in the orders to "Heave away on the cable"—to "Lower the side-ladder," and in urgent requests to me to "Come along, sir! We have been delayed three hours for you. . . . Our time is seven o'clock, you know!"

I stepped on the deck. I said "No! I don't know." The spirit of modern hurry was embodied in a thin, long-armed, long-legged man, with a closely clipped gray beard. His meagre hand was hot and dry. He declared feverishly:

"I am hanged if I would have waited another five minutes Harbour-Master or no Harbour-Master."

"That's your own business," I said. "I didn't ask you to wait for me."

"I hope you don't expect any supper," he burst out. "This isn't a boarding-house afloat. You are the first passenger I ever had in my life and I hope to goodness you will be the last."

I made no answer to this hospitable communication; and, indeed, he didn't wait for any, bolting away on to his bridge to get his ship under way.

The three days he had me on board he did not depart from that half-hostile attitude. His ship having been delayed three hours on my account he couldn't forgive me for not being a more distinguished person. He was not exactly outspoken about it, but that feeling of annoyed wonder was peeping out perpetually in his talk.

He was absurd.

He was also a man of much experience, which he liked to trot out; but no greater contrast with Captain Giles could have been imagined. He would have amused me if I had wanted to be amused. But I did not want to be amused. I was like a lover looking forward to a meeting. Human hostility was nothing to me. I thought of my unknown ship. It was amusement enough, torment enough, occupation enough.

He perceived my state, for his wits were sufficiently sharp for that, and he poked sly fun at my preoccupation in the manner some nasty, cynical old men assume toward the dreams and illusions of youth. I, on my side, refrained from questioning him as to the appearance of my ship, though I knew that being in Bangkok every fortnight or so he must have known her by sight. I was not going to expose the ship, my ship! to some slighting reference.

He was the first really unsympathetic man I had ever come in contact with. My education was far from being finished, though I didn't know it. No! I didn't know it.

All I knew was that he disliked me and had some contempt for my person. Why? Apparently because his ship had been delayed three hours on my account. Who was I to have such a thing done for me? Such a thing had never been done for him. It was a sort of jealous indignation.

My expectation, mingled with fear, was wrought to its highest pitch. How slow had been the days of the passage and how soon they were over. One morning, early, we crossed the bar, and while the sun was rising splendidly over the flat spaces of the land we steamed up the innumerable bends, passed under the shadow of the great gilt pagoda, and reached the outskirts of the town.

There it was, spread largely on both banks, the Oriental capital which had as yet suffered no white conqueror; an expanse of brown houses of bamboo, of mats, of leaves, of a vegetable-matter style of architecture, sprung out of the brown soil on the banks of the muddy river. It was amazing to think that in those miles of human habitations there was not probably half a dozen pounds of nails. Some of those houses of sticks and grass, like the nests of an aquatic race, clung to the low shores. Others seemed to grow out of the water; others again floated in long anchored rows in the very middle of the stream. Here and there in the distance, above the crowded mob of low, brown roof ridges, towered great piles of masonry, King's Palace, temples, gorgeous and dilapidated, crumbling under the vertical sunlight, tremendous, overpowering, almost palpable, which seemed to enter one's breast with the breath of one's nostrils and soak into one's limbs through every pore of one's skin.

The ridiculous victim of jealousy had for some reason or other to stop his engines just then. The steamer drifted slowly up with the tide. Oblivious of my new surroundings I walked the deck, in anxious, deadened abstraction, a commingling of romantic reverie with a very practical survey of my qualifications. For the time was approaching for me to behold my command and to prove my worth in the ultimate test of my profession.

Suddenly I heard myself called by that imbecile. He was beckoning me to come up on his bridge.

I didn't care very much for that, but as it seemed that he had something particular to say I went up the ladder.

He laid his hand on my shoulder and gave me a slight turn, pointing with his other arm at the same time.

"There! That's your ship, Captain," he said.

I felt a thump in my breast—only one, as if my heart had then ceased to beat. There were ten or more ships moored along the bank, and the one he meant was partly hidden away from my sight by her next astern. He said: "We'll drift abreast her in a moment."

What was his tone? Mocking? Threatening? Or only indifferent? I could not tell. I suspected some malice in this unexpected manifestation of interest.

He left me, and I leaned over the rail of the bridge looking over the side. I dared not raise my eyes. Yet it had to be done—and, indeed, I could not have helped myself. I believe I trembled.

But directly my eyes had rested on my ship all my fear vanished. It

went off swiftly, like a bad dream. Only that a dream leaves no shame
behind it, and that I felt a momentary shame at my unworthy
suspicions.

Yes, there she was. Her hull, her rigging filled my eye with a great
content. That feeling of life-emptiness which had made me so restless
for the last few months lost its bitter plausibility, its evil influence,
dissolved in a flow of joyous emotion.

At first glance I saw that she was a high-class vessel, a harmonious
creature in the lines of her fine body, in the proportioned tallness of her
spars. Whatever her age and her history, she had preserved the stamp of
her origin. She was one of those craft that, in virtue of their design and
complete finish, will never look old. Amongst her companions moored
to the bank, and all bigger than herself, she looked like a creature of
high breed—an Arab steed in a string of cart-horses.

A voice behind me said in a nasty equivocal tone: "I hope you are
satisfied with her, Captain." I did not even turn my head. It was the
master of the steamer, and whatever he meant, whatever he thought of
her, I knew that, like some rare women, she was one of those creatures
whose mere existence is enough to awaken an unselfish delight. One
feels that it is good to be in the world in which she has her being.

That illusion of life and character which charms one in men's
finest handiwork radiated from her. An enormous bulk of teak-wood
timber swung over her hatchway; lifeless matter, looking heavier and
bigger than anything aboard of her. When they started lowering it the
surge of the tackle sent a quiver through her from water-line to the
trucks up the fine nerves of her rigging, as though she had shuddered at
the weight. It seemed cruel to load her so. . . .

Half an hour later, putting my foot on her deck for the first time, I
received the feeling of deep physical satisfaction. Nothing could equal
the fullness of that moment, the ideal completeness of that emotional
experience which had come to me without the preliminary toil and
disenchantments of an obscure career.

My rapid glance ran over her, enveloped, appropriated the form
concreting the abstract sentiment of my command. A lot of details
perceptible to a seaman struck my eye, vividly in that instant. For the
rest, I saw her disengaged from the material conditions of her being.
The shore to which she was moored was as if it did not exist. What
were to me all the countries of the globe? In all the parts of the world
washed by navigable waters our relation to each other would be the
same—and more intimate than there are words to express in the
language. Apart from that, every scene and episode would be a mere
passing show. The very gang of yellow coolies busy about the main
hatch was less substantial than the stuff dreams are made of. For who
on earth would dream of Chinamen? . . .

I went aft, ascended the poop, where, under the awning, gleamed the brasses of the yacht-like fittings, the polished surfaces of the rails, the glass of the skylights. Right aft two seamen, busy cleaning the steering gear, with the reflected ripples of light running playfully up their bent backs, went on with their work, unaware of me and of the almost affectionate glance I threw at them in passing toward the companion-way of the cabin.

The doors stood wide open, the slide was pushed right back. The half-turn of the staircase cut off the view of the lobby. A low humming ascended from below, but it stopped abruptly at the sound of my descending footsteps.

III

The first thing I saw down there was the upper part of a man's body projecting backward, as it were, from one of the doors at the foot of the stairs. His eyes looked at me very wide and still. In one hand he held a dinner plate, in the other a cloth.

"I am your new Captain," I said quietly.

In a moment, in the twinkling of an eye, he had got rid of the plate and the cloth and jumped to open the cabin door. As soon as I passed into the saloon he vanished, but only to reappear instantly, buttoning up a jacket he had put on with the swiftness of a "quick-change" artist.

"Where's the chief mate?" I asked.

"In the hold, I think, sir. I saw him go down the after-hatch ten minutes ago."

"Tell him I am on board."

The mahogany table under the skylight shone in the twilight like a dark pool of water. The sideboard, surmounted by a wide looking-glass in an ormulu frame, had a marble top. It bore a pair of silver-plated lamps and some other pieces—obviously a harbour display. The saloon itself was panelled in two kinds of wood in the excellent simple taste prevailing when the ship was built.

I sat down in the armchair at the head of the table—the captain's chair, with a small tell-tale compass swung above it—a mute reminder of unremitting vigilance.

A succession of men had sat in that chair. I became aware of that thought suddenly, vividly, as though each had left a little of himself between the four walls of these ornate bulkheads; as if a sort of composite soul, the soul of command, had whispered suddenly to mine of long days at sea and of anxious moments.

"You, too!" it seemed to say, "you, too, shall taste of that peace and that unrest in a searching intimacy with your own self—obscure as we were and as supreme in the face of all the winds and all the seas, in an immensity that receives no impress, preserves no memories, and keeps no reckoning of lives."

Deep within the tarnished ormulu frame, in the hot half-light sifted through the awning, I saw my own face propped between my hands. And I stared back at myself with the perfect detachment of distance, rather with curiosity than with any other feeling, except of some sympathy for this latest representative of what for all intents and purposes was a dynasty, continuous not in blood indeed, but in its experience, in its training, in its conception of duty, and in the blessed simplicity of its traditional point of view on life.

It struck me that this quietly staring man whom I was watching, both as if he were myself and somebody else, was not exactly a lonely figure. He had his place in a line of men whom he did not know, of whom he had never heard; but who were fashioned by the same influences, whose souls in relation to their humble life's work had no secrets for him.

Suddenly I perceived that there was another man in the saloon, standing a little on one side and looking intently at me. The chief mate. His long, red moustache determined the character of his physiognomy, which struck me as pugnacious in (strange to say) a ghastly sort of way.

How long had he been there looking at me, appraising me in my unguarded day-dreaming state? I would have been more disconcerted if, having the clock set in the top of the mirror-frame right in front of me, I had not noticed that its long hand had hardly moved at all.

I could not have been in that cabin more than two minutes altogether. Say three. . . . So he could not have been watching me more than a mere fraction of a minute, luckily. Still, I regretted the occurrence.

But I showed nothing of it as I rose leisurely (it had to be leisurely) and greeted him with perfect friendliness.

There was something reluctant and at the same time attentive in his bearing. His name was Burns. We left the cabin and went round the ship together. His face in the full light of day appeared very pale, meagre, even haggard. Somehow I had a delicacy as to looking too often at him; his eyes, on the contrary, remained fairly glued on my face. They were greenish and had an expectant expression.

He answered all my questions readily enough, but my ear seemed to catch a tone of unwillingness. The second officer, with three or four hands, was busy forward. The mate mentioned his name and I nodded to him in passing. He was very young. He struck me as rather a cub.

When we returned below, I sat down on one end of a deep, semi-circular, or, rather, semi-oval settee, upholstered in red plush. It extended right across the whole after-end of the cabin. Mr. Burns motioned to sit down, dropped into one of the swivel-chairs round the table, and kept his eyes on me as persistently as ever, and with that strange air as if all this were make-believe and he expected me to get up, burst into a laugh, slap him on the back, and vanish from the cabin.

There was an odd stress in the situation which began to make me uncomfortable. I tried to react against this vague feeling.

"It's only my inexperience," I thought.

In the face of that man, several years, I judged, older than myself, I became aware of what I had left already behind me—my youth. And that was indeed poor comfort. Youth is a fine thing, a mighty power—as long as one does not think of it. I felt I was becoming self-conscious. Almost against my will I assumed a moody gravity. I said: "I see you have kept her in very good order, Mr. Burns."

Directly I had uttered these words I asked myself angrily why the deuce did I want to say that? Mr. Burns in answer had only blinked at me. What on earth did he mean?

I fell back on a question which had been in my thoughts for a long time—the most natural question on the lips of any seaman whatever joining a ship. I voiced it (confound this self-consciousness) in a *dégagé* cheerful tone: "I suppose she can travel—what?"

Now a question like this might have been answered normally, either in accents of apologetic sorrow or with a visibly suppressed pride, in a "I don't want to boast, but you shall see," sort of tone. There are sailors, too, who would have been roughly outspoken: "Lazy brute," or openly delighted: "She's a flyer." Two ways, if four manners.

But Mr. Burns found another way, a way of his own which had, at all events, the merit of saving his breath, if no other.

Again he did not say anything. He only frowned. And it was an angry frown. I waited. Nothing more came.

"What's the matter? . . . Can't you tell after being nearly two years in the ship?" I addressed him sharply.

He looked as startled for a moment as though he had discovered my presence only that very moment. But this passed off almost at once. He put on an air of indifference. But I suppose he thought it better to say something. He said that a ship needed, just like a man, the chance to show the best she could do, and that this ship had never had a chance since he had been on board of her. Not that he could remember. The last captain. . . . He paused.

"Has he been so very unlucky?" I asked with frank incredulity. Mr. Burns turned his eyes away from me. No, the late captain was not an unlucky man. One couldn't say that. But he had not seemed to want to make use of his luck.

Mr. Burns—man of enigmatic moods—made this statement with an inanimate face and staring wilfully at the rudder casing. The statement itself was obscurely suggestive. I asked quietly:

"Where did he die?"

"In this saloon. Just where you are sitting now," answered Mr. Burns.

I repressed a silly impulse to jump up; but upon the whole I was relieved to hear that he had not died in the bed which was now to be mine. I pointed out to the chief mate that what I really wanted to know was where he had buried his late captain.

Mr. Burns said that it was at the entrance to the gulf. A roomy grave; a sufficient answer. But the mate, overcoming visibly something within him—something like a curious reluctance to believe in my advent (as an irrevocable fact, at any rate), did not stop at that—though, indeed, he may have wished to do so.

As a compromise with his feelings, I believe, he addressed himself persistently to the rudder-casing, so that to me he had the appearance of a man talking in solitude, a little unconsciously, however.

His tale was that at seven bells in the forenoon watch he had all hands mustered on the quarterdeck and told them they had better go down to say good-bye to the captain.

Those words, as if grudged to an intruding personage, were enough for me to evoke vividly that strange ceremony: The bare-footed, bare-headed seamen crowding shyly into that cabin, a small mob pressed against that sideboard, uncomfortable rather than moved, shirts open on sunburnt chests, weather-beaten faces, and all staring at the dying man with the same grave and expectant expression.

"Was he conscious?" I asked.

"He didn't speak, but he moved his eyes to look at them," said the mate.

After waiting a moment, Mr. Burns motioned the crew to leave the cabin, but he detained the two eldest men to stay with the captain while he went on deck with his sextant to "take the sun." It was getting toward noon and he was anxious to obtain a good observation for latitude. When he returned below to put his sextant away he found that the two men had retreated out into the lobby. Through the open door he had a view of the captain lying easy against the pillows. He had "passed away" while Mr. Burns was taking this observation. As near noon as possible. He had hardly changed his position.

Mr. Burns sighed, glanced at me inquisitively, as much as to say, "Aren't you going yet?" and then turned his thoughts from his new captain back to the old, who, being dead, had no authority, was not in anybody's way, and was much easier to deal with.

Mr. Burns dealt with him at some length. He was a peculiar man—of sixty-five about—iron gray, hard-faced, obstinate, and uncommunicative. He used to keep the ship loafing at sea for inscrutable reasons. Would come on deck at night sometimes, take some sail off her, God only knows why or wherefore, then go below, shut himself up in his cabin, and play on the violin for hours—till daybreak perhaps. In fact, he spent most of his time day or night playing the violin. That was when the fit took him. Very loud, too.

It came to this, that Mr. Burns mustered his courage one day and remonstrated earnestly with the captain. Neither he nor the second mate could get a wink of sleep in their watches below for the noise. . . . And how could they be expected to keep awake while on duty? He pleaded. The answer of that stern man was that if he and the second mate didn't like the noise, they were welcome to pack up their traps and walk over the side. When this alternative was offered the ship happened to be 600 miles from the nearest land.

Mr. Burns at this point looked at me with an air of curiosity. I began to think that my predecessor was a remarkably peculiar old man.

But I had to hear stranger things yet. It came out that this stern, grim, wind-tanned, rough, sea-salted, taciturn sailor of sixty-five was not only an artist, but a lover as well. In Haiphong, when they got there after a course of most unprofitable peregrinations (during which the ship was nearly lost twice), he got himself, in Mr. Burns' own words, "mixed up" with some woman. Mr. Burns had had no personal knowledge of that affair, but positive evidence of it existed in the shape of a photograph taken in Haiphong. Mr. Burns found it in one of the drawers in the captain's room.

In due course I, too, saw that amazing human document (I even threw it overboard later). There he sat, with his hands reposing on his knees, bald, squat, gray, bristly, recalling a wild boar somehow; and by his side towered an awful mature, white female with rapacious nostrils and a cheaply ill-omened stare in her enormous eyes. She was disguised in some semi-oriental, vulgar, fancy costume. She resembled a low-class medium or one of those women who tell fortunes by cards for half a crown. And yet she was striking. A professional sorceress from the slums. It was incomprehensible. There was something awful in the thought that she was the last reflection of the world of passion for the fierce soul which seemed to look at one out of the sardonically savage face of that old seaman. However, I noticed that she was holding some musical instrument—guitar or mandoline—in her hand. Perhaps that was the secret of her sortilege.

For Mr. Burns that photograph explained why the unloaded ship had kept sweltering at anchor for three weeks in a pestilential hot harbour without air. They lay there and gasped. The captain, appearing now and then on short visits, mumbled to Mr. Burns unlikely tales about some letters he was waiting for.

Suddenly, after vanishing for a week, he came on board in the middle of the night and took the ship out to sea with the first break of dawn. Daylight showed him looking wild and ill. The mere getting clear of the land took two days, and somehow or other they bumped slightly on a reef. However, no leak developed, and the captain, growling "no matter," informed Mr. Burns that he had made up his mind to take the ship to Hong-Kong and dry-dock her there.

At this Mr. Burns was plunged into despair. For indeed, to beat up to Hong-Kong against a fierce monsoon, with a ship not sufficiently ballasted and with her supply of water not completed, was an insane project.

But the captain growled peremptorily, "Stick her at it," and Mr. Burns, dismayed and enraged, stuck her at it, and kept her at it, blowing away sails, straining the spars, exhausting the crew—nearly maddened by the absolute conviction that the attempt was impossible and was bound to end in some catastrophe.

Meantime the captain, shut up in his cabin and wedged in a corner of his settee against the crazy bounding of the ship, played the violin— or, at any rate, made continuous noise on it.

When he appeared on deck he would not speak and not always answer when spoken to. It was obvious that he was ill in some mysterious manner, and beginning to break up.

As the days went by the sounds of the violin became less and less loud, till at last only a feeble scratching would meet Mr. Burns' ear as he stood in the saloon listening outside the door of the captain's state-room.

One afternoon in perfect desperation he burst into that room and made such a scene, tearing his hair and shouting such horrid imprecations that he cowed the contemptuous spirit of the sick man. The water-tanks were low, they had not gained fifty miles in a fortnight. She would never reach Hong-Kong.

It was like fighting desperately toward destruction for the ship and the men. This was evident without argument. Mr. Burns, losing all restraint, put his face close to his captain's and fairly yelled: "You, sir, are going out of the world. But I can't wait till you are dead before I put the helm up. You must do it yourself. You must do it now!"

The man on the couch snarled in contempt. "So I am going out of the world—am I?"

"Yes, sir—you haven't many days left in it," said Mr. Burns calming down. "One can see it by your face."

"My face, eh? . . . Well, put up the helm and be damned to you."

Burns flew on deck, got the ship before the wind, then came down again composed, but resolute.

"I've shaped a course for Pulo Condor, sir," he said. "When we make it, if you are still with us, you'll tell me into what port you wish me to take the ship and I'll do it."

The old man gave him a look of savage spite, and said those atrocious words in deadly, slow tones.

"If I had my wish, neither the ship nor any of you would ever reach a port. And I hope you won't."

Mr. Burns was profoundly shocked. I believe he was positively frightened at the time. It seems, however, that he managed to produce such an effective laugh that it was the old man's turn to be frightened.

He shrank within himself and turned his back on him.

"And his head was not gone then," Mr. Burns assured me excitedly. "He meant every word of it."

"Such was practically the late captain's last speech. No connected sentence passed his lips afterward. That night he used the last of his strength to throw his fiddle over the side. No one had actually seen him in the act, but after his death Mr. Burns couldn't find the thing anywhere. The empty case was very much in evidence, but the fiddle was clearly not in the ship. And where else could it have gone to but overboard?"

"Threw his violin overboard!" I exclaimed.

"He did," cried Mr. Burns excitedly. "And it's my belief he would have tried to take the ship down with him if it had been in human power. He never meant her to see home again. He wouldn't write to his owners, he never wrote to his old wife, either—he wasn't going to. He had made up his mind to cut adrift from everything. That's what it was. He didn't care for business, or freights, or for making a passage—or anything. He meant to have gone wandering about the world till he lost her with all hands."

Mr. Burns looked like a man who had escaped great danger. For a little he would have exclaimed: "If it hadn't been for me!" And the transparent innocence of his indignant eyes was underlined quaintly by the arrogant pair of moustaches which he proceeded to twist, and as if extend, horizontally.

I might have smiled if I had not been busy with my own sensations, which were not those of Mr. Burns. I was already the man in command. My sensations could not be like those of any other man on board. In that community I stood, like a king in his country, in a class all by myself. I mean an hereditary king, not a mere elected head of a state. I was brought there to rule by an agency as remote from the people and as inscrutable almost to them as the Grace of God.

And like a member of a dynasty, feeling a semi-mystical bond with the dead, I was profoundly shocked by my immediate predecessor.

That man had been in all essentials but his age just such another man as myself. Yet the end of his life was a complete act of treason, the betrayal of a tradition which seemed to me as imperative as any guide on earth could be. It appeared that even at sea a man could become the victim of evil spirits. I felt on my face the breath of unknown powers that shape our destinies.

Not to let the silence last too long I asked Mr. Burns if he had written to his captain's wife. He shook his head. He had written to nobody.

In a moment he became sombre. He never thought of writing. It took him all his time to watch incessantly the loading of the ship by a rascally Chinese stevedore. In this Mr. Burns gave me the first glimpse of the real chief mate's soul which dwelt uneasily in his body.

He mused, then hastened on with gloomy force.

"Yes! The captain died as near noon as possible. I looked through his papers in the afternoon. I read the service over him at sunset and then I stuck the ship's head north and brought her in here. I—brought—her—in."

He struck the table with his fist.

"She would hardly have come in by herself," I observed. "But why didn't you make for Singapore instead?"

His eyes wavered. "The nearest port," he muttered sullenly.

I had framed the question in perfect innocence, but his answer (the difference in distance was insignificant) and his manner offered me a clue to the simple truth. He took the ship to a port where he expected to be confirmed in his temporary command from lack of a qualified master to put over his head. Whereas Singapore, he surmised justly, would be full of qualified men.

But his naive reasoning forgot to take into account the telegraph cable reposing on the bottom of the very Gulf up which he had turned that ship which he imagined himself to have saved from destruction. Hence the bitter flavour of our interview. I tasted it more and more distinctly—and it was less and less to my taste.

"Look here, Mr. Burns," I began very firmly. "You may as well understand that I did not run after this command. It was pushed in my way. I've accepted it. I am here to take the ship home first of all, and you may be sure that I shall see to it that every one of you on board here does his duty to that end. This is all I have to say—for the present."

He was on his feet by this time, but instead of taking his dismissal he remained with trembling, indignant lips, and looking at me hard as though, really, after this, there was nothing for me to do in common decency but to vanish from his outraged sight. Like all very simple emotional states this was moving. I felt sorry for him—almost sympathetic, till (seeing that I did not vanish) he spoke in a tone of forced restraint.

"If I hadn't a wife and a child at home you may be sure, sir, I would have asked you to let me go the very minute you came on board."

I answered him with a matter-of-course calmness as though some remote third person were in question.

"And I, Mr. Burns, would not have let you go. You have signed the ship's articles as chief officer, and till they are terminated at the final port of discharge I shall expect you to attend to your duty and give me the benefit of your experience to the best of your ability."

Stony incredulity lingered in his eyes: but it broke down before my friendly attitude. With a slight upward toss of his arms (I got to know that gesture well afterward) he bolted out of the cabin.

We might have saved ourselves that little passage of harmless sparring. Before many days had elapsed it was Mr. Burns who was pleading with me anxiously not to leave him behind; while I could only return him but doubtful answers. The whole thing took on a somewhat tragic complexion.

And this horrible problem was only an extraneous episode, a mere complication in the general problem of how to get that ship—which was mine with her appurtenances and her men, with her body and her spirit now slumbering in that pestilential river—how to get her out to sea.

Mr. Burns, while still acting captain, had hastened to sign a charter-party which in an ideal world without guile would have been an excellent document. Directly I ran my eye over it I foresaw trouble ahead unless the people of the other part were quite exceptionally fair-minded and open to argument.

Mr. Burns, to whom I imparted my fears, chose to take great umbrage at them. He looked at me with that usual incredulous stare, and said bitterly:

"I suppose, sir, you want to make out I've acted like a fool?"

I told him, with my systematic kindliness which always seemed to augment his surprise, that I did not want to make out anything. I would leave that to the future.

And, sure enough, the future brought in a lot of trouble. There were days when I used to remember Captain Giles with nothing short of abhorrence. His confounded acuteness had let me in for this job; while his prophecy that I "would have my hands full" coming true, made it appear as if done on purpose to play an evil joke on my young innocence.

Yes. I had my hands full of complications which were most valuable as "experience." People have a great opinion of the advantages of experience. But in this connection experience means always something disagreeable as opposed to the charm and innocence of illusions.

I must say I was losing mine rapidly. But on these instructive complications I must not enlarge more than to say that they could all be resumed in the one word: Delay.

A mankind which has invented the proverb, "Time is money," will understand my vexation. The word "Delay" entered the secret chamber of my brain, resounded there like a tolling bell which maddens the ear, affected all my senses, took on a black colouring, a bitter taste, a deadly meaning.

"I am really sorry to see you worried like this. Indeed, I am. . . ."

It was the only humane speech I used to hear at that time. And it came from a doctor, appropriately enough.

A doctor is humane by definition. But that man was so in reality. His speech was not professional. I was not ill. But other people were, and that was the reason of his visiting the ship.

He was the doctor of our Legation and, of course, of the Consulate, too. He looked after the ship's health, which generally was poor, and trembling, as it were, on the verge of a break-up. Yes. The men ailed. And thus time was not only money, but life as well.

I had never seen such a steady ship's company. As the doctor remarked to me: "You seem to have a most respectable lot of seamen." Not only were they consistently sober, but they did not even want to go ashore. Care was taken to expose them as little as possible to the sun. They were employed on light work under the awnings. And the humane doctor commended me.

"Your arrangements appear to me to be very judicious, my dear Captain."

It is difficult to express how much that pronouncement comforted me. The doctor's round, full face framed in a light-coloured whisker was the perfection of a dignified amenity. He was the only human being in the world who seemed to take the slightest interest in me. He would generally sit in the cabin for half an hour or so at every visit.

I said to him one day:

"I suppose the only thing now is to take care of them as you are doing till I can get the ship to sea?"

He inclined his head, shutting his eyes under the large spectacles, and murmured:

"The sea . . . undoubtedly."

The first member of the crew fairly knocked over was the steward—the first man to whom I had spoken on board. He was taken ashore (with choleric symptoms) and died there at the end of a week. Then, while I was still under the startling impression of this first home-thrust of the climate, Mr. Burns gave up and went to bed in a raging fever without saying a word to anybody.

I believe he had partly fretted himself into that illness; the climate did the rest with the swiftness of an invisible monster ambushed in the air, in the water, in the mud of the river-bank. Mr. Burns was a predestined victim.

I discovered him lying on his back, glaring sullenly and radiating heat on one like a small furnace. He would hardly answer my questions, and only grumbled. Couldn't a man take an afternoon off duty with a bad headache—for once?

That evening, as I sat in the saloon after dinner, I could hear him muttering continuously in his room. Ransome, who was clearing the table, said to me:

"I am afraid, sir, I won't be able to give the mate all the attention he's likely to need. I will have to be forward in the galley a great part of my time."

Ransome was the cook. The mate had pointed him out to me the first day, standing on the deck, his arms crossed on his broad chest, gazing on the river.

Even at a distance his well-proportioned figure, something thoroughly sailor-like in his poise, made him noticeable. On nearer view the intelligent, quiet eyes, a well-bred face, the disciplined independence of his manner made up an attractive personality. When, in addition, Mr. Burns told me that he was the best seaman in the ship, I expressed my surprise that in his earliest prime and of such appearance he should sign on as cook on board a ship.

"It's his heart," Mr. Burns had said. "There's something wrong with it. He mustn't exert himself too much or he may drop dead suddenly."

And he was the only one the climate had not touched—perhaps because, carrying a deadly enemy in his breast, he had schooled himself into a systematic control of feelings and movements. When one was in the secret this was apparent in his manner. After the poor steward died, and as he could not be replaced by a white man in this Oriental port, Ransome had volunteered to do the double work.

"I can do it all right, sir, as long as I go about it quietly," he had assured me.

But obviously he couldn't be expected to take up sick-nursing in addition. Moreover, the doctor peremptorily ordered Mr. Burns ashore.

With a seaman on each side holding him up under the arms, the mate went over the gangway more sullen than ever. We built him up with pillows in the gharry, and he made an effort to say brokenly:

"Now—you've got—what you wanted—got me out of—the ship."

"You were never more mistaken in your life, Mr. Burns," I said quietly, duly smiling at him; and the trap drove off to a sort of sanatorium, a pavilion of bricks which the doctor had in the grounds of his residence.

I visited Mr. Burns regularly. After the first few days, when he didn't know anybody, he received me as if I had come either to gloat over an enemy or else to curry favour with a deeply wronged person. It was either one or the other, just as it happened according to his fantastic sickroom moods. Whichever it was, he managed to convey it to me even during the period when he appeared almost too weak to talk. I treated him to my invariable kindliness.

Then one day, suddenly, a surge of downright panic burst through all this craziness.

If I left him behind in this deadly place he would die. He felt it, he was certain of it. But I wouldn't have the heart to leave him ashore. He had a wife and child in Sydney.

He produced his wasted forearms from under the sheet which

covered him and clasped his fleshless claws. He would die! He would
die here. . . .

He absolutely managed to sit up, but only for a moment, and when
he fell back I really thought that he would die there and then. I called to
the Bengali dispenser, and hastened away from the room.

Next day he upset me thoroughly by renewing his entreaties. I
returned an evasive answer, and left him the picture of ghastly despair.
The day after I went in with reluctance, and he attacked me at once in a
much stronger voice and with an abundance of argument which was
quite startling. He presented his case with a sort of crazy vigour, and
asked me finally how would I like to have a man's death on my
conscience? He wanted me to promise that I would not sail without
him.

I said that I really must consult the doctor first. He cried out at that.
The doctor! Never! That would be a death sentence.

The effort had exhausted him. He closed his eyes, but went on
rambling in a low voice. I had hated him from the start. The late captain
had hated him, too. Had wished him dead. Had wished all hands dead. .
. .

"What do you want to stand in with that wicked corpse for, sir?
He'll have you, too," he ended, blinking his glazed eyes vacantly.

"Mr. Burns," I cried, very much discomposed, "what on earth are
you talking about?"

He seemed to come to himself, though he was too weak to start.

"I don't know," he said languidly. "But don't ask that doctor, sir.
You and I are sailors. Don't ask him, sir. Some day perhaps you will
have a wife and child yourself."

And again he pleaded for the promise that I would not leave him
behind. I had the firmness of mind not to give it to him. Afterward this
sternness seemed criminal; for my mind was made up. That prostrated
man, with hardly strength enough to breathe and ravaged by a passion
of fear, was irresistible. And, besides, he had happened to hit on the
right words. He and I were sailors. That was a claim, for I had no other
family. As to the wife and child (some day) argument, it had no force.
It sounded merely bizarre.

I could imagine no claim that would be stronger and more
absorbing than the claim of that ship, of these men snared in the river
by silly commercial complications, as if in some poisonous trap.

However, I had nearly fought my way out. Out to sea. The sea—
which was pure, safe, and friendly. Three days more.

That thought sustained and carried me on my way back to the ship.
In the saloon the doctor's voice greeted me, and his large form
followed his voice, issuing out of the starboard spare cabin where the
ship's medicine chest was kept securely lashed in the bed-place.

Finding that I was not on board he had gone in there, he said, to inspect the supply of drugs, bandages, and so on. Everything was completed and in order.

I thanked him; I had just been thinking of asking him to do that very thing, as in a couple of days, as he knew, we were going to sea, where all our troubles of every sort would be over at last.

He listened gravely and made no answer. But when I opened to him my mind as to Mr. Burns he sat down by my side, and, laying his hand on my knee amicably, begged me to think what it was I was exposing myself to.

The man was just strong enough to bear being moved and no more. But he couldn't stand a return of the fever. I had before me a passage of sixty days perhaps, beginning with intricate navigation and ending probably with a lot of bad weather. Could I run the risk of having to go through it single-handed, with no chief officer and with a second quite a youth? . . .

He might have added that it was my first command, too. He did probably think of that fact, for he checked himself. It was very present to my mind.

He advised me earnestly to cable to Singapore for a chief officer, even if I had to delay my sailing for a week.

"Never," I said. The very thought gave me the shivers. The hands seemed fairly fit, all of them, and this was the time to get them away. Once at sea I was not afraid of facing anything. The sea was now the only remedy for all my troubles.

The doctor's glasses were directed at me like two lamps searching the genuineness of my resolution. He opened his lips as if to argue further, but shut them again without saying anything. I had a vision so vivid of poor Burns in his exhaustion, helplessness, and anguish, that it moved me more than the reality I had come away from only an hour before. It was purged from the drawbacks of his personality, and I could not resist it.

"Look here," I said. "Unless you tell me officially that the man must not be moved I'll make arrangements to have him brought on board tomorrow, and shall take the ship out of the river next morning, even if I have to anchor outside the bar for a couple of days to get her ready for sea."

"Oh! I'll make all the arrangements myself," said the doctor at once. "I spoke as I did only as a friend—as a well-wisher, and that sort of thing."

He rose in his dignified simplicity and gave me a warm handshake, rather solemnly, I thought. But he was as good as his word. When Mr. Burns appeared at the gangway carried on a stretcher, the doctor himself walked by its side. The programme had been altered in so far that this transportation had been left to the last moment, on the very morning of our departure.

It was barely an hour after sunrise. The doctor waved his big arm to me from the shore and walked back at once to his trap, which had followed him empty to the river-side. Mr. Burns, carried across the quarter-deck, had the appearance of being absolutely lifeless. Ransome went down to settle him in his cabin. I had to remain on deck to look after the ship, for the tug had got hold of our towrope already.

The splash of our shore-fasts falling in the water produced a complete change of feeling in me. It was like the imperfect relief of awakening from a nightmare. But when the ship's head swung down the river away from that town, Oriental and squalid, I missed the expected elation of that striven-for moment. What there was, undoubtedly, was a relaxation of tension which translated itself into a sense of weariness after an inglorious fight.

About midday we anchored a mile outside the bar. The afternoon was busy for all hands. Watching the work from the poop, where I remained all the time, I detected in it some of the languor of the six weeks spent in the steaming heat of the river. The first breeze would blow that away. Now the calm was complete. I judged that the second officer—a callow youth with an unpromising face—was not, to put it mildly, of that invaluable stuff from which a commander's right hand is made. But I was glad to catch along the main deck a few smiles on those seamen's faces at which I had hardly had time to have a good look as yet. Having thrown off the mortal coil of shore affairs, I felt myself familiar with them and yet a little strange, like a long-lost wanderer among his kin.

Ransome flitted continually to and fro between the galley and the cabin. It was a pleasure to look at him. The man positively had grace. He alone of all the crew had not had a day's illness in port. But with the knowledge of that uneasy heart within his breast I could detect the restraint he put on the natural sailor-like agility of his movements. It was as though he had something very fragile or very explosive to carry about his person and was all the time aware of it.

I had occasion to address him once or twice. He answered me in his pleasant, quiet voice and with a faint, slightly wistful smile. Mr. Burns appeared to be resting. He seemed fairly comfortable.

After sunset I came out on deck again to meet only a still void. The thin, featureless crust of the coast could not be distinguished. The darkness had risen around the ship like a mysterious emanation from the dumb and lonely waters. I leaned on the rail and turned my ear to the shadows of the night. Not a sound. My command might have been a planet flying vertiginously on its appointed path in a space of infinite silence. I clung to the rail as if my sense of balance were leaving me for good. How absurd. I failed nervously.

"On deck there!"

The immediate answer, "Yes, sir," broke the spell. The anchor-watch man ran up the poop ladder smartly. I told him to report at once the slightest sign of a breeze coming.

Going below I looked in on Mr. Burns. In fact, I could not avoid seeing him, for his door stood open. The man was so wasted that, in this white cabin, under a white sheet, and with his diminished head sunk in the white pillow, his red moustaches captured their eyes exclusively, like something artificial—a pair of moustaches from a shop exhibited there in the harsh light of the bulkhead-lamp without a shade.

While I stared with a sort of wonder he asserted himself by opening his eyes and even moving them in my direction. A minute stir.

"Dead calm, Mr. Burns," I said resignedly.

In an unexpectedly distinct voice Mr. Burns began a rambling speech. Its tone was very strange, not as if affected by his illness, but as if of a different nature. It sounded unearthly. As to the matter, I seemed to make out that it was the fault of the "old man"—the late captain—ambushed down there under the sea with some evil intention. It was a weird story.

I listened to the end; then stepping into the cabin I laid my hand on the mate's forehead. It was cool. He was light-headed only from extreme weakness. Suddenly he seemed to become aware of me, and in his own voice—of course, very feeble—he asked regretfully:

"Is there no chance at all to get under way, sir?"

"What's the good of letting go our hold of the ground only to drift, Mr. Burns?" I answered.

He sighed and I left him to his immobility. His hold on life was as slender as his hold on sanity. I was oppressed by my lonely responsibilities. I went into my cabin to seek relief in a few hours' sleep, but almost before I closed my eyes the man on deck came down reporting a light breeze. Enough to get under way with, he said.

And it was no more than just enough. I ordered the windlass manned, the sails loosed, and the topsails set. But by the time I had cast the ship I could hardly feel any breath of wind. Nevertheless, I trimmed the yards and put everything on her. I was not going to give up the attempt.

PART TWO

IV

With her anchor at the bow and clothed in canvas to her very trucks, my command seemed to stand as motionless as a model ship set on the gleams and shadows of polished marble. It was impossible to distinguish land from water in the enigmatical tranquillity of the immense forces of the world. A sudden impatience possessed me.

"Won't she answer the helm at all?" I said irritably to the man whose strong brown hands grasping the spokes of the wheel stood out lighted on the darkness; like a symbol of mankind's claim to the direction of its own fate.

He answered me.

"Yes, sir. She's coming-to slowly."

"Let her head come up to south."

"Aye, aye, sir."

I paced the poop. There was not a sound but that of my footsteps, till the man spoke again.

"She is at south now, sir."

I felt a slight tightness of the chest before I gave out the first course of my first command to the silent night, heavy with dew and sparkling with stars. There was a finality in the act committing me to the endless vigilance of my lonely task.

"Steady her head at that," I said at last. "The course is south."

"South, sir," echoed the man.

I sent below the second mate and his watch and remained in charge, walking the deck through the chill, somnolent hours that precede the dawn.

Slight puffs came and went, and whenever they were strong enough to wake up the black water the murmur alongside ran through my very heart in a delicate crescendo of delight and died away swiftly. I was bitterly tired. The very stars seemed weary of waiting for daybreak. It came at last with a mother-of-pearl sheen at the zenith, such as I had never seen before in the tropics, unglowing, almost gray, with a strange reminder of high latitudes.

The voice of the look-out man hailed from forward:

"Land on the port bow, sir."

"All right."

Leaning on the rail I never even raised my eyes. The motion of the ship was imperceptible. Presently Ransome brought me the cup of morning coffee. After I had drunk it I looked ahead, and in the still streak of very bright pale orange light I saw the land profiled flatly as if cut out of black paper and seeming to float on the water as light as cork. But the rising sun turned it into mere dark vapour, a doubtful, massive shadow trembling in the hot glare.

The watch finished washing decks. I went below and stopped at Mr. Burns' door (he could not bear to have it shut), but hesitated to speak to him till he moved his eyes. I gave him the news.

"Sighted Cape Liant at daylight. About fifteen miles."

He moved his lips then, but I heard no sound till I put my ear down, and caught the peevish comment: "This is crawling. . . . No luck."

"Better luck than standing still, anyhow," I pointed out resignedly, and left him to whatever thoughts or fancies haunted his awful immobility.

Later that morning, when relieved by my second officer, I threw myself on my couch and for some three hours or so I really found oblivion. It was so perfect that on waking up I wondered where I was. Then came the immense relief of the thought: on board my ship! At sea! At sea!

Through the port-holes I beheld an unruffled, sun-smitten horizon. The horizon of a windless day. But its spaciousness alone was enough to give me a sense of a fortunate escape, a momentary exultation of freedom.

I stepped out into the saloon with my heart lighter than it had been for days. Ransome was at the sideboard preparing to lay the table for the first sea dinner of the passage. He turned his head, and something in his eyes checked my modest elation.

Instinctively I asked: "What is it now?" not expecting in the least the answer I got. It was given with that sort of contained serenity which was characteristic of the man.

"I am afraid we haven't left all sickness behind us, sir."

"We haven't! What's the matter?"

He told me then that two of our men had been taken bad with fever in the night. One of them was burning and the other was shivering, but he thought that it was pretty much the same thing. I thought so, too. I felt shocked by the news. "One burning, the other shivering, you say? No. We haven't left the sickness behind. Do they look very ill?"

"Middling bad, sir." Ransome's eyes gazed steadily into mine. We exchanged smiles. Ransome's a little wistful, as usual, mine no doubt grim enough, to correspond with my secret exasperation.

I asked:

"Was there any wind at all this morning?"

"Can hardly say that, sir. We've moved all the time though. The land ahead seems a little nearer."

That was it. A little nearer. Whereas if we had only had a little more wind, only a very little more, we might, we should, have been abreast of Liant by this time and increasing our distance from that contaminated shore. And it was not only the distance. It seemed to me that a stronger breeze would have blown away the contamination which clung to the ship. It obviously did cling to the ship. Two men. One burning, one shivering. I felt a distinct reluctance to go and look at them. What was the good? Poison is poison. Tropical fever is tropical fever. But that it should have stretched its claw after us over the sea seemed to me an extraordinary and unfair license. I could hardly believe that it could be anything worse than the last desperate pluck of the evil from which we were escaping into the clean breath of the sea. If only that breath had been a little stronger. However, there was the quinine against the fever. I went into the spare cabin where the medicine chest was kept to prepare two doses. I opened it full of faith as a man opens a miraculous shrine. The upper part was inhabited by a collection of bottles, all square-shouldered and as like each other as peas. Under that orderly array there were two drawers, stuffed as full of things as one could imagine—paper packages, bandages, cardboard boxes officially labelled. The lower of the two, in one of its compartments, contained our provision of quinine.

There were five bottles, all round and all of a size. One was about a third full. The other four remained still wrapped up in paper and sealed. But I did not expect to see an envelope lying on top of them. A square envelope, belonging, in fact, to the ship's stationery.

It lay so that I could see it was not closed down, and on picking it up and turning it over I perceived that it was addressed to myself. It contained a half-sheet of notepaper, which I unfolded with a queer sense of dealing with the uncanny, but without any excitement as people meet and do extraordinary things in a dream.

"My dear Captain," it began, but I ran to the signature. The writer was the doctor. The date was that of the day on which, returning from my visit to Mr. Burns in the hospital, I had found the excellent doctor waiting for me in the cabin; and when he told me that he had been putting in time inspecting the medicine chest for me. How bizarre! While expecting me to come in at any moment he had been amusing himself by writing me a letter, and then as I came in had hastened to stuff it into the medicine-chest drawer. A rather incredible proceeding. I turned to the text in wonder.

In a large, hurried, but legible hand the good, sympathetic man for some reason, either of kindness or more likely impelled by the irresistible desire to express his opinion, with which he didn't want to damp my hopes before, was warning me not to put my trust in the beneficial effects of a change from land to sea. "I didn't want to add to your worries by discouraging your hopes," he wrote. "I am afraid that, medically speaking, the end of your troubles is not yet." In short, he expected me to have to fight a probable return of tropical illness. Fortunately I had a good provision of quinine. I should put my trust in that, and administer it steadily, when the ship's health would certainly improve.

I crumpled up the letter and rammed it into my pocket. Ransome carried off two big doses to the men forward. As to myself, I did not go on deck as yet. I went instead to the door of Mr. Burns' room, and gave him that news, too.

It was impossible to say the effect it had on him. At first I thought that he was speechless. His head lay sunk in the pillow. He moved his lips enough, however, to assure me that he was getting much stronger; a statement shockingly untrue on the face of it.

That afternoon I took my watch as a matter of course. A great over-heated stillness enveloped the ship and seemed to hold her motionless in a flaming ambience composed in two shades of blue. Faint, hot puffs eddied nervelessly from her sails. And yet she moved. She must have. For, as the sun was setting, we had drawn abreast of Cape Liant and dropped it behind us: an ominous retreating shadow in the last gleams of twilight.

In the evening, under the crude glare of his lamp, Mr. Burns seemed to have come more to the surface of his bedding. It was as if a depressing hand had been lifted off him. He answered my few words by a comparatively long, connected speech. He asserted himself strongly. If he escaped being smothered by this stagnant heat, he said, he was confident that in a very few days he would be able to come up on deck and help me.

While he was speaking I trembled lest this effort of energy should leave him lifeless before my eyes. But I cannot deny that there was something comforting in his willingness. I made a suitable reply, but pointed out to him that the only thing that could really help us was wind—a fair wind.

He rolled his head impatiently on the pillow. And it was not comforting in the least to hear him begin to mutter crazily about the late captain, that old man buried in latitude 8° 20', right in our way—ambushed at the entrance of the Gulf.

"Are you still thinking of your late captain, Mr. Burns?" I said. "I imagine the dead feel no animosity against the living. They care nothing for them."

"You don't know that one," he breathed out feebly.

"No. I didn't know him, and he didn't know me. And so he can't have any grievance against me, anyway."

"Yes. But there's all the rest of us on board," he insisted.

I felt the inexpugnable strength of common sense being insidiously menaced by this gruesome, by this insane, delusion. And I said:

"You mustn't talk so much. You will tire yourself."

"And there is the ship herself," he persisted in a whisper.

"Now, not a word more," I said, stepping in and laying my hand on his cool forehead. It proved to me that this atrocious absurdity was rooted in the man himself and not in the disease, which, apparently, had emptied him of every power, mental and physical, except that one fixed idea.

I avoided giving Mr. Burns any opening for conversation for the next few days. I merely used to throw him a hasty, cheery word when passing his door. I believe that if he had had the strength he would have called out after me more than once. But he hadn't the strength. Ransome, however, observed to me one afternoon that the mate "seemed to be picking up wonderfully."

"Did he talk any nonsense to you of late?" I asked casually.

"No, sir." Ransome was startled by the direct question; but, after a pause, he added equably: "He told me this morning, sir, that he was sorry he had to bury our late captain right in the ship's way, as one may say, out of the Gulf."

"Isn't this nonsense enough for you?" I asked, looking confidently at the intelligent, quiet face on which the secret uneasiness in the man's breast had thrown a transparent veil of care.

Ransome didn't know. He had not given a thought to the matter. And with a faint smile he flitted away from me on his never-ending duties, with his usual guarded activity.

Two more days passed. We had advanced a little way—a very little way—into the larger space of the Gulf of Siam. Seizing eagerly upon the elation of the first command thrown into my lap, by the agency of Captain Giles, I had yet an uneasy feeling that such luck as this has got perhaps to be paid for in some way. I had held, professionally, a review of my chances. I was competent enough for that. At least, I thought so. I had a general sense of my preparedness which only a man pursuing a calling he loves can know. That feeling seemed to me the most natural thing in the world. As natural as breathing. I imagined I could not have lived without it.

I don't know what I expected. Perhaps nothing else than that special intensity of existence which is the quintessence of youthful aspirations. Whatever I expected I did not expect to be beset by hurricanes. I knew better than that. In the Gulf of Siam there are no hurricanes. But neither did I expect to find myself bound hand and foot to the hopeless extent which was revealed to me as the days went on.

Not that the evil spell held us always motionless. Mysterious currents drifted us here and there, with a stealthy power made manifest only by the changing vistas of the islands fringing the east shore of the Gulf. And there were winds, too, fitful and deceitful. They raised hopes only to dash them into the bitterest disappointment, promises of advance ending in lost ground, expiring in sighs, dying into dumb stillness in which the currents had it all their own way—their own inimical way.

The island of Koh-ring, a great, black, upheaved ridge amongst a lot of tiny islets, lying upon the glassy water like a triton amongst minnows, seemed to be the centre of the fatal circle. It seemed impossible to get away from it. Day after day it remained in sight. More than once, in a favourable breeze, I would take its bearings in the fast-ebbing twilight, thinking that it was for the last time. Vain hope. A night of fitful airs would undo the gains of temporary favour, and the rising sun would throw out the black relief of Koh-ring looking more barren, inhospitable, and grim than ever.

"It's like being bewitched, upon my word," I said once to Mr.

Burns, from my usual position in the doorway.

He was sitting up in his bed-place. He was progressing toward the world of living men; if he could hardly have been said to have rejoined it yet. He nodded to me his frail and bony head in a wisely mysterious assent.

"Oh, yes, I know what you mean," I said. "But you cannot expect me to believe that a dead man has the power to put out of joint the meteorology of this part of the world. Though indeed it seems to have gone utterly wrong. The land and sea breezes have got broken up into small pieces. We cannot depend upon them for five minutes together."

"It won't be very long now before I can come up on deck," muttered Mr. Burns, "and then we shall see."

Whether he meant this for a promise to grapple with supernatural evil I couldn't tell. At any rate, it wasn't the kind of assistance I needed. On the other hand, I had been living on deck practically night and day so as to take advantage of every chance to get my ship a little more to the southward. The mate, I could see, was extremely weak yet, and not quite rid of his delusion, which to me appeared but a symptom of his disease. At all events, the hopefulness of an invalid was not to be discouraged. I said:

"You will be most welcome there, I am sure, Mr. Burns. If you go on improving at this rate you'll be presently one of the healthiest men in the ship."

This pleased him, but his extreme emaciation converted his self-satisfied smile into a ghastly exhibition of long teeth under the red moustache.

"Aren't the fellows improving, sir?" he asked soberly, with an extremely sensible expression of anxiety on his face.

I answered him only with a vague gesture and went away from the door. The fact was that disease played with us capriciously very much as the winds did. It would go from one man to another with a lighter or heavier touch, which always left its mark behind, staggering some, knocking others over for a time, leaving this one, returning to another, so that all of them had now an invalidish aspect and a hunted, apprehensive look in their eyes; while Ransome and I, the only two completely untouched, went amongst them assiduously distributing quinine. It was a double fight. The adverse weather held us in front and the disease pressed on our rear. I must say that the men were very good. The constant toil of trimming yards they faced willingly. But all spring was out of their limbs, and as I looked at them from the poop I could not keep from my mind the dreadful impression that they were moving in poisoned air.

Down below, in his cabin, Mr. Burns had advanced so far as not only to be able to sit up, but even to draw up his legs. Clasping them with bony arms, like an animated skeleton, he emitted deep, impatient sighs.

"The great thing to do, sir," he would tell me on every occasion, when I gave him the chance, "the great thing is to get the ship past 8° 20' of latitude. Once she's past that we're all right."

At first I used only to smile at him, though, God knows, I had not much heart left for smiles. But at last I lost my patience.

"Oh, yes. The latitude 8° 20'. That's where you buried your late captain, isn't it?" Then with severity: "Don't you think, Mr. Burns, it's about time you dropped all that nonsense?"

He rolled at me his deep-sunken eyes in a glance of invincible obstinacy. But for the rest he only muttered, just loud enough for me to hear, something about "Not surprised . . . find . . . play us some beastly trick yet. . . ."

Such passages as this were not exactly wholesome for my resolution. The stress of adversity was beginning to tell on me. At the same time, I felt a contempt for that obscure weakness of my soul. I said to myself disdainfully that it should take much more than that to affect in the smallest degree my fortitude.

I didn't know then how soon and from what unexpected direction it would be attacked.

It was the very next day. The sun had risen clear of the southern shoulder of Koh-ring, which still hung, like an evil attendant, on our port quarter. It was intensely hateful to my sight. During the night we had been heading all round the compass, trimming the yards again and again, to what I fear must have been for the most part imaginary puffs of air. Then just about sunrise we got for an hour an inexplicable, steady breeze, right in our teeth. There was no sense in it. It fitted neither with the season of the year nor with the secular experience of seamen as recorded in books, nor with the aspect of the sky. Only purposeful malevolence could account for it. It sent us travelling at a great pace away from our proper course; and if we had been out on pleasure sailing bent it would have been a delightful breeze, with the awakened sparkle of the sea, with the sense of motion and a feeling of unwonted freshness. Then, all at once, as if disdaining to carry farther the sorry jest, it dropped and died out completely in less than five minutes. The ship's head swung where it listed; the stilled sea took on the polish of a steel plate in the calm.

I went below, not because I meant to take some rest, but simply because I couldn't bear to look at it just then. The indefatigable Ransome was busy in the saloon. It had become a regular practice with him to give me an informal health report in the morning. He turned away from the sideboard with his usual pleasant, quiet gaze. No shadow rested on his intelligent forehead.

"There are a good many of them middling bad this morning, sir," he said in a calm tone.

"What? All knocked out?"

"Only two actually in their bunks, sir, but—"

"It's the last night that has done for them. We have had to pull and haul all the blessed time."

"I heard, sir. I had a mind to come out and help only, you know. . . ."

"Certainly not. You mustn't. . . . The fellows lie at night about the decks, too. It isn't good for them."

Ransome assented. But men couldn't be looked after like children. Moreover, one could hardly blame them for trying for such coolness and such air as there was to be found on deck. He himself, of course, knew better.

He was, indeed, a reasonable man. Yet it would have been hard to say that the others were not. The last few days had been for us like the ordeal of the fiery furnace. One really couldn't quarrel with their common, imprudent humanity making the best of the moments of relief, when the night brought in the illusion of coolness and the starlight twinkled through the heavy, dew-laden air. Moreover, most of them were so weakened that hardly anything could be done without everybody that could totter mustering on the braces. No, it was no use remonstrating with them. But I fully believed that quinine was of very great use indeed.

I believed in it. I pinned my faith to it. It would save the men, the ship, break the spell by its medicinal virtue, make time of no account, the weather but a passing worry and, like a magic powder working against mysterious malefices, secure the first passage of my first command against the evil powers of calms and pestilence. I looked upon it as more precious than gold, and unlike gold, of which there ever hardly seems to be enough anywhere, the ship had a sufficient store of it. I went in to get it with the purpose of weighing out doses. I stretched my hand with the feeling of a man reaching for an unfailing panacea, took up a fresh bottle and unrolled the wrapper, noticing as I did so that the ends, both top and bottom, had come unsealed. . . .

But why record all the swift steps of the appalling discovery? You have guessed the truth already. There was the wrapper, the bottle, and the white powder inside, some sort of powder! But it wasn't quinine. One look at it was quite enough. I remember that at the very moment of picking up the bottle, before I even dealt with the wrapper, the weight of the object I had in my hand gave me an instant premonition. Quinine is as light as feathers; and my nerves must have been exasperated into an extraordinary sensibility. I let the bottle smash itself on the floor. The stuff, whatever it was, felt gritty under the sole of my shoe. I snatched up the next bottle and then the next. The weight alone told the tale. One after another they fell, breaking at my feet, not because I threw them down in my dismay, but slipping through my fingers as if this disclosure were too much for my strength.

It is a fact that the very greatness of a mental shock helps one to bear up against it by producing a sort of temporary insensibility. I came out of the state-room stunned, as if something heavy had dropped on my head. From the other side of the saloon, across the table, Ransome, with a duster in his hand, stared open-mouthed. I don't think that I looked wild. It is quite possible that I appeared to be in a hurry because I was instinctively hastening up on deck. An example this of training become instinct. The difficulties, the dangers, the problems of a ship at sea must be met on deck.

To this fact, as it were of nature, I responded instinctively; which may be taken as a proof that for a moment I must have been robbed of my reason.

I was certainly off my balance, a prey to impulse, for at the bottom of the stairs I turned and flung myself at the doorway of Mr. Burns' cabin. The wildness of his aspect checked my mental disorder. He was sitting up in his bunk, his body looking immensely long, his head drooping a little sideways, with affected complacency. He flourished, in his trembling hand, on the end of a forearm no thicker than a walking-stick, a shining pair of scissors which he tried before my very eyes to jab at his throat.

I was to a certain extent horrified; but it was rather a secondary sort of effect, not really strong enough to make me yell at him in some such manner as: "Stop!" . . . "Heavens!" . . . "What are you doing?"

In reality he was simply overtaxing his returning strength in a shaky attempt to clip off the thick growth of his red beard. A large towel was spread over his lap, and a shower of stiff hairs, like bits of copper wire, was descending on it at every snip of the scissors.

He turned to me his face grotesque beyond the fantasies of mad dreams, one cheek all bushy as if with a swollen flame, the other denuded and sunken, with the untouched long moustache on that side asserting itself, lonely and fierce. And while he stared thunderstruck, with the gaping scissors on his fingers, I shouted my discovery at him fiendishly, in six words, without comment.

V

I heard the clatter of the scissors escaping from his hand, noted the perilous heave of his whole person over the edge of the bunk after them, and then, returning to my first purpose, pursued my course on the deck. The sparkle of the sea filled my eyes. It was gorgeous and barren, monotonous and without hope under the empty curve of the sky. The sails hung motionless and slack, the very folds of their sagging surfaces moved no more than carved granite. The impetuosity of my advent made the man at the helm start slightly. A block aloft squeaked incomprehensibly, for what on earth could have made it do so? It was a whistling note like a bird's. For a long, long time I faced an empty world, steeped in an infinity of silence, through which the sunshine poured and flowed for some mysterious purpose. Then I heard Ransome's voice at my elbow.

"I have put Mr. Burns back to bed, sir."

"You have."

"Well, sir, he got out, all of a sudden, but when he let go the edge of his bunk he fell down. He isn't light-headed, though, it seems to me."

"No," I said dully, without looking at Ransome. He waited for a moment, then cautiously, as if not to give offence: "I don't think we need lose much of that stuff, sir," he said, "I can sweep it up, every bit of it almost, and then we could sift the glass out. I will go about it at once. It will not make the breakfast late, not ten minutes."

"Oh, yes," I said bitterly. "Let the breakfast wait, sweep up every bit of it, and then throw the damned lot overboard!"

The profound silence returned, and when I looked over my shoulder, Ransome—the intelligent, serene Ransome—had vanished from my side. The intense loneliness of the sea acted like poison on my brain. When I turned my eyes to the ship, I had a morbid vision of her as a floating grave. Who hasn't heard of ships found floating, haphazard, with their crews all dead? I looked at the seaman at the helm, I had an impulse to speak to him, and, indeed, his face took on an expectant cast as if he had guessed my intention. But in the end I went below, thinking I would be alone with the greatness of my trouble for a little while. But through his open door Mr. Burns saw me come down, and addressed me grumpily: "Well, sir?"

I went in. "It isn't well at all," I said.

Mr. Burns, reestablished in his bed-place, was concealing his hirsute cheek in the palm of his hand.

"That confounded fellow has taken away the scissors from me," were the next words he said.

The tension I was suffering from was so great that it was perhaps just as well that Mr. Burns had started on his grievance. He seemed very sore about it and grumbled, "Does he think I am mad, or what?"

"I don't think so, Mr. Burns," I said. I looked upon him at that moment as a model of self-possession. I even conceived on that account a sort of admiration for that man, who had (apart from the intense materiality of what was left of his beard) come as near to being a disembodied spirit as any man can do and live. I noticed the preternatural sharpness of the ridge of his nose, the deep cavities of his temples, and I envied him. He was so reduced that he would probably die very soon. Enviable man! So near extinction—while I had to bear within me a tumult of suffering vitality, doubt, confusion, self-reproach, and an indefinite reluctance to meet the horrid logic of the situation. I could not help muttering: "I feel as if I were going mad myself."

Mr. Burns glared spectrally, but otherwise was wonderfully composed.

"I always thought he would play us some deadly trick," he said, with a peculiar emphasis on the *he*.

It gave me a mental shock, but I had neither the mind, nor the heart, nor the spirit to argue with him. My form of sickness was indifference. The creeping paralysis of a hopeless outlook. So I only gazed at him. Mr. Burns broke into further speech.

"Eh! What! No! You won't believe it? Well, how do you account for this? How do you think it could have happened?"

"Happened?" I repeated dully. "Why, yes, how in the name of the infernal powers did this thing happen?"

Indeed, on thinking it out, it seemed incomprehensible that it should just be like this: the bottles emptied, refilled, rewrapped, and replaced. A sort of plot, a sinister attempt to deceive, a thing resembling sly vengeance, but for what? Or else a fiendish joke. But Mr. Burns was in possession of a theory. It was simple, and he uttered it solemnly in a hollow voice.

"I suppose they have given him about fifteen pounds in Haiphong for that little lot."

"Mr. Burns!" I cried.

He nodded grotesquely over his raised legs, like two broomsticks in the pyjamas, with enormous bare feet at the end.

"Why not? The stuff is pretty expensive in this part of the world, and they were very short of it in Tonkin. And what did he care? You have not known him. I have, and I have defied him. He feared neither God, nor devil, nor man, nor wind, nor sea, nor his own conscience. And I believe he hated everybody and everything. But I think he was afraid to die. I believe I am the only man who ever stood up to him. I faced him in that cabin where you live now, when he was sick, and I cowed him then. He thought I was going to twist his neck for him. If he had had his way we would have been beating up against the Nord-East monsoon, as long as he lived and afterward, too, for ages and ages. Acting the Flying Dutchman in the China Sea! Ha! Ha!"

"But why should he replace the bottles like this?" . . . I began.

"Why shouldn't he? Why should he want to throw the bottles away? They fit the drawer. They belong to the medicine chest."

"And they were wrapped up," I cried.

"Well, the wrappers were there. Did it from habit, I suppose, and as to refilling, there is always a lot of stuff they send in paper parcels that burst after a time. And then, who can tell? I suppose you didn't taste it, sir? But, of course, you are sure. . . ."

"No," I said. "I didn't taste it. It is all overboard now."

Behind me, a soft, cultivated voice said: "I have tasted it. It seemed a mixture of all sorts, sweetish, saltish, very horrible."

Ransome, stepping out of the pantry, had been listening for some time, as it was very excusable in him to do.

"A dirty trick," said Mr. Burns. "I always said he would."

The magnitude of my indignation was unbounded. And the kind, sympathetic doctor, too. The only sympathetic man I ever knew . . . instead of writing that warning letter, the very refinement of sympathy, why didn't the man make a proper inspection? But, as a matter of fact, it was hardly fair to blame the doctor. The fittings were in order and the medicine chest is an officially arranged affair. There was nothing really to arouse the slightest suspicion. The person I could never forgive was myself. Nothing should ever be taken for granted. The seed of everlasting remorse was sown in my breast.

"I feel it's all my fault," I exclaimed, "mine and nobody else's. That's how I feel. I shall never forgive myself."

"That's very foolish, sir," said Mr. Burns fiercely.

And after this effort he fell back exhausted on his bed. He closed his eyes, he panted; this affair, this abominable surprise had shaken him up, too. As I turned away I perceived Ransome looking at me blankly. He appreciated what it meant, but managed to produce his pleasant, wistful smile. Then he stepped back into his pantry, and I rushed up on deck again to see whether there was any wind, any breath under the sky, any stir of the air, any sign of hope. The deadly stillness met me again. Nothing was changed except that there was a different man at the wheel. He looked ill. His whole figure drooped, and he seemed rather to cling to the spokes than hold them with a controlling grip. I said to him:

"You are not fit to be here."

"I can manage, sir," he said feebly.

As a matter of fact, there was nothing for him to do. The ship had no steerage way. She lay with her head to the westward, the everlasting Koh-ring visible over the stern, with a few small islets, black spots in the great blaze, swimming before my troubled eyes. And but for those bits of land there was no speck on the sky, no speck on the water, no shape of vapour, no wisp of smoke, no sail, no boat, no stir of humanity, no sign of life, nothing!

The first question was, what to do? What could one do? The first thing to do obviously was to tell the men. I did it that very day. I wasn't going to let the knowledge simply get about. I would face them. They were assembled on the quarterdeck for the purpose. Just before I stepped out to speak to them I discovered that life could hold terrible moments. No confessed criminal had ever been so oppressed by his sense of guilt. This is why, perhaps, my face was set hard and my voice curt and unemotional while I made my declaration that I could do nothing more for the sick in the way of drugs. As to such care as could be given them they knew they had had it.

I would have held them justified in tearing me limb from limb. The silence which followed upon my words was almost harder to bear than the angriest uproar. I was crushed by the infinite depth of its reproach. But, as a matter of fact, I was mistaken. In a voice which I had great difficulty in keeping firm, I went on: "I suppose, men, you have understood what I said, and you know what it means."

A voice or two were heard: "Yes, sir. . . . We understand."

They had kept silent simply because they thought that they were not called to say anything; and when I told them that I intended to run into Singapore and that the best chance for the ship and the men was in the efforts all of us, sick and well, must make to get her along out of this, I received the encouragement of a low assenting murmur and of a louder voice exclaiming: "Surely there is a way out of this blamed hole."

* * *

Here is an extract from the notes I wrote at the time.

"We have lost Koh-ring at last. For many days now I don't think I have been two hours below altogether. I remain on deck, of course, night and day, and the nights and the days wheel over us in succession, whether long or short, who can say? All sense of time is lost in the monotony of expectation, of hope, and of desire—which is only one: Get the ship to the southward! Get the ship to the southward! The effect is curiously mechanical; the sun climbs and descends, the night swings over our heads as if somebody below the horizon were turning a crank. It is the prettiest, the most aimless! . . . and all through that miserable performance I go on, tramping, tramping the deck. How many miles have I walked on the poop of that ship! A stubborn pilgrimage of sheer restlessness, diversified by short excursions below to look upon Mr. Burns. I don't know whether it is an illusion, but he seems to become more substantial from day to day. He doesn't say much, for, indeed, the situation doesn't lend itself to idle remarks. I notice this even with the men as I watch them moving or sitting about the decks. They don't talk to each other. It strikes me that if there exists an invisible ear catching the whispers of the earth, it will find this ship the most silent spot on it. . . .

"No, Mr. Burns has not much to say to me. He sits in his bunk with his beard gone, his moustaches flaming, and with an air of silent determination on his chalky physiognomy. Ransome tells me he devours all the food that is given him to the last scrap, but that, apparently, he sleeps very little. Even at night, when I go below to fill my pipe, I notice that, though dozing flat on his back, he still looks very determined. From the side glance he gives me when awake it seems as though he were annoyed at being interrupted in some arduous mental operation; and as I emerge on deck the ordered arrangement of the stars meets my eye, unclouded, infinitely wearisome. There they are: stars, sun, sea, light, darkness, space, great waters; the formidable Work of the Seven Days, into which mankind seems to have blundered unbidden. Or else decoyed. Even as I have been decoyed into this awful, this death-haunted command. . . ."

The only spot of light in the ship at night was that of the compass-lamps, lighting up the faces of the succeeding helmsmen; for the rest we were lost in the darkness, I walking the poop and the men lying about the decks. They were all so reduced by sickness that no watches could be kept. Those who were able to walk remained all the time on duty, lying about in the shadows of the main deck, till my voice raised for an order would bring them to their enfeebled feet, a tottering little group, moving patiently about the ship, with hardly a murmur, a whisper amongst them all. And every time I had to raise my voice it was with a pang of remorse and pity.

Then about four o'clock in the morning a light would gleam forward in the galley. The unfailing Ransome with the uneasy heart, immune, serene, and active, was getting ready for the early coffee for the men. Presently he would bring me a cup up on the poop, and it was then that I allowed myself to drop into my deck chair for a couple of hours of real sleep. No doubt I must have been snatching short dozes when leaning against the rail for a moment in sheer exhaustion; but, honestly, I was not aware of them, except in the painful form of convulsive starts that seemed to come on me even while I walked. From about five, however, until after seven I would sleep openly under the fading stars.

I would say to the helmsman: "Call me at need," and drop into that chair and close my eyes, feeling that there was no more sleep for me on earth. And then I would know nothing till, some time between seven and eight, I would feel a touch on my shoulder and look up at Ransome's face, with its faint, wistful smile and friendly, gray eyes, as though he were tenderly amused at my slumbers. Occasionally the second mate would come up and relieve me at early coffee time. But it didn't really matter. Generally it was a dead calm, or else faint airs so changing and fugitive that it really wasn't worth while to touch a brace for them. If the air steadied at all the seaman at the helm could be trusted for a warning shout: "Ship's all aback, sir!" which like a trumpet-call would make me spring a foot above the deck. Those were the words which it seemed to me would have made me spring up from eternal sleep. But this was not often. I have never met since such breathless sunrises. And if the second mate happened to be there (he had generally one day in three free of fever) I would find him sitting on the skylight half senseless, as it were, and with an idiotic gaze fastened on some object near by—a rope, a cleat, a belaying pin, a ringbolt.

That young man was rather troublesome. He remained cubbish in his sufferings. He seemed to have become completely imbecile; and when the return of fever drove him to his cabin below, the next thing would be that we would miss him from there. The first time it happened Ransome and I were very much alarmed. We started a quiet search and ultimately Ransome discovered him curled up in the sail-locker, which opened into the lobby by a sliding door. When remonstrated with, he muttered sulkily, "It's cool in there." That wasn't true. It was only dark there.

The fundamental defects of his face were not improved by its uniform livid hue. The disease disclosed its low type in a startling way. It was not so with many of the men. The wastage of ill-health seemed to idealize the general character of the features, bringing out the unsuspected nobility of some, the strength of others, and in one case revealing an essentially comic aspect. He was a short, gingery, active man with a nose and chin of the Punch type, and whom his shipmates called "Frenchy." I don't know why. He may have been a Frenchman, but I have never heard him utter a single word in French.

To see him coming aft to the wheel comforted one. The blue dungaree trousers turned up the calf, one leg a little higher than the other, the clean check shirt, the white canvas cap, evidently made by himself, made up a whole of peculiar smartness, and the persistent jauntiness of his gait, even, poor fellow, when he couldn't help tottering, told of his invincible spirit. There was also a man called Gambril. He was the only grizzled person in the ship. His face was of an austere type. But if I remember all their faces, wasting tragically before my eyes, most of their names have vanished from my memory.

The words that passed between us were few and puerile in regard of the situation. I had to force myself to look them in the face. I expected to meet reproachful glances. There were none. The expression of suffering in their eyes was indeed hard enough to bear. But that they couldn't help. For the rest, I ask myself whether it was the temper of their souls or the sympathy of their imagination that made them so wonderful, so worthy of my undying regard.

For myself, neither my soul was highly tempered, nor my imagination properly under control. There were moments when I felt, not only that I would go mad, but that I had gone mad already; so that I dared not open my lips for fear of betraying myself by some insane shriek. Luckily I had only orders to give, and an order has a steadying influence upon him who has to give it. Moreover, the seaman, the officer of the watch, in me was sufficiently sane. I was like a mad carpenter making a box. Were he ever so convinced that he was King of Jerusalem, the box he would make would be a sane box. What I feared was a shrill note escaping me involuntarily and upsetting my balance. Luckily, again, there was no necessity to raise one's voice. The brooding stillness of the world seemed sensitive to the slightest sound, like a whispering gallery. The conversational tone would almost carry a word from one end of the ship to the other. The terrible thing was that the only voice that I ever heard was my own. At night especially it reverberated very lonely amongst the planes of the unstirring sails.

Mr. Burns, still keeping to his bed with that air of secret determination, was moved to grumble at many things. Our interviews were short five-minute affairs, but fairly frequent. I was everlastingly diving down below to get a light, though I did not consume much tobacco at that time. The pipe was always going out; for in truth my mind was not composed enough to enable me to get a decent smoke. Likewise, for most of the time during the twenty-four hours I could have struck matches on deck and held them aloft till the flame burnt my fingers. But I always used to run below. It was a change. It was the only break in the incessant strain; and, of course, Mr. Burns through the open door could see me come in and go out every time.

With his knees gathered up under his chin and staring with his greenish eyes over them, he was a weird figure, and with my knowledge of the crazy notion in his head, not a very attractive one for me. Still, I had to speak to him now and then, and one day he complained that the ship was very silent. For hours and hours, he said, he was lying there, not hearing a sound, till he did not know what to do with himself.

"When Ransome happens to be forward in his galley everything's so still that one might think everybody in the ship was dead," he grumbled. "The only voice I do hear sometimes is yours, sir, and that isn't enough to cheer me up. What's the matter with the men? Isn't there one left that can sing out at the ropes?"

"Not one, Mr. Burns," I said. "There is no breath to spare on board this ship for that. Are you aware that there are times when I can't muster more than three hands to do anything?"

He asked swiftly but fearfully:

"Nobody dead yet, sir?"

"No."

"It wouldn't do," Mr. Burns declared forcibly. "Mustn't let him. If he gets hold of one he will get them all."

I cried out angrily at this. I believe I even swore at the disturbing effect of these words. They attacked all the self-possession that was left to me. In my endless vigil in the face of the enemy I had been haunted by gruesome images enough. I had had visions of a ship drifting in calms and swinging in light airs, with all her crew dying slowly about her decks. Such things had been known to happen.

Mr. Burns met my outburst by a mysterious silence.

"Look here," I said. "You don't believe yourself what you say. You can't. It's impossible. It isn't the sort of thing I have a right to expect from you. My position's bad enough without being worried with your silly fancies."

He remained unmoved. On account of the way in which the light fell on his head I could not be sure whether he had smiled faintly or not. I changed my tone.

"Listen," I said. "It's getting so desperate that I had thought for a moment, since we can't make our way south, whether I wouldn't try to steer west and make an attempt to reach the mail-boat track. We could always get some quinine from her, at least. What do you think?"

He cried out: "No, no, no. Don't do that, sir. You mustn't for a moment give up facing that old ruffian. If you do he will get the upper hand of us."

I left him. He was impossible. It was like a case of possession. His protest, however, was essentially quite sound. As a matter of fact, my notion of heading out west on the chance of sighting a problematical steamer could not bear calm examination. On the side where we were we had enough wind, at least from time to time, to struggle on toward the south. Enough, at least, to keep hope alive. But suppose that I had used those capricious gusts of wind to sail away to the westward, into some region where there was not a breath of air for days on end, what then? Perhaps my appalling vision of a ship floating with a dead crew would become a reality for the discovery weeks afterward by some horror-stricken mariners.

That afternoon Ransome brought me up a cup of tea, and while waiting there, tray in hand, he remarked in the exactly right tone of sympathy:

"You are holding out well, sir."

"Yes," I said. "You and I seem to have been forgotten."

"Forgotten, sir?"

"Yes, by the fever-devil who has got on board this ship," I said.

Ransome gave me one of his attractive, intelligent, quick glances and went away with the tray. It occurred to me that I had been talking somewhat in Mr. Burns' manner. It annoyed me. Yet often in darker moments I forgot myself into an attitude toward our troubles more fit for a contest against a living enemy.

Yes. The fever-devil had not laid his hand yet either on Ransome or on me. But he might at any time. It was one of those thoughts one had to fight down, keep at arm's length at any cost. It was unbearable to contemplate the possibility of Ransome, the housekeeper of the ship, being laid low. And what would happen to my command if I got knocked over, with Mr. Burns too weak to stand without holding on to his bed-place and the second mate reduced to a state of permanent imbecility? It was impossible to imagine, or rather, it was only too easy to imagine.

I was alone on the poop. The ship having no steerage way, I had sent the helmsman away to sit down or lie down somewhere in the shade. The men's strength was so reduced that all unnecessary calls on it had to be avoided. It was the austere Gambril with the grizzly beard. He went away readily enough, but he was so weakened by repeated bouts of fever, poor fellow, that in order to get down the poop ladder he had to turn sideways and hang on with both hands to the brass rail. It was just simply heart-breaking to watch. Yet he was neither very much worse nor much better than most of the half-dozen miserable victims I could muster up on deck.

It was a terribly lifeless afternoon. For several days in succession low clouds had appeared in the distance, white masses with dark convolutions resting on the water, motionless, almost solid, and yet all the time changing their aspects subtly. Toward evening they vanished as a rule. But this day they awaited the setting sun, which glowed and smouldered sulkily amongst them before it sank down. The punctual and wearisome stars reappeared over our mastheads, but the air remained stagnant and oppressive.

The unfailing Ransome lighted the binnacle lamps and glided, all shadowy, up to me.

"Will you go down and try to eat something, sir?" he suggested.

His low voice startled me. I had been standing looking out over the rail, saying nothing, feeling nothing, not even the weariness of my limbs, overcome by the evil spell.

"Ransome," I asked abruptly, "how long have I been on deck? I am losing the notion of time."

"Twelve days, sir," he said, "and it's just a fortnight since we left the anchorage."

His equable voice sounded mournful somehow. He waited a bit, then added: "It's the first time that it looks as if we were to have some rain."

I noticed then the broad shadow on the horizon, extinguishing the low stars completely, while those overhead, when I looked up, seemed to shine down on us through a veil of smoke.

How it got there, how it had crept up so high, I couldn't say. It had an ominous appearance. The air did not stir. At a renewed invitation from Ransome I did go down into the cabin to—in his own words— "try and eat something." I don't know that the trial was very successful. I suppose at that period I did exist on food in the usual way; but the memory is now that in those days life was sustained on invincible anguish, as a sort of infernal stimulant exciting and consuming at the same time.

It's the only period of my life in which I attempted to keep a diary. No, not the only one. Years later, in conditions of moral isolation, I did put down on paper the thoughts and events of a score of days. But this was the first time. I don't remember how it came about or how the pocketbook and the pencil came into my hands. It's inconceivable that I should have looked for them on purpose. I suppose they saved me from the crazy trick of talking to myself.

Strangely enough, in both cases I took to that sort of thing in circumstances in which I did not expect, in colloquial phrase, "to come out of it." Neither could I expect the record to outlast me. This shows that it was purely a personal need for intimate relief and not a call of egotism.

Here I must give another sample of it, a few detached lines, now looking very ghostly to my own eyes, out of the part scribbled that very evening:

* * *

"There is something going on in the sky like a decomposition; like a corruption of the air, which remains as still as ever. After all, mere clouds, which may or may not hold wind or rain. Strange that it should trouble me so. I feel as if all my sins had found me out. But I suppose the trouble is that the ship is still lying motionless, not under command; and that I have nothing to do to keep my imagination from running wild amongst the disastrous images of the worst that may befall us. What's going to happen? Probably nothing. Or anything. It may be a furious squall coming, butt end foremost. And on deck there are five men with the vitality and the strength of, say, two. We may have all our sails blown away. Every stitch of canvas has been on her since we broke ground at the mouth of the Mei-nam, fifteen days ago . . . or fifteen centuries. It seems to me that all my life before that momentous day is infinitely remote, a fading memory of light-hearted youth, something on the other side of a shadow. Yes, sails may very well be blown away. And that would be like a death sentence on the men. We haven't strength enough on board to bend another suit; incredible thought, but it is true. Or we may even get dismasted. Ships have been dismasted in squalls simply because they weren't handled quick enough, and we have no power to whirl the yards around. It's like being bound hand and foot preparatory to having one's throat cut. And what appals me most of all is that I shrink from going on deck to face it. It's due to the ship, it's due to the men who are there on deck—some of them, ready to put out the last remnant of their strength at a word from me. And I am shrinking from it. From the mere vision. My first command. Now I understand that strange sense of insecurity in my past. I always suspected that I might be no good. And here is proof positive. I am shirking it. I am no good."

* * *

At that moment, or, perhaps, the moment after, I became aware of Ransome standing in the cabin. Something in his expression startled me. It had a meaning which I could not make out. I exclaimed: "Somebody's dead."

It was his turn then to look startled.

"Dead? Not that I know of, sir. I have been in the forecastle only ten minutes ago and there was no dead man there then."

"You did give me a scare," I said.

His voice was extremely pleasant to listen to. He explained that he had come down below to close Mr. Burns' port in case it should come on to rain. "He did not know that I was in the cabin," he added.

"How does it look outside?" I asked him.

"Very black, indeed, sir. There is something in it for certain."

"In what quarter?"

"All round, sir."

I repeated idly: "All round. For certain," with my elbows on the table.

Ransome lingered in the cabin as if he had something to do there, but hesitated about doing it. I said suddenly:

"You think I ought to be on deck?"

He answered at once but without any particular emphasis or accent: "I do, sir."

I got to my feet briskly, and he made way for me to go out. As I passed through the lobby I heard Mr. Burns' voice saying:

"Shut the door of my room, will you, steward?" And Ransome's rather surprised: "Certainly, sir."

I thought that all my feelings had been dulled into complete indifference. But I found it as trying as ever to be on deck. The impenetrable blackness beset the ship so close that it seemed that by thrusting one's hand over the side one could touch some unearthly substance. There was in it an effect of inconceivable terror and of inexpressible mystery. The few stars overhead shed a dim light upon the ship alone, with no gleams of any kind upon the water, in detached shafts piercing an atmosphere which had turned to soot. It was something I had never seen before, giving no hint of the direction from which any change would come, the closing in of a menace from all sides.

There was still no man at the helm. The immobility of all things was perfect. If the air had turned black, the sea, for all I knew, might have turned solid. It was no good looking in any direction, watching for any sign, speculating upon the nearness of the moment. When the time came the blackness would overwhelm silently the bit of starlight falling upon the ship, and the end of all things would come without a sigh, stir, or murmur of any kind, and all our hearts would cease to beat like run-down clocks.

It was impossible to shake off that sense of finality. The quietness that came over me was like a foretaste of annihilation. It gave me a sort of comfort, as though my soul had become suddenly reconciled to an eternity of blind stillness.

The seaman's instinct alone survived whole in my moral dissolution. I descended the ladder to the quarter-deck. The starlight seemed to die out before reaching that spot, but when I asked quietly: "Are you there, men?" my eyes made out shadow forms starting up around me, very few, very indistinct; and a voice spoke: "All here, sir." Another amended anxiously:

"All that are any good for anything, sir."

Both voices were very quiet and unringing; without any special character of readiness or discouragement. Very matter-of-fact voices.

"We must try to haul this mainsail close up," I said.

The shadows swayed away from me without a word. Those men were the ghosts of themselves, and their weight on a rope could be no more than the weight of a bunch of ghosts. Indeed, if ever a sail was hauled up by sheer spiritual strength it must have been that sail, for, properly speaking, there was not muscle enough for the task in the whole ship let alone the miserable lot of us on deck. Of course, I took the lead in the work myself. They wandered feebly after me from rope to rope, stumbling and panting. They toiled like Titans. We were half-an-hour at it at least, and all the time the black universe made no sound. When the last leech-line was made fast, my eyes, accustomed to the darkness, made out the shapes of exhausted men drooping over the rails, collapsed on hatches. One hung over the after-capstan, sobbing for breath, and I stood amongst them like a tower of strength, impervious to disease and feeling only the sickness of my soul. I waited for some time fighting against the weight of my sins, against my sense of unworthiness, and then I said:

"Now, men, we'll go aft and square the mainyard. That's about all we can do for the ship; and for the rest she must take her chance."

VI

As we all went up it occurred to me that there ought to be a man at the helm. I raised my voice not much above a whisper, and, noiselessly, an uncomplaining spirit in a fever-wasted body appeared in the light aft, the head with hollow eyes illuminated against the blackness which had swallowed up our world—and the universe. The bared forearm extended over the upper spokes seemed to shine with a light of its own. I murmured to that luminous appearance:

"Keep the helm right amidships."

It answered in a tone of patient suffering:

"Right amidships, sir."

Then I descended to the quarter-deck. It was impossible to tell whence the blow would come. To look round the ship was to look into a bottomless, black pit. The eye lost itself in inconceivable depths. I wanted to ascertain whether the ropes had been picked up off the deck. One could only do that by feeling with one's feet. In my cautious progress I came against a man in whom I recognized Ransome. He possessed an unimpaired physical solidity which was manifest to me at the contact. He was leaning against the quarter-deck capstan and kept silent. It was like a revelation. He was the collapsed figure sobbing for breath I had noticed before we went on the poop.

"You have been helping with the mainsail!" I exclaimed in a low tone.

"Yes, sir," sounded his quiet voice.

"Man! What were you thinking of? You mustn't do that sort of thing."

After a pause he assented: "I suppose I mustn't." Then after another short silence he added: "I am all right now," quickly, between the tell-tale gasps.

I could neither hear nor see anybody else; but when I spoke up, answering sad murmurs filled the quarter-deck, and its shadows seemed to shift here and there. I ordered all the halyards laid down on deck clear for running.

"I'll see to that, sir," volunteered Ransome in his natural, pleasant tone, which comforted one and aroused one's compassion, too, somehow.

That man ought to have been in his bed, resting, and my plain duty was to send him there. But perhaps he would not have obeyed me; I had not the strength of mind to try. All I said was:

"Go about it quietly, Ransome."

Returning on the poop I approached Gambril. His face, set with hollow shadows in the light, looked awful, finally silenced. I asked him how he felt, but hardly expected an answer. Therefore, I was astonished at his comparative loquacity.

"Them shakes leaves me as weak as a kitten, sir," he said, preserving finely that air of unconsciousness as to anything but his business a helmsman should never lose. "And before I can pick up my strength that there hot fit comes along and knocks me over again."

He sighed. There was no reproach in his tone, but the bare words were enough to give me a horrible pang of self-reproach. It held me dumb for a time. When the tormenting sensation had passed off I asked:

"Do you feel strong enough to prevent the rudder taking charge if she gets sternway on her? It wouldn't do to get something smashed about the steering-gear now. We've enough difficulties to cope with as it is."

He answered with just a shade of weariness that he was strong enough to hang on. He could promise me that she shouldn't take the wheel out of his hands. More he couldn't say.

At that moment Ransome appeared quite close to me, stepping out of the darkness into visibility suddenly, as if just created with his composed face and pleasant voice.

Every rope on deck, he said, was laid down clear for running, as far as one could make certain by feeling. It was impossible to see anything. Frenchy had stationed himself forward. He said he had a jump or two left in him yet.

Here a faint smile altered for an instant the clear, firm design of Ransome's lips. With his serious clear, gray eyes, his serene temperament—he was a priceless man altogether. Soul as firm as the muscles of his body.

He was the only man on board (except me, but I had to preserve my liberty of movement) who had a sufficiency of muscular strength to trust to. For a moment I thought I had better ask him to take the wheel. But the dreadful knowledge of the enemy he had to carry about him made me hesitate. In my ignorance of physiology it occurred to me that he might die suddenly, from excitement, at a critical moment.

While this gruesome fear restrained the ready words on the tip of my tongue, Ransome stepped back two paces and vanished from my sight.

At once an uneasiness possessed me, as if some support had been withdrawn. I moved forward, too, outside the circle of light, into the darkness that stood in front of me like a wall. In one stride I penetrated it. Such must have been the darkness before creation. It had closed behind me. I knew I was invisible to the man at the helm. Neither could I see anything. He was alone, I was alone, every man was alone where he stood. And every form was gone, too, spar, sail, fittings, rails; everything was blotted out in the dreadful smoothness of that absolute night.

A flash of lightning would have been a relief—I mean physically. I would have prayed for it if it hadn't been for my shrinking apprehension of the thunder. In the tension of silence I was suffering from it seemed to me that the first crash must turn me into dust.

And thunder was, most likely, what would happen next. Stiff all over and hardly breathing, I waited with a horribly strained expectation. Nothing happened. It was maddening, but a dull, growing ache in the lower part of my face made me aware that I had been grinding my teeth madly enough, for God knows how long.

It's extraordinary I should not have heard myself doing it; but I hadn't. By an effort which absorbed all my faculties I managed to keep my jaw still. It required much attention, and while thus engaged I became bothered by curious, irregular sounds of faint tapping on the deck. They could be heard single, in pairs, in groups. While I wondered at this mysterious devilry, I received a slight blow under the left eye and felt an enormous tear run down my cheek. Raindrops. Enormous. Forerunners of something. Tap. Tap. Tap. . . .

I turned about, and, addressing Gambrel earnestly, entreated him to "hang on to the wheel." But I could hardly speak from emotion. The fatal moment had come. I held my breath. The tapping had stopped as unexpectedly as it had begun, and there was a renewed moment of intolerable suspense; something like an additional turn of the racking screw. I don't suppose I would have ever screamed, but I remember my conviction that there was nothing else for it but to scream.

Suddenly—how am I to convey it? Well, suddenly the darkness turned into water. This is the only suitable figure. A heavy shower, a downpour, comes along, making a noise. You hear its approach on the sea, in the air, too, I verily believe. But this was different. With no preliminary whisper or rustle, without a splash, and even without the ghost of impact, I became instantaneously soaked to the skin. Not a very difficult matter, since I was wearing only my sleeping suit. My hair got full of water in an instant, water streamed on my skin, it filled my nose, my ears, my eyes. In a fraction of a second I swallowed quite a lot of it.

As to Gambril, he was fairly choked. He coughed pitifully, the broken cough of a sick man; and I beheld him as one sees a fish in an aquarium by the light of an electric bulb, an elusive, phosphorescent shape. Only he did not glide away. But something else happened. Both binnacle lamps went out. I suppose the water forced itself into them, though I wouldn't have thought that possible, for they fitted into the cowl perfectly.

The last gleam of light in the universe had gone, pursued by a low exclamation of dismay from Gambril. I groped for him and seized his arm. How startlingly wasted it was.

"Never mind," I said. "You don't want the light. All you need to do is to keep the wind, when it comes, at the back of your head. You understand?"

"Aye, aye, sir. . . . But I should like to have a light," he added nervously.

All that time the ship lay as steady as a rock. The noise of the water pouring off the sails and spars, flowing over the break of the poop, had stopped short. The poop scuppers gurgled and sobbed for a little while longer, and then perfect silence, joined to perfect immobility, proclaimed the yet unbroken spell of our helplessness, poised on the edge of some violent issue, lurking in the dark.

I started forward restlessly. I did not need my sight to pace the poop of my ill-starred first command with perfect assurance. Every square foot of her decks was impressed indelibly on my brain, to the very grain and knots of the planks. Yet, all of a sudden, I fell clean over something, landing full length on my hands and face.

It was something big and alive. Not a dog—more like a sheep, rather. But there were no animals in the ship. How could an animal. . . . It was an added and fantastic horror which I could not resist. The hair of my head stirred even as I picked myself up, awfully scared; not as a man is scared while his judgment, his reason still try to resist, but completely, boundlessly, and, as it were, innocently scared—like a little child.

I could see It—that Thing! The darkness, of which so much had just turned into water, had thinned down a little. There It was! But I did not hit upon the notion of Mr. Burns issuing out of the companion on all fours till he attempted to stand up, and even then the idea of a bear crossed my mind first.

He growled like one when I seized him round the body. He had buttoned himself up into an enormous winter overcoat of some woolly material, the weight of which was too much for his reduced state. I could hardly feel the incredibly thin lath of his body, lost within the thick stuff, but his growl had depth and substance: Confounded dump ship with a craven, tiptoeing crowd. Why couldn't they stamp and go with a brace? Wasn't there one Godforsaken lubber in the lot fit to raise a yell on a rope?

"Skulking's no good, sir," he attacked me directly. "You can't slink past the old murderous ruffian. It isn't the way. You must go for him boldly—as I did. Boldness is what you want. Show him that you don't care for any of his damned tricks. Kick up a jolly old row."

"Good God, Mr. Burns," I said angrily. "What on earth are you up to? What do you mean by coming up on deck in this state?"

"Just that! Boldness. The only way to scare the old bullying rascal."

I pushed him, still growling, against the rail. "Hold on to it," I said roughly. I did not know what to do with him. I left him in a hurry, to go to Gambril, who had called faintly that he believed there was some wind aloft. Indeed, my own ears had caught a feeble flutter of wet canvas, high up overhead, the jingle of a slack chain sheet. . . .

These were eerie, disturbing, alarming sounds in the dead stillness of the air around me. All the instances I had heard of topmasts being whipped out of a ship while there was not wind enough on her deck to blow out a match rushed into my memory.

"I can't see the upper sails, sir," declared Gambril shakily.

"Don't move the helm. You'll be all right," I said confidently.

The poor man's nerves were gone. Mine were not in much better case. It was the moment of breaking strain and was relieved by the abrupt sensation of the ship moving forward as if of herself under my feet. I heard plainly the soughing of the wind aloft, the low cracks of the upper spars taking the strain, long before I could feel the least draught on my face turned aft, anxious and sightless like the face of a blind man.

Suddenly a louder-sounding note filled our ears, the darkness started streaming against our bodies, chilling them exceedingly. Both of us, Gambril and I, shivered violently in our clinging, soaked garments of thin cotton. I said to him:

"You are all right now, my man. All you've got to do is to keep the wind at the back of your head. Surely you are up to that. A child could steer this ship in smooth water."

He muttered: "Aye! A healthy child." And I felt ashamed of having been passed over by the fever which had been preying on every man's strength but mine, in order that my remorse might be the more bitter, the feeling of unworthiness more poignant, and the sense of responsibility heavier to bear.

The ship had gathered great way on her almost at once on the calm water. I felt her slipping through it with no other noise but a mysterious rustle alongside. Otherwise, she had no motion at all, neither lift nor roll. It was a disheartening steadiness which had lasted for eighteen days now; for never, never had we had wind enough in that time to raise the slightest run of the sea. The breeze freshened suddenly. I thought it was high time to get Mr. Burns off the deck. He worried me. I looked upon him as a lunatic who would be very likely to start roaming over the ship and break a limb or fall overboard.

I was truly glad to find he had remained holding on where I had left him, sensibly enough. He was, however, muttering to himself ominously.

This was discouraging. I remarked in a matter-of-fact tone:

"We have never had so much wind as this since we left the roads."

"There's some heart in it, too," he growled judiciously. It was a remark of a perfectly sane seaman. But he added immediately: "It was about time I should come on deck. I've been nursing my strength for this—just for this. Do you see it, sir?"

I said I did, and proceeded to hint that it would be advisable for him to go below now and take a rest.

His answer was an indignant "Go below! Not if I know it, sir."

Very cheerful! He was a horrible nuisance. And all at once he started to argue. I could feel his crazy excitement in the dark.

"You don't know how to go about it, sir. How could you? All this whispering and tiptoeing is no good. You can't hope to slink past a cunning, wide-awake, evil brute like he was. You never heard him talk.

Enough to make your hair stand on end. No! No! He wasn't mad. He was no more mad than I am. He was just downright wicked. Wicked so as to frighten most people. I will tell you what he was. He was nothing less than a thief and a murderer at heart. And do you think he's any different now because he's dead? Not he! His carcass lies a hundred fathom under, but he's just the same . . . in latitude 8° 20' north."

He snorted defiantly. I noted with weary resignation that the breeze had got lighter while he raved. He was at it again.

"I ought to have thrown the beggar out of the ship over the rail like a dog. It was only on account of the men. . . . Fancy having to read the Burial Service over a brute like that! . . . 'Our departed brother' . . . I could have laughed. That was what he couldn't bear. I suppose I am the only man that ever stood up to laugh at him. When he got sick it used to scare that . . . brother. . . . Brother. . . . Departed. . . . Sooner call a shark brother."

The breeze had let go so suddenly that the way of the ship brought the wet sails heavily against the mast. The spell of deadly stillness had caught us up again. There seemed to be no escape.

"Hallo!" exclaimed Mr. Burns in a startled voice. "Calm again!"

I addressed him as though he had been sane.

"This is the sort of thing we've been having for seventeen days, Mr. Burns," I said with intense bitterness. "A puff, then a calm, and in a moment, you'll see, she'll be swinging on her heel with her head away from her course to the devil somewhere."

He caught at the word. "The old dodging Devil," he screamed piercingly and burst into such a loud laugh as I had never heard before. It was a provoking, mocking peal, with a hair-raising, screeching over-note of defiance. I stepped back, utterly confounded.

Instantly there was a stir on the quarter-deck; murmurs of dismay. A distressed voice cried out in the dark below us: "Who's that gone crazy, now?"

Perhaps they thought it was their captain? Rush is not the word that could be applied to the utmost speed the poor fellows were up to; but in an amazing short time every man in the ship able to walk upright had found his way on to that poop.

I shouted to them: "It's the mate. Lay hold of him a couple of you. . . ."

I expected this performance to end in a ghastly sort of fight. But Mr. Burns cut his derisive screeching dead short and turned upon them fiercely, yelling:

"Aha! Dog-gone ye! You've found your tongues—have ye? I thought you were dumb. Well, then—laugh! Laugh—I tell you. Now then—all together. One, two, three—laugh!"

A moment of silence ensued, of silence so profound that you could have heard a pin drop on the deck. Then Ransome's unperturbed voice uttered pleasantly the words:

"I think he has fainted, sir—" The little motionless knot of men stirred, with low murmurs of relief. "I've got him under the arms. Get hold of his legs, some one."

Yes. It was a relief. He was silenced for a time—for a time. I could not have stood another peal of that insane screeching. I was sure of it; and just then Gambril, the austere Gambril, treated us to another vocal performance. He began to sing out for relief. His voice wailed pitifully in the darkness: "Come aft somebody! I can't stand this. Here she'll be off again directly and I can't. . . ."

I dashed aft myself meeting on my way a hard gust of wind whose approach Gambril's ear had detected from afar and which filled the sails on the main in a series of muffled reports mingled with the low plaint of the spars. I was just in time to seize the wheel while Frenchy who had followed me caught up the collapsing Gambril. He hauled him out of the way, admonished him to lie still where he was, and then stepped up to relieve me, asking calmly:

"How am I to steer her, sir?"

"Dead before it for the present. I'll get you a light in a moment."

But going forward I met Ransome bringing up the spare binnacle lamp. That man noticed everything, attended to everything, shed comfort around him as he moved. As he passed me he remarked in a soothing tone that the stars were coming out. They were. The breeze was sweeping clear the sooty sky, breaking through the indolent silence of the sea.

The barrier of awful stillness which had encompassed us for so many days as though we had been accursed, was broken. I felt that. I let myself fall on to the skylight seat. A faint white ridge of foam, thin, very thin, broke alongside. The first for ages—for ages. I could have cheered, if it hadn't been for the sense of guilt which clung to all my thoughts secretly. Ransome stood before me.

"What about the mate," I asked anxiously. "Still unconscious?"

"Well, sir—it's funny," Ransome was evidently puzzled. "He hasn't spoken a word, and his eyes are shut. But it looks to me more like sound sleep than anything else."

I accepted this view as the least troublesome of any, or at any rate, least disturbing. Dead faint or deep slumber, Mr. Burns had to be left to himself for the present. Ransome remarked suddenly:

"I believe you want a coat, sir."

"I believe I do," I sighed out.

But I did not move. What I felt I wanted were new limbs. My arms and legs seemed utterly useless, fairly worn out. They didn't even ache. But I stood up all the same to put on the coat when Ransome brought it up. And when he suggested that he had better now "take Gambril forward," I said:

"All right. I'll help you to get him down on the main deck."

I found that I was quite able to help, too. We raised Gambril up between us. He tried to help himself along like a man but all the time he was inquiring piteously:

"You won't let me go when we come to the ladder? You won't let me go when we come to the ladder?"

The breeze kept on freshening and blew true, true to a hair. At daylight by careful manipulation of the helm we got the foreyards to run square by themselves (the water keeping smooth) and then went about hauling the ropes tight. Of the four men I had with me at night, I could see now only two. I didn't inquire as to the others. They had given in. For a time only I hoped.

Our various tasks forward occupied us for hours, the two men with me moved so slow and had to rest so often. One of them remarked that "every blamed thing in the ship felt about a hundred times heavier than its proper weight." This was the only complaint uttered. I don't know what we should have done without Ransome. He worked with us, silent, too, with a little smile frozen on his lips. From time to time I murmured to him: "Go steady"—"Take it easy, Ransome"—and received a quick glance in reply.

When we had done all we could do to make things safe, he disappeared into his galley. Some time afterward, going forward for a look round, I caught sight of him through the open door. He sat upright on the locker in front of the stove, with his head leaning back against the bulkhead. His eyes were closed; his capable hands held open the front of his thin cotton shirt baring tragically his powerful chest, which heaved in painful and laboured gasps. He didn't hear me.

I retreated quietly and went straight on to the poop to relieve Frenchy, who by that time was beginning to look very sick. He gave me the course with great formality and tried to go off with a jaunty step, but reeled widely twice before getting out of my sight.

And then I remained all alone aft, steering my ship, which ran before the wind with a buoyant lift now and then, and even rolling a little. Presently Ransome appeared before me with a tray. The sight of food made me ravenous all at once. He took the wheel while I sat down of the after grating to eat my breakfast.

"This breeze seems to have done for our crowd," he murmured. "It just laid them low—all hands."

"Yes," I said. "I suppose you and I are the only two fit men in the ship."

"Frenchy says there's still a jump left in him. I don't know. It can't be much," continued Ransome with his wistful smile. "Good little man that. But suppose, sir, that this wind flies round when we are close to the land—what are we going to do with her?"

"If the wind shifts round heavily after we close in with the land she will either run ashore or get dismasted or both. We won't be able to do anything with her. She's running away with us now. All we can do is to steer her. She's a ship without a crew."

"Yes. All laid low," repeated Ransome quietly. "I do give them a look-in forward every now and then, but it's precious little I can do for them."

"I, and the ship, and every one on board of her, are very much indebted to you, Ransome," I said warmly.

He made as though he had not heard me, and steered in silence till I was ready to relieve him. He surrendered the wheel, picked up the tray, and for a parting shot informed me that Mr. Burns was awake and seemed to have a mind to come up on deck.

"I don't know how to prevent him, sir. I can't very well stop down below all the time."

It was clear that he couldn't. And sure enough Mr. Burns came on deck dragging himself painfully aft in his enormous overcoat. I beheld him with a natural dread. To have him around and raving about the wiles of a dead man while I had to steer a wildly rushing ship full of dying men was a rather dreadful prospect.

But his first remarks were quite sensible in meaning and tone. Apparently he had no recollection of the night scene. And if he had he didn't betray himself once. Neither did he talk very much. He sat on the skylight looking desperately ill at first, but that strong breeze, before which the last remnant of my crew had wilted down, seemed to blow a fresh stock of vigour into his frame with every gust. One could almost see the process.

By way of sanity test I alluded on purpose to the late captain. I was delighted to find that Mr. Burns did not display undue interest in the subject. He ran over the old tale of that savage ruffian's iniquities with a certain vindictive gusto and then concluded unexpectedly:

"I do believe, sir, that his brain began to go a year or more before he died."

A wonderful recovery. I could hardly spare it as much admiration as it deserved, for I had to give all my mind to the steering.

In comparison with the hopeless languour of the preceding days this was dizzy speed. Two ridges of foam streamed from the ship's bows; the wind sang in a strenuous note which under other circumstances would have expressed to me all the joy of life. Whenever the hauled-up mainsail started trying to slat and bang itself to pieces in its gear, Mr. Burns would look at me apprehensively.

"What would you have me to do, Mr. Burns? We can neither furl it nor set it. I only wish the old thing would thrash itself to pieces and be done with it. That beastly racket confuses me."

Mr. Burns wrung his hands, and cried out suddenly:

"How will you get the ship into harbour, sir, without men to handle her?"

And I couldn't tell him.

Well—it did get done about forty hours afterward. By the exorcising virtue of Mr. Burns' awful laugh, the malicious spectre had been laid, the evil spell broken, the curse removed. We were now in the hands of a kind and energetic Providence. It was rushing us on. . . .

I shall never forget the last night, dark, windy, and starry. I steered. Mr. Burns, after having obtained from me a solemn promise to give him a kick if anything happened, went frankly to sleep on the deck close to the binnacle. Convalescents need sleep. Ransome, his back propped against the mizzen-mast and a blanket over his legs, remained perfectly still, but I don't suppose he closed his eyes for a moment. That embodiment of jauntiness, Frenchy, still under the delusion that there was a "jump" left in him, had insisted on joining us; but mindful of discipline, had laid himself down as far on the forepart of the poop as he could get, alongside the bucket-rack.

And I steered, too tired for anxiety, too tired for connected thought. I had moments of grim exultation and then my heart would sink awfully at the thought of that forecastle at the other end of the dark deck, full of fever-stricken men—some of them dying. By my fault. But never mind. Remorse must wait. I had to steer.

In the small hours the breeze weakened, then failed altogether. About five it returned, gentle enough, enabling us to head for the roadstead. Daybreak found Mr. Burns sitting wedged up with coils of rope on the stern-grating, and from the depths of his overcoat steering the ship with very white bony hands; while Ransome and I rushed along the decks letting go all the sheets and halliards by the run. We dashed next up on to the forecastle head. The perspiration of labour and sheer nervousness simply poured off our heads as we toiled to get the anchors cock-billed. I dared not look at Ransome as we worked side by side. We exchanged curt words; I could hear him panting close to me and I avoided turning my eyes his way for fear of seeing him fall down and expire in the act of putting forth his strength—for what? Indeed for some distinct ideal.

The consummate seaman in him was aroused. He needed no directions. He knew what to do. Every effort, every movement was an act of consistent heroism. It was not for me to look at a man thus inspired.

At last all was ready and I heard him say:

"Hadn't I better go down and open the compressors now, sir?"

"Yes. Do," I said. And even then I did not glance his way. After a time his voice came up from the main deck.

"When you like, sir. All clear on the windlass here."

I made a sign to Mr. Burns to put the helm down and let both anchors go one after another, leaving the ship to take as much cable as she wanted. She took the best part of them both before she brought up. The loose sails coming aback ceased their maddening racket above my head. A perfect stillness reigned in the ship. And while I stood forward feeling a little giddy in that sudden peace, I caught faintly a moan or two and the incoherent mutterings of the sick in the forecastle.

As we had a signal for medical assistance flying on the mizzen it is a fact that before the ship was fairly at rest three steam launches from various men-of-war were alongside; and at least five naval surgeons had clambered on board. They stood in a knot gazing up and down the empty main deck, then looked aloft—where not a man could be seen, either.

I went toward them—a solitary figure, in a blue and gray striped sleeping suit and a pipe-clayed cork helmet on its head. Their disgust was extreme. They had expected surgical cases. Each one had brought his carving tools with him. But they soon got over their little disappointment. In less than five minutes one of the steam launches was rushing shoreward to order a big boat and some hospital people for the removal of the crew. The big steam pinnace went off to her ship to bring over a few bluejackets to furl my sails for me.

One of the surgeons had remained on board. He came out of the forecastle looking impenetrable, and noticed my inquiring gaze.

"There's nobody dead in there, if that's what you want to know," he said deliberately. Then added in a tone of wonder: "The whole crew!"

"And very bad?"

"And very bad," he repeated. His eyes were roaming all over the ship. "Heavens! What's that?"

"That," I said, glancing aft, "is Mr. Burns, my chief officer."

Mr. Burns with his moribund head nodding on the stalk of his lean neck was a sight for any one to exclaim at. The surgeon asked:

"Is he going to the hospital, too?"

"Oh, no," I said jocosely. "Mr. Burns can't go on shore till the mainmast goes. I am very proud of him. He's my only convalescent."

"You look—" began the doctor staring at me. But I interrupted him angrily:

"I am not ill."

"No. . . . You look queer."

"Well, you see, I have been seventeen days on deck."

"Seventeen! . . . But you must have slept."

"I suppose I must have. I don't know. But I'm certain that I didn't sleep for the last forty hours."

"Phew! . . . You will be going ashore presently I suppose?"

"As soon as ever I can. There's no end of business waiting for me there."

The surgeon released my hand, which he had taken while we talked, pulled out his pocket-book, wrote in it rapidly, tore out the page and offered it to me.

"I strongly advise you to get this prescription made up for yourself ashore. Unless I am much mistaken you will need it this evening."

"What is it, then?" I asked with suspicion.

"Sleeping draught," answered the surgeon curtly; and moving with an air of interest toward Mr. Burns he engaged him in conversation.

As I went below to dress to go ashore, Ransome followed me. He begged my pardon; he wished, too, to be sent ashore and paid off.

I looked at him in surprise. He was waiting for my answer with an air of anxiety.

"You don't mean to leave the ship!" I cried out.

"I do really, sir. I want to go and be quiet somewhere. Anywhere. The hospital will do."

"But, Ransome," I said. "I hate the idea of parting with you."

"I must go," he broke in. "I have a right!" . . . He gasped and a look of almost savage determination passed over his face. For an instant he was another being. And I saw under the worth and the comeliness of the man the humble reality of things. Life was a boon to him—this precarious hard life, and he was thoroughly alarmed about himself.

"Of course I shall pay you off if you wish it," I hastened to say. "Only I must ask you to remain on board till this afternoon. I can't leave Mr. Burns absolutely by himself in the ship for hours."

He softened at once and assured me with a smile and in his natural pleasant voice that he understood that very well.

When I returned on deck everything was ready for the removal of the men. It was the last ordeal of that episode which had been maturing and tempering my character—though I did not know it.

It was awful. They passed under my eyes one after another—each of them an embodied reproach of the bitterest kind, till I felt a sort of revolt wake up in me. Poor Frenchy had gone suddenly under. He was carried past me insensible, his comic face horribly flushed and as if swollen, breathing stertorously. He looked more like Mr. Punch than ever; a disgracefully intoxicated Mr. Punch.

The austere Gambril, on the contrary, had improved temporarily. He insisted on walking on his own feet to the rail—of course with assistance on each side of him. But he gave way to a sudden panic at the moment of being swung over the side and began to wail pitifully:

"Don't let them drop me, sir. Don't let them drop me, sir!" While I kept on shouting to him in most soothing accents: "All right, Gambril. They won't! They won't!"

It was no doubt very ridiculous. The bluejackets on our deck were grinning quietly, while even Ransome himself (much to the fore in lending a hand) had to enlarge his wistful smile for a fleeting moment.

I left for the shore in the steam pinnace, and on looking back beheld Mr. Burns actually standing up by the taffrail, still in his enormous woolly overcoat. The bright sunlight brought out his weirdness amazingly. He looked like a frightful and elaborate scarecrow set up on the poop of a death-stricken ship, set up to keep the seabirds from the corpses.

Our story had got about already in town and everybody on shore was most kind. The Marine Office let me off the port dues, and as there happened to be a shipwrecked crew staying in the Home I had no difficulty in obtaining as many men as I wanted. But when I inquired if I could see Captain Ellis for a moment I was told in accents of pity for my ignorance that our deputy-Neptune had retired and gone home on a pension about three weeks after I left the port. So I suppose that my appointment was the last act, outside the daily routine, of his official life.

It is strange how on coming ashore I was struck by the springy step, the lively eyes, the strong vitality of every one I met. It impressed me enormously. And amongst those I met there was Captain Giles, of course. It would have been very extraordinary if I had not met him. A prolonged stroll in the business part of the town was the regular employment of all his mornings when he was ashore.

I caught the glitter of the gold watch-chain across his chest ever so far away. He radiated benevolence.

"What is it I hear?" he queried with a "kind uncle" smile, after shaking hands. "Twenty-one days from Bangkok?"

"Is this all you've heard?" I said. "You must come to tiffin with me. I want you to know exactly what you have let me in for."

He hesitated for almost a minute.

"Well—I will," he said condescendingly at last.

We turned into the hotel. I found to my surprise that I could eat quite a lot. Then over the cleared table-cloth I unfolded to Captain Giles the history of these twenty days in all its professional and emotional aspects, while he smoked patiently the big cigar I had given him.

Then he observed sagely:

"You must feel jolly well tired by this time."

"No," I said. "Not tired. But I'll tell you, Captain Giles, how I feel. I feel old. And I must be. All of you on shore look to me just a lot of skittish youngsters that have never known a care in the world."

He didn't smile. He looked insufferably exemplary. He declared:

"That will pass. But you do look older—it's a fact."

"Aha!" I said.

"No! No! The truth is that one must not make too much of anything in life, good or bad."

"Live at half-speed," I murmured perversely. "Not everybody can do that."

"You'll be glad enough presently if you can keep going even at that rate," he retorted with his air of conscious virtue. "And there's another thing: a man should stand up to his bad luck, to his mistakes, to his conscience and all that sort of thing. Why—what else would you have to fight against."

I kept silent. I don't know what he saw in my face but he asked abruptly:

"Why—you aren't faint-hearted?"

"God only knows, Captain Giles," was my sincere answer.

"That's all right," he said calmly. "You will learn soon how not to be faint-hearted. A man has got to learn everything—and that's what so many of them youngsters don't understand."

"Well, I am no longer a youngster."

"No," he conceded. "Are you leaving soon?"

"I am going on board directly," I said. "I shall pick up one of my anchors and heave in to half-cable on the other directly my new crew comes on board and I shall be off at daylight to-morrow!"

"You will," grunted Captain Giles approvingly, "that's the way. You'll do."

"What did you think? That I would want to take a week ashore for a rest?" I said, irritated by his tone. "There's no rest for me till she's out in the Indian Ocean and not much of it even then."

He puffed at his cigar moodily, as if transformed.

"Yes. That's what it amounts to," he said in a musing tone. It was as if a ponderous curtain had rolled up disclosing an unexpected Captain Giles. But it was only for a moment, just the time to let him add, "Precious little rest in life for anybody. Better not think of it."

We rose, left the hotel, and parted from each other in the street with a warm handshake, just as he began to interest me for the first time in our intercourse.

The first thing I saw when I got back to the ship was Ransome on the quarter-deck sitting quietly on his neatly lashed sea-chest.

I beckoned him to follow me into the saloon where I sat down to write a letter of recommendation for him to a man I knew on shore.

When finished I pushed it across the table. "It may be of some good to you when you leave the hospital."

He took it, put it in his pocket. His eyes were looking away from me—nowhere. His face was anxiously set.

"How are you feeling now?" I asked.

"I don't feel bad now, sir," he answered stiffly. "But I am afraid of its coming on. . . ." The wistful smile came back on his lips for a moment. "I—I am in a blue funk about my heart, sir."

I approached him with extended hand. His eyes not looking at me had a strained expression. He was like a man listening for a warning call.

"Won't you shake hands, Ransome?" I said gently.

He exclaimed, flushed up dusky red, gave my hand a hard wrench—and next moment, left alone in the cabin, I listened to him going up the companion stairs cautiously, step by step, in mortal fear of starting into sudden anger our common enemy it was his hard fate to carry consciously within his faithful breast.

THE END

www.ingramcontent.com/pod-product-compliance
Lightning Source LLC
Chambersburg PA
CBHW032250020726
47495CB00001B/49